I0831541

PETER DOMANIG

PETER DOMANIG

Morning in Vienna

by

VICTOR WHITE

Cherokee Publishing Company
Atlanta, Georgia

White, Victor Francis, 1902–
Peter Domanig; morning in Vienna, by Victor White. Indianapolis, New York, The Bobbs-Merrill company [1944]

704 p. 22 cm.

A novel.
"First edition."

I. Title.

PZ3.W5855Pe 44–3822 rev

Library of Congress [r57h½]

This book is printed on acid-free paper which conforms to the American National Standard Z39.48-1984 *Permanence of Paper for Printed Library Materials.* Paper that conforms to this standard's requirements for pH, alkaline reserve and freedom from groundwood is anticipated to last several hundred years without significant deterioration under normal library use and storage conditions.

Manufactured in the United States of America

ISBN: 978-0-87797-361-4 Hardcover
ISBN: 978-0-87797-362-1 Paper

Cherokee Publishing Company
P O Box 1730, Marietta, GA 30061

To

CALVIN L. ZERBE

"There are children who brood from their earliest years over their family through being humiliated by the unseemliness of their surroundings and of their parents' lives. I noticed these brooding creatures while I was still at school, and I concluded then that it all came from their being prematurely envious. . . . It is sad for those natures who are flung back on their own resources and dreams, especially when they have a passionate, premature and almost vindictive longing for seemliness—yes, 'vindictive.' "

—Dostoevski

"Then, because one bastard itches, all the rest of us have to scratch!"

"Invariably. You are dealing there with spiritual insecurity. And in case you mean 'bastard' literally, you're only picking the most obvious example. . . . That type has a lust for power. Society is lucky every time one of them turns only into an ordinary crank or criminal—the chances are he'll want to dominate an industry or found an empire. Occasionally one of them outgrows his fear and becomes whole, but that's rare, for where there's self-pity there can be no growth. . . ."

—From a conversation

PART I

Chapter One

THE first beams of the afternoon sun poked slyly between the partially lowered blind and the tops of the potted plants on the window sill. They kindled the fuchsia blossoms into pulsing red, then slanted in a trembling, silvery column to the floor where they formed a bright patch behind the boy who was too absorbed in the tower he was building with his blocks to notice any of it.

The rest of the room was drowsy with a cool half-light. The Venetian blind on the other window, above the head of the divan, was down and the slats folded tight to keep the light out of the eyes of the man who lay asleep there.

The man looked heavier lying down than he really was. That was partly the fault of his unbuttoned vest which showed a great expanse of starched white shirt buckling capriciously around his chest. His red face looked purple in the shadow and severe with its bristly, graying mustaches. His thin lips were tightly shut. His hands were folded peacefully on his stomach.

The man gave a sudden snore which startled the boy. He raised himself cautiously on his knees to see whether the man was awake. When he had made sure that the man was still asleep and after he had watched the loose, lower hairs of his mustaches which quivered softly for a minute with each breath the man took, he lowered himself back on his heels again.

The square tower was nearly finished. The boy leaned forward intently to inspect it. His hand moved toward it once as if to change a block but stopped halfway.

The tower was real again! It was just like the tower in the motion picture about Roland and Oliver and all the other knights he and Rudi had seen in school on Tuesday. It stood high in the mountains, set defiantly among barren, forbidding crags . . .

The boy's eyes became dreamy as the ferment of imagination began to work in him.

. . . he would bring Roland to the tower after he had rescued him from the Saracens in the pass. He would get mountain water from a spring he knew and herbs for Rudi's wounds from an old woman who lived in the mountains . . .

He could see Rudi Martin stretched out on a bed of moss and heather and himself beside Rudi putting cold compresses on Rudi's head.

. . . and in between nursing Roland, he would stand off the Saracens who had followed them to the tower. His body tensed and strained as he saw himself fighting them, first in single combat, one by one, then a whole horde of them all at once. They were all around him now, slashing and stabbing at him from every side. He could hear their hoarse cries, the clatter of steel on steel, see their ferocious faces . . .

Then the whole scene shifted suddenly. He was in the pass at Roncesvaux. He was still fighting the Saracens, hundreds of them. But it was he who was Roland now and Oliver was miles away. A fierce exultation possessed him at the thought of dying for Rudi who was already hastening to the rescue but would arrive too late. . . .

The magic violence of his reverie had exhausted itself and left only a sweet poignancy behind. A discreet clinking of dishes from beyond the closed kitchen door scattered the last, lingering shreds of his daydream.

A sudden scorn of the battered blocks seized him. He was too big to play with blocks! Next fall he would begin to study Latin and algebra out of big books like the ones Franz had on the bottom shelf of his bookcase in his room. He would be in the *Gymnasium* with the big boys—he and Rudi.

Thinking of Rudi made him sharply aware of the man on the divan again. If only he would take him along this afternoon! Rudi had said that his father had promised to take him to the fireworks in Hütteldorf. Perhaps he could persuade Father to go to Hütteldorf too. . . . But it depended on *her* out there in the kitchen. *She* might not let him go—like last Sunday.

Please, God, make her let me go! he prayed quickly.

He started to put away the blocks in the flat, wide box which held all his treasures: an old, rusty padlock, locked and without key;

three short pieces of electric cable; a broken nickel watch; two elastic bands; several screws and bolts; and a brass pulley. He was careful not to make any noise. When he had wedged the last block into the box, he lifted it clear of the floor and slid it cautiously under the big mahogany chest of drawers opposite the foot of the divan. Then he stood up and looked at the man. He was still asleep.

At a loss for what to do next, his eyes roved around the room and finally came to rest on an envelope with a foreign stamp, which stood propped up against the heavy bronze inkwell on top of the chest of drawers.

That was the letter from Mizzi—from America—and the stamp was an American stamp. It was much smaller than Austrian stamps and looked odd. The letter had had a bank draft in it—that was what Franz had called the pink piece of paper which *she* had taken to the bank in the Burggasse the very same day. She had got a lot of money for it. He knew because he had seen her take it out of her purse when she came home.

It was funny to think that Mizzi was his mother. Yet they all said so, even Franz. It gave him a queer feeling to think of it as if it might be true somehow and still not real, like the big ships on the ocean Franz had told him about which were as high as a house. He suddenly remembered the photographs of Mizzi in the album and how strange and foreign Mizzi looked in them. But Poldi had forbidden him to say so. Poldi said that it was only the clothes Mizzi wore, because clothes were different in America than in Vienna, just as people in America lived in houses that were as tall as a church steeple and ate tomatoes raw.

He tried to imagine what it would be like if Mizzi were here. He forgot the photographs and pictured her as elegant and smiling like Rudi's mother. Perhaps she would be nice too, like Rudi's mother, and always have chocolate in the dining room—for, of course, they would live in a big apartment in the Westbahnstrasse like Rudi. At any rate—he was suddenly angrily sure of that—she would not make him go to church all the time and she would let him go along with Father Sunday afternoons. . . .

Through the door beside the chest of drawers came the sound of swishing water. He listened attentively for a few seconds. *She* must be almost through with the dishes. He wondered whether Poldi had already left for her congregation. Then he heard Poldi talking. He could not make out what she was saying but her voice told him that she was asking *her* for something. There followed a brief altercation which ended with Poldi's impatient, "Oh, Mother!" He wondered what Poldi had wanted from *her*—it must have been important, for Poldi had offered to wipe the dishes; it was usually he who had to do it.

There was nothing he could do now but wait for Father to wake up. He tiptoed with elaborate caution across the room and pulled a footstool from under one of the two beds which stood end to end along the wall. He brought it back to the window and stood on it. By thrusting his head as far as he could between the fuchsia and geranium plants he was able to see all the way down the three-story façade across the courtyard. Poldi was standing near the entry with Lili Breitner.

Poldi was wearing the new horsehair hat she had bought yesterday. She looked very trim, almost tall, in her tight blue skirt and the white batiste blouse. Beside her, Lili Breitner in a flouncy pink dress seemed plump and ungainly. It occurred to him suddenly that he was always proud of Poldi when he saw her anywhere away from home. Perhaps it was, he told himself, because Poldi was always asking him about his homework and making him do things he did not want to do. It was even worse now since Poldi had finished commercial school and had started to work in an office. . . .

Fräulein Gisl came in from the street and joined Poldi. He saw that Fräulein Gisl had on a black horsehair hat too. She and Poldi and two or three other girls in their congregation were always buying the same things and dressing alike when they went out together Sunday afternoons. He found himself wishing that Poldi had waited for Fräulein Gisl in the kitchen instead of meeting her in the courtyard. He liked to be near Fräulein Gisl. She was tall and soft with beautiful gray eyes and a lilting voice, in contrast with Poldi who was dark and brusque and always made him think of the time when she had taken the part of a heroic, flashing-eyed boy in a play her congregation put on a year ago. He dreamed for a minute of having Fräulein Gisl at home all the time instead of Poldi, then remembered the candy Poldi had brought him on Thursday and instantly felt guilty.

The springs of the divan creaked suddenly. He turned around to look. The man on the divan grunted and swung his legs down to the floor.

He got hurriedly off the footstool.

"Shall I get your shoes, Father?"

The man reached for the pince-nez on top of a half-open newspaper on the table beside the divan and jiggled it into place on his nose. His eyes looked small and pale blue behind the nickel-rimmed pince-nez. He looked much less severe now that he was awake.

"The ones with the shoe trees in them." His voice was gruff but not unkind.

The boy hurried to the night-table beside the bed and got out a pair of shoes. He brought them back to the divan and was about to set them down when the man said: "Not those—the ones with the elastic sides."

"I'll get them," the boy said eagerly.

He brought the shoes and started to tug at the shoe trees.

"Here! I'll do that." A tinge of amusement had come into the man's voice. He took the shoes and slipped the trees out easily. "Where's Poldi?"

"She's gone to her congregation. You know, the Children of Mary." He felt a little guilty when he had said it as if he had betrayed Poldi somehow.

"Children of Mary!" the man half sneered and half chuckled. "Running to the priests like the old woman."

"Are you going out on the Schmeltz, Father? Can I come with you?"

The man pulled on the second shoe with a little grunt. He stopped to measure the boy who was busily picking up the red carpet slippers. A brief twinkle flickered in his pale blue eyes.

"I guess so," he said. "But I don't want to hear any whining that your feet hurt you again."

"I won't say anything," the boy promised. "Please, Father!"

"All right. You shine your shoes and brush your hair."

The boy forced himself to open the door into the kitchen very quietly. The hardest part lay still ahead of him. It all depended on *her* now.

The woman he was looking for sat in front of the sewing machine by the window, rummaging in a small basket filled with odds and ends of cloth and linen in her lap. She was a small woman with a round face which had once been apple-cheeked but now was merely a sallow red and faintly wrinkled with middle age. A faded blue apron hid most of the high-necked brown velvet blouse and of the voluminous black skirt she wore.

Small as she was, to the boy her power to blight his Sunday afternoon made her loom enormous.

"Father is up," he said as casually as he could.

The woman was holding a linen patch against a worn spot in a shirt.

"Father said I could come along."

Without looking up, the woman said tartly: "To watch him drink wine, I s'pose."

"I have to shine my shoes."

"You aren't so anxious to shine your shoes when you are going to church!"

"Father said I had to . . ."

He pulled out the box with the shoebrushes from under the kitchen cabinet and went out on the landing. He started to brush hard at his shoes.

"How often do I have to tell you not to use the polish?" She had come out on the landing behind him without his hearing her. "As if the blacking weren't good enough for your shoes!"

"I was only using it on the tips," he defended himself. He hated to use the blacking because it was so much harder to get his shoes to shine with it, but he did not dare use the polish again for fear that she might be watching him.

When he came back into the kitchen, she had begun to sew the patch on the shirt. Father came out from the living room and opened the washstand. He blustered a little as he washed his face. His face looked very red after he dried it. Then he proceeded to gargle into the enamel pail on the floor. His gargling was a little ostentatious, ponderous like everything else about him.

"Month of May, month of Mary, my mother always said," the woman asserted suddenly. She seemed to be speaking neither to the man nor to the boy so that her voice sounded oddly monotonous and irritating. "Children should be in church on Sunday, not gallivanting to the *Heurigen* to learn winebibbing."

Apprehension made the boy's throat go raw and prickly.

"Can't I go, Mother?"

"Children belong in church on Sunday," she said stubbornly.

"But Father said I could go with him——"

"If he wants to go, he can go!" the man said. "It won't do him any harm to get out in the open air once a week."

"Open air!" the woman scoffed. "I know your open air all right—sitting at the *Heurigen* all afternoon. He can get all the fresh air he needs on the way to church."

The man bridled suddenly. He slid his pince-nez out of his vest pocket and clapped it on his nose. "If I say Peter goes with me, he goes with me! Time enough for him to run to the priests when he is older."

"That's what you said about his mother too. I listened to you once and once was too often. A boy like him needs all the grace he can get. As the twig is bent, so is the tree inclined—and it wouldn't do some other people I know any harm either to go to church once in a while. Pater Alfred said——"

"To hell with your Pater Alfred!" the man exploded. "When I want his advice I'll ask for it. You keep your priests to yourself." He shut the lid of the washstand with a bang and stamped into the living room.

Fear turned into anguished certainty in the boy.

"Can't I go just this once? I'll go to vespers every night next week."

Still without looking up from her sewing, she said dryly: "You are going to church with me where every Christian belongs on Sunday."

He knew then that it was no use.

He followed the man into the living room and sat on the edge of the divan to watch him dress. His eyes burned with scalding resentment of the woman, but he forced back his tears and silently ground his teeth until they hurt. His disappointment made him picture the outing in the glamorous colors of deprivation—first the leisurely stroll across the Schmeltz where there were always some soldiers drilling even on Sunday, then Hütteldorf with its grassy sidewalks and old trees everywhere and the cool little villas half hidden in the gardens, the fireworks in the evening, and then best of all, the *Heurigen* with hundreds of people laughing and joking at tables and Chinese lanterns and an orchestra, and raspberry juice and soda for him. . . .

The man had taken a pair of clean cuffs from the top drawer in the big chest and was snapping in the cuff links. When he had slid on the cuffs and pulled his coat sleeves meticulously straight over them, he picked up his rings one by one from a glass tray. He wore two rings on each hand, one with a big amethyst which Peter liked particularly. There was a finicky precision to the way the man dressed.

The boy watched each step with a further dashing of his hopes. When the man had put his leather cigar case in one inside coat pocket and the thick billfold with the elastic around it in the other, he had finished at the mahogany chest. He crossed the room to the wardrobe beside his night-table and got out a light gray hat and his best cane with the bone handle. Every detail pointed to a particularly fine outing.

"Can't I come?" the boy made another, final attempt.

The man tucked the black ribbon of his pince-nez behind his ear. "You do as Mother says," he said irritably. Then, as if sorry for his gruffness: "I'll take you next week." He went out into the kitchen. A second later the door on the landing slammed shut.

A surge of desolation went through the boy. He had the feeling again that all this was unreal, that somebody would come to rescue him. The room had become unbearably drab. He stared across at the picture of Jesus over *her* bed and then at the companion picture of Mary over Father's bed and he hated them.

Chapter Two

A GREAT city is not unlike a woman.

There comes a time when a well-grown woman reaches a point of languorous, vibrant maturity when body and spirit are so nearly one, so interfused that no part of her is so insignificant as to be safely negligible. Far from being flattered, she is apt to be merely bored by praise that would romantically limit her to her obvious excellencies—her eyes perhaps, or her ravishing mouth, or her beautiful figure. Such praise will merely remind her of all that has been left out. For at the very moment when she is most harmoniously one, every part of her has also become most fully itself and most unique in its contribution to the whole. Woe to the artist or lover who misses the dimple in her thigh, the unexpected stop in the curve of her instep, the infinitesimal birthmark on her shoulder. He does not know the woman and she will never forgive him.

Vienna in 1912 had come to this triumphant maturity. Superficially one, easily romanced about by the makers of popular songs and by tourists, Vienna contained in reality a dozen cities. And not cities only, but villages and towns, whose boundaries zigzagged across Vienna without regard for street signs and other artificial boundaries. Barely a house whose six or a dozen families were not subtly bound together by their own little provincialisms, their pet sayings and pleasant little prejudices, which might or might not be shared by the equally snug little world in the house next to it.

But it took the children to be aware of that. For children are the true lovers of a city. To them, turning the corner of a street is an adventure into another continent, and crossing into an unfamiliar ward becomes an excursion into another dimension. They alone know the city for they see it with the frightening insight of childhood. They see at once the intimate detail which the artist strives after and jealously knows not to be a detail at all but the very essence of the thing, the iceberg on which his ambition founders.

After they had turned into the Burggasse, Peter managed to draw away from *her* little by little until he had put half of the width of the sidewalk between them. As long as they had been in the Schottenfeldgasse where everybody knew them there had been no use in pretending that he was not with her. But the Burggasse was different. He kept his eyes glued on the corrugated steel shutters over the shop windows to show that it was merely an accident that she and he were on the same sidewalk together.

He was ashamed of her. The prim dowdiness of her clothes and a certain stubborn humility in her bearing exasperated him. He knew every detail of her appearance by heart, resentfully, with the precision of utter dislike: her squashy little black hat with the bunch of silk violets and the tufts of black organdy and the shiny glass spangles; the black lace fichu over her black satin blouse; the filigree gold brooch at the collar; her black net gloves; her parasol with the white and gray stripes and the broken amber handle; the gray reticule in her other hand. . . .

Why couldn't he have a mother like Rudi's mother—or like the woman just ahead of them straightening the little boy's sailor collar in front of the confectionery shop! He watched with envy the woman's affectionate fussing over the boy who paid attention only to the gold-lettered box of candy in his hand. The woman looked cool, elegant, lovely.

They passed the woman and the confectionery shop. Both windows of the shop were crowded with glass shelves laden with pastries and trays of chocolates. Through the open door he saw the table where he had sat with Poldi one time last September when Poldi had bought him an ice. Someday he would have lots of money and he would go into a confectionery shop whenever he wanted to, and he would wear clothes that came from a store the way the other boys in school did—not made-over things that *she* had cut down from Franz's old clothes—and he would be free from her. . . .

The more familiar part of the Burggasse was behind them now. Across the street was the enclosed market with the sloping glass roof where she went shopping every morning after Mass. And there was the church of St. Ulrich with its funny steeple. The shops became sparser; the houses were smaller and more reserved. They came to the iron fence in front of the girls' school. He read the legend above the entrance: LYCÉE DU SACRÉ COEUR. Poldi said that it was a school for very rich girls. He had seen the girls come out of the school once—they had all been dressed alike in dark blue dresses and black patent-leather hats. Poldi said that it was a French school. He wondered whether it would be hard to learn French. If he went to the *Gymnasium* next year with Rudi, he would study French and Latin, too. Franz said that Latin wasn't hard but Greek was. Still, you didn't take Greek until you were older. . . .

One of the new double-decker streetcars went by. It was marked "Hütteldorf." If he had gone with Father he might have got him to ride home in it. Father was probably sitting in the garden of a *Heurigen* by now. . . .

They were getting near the Volkstheater and the traffic in the street was heavier. There were private carriages and *Fiaker* with two horses and the humbler hacks with only one. Most of the hacks had their roofs down, and the cabbies had decorated their whips and the shiny black harness on the horses' heads with little bunches of flowers. The people in the carriages looked gay, elegant, enviable.

He felt exhilarated as he always did when he approached the fashionable heart of the city. Something within him thrilled to the well-dressed people in the streets, to the uniforms of the officers, the hum of the carriages, the great electric arc lights with baskets of geraniums halfway up the mast, to the luxuriance of the huge chestnut trees that lined the streets.

They had come to the Ring, the wide boulevard which circled the Innere Stadt. Peter stiffened in anticipation of what he knew was going to happen. There it was! She reached out for his hand. He felt the black net glove burning into his hand and tried to free himself from her grasp.

"You are going to wait until the carriages have gone by!" she warned and held him tighter.

"I know how to cross a street. I'm not a little child."

"When you're with me, you're going to take my hand."

He submitted furiously.

"Now we can go, can't we?" he urged, exasperated by her caution when the street was for a moment clear of carriages. She did not answer but waited until an automobile which was still a hundred yards away had gone by as well.

Only when they had crossed the bridle path beyond the street did she finally let go of his hand. He drew away from her immediately. They entered the Volksgarten alongside of the Imperial Palace. Around the gate were clustered half a dozen flowerwomen with their wide baskets on camp stools. From the terrace of the restaurant in the park the strains of a waltz came floating through the trees. The languid music seemed to him all at once as precious as the millions of white and pink chestnut blossoms that carpeted the ground. He loved the endless rows of lush chestnut trees which he had come to associate with the Ring as much as the elegant terraces of the coffeehouses and the muffled murmur of carriage wheels on the asphalt.

When he grew up he would spend all his time on the Ring! He would sit at a table on the sidewalk, discreetly shielded from view by the screen of potted oleanders and the trellises of ivy, and leisurely drink coffee with *Schlagobers* and watch the people strolling by on the sidewalk and the carriages in the street.

Reluctantly he left the Ring and followed her into the park. Children were playing in the sand or rolling hoops or playing ball or diavolo. Most of them were with nurses and wore better clothes even than the children in school. They probably lived in fine hotels or in the aristocratic apartment houses along the Ring. He wondered whether they were really as unhappy as Franz had said. Franz had told him one time that rich children got beaten by their governesses and had to learn three languages and never saw their parents. They did not look unhappy and the governesses spoke very politely to them, he noticed. Anyhow, he would not mind having to study all the time and getting beaten if he could live in a beautiful house and wear fine clothes.

They had reached the end of the park.

"Can't we stay a little?" he pleaded. "I'm tired. I'd like to sit down on a bench."

"You can sit down in church. I don't want to get there when it's all filled up and have to stand in back. I want to hear Pater Poissl."

She hastened her pace and walked out through the tall wrought-iron gate. They were in the inner city. Old buildings now, and narrow, heavily shadowed streets. Now and then they came out on an open square only to plunge into another narrow, silent street again. Peter glanced through the plate-glass window of a coffee-house on the Graben. He saw the luxuriously upholstered benches against the walls, the abundance of silver and crystal on the glass tiers of the sideboard, the stack of newspapers a waiter placed before an elderly man near the window. At one of the tables two men were playing chess.

They entered another alley that ended in a stair with smoothly worn granite treads, and then they were in the big square on one side of which frowned the Palladian façade of the church they were heading for.

The church was already well filled even though they were half an hour early. The two long rows of heavy oak pews down the middle were packed to overflowing, and there was a press of people in the upper half of the left aisle where the red marble pulpit was.

She made her way up the far aisle and knelt down at the communion rail of the side altar of St. Joseph. The altar was directly across from the pulpit and they would be able to see Pater Poissl and hear well, but Peter was annoyed by her choice. If she had gone up the left aisle he could have sat down on the stoop that ran along the wall. Some people were already sitting there, he saw. Here he would have to kneel until the sermon started and perhaps she would not let him sit down even then.

Someday he would be able to go riding in an automobile like Franz with his friend, the Baron, on Sunday and go to theaters in the evening and come home late. He would pay the janitor two kronen a month the way Franz did and have his own key to the big door on the street and come home after ten when the gas lamps had been turned out on the landings. One time Franz had stayed out all night and *she* had been worried. But she never scolded Franz—he was too big—but there was another reason: she did not want to scold Franz; it was only he who never did anything right; it was something to do with Mizzi. . . .

His knees were hurting already. He tried shifting all his weight first on one knee and then on the other.

If she did not make him kneel so much there would be no

danger of his wearing out his stockings and he would not have to wear pants that hung down over his knees like a yokel's!

Out of the corner of his eye he watched her slip the beads of her rosary through the tips of her fingers. Her lips moved faintly as she prayed. He looked away from her and his eyes wandered over the altar and the statue of St. Joseph. As always when he had to be in church with her, an inexorable boredom tortured him like a strait jacket. He tried to pray, then he tried to think of Rudi. It was no use. His thoughts chased aimlessly in circles in a vast sodden emptiness.

She had noticed that he was not praying and whispered hoarsely:

"God sees you all right! He knows that you don't show any respect in His house."

Startled, he folded his hands tighter and stared hard at the statue of St. Joseph. The resentment he had felt against her all afternoon flared into burning hatred. He said two "Our Father's" passionately to St. Joseph to make him grow up quickly so that he would be free. He started a third and then had a feeling that it was wrong to pray against her. Besides, it wasn't any use because he wasn't good. At the same time doubt assailed him whether St. Joseph could help anyhow—she was too strong. . . .

There was a discreet stir around them. People were craning their heads toward the sacristy door. Girls were coming in from the sacristy two by two and taking their places at the phalanx of *prie-dieux* in the front part of the church. They were all wearing white blouses and had around their necks broad light-blue ribbons from which hung silver medallions.

He risked her disapproval and stood up. There were about a hundred girls and he tried to see Poldi and Fräulein Gisl among them. It was too dark and he was too far away to make out faces distinctly, but he noticed one girl who limped. They knelt down at the *prie-dieux* and there was nothing more to see for the moment. The sacristan lighted six candles at the high altar. Another five minutes passed, then the preacher appeared through the sacristy door. He was preceded by the sacristan who made a lane for him through the crowd.

The priest climbed the stair into the pulpit, knelt down and said an "Our Father" and a "Hail Mary" in a resonant voice. Then he rose and switched on the small cluster of electric bulbs that hung from the canopy over the pulpit. He was a middle-aged man with a great shock of dark hair, a ruddy face and beetling eyebrows which made him look formidable and austere. But his voice was tender and melodious when he started to speak. He was describing the Virgin as a little child. . . .

Peter listened attentively at first, then began to wonder whether Pater Poissl was really as kind as Poldi said. She always raved about the wonderful times they had when he went on an excursion with them. Peter was afraid of priests or at best ill at ease with them. Even Pater Alfred, whom he had had for catechism for four years now, made him feel uncomfortable.

He wanted to sit down. He pulled at her lace fichu.

"Now may I sit down?"

She did not answer and he sat down on the worn marble stoop where he had been kneeling before. He could not see Pater Poissl now and his voice seemed to come from another part of the church. He found it impossible to keep his mind on what the voice was saying. To give himself something to do he started to study the people around him. They were mostly elderly women with only a sprinkling of men. One distinguished-looking man standing beside a pillar struck his attention. He was still young but his elegant clothes and the way he held himself made him look like someone of importance. The man was listening attentively to Pater Poissl, and because the man impressed him, Peter began to listen too.

Pater Poissl was talking about Mary as the Queen of Heaven. His voice was impassioned. Peter thought he recognized the crescendo that preceded the end of a sermon. Yet there was no sign of the sacristan at the high altar to light up the rest of the candles for the Benediction.

The word "mother" recurred with the regularity of rhythm in the preacher's mouth. Peter's mind fastened on it and began to turn it over and over. Why did grownups and books always use that reverent tone for the word? Maybe they had had nice mothers, though, like Rudi. Rudi's mother kissed him when he came home from school and bought him anything he wanted. Not that he would have wanted *her* to kiss him!

There was something peculiar about him. *She* was his mother but there was also Mizzi. Mizzi was far off in America, somewhere beyond Germany and England even, across the ocean—and she was his mother, too. But she had her own children, a boy and a girl. He could not see how she could be his mother and so far away. Yet *she* insisted that Mizzi was his mother; only, whenever he asked her to explain the puzzle she told him to wait until he was older. All he knew was that Mizzi was her sister and that *she* had brought her up, too, and that Mizzi had been vain and had done something wrong, and that Father always defended Mizzi when they talked about her. . . .

There! he had missed the sacristan coming out. The candles on the altar were all lighted and presently the great crystal chandeliers above the altar flashed on. The rich cadences of the priest's voice pyramided to a climax and the sermon was over.

Behind them up in the organ loft the organ rose and he felt quickened with exhilaration. He liked the vesper service here because the girls sang the litany in Latin and it did not seem boring then. He stepped up on the stoop to get a better view. The altar was banked with white lilac and lilies. A double wreath of electric bulbs around the picture of the Virgin combined with the sparkling chandeliers to make the whole apse look resplendent and festive.

A minute later Pater Poissl came out in the heavy gold-embroidered cope from the sacristy and followed the two altar boys to the altar and the service began. The man whom Peter had noticed during the sermon was standing a little closer now. He was joining softly in the "*ora pro nobis*" when the full choir of girls up front chanted the responses. The man's singing annoyed him at first. The singing was supposed to be done by the choir! But after a while the temptation was too much for him and he started to hum the responses himself. Pretty soon he was singing quite boldly—after all, why shouldn't he sing if the man could? Wasn't he in the last year of choir school and wasn't he going to be in Herr Granini's choir next fall? He noticed that a few of the women glanced at him with approval, and once the man winked at him encouragingly and smiled.

A curious exaltation seized him and made him feel warm and very virtuous. It was as if the thin, faintly acrid fragrance of incense coming from the altar, the organ and the voices of the girls up front singing "*O Stern des Meeres,*" and his consciousness of the man in the gray suit all fused in the single desire in him to be desperately good. He started to pray fervently: "Please, God, let me be good . . . pure. . . ."

The moment had assumed a mystic significance and he did not want it to end. He felt light, bodiless—"My knees don't hurt at all now!" he told himself triumphantly. Even *she* was included in his sudden burst of affection.

The service had come to an end. The girls were beginning to file out through the sacristy. He had to get up to follow her to one of the pews up front which had emptied already. The sacristan was slowly extinguishing the candles on the altar.

He knelt rather than sat down in the pew and started to pray again in a rush of devout fervor. He prayed for Rudi and remembered that their first communion was only three weeks away. He pictured himself kneeling beside Rudi in the Schottenfeld Church and began to wish that it were now. He might not be able to feel so pure then! If only something would happen in the next three weeks so that he could prove his purity and prove himself worthy of Rudi . . .

It was she who finally nudged him to go.

Outside in the square a few people were waiting. Among them was the man in the gray suit. Peter saw with a tremor of excitement that the man was coming toward them. He stopped directly in front of her and raised his hat.

"This is a very fine boy!" he said to her. "And what is your name, young man?"

The man's slightly saccharine smile and the gray-gloved hand he had put on his shoulder made him uneasy. He hated to have people touch him. But he was flattered by the man's attention.

"Peter Domanig . . ."

The man's fingers tightened on his shoulder as he turned to her and said earnestly:

"Your son has a very promising voice, Frau Domanig."

She shook the folds of her parasol a little. Peter knew the gesture. She was nervous with the distinguished-looking man.

"He can sing all right if the notion takes him. That's all he cares about in church. He's not like my own children," she complained with a little sigh.

Peter suddenly found the stranger's touch unbearable. He wanted to run away from both of them and hide somewhere. His whole being stiffened as he recognized the special tone of voice she always used in explaining about him.

"Trouble enough bringing up your own," she went on. "He's my sister's boy. I'm Frau Bartsch. I'm bringing him up."

Peter wriggled his shoulder so that the man took away his hand. He felt embarrassed at the man's sympathetic glance and furious with her for humiliating him.

"Oh, I see," the man said quickly. "Well, I think Peter deserves something for singing so well——" He brought out a brown pocketbook and opened it. "How would you like a ten-heller piece?" He held the coin teasingly in front of Peter.

Peter hesitated. He did not like to accept things from people, yet the coin tempted him.

"Well, take it and thank the gentleman!" she said querulously.

He took it then and said stiffly, "Thank you."

"That's all right, young man. Buy yourself some candy with it." The man said good evening, smiled, and walked away.

"May I keep it?" Peter asked her after a few steps. The coin in his pocket felt cool and new and had made him forget his anger with her.

"You better save it toward a new cap instead of wasting it on candy."

"I won't buy any candy for myself," he promised. "Only, I'd like to keep it."

She did not answer. They were following a different route this time and walked along outside the tall iron fence of the park.

The coin and the memory of the man's praise had brought back the mood in church.

"I'd like to be a priest," he said quickly. He clutched the coin in his pocket like a talisman. "I'd like to preach like Pater Poissl."

"You'd make a fine priest. A boy like you that doesn't even want to go to church."

"But don't you think I could be? If I studied hard and went to church every day?"

"Well, maybe, if God gives you grace," she admitted grudgingly. He could tell that she was pleased.

They walked along for several minutes in silence. The yellow stucco on the buildings across the street had taken on a soft amber glow except where the street lamps projected brittle medallions of silver-gray on the façades. On their left, the globes of light in the park gleamed warmly through the foliage of the trees.

He loved the evening in the Innere Stadt. The gay tune of the hymn to the Virgin Mary which the girls had sung started to run through his head. He began to hum it softly to himself.

He was walking quite close to her now. The rebelliousness which he had felt all afternoon and which had flared up for a second when she had talked to the man about him had exhausted itself. He was aware only of a wistful desire for approval.

They crossed the square in front of the Burgtheater and came out on the Ring. The many double doors along the curved façade of the theater were all closed, but through the panes he could see the liveried attendants talking together in the lobby. On the second floor the row of tall windows also showed light. The building had the smug, secretive air that only a theater with a performance going on inside can achieve.

"Has Father always been in the Burgtheater?" he asked suddenly.

"Ever since we got married twenty-three years ago."

"But I thought Father worked for Herr Gregor then?"

"Father never worked for Herr Gregor anywhere. Herr Gregor was nothing more than a simple cabinetmaker. I said they were working in the same shop together."

He tried to imagine Herr Gregor who was so rich and had the big shop in the Kandlgasse as a simple cabinetmaker who worked with Father.

"Why didn't Father get rich, too, like Herr Gregor?"

"Because God didn't want it that way," she said curtly.

"But why didn't Father stay with Herr Gregor?"

"Because! . . . Do you have to know everything?" But she went on suddenly of her own accord: "Because when I met Ludwig he and Herr Gregor used to go to the *Heurigen* every Sunday and holiday and get drunk. I wasn't going to marry a man who carried on like that even before he was married. It was either the *Heurigen* or me. That's why I got Wetti's husband to get him into the Burgtheater. Man proposes and God disposes," she ended with a sigh.

"Why did you want Father to be in the Burgtheater?"

"Why does anybody want a government job? Because of the salary and the pension when you're too old to work, and because I wanted to get him away from all his cronies who thought the Lord's Day was made only for going to the *Heurigen* and having a good time. I didn't know then that Herr Gregor would settle down into a fine, steady man—I might have known, though, that anything Wetti had a hand in would turn out wrong."

He knew why she did not like Wetti. Aunt Wetti was rich and didn't go to church either, and Aunt Wetti had had something to do with Mizzi's being in America. That was why they never went to see her except that one time when Franz had been in some mysterious trouble in the *Gymnasium*, a long time ago, and Aunt Wetti's husband had to see about getting Franz reinstated.

Aunt Wetti had been very nice to him. She had given him cake and a funny kind of candy that had puckered his mouth and really tasted bitter after you licked the sugar off. Poldi had said that it was candied ginger when he had asked her about it afterward. He also remembered that Aunt Wetti was tall and had worn a frilly, light-green dress and that Aunt Wetti's husband had a white beard like a doctor and wore gold-rimmed spectacles.

They had almost reached the Burggasse. Now that they were shortly going to cross the Ring, he became again sharply aware of the sights and sounds of the boulevard and of the smell of the chestnut blossoms in the air. He did not want to leave the Ring yet. When she started to cross the bridle path, he bent down quickly and swept together a little heap of the fluffy white blossoms. He called to her from the ground:

"I want to take these home, Mother! May I?"

"What for? To make a mess in the house?"

"Just a few. I could put them on the little altar in the kitchen."

"I got a peony this morning for the altar. You don't need trash like that."

He contented himself with scooping up a handful of the blossoms and carrying them loosely in his free hand. She had taken hold of his other hand again as she prepared to cross the street.

After they had walked along the Burggasse for several minutes and he had got tired of smelling the blossoms, he remembered Aunt Wetti again. Did Mizzi look like Aunt Wetti? He suddenly felt that he had to know.

"Was Mizzi nice-looking like Aunt Wetti?"

"Why shouldn't she be? She's her sister."

"But you don't look like Aunt Wetti. . . ." He realized that he had made a blunder when she said tartly:

"Handsome is as handsome does. God looks at the heart, not at the face."

"Did you think Mizzi was pretty?"

"Frau Wimmer used to say she was the prettiest girl in the whole parish," she said, not without an unexpected note of pride. "That was her ruin, too. If she hadn't had a pretty face, Ludwig wouldn't have spoiled her the way he did. Nothing good enough for her: she had to have shoes from the Kärtnerstrasse and dresses from a dressmaker—he's the one who put all those highfalutin ideas into her head, he and Wetti. Between them they fixed her all right. 'Pride goeth before a fall!' Everything for show and every heller she ever made had to go on her back. Just like Wetti!"

"But Aunt Wetti is happy, isn't she?"

"God's mill grinds slow but sure! He's shown her with her children."

"But Aunt Wetti hasn't any children!"

"She had them all right: three of them and all of them dead before they were a year old. God's shown her who's boss."

"Didn't you like Mizzi?" he asked now, still intent on finding out as much as he could while she was in this communicative mood.

"Would I have raised her ever since she was eight years old, if I hadn't? But if I hadn't promised my mother on her deathbed and if I'd known that I'd have to bring up her child someday too, I'd have thought twice about it."

"Did Mizzi really act in the theater?"

"You'll have to ask Father about that. I had nothing to do with her after she left my roof. That was his doing and Wetti's. I knew nothing good would come of it, but no, he had to send her to the conservatory and Wetti had to doll her up like a young lady. I wasn't good enough for her after that. Wetti was just right for her, and Herr von Garnhaft had nothing better to do than to get her into the theater. I was good enough again to look after her brat. She didn't go to Wetti then! She came crying and sobbing to me."

"But you said the stork only brought children to married people and you said she wasn't married then?"

"Ask me no question and you'll hear no lies," she said abruptly.

He realized that he had got as much information out of her as he was going to. It was only rarely that he could get her to talk about the past and he had been luckier than usual this evening.

They passed the confectionery shop where he had seen the woman and the little boy that afternoon. He began to feel hungry.

"Is there going to be meat for supper?" he cajoled.

"Children don't need meat all the time. The meat is for Franz and Poldi. You're going to have polenta."

His heart sank at the thought of the yellow corn-meal pudding with lumps in it.

"May I have some jam on it?"

"You'll see when you get home."

That meant that he probably would. He felt a little cheered by the prospect of jam.

Chapter Three

In Hütteldorf the fireworks were still going. Rockets crisscrossed in the sky and burst into sheaves of red and yellow sparks which hung there for a minute, suspended above the dark trees, then did not so much die as suddenly turn into a magnificently spluttering Catherine wheel or that comet's tail over there blazing a crimson parabola across the blue night, straight at you, until you were sure the comet's tail was going to land right in your lap.

A fine sight but not even the children paid attention to the fireworks any more. They were more interested in the three acrobats and the clown who was aping them down there on the stage. The stage, brilliantly lighted with acetylene flares and long strings of many-colored electric bulbs, was at the far end of the garden where everybody could see it. In front of it where the tables were thickest and the noise loudest, the orchestra was playing for all it was worth to make itself heard above the hubbub of voices and laughter.

A huge garden this *Heurigen*, seating easily two thousand people at its rows on rows of long, green tables in back and along the sides and at the preferred round tables down the center. Handsome kerosene lamps on cast-iron poles diffused a mild, friendly light and hundreds of Chinese lanterns had been strung between the trees and swayed softly with the breeze.

It was old, too, this *Heurigen*. Many of the linden trees it would have taken three men to span and the porcelain beer saucers proclaimed proudly: Founded in 1768. Schubert might well have sat here some Sunday evening like this, and Beethoven before he moved out to Heiligenstadt which has its own vintners who sell *heurigen* wine.

The vast garden was getting noisier by the minute and more gay. The hum of voices blended into an exhilarating fabric of sound with the strains of the orchestra, the sudden bursts of laughter, and the tinkle of glass as waiters expertly swooped up whole armfuls of empty glasses to dash off for more wine.

The aisles between the tables were alive with a milling crowd: latecomers craning their necks to find a vacant table, perspiring waiters balancing enormous trays above their heads, girls in dirndl costume crying "*Zigarren, Zigaretten,*" more girls in pert black dresses and dainty white aprons selling pastry, men selling toy balloons and freak-shaped candy sticks, peddlers with outlandish trinkets pinned all down the front of their vests and coats, pretzel vendors and frankfurter-men—all of them laughing and talking, and all of them ready for a minute of amiable chitchat or a little bout of hilarious repartee.

Gay! Gay! One had the feeling that all this was going to go on forever. Security breathed like a benediction from the ancient trees, lifted like a sigh of content from the happy confidence of these people. And if you had told the jovial master-locksmith sitting with his wife and his three pink-cheeked children, or that handsome Uhlan sergeant over there who was going to finish his military service in November that there was going to be a war within little more than a year, a grim war which would mean the end of Vienna, either one would have enjoyed the joke hugely and would have assumed that you were some new kind of *Heurigen* entertainer. And master-locksmith or Uhlan sergeant, they would have insisted that you sit down at their table and share their wine so that you could all have a good laugh together over your brainstorm.

At the end of one of the long tables sat a solidly built man with a pince-nez clamped firmly on the puckered bridge of his nose. His left hand with the large amethyst ring was folded loosely around the half-empty wineglass in front of him. His small, alert, pale-blue eyes were on the stage where the clown was making fun of the acrobats. The two little girls who belonged to the man and the woman at the same table with him were screaming with delight at the antics of the clown.

"The clown is the best acrobat of the lot," Herr Bartsch was thinking. "Too bad the boy isn't here. Peterl would have enjoyed all this. Mizzi used to be crazy about the *Heurigen*, too. I'll have to get a *Salzstangl* when I go and take it home to him."

Then he happened to look down on his hand that was holding the cigar and a frown appeared on his forehead. He twisted the hand so as to see his fingernails.

The nails were worrying him. They had been growing thicker and thicker in the last six months. They were as thick as a peasant's toenails and they had an unhealthy yellow color. It was some disease all right. Thursday, he decided, he was going to go to the clinic in the *Allgemeinen* hospital. See what they'd say. . . .

What worried him most was that his finger tips had lost nearly all sense of touch. He had been getting into the habit lately of using the upper part of his fingers to feel surfaces and joints in the shop. It was a nuisance. He'd been bathing his nails in formaldehyde twice a day the way a fellow had told him, but that hadn't seemed to do much good. Perhaps he ought to have gone to the clinic before. There was the doctor in the theater, of course, but he was out of the question. They were too fussy about things like that in the theater—there was the stage electrician they had pensioned just because he'd had a rash. After all, he'd been very careful at home and in the shop just in case it was something contagious. . . .

He realized suddenly that the stringy, tall man standing up at one of the round tables near the stage was flourishing his red and white checked napkin at him and calling his name. Then he saw that it was Schani—Schani Gregor. He raised his glass hastily by way of greeting and grinned uneasily. Schani waved even more violently. He was signaling him to come over to his table. Herr Bartsch pretended not to understand and raised his glass once again, then quickly looked the other way.

He had been feeling uneasy with Schani Gregor for more than twenty years now. Uneasy and a little sheepish. It was all Kathi's fault.

Thirty years ago almost, he and Schani had come up from Styria together after they had finished their apprenticeship in Graz. They had worked, planned, saved, and occasionally gone on a spree together. Their plan had been to start a shop of their own as soon as they had saved enough. Then Kathi had come along.

Kathi had been from the country, too, but she had had different ideas. In the first place, she had always distrusted the city. She had been afraid of the risk and she had disliked Schani. In the end, like a fool, he had given in to her and had let her brother-in-law pull strings to get him the job in the Burgtheater. The big wages and the glamour of working in the theater had appealed to him, too—no use denying it. And when he was sixty, there would be the pension. But if she hadn't been so scared of taking a chance, it she'd had a little more gumption, he'd be Schani's partner now. Schani had nine men working for him, to say nothing of the apprentices, and he owned the big corner house in the Kandlgasse.

Herr Bartsch pulled himself together with a start: Schani was coming toward his table. No question about it! He stiffened with sudden alarm and knew that he was looking ludicrously belligerent because of his uneasiness.

Herr Gregor, spare and tall and wooden-jointed, something boyish about his eagerness in spite of the bald head and the heavy gold chain across his flat stomach as became a landlord who owned a three-story corner house, came to a fidgety stop beside Herr Bartsch. His homely face, all bulging bones and hollows, wore a conciliatory grin and his pale eyes pleaded curiously with Herr Bartsch who sat in wary compactness:

"*Du*, Ludwig, how about coming over to our table? Lots of room where we are."

Herr Bartsch squinted at the other uncertainly, then recognized the tall man's anxiousness to bridge the years. His firm-lipped mouth loosened in a smile.

"All right, Schani."

In a flash, the tall man had become all eager impatience to get Herr Bartsch to his table. He urged him forward with friendly little shoves and chattered happily:

"My sister-in-law is with us. I don't think you've ever met her—you'll like Liesel. . . ."

The two women at his table received them with welcoming smiles. The stout one in the black and rose striped dress promptly held out her hand and cried:

"Well, hello, Herr Bartsch! How are you? How do you like the fun? It's been ages since we have been at the *Heurigen* together. I guess being in the theater and knowing all those actresses has spoiled you for plain people like us—we aren't good enough for him any more!" she explained to the woman beside her with an infectious, bell-like laugh surprising in such a stout woman.

She was still holding his hand and Herr Bartsch had to laugh, too, especially when she put on a reproachful pout which gave way at once to another burst of laughter. He was feeling good already, glad that all this was happening.

"This is my sister—Frau Oliva," she said now and he got his first good look at the other woman. Liquid brown eyes smiled up at him from beneath the wide brim of her straw hat. He knew a quickening little glow of pleasure as he took in her trim figure and the fresh, firm column of her throat exposed by the white lace waist. And he liked the frank way she shook hands and said: "Delighted, Herr Bartsch."

"Sit down, sit down!" Schani urged and pulled him down in the empty chair beside Frau Oliva.

"You wouldn't think she was my sister, now would you?" Frau Gregor laughed her bell-like laugh again. "Schani says if I get any fatter he is going to put me in the circus."

"Waiter! Another liter of Gumpoldskirchner," Schani ordered.

Herr Bartsch met the smiling brown eyes of Frau Oliva again. For a second or so they explored each other, then they both had to smile.

"A real woman!" Herr Bartsch told himself excitedly. He thought he could discern lots of spirit behind those mischief-flecked eyes.

"You better watch out, Ludwig! She's a widow," Schani warned, then turned to her with a broad wink: "And you want to watch yourself too, Liesel! Ludwig's an old sinner—I know!"

"Why didn't you bring Frau Bartsch?" Frau Gregor asked politely and a little mischievously, since she knew as everybody else in the neighborhood did that she never went anywhere but to church.

"She's with the priests," Herr Bartsch chuckled, "praying for me."

"It hasn't done much good so far, has it?" Schani said with a great guffaw. "Do you remember that time in Grinzing at the trapshoot when she made you go to Mass first? I've always said she prayed me out of winning from you—Ah, here's our wine. . . ."

While Schani was busy filling their glasses, Frau Oliva turned to Herr Bartsch.

"Do you always look so grumpy?" she teased.

"Maybe it's because I'm not used to good company any more—and pretty women."

It had been a long time since he had felt so exhilarated by a woman. From sheer pleasure at her nearness he laughed a deep laugh.

"Are you from Styria, too, like Schani?"

"Yes, I'm a *Steirer*. And you? You look like a real *Wienerin* to me. . . ."

"I am! Born and bred in Vienna. Oh, look! They're dancing a *Schuhplattler*—I wish I could be up there dancing; I'm just in the mood for it, but you'd have to show me how."

He looked at her appreciatively. Yes, she'd look good up there on the stage with her slim waist and swelling bosom and her melting, roguish eyes that drew you like a magnet. She'd look good anywhere. A man'd be proud to be seen with her. Now, if he'd only had a woman like her instead of a whining old biddy who thought of nothing but running to church all day long, he might have been somebody, got somewhere. He felt the old surge of ambition inside him again which had lain dormant for years. But it was too late now. In another ten, twelve years he'd be eligible for his pension.

He forced himself to break off his gloomy speculation and look at the stage like the others. Might as well have a good time. . . .

"Listen, Herr Bartsch! She's singing the song from the *Fledermaus!* That's my favorite song. . . ."

Frau Oliva had put her hand on his arm and was letting it stay there for a minute. Her eyes shimmered moistly and her face glowed from all the wine they had drunk and from laughter. Herr Bartsch felt a little dizzy with the consciousness of the warmth and fragrance of her body so close to him. His eyes could not help straying to the softly rounded shoulders and the firm curve of her breasts beneath the white blouse.

She became aware that he was watching her. Her cheeks flushed a richer pink.

"You aren't listening," she chided. "Don't you like it?"

"I'd like anything right now."

"I've seen the *Fledermaus* eleven times. I think there's nothing like a good operetta, though I like a good drama too, once in a while."

He hesitated for a second, not sure whether she might not snub him. She couldn't be a day over thirty-five—if she was that.

"I can get you tickets for the Burgtheater any time you want."

"That's awfully nice of you, Herr Bartsch. But what would I do with tickets? I wouldn't have anyone to go with. Neither Schani nor my sister likes serious plays. I used to go with my other sister all the time, but she's in Germany now. And I don't think it's proper for a woman to go alone to the theater, do you?"

Herr Bartsch decided to risk it:

"Well, how'd I do?"

She measured him tentatively.

"All right, let's!" Her laugh had a reckless edge that caused his blood to tingle. "That is, if your wife won't scold you?"

It was his turn to laugh carelessly:

"Oh, she! She doesn't have to know everything, and what she doesn't know won't hurt her."

Frau Oliva sipped her wine with well-bred little sips. Her eyes followed a woman who was wearing an extravagantly large hat.

"Did you see that hat!" she invited him to look. "If that's going to be the fashion, I'd just as soon wear a kerchief over my head."

"Looks like she had half the menagerie from Schönbrunn on it," he chuckled.

"Doesn't it? And look at those heels! Just like stilts. Not for me! I like simple things, but good."

Appreciatively again, he glanced at her own straw hat with only a red velvet ribbon around it. Simple all right, but very stylish. She knew what was what—any fool could see that. Sensible, too. . . . He wondered whether it would be too soon to ask her for Thursday. Thursday he would not be working. . . .

Frau Oliva took his arm with engaging spontaneity, as if it were the most natural thing in the world for her to do, when they finally left the *Heurigen*. Schani and his wife were just ahead of them and paused from time to time to throw some joking remark over their shoulders. A laughing, chattering, straggling procession stretched all the way up to the streetcar terminus along the rustic sidewalk.

In front of the waiting-shed a crowd was already waiting for the next train of red and white cars to be made up and come slowly swaying around the loop. As each train came to a stop, there was a good-natured stampede for the cars until the conductors shouted "*Komplett*" and what was left of the crowd had to draw back and wait for the next train.

When they had finally got to the front of the platform and just as he was about to help Frau Oliva up on a car, a mountainously fat woman with a big bunch of wilted wild flowers crowded Frau Oliva against him, so that her breasts pressed against his chest and he could feel her warm thigh against his leg. Frau Oliva drew away immediately, flushed just like a girl, then gave him a quick smile that had nothing of the little girl in it at all. Emboldened by the brief contact, he passed his arm around her waist and gave it a little squeeze. Her fingers seized on his hand in instant reproof, but relented almost immediately and even responded with an unmistakably forgiving pressure as she stepped up on the car.

Inside the car there was another rush for seats. By the time he had got on behind her there were only two vacant ones left. Herr Bartsch managed to reach one seat together with an anemic-looking youth who said "Pardon" in an affected, nasal voice. Angered, Herr Bartsch grasped the boy's elbow and lifted him off balance and to one side.

The maneuver had not escaped Frau Oliva. She rewarded him with a ravishing smile as he handed her to the seat. He himself held on to the leather strap above her. From time to time their eyes locked in a half-mocking exchange of glances, because they were after all grown people, but their communion seemed nevertheless delightfully intimate and made Herr Bartsch feel warm all over. He had completely forgotten about the Gregors who were probably in one of the cars up front. By the time they had passed Baumgarten and the reservoir, his mind was made up. He bent down toward her:

"They are giving *Don Carlos* in the Burgtheater this Thursday. Would you like to see that?"

Her eyes answered him before her mouth did.

"Why, that would be lovely, Herr Bartsch!"

Chapter Four

He was sure without looking that the sun outside was playing over the roof across the yard and on the Breitner windows. It was going to be a beautiful day.

He knew he should get up or *she* would come in again and scold, but he lay there clutching at the tantalizing fragments of the dream she had scattered when she woke him, hoping they would fall into a pattern again.

All sorts of pleasant images chased each other across his consciousness: himself and Rudi in a toy train big enough for them to ride on in the garden of a villa in Hütteldorf, then Rudi's mother coming to call them to a delicious *Jause* in a summerhouse. Then it wasn't Rudi's mother any longer but Aunt Wetti, and then some woman he didn't know at all. She was beautiful and she had come from very far to take him away with her, and she had bought him many boxes with presents in them. . . . Next it was a man who had given him a box with a lot of money in it: he had bought a beautiful gray automobile like the one Franz's friend, the Baron, had and he and Rudi were riding through the Mariahilferstrasse——

The creaking of the door cut short his dream.

"Are you going to get up now! I'm not calling you again!"

He sat up guiltily. She was gone before he could promise, "I'm getting up."

He started to pull on his stockings, then remembered the coin the man had given him last night. He reached for his pants to see whether it was still there. It was. Relieved, he hurriedly pulled on his stockings, then his shoes, and then the rest.

He slipped off the couch and peered toward the bed against the short wall of the long, narrow room. Franz was still asleep. His soft, blond mop of hair had fallen down over his forehead; the thrown-off blanket revealed the upper part of his chest and his muscular shoulders. When he was sure that Franz was still asleep,

Peter stole to the desk opposite the couch. The automobile goggles were there beside Franz's pocketbook and watch. He tried on the goggles and looked out through the window. He was a little disappointed when he found that the roof and the Breitner windows looked much the same as they always did. He had somehow expected things to look different. Still the feel of the heavy goggles thrilled him. He wished that he could take them to school to show to the other boys.

The clatter of a pan out in the kitchen made him take off the goggles hurriedly. He put them back on the desk and went out into the living room.

Father was by the chest of drawers brushing his mustaches. He looked all ready to leave except for putting on his coat and hat. His neck still shone ruddily from recent scrubbing. Peter could not tell whether he was in a good humor or not and slipped by him with a hasty, "Good morning, Father," into the kitchen.

Poldi was still at the washstand. Her arms and shoulders were bare and she snatched up her towel and held it against her.

"You turn to the window!" she commanded. When he had turned around, she fumed: "One can't even wash decently in this place! I don't see why we can't have an apartment big enough for me to have a room to myself. I want a room of my own."

"You and your fancy notions!" *she* scoffed from the stove. "I guess we're going to rent a villa just for you—as if that boy were going to hurt you."

"Other people can live in decent apartments. I can't see why we can't!"

"I guess this flat is good enough for you," *she* said more acridly now. Her voice became a curious dry hiss when she was irritated. "It's done us for twenty years and nobody ever complained until you came along with your big ideas."

"I don't care. Franz has a room he can call his own. I want some privacy, too."

"You'll get your privacy in a minute if you don't stop this!" Father had appeared in the door from the living room. Peter turned around to watch.

"Mother!" Poldi appealed to her shrilly. She was holding the towel over her throat and shoulders again. "Tell Father to go away."

Poldi had brown eyes like *she* had. They flashed angrily at Father now.

"One more word out of you," Father threatened, "and I'll give you something else to think about."

Watching him, Peter had a feeling that Father was not really angry at all. You could not always tell with Father when he frowned like this. Sometimes he pretended to be stern and Peter was sure that Father was really secretly laughing. It was a kind of play acting because Father felt he ought to be stern. Just like Father's threats to get the strap—he had never beaten him yet, and he had only slapped Poldi once, a long time ago, because Poldi had kept on talking back to him. On the other hand, it was easy for Father to get really angry if anyone irritated him when he was in this mood—as now when *she* said peevishly from the stove: "You leave her alone. She wasn't talking to you." Father at once gave the impression of planting his feet more solidly on the floor. His eyes which had been merely stern before had become a hard, brittle blue. Poldi who was still holding the towel over her shoulders had started to cry from exasperation. Father looked at her briefly, then turned and stamped back into the living room. A minute later he came out through the kitchen and left without another glance at anyone.

Poldi had gone into the living room to dress.

"You get on with your washing," *she* said to him. "Here, get some water."

He picked up the water can and went out on the landing to the tap. When he came back, she was setting out Poldi's coffee on the kitchen cabinet in the pink-flowered cup that had always been Poldi's.

He started to wash. Poldi came out wearing her white blouse with the small blue dots which she had so far worn only on Sundays.

"Did you brush your teeth?" Poldi asked. "Where is the toothbrush I bought you?"

"Here." He got it down from the shelf above the washstand and started to brush his teeth.

"And, Mother, he needs a haircut. Can't you send him to the barber today?"

"You send him if you've got so much money. Time enough if he goes before his first communion."

"I hope you aren't going to let them use the clippers again so that he looks like a yokel."

"No, I'm going to have him fixed up to suit you! As if a haircut that's good enough for other boys weren't good enough for him."

"Other boys don't get their hair cut like that either. There's no need for him to look like a peasant. Where's the strainer, Mother?"

"A little skin isn't going to hurt you. The best part of the milk. You'll be sorry someday, you mark my words!"

"Oh, Mother!" Arguments between them invariably ended on this note of exasperation.

Peter sat on the chair by the sewing machine and waited until Poldi had finished her roll and coffee, then he went to take her place at the kitchen cabinet. *She* brought him his coffee in his white enamel cup. There were several bits of skin floating on top; he looked at it with revulsion.

"Mother, there's skin on the coffee," he complained.

She went on rinsing Poldi's cup.

"I don't like skin."

"You drink your coffee or I'll show you," she said angrily.

"But I don't like it."

"Whether you like it or not, you're going to drink it."

He looked dolefully at the strainer she had just rinsed, then at the skin. He hated skin on coffee. It made him sick just to look at it. It was like the horse-radish sauce she was always making him eat. Tears bit at his eyes but he did not dare protest any longer. He moved as many bits of skin as he could to the rim of the cup with his spoon, then forced himself to drink it by closing his eyes and stuffing his mouth with pieces of roll to kill the taste.

Poldi stopped on her way out.

"Did you memorize the poem?"

"Yes," he said sulkily. He did not like to be asked about his homework.

"You'll have to get nothing but 'ones' in your report if you want to go to the *Gymnasium*. They only take boys who stand high."

"*Gymnasium!*" *she* broke in. "He needs to go to a *Gymnasium!* He is going to public school like all the other boys. You just go on putting ideas in his head! He's going to the *Bürgerschule.*"

"We'll see about that!"

"Who's going to pay for it, I'd like to know?"

"I am. And I'm going to write his mother. The least she can do is to see that he gets an education."

"You leave Mizzi alone," *she* said threateningly. "I've brought him up so far and I don't need anything from her now."

"Brought him up! If he goes to the *Bürgerschule* all he'll be fit for is a counterjumper!"

"And what's wrong with that, I'd like to know? An honest trade——"

"We'll talk about that later," Poldi said haughtily from the door. "Good-by."

He wondered as he went down the stairs on his way to school whether *she* was serious about not wanting him to go to the *Gymnasium.* He had assumed all along that he would go to school in the big white granite building with the imposing columns in the Kandlgasse. Franz had gone there! Why else had they all been after him all the time to get good marks? Not that he was at the head of his class. The best he had been able to do was to get a respectable mixture of "ones" and "twos." There were at least five boys in class who had more "ones" than he had. It was his handwriting that stood in the way. Herr Renzl always marked him off for it. He never could make an arithmetic exercise or an essay look as neat as Rudi, for instance, no matter how hard he tried. It was as if some perverse genius dogged him and made any written work he did look sloppy.

He crossed the cobblestone courtyard to the tunnel-like entranceway which led out into the street. Frau Schreier, the janitor's wife, was talking to the gigantic man who worked for the express company several houses farther up the street. There was something queer about the man and Frau Schreier. He had heard people refer to it several times when they had talked to *her* about Frau Schreier. It was one of those things he did not understand and she refused to tell him about, but he knew that it was something wrong. So he felt vaguely uncomfortable when Frau Schreier called cheerfully, "Good morning, Peterl."

He returned her greeting and hurried past them out to the street. Karl Breitner was waiting for him on the sidewalk.

"Where've you been? I've been waiting for half an hour," Karl boasted.

"I just got up," Peter lied. He did not like to admit to Karl that he was not allowed to come downstairs any earlier. He felt at once superior to Karl and inferior to him—superior, because Karl was in 5-b, the slower section of the grade, and inferior, because Karl was allowed to play in the street and go to the park and knew lots of older boys in the house.

"I played soccer yesterday," Karl announced. "On the Schmeltz. Then we had a rock fight with a gang from Ottakring and then I went to the movies."

"I saw a horse shy on the Ring," Peter invented on the spur of the moment so that Karl would not think that nothing exciting had happened to him yesterday. "It ran away and almost killed a woman."

"Was she hurt?"

"Sure she was hurt. She was almost dead."

"I bet it wasn't dangerous. We played until dark; then was when we had the fight. One of the boys had a hole as big as this in his head—" Karl stuck out his fist to show the size of the hole—"and they had to take him to a doctor. I bet you had to go to church again with your mother!"

"I didn't! We went for a walk to the Burgtheater." Peter was glad that he could mention the theater because Karl knew that Father worked there and it sounded as if he had been inside.

"Did you see the play?"

"No, but we were in back where the stage is."

"I can go backstage, too, in the Raimund Theater, any time I want to. My father knows a man there. I'd rather go to the movies. It's much more exciting than the theater."

They had turned into the Kandlgasse. The sidewalks on either side of the street were crowded with children and with mothers taking the smaller children to school. Two blocks farther up the street was the Gymnasium. When they stood outside on the steps of their school, Peter could see its big white bulk which towered a whole story above the other buildings near it.

The warning gong rang inside and he turned to go in.

"What do you want to go in for already?" Karl jeered. "Afraid of the teacher?"

"I have some homework I've got to finish," Peter lied again. He was anxious to get upstairs to see whether Rudi had come. He left Karl on the steps and went upstairs.

It was still several minutes before the final gong and Herr Renzl was not yet in the room. He looked around for Rudi and did not see him anywhere. Disappointed, he stowed his schoolbag on the shelf under his desk and drifted over to the group of boys around Fröschl. Fröschl had a new ivory penholder and the boys around him were taking turns looking through a tiny lens in it. It appeared that one could see a panorama of Munich by looking through it. Fröschl's father owned a silk factory and was always going on long trips to Germany and even to Denmark and England, from which he brought back souvenirs which Fröschl showed off in school. While he waited for his turn to look through the penholder, Peter kept on the edge of the eagerly talking group. He did not feel shy with them usually, but when they were talking about their parents' plans for the vacation or about their new stamp catalogues—as now—he felt suddenly left out and inferior. And he became acutely conscious of his clothes.

All the other boys were wearing either sailor suits with blue or white blouses or Norfolk suits which had obviously come from a store and contrasted sharply with his homemade brown jacket and the patched, gray pants which hung below his knees. He hated the way *she* always cut the pants she made for him. Looking at the other boys around him, it seemed to him that he would never want anything quite as much as a pair of blue, snug-fitting pants which ended elegantly above the knees. Then there were his stockings and his old, high shoes—all the other boys had been wearing sandals and gaily colored socks ever since April. . . .

Herr Renzl had come into the room. The group broke up abruptly and Peter went to his desk. Herr Renzl, too, Peter saw, wore sandals—brand-new, shiny, black ones.

The gong shrilled in the corridor. Rudi still had not come. They rose and said the "Our Father" and the class began. It was a reading lesson. Madenski, who was one of Herr Renzl's favorites and who never had anything but "ones" on his report card, was called to the platform out front. He recited the first two stanzas of the poem they had had to memorize, was praised, and came back to his seat. Herr Renzl's eyes wandered over the class. Peter hoped that he would not call on him. He did not want to stand up there on the platform where they could all see the new patch on his left knee. He sat very straight with his hands folded on the desk so as not to attract the teacher's attention. Around him several hands were raised.

"Domanig!"

There it was! He fought down the constriction at the pit of his stomach and went up to the platform. He did not mind reciting. If he had only had sandals like Madenski and gay red socks, he was certain he would even have liked it. As it was, after he had gone through one stanza he forgot about his clothes and did the next one as he had done it at home when he had memorized the poem. Herr Renzl seemed to be pleased. He made him do three stanzas in all before he sent him back to his seat.

He tried to see what mark Herr Renzl was putting down in his book. He could not tell whether it was a "two" or a "one" from where he sat, but Lembacher in the front row surreptitiously stuck out two fingers into the aisle.

He was disappointed. He felt that he had deserved a "one." He wondered whether his clothes had anything to do with the fact that Herr Renzl did not like him the way he did eight or nine other boys. With the exception of Heindl, whose father was only a janitor, all of Herr Renzl's favorites were boys whose parents were rich, it occurred to him suddenly.

The poem had been recited all the way through once and Fröschl started from the beginning again. He had hardly got started when the door opened softly and Rudi came in.

Peter watched him proudly as he walked from the door to Herr Renzl's desk to present his note. His heart had begun to pound a little with excitement. Everything about the familiar classroom had taken on a subtle significance that made the moment seem memorable.

Rudi was still waiting beside the desk. He was a handsome, healthy-looking boy with long, dark eyes and soft, brown hair. A certain languor in his movements gave him an engaging, almost dainty awkwardness. This impression was at least partly due to his immaculate grooming, and Peter could not have said whether it was the white blouse with the blue sailor collar and the blue and white striped socks and brown sandals, or Rudi's slow way of speaking, or the way Rudi always managed to remain miraculously clean even when they wrestled or played soccer before choir class in the afternoons that drew him to Rudi. He only knew that ever since Christmas he had been happiest when he had been able to be with Rudi. . . .

Herr Renzl nodded to Rudi now—a friendly, intimate nod such as only his favorites got—and Rudi came toward his seat. He smiled at Peter as he came down the aisle. The smile completed Peter's happiness. Out of the corner of his eye he watched Rudi slide his leather bag under his desk and sit down. Only the fear of Herr Renzl's disapproval kept him from trying to catch Rudi's eye during the remaining half-hour. He could hardly wait for the end of the class.

"Did you see the fireworks?"

"I looked for you," Rudi said earnestly. "Mama did, too."

"I couldn't go—did you see the diver? Was it high?"

"As high as our house. Only, Mama said it wasn't quite as high. I started the railroad in the garden. We can build a bridge over the brook and a tunnel—can you come next Sunday? Mama said you could come every Sunday. . . ."

"I'll have to ask. . . ."

It seemed to him that he was always having to ask for things that other boys took as a matter of course, and that he was always being turned down. That day, after lunch, while he was drying the dishes, he said:

"Rudi Martin is going to the park, Mother, after school—can I go with him?"

"You are coming home where you belong and not going gallivanting around the streets like that Breitner boy."

"But it isn't Karl! It's Rudi and his mother is taking him to the park."

"His mother can do what she wants. You're coming home after school."

The whole afternoon went wrong after that. Herr Renzl caught him drawing pictures—he always drew when he was angry or sad, almost without being aware of it—and Herr Renzl had made a note in the big register. Now he would probably get a bad mark in deportment and Father would really beat him with the strap. And to make matters worse, he got mixed up on a question in catechism and Pater Alfred not only wrote something in his record book but made a remark that showed that Herr Renzl had told him about the drawing. Pater Alfred would probably tell her when she went to confession to him on Saturday.

He was even more miserable when he found that Rudi's mother was waiting for them in front of the school. She carried a gay parasol tilted over one shoulder and in her other hand held a fashionable rattan bag with Rudi's *Jause* and his ball in it. He experienced a pang of envy as he watched her bend down to kiss Rudi.

He shifted uneasily when she turned to him with a smile:

"Rudi said you were coming to the park with us, Peter?"

He stammered: "I can't—I'd like to, but I have to go home."

"Oh, I'm sorry. I brought some *Jause* for you—see?" She held the rattan bag open so that he could see the buttered rolls and the paper bag full of cherries. "Would you like some cherries?"

"No, thank you," he said hastily. "I'll get my *Jause* at home."

"But you can take some cherries all the same," she urged. "Rudi can't eat them all. I got them for you."

He had not had any cherries yet that spring and perhaps he would not get any later either, except maybe one or two when *she* bought some for cooking. But his pride would not let him give in.

He turned once or twice to watch Rudi and his mother walk up the Kandlgasse toward the *Gymnasium* and the park. He himself walked along slowly, his feet leaden with unwillingness to go home. By the time he entered the house and crossed the courtyard, the afternoon stretched ahead of him drab and desolate. Tomorrow was washday—she would be starting to take the washing down into the laundry in the cellar to soak. . . .

But in the kitchen there was no sign of the usual preparations for washday yet. She was working on the wide board which folded down over Poldi's bed during the day, chalking marks on a piece of blue serge.

All his grievances against her were suddenly forgotten—he *was* getting a new suit for his first communion! He could hardly contain his excitement.

"Is it for me, Mother?" he asked, before he had even got his schoolbag off his back.

"Don't ask so many questions. You'll find out in due time."

Then he saw something that made his heart sink again. She was measuring the length of the pants he had worn yesterday. Was she going to make the new pants hang down over his knees like all the others?

"Mother, can I have short pants like all the other boys?"

She had some pins between her lips and did not answer him.

"Can I have them short, Mother?"

"You take what you get and be grateful that you are getting a new suit at all."

He did not dare insist. If she thought that he was set on having the pants short, she would only make them hang down even farther over his knees. She always did things contrary to what he begged her for.

"Am I going to have a blue collar?"

"If you don't stop bothering me, you won't get anything. If it had been for me, you wouldn't have had a new suit anyhow. You can thank Poldi for that."

He drifted into the living room. At a loss for something to do, he decided to sneak into Franz's room. He had to do it stealthily for she did not allow him to be there during the day. Getting the ruler from Franz's desk for his homework was the excuse he usually used when she caught him.

He lingered at the ornate desk which like the upholstered chairs and the chest of drawers in the living room had once been stage properties and had been brought home by Father. There was a disturbing discord in Franz's room between the arrogant elegance of the desk and the drabness of the rest of the furniture. The washstand with some of its veneer peeled off suffered most by the comparison, but to Peter, his eyes roving scornfully around the room, the bed seemed an even worse offender against the standard set by the desk, even though its walnut veneer was quite without blemish. What exasperated him about the bed was its dull, heavy lines which suggested a complacent bourgeois humility. It was as if the bed were saying: "I make no pretense—I am what I am—I know my place!" It struck him that the bed was just like her:

stubborn to the point of immovability and exasperatingly humble.

His eyes went to the crossed sabers on the wall above the bed. They had been there ever since Franz had finished his military service last fall. Still thinking of her, it struck him now that Franz was a little like her, too. Even though Franz had been a second lieutenant, an officer, and worked in the War Ministry now, and had a baron for his friend, he did not seem to mind being poor. Franz did not even seem to notice how dowdy she always looked. Had he not brought Baron Ortner upstairs one Sunday so that Peter had winced every time Baron Ortner had addressed her as *Gnädige Frau?*

Yet he loved Franz! Franz was always making people laugh, and when he went out the flat seemed empty and cheerless. And he had dozens of friends and he was always going to parties with them and looking much handsomer than they did even though he did not have such good clothes.

It was funny, but Poldi whom he did not like half so much, he understood much better. Poldi was constantly irritated by the same things he found unbearable. Poldi nagged at *her*, for instance, about the way she dressed, about the homely expressions she always used, about the way she seemed almost to enjoy being poor.

Someday, he resolved passionately, he would be free from all this! He would live on the Ring—or better still, in one of those haughtily retiring villas in Hütteldorf or in Mödling—and he would wear elegant clothes like Baron Ortner and have an automobile, and he would go to church only when he wanted to. . . .

Carried away by his ambitious daydream, he had not heard her come through the living room.

She squinted at him suspiciously from the door.

"I thought I'd told you that you weren't supposed to come in here?"

He picked up Franz's ruler hurriedly.

"I was just getting the ruler."

She waited until he had sat down at the big table beside the divan in the living room, then she went back into the kitchen. He opened his schoolbag. There was a composition he had to write for tomorrow. He decided against it. There'd be plenty of time in the evening. He got out the drawing pad instead, took down the blue vase from Father's wardrobe, and started to draw. The drawing was not due until Thursday, but as always when he did not feel like doing any other homework, he chose drawing. It was easy and exciting and the only subject in which he was easily at the head of the class. Herr Renzl did not even hold his clumsy lettering of the titles against him enough to give him less than a "one."

He had nearly finished drawing the vase when the sound of footsteps on the landing made him pause. The front door was flung open boisterously.

"Light! Food! I'm hungry!" in a deep voice, buoyant with laughter.

It was Franz! Peter climbed down from the chair as fast as he could and went to the kitchen door to watch. Franz had come up behind her by the stove and was sniffing the air with pretended scorn.

"Kale! What else have you got for me, you old dragon?"

He towered above her by a whole head and now made as if to lift her off the floor by the elbows. She turned and slapped his hand.

"You get away from here! You'll find out when it's on the table."

"Be sure it's something more than kale or I'll tell Pater Alfred what a raven mother you are."

To Peter the spectacle of Franz jollying her never lost its element of surprise and of faint impropriety. What made it even more puzzling was that she actually seemed to like it.

He drew aside to let Franz pass, even though the door was a wide one. It always seemed to him as if Franz needed lots of room.

"How are you, shrimp?" Franz called to him.

The bric-a-brac on the two wardrobes quavered softly with the vibration of his long strides. Peter wanted to follow him into his room but did not dare because of her. He went back to his drawing and started to niggle at this line and that. He wanted it to be perfect; perhaps Franz would look at it.

She appeared suddenly in the kitchen door.

"You clear off the table now," she commanded. "Right away! Franz has to eat."

"Just one more minute," he begged. "I've only a little more——"

"I said right away!"

He was hoping desperately that Franz would come out from his room. He wanted Franz to see the drawing but he did not want to ask him to come and look. When he had stalled as long as he dared, he picked up the vase to put it back on top of Father's wardrobe. On his way past Franz's door, he stopped to peer in at him. Franz was taking off his necktie and the stiff collar. Franz saw him and grinned.

"What have you been up to today?" Then he saw the drawing things on the table and came to look. He pinched Peter's shoulder before he bent over the drawing.

"Not bad, shrimp. But where's all the gold business?" Franz pointed to the gold filigree on the indigo blue background of the vase.

"I thought it looked better without it."

"You sure that was the reason?" Franz asked, and Peter felt guilty even though he had decided that he did not like the gold ornamentation and had left it out deliberately. It seemed terribly important that Franz believe him.

"I'll draw it again for you," he said breathlessly. "I'll draw it just as it is."

Franz squeezed his shoulder. "All right, I believe you. Did you know that artists often leave out things?"

Peter shook his head. He hadn't known that. All that mattered was that Franz mustn't think that he could not have put in the gold business if he had wanted to.

"That's called composition," Franz said. "Composition is very important in painting. Maybe someday you'll be an artist like——"

"Don't you, too, go putting ideas in his head," she interrupted irritably from the kitchen. "He better learn to write a decent hand without making blots all over the paper."

"Never mind," Franz consoled him. "You work hard at your drawing and some Saturday I'll take you to the museum and we'll look at some real pictures. Ask Mother for some hot water for me, will you?"

Flushed with excitement at Franz's praise, he put away the drawing and the paintbox which had once belonged to Franz. Then he hurried into the kitchen for the hot water.

He still had to set the table, but he also wanted to watch Franz shave. He quickly laid the four places—Father was not coming home tonight; it was one of the nights when he worked in the theater—then got the bread out of the breadbox in the kitchen and the big bread knife and took them in to the table.

Franz was in his undershirt when Peter edged into his room. He was lathering his face. Peter watched silently while he slapped on great dabs of soap and rubbed it around his chin. He wanted to ask Franz where he and Baron Ortner had gone in the automobile on Sunday but he thought it wiser to wait until Franz spoke first.

Franz started to strop his razor.

"When are you going to have your examination for the choir?" he asked.

"I don't know, Franz. I think in June. That's what Professor Wessely said Herr Granini said."

"Granini is a great man," Franz said enthusiastically.

"Are the examinations hard?"

Franz grinned at him.

"Not very. Herr Granini only wants to see what kind of a voice you've got."

"Were you in the choir long, Franz?"

"Until my voice broke."

"Why does one's voice break?"

"Everybody's voice breaks. Then you get a deeper voice and you are all set."

"Will your voice break again?"

Franz chuckled. "I hope not."

"Did you go far in the automobile yesterday, Franz?"

"Up on the Kobenzl."

"All the way up?"

"To the very top where the restaurant is."

"Franz, is it dangerous riding in an automobile?"

Franz had understood what he meant. "Yes, it's exciting," he said. "When you are older, you'll see."

He had started to shave. Peter knew that he must not talk now or Franz might cut himself. He watched intently while Franz pulled at the skin around his Adam's apple, which always seemed to him one of the strange, mysterious things about grown men, like the hair on their chests and legs.

Franz lathered his whole face again and went all over it a second time with the razor. Then he poured more water into the porcelain basin and washed with much spluttering. The spluttering and splashing when he washed seemed to Peter as inseparable from Franz as his mop of soft, blond hair, or his long stride, or his friendly blue eyes with the pale blond eyebrows over them. Nobody else was allowed to splash by *her*. When Poldi did it in the kitchen, *she* scolded at once and made Poldi wipe up the water on the floor.

Franz was rubbing his face and neck vigorously with the big towel. His face glowed a cheerful pink. Peter was suddenly aware of how different Franz looked from all the rest of them. Father's face was red and solid, *hers* was almost round with knobbly cheeks, and Poldi's was oval and much darker than Franz's face, which was long and bony with a wide mouth and brilliant teeth. But it was his eyes that were most different. *She* and Poldi had brown eyes which were always serious—Franz's were a light, clear blue. Father had blue eyes, too, but they were so small and pinched behind his pince-nez that they seemed hardly blue at all but gray, while Franz's were large and always so wide open that one saw a little of the white above and below the pupil. One had the impression that Franz was constantly laughing at something.

Franz noticed that he was looking at him and grinned.

"How about washing the brush for me, shrimp, and emptying the washbowl?"

"Yes, Franz." Anything that would allow him to stay in the room with him a little longer. Franz, however, tucked in the tail of the clean shirt he had just put on and went out into the kitchen.

"Mother, can you spare me five kronen?" Peter heard him ask her.

"You must think I'm made of money," she complained. "The rent is due next week. What did you do with the two kronen I gave you yesterday?"

"Gone, Mother!" Franz sighed dramatically. "Now, you know you've got lots of money. I'll give it back to you on the first."

"You're not coming to any good running around with barons and going to the opera every night! And driving around in automobiles on Sunday instead of being in church."

"Who said we weren't in church? Why, Heinrich's mother has her own chapel in Baden, right inside the castle. Now could anything be more religious than having your own chapel right in the house?"

"You can't fool me," she grumbled. "Chapel or no chapel. You mark my words: nothing good can come out of all this riding around in automobiles. Someday you'll have an accident like the boy on the corner and they'll bring you home in an ambulance."

"Not with all the praying you do for me," Franz teased. "Not a chance."

When he came back into the room, Peter saw him put down the silver coins beside his wallet on the desk.

"Are you going to the opera tonight, Franz?"

"Yes, shrimp. I'm going to hear some great music tonight."

"Is it better than Herr Granini's choir?"

"It's different, Peter. More like the theater, only the actors sing instead of talking."

"Will I be able to go to the opera when I get to the *Gymnasium?*"

"Well, after you've got on a little way, I'll take you sometime. But you'll have to get good marks."

"Oh, I will, Franz," he promised fervently.

Poldi stopped in the kitchen while he was wiping the dishes after supper.

"I'm going to Mama's," she announced. "We're having an Italian lesson."

Mama was the tall woman with the gold-rimmed glasses and the gray hair at whose apartment in the Kaiserstrasse Poldi and her friends were always meeting.

"You and your 'Mama'!" she grumbled. Her voice conveyed her unshakable suspicion of anything touched with refinement. But she did not say anything more. Mama was one of the patronesses of the congregation to which Poldi belonged and immensely devout. There was no foothold there for criticism.

Poldi took a glass and went out on the landing to draw a drink of water. When she came back she said: "Mama is taking us on an excursion to Mödling next Sunday."

"Well, don't expect one heller from me. I don't know now how I'm going to get the rent together this month."

"I won't need any money. Mama is treating us," Poldi said haughtily. "I'll be home at ten."

When he had finished with the dishes, he went into the living room where the lamp was still burning from supper and started to read the book Rudi had lent him. It was a collection of hunting stories illustrated with many photographs. The stories really bored him but he read on doggedly because Rudi had liked the book.

She came in to close the windows. Out of the corner of his eyes Peter saw that she had changed her blouse and had put on the black sateen apron she wore to go out on weekdays.

"Get your cap. We're going out."

"Can't I stay and read?"

"You're not going to stay here alone with the lamp."

He put down the book and went to get his cap.

"Where are we going?"

"We're going to see Frau Gerstecker because she's sick."

"Oh, I don't like sick people. Can't I stay in the courtyard till you come back?"

"And play with all the roughnecks from the street! You're coming with me. It isn't going to hurt you to visit a sick woman who's all alone in the world, for a few minutes!"

The visit ahead of him filled him with dismay. He had never liked Frau Gerstecker, a big, rawboned old woman who was very poor and who came every Thursday afternoon for something to eat. The fact that she was ill only added to his aversion as they approached the Neustiftgasse. Sick people repelled him almost as much as the funerals to which she was always taking him.

Frau Gerstecker lived in an old single-story house which was gloomy even in the daytime. A single gas flame flickered in the entranceway now and cast eerie shadows. The gas jet burned at the tip of a resplendent torch held aloft by a blackened bronze figure of a naked boy. Just beyond him a door with varicolored panes led out into a small, dank courtyard. They crossed the yard and climbed an outside stone stair with a rusty cast-iron railing. The door at the head of the stair stood half open. She knocked and was answered by a groan.

The door opened into a kitchen which was dark. A musty, acrid smell came from the room beyond, where Frau Gerstecker was lying. It was the stench he had come to associate with sickrooms.

She had already gone into the room and turned up the kerosene lamp. He ventured timidly as far as the door. The room was crowded with dilapidated furniture. Frau Gerstecker was wearing a rumpled white flannel jacket, he saw, and her gray hair was lank with perspiration and hung down over her temples and forehead. On the night-table beside the bed was a confusion of medicine bottles with stained, messy labels.

"I brought you some nice, strong broth," *she* was saying as she straightened Frau Gerstecker's pillows. "That's what you need, not all those pills that doctor feeds you."

"God bless you, Frau Bartsch. I'll never——"

"I brought the boy along." She cut short Frau Gerstecker's thanks. "He only gets into mischief if I leave him home alone."

Frau Gerstecker turned her head to look at him. He felt uncomfortable with her burning, deeply sunken eyes searching for him. He saw that her face had a sickening yellow color that was broken by big brown splotches.

"Hello, Peterl," she said. "Come to see a sick, old woman——" She made a sound that was half a groan and half a chuckle. "Come and sit down. Don't be afraid. . . ."

Reluctantly he went and sat on the edge of an ancient easy chair. The heavy, stale air nauseated him. He tried to hold his breath so that he would not have to breathe.

Frau Gerstecker was drinking the soup *she* had brought. When she had finished it, they started to talk about Frau Gerstecker's illness and then about some people who had had the same illness, and he lost interest. He looked around the room. There was only the rickety furniture which cluttered up every bit of space: old-fashioned chairs with curved legs which were broken and had been clumsily wired to the seat, a chest of drawers with most of the handles missing, a blind mirror—the only object in the room which even faintly interested him was a bronze clock on a table: the clock face was part of a globe which was supported by two elephants.

She was talking about religion. Her voice had taken on that impersonal dreariness which at once bored and exasperated him. He longed to escape from the oppressive air that filled the room, from the sight of the old woman with her yellow face, from his uncomfortable position on the dilapidated chair. When *she* mentioned the words "extreme unction" for the second time, Frau Gerstecker groaned. Her eyes, which seemed to him to be even brighter than before, rolled around the room, then came to rest on him. She croaked:

"Peterl, will you pray for me?"

Embarrassed, he nodded.

"Can't you say anything?" *she* said peevishly.

He swallowed hard. "Yes, Frau Gerstecker."

Frau Gerstecker suddenly whispered something to her, and *she* turned to him:

"You go downstairs in the yard and wait for me. I'll be down in a few minutes."

He was relieved to get out of the room and down into the yard. The moon was up and a pale light picked out the weather-worn granite fountain against the wall. The fountain was almost completely overgrown with a rank, tumbling mass of ivy. He tried to pass the time by examining the heart-shaped flower bed in front of the fountain. He found two terra-cotta dwarfs among the geranium plants and several colored glass globes on sticks. The stone border around the bed was covered with moss. . . .

It was a long time before she came downstairs.

When they were safely out in the street, he asked:

"Is Frau Gerstecker going to die?"

She hunched her shoulders forward a little as if to shake off his question.

"We all have to die. The important thing is to live so as to be ready to meet our Maker any hour of the day or night."

Something in her voice implied that Frau Gerstecker was not ready to meet her Maker.

"Has Frau Gerstecker done something very bad?"

"That's for God to decide," she said curtly. "We're all poor sinners and nobody knows the day of reckoning."

It was all he could get out of her. Lying in bed that evening, just before he fell asleep, he wondered what the crime was Frau Gerstecker had committed since she was so afraid of having *her* call Pater Alfred, and whether she was really going to die, and whether she would be buried in the Baumgarten cemetery if she died.

Chapter Five

ONLY a vaguely disagreeable memory of the visit to Frau Gerstecker remained with him the following afternoon, but he was glad all the same that it was the day for choir class so that he would not have to go back with her to the dreary, ill-smelling sickroom in the Neustiftgasse.

He still had the shiny ten-heller piece the stranger had given him on Sunday. But it no longer seemed like the same coin to him. All day the temptation to spend it had gnawed at him until the coin had assumed the combined glamour of all the things he might have bought with it. There had been the *Sacher-Torte* at the confectioner's in the Westbahnstrasse—he gave you a great big piece if you asked for stale pastry, and sometimes a piece of candy besides. Then there had been the cherries at the grocer's and the tin of sardines, then the marbles Karl had—but worst of all had been the temptation to buy a piece of real movie film a boy had shown him in school. He had almost succumbed then because he had told himself hypocritically that he might give the film to Rudi. . . .

By five, half an hour before she would allow him to leave for choir class in the Verein, the memory of all his furious self-denials had wrought him up to a feverish anticipation of the moment when he would be alone with Rudi and could casually invite him to the confectioner's to buy some candy.

To make the time go faster, he opened the text they used in choir class and practiced the voice exercises in back. He was alone in the flat; she was still downstairs in the laundry. When he had finished the exercises a bare five minutes had gone by. She had only an old watch which was always fast down in the cellar—he decided to risk it. But he killed as much time as he could in locking the door and on his way down the stairs.

The laundry was still steamy although she and Frau Werner, who helped her with the washing every week, had started to rinse the wash in cold water. Frau Werner wore an apron made of oilcloth that went from her neck clear down to her shoes. *She* had on an old blue flannel blouse and she wore two old aprons one on top of the other. He lingered for a minute by the wringer as if fascinated by its mechanism before he put the key to the flat on the long deal table. He was relieved when she did not look at the watch and merely said:

"I want you home right after the choir. I'm going to Frau Gerstecker's and I'm not waiting for you. If I'm not home, the key is under the mat. . . ."

That meant that Frau Gerstecker was worse and that *she* might not even come back for supper and he would be alone at home in the evening: he would be able to finish the novel about the Italian count that Poldi was reading, unless Poldi came home early. . . .

"Yes, Mother," he said meekly.

"And you be careful when you light the lamp. You don't have to turn it up until the chimney gets all smoked up."

Relieved at getting away, he hurried up the cellar stair and out into the street. The expressman on the far corner of the Kandlgasse was loading some queer-shaped boxes. The labels on the boxes said: Innsbruck. He wondered as he walked past the glover's shop next door what Innsbruck was like. Someday he would go to Innsbruck and Munich and to Paris where they spoke French. It must be fun to travel. Franz had been in Switzerland and in Italy. . . .

He passed the rest of the familiar house fronts and shops: the umbrella-maker's and then the window of the delicatessen store which was always crowded with foreign-looking tins and boxes, with print on it which he could not read and with strange fruits in gaily decorated baskets. He had been inside the store only once when Poldi had sent him for some *Wurst* one morning when she was going on an excursion. But even Poldi bought things there only on special occasions: the delicatessen shop was for people like Rudi's parents and Frau Frank, the Jewish lady on the second floor, who had lots of money.

He hastened his step after he had turned the corner into the Westbahnstrasse to get to the apartment house where Rudi lived. Merely to enter the cool, wide entrance hall with its black and brass elevator in back always filled him with exhilaration. He loved the red coco-fiber carpet on the stair and the shiny brass rods that fastened it to the treads, the impressive double doors, the spacious landings. He faltered a little before he pushed the bell at Rudi's door. As he had feared, it was the maid that let him in. She was a plump, brisk woman with a white lace apron over her black dress and a black bow in her hair. He was more in awe of her than of Rudi's mother.

She said:

"Come in. Rudi is just getting ready."

He heard the condescension in her voice and quivered with humiliation. She wouldn't dare to talk to him in that tone if only he were dressed like Rudi! He waited uneasily in the vestibule while she went into the drawing room. Through an open door he could see the shiny white cupboards and the gleaming nickel taps of the sink in the kitchen. The door behind him led, he knew, into the bathroom. It always seemed to him the greatest luxury of all.

More to take his mind off the humiliating fact that they had no bathroom at home than because he was interested, he examined the two lithographs of old Vienna which hung on either side of the wide hall mirror. He was still looking at one of them when Rudi came out of the drawing room. He had, Peter saw, changed his clothes since earlier in the afternoon. He had been wearing a blue sailor suit in school: now he had on a brown Norfolk jacket. His shirt collar was open at the throat and his hair was still wet from brushing.

"You're late," Rudi reproached him. "You said you'd come before five. Now we can't draw the plan for the tunnel." The next moment a charming eagerness routed the disappointment from his pink, soft, almost girlish face. "Hurry, I want to show you the new signals."

As he followed Rudi with a renewed access of shyness across the drawing room, Peter marveled once again at the negligent forgetfulness with which Rudi moved among the beautiful furniture. If he lived here, he felt, he would treat each object with reverence. He hesitated for a fraction of a second before he stepped on the thick-pile rug, and he did so only because the floor around it was so highly polished that it seemed somehow precious too, and because the grand piano extending far out into the room left him no other alternative.

Rudi's room was easily as large as Franz's room at home. The walls were covered with a gay paper. It had a real, grown-up bed, a desk, chests of drawers. . . . On the walls were framed scenes from *Don Quixote* and *Gulliver's Travels.*

Rudi brought a cardboard box from under his desk and one by one took out the new signal lights for his railroad. He hooked them up to the battery and turned the switch. He pointed to the smallest of the red lights:

"This one is for inside the tunnel. I'm going to make a lake too and build a bridge over that. Papa is going to help us with the bridge. Are you coming this Sunday?"

"I haven't asked yet," Peter admitted. He knew that *she* would never let him go to Hütteldorf alone and he was unconsciously intending not to ask her until the very last moment so that he could make believe that he would actually go.

He heard a faint, intimate rustle behind him. It was Rudi's mother. She smiled at him as he scrambled to his feet.

"How do you do, Peter? Do you like Rudi's signals?"

He felt himself blushing. Frau Martin's friendliness always embarrassed him. "They are wonderful," he stammered.

"You must come to Hütteldorf often this summer and play with Rudi—Rudi, isn't it time for your choir class?"

"Yes, Mama," Rudi said evenly.

And here was another thing that struck him as part of the magic that adhered to everything connected with Rudi: Rudi was never even ruffled when his mother mentioned school or homework, to say nothing of being actually afraid as he was when anyone at home spoke of his coming report card. . . .

Rudi's mother was waiting for them in the vestibule. She had a large bar of chocolate which she held out to him. He broke off one of the small squares and thanked her, only to have her protest:

"But you haven't taken any, Peter. You must take a bigger piece."

"No, thank you, Frau Martin. That is all I want." He was glad that she did not urge him again. To him—almost unbearably aware as he was of the beautiful dress she wore, of the cool freshness of her face and hands, of the faint perfume that hung about her—there had been something almost sacramental in her gesture of offering him chocolate just as she did now to Rudi. He watched her straighten Rudi's cap and smooth the shirt collar over Rudi's coat.

"Don't run, Rudi," she admonished them as they left, for Peter felt that her tone of voice miraculously included him too.

The little piece of chocolate was beginning to melt between his fingers and he stuck it hastily into his mouth. He felt an uncontrollable urge to tell Rudi that his mother was wonderful, but because he was aware of a vague impropriety in doing so, he said instead: "The chocolate is wonderful!"

He saw that Rudi glanced at him curiously. He added quickly and with studied casualness:

"I've finished my drawing. I drew a blue vase."

"I'm going to do mine tonight. Anyhow, the color doesn't make any difference. You can't tell from a drawing."

"Yes, you can," Peter defended himself. "You can tell from the shading. I shaded it the way blue is."

"Papa is going to help me with mine tonight," Rudi said.

A pang of jealousy stabbed Peter. He was jealous of Rudi because he had a father who helped him with his drawing, and then jealous of Rudi's father because he could be with Rudi all evening. He felt a poignant desire to help Rudi with this particular drawing. Rudi drew awkwardly, but he always got good marks because his lettering looked very neat.

They were down in the street. Instantly Peter reached into his pocket to feel the coin. There was the confectionery shop just a little farther up the street!

"I've got ten heller: let's go to the confectioner's and get some chocolate."

"But we've just had some," Rudi objected. "Why didn't you take a bigger piece?"

For a second all his anticipation of this moment was dashed. Then he had an idea.

"I didn't mean chocolate, really. I want to get some of those green eucalyptus drops Herr Granini hands out to the choir sometimes. All the singers use them. Franz said so; they clear the throat."

They crossed the street to the shop. The coin in Peter's hand while he watched the woman weigh out the green gumdrops had become important again. For just a second, however, he could not help wishing that he could have had some of the chocolate candy on the glass trays in front of him on the counter instead of the eucalyptus drops; then the consciousness of his self-denial in buying them just to please Rudi and the fact that the drops were not sweet at all except for the fine powdering of crystal sugar on top made his gesture seem austere and aristocratic and gave him back the happiness he had been looking for.

He opened the little paper bag on the sidewalk. Each put one of the pungent, aromatic drops into his mouth and then they crossed the street toward the Verein.

The Verein was really a club for young men like Franz. Peter knew dimly that it had started as a sodality in the Schottenfeld Church and that a few wealthy sponsors had furnished the money to buy the big building with the garden. It was hard for Peter to imagine that the building had ever been an apartment house, had ever been different from the Verein as he had always known it, with its huge garden in back, the clubroom downstairs, the big music room on the second floor where the choir rehearsed with Herr Granini and which was used for all sorts of entertainments, the cosy chapel on the third floor, and on the fourth the two classrooms where he had had choir class for three years now.

There were, he knew, any number of subsidiary clubs for members of the Verein like Franz. There was a ski club, a mountain-climbing club, a fencing club, a dramatic club, and a dozen others he did not even know about. For him the Verein meant the choir, which in a way was not even part of the Verein since only the tenors and baritones and basses were old enough to be members. The only reason it was housed there, Franz had explained to him one time, was that Herr Granini had given a great deal of money to the Verein at various times and because everybody was very proud of the choir, which some people claimed was even better than the boys' choir in the Imperial Chapel.

If only, Peter told himself as he entered the building with Rudi, they could pass the examination in June they would be in the choir together. Exultation seized him at the thought of Rudi and himself going upstairs into the big music room every evening for rehearsal with the black-locked, burning-eyed Herr Granini instead of just having choir class with Professor Wessely. They would sing at concerts and in many different churches and go on all the wonderful excursions Herr Granini was said to take the choir on all through the summer.

They still had a few minutes before class. They went out into the garden. A group of older boys from the choir were playing soccer. At the far end of the garden several men were watching the bowling in the two alleys under the mulberry trees. A few boys from their class were playing tag near the seesaw. It would be much gayer in the garden later on, Peter knew from the times when he had come to the vesper service upstairs in the chapel with her.

He and Rudi watched the soccer game. He held out the bag with eucalyptus drops to Rudi.

"They make my nose tingle," Rudi said. "It's like when you smell snow."

Peter could tell that he liked the drops. He held out the entire bag to Rudi. "You take them——"

"But they are yours!"

"I don't really like them."

"Then why did you buy them?"

He ached to tell Rudi that he had bought them for him, that he would have liked to be able to present the whole confectionery store to him. To hide his emotion, he said brusquely: "I couldn't think of anything else to get." He turned away from Rudi as if the two boys on the seesaw had suddenly absorbed all his attention.

The happiness that had flooded through him when Rudi had taken the bag stayed with him until they went upstairs. Professor Wessely had not yet come. One of the other boys asked Rudi what he was eating and Rudi started to pass the candy to all the boys in the class. Peter hated that. He had a feeling that the other boys were violating the infinitely private bond between him and Rudi. Only when on the way home from class Rudi brought out the bag again and said: "Don't you want one now?" did he feel happy again.

He said stolidly: "I don't care. . . ."

The pungent taste of the eucalyptus drop made him feel closer to Rudi than he had ever felt before.

Chapter Six

FRAU GERSTECKER'S funeral was on a Saturday. "Do I have to go and look at her?" Peter complained when she told him to get dressed. "I don't want to look at dead people. Why can't I wait for you in church?"

"Because you are coming with me, that's why! It won't hurt you to look at Frau Gerstecker once more—she won't bite you."

"Dead people smell funny. . . ."

"You'll smell funny too, when you're dead. The worms aren't so particular—ashes to ashes, and dust to dust." She sighed piously. "You just remember to keep your soul sweet and fragrant, that's more important."

She poked a hatpin through the dreary black hat with the bit of black veil hanging down behind which she always wore to funerals. He watched her put a little bottle with holy water in the black reticule, then add two folded paper bags and a small garden trowel. The trowel meant that she intended to stay in the cemetery afterward to tend the three or four graves she took a special interest in.

He minded the trips to the cemetery much less than going to church with her. There was always the chance of seeing something interesting on the way, and he rather liked the long ride in the blue-and-black busses. The busses were iron-tired and uncomfortable, but he always forgot about that after the first few jolts if he could sit by a window. And they usually rode in the last or next to last bus, since she had often known the dead person only by sight, so that there was rarely anybody really sad in the bus and the conversations were sometimes quite cheerful. What he did mind was going into the room where the coffin was. . . .

When they got to the Neustiftgasse a hearse and several busses were already lined up in front of the house. A few children and grownups from the neighborhood were idly watching on the sidewalk. He could not suppress a little thrill of importance as he walked past them into the house and out into the courtyard. A group of old women he had often seen in church were clustered around the foot of the stair. Their ridiculously bedizened hats bobbed with absurd animation as they whispered together. All of them wore either black fichus or ancient little capes around their shoulders and carried umbrellas. In church it was always they who prayed loudest and made a great show of their rosaries. Poldi referred to them scornfully as "those parish gossips."

They received *her* with sibilant enthusiasm and tried to draw her into a conversation. She refused to stay. It was the only thing about her which even faintly reconciled Peter to her piety, for she never did more than barely respond to their syrupy greetings. He sensed that in spite of all her humility, she held herself superior to them. What he could not forgive her was that her constant running to church and her dowdiness made her seem so much like the gossips that he was sure all the people in their neighborhood thought of her as one of them.

Two of the women started to paw his head and shoulders and simpered: "My, what a nice boy, Frau Bartsch—all dressed up like a little gentleman—your youngest, isn't he, Frau Bartsch?"

He squirmed away from their repulsive fingers and ran up the stairs ahead of her.

On the landing the fat janitor and his wife were waiting importantly.

"The nephew and his family are inside, Frau Bartsch," the janitor said. "They're waiting for the nephew's son before they nail up the coffin." The janitor wiped his bald head with a black-bordered handkerchief. "You and the wife did a beautiful job laying her out, I must say. You'd think she was only sleeping, the way she looks. I guess you'll want to have another look at her?"

He stood aside to let them pass.

Peter followed her with the mingled feeling of curiosity and revulsion which he always experienced when he was about to enter a room with a dead person in it. The room had been darkened with black hangings over the windows. Three tall candles burned steadily on each side of the coffin which rested on a black-covered table. As usual, the coffin was slightly tilted so that he saw the yellow face with its closed eyelids at once. The face drew him like a magnet in spite of the stealthy, evil stench that came from the coffin. The horrible odor was so pervasive that he had a feeling that even the flowers in the room shared in it.

A clumsy-bodied man with a good-natured, stupid face hovered near the foot of the coffin. He wore an ill-fitting, obviously new black suit. Beside him was a thin woman in ostentatiously deep mourning who had started to cry noisily the moment they had entered the room. A boy of about Peter's own age stood picking his nose behind them, when he was not busy fingering the surface of the coffin lid which was leaning against the wall.

Peter kept behind *her* when she went up to the coffin to pray. He could get a good look at Frau Gerstecker now. Her hands were clasped over a silver crucifix on her chest; they looked waxen and unreal.

He wondered how much longer *she* was going to stay. She wiped her eyes once or twice and turned around to him:

"Did you say an 'Our Father' for Frau Gerstecker?"

"Yes. I want to go outside."

"Say good-by to Frau Gerstecker."

She herself made the sign of the cross over the dead woman's face and chest, then went to the silver urn on a little stand, picked up the sprinkler and sprinkled holy water on her. Then she handed the sprinkler to him. The thin woman with the heavy black veils had started to bawl much louder again. She followed them out into the kitchen.

"Such a good soul," she said in a whiny, hypocritical voice.

Peter saw *her* lips set grimly. He sensed her disapproval of the woman for not having looked after Frau Gerstecker when she was ill.

"God knows what's best," she said primly.

The man in the black suit said helplessly: "They want to nail up the coffin and my oldest boy hasn't shown up yet. He's doing his military service in Stockerau. What do you think, Frau Bartsch?"

Peter took advantage of the man's question to slip out of the kitchen and go downstairs into the yard. He saw that the little group of gossips had had several additions and that there were also more people out in front of the house. He went to the ivy-overgrown fountain to wait for the coffin to be carried downstairs. Once they were out of the house, the afternoon would be less dull. There would only be the stop at the church and then they would be on their way to the cemetery. . . .

The coffin had been lowered into the grave and Frau Gerstecker's nephew and his thin wife scattered a few crumbs of red dirt down on top of it with the trowel the undertaker's man handed them. When her turn came, she took out the little bottle with holy water and emptied it into the grave as well. The thin woman was sobbing so loudly that the janitor's wife felt it necessary to console her:

"There, there. She doesn't feel anything any more. She's better off now than we are."

The nephew cleared his throat.

"I think it wouldn't do us any harm," he said awkwardly as if he were reciting a speech he had learned by heart, "to have a drop of wine down there in Baumgarten—in honor of my aunt."

It was what most of the mourners had been waiting for, Peter knew from the conversation in the bus on the way out. The fat janitor in particular had said at least twice: "I hope the Herr nephew knows what's what and is going to stand us a couple of liters of something afterward. With all the money he's come into . . ."

She was still lingering by the grave as if she intended to watch the two gravediggers finish the job of filling it up with dirt. Her lips moved faintly as she prayed. The others were already quite a little distance away when the nephew suddenly came back, shifted apologetically from one foot to the other, and said:

"I hope you'll do us the honor, Frau Bartsch, of taking a little glass with us."

Peter half dreaded some pious reproof from the way she looked at him.

"I'm just going to look up a few acquaintances," she said. "Maybe if you're still there when we go home, I'll drop in."

"We'll wait for you," the nephew said, clearly relieved that he had not been rebuffed. It was easy to see that he felt guilty about having neglected Frau Gerstecker and was anxious to make a good impression.

When he had gone, she started up the avenue toward the older part of the cemetery. The part where Frau Gerstecker had been buried looked poor, raw, depressing. It did not have fine tombstones and beautiful flowers, and the trees in the avenues were still young and scraggly.

"Why didn't they bury Frau Gerstecker over where Frau Wimmer is?" Peter asked.

"You'll have to ask him," she said curtly, but after they had walked a few steps she added of her own accord: "Fine relations they are! I'd be ashamed to show my face. First they don't bother about poor Frau Gerstecker from one year's end to the next, then they come running when they hear she's left them some money—then they can remember their aunt quick enough! And they haven't even the decency to buy her a plot of her own. . . ."

"How much money did Frau Gerstecker leave?"

"Enough! Enough so they could have bought her a private plot instead of burying her with the paupers where they can dig her up after a few years."

"Did she leave you anything?"

"Don't be so nosy—if she left me anything it's going to pay off the debts your mother made and never paid. She can wear fine clothes and ride around in an automobile, but pay her debts, no! Kathi is good enough for that."

They had reached the monument to the nuns who had died in a fire. It was only a few steps from here to Frau Wimmer's grave. Except for a few landmarks he was completely lost in the huge cemetery. He had often wondered how she could find her way in the maze of avenues and lanes, but if pressed she knew stories about an enormous number of people who lay buried everywhere—from the opera singer who had committed suicide and who had a huge black marble angel bending over her tomb to the simple grave of Herr Laub which had a miniature rock garden and strawberries on it, because he had been very fond of strawberries.

Frau Wimmer's grave was unpretentious but well kept. It had a tall granite headstone with simple gold lettering. On either side of the stone, rambler roses had been trained up an iron trellis so that they formed a green arch over the stone. She took the trowel from her reticule and started to work on the grave. The pansies and the outer border of geraniums were already in bloom. He knew where the pansies had come from—she had got several plants the year before from a grave in the next lane and had transplanted them. She was always doing that. . . .

She made him take the watering can which she kept hidden behind the rambler bush and get water from the tap a little farther up the avenue. After he had made several trips with the watering can, she was satisfied with the results of her gardening and she prepared to leave. She stood and said another prayer for Frau Wimmer, then they started for the big avenue which led to the main entrance.

The street outside the cemetery had a number of wineshops along it, scattered between the stonecutters' establishments with their forests of tombstones and crosses and the gardeners with their displays of potted plants and bushes. They looked into the gardens of three wineshops from the sidewalk before he saw Frau Gerstecker's nephew and the other mourners. The nephew hailed *her* enthusiastically. He insisted that they sit at his table and ordered a carafe of wine for her and raspberry juice and soda for him.

Peter heard the fat janitor laugh boisterously at another table. Presently the nephew was laughing, too, at something the janitor called to him. It was clear that for a minute their arrival had interrupted everybody's mirth. Peter saw that the thin wife of the nephew no longer made any pretense of being sad. She had thrown back her veil over her shoulders and was busily munching a roll and sausage. The boy whom Peter had noticed in the Neustiftgasse was eating candy out of a sticky-looking paper bag.

Something about the scene and the now uproarious mirth of the nephew struck Peter as indecent. Then the nephew asked him whether he wanted a piece of cake and he forgave him his uncouthness which had offended him.

Chapter Seven

"TODAY, today is my first communion!" he thought exultantly.

Consciousness had at last burst the shimmering bubble in which he had been almost unbearably suspended, in a sucking vacuum of mingled alarm and delicious anticipation. Now that he knew himself awake, he lay there for a minute reveling in the cool, silvery tremulousness which made everything he could think of excitingly significant. Even the stucco medallion in the center of the ceiling when he opened his eyes seemed to have become other than it had been. The design struck him as lacy and wonderfully pure. Franz was breathing softly as he slept. He could hear *her* moving in the kitchen.

"Mother is getting ready for breakfast," he thought. He persisted dutifully: "She *is* my mother—she made me a new suit." But he could not work up any warmth for her and he thought of Father instead. Instantly he could feel Father's bristly, rough, red cheek against his face, and a pleasantly vivid memory of Father carrying him home pickaback over the Schmeltz was succeeded by the enchanting taste and fragrance of the chocolate lions Father always put on the white tablecloth in front of everybody's coffee cup on Christmas morning. Then he thought of Poldi who was gruff, too, like Father and who was always doing things for him, but he had to force himself to think of Poldi affectionately, as he had to force himself with *her*—with "Mother," he corrected himself quickly.

He had saved Franz until last. Quick affection welled up in him as he listened to Franz's breathing. He felt an impulse to go and climb into Franz's bed the way he had done when he was small and Franz had drawn ships for him on big pieces of cardboard.

Alarm suddenly seized him. He would have to ask Franz's pardon for talking back and for being disobedient. He would have to do it with all of them. Pater Alfred had said so. They must be absolutely pure when they received their first communion. It would not be so hard with Franz, only embarrassing, for he had never been fresh with Franz or Father, only with her and Poldi. To put off the dreaded prospect of asking *her* forgiveness, he started to think about the rest of the morning. He saw himself walking to school, where they were to assemble, then marching to church. He wondered whether they would go by way of the Kaiserstrasse or the Kandlgasse and whether Father would come to church. Then he remembered his new suit.

He leaned out of bed to look at it on the chair and to touch the sleeve of the blouse. Once he had felt the stiff newness of the blue serge, the temptation to put it on became overpowering. He dressed slowly, almost reverently. It was the first new suit he had ever had except for the brown velvet one when he was small. He pulled up the pants as far as he could. They still hung over his knees but the starched-looking crease made them look almost like the other boys' pants, he told himself. Then he put on the new black stockings which stretched taut around his legs, and then the shoes. The new shirt would have to wait until after he had washed. He put on the one he had worn to confession the night before and softly opened the door into the living room. Father was still in bed. He tiptoed out into the kitchen.

Poldi was washing. He turned his back quickly, expecting to get scolded, and said shyly, "Good morning."

She was sitting by the sewing machine. Without looking up from the stocking she was darning, she asked: "Did you say good morning to Jesus, too? That's more important!"

He faced quickly toward the statue of the Sacred Heart in the corner between the window and the front door and started to say his morning prayer. Poldi's presence embarrassed him. He did not mind saying his prayers out loud before *her*, but Poldi and Franz made him nervous. He forced himself to think of the first communion and to be very devout.

By the time he had finished, Poldi had put on a blouse and was brushing her hair.

"He isn't going to wear *that* shirt, is he, Mother?" Poldi asked.

"No, I've been waiting for you to make him one," she said tartly.

"Wash yourself good. Behind the ears too," Poldi admonished him.

The new meekness he felt would not allow him to protest that he had scrubbed himself very carefully the night before when he had taken his bath. He washed his ears with soap as if he had not done it the night before and brushed his teeth twice. When he was through, Poldi said: "Bring your collar and things out here; I'm going to fix your scarf."

He went into Franz's room to put on the new shirt. When he came back into the kitchen, Poldi put on his collar and the black silk scarf. He held himself quietly while she fussed over him. Only when she made him sit down in front of the mirror he protested.

"I don't want curls."

"You're going to sit still," Poldi threatened. She was testing the curling iron on a piece of paper. "Hold still now unless you want me to burn you."

He was torn between his loathing of curls and the fear of perhaps committing a sin by disobeying Poldi and quarreling with her. So he confined himself to pleading: "That's enough, Poldi. Please, don't do any more. I don't want any more."

Poldi finally let him go. "Now go and sit down somewhere and don't get yourself mussed up. You've got a whole half-hour yet."

In Franz's room he went straight to the mirror above Franz's washstand. The stiff Eton collar felt uncomfortable around his neck but he liked the way it looked with the bowknot Poldi had tied in the black scarf. Poldi's efforts with the curling iron, however, worried him. His hair was mouse-colored and naturally straight. He hated the curls Poldi had made in front. He dipped his hand quickly into the water jug and smoothed down his hair furiously in an attempt to get rid of them.

"What are you doing there in front of the mirror?"

He spun around guiltily. Franz was awake and must have been watching him.

"Don't you know that vanity is a sin?" Franz's eyes were laughing at him.

"I wasn't looking. I was only trying——"

"What, the curls?"

He nodded, glad that Franz understood.

"Who did it? Poldi?"

"I didn't want to, but she made me."

"We'll soon fix that." Franz had sat up in his bed. "Get me the hair pomade on the desk."

The twinkle in Franz's eyes made it seem like a gay conspiracy. He went to get the little glass jar which smelled faintly of lilac, but when Franz unscrewed the lid he was a little afraid.

"Poldi is going to be mad."

Franz laughed.

"That's why we are doing it, shrimp. Hold out your hand. . . . Now rub it in your hair."

He did as Franz had told him to do, then tried to comb himself, but the mirror hung too high and he could not get the part straight. After he had tried several times, Franz said: "Come here. I'll do it for you."

He sat on the edge of the bed while Franz raked the comb over his scalp this way and that.

"There you are, milord. The perfect little gentleman. Poldi won't even know you." Franz leaned back against his pillow and smiled at him. "How do you feel about today? Happy? One's first communion is pretty important, you know."

Peter had got up from the edge of the bed and stood awkwardly beside it. Franz's mention of his first communion had reminded him that he still had to ask his pardon.

"I know," he said shyly. "Franz, I'm supposed to ask your pardon for . . . will you forgive me for being fresh and . . ."

Franz reached out and cuffed his head playfully so that he had to stop.

"All right, shrimp, all right. If you ever get fresh with me I'll bounce you off the ceiling and catch you on these—" he looked meaningly at the sabers on the wall—"like a sausage." Peter had to laugh even though he still felt a little awkward. "I guess it's Mother's pardon you're supposed to ask. Run along now. And you might open the package on the desk. It's for you."

"For me?"

"It's not anything to eat so don't get excited. Run along now."

Franz had closed his eyes as if he were already asleep so that Peter did not dare to say any more and thank him. He tiptoed to

Franz's desk and saw the flat package propped up against the wall. He took it down gingerly and removed the wrapping. Inside was a fine, thick, new book. It was called *The Three Musketeers* and had lots of beautiful, exciting-looking illustrations. Gratitude and affection for Franz made him feel shy again. He looked at Franz intending to thank him and tell him how wonderful the book was, but Franz had thrown one arm over his face. Perhaps he was really asleep. He sat down and started to look at the illustrations.

In a little while Poldi opened the door. She saw his hair and gasped.

"Did you do that?"

From Franz's bed came a deep chuckle. Poldi turned angrily toward Franz.

"Franz, you are a beast, a beast!" She was really angry, Peter could tell. He took the opportunity to sneak out into the living room. Behind him he heard Franz say, his voice choked with laughter: "Go away. Can't you see I'm asleep?"

Father was at the big table eating his breakfast with the morning paper spread out in front of him. It was not safe to disturb Father when he was reading, but he had to risk it. He shifted uneasily from one foot to the other until Father looked up from the paper and asked gruffly: "What is it?"

"Father," he stammered finally, "please forgive me for being bad and disobedient. I won't do it any more."

"What in the three devils' name!"

"Well, you don't have to bark at him," Poldi said from the kitchen door. "He has to do it for his first communion."

Father turned and glowered at her. "You speak when you are spoken to," he growled. But when he turned back to Peter his voice had an unmistakable tenderness in it.

"That's all right, Peterl! You just behave yourself and get good marks in school." He turned abruptly back to his paper and when Peter said, "Thank you, Father," dismissed him with another gruff, "That's all right now."

He swallowed hard and turned to Poldi by the kitchen door, but Poldi would not even let him get started and he was grateful for that.

It was *her* turn next. He forced himself to go up to her and fought down his reluctance to utter the formula to her.

She wiped one eye with the corner of her apron.

"It's God you must ask for forgiveness," *she* said. He felt that she was going to say something else. He waited in an agony of embarrassment while she wiped her eyes again. "Be sure you pray for all of us and for your mother, too. A child's prayer when he first holds the Lord on his tongue goes straight up to Heaven."

Confusion suddenly prompted him to reach out his arms and kiss her. He never kissed her ordinarily except at Christmas and she mistook what had merely been a desperate reaction against the strain of the situation for affection and said: "It's afterward you want to kiss me when you've had the wafer in your mouth."

"All right, come on now. It's time to go," Poldi said from the door. She was already holding his new cap in her hands, waiting to take him to the school.

Now it was coming, now!

Pater Alfred bent low over the altar so that his gold-embroidered, bright-green vestment stood stiffly out behind. The altar boy gave a dry, peremptory shake to the silver hand bell. Stillness settled around the altar. The organ had dwindled into a devout, far-off humming. The sacristan hastily finished folding the communion cloth over the altar rail, genuflected, and disappeared into the sacristy. In a minute now they would have to start the prayer they were to recite in unison.

"I must be reverent! I am supposed to be contrite and very pure," Peter told himself in sudden panic. He had been caught up in a wave of happiness where his attention had wandered dreamily from the flower-banked altar to the quivering shafts of sunlight which slanted down from the square, baroque windows on top, and back again to the new chasuble Pater Alfred wore. He was glad that the walls and pillars had already been hung with the bright red damask in preparation for Corpus Christi day. The familiar Schottenfeld Church seemed to him to be the very center of the spring morning. He wondered whether Franz had got up and was somewhere behind him in the crowded church. He had seen Poldi over on the right when they had marched in. *She*—Mother, he corrected himself quickly—was somewhere, he was sure. Perhaps even Father had come—he would be far in back, near the holy water stoup, where he always was when some special occasion took him inside a church. Then all his tingling sense of happiness flowed into affection for Rudi beside him.

Rudi's face looked pink and calm. His eyes were on the altar. He did not look devout so much as placidly attentive.

"I love Rudi!" he thought passionately. "Please, Jesus, make me be like Rudi——" But when he glanced sideways at Rudi's hands which were holding open his prayerbook, something about Rudi's pink, stubby thumbs and the soft, square wrists made him realize that he could never be like Rudi. The slow, deliberate gestures of Rudi were as unattainable for him as the pink freshness of his face and the way his soft brown hair looped down his forehead. "At least," he changed his prayer, "make us always be friends. . . . I want to do something to make Rudi be proud of me . . . something big, like building a huge bridge or being an artist like Herr Granini, or maybe I could be a famous painter. . . . Franz said I might be, perhaps, if I studied painting later. . . . I want to do something important . . . something!"

He felt for a minute equal to anything.

The mellow spring morning, luscious and golden like a superlative peach, glowed with an infinite promise of fulfillment. The next moment the fear of not being reverent enough assailed him again . . . he was not supposed to be as happy as this before the communion; he was supposed to be contrite and humble. . . .

He started to read hastily in the handsome new prayerbook Poldi had given him, but it was difficult to compel the words into sense. The future kept tantalizing him with its shimmering certainties. He had read only half of what he was supposed to read when the teacher started the prayer they were to say out loud. Really scared now because he had suddenly remembered what Pater Alfred had said about sacrilege, he bent every fiber on saying each sentence devoutly. Yet even so he could not achieve the mystic concentration he felt he ought to feel; the prayer merely made him feel solemn and tremulous.

Pater Alfred had left the altar with the chalice in his hand and was coming down to the communion rail. In just a few seconds now it would be their turn. He shuddered a little as he lifted the cool, starched communion cloth to his chin. "Please, God, let me be worthy—please, Jesus . . ." He tried to visualize Jesus in the manger because that was the only way he had ever been able to think of God and get any sort of picture of Him. The murmur of Pater Alfred's voice was rapidly coming nearer. Now he was in front of the boy next to Rudi.

He wanted to look at Rudi to reassure himself but he did not dare: he mustn't think of Rudi now, only of God. He kept his eyes lowered on the communion cloth while Pater Alfred stopped in front of Rudi—then the green and gold brocade of Pater Alfred's chasuble was already in front of him. Again the murmur of the Latin words and he felt the wafer—and for an instant the tip of Pater Alfred's finger—on his tongue. He closed his mouth carefully as they had been told to do. Awe and the strange sensation of the wafer intruded into his consciousness in spite of his effort to think only of the words of the prayer they had memorized for this particular moment.

They had to leave the communion rail to make room for the row of boys behind them. By the time they had knelt down again, the wafer was beginning to dissolve on his tongue. He had grown accustomed to it and the awe he had felt at first had given way to exultation. Jesus was really inside him now. *She* had said that God listens particularly to children who were making their first communion.

"Please, Jesus, let me always be together with Rudi. Please let me pass the examination for the choir, and Rudi, too. Then Rudi and I can go on all the trips Herr Granini takes the choir on." He almost added: "And I won't have to go to vespers with her every night," because the choir rehearsals came in the late afternoon just when she usually went to vespers. "And dear Jesus, please make her let me go to the *Gymnasium* so that I can be with Rudi."

The wafer was almost completely gone and he realized guiltily that he had asked for things only for himself. He started to pray for Franz and Poldi and Father, and for *her*. When he thought of Mizzi in America, who was really his own mother, he had a vague and fantastic picture of skyscrapers as always when he thought of her.

The organ had started to play again. The Mass was coming to its end. Once Rudi turned to him and smiled, just before they started to sing the final hymn. He suddenly felt very hungry and he wanted to be outside. He was too happy to stand still. He wanted to move and talk to Rudi.

When they finally marched out down the center aisle he saw both Franz and Father. Franz grinned at him and nodded his blond mop vigorously. Father, who was a little behind him not very far from the door, looked redfaced and truculent until he saw him, then his face relaxed into the beginning of a smile.

They stood on the sidewalk in the sun for a minute before the teacher dismissed them.

"Mama and Papa are taking me to Baden right after breakfast to see Grossmama. I wish you were coming too."

"I wish I were." Peter felt awkward with Rudi now after the fervor he had felt for him in church. It puzzled him that Rudi's voice should sound the way it always did.

"Grossmama promised to let me drive the horses," Rudi said in his calm voice, without sounding boastful. "You'd like them. I feed them sugar."

"In your hand?"

"Of course."

Parents, sounding gay and excited in unaccustomed contrast with the children who were still subdued and solemn, began to crowd around them. Rudi's mother appeared with his hat which she had been carrying. She looked especially elegant and young this morning, Peter thought, and wondered once again at Rudi's casual way of accepting her caresses, as now when Frau Martin bent over to kiss him and Rudi barely did more than raise his face toward hers. It seemed to Peter that if he had been in Rudi's place he would have thrown his arms around her to let everybody see that this charming woman was his mother.

Frau Martin turned to him with a friendly smile. "Is your aunt here, Peter? Would you like to come and have breakfast with Rudi?"

He felt himself flush at her graciousness. "No, thank you," he said quickly. "Poldi is here . . . and my father."

"Oh, *schön*. Well, shall we go, Rudi? Papa is waiting for us." Rudi said good-by and went away with his mother.

He turned to look around for Poldi or Franz and saw that Poldi was coming toward him. She said: "You had to plaster down your curls, didn't you?"

"I don't want the other boys to make fun of me," he excused himself and sounded very meek.

"And your scarf," she chided. "It's all lopsided." She pulled it straight. "There. Now we'd better start. Mother is waiting."

"I saw Franz and Father," he said quickly, hoping to make her stay a little longer. He did not want to leave the cheerful confusion of voices and the bright bustling crowd in front of the church. It seemed to him that once he left it he would be engulfed in the drabness of everyday again. He looked back several times after Poldi had taken his hand and started for home.

She was basting a roast in the oven of the kitchen stove when they came in, but she was wearing one of the Sunday blouses and he could tell that she had been in church. Her eyes were red as if from recent crying. When he hung around by the sewing machine, she said: "Now you can come and kiss me with the Jesus Child fresh in your mouth." He went back toward the stove where she was and stretched up to kiss her. "Now remember to keep Jesus in your heart the rest of your life," she warned. He could tell that she was deeply moved by the harsh, clipped way she talked. "And I want you to take off your new suit right away before you drink your coffee."

Reluctantly he started toward the living room. He did not want to take off his new suit. He was afraid that the day would lose some of the special quality that lifted it out from among all the other days once he parted with any of the trappings that accompanied it. But a new shyness was upon him still from church and he did not dare protest. Then he saw that she had set the table in the living room for him and that there were *Nusskipfl* for breakfast. There was even a bouquet of roses and forget-me-nots and baby's breath, and she had used one of her best white damask tablecloths. He felt touched by this unheralded display of kindness on her part. He hurried to change into his ordinary Sunday clothes.

Chapter Eight

SHE had put on the brown skirt that belonged to her best suit, the white organdy blouse with its rows on rows of ruffles and the cream-colored ruche down the front of it, and the brown straw hat which had none of the dowdiness of the hats she usually wore. It was the costume she reserved for two or three important occasions during the summer, such as the Corpus Christi procession and the annual excursion to Maria-Enzersdorf. That the visit to Aunt Wetti was important to her, Peter had also been able to sense from the care and dispatch with which she had started to dress immediately after dinner. The visit had something to do with the money she had got from Frau Gerstecker, for when Franz had teased her during the dinner: "What are you going to do with all the money Frau Gerstecker left you, Mother? Hoard it?" she had bridled immediately and said: "That money is going to Aunt Wetti. I'm thankful God's given me a way to pay her back." And when Father had said something about Aunt Wetti's not needing their money, she had turned on him with unaccustomed defiance:

"That money was left to me. It's my money and I'm going to do with it as I see fit."

For just one moment Peter had been afraid that Father would flare up, but Father had contented himself with glaring at her and then had seemed to forget about the money. Except for that one moment of tension, the dinner had been lovely.

She had had all the things he liked: liver-dumpling soup, roast pork with baked apples and rice, watercress and potato salad, and best of all—wine château and ladyfingers. The wine sauce in particular had moved him with sudden tenderness for her.

The entire day so far had been wonderful. After breakfast he had started to read the book Franz had given him, and then Poldi had mysteriously gone out and had come back with a huge box of chocolates for him. Only Father had not really given him anything, but just before dinner he had suddenly promised to take him to the Prater soon and to let him ride on the scenic railway.

Father's promise sufficed to round out his happiness. He had secretly been worrying whether Father was not ever going to take him along with him any more. Ever since the Sunday of the fireworks Father had refused to let him come along; yet Father had seemed to go to fascinating places for he dressed more meticulously than ever and he did not even stop to take a nap after dinner any more.

But he did not mind going with her today. He was curious to see Aunt Wetti again.

They got off the streetcar near the big sun-washed square in front of the Karlskirche. She opened her gray and white striped parasol and tilted it over her shoulder. Her left arm with the brown jacket folded over it was pressed against her side. It seemed to Peter that she held herself more erect than usual and that there was a subtle new note of self-assurance about her.

When they came to the Kolowat-Ring, she said:

"It's number 21. I'll remember the house when I see it, but you might as well watch the numbers."

He was already delightfully engrossed by the houses on both sides of the street. They were tall houses with reserved, haughty façades and with balconies on every floor. There were only a few houses in the Schottenfeldgasse with balconies. Even the apartment where Rudi's parents lived did not have a balcony. He felt a thrill of pride at the thought that Aunt Wetti lived in this cool, elegant street which did not have a single shop in it and which was paved with silk-smooth asphalt, so that the wheels of carriages made hardly any noise at all and only the discreet clop-clop of the horses broke the aristocratic quiet.

"There it is." He tried not to betray his excitement. "This is number 19; it's the next one."

"I remember it."

She stopped in the high, handsome doorway to admonish:

"You remember your manners now! I don't want her to think that you haven't had any bringing-up."

"Shall I kiss Aunt Wetti's hand?"

"Nobody said anything about kissing her hand. You say how-do-you-do and that's enough."

They entered the marble-paneled hall which led to a gold and black wrought-iron elevator cage from which an oval plate-glass cylinder shot high up in the air.

"Can't we ride in the elevator—just once?"

"You're going to walk same as I am."

He followed her up the red-carpeted stairs. On the third floor she turned right and stopped in front of one of two adjoining double doors to disentangle the reticule from her jacket and to pat the ruche on her blouse. Peter raised himself on his toes to read the brass plate above the buzzer.

"It's Aunt Wetti's door all right," she said. "You don't have to look."

The brass plate announced with arrogant simplicity: VON GARNHAFT. It seemed to scorn to give any information beyond that. In their own street or in any other street in their neighborhood, the little plate on the door always gave the Christian name as well as any title the occupant might possess, such as: master carpenter, or merchant, or municipal music teacher. . . .

"May I ring the bell?"

She had already shifted the parasol into her left hand.

"No. I'm going to knock."

He fought down his irritation at her obstinate humility which together with her distrust of modern appliances made her knock now rather than use the electric buzzer. No wonder the maid peered at them suspiciously when she opened the door and seemed subtly insolent even after she had told her that she was Frau von Garnhaft's sister.

The maid had left them standing in the hallway of the apartment. He felt himself go hot and cold at the mere thought that Aunt Wetti might not receive them, even though he had on his new suit. The next minute his fears were pleasantly scattered by the somewhat breathless entrance of a tall, handsome woman in a wine-colored dress which shimmered green when she moved. The silk of her dress whispered caressingly as she rushed toward her.

"Well, Kathi!" she exclaimed. "It's about time you showed your face again. How are you?"

Aunt Wetti had thrown both arms around her and was kissing her. He noticed that *she* only pecked at Aunt Wetti's cheek and immediately started to push Aunt Wetti away with little defensive nudges of her arm.

Aunt Wetti did not seem to have noticed it. She turned to him and cried:

"And this is Peter! But how he has grown!"

Then he felt himself drawn against the rustling silk of Aunt Wetti's dress and somewhat alarmingly soft lips touched his mouth.

"But come in," Aunt Wetti urged. "You're just in time for some *Jause*."

Peter hesitated when they had got inside the door of the drawing room. He did not dare penetrate any farther without some further encouragement into the magnificence everywhere in the room. He took in the heavy Oriental carpet, the gleaming grand piano by the window, the dainty Biedermeier chairs and settees, the bric-a-brac on the mantle, the paintings. Only when Aunt Wetti came back for him and took his hand with an inviting, "Come and sit by me, Peter, and tell me all about yourself!" did he feel that he really belonged in this room. He sat down gingerly on the needle-point sofa beside her.

Aunt Wetti turned to the maid: "We'll have coffee right away, Trude. And see whether there are any of the cakes Marie made yesterday left over for this young man. . . ."

She had sat down on a straight chair opposite them. She was still folding her brown jacket and the reticule in her lap and leaning the parasol against her thigh.

"We didn't come for coffee," she said defensively.

"But surely you're at least going to have a cup of coffee when you only come once every ten years. One'd think you live on the North Pole, you come to see me so seldom."

"It's just as far from you to me as it's from me to you."

"I know," Aunt Wetti sighed. "It's a shame. We must get together oftener. How is Ludwig?"

"He goes to the *Heurigen* the way he always did."

It seemed to Peter, watching Aunt Wetti surreptitiously, that the corners of her mouth flicked as if she were about to laugh. Then he saw that her eyes were serious and that the infinitesimal quivering of her mouth had betrayed irritation rather than amusement. He wondered why, but had no time to think about it for Aunt Wetti was looking at him and saying:

"And Peter: what a big boy he is getting to be!"

"He made his first holy communion today."

"No! Really?" He shrank a little from Aunt Wetti's too friendly, inquisitive glance which was swiftly traveling over him. "No wonder he is all dressed up like a little gentleman!"

He had a feeling that she had said that for *her* benefit, that she had been able to tell at a glance that his new suit had not come from a store, and that she pitied him. A flash of hope that she might feel so sorry for him that she would ask him to stay with her shot through him. He tried to imagine what it would be like to live in this beautiful room and all the other rooms there must be. But her expression gave him no encouragement to pursue the brief dream. She was already looking at him with that same shallow, patronizing and insistent warmth with which Poldi's friends always asked him about school.

"How old are you, Peter?"

"I'll be eleven in September."

"Then you'll finish the lower school this year?"

"Yes, Aunt Wetti."

"Why, then you'll be in the *Gymnasium* next fall!"

"I . . . I don't know yet."

"We'll see," *she* broke in. "There's time enough to think about that yet. I had enough worry to get my own through school. Public school is good enough for anybody, and then if he learns an honest trade . . . It isn't as if he were getting nothing but 'ones.' "

That was unfair, he felt. He couldn't help it if Herr Renzl didn't like him because he was poor and his handwriting was bad.

"What kind of report card have you been getting?" Aunt Wetti asked.

"I had three 'twos' and four 'ones.' "

"Why, that's pretty good, I should say. Most of the children of the people I know have 'threes' and have to take an entrance examination."

"They have parents to pay for them. I had enough worry with Franz when he lost his scholarship for a year."

Aunt Wetti ignored the objection. She seemed really interested in him now.

"Do you like to study, Peter?"

"Yes, Aunt Wetti."

"What subject do you like best?"

"I like reading . . . and singing."

"He's always having his head in a book, only it's storybooks," *she* said. "And the teacher complains that he's all the time drawing in school instead of learning something."

"Drawing?" Aunt Wetti looked suddenly very alert. "Does he know about . . . ?"

"No, he doesn't! And I'm not going to have any notions put in his head. He's got enough of them already."

Aunt Wetti ignored her. "Do you like to draw pictures, Peter?"

"Yes, sometimes, Aunt Wetti, but I'd rather sing."

"He's in the Verein in the choir class."

"How nice." Aunt Wetti sounded indifferent to the information and appeared to be thinking of something else. "It may come out later," she said suddenly. "Kathi, if you need anything for him I'd like to help you. If he's going to the *Gymnasium* he'll need a lot of things. I'd like to do something for him."

She pulled the reticule in her lap over to one side and pressed it against her leg. "I don't need your help. I've brought him up so far without anything from you and I don't need any help now."

The maid was softly opening the double door from the dining room. . . .

"Shall we have coffee?" Aunt Wetti asked with glib graciousness, as if she had not just a moment ago suffered a rebuff from *her*. He admired the silken calm with which Aunt Wetti had got up and stood smilingly waiting for them. At home there would have been an argument or even a quarrel, but Aunt Wetti was talking now about the cook's day out as if nothing had happened.

She made them sit on either side of her at one end of the long dining-room table. Then she cut a big slice of *Gugelhupf* for him and handed him the plate with a smile that made him lower his eyes; he was not used to as intimate a smile as hers; it made him feel crowded and embarrassed. He busied himself with the coffee which had an enticing layer of *Schlagobers* on top. When he finally lifted the cup he did so with great precautions for fear that he might break the fragile china.

His eyes wandered guardedly around the room while he ate. Rudi's parents had a dining room but it was not nearly so beautiful. The vast sideboard gleamed with crystal and beautifully ornamented plates. One leaf of the French window stood open so that he could see the great mass of flowers in porcelain pots on the floor of the balcony. There were oil paintings on the walls here too and a lovely rose and green rug that ran clear to the walls.

Aunt Wetti was gaily talking about the weather, the summer, and about the villa she and Uncle von Garnhaft had rented in Ischl the year before. *She* listened silently, her head lowered as if in disapproval. When he had finished the slice of *Gugelhupf*, Aunt Wetti passed him the plate with the delicious-looking cakes such as he had only seen at the confectioner's before. He did not dare help himself for fear that *she* might scold him afterward; Aunt Wetti briskly put out five little cakes on his plate.

"You don't want to make me think that you don't like cakes, do you? Finish them quickly and there'll be some chocolates for you."

"I don't want him to get sick!" *she* objected.

"Oh, bother! He won't get sick from a few cakes." And again he was conscious that Aunt Wetti gave him a sideways glance as if she felt sorry for him. Suddenly exacerbated pride made him sit up very straight and finish the cakes with forced deliberateness; and when she offered him chocolates out of the silver and crystal *bonbonnière* which stood in front of her place, he said haughtily:

"No, thank you, Aunt Wetti."

Aunt Wetti took the *bonbonnière* into the drawing room when they went back and put it down on a little table.

"These are for you, Peter. Reach in, and what you don't eat I'll wrap up for you to take home. Would you like to look at pictures?" She reached over to a table behind the sofa and handed him a sheaf of illustrated magazines. "Perhaps you'd like to sit on my chaise longue over there. . . ."

He went and sat down on the chaise longue which had been placed between the open glass doors and extended out on the balcony. Aunt Wetti had gone back to the sofa. He wished now that he had stayed near her. If he had, she might have offered him chocolates again and now he'd probably never get any of them. She had no doubt only been joking about the chocolates; she'd never give them to him. They were much too expensive-looking.

He started to look at the magazines, but when he heard *her* say: "I came to pay back the three hundred kronen," all his attention was instantly on the two women.

"What three hundred kronen?" Aunt Wetti asked.

"The money Mizzi borrowed from you to go to America on. You needn't think I have forgotten."

"Oh, that! That's much too trivial to talk about."

"It isn't trivial to me," *she* persisted.

There was a pause in which Peter could feel Aunt Wetti grow tense all of a sudden. Her voice when it came showed traces of her effort to keep from getting angry.

"How do you know that she hasn't paid me back long ago?"

"Because I know Mizzi. I wrote her and she wouldn't even answer me. It's just like her to have plenty of money and ride around in automobiles, but look after her child or pay back her debts—no!"

Aunt Wetti said coldly:

"Why should you feel called on to pay me that money? Whatever happened was between Mizzi and me. Really, Kathi, it's no concern of yours."

"It is my concern because I promised my mother to look after her."

Peter listened intently now. He knew that she had some mysterious grievance against Aunt Wetti which went back even before the time when Mizzi had gone to live with Aunt Wetti. It had to do with Aunt Wetti's coming to Vienna when *she* had still been in the Tyrol.

"Don't forget she was my mother, too," Aunt Wetti said.

"Much you cared about your mother! All you could think of was to get away to Vienna. I didn't see you remembering she was your mother when she lay on her deathbed. No, you came like a fine lady in time for the funeral."

"That's because I was working and couldn't get away. Really, Kathi! . . ." Peter was astonished at her uncertain voice and even more at the placating note that came into it with the next sentence.

"Kathi, aren't you ever going to forget the few years earlier I got away to Vienna? Somebody had to stay home and after all I was the eldest. I simply wasn't cut out to spend my life in a village."

"Nobody asked you to."

"You act as if I had committed goodness knows what crime. It isn't my fault that we never see each other except once every five years."

"Better the way it is. You go your way and I'll go mine. Here's the money."

He saw that it was Aunt Wetti, the more glamorous and more powerful of the two, who had lost. His sympathies had shifted back and forth from one to the other. He could not understand why Aunt Wetti did not defend herself better and why she had resorted to pleading instead of becoming angry the way Father did with *her.*

Aunt Wetti had been forced to take the envelope with the money, but she held it out toward *her* again. "Why don't you use it for him?" she asked. "I don't need it. I'm sure you can use it. I'd love to do something for him."

She pinched her lips and groped for her reticule and the parasol with the prim gesture he knew so well. "And I don't need it either," *she* said. "I can bring him up without your help."

"All right. But if you won't let me help with money, then how about this: Felix and I are leaving for Denmark next week for the summer. Felix' uncle has a beautiful estate there. Why don't you let him come along with us? Felix loves children and he's always talking about Peter. It would do him so much good—how would you like to come to Denmark with us, Peter?" Aunt Wetti turned to him. "There are horses and cows and I'll show you the big steamers that go across the ocean——"

"He'll stay here in the Schottenfeldgasse with us," *she* cut Aunt Wetti short. "It doesn't hurt us and it won't hurt him, either."

"Honestly, Kathi, you're just determined to keep me from doing anything for him."

"You had plenty of chance years ago, but did you do anything for him then—no! For all you cared he'd still be with the peasants in Styria today. You and Mizzi—you'd have let him be brought up on cider and *Sterz,* and eaten up by lice, the way Ludwig found him. Now that he's growing up, he interests you again."

She had already got up and he saw that the end of their visit had come. Regretfully, he put down the magazines and went to join her just as she faced toward the door into the hall.

Aunt Wetti said softly: "You are hard, Kathi," and then: "Wait a minute——" She went to the drawer of a secretary, took out some small object and wrapped it in a piece of tissue paper; then she went into the dining room and appeared a minute later with a confectioner's carton into which she emptied the contents of the *bonbonnière*.

"Here, Peter! Here are the chocolates I promised you—and this is a little present for your first communion. Don't lose it. It's a gold piece."

She bent down and kissed him before he had a chance to stammer out his thanks. He thought he saw a tear glistening in one eye, but he could not be sure. They went out into the hall. They stopped awkwardly at the front door. Aunt Wetti was saying:

"Don't wait years again before you pay me another visit. . . ."

Then they were going down the stairs. He carried the cardboard box with the candy gingerly in his hand.

"May I keep the gold piece?" he asked as soon as they were out in the street.

"Not to spend! I'll put it in the bank. Goodness knows when you'll need something. It'll come in handy."

Bits of the conversation between them came back to him as they walked back toward the Mariahilferstrasse. Why hadn't she let him go to Denmark with Aunt Wetti? Would she let him buy the sandals he wanted with the ten kronen Aunt Wetti had given him? And why couldn't *she* have taken the three hundred kronen Aunt Wetti had wanted to give her for him?

Irritation struggled with loyalty in him. The tenderness he had felt for her at noon had not altogether left him and he found himself alternately siding with her and with Aunt Wetti. One thing was clear, though, and that was that neither Mizzi nor Aunt Wetti had wanted him when he had been small and that *she* had sent for him. He wondered why she had not left him in Styria with the peasants since she was always saying what a burden he was.

He asked:

"Why was I in Styria?"

"Because Mizzi sent you there."

"Why?"

"Because she didn't want you with her, that's why! She and Wetti with their highfalutin notions . . . I knew how it was all going to end. And then when there was a child, only quickly away somewhere into the country with it."

Styria was somewhere to the east of the Tyrol, he knew. He remembered seeing a picture somewhere of a kermess in a Styrian village with peasants in national costume dancing in front of an inn.

"Was it a nice place?"

"Nice!" she sneered. "Father found you with a girl's dress on, crawling around in the dirt among the chickens, and full of rash from the cider they'd been giving you. They took the money Mizzi paid for you and that's all they cared about."

"Why did you send for me?"

"I sent for you because I felt sorry for you, that's why. I wasn't going to let you grow up with a lot of Styrian yokels, even if your mother would."

"Did you go yourself?"

"Go where?"

"To Styria."

"Father and Franz went the summer after I found out where you were."

"Was it because you liked me?"

"I guess I must have or I wouldn't have kept you."

There was a gruff warmth in her voice which was as close to a show of affection as she ever came, but it was the information itself which moved him and drew him to her. Aunt Wetti and Mizzi had not cared! Someday he would be rich and powerful and he would pay *her* back for having been good to him—for the moment he had a warm illusion that she was being good to him—and he would make Mizzi feel sorry. . . .

Chapter Nine

GRADUALLY his resentment of *her*, the restiveness he felt under her constant restraint, came back again.

He had been elated by the signs of affection he had thought he detected in her manner toward him on the day of his first communion. The vehemence of his own answering tenderness had persuaded him that she had suddenly changed, that everything would be different. But a few days later she had again become the gray, exasperating obstacle that stubbornly blocked him from every promise of joy. It was, he thought desperately, as if she were determined to punish him for some misdeed she was sure he would commit later on.

He felt cheated and unhappy when he was not merely bored. And boredom was in some ways the worst of the lot. To have to sit on a divan in the living room and try to read when he could hear the voices of the boys who were playing down in the courtyard and knew that other boys were free to play in the park and on the Schmeltz was torture. He felt at such times that he hated her.

But he was careful not to show his feelings. Nothing had as yet been decided about the *Gymnasium*. He felt sure that as long as he did not irritate her she would give in and allow Poldi to matriculate him. And as long as he could look forward to going to the *Gymnasium* with Rudi next fall he would not mind going to church with her twice a day throughout the summer, and having to stay indoors here in the Schottenfeldgasse while all the other boys in the class would be away in the country for the vacation.

He had put all his hope in Poldi. Poldi, he knew, was his only champion. She was set on having him get an education. Franz liked him but he was rarely at home now and busy with his own affairs, and Peter distrusted his incomprehensible, playful affection for his mother which would make him side with her in any quarrel between her and Poldi. As for Father, there was no way of telling what he might say. He sensed a subtle danger to his dreams of the *Gymnasium* from the business of his fingernails.

It was a whole week now that Father had been wearing the white gloves. He wore them all the time, even to eat. They were ordinary cheap, white cotton gloves and they were everywhere. Father kept several clean pairs on top of the dresser. He had a supply of new ones in the top drawer and there was a cardboard box in his night-table where he threw the old ones. Every few days *she* boiled out the soiled ones in a special pot and then she hung them up to dry on a line across the kitchen window above the fuchsias. Once, at night, when they came home after dark and he had not yet grown accustomed to the sight of the gloves, he had been startled by them: they seemed like a row of ghostly hands reaching out for something he had. Ever after the gloves were a sinister symbol of some indefinable threat.

The gloves had to do with Father's fingernails, as did the pungent-smelling fluid in which he bathed his finger tips every morning. He had known that Father's fingernails were peculiar as far back as he could remember. They were very thick, and he had watched with a kind of fascination when Father trimmed them. Father did not use scissors like everybody else, but clippers that were as big as wire cutters.

But it turned out now that Father's nails were not only peculiar; they were sick. That was why he did not go to the theater now and was home so much. He had a sick leave and Peter had heard the baker who brought the rolls every morning tease Father about his fine three-months vacation. But there was something dangerous about the vacation. *She* was worried that Father might get pensioned. That would mean less money for her housekeeping. It would make her more cautious than ever and less inclined to let him go to the Gymnasium.

Everything depended on Poldi. He waited anxiously for her to say something about the *Gymnasium*. There were only two weeks left for matriculation. He wondered whether she was biding her time because she felt that she could somehow strengthen her case.

Then one day, when his impatience would barely let him wait any longer without asking Poldi whether she had forgotten, Poldi made him put on his new suit after lunch. He changed his clothes in a fever of anticipation. Poldi must have won in the argument she had had with her. He could tell that there had been an argument by the brusque, impetuous way Poldi tossed her head as she went back and forth in the living room. *She* was sitting by the sewing machine, small, compact and disapproving.

"Pride goeth before a fall," she said in a deadened, ominous voice as Poldi held the door on the landing open for him and pushed him through it.

"All right, Mother, you and your proverbs. . . . Good-by!" and she slammed the door gaily. But Peter had a foreboding that *she* would not yield so easily.

As they approached the big stone building in the Kandlgasse he became a little scared. He had never been inside the *Gymnasium*.

"Will they examine me right away?" he asked.

"Don't be such a coward," Poldi said scornfully. "Nobody's going to bite you. All we're going to do is to get the application blanks and some information."

"They look very stern, the professors do," he excused himself. Poldi always made him feel ashamed of seeming afraid.

"Next year you'll see them every day, and believe me, if you don't study after all this you'll hear from me."

"Oh, I'll study hard, Poldi."

"You better."

Classes were still in session in the building. The big lobby with its monumental staircase and high windows and the white marble statue of a man holding a book and a pair of calipers brought back a delicious fear again. It was several degrees cooler in here and very quiet. From somewhere in the building came snatches of a stern, monotonous voice. He walked automatically on tiptoe over the stone floor as he followed Poldi to the glass-enclosed lodge of the janitor.

While the janitor explained the intricate forms to her, he tried to hear what the voice which came from some upper story was saying. He could only make out an occasional "gentlemen" and the words "elective affinities." The words recurred again and again. He did not know that they meant but like a ritual formula they suddenly became a mysterious, verbal symbol of the whole enticing world of the *Gymnasium*.

Poldi was still talking to the man inside the glass door of the lodge. He was a big man with a bushy red beard and arrogant eyes. The tall uniform cap shoved back a little on his forehead made him seem gigantic. He was explaining the application for a scholarship now and a note of impatient condescension had come into his voice. Peter knew the tone and he squirmed under it. It was the same special voice he heard when *she* took him to be measured for shoes in November at the charity league for poor children.

He was glad when Poldi finally folded up the forms and put them in the envelope the man had given her. Once outside and walking down the steps of the building he remembered only the cool hall and the mysterious voice he had heard.

"That's that," Poldi said. "Now Father has to fill it out and then you take it to school and get the principal to sign it, and on Saturday I'll get the other signatures from the Poor-Mother and the rest."

"And then will I really get in?"

"If you behave yourself and get good marks on your last report."

"Poldi, what does 'elective affinities' mean?"

"What?"

He repeated the words for her.

"Where did you read them?"

"I heard a man say it in the *Gymnasium*."

"Oh—I guess it's something to do with science. You'll have to ask Franz. And I don't want you to read my books again. You were reading the novel I left on the chest of drawers."

"I only looked at it."

"Don't lie. You've only just made your first communion and anyhow a gentleman doesn't lie. You have enough books to read in the trunk."

The trunk was in the attic and contained Franz's and her old books.

"But I've read them all, and they are all fairy tales."

"Well, you have your schoolwork. If you get good marks this term I'll take out a library card for you in the summer."

"Really, Poldi?"

"Yes, really! And stop saying 'really' all the time like a baby. Come on, we're going in here." She took his hand and pulled him into the confectionery shop.

They sat down at one of the little marble tables and Poldi ordered an ice for each of them—vanilla and raspberry ice! He felt warm and happy inside, and grateful to Poldi. It was true that Poldi was always nagging him about all sorts of things, such as the way he held his fork, or the way he wrote, or about the things he said; it was also true that when Franz felt gay and paid attention to him, he was much happier with Franz than he ever felt with her, but Franz was always going off somewhere and sometimes weeks went by when Franz hardly noticed him. In the end, Poldi was the only one whom he could always count on for help against *her!* The consciousness of having been ungrateful to Poldi by even thinking of the fun he had with Franz sometimes, made him feel guilty. He said virtuously:

"I'll study very hard, Poldi. I'll get nothing but 'ones' next year."

"I should hope so."

He was laying the table for supper when Father came in.

Poldi had put the big blotter which Father always used when he had any writing to do in front of his place and the application blanks on top of it. Peter watched him anxiously for any sign that might give a clue to the humor he was in, but Father's "*Grüss Gott*" was noncommittal. If it sounded a little bit abrupt, that might only be because he was impatient for his supper.

Poldi brought in the lamp and set it on the table. A minute later Father brought his newspaper from the chest of drawers and prepared to sit down at the table.

"What's this?"

"It's the matriculation form for Peter. For the *Gymnasium*," Poldi explained. "I thought you might fill it out before supper."

He eyed the blanks uncertainly for a second, then shoved the blotter to one side.

"I'm filling out nothing until I've eaten. I want my supper."

"But it'll only take you a minute, Father. I don't see why you can't do it now."

It had been the wrong moment to insist, Peter saw at once. Father's small blue eyes glittered dangerously behind the pince-nez.

"Whether it takes a minute or not, I'm not doing any writing now. You move this junk off the table and faster than that."

Poldi had taken the usual approach to getting him to sign documents. Franz and Poldi when they had something that needed his signature always gave it to him before lunch or supper. It had become a custom. Poldi, he excused her, could not have known that Father would be irritable this particular evening.

"Here, put the inkstand where it belongs," Poldi commanded him. He hurried to obey her for fear that Father might get angry again. Poldi herself moved the blotter with the application blanks over on one of the beds. Then she straightened out the tablecloth in front of his place.

"Will you sign it after supper, Father?" she asked him. "There isn't much time left. The blanks have to be in by July first."

"If you don't give me peace pretty soon, I'll teach you a few manners. I'll sign them when I get good and ready. Where's my soup?"

She came in with his plate of soup, then she and Poldi went out for the other plates. They ate in silence. Poldi looked sulky. Father was still reading his paper and crackling it threateningly from time to time. Only when *she* had brought in the platter with the boiled beef and carrots and potatoes and Poldi had brought the platter of string beans and he had helped himself, was the silence broken.

This time it was *she* who was talking. She spoke in the low, flat monotone that always made her sound most exasperating to Peter because he knew from experience how hopeless it was to argue with her then.

"That boy needs to go to a *Gymnasium!* A boy without parents. As if I didn't have enough to worry about without having to worry about fines."

"Oh, Mother! There aren't going to be any fines. He gets a scholarship and it doesn't cost any more than it does to send him to public school."

"As if I didn't know! What about the hundred kronen Father had to pay for Franz?"

"That's because he hadn't studied that term and lost his scholarship."

"As if Father hadn't had to run from Pontius to Pilate to get him his scholarship back again," *she* droned on as if Poldi had not said anything.

"But now Franz has finished and he has a career ahead of him instead of having to work as a counterjumper in some shop."

"A trade was good enough for my father and good enough for your father. There is no reason why he shouldn't learn a good, honest trade."

"There's every reason in the world," Poldi countered hotly. "He's not going to be a day laborer like the Breitner boy."

"As if some good, honest trade weren't good enough for him! You and his mother with your highfalutin notions! The Breitner boy has at least got a father who makes a good wage."

"Mother! Not in front of him."

"I'll say what I like. Where's the money coming from, I'd like to know? Everything going up all the time and no more coming in."

"Well, I'm earning money now."

"Your salary! We can live high on *that!*" *she* sneered.

"Silence!"

Peter cowered involuntarily at the thundering blow of Father's fist. It was the first sign Father had given that he had been listening. Now he was angry and perhaps everything was lost. He got up from the table and went to the chest of drawers to put his pince-nez and the cigar case away in his pockets.

Just before he put on his hat to go out, Poldi said cajolingly: "You will look at it tomorrow, Father, won't you, and sign it?"

"I'll do as I see fit and there's an end to it!"

He left on that note. Peter thought he could discern a glimmer of hope in it, but he also remembered *her* treacherous opposition during supper. She had committed herself now. He knew her well enough to know that she would not change her mind—unless, indeed, Franz decided to talk to her.

Poldi flung out of the apartment a minute later and he was left alone with *her*. His dislike of her was so intense that he wondered whether she was not aware of it.

A kind of numbness kept him from realizing too sharply what not being able to go to school with Rudi would mean by the time fall came. He had still a child's defenses against grief, a kind of fairyland cynicism of fact and the unshakable hope that the world of the Schottenfeldgasse might at any moment expand into something strange and wonderful. This vague hope was his cushion against disappointment.

During the days that followed he told himself more than once: "This is only a trial. I'm being tried. All of a sudden everything is going to clear. I'll be in the *Gymnasium* with Rudi and I'll live in a fine house and have sandals and red socks, and I'll have a pony and invite Rudi to come and spend the Sunday and ride my pony."

At such moments he saw Mizzi arriving in the courtyard in a fine carriage, beautifully dressed and haughty to everybody but himself. She would come slowly up the stairs to claim him. He would hang back at first because she would be so magnificent, but she would bring a wonderful certitude with her. He would feel absolutely secure when she kissed him. After that he would never feel afraid again . . . and later he would come back alone—still in the carriage—and bring them all presents, even to *her*, and she would be ashamed.

This particular daydream was his escape from what he had come to feel as her tyranny. He had had it as far back as he could remember. At first, before he had even known about Mizzi in America, the woman in the carriage had been a great lady, half fairy and half a composite of the beautiful women he saw in the Innere Stadt. Then, later, the woman was his mother—not the Mizzi that she made out a rather foolish, giddy girl, but the Mizzi other people always referred to with a mixture of envy and admiration when they asked about her.

The daydream flowed over into his actual behavior, as now when he might have pleaded with her. It was true that there was no end to her stubbornness, but he knew that somehow she expected him to come and beg. He realized that if he had pretended that he wanted to become a priest, she might have softened. But his pride would not let him. He felt almost like a bystander watching the silent struggle that went on between Poldi and her for the next two weeks.

The matriculation blanks continued to lie on the chest of drawers, unsigned. He felt that Poldi's campaign was doomed but he could not give up hope. Once or twice he was on the point of asking

Father to sign the blanks. He didn't, partly because he felt too much in awe of him and partly because he knew that without *her* consent even the signature would somehow be meaningless. In the end she would always have her own way.

What disturbed him most was that Father did not assert himself. Father had always warned him to study hard and had talked of the importance of having an education. Now he seemed suddenly to have lost interest. He was changed. On the one hand, the business of his fingernails had made him more quick-tempered around the house; on the other, he seemed gayer and somehow more alive. But the cause of his higher spirits lay outside the house. Now that Father had the whole day to himself he was home much less than formerly when he had gone to the theater. He dressed with extra care and wore his best suits. Several times when he met him in the street on the way home, Peter noticed that he was in very high spirits with people he met, only to become dark and glowering the moment he entered the apartment. And he never took him with him any more. Peter felt that Father had somehow lost his interest in him.

On the third morning Poldi filled out the application blanks herself and made him take them to school to be signed by the teacher and the principal. Then she spent two days in getting all the other necessary signatures and endorsements. One day at lunch she again put the blanks on the table beside Father. They were folded in the envelope this time. Father promised to look them over after lunch. That meant that he was going to sign them.

But after Poldi had left for her office, Peter listened with frozen dismay while *she* brought up again all the arguments that she had used before. She made much of Father's sick-leave and the danger that he might be pensioned.

"And if he doesn't pass the examinations who's going to pay the fine I'd like to know? I'm not. You can't draw blood from a stone. I don't know how I'm going to make ends meet now with everything going up and the few heller I get. . . ."

Father was bathing his nails with the bowl held between his legs on the divan. He looked merely irritated at her insistent low-voiced monologue. "Don't talk so much," he said finally, but he went out without taking the blanks out of the envelope.

The following day Poldi tried to enlist Franz on her side. She appealed to him at dinner:

"Franz, don't just sit there and say nothing! Don't you think it's a crime not to send him to the *Gymnasium?*"

Franz looked uncomfortable. The fine skin below his blond mop creased worriedly.

"Well, if Mother would rather not this year. . . ."

"But he'll lose a whole year! Why make him lose a year?"

"I don't see that that's so tragic," Franz temporized. "What's a year after all? He'll only be better prepared."

"Oh tommyrot! You know as well as I do that next year it'll only be the same story all over again. . . ."

"Well, suppose it is? Perhaps Mother is right if she wants him to go to public school. He can always go to an arts and crafts school afterward . . . especially with his talent for drawing. . . . Just look at Hans Huber: he's assistant superintendent of some factory in Währing. In a few years he'll probably be as well off as an engineer with a diploma. He only went to public school."

"He's still only a machinist," Poldi said scornfully, "and not an engineer. It's all right for you to talk. You *did* go to the *Gymnasium*. What do you suppose his mother'll say when she hears about this?"

"His mother!" *she* broke in rancorously. "Who cares about what his mother thinks? She isn't supporting him—*I* am. All she has ever done is to play the grand lady and send pictures of herself in an automobile and a few dollars now and then. If it were up to her, he'd still be in Styria with the peasants."

"But he isn't and we have a responsibility to bring him up decently."

"My only responsibility is to bring him up into a good Christian," she lashed at Poldi.

There was a scene. Poldi threatened to write Mizzi. Father, who so far had said nothing and had only frowned, exploded suddenly and threatened to slap Poldi's face if she did not stop arguing. Poldi had turned red with anger and looked as if she were going to cry. She did not dare talk back to Father, but her eyes snapped with rage and she fled into the kitchen. Franz looked serious and uncomfortable; then the frown on his forehead smoothed out and his blue eyes appealed to them all to laugh:

"I'll wire Uncle Florian to hurry up and die," he said loud enough for Poldi out in the kitchen to hear. Uncle Florian had a big sawmill in the Tyrol and was a bachelor; his death and the money he was going to leave them were a standing joke in the family. But nobody laughed this time. Franz excused himself hastily and went into his room. *She* started to clear the table. There was a subtle note of silent, stubborn triumph about her movements to Peter; his hatred fastened on the way her long black skirt brushed the floor as she went out into the kitchen with the empty plates.

When the last day for submitting the application came and Poldi angrily tore up the blanks and tossed them into the coal scuttle, he knew that there was no more room for hope. The finality of the torn application blanks made his throat ache and his eyes burn. He wanted to cry, but couldn't. He could only remember two occasions when he had really cried: once, when he had fallen out of a swing at the *Heurigen*, and once, when a wasp had stung him in the foot.

But he ground his teeth all the way to school and he found it hard to talk with Rudi, who was very gay because his grandmother had promised to give him a pony. He could not keep from brooding on the vindictiveness with which *she* had set herself against his entering the *Gymnasium*. As always when his attention wandered, his hand reached out automatically for the pencil and he started to draw. He drew dozens of monsters—invariably women with round cheeks and absurd little hats—without even being aware of what he was drawing. Herr Renzl caught him twice on the same day and the second time announced before the whole class that he was going to have a bad conduct mark.

He found he hardly cared. A stubborn indifference had taken the place of his first fury.

He had also told Rudi, and Rudi had been sympathetic but not upset. They would still be in the choir together and see each other every day, Rudi said, and suggested that he could tell him every evening what they were studying in the *Gymnasium* so that Peter would be able to keep up with them in Latin and all the other subjects and perhaps take an examination and join him in the *Gymnasium* later on. The prospect of getting into the *Gymnasium* later on seemed faraway and slight, but Rudi's loyalty cheered him somewhat. He realized that it was the choir that would be the link between Rudi and him.

After that all his ambition centered on passing the examination Herr Granini was to give them and on getting into the choir. He spent hours reviewing the textbook they had used in choir class that year and in practising the voice exercises.

Herr Granini's examination came the week before school closed. He had thought about it so much that he looked forward to it with a good deal of trepidation. Once again he had occasion to wonder at Rudi's calm-eyed composure while they waited for Professor Wessely in the music room in the Verein to take them to Herr Granini's house. There were twelve boys altogether and most of them were nervous and talked almost in whispers.

Professor Wessely was late. When he came, he promptly hurried them downstairs. They crowded into the two waiting taxis and started for the Mariahilferstrasse.

The taxis stopped in front of an old-fashioned two-story house in the Mariahilferstrasse, only a stone's throw away from the Ring and the Opera. This was Herr Granini's house, Peter knew, and the two houses adjoining it belonged to Herr Granini too. He had often looked curiously into the friendly, patrician entranceway and wondered whether he would ever get inside the house and to one of the famous parties Franz and his friends were always going to after the opera.

Professor Wessely took them to the second floor. An elderly, big-bosomed woman in a beige dress answered the bell. She addressed Professor Wessely in a peremptory manner—almost as if he had been a boy like themselves. Peter recognized her at once from Franz's descriptions: this was the famous housekeeper who made even opera stars go back and wipe their feet on the mat before she would let them come in.

They were taken into a large drawing room.

"Let's sit over there," Rudi said. He pointed to a silk-upholstered armchair large enough to hold both of them. But when they got to the chair Peter preferred to stand. The furniture in the room seemed to him too precious to be touched. He called Rudi's attention to the music room they could see through an open door:

"Look at the violins."

In a glass case on the wall dozens of violins hung side by side. Professor Wessely saw them looking, and said:

"Those are very old violins. Some of them are two hundred years old."

"Does anybody play them?" Mathuschek, who claimed that he was going to be a violin virtuoso, asked.

"Herr Granini lets his friends play them sometimes. When you get to be a famous violinist, he'll let you play them, too."

The violins, the fact that there were two grand pianos standing tail to tail in the music room, the beautiful furniture all around him, filled Peter with a mixture of awe and joy. He loved the mellow, casual luxury of the drawing room. The room, he felt, had something beyond elegance, just as Herr Granini, who everybody knew was very rich, never impressed one because of the fine clothes he wore but rather because of a fascinating intensity about him that stemmed from his lustrous, black eyes and had to do with his rich, soft voice and the knowledge that he was at the heart of such things as the Opera and the Philharmonic Orchestra and the choir.

"Did you parse the sentences for tomorrow?" Rudi asked. Peter had just time enough to wonder how Rudi could think of anything as commonplace as schoolwork now, when Herr Granini entered the room.

Herr Granini's deep-socketed eyes swept over them and came to rest on Professor Wessely. A faint frown which had sat on his forehead smoothed out. His firm, full-lipped mouth softened with a smile.

"Hello, boys," he said. His eyes traveled more slowly back over them. "So this is the day when you're going to show off! Wessely, I think we'll sing first and have some *Jause* afterward—how does that sound to you, boys?"

Peter, when Herr Granini's eyes came to him as if to ask his opinion, could only nod. Rudi said very distinctly: "*Danke schön, Herr Granini.*" So did Mathuschek and one or two others following Rudi's lead. Professor Wessely, looking friendlier than Peter had ever seen him in class, said:

"I'm sure they won't turn down the *Jause.*"

Herr Granini smiled. "Schön. Well, whom do we take first?"

"Seiffert!"

The atmosphere immediately became taut, almost as if they were in school. Peter felt apprehensive and alert. If only his turn wouldn't come right away, so that he could see first what happened to the others. He felt a little reassured when he saw the friendly way in which Herr Granini put his hand on Seiffert's shoulder and said:

"All right, Seiffert, let's see whether you are better than Rittmeyer."

They all knew Rittmeyer—by sight, of course, for he was years older and would not talk to them except once in a while to settle a fight in the garden in the Verein. Rittmeyer was the soprano soloist in the choir and in the third year of the *Gymnasium* and a good soccer player.

"Let's move over there," Rudi suggested. They moved a little to the left where they could see the whole corner of the music room. Herr Granini had sat down at the piano and started to run over a scale.

"Start with 'ah-ah-ah,'" Herr Granini said, and Seiffert sang "ah-ah-ah-ah" up and down the scale. Then Herr Granini changed to another key and urged Seiffert to go up as high as he could.

This wasn't so bad, Peter told himself. It was just like the voice exercises they always did at the beginning of class. Even when Seiffert was given a sheet of music and asked to read at sight, Herr Granini's voice was friendly. And once when Seiffert got stuck on a difficult phrase Herr Granini's voice took up the phrase and helped him through it.

Watching Herr Granini at the piano and Professor Wessely standing on the other side of it by the window, Peter realized that he was more afraid of Professor Wessely than of Herr Granini. There was something about the man that gave him confidence; he suddenly knew that he would sing all right. He even began to wish that it would be his turn next.

He did not get his wish. Rudi was called in before him and came out with his pink face a little more flushed than usual.

"What did he say?" Peter asked him eagerly.

"He said I'd be all right, and he asked about Papa."

While he waited and watched boy after boy go into the other room and stand by the piano, Peter had abundant opportunity to study Herr Granini. He was not a tall man but he had a powerful chest and powerful shoulders which showed under the black mohair coat he wore. What struck Peter most about him, however, was his head. It was a beautifully shaped head with long, black hair which curled up just above the coat collar, so that Peter was reminded of the busts of the great composers he had seen in parks. He marveled again at the simplicity with which Herr Granini was dressed. Franz said that he was very rich; yet he wore a simple mohair suit like several teachers in school, and black sandals. Only his extraordinary calm and his striking head gave any clue that he was no ordinary man. All of a sudden Peter knew that he was as anxious to get into the choir because of Herr Granini as because of Rudi.

When his turn came at last, he felt all choked up and shy again.

Professor Wessely said: "This is Franz Bartsch's cousin."

Herr Granini smiled at him.

"Are you as good as your cousin?"

"I don't know, Herr Granini," he said flusteredly.

"Well, shall we see? Let's try a few scales. . . ."

He took a deep breath as they had been taught. When Herr Granini changed to another key he nodded encouragingly. Peter felt his voice getting clearer. Once he reached high 'F,' which he knew was good for an alto, and he had no difficulty with his lower register. But he did badly when Herr Granini tested him for pitch. He had to identify chords and then he had to sing half a page of a song he had never seen before. All his confidence left him and he was afraid. Then Herr Granini handed him a *Sanctus* they had rehearsed in class. He made a desperate effort to fight down his fear and after a few bars he felt his voice getting loose again.

He felt exultant when Herr Granini took his hands off the keyboard and said earnestly:

"You've got the makings of a voice, Domanig. We'll work on it. Say hello to Franz."

That meant that he had passed! An immense gratitude to the man with the suave, low-pitched voice seized him. He would be in the choir now and go on all the trips—sometimes they stayed away overnight even—and he would be with Rudi. He whispered hurriedly to Rudi what Herr Granini had said before the next boy started to sing. . . .

The last boy came out of the music room. Herr Granini came in behind him and asked:

"Who wants some chocolate?"

"I—I!" Peter joined in the chorus. The strain of the examination had been broken. By the time they had sat down around the long table in the dining room they were all talking noisily. It occurred to Peter that four out of the twelve boys would not be taken into the choir. Professor Wessely had said that only eight of them would pass. It seemed to him a part of Herr Granini's compelling warmth that the four who would be dropped were as gay as the rest.

There was chocolate with whipped cream and delicious cake. The housekeeper in the beige dress was urging them to have a third piece. At the upper end of the table, Herr Granini was talking with Professor Wessely. Rudi looked at him from across the table and smiled.

The *Gymnasium* seemed suddenly unimportant.

Chapter Ten

THE CHOIR opened a new world for him. Every morning when he awoke his first thought was of the rehearsal that afternoon. He could hardly wait for five o'clock when he could at last hurry to the Verein.

He loved the routine of rehearsals. They would usually play soccer or tag in the garden until Herr Granini came strolling out to watch them for a few minutes before he gave the signal to go upstairs. Once Peter had happened to be near the little group of older boys who invariably gathered around Herr Granini; he had edged as close to them as he dared. Herr Granini was talking of a Bach cantata which they had recently started rehearsing and of a famous Spanish choir and its performance of the same cantata, then in his warm, husky, curiously seductive voice he had said: "Well, shall we start?" The older boys had called to the rest and they had all trooped upstairs.

In the music room they took their places in the double row of chairs arranged in a half-circle around Herr Granini's music stand. Herr Merz or some other accompanist went to the piano; one of the soloists handed out the music; Herr Granini hoisted himself up on the high stool behind his desk and the rehearsal would start.

He came to look forward to Herr Granini's mannerisms—the way he tossed his manelike locks or brushed them back over his ear with the cork handle of his baton, the way his smoldering eyes swept over them before an attack, the way Herr Granini listened sometimes to a phrase with bent head, his baton drooping in front of his chest. He could not get enough of the man. There was in Herr Granini a commanding, deep-toned respect for the music they sang, which made every minute exciting and taut with joy. Once or twice, indeed, Peter had observed Herr Granini's eyes flash dangerously when one of the older boys had bungled an attack—the aspenwood stick hissed through the air then and caught the culprit on the chest. Herr Granini always had two or three extra sticks on the ledge of his desk. Later the stick would be quietly passed up front; Herr Granini would take it with a grin and they would all be glad that his anger had passed. And he would be warm with praise if they had sung some passage particularly well.

But the rehearsals were only a prelude to Sunday. Peter had always dreaded Sunday before; now it came to be the day he looked forward to most. They usually sang for High Mass in the Lazarist Church at nine. As soon as they had finished, there would be a gay rush to a coffeehouse in the Kaiserstrasse for coffee or chocolate and cake. There were always a dozen or more men who sang the tenor and bass and baritone parts, and sometimes when Herr Granini used an orchestra there were more men than boys and the coffeehouse hummed with their deep voices and laughter.

It was the brightest spot of the morning for him. He had never been in a coffeehouse before. He loved the good coffee with whipped cream, the white marble-topped tables and the red plush upholstered seats.

After this second breakfast they would crowd into taxis and ride into the Innere Stadt to sing at the University Church. Then they would either stroll home through the Mariahilferstrasse or stop at the Palace Chapel to listen to their rival choir there.

The choir kept him from thinking much about the *Gymnasium*. He saw Rudi every day. They stood side by side at the end of the alto section and they often sang from the same sheet of music. They walked home together from rehearsal and always lingered for a few minutes in the doorway of Rudi's house, for there were always so many things they had to tell each other just then that it was hard to say good-by. These few minutes at the end seemed most precious of all to Peter; they seemed momentous and full of a consuming sweetness. He did not dare to think of the vacation when Rudi's parents would move to their villa in Hütteldorf and Rudi would be away. He caught himself hoping secretly that something would happen to force Rudi's parents to stay in town.

School was rapidly drawing to a close. He tried hard to efface the bad impression he had made on the teacher, but he realized that it was already too late. His first glance when he was handed his report card on the last morning of school showed him that Herr

Renzl had given him a "two" in deportment. Fear of what Father would say made him feel weak for a moment. The conduct mark was always the first thing Father looked for, just as she always looked first to see whether he had a "one" in religion.

He waited until after lunch before he brought out the card. He hardly dared to believe his ears when Father merely asked:

"Where's the pen and ink?"

He thought that Father had not noticed the conduct mark. But when he said, timidly enough, "The teacher said you didn't have to sign it this time, because it's the last one," Father flared up immediately: "I suppose that's how you got that 'two' in conduct, for talking back. If that happens again, you'll get a taste of the strap."

He wanted badly to explain how he had got the bad mark, that it had been for drawing and that each time the teacher had caught him he had not even been aware that he was drawing. But on the whole he was grateful that things had gone off so well—grateful, and a little surprised.

Father had changed! There could no longer be any doubt about it. He had come in several times long after Peter had already been asleep and he had made so much noise that Peter had waked up. She had said the day after that Father had been drunk, but Father on those occasions seemed to Peter only exceptionally gay. He laughed a lot and sang snatches of songs and took a long time getting undressed. Peter would listen intently, a little afraid of Father's unaccustomed hilarity. Once, when he had crept to the door to peer out into the living room, he had seen Father standing by the chest of drawers, winding his watch and singing softly and, Peter thought, quite pleasantly to himself. He was swaying a little and when he started to walk toward his bed he would have fallen down if she had not caught him under the arm. Then when he had safely sat down on the bed, she began to unlace his shoes to a running accompaniment of scolding. Only, Father did not take her seriously and kept on laughing at her. She was wearing a long white nightgown and the white petticoat in which she had waited up for him. At one point, Peter saw him reach up as if to pull her toward him. She had pushed him away angrily and hissed: "Don't you dare touch me!" Father had merely laughed again and said:

"Who'd want to touch you?" Then Father was singing again to himself, until he suddenly fell asleep and began to snore softly. In between his noisy breathing Peter could hear her pray.

The morning after, Poldi greeted Father coldly and went about with a scowl all day. Peter thought at first that Poldi was merely angry because Father had been drinking too much wine and because she resented not having a room of her own, instead of sleeping in the kitchen and having Father and Franz walk through when they came home.

Then one evening toward the end of July he was sitting on the divan in the living room, reading. It was almost dark and he sat crouched forward toward the window, anxious to finish one of Poldi's books before Poldi came home. The book had to do with an Italian *contessa* who was dying of tuberculosis and a broken heart. The broken heart and the tuberculosis seemed both to have been caused by the unfaithfulness of her fiancé, but there had been indications that he was repentant. For several chapters now there had been mysterious baskets of white roses. Presumably the fiancé would show up on any page now, bearing a basket of white roses.

His eyes raced over the pages. His ears remained alert to the noises out in the kitchen. *She* was fixing supper. If she saw him with one of Poldi's books, *she* would be sure to tell her. He had guarded against discovery by having one of his own books on his lap which he could pretend to be reading in case she came in.

He had reached the last chapter. A man with a basket of white roses stepped out of a carriage in front of the sanitarium. . . . There it was! He felt irritated at the romantic patness of it. The book struck him as mawkish and turgid like most of the books Poldi brought home. Still he could not resist reading them even at the risk of getting punished. A passionate curiosity drove him to the books. The worst of it was that the books rarely gave him a glimpse of light, as now: Why had the fiancé broken his engagement to her if he loved her? It was all vague and senseless.

He heard someone at the front door. It was Poldi. Quickly he closed the book and put it back on top of the chest of drawers. But his precaution had not been necessary. Poldi did not even come into the living room; she started talking to *her* at once in an angrily lowered voice:

"I saw him again, Mother! You've got to do something. It's a disgrace. They were walking up the Westbahnstrasse together just as I got off the streetcar. What are you going to do?"

He realized suddenly that Poldi was talking about Father. It flashed on him that what made Poldi so angry was the lady he had seen with Father in the Kandlgasse about a week ago.

There followed a tense silence. He was careful not to make any noise. Perhaps now he would discover why Father had been so different lately and had not wanted to take him with him Sunday afternoons. The silence continued, fragile as a bubble. He knew that *she* was grimly gathered into herself the way she got when she was worried, like the time when Franz had been out all night.

"What are you going to do, Mother?"

"What is there to do except bear the cross God sends me? God'll show him. . . ."

"Well, I'm going to do something about it, if you aren't. Where is Franz?"

"You let Franz alone. He isn't home yet."

"I will *not* let him alone. Franz has got to talk to Father or I will!"

Poldi came into the living room. Her face and throat were flushed. He pretended to be engrossed in his book.

"What are you doing here?"

"Reading."

He could tell that she was annoyed that he had overheard what she had said.

"I've told you not to read in this light."

"I was only finishing this page."

"You aren't finishing any page. Here——" She took hold of the book and tried to get it away from him. He clung to it for a second and struggled with her as part of the comedy he was playing to make her believe that he had not heard her angry outburst in the kitchen. But during the rest of the evening he watched Poldi and her intently.

When Father came home, Poldi dashed into Franz's room and pretended to be busy writing a letter. She did not come out until supper was already on the table. Her face still wore a dark flush. Twice when Father addressed her—he was unusually talkative this evening—she refused to answer. The second time, Father flared up: "Can't you answer when you are spoken to? Or do I have to teach you manners?" He finally sensed that something was wrong when *she* also confined herself to grudging monosyllables. He hammered on the table with his fist so that all the plates danced——

"God-damned females! I want some manners in my house!"

Poldi got up defiantly and went into Franz's room. Peter heard her turn the key on the inside. *She* sat for a minute longer, then she went into the kitchen as if to fetch something and did not come back. Peter was left alone with him. Several times Peter tried to speak, but fear made his throat feel dry. Angry as he was now, Father might not like it if he broke into the sullen silence. Yet he felt tremulous with an uneasy affection for him and wanted to let him know somehow that he disapproved of the conspiracy between Poldi and her.

A minute later his opportunity was gone, for Father pushed back his plate, got up and was out of the flat almost before Peter could get his breath. He had been gone only a minute or two when Franz flung open the front door and called:

"Light! Food! I'm hungry. Hello, everybody."

Peter saw him go to her beside the stove.

"What's the matter?" Franz said gaily. "Do you hear? What's up?"

She was wiping her eyes with the corner of her apron.

"Go away. Let me alone. Your supper is getting cold."

Franz seized her by the shoulders and was shaking her playfully. "I want to know, you old witch, do you hear? I just met Father in the yard and he just barely said hello." The soft blond skin on Franz's forehead was creasing into troubled wrinkles. "What is it?"

"I'll tell you in a minute—" Poldi had come out through the living room—"Peter, you take this book to Gisl!"

"Now?"

"Yes, now!"

He had to go.

Ordinarily, he would have jumped at the chance to run an errand to Fräulein Gisl who lived on the Gürtel. Fräulein Gisl was tall and pretty and she usually gave him a piece of chocolate or some cake. Besides, the trip to her house allowed him to walk through the park where some boys from school were always sure to be playing. . . .

He went reluctantly down the stairs and out through the yard. For a minute he toyed with the idea of climbing back up the stairs and listening at the door, but he resisted the temptation. Eavesdropping was for old women, not for heroes. Then, just as he walked out through the entranceway of the house, the sight of Frau Schreier brought his mind back to Father and to what Poldi had been saying.

He remembered the remarks he had heard different women make about Frau Schreier to *her*. He had paid no attention at the time, but now the remarks suddenly seemed significant. Frau Schreier was "carrying on" with the enormous man who worked for the expressman up the street, and Herr Schreier was "carrying on" with the widow lady who lived on the third floor on the back stairs. He had seen Herr Schreier come down the back stairs several times—Herr Schreier must have been to see the widow lady and that was what the women meant by "carrying on."

So that was what Father was doing! He had a vague feeling that it was wrong for Father to be seen with another woman, but when he tried to figure out why it was wrong, he failed. After all, Father never went out with *her* and the lady he had seen him with that day had looked so nice that he felt rather proud at the thought that Father should be with her. If he were in Father's place he would not want to be seen with *her* either. Still, there must be something wrong about it, something that had to do with the vague realm of the impure that Pater Alfred had explained to them in catechism before they had made their first confession. It had all seemed quite clear to him at the time, but now he wondered whether there had not been something he had missed.

He puzzled about it until he reached Fräulein Gisl's house. Then he decided to ask Franz sometime. Perhaps Franz would tell him. In the meantime he resolved to watch very carefully to find out just what it was Poldi had against the lady.

The tension Poldi's angry remarks in the kitchen had started grew more oppressive every day. He began to dread the times when they were all home together. The excitement which he had felt at first had given way to resentment. He was aware of a vague fear, and he fled with relief to the Verein on the mornings when Herr Granini was taking them on an excursion for the whole day.

But there were still the evenings, and the days when he had to stay at home. He tried to make himself as unobtrusive as possible. Even Franz who had always been so gay was apt to be impatient with him when he tried to ask him questions in the hope of starting a conversation. He suffered most from the change that had come over Franz. Franz never smiled now. His forehead was creased and his blue eyes which had always laughed at people looked stern and embarrassed somehow.

As for Poldi, she seemed angry and determined. She got up earlier in the morning and was out of the house before Father was up, and she had changed her lunch hour so that she ate later than Father did and could eat in the kitchen. When she did eat with Father, her face invariably wore a flush.

Only Father appeared not to have changed. But that, Peter realized, was just on the surface. Father was really asserting his indifference to Poldi and to her by emphasizing the ponderous rhythm of his daily routine. Where formerly he had merely been irritated if his stiff shirts had not come back from the laundryman in time, he would shout at her now over such a trifle as moving a cuff link on the chest of drawers. At meals he brought his newspaper and read steadily while he ate. If she was slow in bringing on the next course, he would rap on his plate with the knife and growl:

"What about the meat? Do I have to wait all day?"

She in turn had made a habit of never sitting down at the table any more. Although Peter laid her place, she used her cooking as an excuse to stay by the stove and eat in the kitchen.

One Sunday noon while he was drying the dishes, he watched Father getting ready to go out. Through the living-room door he could see him brush his mustache, then fill his cigar case from the cedarwood box in which the cigars came from the tobacco shop.

She suddenly dried her hands and went to the door of the living room.

"I hope you aren't forgetting that the rent's due tomorrow," she said in her muffled, clipped voice which had grown even more impersonal and more reproachful and sardonic in its hushed meekness in the last few weeks.

Father gave an impatient grunt, picked up his keys and went to the mahogany table in front of the two beds and unlocked the drawer. He tossed two banknotes on top of the table, locked the drawer, and came back to the window.

Peter crossed the kitchen to see what was going to happen. Father was calmly hooking his watch chain through the buttonhole in his vest. She went to the table, then came to the chest of drawers and held the banknotes out to him:

"What am I going to pay the rent with?"

"You can count, can't you? That's the rent."

"And what are we going to eat on?"

He did not answer.

"Do you think the grocer and the butcher are going to give us things for nothing?"

Father was pulling his coat straight in front of the mirror. "What about the money Frau Gerstecker left you? I suppose that's going to the priests?"

"That money went to Wetti, and the few kronen that were left over are going to be used to have a few Masses said for Frau Gerstecker's soul."

"Masses! If you didn't give all the money to the priests—"

"Yes, I have money to give to the priests with what you give me. There's a lot left at the end of the month!"

Poldi had appeared in the door from Franz's room where she had gone immediately after dinner. Franz was away on an excursion with Baron Ortner for the day. . . .

"You ought to be ashamed of yourself, Father," Poldi said angrily, "to say things like that about Mother after the way—"

Father had spun around to face her. "You shut your mouth or I'll teach you to butt in."

But Poldi was too wrought up to stop.

"The whole neighborhood is talking!"

"Talking about what?" He took two threatening steps toward her.

"About you and that woman. It's a—"

The impact of Father's hand on Poldi's face sent her back against the door.

"Don't you dare hit her in the head!" *she* spat. The restraint that habitually muted her voice kept her even now from shouting.

"I'll teach her to talk to me like that!"

Poldi was sobbing defiantly. She drew herself up very straight. "It's true and I'll say it as long—"

Peter, quivering with excitement and fear, saw him raise his hand to hit Poldi again. But he did not strike. She had pushed Poldi to one side and blocked his way.

"You hit her again!" she threatened. For a moment Peter thought that Father was going to strike *her*, too. They stood there facing each other, his hand with the two rings on it still poised by his shoulder. "You just hit me!" she dared him. "Herr Herzig beats his wife, but you aren't going to put your hands on me."

To his astonishment Peter saw Father turn away abruptly and merely mutter, "Priest-slut!" Poldi had flung into Franz's room and was sobbing there. *She* had come back out into the kitchen and Peter hastily busied himself with the remaining dishes. He could see that she was crying. . . . A few minutes later Father stamped out through the kitchen and slammed the front door hard.

As soon as he was finished with the dishes, he hurried into the living room. Seeing her cry made him feel uneasy and embarrassed, and he wanted to be alone to think about what had just happened. He felt that all the values that had always seemed as unchangeable a part of home as the chest of drawers or the divan had suddenly been upset. Poldi who was a grownup—she had been eighteen in the spring—had been slapped by Father just as he might have been. And *she*, who was smaller than Poldi and barely came up to Father's shoulders, had somehow made him back down. He had a feeling that while she had not got the money she wanted—how was she going to buy them food if she had no money?—she had yet somehow come out on top. He remained puzzled and upset, and doubly grateful for the choir that afternoon.

The excursions on which Herr Granini took them almost every day now were an escape into a world where everything was laughter and joyful surprise. He lived only for the excursions, and during the hours he had to spend at home he tried to numb himself against the constant threat of another set-to by thinking of the next outing.

Only about half of the boys were left; the rest had gone into the country with their parents. That had its advantages. The older boys who were left were less standoffish with him and with the other new boys than they had been at first. Rittmeyer, in particular, who was the soprano soloist and acknowledged to be the best soccer player as well, had gone out of his way to be friendly to him. His attention had almost made Peter forget about Rudi's absence.

They usually started out early in the morning from the Verein. They would ride to the end of the streetcar line, then walk through the woods to some rustic restaurant where they had lunch. In the afternoon they either played soccer, if they could find a smooth enough meadow, or they divided up into two groups and played a complicated form of tag which consisted in getting into the enemy's territory and touching a tree before one got tagged. It was exciting. The fragrance of the forest meadows, the drowsy butterflies hovering over the flowers, the consciousness of having been singled out by Rittmeyer for all kinds of flattering attention, the good food in the restaurants—all blended into the intoxicating happiness he had come to associate with the excursions.

And there was always Herr Granini!

Half shyly and half brazenly, he watched him as he sat under a tree with a few men of about Franz's age, and he found himself wishing that he might grow up quickly so that he too could be near Herr Granini like the men and listen to his fascinating voice which could be so thrillingly serious and so rich with laughter.

It was almost the middle of August and he could not help thinking now and again, bleakly, about the fall when he would have to stay home with her except for the few hours of choir rehearsal. The atmosphere at home was still tense. Father came and went with a kind of belligerent self-complacency—aimed, it seemed to Peter, at keeping Poldi and Franz at bay. And Father had never given her the rest of the housekeeping money. She went around swollen-eyed and mute, and Peter knew that she cried at night while she lay in bed. Sometimes before he fell asleep he could hear her praying.

Franz's efforts to tease her out of her worry were half-hearted and no longer successful. Franz himself had come to wear a frown most of the time. Peter noticed that he stayed away from home more and more.

But it was of what Poldi might do that Peter was most afraid. She moved about the house with her bottled-up indignation which threatened to explode at any moment. One evening when they thought him asleep, Peter heard her say:

"I waited for two hours and then I saw them come out—together!"

She mumbled something which made Poldi burst out angrily:

"I don't care! I'm going to talk to that woman; I'm going to tell her what I think and you can't stop me!" There was a mumble again and then Poldi's voice: "We'll see about that! He has no right——"

Chapter Eleven

Herr Bartsch sauntered around the corner of the Kandlgasse and turned right on the Gürtel. His walking stick beat out a leisurely tattoo on the sidewalk. His sharp blue eyes with their pinched corners at the base of his nose moved alertly this way and that behind the nickel-rimmed pince-nez. He looked like a well-to-do burgher out for an afternoon stroll, anxious not to miss any interesting sight on either side of the street.

When he came to the square, cut-stone doorway of a modern-looking apartment house whose imposing three-story façade had been recently done over in stippled gray stucco, he slowed down and stepped into the shelter of the doorway, ostensibly to light his pipe. With the same leisurely deliberation with which he had been walking he now hooked his cane over his arm, stripped off his pearl-gray cotton gloves, and brought out a pipe and a worn leather pouch from his coat pocket.

Liesel liked him to smoke a pipe! Since he had known her he had almost given up smoking cigars. She said they smelled bad. "Women!" he told himself with amused indulgence as he lighted his pipe. After two or three experimental puffs, his eyes swept briskly over the tree-lined promenade across the street and the narrow park beyond it from which came the shrill cries of children.

Not that he cared whether anybody saw him or not. What he did was his business. He was his own master. Still, with the children and all . . .

Quite suddenly but still without haste, he grasped his stick more firmly, turned on his heels and walked down the pleasantly dusky entranceway of the house. He did not look back as he climbed the half-dozen steps on the left that led to the ground floor. By the time he had started up the staircase and reached the second floor a surprising change had come over him. The habitually taut muscles of his red face which made him look stern had relaxed and he looked eager and almost boyish. His step as he walked to the end of the second-floor landing had lost its measured dignity. There was a springiness in it now. When he came to a halt in front of the door which bore a discreet bronze plate with FRAU BETTY OLIVA engraved on it his expression changed again. He looked faintly mischievous as he pushed the electric buzzer four times in quick succession. Three rings was the signal Liesel and he had agreed upon.

From behind the door came the muffled crescendo of approaching steps. There was the dull click of a guard chain being unhooked and the door opened softly. He stepped inside at once with the assurance of habit and said gaily, "*Servus*, Liesel," to the woman holding open the door.

The woman wore a smart white batiste blouse that clung caressingly to the bold rise of her breasts, and a close-fitting navy-blue skirt that molded her trim waist. She looked as if she had been on the point of getting ready to go out. She said, "*Servus, Du!*" and smiled at him briefly, almost hastily. Her eyelids lowered immediately over her liquid brown eyes, but the effect was more evasive than seductive. She closed the door very softly.

Herr Bartsch watched her with an amused grin as she hooked the guard chain into place.

"Afraid somebody'll come and steal you?"

Without looking at him, she said: "You can't be too careful these days."

He had slipped one arm around her waist and was drawing her to him. "I didn't know you were such a scaredy-cat. . . ." His mouth sought her lips. She had yielded to the pressure of his arm and now kissed him quickly as if anxious to get free again. But he did not let her go. "Well, how's the Emperor's girl today?"

It was a joke they had had between them ever since the day when Franz Joseph had waved back to her from his carriage in Hietzing one afternoon. But it did not draw a soft laugh from her today, not even a smile. He realized that something was wrong and took away his arm.

"That peasant theater you liked so much is playing tonight in Sievering—at Schrantzer's. . . ."

"Schrantzer's?" she repeated absent-mindedly.

"It's out-of-doors. It'll be nice out there tonight."

She had stood waiting for him to put his hat and his walking stick on the narrow hall table beneath an ornate Venetian mirror. She turned now to go into the living room.

It was really a drawing room, as he had often before told himself proudly, for her apartment boasted a dining room and another sitting room, where she kept her accounts and which she called her office. The room breathed a comfortable, sprightly elegance. His experienced cabinetmaker's eye reapproved for the twentieth time the subtly deprecated solidity of the modern Biedermeier furniture; he missed few of the little touches with which she had given the room an air of gay informality. It was precisely the sort of room he had once dreamed of having and now would never have. You had to have money to afford this sort of thing; you had to be a *Hausfrau* like Liesel! So that even after months of coming here every day, he never entered this room without the secret, exhilarating consciousness that Liesel owned the whole big apartment house. The thought did not make him envious; it merely added to his pride that Liesel should be in love with him.

"Well, what do you think? Are we going to Schrantzer's tonight?"

"I hadn't thought . . . we'll see, Ludwig."

She had gone to one of the tapestry-upholstered armchairs across the room and picked up the slip cover on which she had been sewing. He noticed then that the sofa and two of the chairs already had covers over them.

"Why the dust covers? You going away somewhere?" he chuckled complacently.

"I thought I'd better put them on."

Her voice sounded evasive but it was her eyelids that caught his attention. They were lowered until the brown, soft lashes almost rested on her cheeks as she sewed. Together with the unusually heightened color she had today, they reminded him of his first evening in this room. It was the way she had looked when she had finally given in after the laughing, playful tussle with which she had defended herself and had let him carry her into the bedroom.

The memory kindled his blood. He crossed the rug and drew her up from the chair. In his passion he barely noticed her reluctance. His left hand had slid caressingly down to her thigh, when she twisted away from him.

"Look out for the needle! D'you want me to stick you?"

He held her only more closely. Her body felt soft and yet firm against him and he bent over her greedily to kiss her mouth. Only when her body stiffened with resistance and she murmured almost fiercely, with her head strained far to one side: "Not today, Ludwig," did he finally let her go.

Her resistance puzzled him. He stepped away from her and watched her with a faint frown.

"What's the matter with you today, Liesel?"

Her head bent still more resolutely over her sewing. The flush still crimsoned her face and throat. It was finally borne in on him that something was wrong. This subdued drawing back from him was not like her. It was usually she who teased him with caresses, and she had not once called him "Putzi" today. The slip covers suddenly assumed a sinister significance.

"Why are you putting on those covers?"

"I'm going to Germany tomorrow, Ludwig. To Dresden to visit my sister."

He stood silent for a minute as if he had not heard. To hide his alarm, he joked: "This is the first I hear about it! That doesn't give me much time to get ready. . . ."

"You aren't coming, Ludwig."

"Now, what's all this about?" Anger had come into his voice. "Do you mind letting me in on it?"

She looked up quickly. Her eyes looked troubled, pleading.

"Putzi, you knew this couldn't go on forever. You knew there had to be an end sometime."

"Why does there have to be an end? Unless——"

"It isn't me, Ludwig. You know that! It's your family."

"What's my family got to do with it? You said yourself you didn't want to marry again."

"It isn't that, Putzi."

His hand pressed down so hard on the back of the chair that the chair creaked. "Then, what is it?"

"Your daughter was here today, this noon."

"What!"

She smiled a little.

"She's a regular spitfire, that daughter of yours. I'd say a chip off the old block."

His scowl had made the pince-nez slip off his nose. He left it dangling on the black silk string.

"I'll give that brat such a hiding!"

"No, you won't. Putzi, you must promise me!" She had come toward him to put one hand on his arm. "She couldn't help it. Girls at that age take things like that hard. We had a good time while it lasted. Let's remember the good times we had together."

He could feel the warmth of her body as she bent forward pleadingly. The troubling fragrance of her hair and skin finished turning his anger into panic.

"Liesel," he said hoarsely, "you can't! Not now, after—I've got to have you! I'll go to Germany with you and get a divorce. I can start all over again. I've got my trade. . . ." His hand fumbled against her arm and around to her back.

Moved as she was by his hoarse, half-stammered appeal, almost ready to change her mind about going, she yet experienced a sudden sense of revulsion at the thought of his horny fingernails. She realized that the revulsion had been growing on her for several weeks. It was curious about his nails: she remembered the morbid fascination the thick, yellow nails had had for her at first, the shuddering voluptuousness with which she had first felt his fingers on her naked skin.

She forced herself to draw away from him gently.

"It wouldn't work, Ludwig. We're both Catholic and you couldn't get a divorce anyway."

"To hell with being Catholic. I'll turn Protestant in Germany."

"No, Putzi. I don't think I'd like to do anything like that. Besides, there is your son. . . ."

He sneered: "Was he here, too?"

"No, but Poldi told me how he felt and you needn't tell me how much Franz means to you."

He had fallen silent at the mention of Franz. Then a new idea made his eyes flash with hope——

"Why couldn't you rent a villa in Hütteldorf like we said?"

"It's too late. It wouldn't work. I didn't want to tell you but this wasn't the first time I heard from Poldi. About a week ago she wrote me a letter. I didn't pay much attention to that because—well, you know, a letter—but today was different."

"Where's that letter?"

"I won't show it to you."

"I'll kill that old bitch! She's the one that put her up to that." His rage gave way to pleading again: "What do you care about the damned girl?"

"I do care. She threatened to make a scene in the street next time she saw us together. I've got my good name to think of. No, Ludwig, let's call it quits! It was too nice to spoil it that way."

He recognized the determination in her voice and gave up arguing. Instead, he tightened his hold around her waist and drew her to him. She yielded at first and kissed him with parted lips, but when he made a move to draw her toward the bedroom she pushed him away with all her strength—"No!"

"You might at least leave me that to remember."

She patted her hair and then pulled at her blouse. "What's the use? It'll only make it harder for both of us."

"The other's really an excuse, isn't it? The truth is you don't give a damn about me any more!"

"You said that—not I! It's just as hard for me as it is for you. Oh, Putzi, let's be sensible! Let's say good-by and remember all the fun we had——" She kissed him quickly, caressed his arm, then kissed him once more.

He remained wooden under her caresses.

"When are you coming back?"

"I don't know, Putzi. I may stay all winter. Believe me, it's better that way."

"Then it's all over?"

"It's got to be—don't you see?"

"All right," he said finally, "good-by, Liesel."

She followed him out into the hall. He picked up his hat and walking stick without looking at her.

"One thing more, Putzi: promise not to take this out on your family. They couldn't help it. It's only natural——"

He had already unhooked the guard chain.

She whispered, "Good-by, Putzi," from where she stood and blew him a kiss.

He did not see it. . . .

He walked away from the house and up the Gürtel. His legs

moved stiffly as if he were struggling through the wet loam of a new-plowed field. His stick made a dull, cheerless clatter every time it hit the sidewalk. When he came to the terrace at Wimberger's with its blue-striped awnings, he went inside and sat down at the farthest table. A bandy-legged waiter came flicking his napkin with exasperating cheerfulness and tried to make conversation. He was only barely polite and ordered a glass of Gumpoldskirchner.

When he had his wine and was alone again, he sat looking down on the blue and white checked tablecloth. His mind kept teasing him with bright, torturing details of his life with Liesel. There seemed to be no end to the things he remembered. Then he fell back into the stupor that told him that all was finished—not only Liesel but his life as well. For Liesel had made the future seem as bright and promising as coming out of a tunnel. He had been making plans. If they pensioned him in the theater, he was going to go to Schani and ask him to lend him the money to buy old Himmelreiter's shop in the Kaiserstrasse. He was going to start all over again. He wasn't old yet. In fact, Liesel had made him feel that things were only just beginning for him.

Remembering how he had felt only this morning plunged him back into despair. Two men and a woman entered between the potted oleander trees and sat down a few tables away from him. He raised his glass to his lips and found that he had finished the wine without realizing it. He signaled the waiter and ordered another half-liter. More people kept coming in. It was getting on toward evening. A party of four were laughing boisterously at the far end of the terrace. . . .

Supposing Liesel had only been excited! She had been as crazy about him as he had been about her. After she'd have been away for a few weeks she'd decide to come back and everything would be as before. But an instant later he knew that he was deluding himself. Liesel wasn't like that. If she said a thing she meant it. That was one of the reasons why he'd been so taken with her. No, it was finished all right!

His dull despair suddenly found relief in a rage that made him twitch with its violence.

It was all her fault, the priest-ridden bitch! She had sicked Poldi on to it. She had spoiled it for him the way she always had spoiled everything for him, but he'd show her! His nails dug convulsively into his palms. She'd pay for this!

Peter awoke with a start and was instantly and quiveringly alert. It seemed to him that the uproar in the other room had been going on for hours. Father was shouting in an angry, reckless voice. He could not at first make out what he was shouting but he knew at once that it was about *her*. Franz was talking to Father cajolingly—he sounded worried.

It was very dark. The door into the living room was closed; underneath it, on the floor, shone a narrow strip of light.

A chair crashed on the floor. Someone lunged against a wardrobe.

"Jesus, Mary, and Joseph! Now he's wrecking the furniture!"

"Sure I'll wreck it. I'll wreck every God-damn bit of it. Where's the ax? I want the ax——"

"We'll do that tomorrow, Father," Franz tried to humor him; "first thing in the morning. Let's go to bed now."

There came the sounds of another struggle.

"I'm going to get the ax. I'll show her!"

Peter cowered in frozen alarm, his knees and the blanket drawn up to his chin. Fear sharpened his ears until even the slightest noise from beyond the door was infinitely menacing.

"O Sacred Heart of Jesus," she was half praying and half scolding, "what a disgrace after twenty years in the house. He'll wake up all the neighbors!"

"Come on to bed, Father. Time to get some sleep—there's a good fellow. . . ." Peter could hear Father sit down heavily on his bed.

". . . . bitch . . . whoring after the priests . . ."

"Sure, Father! Women are all alike."

Peter listened hopefully. Franz sounded almost as he did when he teased *her*. Presently there came the sound of a shoe being set on the floor. Father was quieter now. Peter found time to wonder what he had meant when he had said that she went "whoring after the priests."

Then Father was shouting again.

"Sacred Heart of Jesus!" he mimicked with a roar. "You can't fool me! Did you have your date with your black priest today?"

Even Franz did not appear to be able to calm him this time. He was determined to get the ax from the woodbox in the kitchen. For a second Peter's terror conjured up a picture of Father swinging the ax wildly over her head. He heard Poldi say angrily:

"Do close the windows, Mother! Do you want all the neighbors to hear?"

Father had evidently heard her, too.

"The windows stay open! To hell with the neighbors! I want them to know what a priest-ridden bitch I've got."

"I won't have you talk about Mother that way!" Poldi burst out.

"Oh, be quiet!" from Franz.

There followed a fiercer struggle than any before. Peter could feel the floor shake even in his room. Father was threatening to beat Poldi and he was evidently trying to free himself. *She* was closing the windows and praying out loud.

It seemed to Peter to go on for an endless length of time. His heart pounded with noisy thumps. Once he resolved to go out into the other room and plead with Father to go to bed and he had actually got his feet down on the floor, but Franz must have heard the sofa creak for he said quickly to Father: "You are going to wake up Peter!" His heart beat louder than ever then and he crawled back into bed. Twice he started to pray but he was unable to finish even a single "Our Father" because some new alarm from the other room made him forget where he was with his prayer.

Franz finally opened the door. It had been quiet in the living room for some time. Franz went to bed. Peter could hear him turning this way and that. He could also hear Father's breathing in the other room and the dry tinkling of the beads of *her* rosary. Limp and with his brain still crowded with terrifying images of Father brandishing the ax, he lay awake for a long time.

Chapter Twelve

HERR GRANINI took them on an especially fine outing the following day. They were free to climb around among the ruins of an old castle all morning long, and after lunch they played Indians and Trappers in an eerie ravine. By dint of playing with a kind of desperate abandon, Peter managed to shut out the memory of the night before, but he could not rid himself of a vaguer but more persistent anxiety which had become coupled with his dread of going home.

He lingered in the garden of the Verein in the evening as long as he dared. In the end, it was his hunger and a sudden curiosity to see what had happened since morning that made him go home, rather than his usual fear of her scolding when he had stayed out too late.

She was alone in the flat. He noticed that her eyes were still swollen. She hurried him through his supper and made him come with her to the little convent church in the Kaiserstrasse where there was a vesper service at eight. He saw as he knelt beside her that a certain pious self-assurance was missing from the way she held her head as she prayed. The discovery filled him with malicious satisfaction at first; but a little later when she wiped her eyes with her already damp handkerchief, he felt ashamed of his vindictiveness.

He forced himself to stay awake after he had gone to bed. He heard Poldi come home and then Franz. They were talking in the kitchen about Father. After a long while Franz opened the door. He was holding a lamp in one hand and he came over to the sofa to look.

"Why don't you go to sleep?"

"I can't."

"Why can't you?"

"I'm afraid. Because of Father . . ."

He could see the fine, golden hairs that fringed Franz's pale eyebrows bristle with his frown.

"Never mind Father. He isn't going to hurt you. He just had a glass too much last night."

"But he was so angry!"

"People get that way when they've had too much to drink. Go to sleep now. Good night."

He said "Good night" and turned his face to the wall where he could see the soft reflection cast by the lamp. Franz had sat down at his desk and had opened a book. Presently Father came home. An ominous silence, broken only by Father's footsteps and the opening and closing of a drawer as he got ready to go to bed, emanated from the other room. Father did not seem drunk, but all of a sudden he was shouting again. In almost no time he had worked himself into a savage rage. Franz shifted irritably in his chair, then suddenly closed the book and got up from the desk. Peter watched him put some underwear into the little leather bag Franz always took when he went away on short trips. Franz closed the bag with a sharp snap, blew out the lamp on his desk, and went out into the living room.

Her voice was squeaky with alarm:

"Where are you going, Franz?"

"I'm going to a hotel. I can't sleep here with a drunk raving all night."

"Who's drunk?" Father growled. "Perhaps I've got to teach you some manners, too!"

"You taught me manners all right, Father, but not for a situation like this!"

"This is my house and I'll do as I please in it. If you don't like it, you can get out and stay out and the devil take you!"

Franz closed the front door.

She sobbed:

"O dear Jesus, what have I done to deserve this? Now he's even driving the children out of the house. . . ."

It was enough to set Father off again. Peter listened with stifled breath while Father swore at her. Yet Franz's startling departure seemed to have had a chastening effect on him and half an hour later the flat had become quiet. Only, it seemed to Peter a menacing stillness that might explode at any moment into some new, unimaginable violence again. The fact that Franz was no longer there made him feel both more fearful and more brave. It was up to him now to protect Poldi and her. . . .

There followed a whole week like that. He was gradually growing less afraid and he tried to fight off the anxiety that seized him when evening came. Franz, who had slept home again after that one night when he had gone to a hotel, left once more in the middle of the night and this time did not come home again for two whole days.

On the morning of the second day, Poldi made him stop in the middle of breakfast and come out on the landing. She looked very important.

"You're to tell Herr Granini that you won't be back in the choir until school opens again—you're going to Almzell tomorrow with Mother and Franz. And you're not to say anything about it in front of Father, do you hear?"

He could hardly believe his ears. He was going to Almzell where *she* and Aunt Wetti and Mizzi had been born, and where there were high mountains and real forests and wild deer, and he would be riding on the train all day, because Almzell was in the Tyrol—far away! Franz must have changed his plans for his vacation, for Franz had said that he was going to Switzerland only a few weeks ago. And Poldi was staying behind—he wondered for an instant whether she was not afraid to be all alone with Father—and there was a secret about their going away!

For once, the day with the choir dragged unbearably. Herr Granini had taken them to an island in the Danube to bathe. He picked a moment when Herr Granini was alone under his beach umbrella to tell him about the trip; then he hurried back into the water to tell Rittmeyer and some of the boys with whom he had grown particularly friendly during the summer. They were all boys whom he ordinarily envied, either because of the handsome clothes they wore, or because of the pocket money they got from home, or simply because they were going to the *Gymnasium* in the fall; it was the first time that he had ever been able to boast of anything himself.

He found it hard to control his exultation when he got home. The two wicker suitcases from the attic were standing side by side by the sewing machine and were already packed. On Franz's bed lay his new cowhide bag, still open but bulging with clothes and ready to shut. Scattered on the floor was Franz's mountain-climbing gear. They were really going! He tried not to pay any attention to her protests that she did not want to go.

"Who is going to look after him if anything happens?" she began again after supper.

"Nothing is going to happen," Poldi said impatiently. "Stop worrying. I'm going to be here."

"Much good you can do——"

"I don't see that you are able to do anything about it as long as he is like this. Maybe if you and Franz are away for a few weeks that'll bring him to his senses."

"And who's going to pay for all this? I haven't any money. He gave me only enough to pay the rent, and the few heller Frau Gerstecker left me are gone."

"Oh, stop worrying, Mother! Franz is going to pay for the railroad tickets and the first two weeks. After that, Father will have to give you the money."

"Yes, he sounded like it today!"

"I'll talk to him all right. I'm not afraid of him."

"If only he doesn't get pensioned! That'd be the end."

"Oh, you're always worrying, Mother."

"As if I hadn't plenty to worry about!"

But Peter saw that she had resigned herself to going. If only Father now did not make them stay, for Father came home and immediately burst out:

"You are staying here! Those bags are going to be unpacked first thing in the morning. I suppose you thought you were going to meet your fat priest down there? But I'll fix that! You aren't going anywhere unless I say so!" He stormed for a long time and Peter began to lose hope. Only the memory of Poldi's determination and the knowledge that Franz would be coming for them in the morning still left him a glimmer of hope.

He woke up jubilantly the next morning and yet afraid. He noticed that Poldi had stayed home from her office. Father was up unusually early, too, and sat eating breakfast and reading the morning paper. He had not spoken to anybody so far. A few minutes later Franz arrived. Franz went straight to his room to finish packing. Peter followed him anxiously.

"Are we really going, Franz?"

"Is your rucksack packed?"

"It's all ready, Franz. Are we going?"

"We're as good as on our way!" It was the first time Franz had grinned at him in weeks.

But it turned out not to be as easy as all that. After she had already put on her hat and was trying to tell Father about the keys, Father flew into another rage. There was a set-to between Father and Franz from which Franz emerged the victor, and then—miraculously—they were down in the courtyard and walking out through the cobblestone entranceway. Franz had got a man and a boy to help carry the suitcases down the street. Frau Schreier stopped them for a precious minute to wish them a good trip. All the way down to the corner, Peter hurried ahead in an effort to make them walk faster. He felt that once they were in the streetcar they would be safe. But even after they had transferred to another line and when they were almost at the railroad station, he was still dogged by his secret terror that Father might catch up with them and somehow keep them from getting on the train. And only when they were really on the train and it was at last moving out of the station, long after they had stowed away their suitcases on the baggage racks in the compartment they shared with an elderly couple, and Poldi was growing smaller on the platform, was he able to believe that they were safe. The last remnant of his fear gave way to joy.

The train pulled past Mödling and the fields broadened out. The meadows glistened with morning freshness, unbelievably green and still wet with dew. Cows stared at the train and looked like animals out of a toy box. Here and there a tongue of forest ate into the placid checkerboard pattern of the fields and lent a note of gay irresponsibility to the landscape. A squat, yellow-stuccoed village church drew slowly past and sank out of sight behind a hill.

There were a dozen questions he wanted to ask Franz: what the brilliant red berries were on that row of trees, what the brass lever was for above the window—but he could not ask Franz anything now. Franz was talking to the elderly gentleman about some trouble in the Balkans.

She was sitting in the corner by the compartment door. The lady who was the elderly gentleman's wife had talked with her for a while, then the conversation had lapsed and the lady had started to look at the magazines in her lap. The lady was very friendly: she had already offered him a piece of candy from a confectioner's cardboard box and she had put the box on the window ledge beside him and told him to help himself. He wondered whether it would be all right if he took another candy, then decided against it. *She* would not like it. Instantly he felt ashamed of her again. If only he could have been alone on the train with Franz!

Franz was talking along easily in his deep voice with its engagingly cultured inflections. Peter wondered whether one learned to talk like that in the *Gymnasium,* then remembered some of Franz's friends and decided that it was rather a part of the golden grace that was like an aura around Franz. He felt a thrill of pride at how handsome Franz looked as he talked. When he was serious, Franz's long pale eyebrows beetled and his frown seemed to run in waves up his soft forehead to the heavy silvery-blond mop of hair. He looked so deeply concerned when he frowned that you wanted to do anything to make Franz happy again. But always when the creases in Franz's forehead were deepest, he would suddenly find something amusing to say, his blue eyes laughed at you and you were glad that everything was all right again and you felt quite extravagantly happy.

If only he could have been alone with Franz! But there she sat, immovable and humiliating in her brown skirt with the brown cloth belt which did not fit elegantly around her waist the way the other woman's skirt did, and in her cream-colored blouse with the ridiculous jabot pinned to her old-fashioned, high collar.

To forget her, blot her out of his consciousness, he stuck his head all the way out through the window. A little girl was driving three cows up a hillside. While he was still watching the girl and the cows, a stiff object poked his leg. It was her parasol.

"You'll get a cinder in your eye," she muttered in her inexorable voice which seemed to him apologetically lowered for everybody else's benefit but his own. "You've been looking out of the window long enough. Tomorrow you'll have sore eyes."

He sat down between her and the elderly lady, who smiled at him and started to ask about school. They were the usual irksome questions grownups asked, but he could not help liking her. She made him take another piece of candy and gave him a magazine to look at.

They were approaching the Semmering. Mountains began to crowd on the horizon, high mountains. He felt excited again. He would see real glaciers, Franz had said in the station, and they would have to have two engines on the train. It was getting warm in the compartment. Franz and the other man had gone out into the corridor and stood leaning with their backs against the glassed-in partition. There were bigger windows on the other side of the car, and he wanted to go out into the corridor, but he knew that it would be useless to ask her. He was also beginning to be hungry! It seemed to him that they had been in the train a long time, but she said that it was too early for lunch.

"Is this the Tyrol yet?" he asked Franz.

He was at last out in the corridor. It was afternoon and they had had the lunch she had brought along hours ago, or so it seemed. The elderly couple had got off shortly after the Semmering.

Franz smiled. "This is it."

"When do we come to the high mountains, Franz?"

"Oh, that'll take a couple of hours yet."

"Can you see them from the train?"

"You can even smell the snow."

He was not sure whether Franz was joking or not. Still, he might not be, though it did sound impossible that one should be able to "smell" snow.

He felt very grown-up, standing there beside Franz in the corridor where people constantly passed and said "Pardon" very formally to you. He tried hard to lean as casually as Franz against the glass partition of the compartment, but was not altogether successful because his legs were not long enough to put one foot up on the brass ledge below the window. But he forced himself not to ask any more questions nor to move up close to the window, because he felt that it gave him more the air of an experienced traveler to look silently out on the masses of pine trees that grew almost down to the track. He wished that he could have had a Loden suit like Franz with a Norfolk jacket and knickers and rough wool stockings. Someday he would have a suit like that and go traveling to the Tyrol all by himself——

"See the doe?"

"Where—where, Franz?"

"Look!" Franz shoved him toward the window. He caught just a glimpse of a gray, smooth-furred animal before the train rounded a curve. The sight of the doe made him forget his resolve to be silent and grown-up.

"Are we going to see deer in Almzell, Franz?"

Franz laughed. "Loads of them. Mother says our grandfather used to go out on moonlight nights and shoot stags right in front of the house. In the winter when they get hungry, the deer come down from the woods into the orchard."

"Big stags—honestly, Franz?"

But he was not thinking of the stags, fascinating as it was to try and imagine real stags so close to where they were going to stay. Franz had said "our grandfather"! The words were disturbing, but also curiously comforting. It was as if Franz and he were suddenly very close together in a small shelter, like the time they had stepped into an empty sentry box in Schönbrunn during a cloudburst. It was the first time he had ever thought of the connection between himself and Almzell.

"They call the meadow above the house the 'Hirschenwies' because there are so many deer there in the winter," Franz was saying.

"Did you ever knew Mother's father, Franz?" He could not get himself to say "our grandfather."

"Sure I knew him. He gave me an awful thrashing one time because I stopped up the water pipe that comes down from the spring." Franz laughed as he remembered it. "And he used to make slingshots for me and he made me a small water mill—it's probably still there if Karl hasn't ruined it."

"Is Karl very big?" Karl was his cousin, he knew, and a whole year older than he.

"I haven't been in Almzell for three years. I guess you're about the same age. Pity you didn't know Grandfather. He was a real Tyroler."

"Did he climb mountains, Franz?"

"No, I don't think he climbed around in the mountains any more than he had to. People who live in the mountains get enough climbing just getting their wood down, and Grandfather had to go to the quarries for his stones."

It had been a long time since he had had such a good talk with Franz. The warm intimacy he felt between them encouraged him to ask:

"Are you sorry, Franz, you didn't go to Switzerland?"

"Sorry? No, I don't think so. Switzerland is a beautiful country, but so is the Tyrol. Wait till you see it! It's a fine country to come from. We had a professor in the *Gymnasium* who used to say that most of the great men in Vienna were Tyroleans."

"Will you take me along sometime when you go mountain climbing, Franz?"

Franz grinned. "Well, if I climb a little one, maybe."

Chapter Thirteen

A SHATTERING noise blasted his sleep and made him cower in the big bed. There it was again: a long-drawn-out bellow, sounding impossibly outraged and making him want to laugh all of a sudden, followed by a more distant lowing and the broken jingle of bells.

Cows, of course! And that was a cock crowing. . . .

He opened his eyes cautiously and looked. He was in a low-ceilinged room. In one corner was a high porcelain stove, in the other a massive clothespress with a huge lock. There were two small, square windows with red-flowered muslin curtains which swung softly in the breeze. Behind him, at a right angle to his own bed, was another four-poster with Franz in it.

He was really in Almzell, at Aunt Resi's!

Impatient now that he was awake to see the rest of the house, he slid carefully down on the floor from the high bed. It was cold; yet in Vienna yesterday—was it really only yesterday?—it had been hot. He got dressed quickly and let himself out through the door. He walked timidly toward the light along the narrow, dusky corridor that felt like a cellar, until he saw a good-sized yard that was paved with irregular flags. He recognized it after a second of taking stock. Over there was the gate through which they had come in, and there in the corner was the door through which Aunt Resi had taken them into the kitchen and the parlor.

The yard was oblong and swept very clean, except for a fresh trail of grass that led from the big gate to a roughly timbered door in the wall at the far end. He remembered that she had pointed to the door the night before and had said something about a barn.

The house itself formed two sides of the yard. Along the shorter of the two sides was an enormous trough hewn out of a single rock into which water murmured steadily from a wooden pipe. He went to the trough and dipped his finger into the water—the water was ice-cold. His eyes fell on the inscription on the side of the trough: A. D. 1827, in curious, old-fashioned letters.

Just then, the door from the barn was pushed open and one of the two girls he had seen last night came out with a pail of milk in each hand. She wore no stockings, only wooden shoes that clattered as she walked across the yard, and her skirt was gathered up in front and tucked in behind so that she stood in her red petticoat which was as short as the skirts of the cigarette girls he had seen at the *Heurigen*. And he noticed that the kerchief over her head was tied at the nape of her neck instead of under her chin, as he had always imagined peasant girls wore them.

He realized that he must have looked foolish staring at her, for when she came up to him her smile broadened into an open laugh.

"Well, you do stare like a calf without a mother," she said gaily. "I didn't know boys got up so early in the city."

"I couldn't sleep any more," he defended himself.

"Did the animals wake you up? You'll get used to them in a few days."

"No, I slept fine," he assured her quickly, afraid she might somehow guess that the bellowing of the cows had scared him at first.

She had set the pails of foaming milk down beside her, so that he could smell the sweetish, almost sickening odor of the milk.

"Can I watch you milk sometime?"

"Sure. Haven't you ever seen anybody milk before? You can watch tonight."

He felt a little nettled by her obvious amusement at his ignorance, but he had already made up his mind that he liked her.

"Are you Gretl?"

"No, I'm Lisl. You better come inside and I'll give you some milk."

"I don't think I like milk."

"You don't like milk? Even if it's fresh from the cow, like this?"

"I guess I'll try some," he said hastily, anxious to please her, although the sight of the foam in the pails filled him with revulsion.

Lisl pushed open the door into the brick-paved hall. Along the wall was a long, low chest with two rows of pails on it. Lisl reach up on a shelf and took down an earthenware cup. She filled it with milk and handed it to him.

"There," she said.

He forced himself to take a sip, then made a violent effort to swallow the mouthful of milk. He thought that he was going to be sick.

Lisl reached for the cup. "Here! You don't have to drink it if you don't want to," she laughed. "But you'll never get to be as big as Franz if you don't drink lots of milk. Come on, I'll get you some coffee."

She had taken his hand as if he were a little boy and was leading him to the stone-framed door where one stepped down into the kitchen. He did not mind her taking him by the hand, nor did he mind when she warned: "Look out for the step!" She was much nicer than Poldi was!

Aunt Resi was standing with her back to them, stirring something in a cast-iron pot on the huge brick range. She turned around when Lisl called:

"Mother, he doesn't like milk. I gave him some fresh from the cow and he wouldn't drink it."

Aunt Resi's gaunt face remained without a smile.

"Grüss Gott, Peterl," she said. "The coffee will be ready right away. Cut some bread, Lisl. I'll bring the coffee in a minute." Her voice was friendly but weary. He wondered why she sounded so tired. He felt shy with her, partly because her large, gaunt body intimidated him, and partly because he had difficulty in understanding her when she spoke. Now, he could understand everything Lisl said. Lisl spoke to him in a kind of High German that was neither the Viennese speech he was accustomed to nor the Tyrolean dialect. It sounded stiff and artificial. He resolved while he stood waiting in the parlor, watching Lisl cut off slices from the big loaf of black bread, that he would learn to speak Tyrolese so that Lisl wouldn't have to talk to him in that funny way.

The parlor where they had all sat and eaten cookies and drunk buttermilk the night before looked less formidable this morning. The dark, heavy chests and the carved wood crucifix on the wall had lost their sinister quality. He no longer had the feeling that someone might be hiding in the big cupboard with the monstrous iron lock. There were windows on two sides of the room—square windows with stone frames and cheerful curtains—through which he could see grass and scattered trees outside.

Aunt Resi came and hovered at one end of the white deal table while he ate the dark, juicy bread Lisl had buttered for him and drank the coffee which tasted so different from the coffee *she* made. He waited for Aunt Resi to speak; he felt uneasy all alone with her, for Lisl had left the room.

"Is the coffee all right?"

"It's very good, Aunt Resi."

"We don't make it the way city folks do. Coffee is very dear." She did not look at him when she spoke. Her eyes rested somewhere on the table in front of him. "Did you like your bed?"

"Oh, yes. It's the first time I ever slept in such a big bed." He felt increasingly embarrassed by her deference.

"Do you hear much from your mother?"

Her question took him unawares and made him feel uncomfortable, as did any mention of Mizzi. Then he remembered the last letter from America. It had had one of those checks in it which *she* had gone to the bank to cash. He had only seen the last page where it said that Mizzi sent him "a thousand kisses." That had been right after school closed. Mizzi's letters had a cold, foreign unreality for him, and when she referred to him it always seemed to him as if it were some other Peter she was talking about. But he did not want to admit to Aunt Resi that there was such a tenuous bond between Mizzi and him. Mizzi was obviously important to her. He lied:

"Yes, she writes long letters often. There was a long letter just a little while ago."

"I guess she doesn't remember us poor Almzellers any more," Aunt Resi said with a little sigh.

"Oh, I'm sure she wrote something about you, Aunt Resi," he assured her quickly, but he was glad that she changed the subject to say:

"Kathl has gone to church, to Mass. I wish I could go, but I can't with all the work. There's a lot of work for a woman without a man in the house. I hope you like it here. We do things in a rough way, not like they do in the city. . . ."

Her voice trailed off and her long arms which had been hanging stiffly by her sides crooked at the elbows with a twitch of mingled helplessness and apology.

"I think it's wonderful here, Aunt Resi," he said with shriller enthusiasm than he meant to, for he was at a loss to explain her humility. The house was so big and there were so many things to see that she seemed wealthy to him when he thought of their small flat in the Schottenfeldgasse. He had finished the second slice of bread and butter and could not eat any more. Anxious to get away from her now, he asked: "Is it all right if I go outside, Aunt Resi?"

"Sure. Karl is up in the pasture with the cows."

He hurried through the yard, impatient to see what was outside. Ahead of him lay a small orchard of some thirty scattered trees. The fruit on them was still green except for a few apples which were beginning to turn red. He picked up an apple from the grass and brushed off the ants; it tasted tart and sour.

When he had inspected all the trees he started for the rocky path which wound past the two barns up the hill. He saw that what had shimmered yellow through the trees was a big wheat field and that it sloped gently upward. Above it was another field with some other kind of grain that was still green, and still higher up the slope that was rising more steeply at that point, there were rows and rows of little bushes. By shading his eyes against the sun he could make out a stone wall which described an irregular arc and gave the effect of a dam holding back the dark woods which seemed to surge down from the hill above. The stone wall continued down on either side of the cultivated land.

He stopped at the larger of the two barns to look in through the gaping doors. The other girl—the one who was Gretl—was shaking grain in a sieve. She saw him and called:

"Grüss Gott, you."

"Hello!" he called back, bold because he was so far away from her.

She had straightened up and was resting the sieve against her stomach.

"What are you up to?"

"I'm going to climb the mountain."

She laughed boisterously.

"That's not a mountain. That's just the Hirschenwies."

"Well, I'm going to climb it anyway."

"Look out the wolves don't get you."

"Are there wolves up there?" He realized as soon as he said it that he had fallen into a trap. He had already decided that he liked Lisl better.

"There aren't any wolves. You don't have to be afraid. Karl's up there." Her head indicated the woods above the fields. . . .

The path up the slope was steeper than he had thought. After he had passed the two grain fields, he had to stop to get his breath. From where he was he could look down on the house and the barns; he saw that the village was even farther below. The fact that Aunt Resi's house lay so high filled him with pride. Down in the long, troughlike valley the fields sloped away from the village up the mountainsides. And beyond the woods and the nearer hills, only a little distance away, there were the unmistakably snow-covered peaks Franz had shown him last night.

A field mouse darted out from a crevice in the stone wall on his left and startled him. He loved the rough stone wall which ran parallel with the path. Parts of it were completely overgrown with brambles and blackberry vines. Flowers grew between the stones, and on one rock there was a big cluster of hen-and-chickens—and a snake! It was gray, and it had been lying there on the rock all the time. It frightened him, but he watched it for a few minutes until it suddenly slithered down over the edge of the rock and disappeared.

He reached the beginning of the woods. Bushes and young beech trees hemmed in the path on both sides. He wondered whether he had not better turn back. Perhaps he had missed Karl or perhaps this wasn't the right path, although he hadn't noticed any other. The mysterious rustling of the leaves all around him worried him, as did the fact that he could not see the house any more. Then he heard the jangling of a cowbell quite close by—a cow stared out at him from behind a bush. Presently he saw another cow and a calf. On his left the bushes grew sparser and behind them was a meadow strewn with rocks. He made his way out into the meadow until he saw Karl on top of one of the boulders.

Karl watched him approach without a word. His "*Grüss Gott*" sounded cautious, almost hostile. But when Peter attempted to climb up beside him, Karl said: "You have to come up over here." He saw then that there was a smaller rock from which it was easy to climb up.

Sitting beside Karl now, he found himself at a loss for something to say. Karl went on whittling on a piece of wood.

"What's that you're making?"

"A dowel."

"What's that?"

"It goes into a wheelbarrow."

Peter did not press him any further from fear of seeming ignorant. After a while he said: "I saw a snake. On the wall. It was gray and so long——"

"That's only a grass snake."

"Don't they bite?"

"They don't bite."

"Have you ever killed one?"

Karl's eyes became blunt with scorn. "We don't kill them. They are good for the field; they get the mice."

After another silence, he ventured:

"Franz found some blueberries last night."

Karl shrugged. "We've got lots of blueberries."

"Where?"

"Up there." Karl pointed in back of him into the woods.

"Is it far?"

"You follow the path up to the crossways. That's where they start. . . . You like strawberries?"

"Are there strawberries?"

Karl slid down from the boulder and walked toward the edge of the woods. Peter followed him. After only a few steps Karl bent over and then he saw them, too! They were everywhere among the grass. He had never seen so many strawberries before.

"They're little ones," Karl said. "That's because it's late for them. Here——" He had already picked a small handful and poured them into Peter's hand.

"Don't you like them?"

"I've eaten my fill this year."

Peter realized suddenly that Karl had not meant to be patronizing, and that if he was curt it was because he was shy.

"Thanks for showing me the strawberries, Karl," he said.

"I can show you where there are raspberries. They're harder to find. You've got to know the spots."

"Will you really? I'll just take these down to Franz, then I'll come right back. Are you going to be here?"

"Sure."

"I'll be right back." He hurried out toward the path with the little bunch of strawberries he had picked with the stems to take down to Franz. Once on the path, he started to run because already he wanted to be back with Karl to find out where the raspberries were. . . .

It was *she*, however, who knew about the enormous raspberry patch in back of the quarry. Karl had known only about the clearing above the crossroads—breathtaking enough until he had seen the other. To get to her place you followed the wagon trail through the woods to Grandfather's quarry, then climbed in and out among the towering, weird-shaped rocks until you came to a sudden drop. Down below, growing among the boulders, was where they were: thousands of yellow-leafed bushes, all unbelievably red with berries when you got close to them. It had been like standing in the midst of inexhaustible wealth the first day. When you had eaten all you wanted and had been picking for hours into the pails, there were still red-twinkling bushes all around.

They went back the next day and Lisl and Gretl had come along too. He had had fun vying with Lisl who could get a pailful first. Lisl was much nicer than Gretl. She laughed all the time and she did not treat him as if he were a little boy. Gretl did. She had made him get out of the barn when he was examining the fodder-cutting machine and she would not let him chop wood behind the barn.

It had surprised him at first that neither Lisl nor Gretl nor Karl had known about the big raspberry patch. It made him see *her* in a new light. She knew about other places, too, and about cranberries and all sorts of mushrooms that grew in the woods. He became accustomed to seeing even Aunt Resi defer to her constantly; Aunt Resi consulted her about a calf that had something the matter with its foot and about drying poppy seed.

Imperceptibly, the stubborn, querulous humility that had always exasperated him so in her, turned into a low-voiced, undeniable air of authority. It was nothing that he could put his finger on exactly; she did not try to tell Aunt Resi how to do things. It was rather that her connection with Grandfather seemed to make Aunt Resi afraid of her.

Once, when she made him go calling on some people in the village with her, she stepped into the shed where the plows and the wagons were and after looking around for a minute, she said heavily: "I'm glad Grandfather isn't here to see this! All his wagons he made himself broken down and the whole place going to wrack and ruin." Another time when he had followed her up the ladder to the attic where the big loaves of bread were stored between baking time, she pointed to a rift between the shingles and muttered tartly: "If my poor mother, God rest her soul, had seen that!"

But it was usually Grandfather she invoked in these criticisms. One morning when he went into the kitchen for a piece of bread and butter, he heard Aunt Resi say something to her about a tract of forest land. He gathered that Aunt Resi had sold it because she had needed the money to pay some debt. Aunt Resi sounded apologetic as she explained about the piece of forest and he felt sorry for her because he had a feeling that *she* disapproved. There was a long, grim pause when Aunt Resi had finished, then *she* said slowly:

"Grandfather would turn in his grave if he knew that you had sold that forest. He had to wait ten years before he could buy it. He would have lost his right arm rather than sell that timber stand."

Aunt Resi had cried then. Through the door he could see her gaunt shoulders sag with despondency. After a minute, she had said piteously:

"What was I to do? I had to pay the interest and the potatoes were bad—it rained for six weeks without letting up. There weren't more than a couple of bushels for the pigs when we dug them."

He hated her for making Aunt Resi cry. It was the way she treated him in Vienna when he wanted to go out and play with the other boys. But he could not help thinking about the forest and wondering which piece of forest it was Aunt Resi had sold. That afternoon while *she* was spreading blueberries on sheets of wrapping paper to dry, he asked about the quarry in the hope of getting her to say something about the forest. But she would talk only about the quarry itself and the strip of woods that the wagon trail led through. All he could find out was that Aunt Resi had already sold the timber that stood on it to the man who had the next house below them. His name was Flurl, Peter knew, and he had a little girl whom he had seen several times.

She was always making remarks that referred to the place as it had been when Grandfather was alive. They would be out picking blueberries and she would indicate with a little jerk of her chin some clearing or a clump of trees: "Grandfather set out those trees. . . ." Then there would follow a silence which implied that Aunt Resi had somehow betrayed Grandfather by selling the timber too young or by selling the land on which it stood as well. Or they would be going to church on Sunday and she would look sideways at the buggies around the church and sigh: "Grandfather always had two teams of horses in the stable." Aunt Resi, he knew, had no horses and hired other farmers to plow her fields.

Gradually he began to form a picture of Grandfather from the odds and ends he pieced together from what she said and from the house itself. On the wall in the room where *she* slept there was a faded daguerreotype of a man with a heavy jaw and tousled, curly gray hair in Tyrolese costume. He studied it interestedly one day, but it seemed pale and trivial alongside his own impression of him. Grandfather had rebuilt the house. The heavy stones had been carted down from the quarry and hewn by Grandfather's hands. He had hammered out the long iron hinges, with the vine tendrils traced on them, on the anvil in the shed. Grandfather had also made the altar rail and the stone altar in the church, and he had cut stone for the big church in Lienz and for buildings as far as Villach and Meran.

An aura of power and determination surrounded the memory of Grandfather. Everywhere there were reminders of him in granite that his hand had touched—even though it was only a stone wall around a field, built from rocks that had been blasted and clawed out of the soil and laboriously tugged to the side. He could feel something ruthless and violent in Grandfather that appealed to a craving for violence in him. He listened with sharpened ears when he went visiting people in the valley with *her* and when they reminisced about Grandfather's drinking bouts and how Grandfather had bent horseshoes with his bare hands at a kermess one time.

He was careful not to let her see how eager he was for every shred of information about him. Even now when he thought about him, he did not say "my grandfather" but "Grandfather," just as he would have used any other name. The fact that he had been Mizzi's father was as distant and meaningless as that other fact that Mizzi was his mother. He had, indeed, felt suddenly warm and grateful when Franz had said "our grandfather" that time on the train, but more because the words had established a bond that had seemed to draw him closer to Franz. . . .

Gradually, too, he began to piece out the past when *she* had still been on the farm. There had been four children, he knew: Aunt Wetti and *she* and Karl and Mizzi. Karl had been Aunt Resi's husband. Aunt Wetti had been the oldest and Grandfather's favorite. When Aunt Wetti was sixteen she was allowed to go off to Vienna to learn cooking with another girl from the village. *She* had helped her mother in the house and with the dairy, and sometimes she had even had to help Grandfather in the fields. She had dug potatoes, for instance, and cut fodder for the cows. Karl had been much younger and Mizzi very small. Then *her* mother had died and Wetti had not come until the funeral. That was one of the grudges she held against Aunt Wetti. And Grandfather had married a woman within six months of *her* mother's death and that had been wrong somehow, and *she* had gone to Vienna into service and had married Father, and later she had come for Mizzi. And still later, much later, Uncle Karl had married Aunt Resi who was not a good housekeeper. Uncle Karl had drunk a great deal and he had neglected the farm and then Uncle Karl had died—had been killed by being thrown from a wagon. Every time Peter thought of Uncle Karl he saw a man with a bloody head lying on the side of a road. And since then Aunt Resi had had the place and had let it run to "wrack and ruin."

Yet he could not get himself to share her disapproval of Aunt Resi. Aunt Resi was friendly and she worked all the time. Something pathetic about her deference toward *her* aroused his sympathy. He liked Aunt Resi, just as he liked Lisl who let him help her with hoeing potatoes and cutting grass with the big scythe in the evenings, and Gretl and Karl with whom he was beginning to make friends, although it was more difficult than with Lisl because they said little and were not as gay as she. All in all, he told himself, he had never been so happy as he was here. He wished that he could stay all winter, all the time. But the end of the vacation was drawing inexorably close.

His birthday fell just a few days before they had to leave. It came on a Friday. On Wednesday the mailman brought a big parcel from the post office in Lienz. The parcel was for him and it was from America. There was his name—Peter Domanig—just above their Vienna address which Poldi had crossed out to write "Almzell, Tyrol." It was the first parcel that had ever come addressed to him alone. He was torn between taking it into the room where he and Franz slept so that he could look at it for a long time all by himself, and impatience to see what was inside.

They all stood around the big table in the parlor while he opened it. Even Aunt Resi had come to the door to watch. Only *she* went pointedly out into the kitchen and stayed there. He started to untie the string. The knots were stubborn, but when Franz laughingly offered to cut the string, he was in a panic that Franz might really get a knife. He wanted to preserve everything about the parcel as intact as possible. He folded back the wrapping and came upon a carton, then a layer of excelsior, and then some long tin boxes. Franz sniffed one of the tins and said they contained cookies. Next he found two glass jars with delicious-looking candy inside. Then came an Erector set which was larger than Rudi's, then two sweaters—a gray one which buttoned down in front and looked very foreign, and a white one to pull over your head such as he had often seen in the windows of sports shops. At the very bottom of the carton were two little stacks of books, fairy tales with bright covers—the sort of books, he noted unconsciously, that he had read when he was still very small.

Franz had picked up the gray sweater with the pockets and was holding it against his chest. "Just what I need for skiing," Franz joked. "You're going to let me have that, aren't you?"

They were all handling his treasures, except Karl, who was too proud to do more than stand and look. Franz was still turning the gray sweater this way and that, pretending to put it on. It was Lisl who noticed the bulge in one of the pockets and the safety pin over it. The bulge turned out to be a shiny brown pocketbook; inside it was a folded note and all kinds of coins. Franz said that the coins were American coins and that he could change them at the bank. Franz was urging him to read the note. He finally unfolded it and read:

> MY DARLING PETER:
> A thousand kisses from your mother on your birthday. Do you think of me often? I think of you every day. I hope you like the books and the candy. Your little brother and sister send you many kisses, and so does
> YOUR LOVING MOTHER

He handed the note to Franz who glanced through it and said:

"Well, aren't you glad? You must write your mother a nice long letter for all this. It isn't everybody who has a mother in America that sends them things!"

The parcel remained in the foreground of his consciousness. It was a foreign, strangely irresistible island in the ocean of by now familiar things in Aunt Resi's house. He went back to it a dozen times a day to handle each object.

He opened the pocketbook every time he opened the parcel, and he fingered the coins but he did not take out Mizzi's note again. A kind of shyness kept him from rereading it. Yet he remained aware of the folded white paper in the pocketbook. It was Mizzi who had written the note and who had sent the parcel! As often before, he tried to imagine what Mizzi was like, but he did not succeed in calling up any other image than that of the foreign-looking woman in the photograph which Mizzi had sent last Christmas.

Everything about the parcel remained strange and foreign to him: the books, the flat tins, the wrapping, the string—even the smell of the sweaters was peculiar. He knew how new socks and jerseys smelled in the stores in Vienna; that smell was enticing and insinuatingly familiar, but this smell was different. Just as the sweaters looked outlandish, too. He would not want to be seen in either of them in school and especially not in the choir. The boys might laugh and he would feel as mortified as he did in the pants that hung down over his knees, or in the shoes which *she* had got for him from a charity organization last winter. And the books were strange, too, and not only strange but stupid. He felt more scornful every time he looked at them. Did Mizzi think that he was still reading about

Snow White and Tom Thumb? Why, he had been reading novels, real novels, even though Poldi did not know that he had.

Sometimes when he was alone with the parcel, he suddenly remembered Mizzi's mention of a little brother and sister—it would be nice to have a younger brother and sister! He wondered whether this little sister was as nice as Mali Flurl, the little girl in the house below Aunt Resi's. Not that Mali was really so little, although she was a whole year younger than he, so that he always felt an urge to protect her from some vague danger. Mali had mischievous, cornflower-blue eyes and very pink cheeks and she liked to pick up lizards and even snakes and pretend to stick them down his neck, ever since she had found out that he was afraid of snakes. . . .

The evening before his birthday, Franz called him into their room and got him to open the parcel again. He was puzzled. Franz had already seen everything there was to see. Then, suddenly, there was a great din out in the yard. It sounded as if a whole wagon of scrap iron were being dumped all at once.

"Your friends are wishing you a happy birthday," he said. "It's one of their Almzell customs. They want some of your candy."

A minute later they came crowding into the room. There were at least fifteen of them: Karl and some of Karl's friends, Mali, two other girls he had seen now and again on the way to the village, Lisl and Gretl, and even Aunt Resi. They all had iron or copper pans and were beating on them with spoons, and they were shouting: "Happy Birthday! We want candy!"

He felt himself flushing with embarrassment and joy. He reached blindly for the tins of cookies and the jars of candy Franz opened for him and poured candy and cookies into the outstretched pans until Franz finally warned:

"Here, you better go easy or there won't be any left for me!"

He did not have more than a handful of candy and four or five cookies when they were gone, but he felt extravagantly happy, especially when he remembered afterward as he lay in bed that he had given Mali at least twice as much as anyone else. . . .

Chapter Fourteen

THE big arc lights high under the iron-ribbed glass roof of the station hung like sullen tears on the face of a slattern. They threw a thin, watery light into the farthest corners. Peter could not have said why the lamps reminded him of the screeching woman he had seen rushing out of a shabby old house in Ottakring one night when he was coming home with Father, except that the arc lights spread the same brittle, importunate drabness from which he wanted to flee.

It could not be the same station where they had waited for the train less than a month ago! Yet there was the bookstand where Franz had bought his newspaper and the bag of mints. Everything about the station now seemed ruthless and subtly hostile: the porters trundling their clattering baggage carts, people knocking against one's legs with sharp-cornered suitcases, the clangor of the streetcar gongs outside, the locomotive behind them from which hissed clouds of ruddy steam.

"I wish I could go back!" he thought in a sudden panic.

They had piled their suitcases and the baskets in which *she* had packed the dried berries and jars of preserves just inside the tall iron grill where Poldi had been waiting for them. Poldi was wearing a new hat with a very wide brim. It was blue and had a pink ribbon around it and a large bow on one side. It made Poldi look very self-assured and pretty, too, he thought, but also different from the way he remembered her.

Poldi poked one of the baskets with the tip of her shoe. "Goodness, what a lot of junk!"

She leaned down quickly and pulled the basket closer beside her.

"You better be careful what you say about that basket," Franz warned. "It's got Mother's sacrosanct fresh eggs in it. She's been guarding them like a lioness all the way from Almzell." Franz stood with his shoulders pulled forward against the weight of his bulging rucksack and grinned.

"You'll be mighty glad of the *junk* when it comes to eating it," she said tartly.

"All right, Mother, all right! Let's get started. I'm going to get a cab."

"We need a cab! Why don't you get half the porters in the place, too? You and your big ideas!"

"Well, if you think I'm going on the streetcar with all those bundles, looking like a bunch of gypsies, you're mistaken, Mother!"

"Nobody asked you to. You can go by yourself if you're such a grand lady."

"I don't suppose a cab will be so much more," Franz put in diplomatically. "By the time we pay four fares . . ."

"If you've got money to throw out the window, I haven't. I'm going on the streetcar."

Poldi picked up the leather suitcase and started for the street. She did not speak to any of them until they were in the streetcar and then she pointedly spoke only to Franz. Poldi's voice became deeper and a little husky when she was angry, Peter noticed again. She was telling Franz about meeting his friend, Herr Schmidtmeyer, on an excursion to Klosterneuburg, and Franz started to tease her about him. So far Poldi had not once mentioned Father. Was that because Father was all right again or was it because—Peter realized suddenly that the formless fear he had felt that morning when they got on the train at Villach had had to do with Father—because Father had been drunk again?

They were almost at the Westbahnstrasse before Franz asked: "How's Father?"

"Oh, he's all right," Poldi said.

She sat holding the basket with the eggs on her lap and gave no sign that she had heard. Only when they got off to change trams she asked suddenly:

"Has anything come from the theater?"

"How should I know, Mother? Father and I didn't go in much for conversation—just the necessary things. But I made him toe the mark. He wasn't drunk once, not once!"

"If only he doesn't get pensioned!" she sighed.

"Oh, stop worrying, Mother. He isn't going to get pensioned."

"It's easy enough for you to talk. Herr Hügel got pensioned just because he had a little bit of rash."

"Well, suppose he does! The world isn't going to come to an end just because Father gets pensioned." Poldi turned away from her to Franz and lowered her voice to a whisper. Her eyes indicated the big apartment house half a block down on the Gürtel. "Gisl says she's still in Germany. We won't have to worry about *that* any more anyway!"

Poldi, he knew, was talking about the lady he had seen Father with once. Perhaps if the lady was in Germany now everything would be again as it had been before Poldi had started to whisper angrily to Franz and *her* every evening in the kitchen. But he did not feel very confident about it. Franz was worried, too. His forehead had folded into soft creases as he looked up the street to see whether their streetcar was coming.

It was strange, he puzzled once again, that Poldi should have dared to go to the lady who was Father's friend and should have caused her to go away, as Franz had said to *her* after reading one of Poldi's letters in Almzell. Germany was far away. . . . He wondered what she had said to the lady to make her go all the way to Germany. And why had Father let Poldi do it? Father had been very angry but he had also seemed helpless. What had given Poldi this unexpected power to go against Father when Father could still slap her and make her cry?

He was still thinking about it when they got on the streetcar. Poldi's assurance had done nothing to allay his anxiety. Poldi was very brave: he remembered the gymnastics festival at Schönbrunn when Poldi had jumped over four horses and had done the giant swing on the high bar. Everybody, even the girls in her own Turnverein, had applauded and Poldi still had the laurel wreath and the medal they had given her. He tried to imagine himself doing the giant swing, swinging with his body perfectly straight, actually standing on his hands for a second. His arms stiffened involuntarily. No, he would not be able to do it! Perhaps when he was bigger, though, or if Poldi called him a coward like the time she had taken him to have his tooth pulled. He had not cried at all even though the dentist had had to change pliers and it had hurt terribly.

This was different, though. It had nothing to do with a sharp pain where you could clench your fists and feel very brave. If Father was shouting again and knocking against furniture—a gray, hopeless procession of leaden days suddenly stretched ahead of him into the future. And then there would be the gloomy-looking school in the Ziegelgasse every day instead of the bright, new *Gymnasium* and he would never see Rudi except in the evenings in the choir. . . .

They were riding down the Westbahnstrasse now where every shop and building was familiar. There was the store where they sold playing cards, then the coffeehouse where Franz often went, and there was the confectionery shop where he had bought the eucalyptus drops with Rudi. His eyes leaped ahead to the entranceway of the Verein: lights were still on out in the garden and on the second floor. He felt relieved. As long as he had the choir and could be with Rudi and Herr Granini—here was Rudi's house! He looked quickly to see whether there were any lights. The windows were dark. But perhaps Rudi's parents were out or perhaps they had already gone to bed. It was late: almost ten o'clock. . . .

Father was not home yet, he saw at once when Poldi tried the door. Poldi had to get out her key and unlock the door. The flat was dark and felt strangely empty. She jiggled the two pins out of her hat and lifted the hat off her head with the quick, mousy movements Peter knew so well; then she started to light the lamp. Franz was walking through the living room which was still dark and bumped into a chair.

"I changed the table around," Poldi said to his back.

She had turned up the wick and carried the lamp into the living room to look. The big table was out in the middle of the room and away from the divan.

"I suppose that table wasn't good enough for you where it was," she said. "It's been there twenty years and nobody ever saw anything wrong with where it was."

"Well, it was about time somebody moved it. It looks much better where it is. I thought you'd like what I had done to the room!" Poldi had turned to the chest of drawers and looked at them expectantly.

Peter saw that Poldi had put out the crocheted runner and that she had taken away Father's bronze inkstand and had replaced it with the blue and gold vase which usually stood on top of Father's wardrobe.

"My best runner out on a weekday!" *she* gasped. "And you had to take the vase down, too, so that it can get broken, I suppose? You wait until Father comes home and sees what you have done with his inkstand and all his other things. . . ."

"Father's seen it already and he never said a word," Poldi said triumphantly. "It's been like this all week. No reason why this place has to look like a dump all the time."

"That table is going back tomorrow where it's always been."

"All right—if you want the place to look like a dump!"

"Maybe you'll be glad someday if you have a 'dump' like this to bless yourself with!" She had started to turn down the beds. "It would have been a whole lot better if you'd aired the bedding once in a while. I bet these bedclothes haven't seen any sun since I left this house!"

"Well, you're wrong. They were aired every morning, before I went to the office."

"I'd like to believe it."

"Well, you can."

Franz was already unpacking in his room. He had not said a word since Poldi and she had started bickering about the table and Peter could hear him whistling softly to himself. He would have liked to go into Franz's room right now, before Father came home, but he knew that *she* would want him to unpack his rucksack first out in the kitchen. Besides, Franz had spread out his suitcase on the couch and she had not yet made up his bed. There was nothing for it but to wait until she allowed him to unpack his things.

She had only taken off the lid from the round fruit basket which contained the eggs, when Father's footsteps sounded out on the landing. She had heard Father, too, for she got up hastily from the floor to pull the wicker suitcase farther away from the door.

Father was wearing his light tan suit with the small checks which he usually wore when he went on an outing, but he carried the smooth walking stick which he used only in town. He was not drunk, Peter saw with instant relief. Reassured, he pushed forward a little toward Father and called louder than he would have dared ordinarily, "Good evening, Father."

Father glanced at him briefly and said, "*Servus.*" Then he walked straight into the living room without even looking at *her*. Father ignored Poldi as well. It was as if he had seen neither of them, as if he did not even know they were there. He put his walking stick and his hat in the wardrobe, then went to the chest of drawers and took out his cigar case from his pocket.

Franz had come to the door of his room. He said gaily: "Hello, Father. Well, we're back."

Father turned around and said, "*Servus.*" It sounded no gruffer than usual. What worried Peter was that there seemed to be something absent-minded about Father's voice. Father had turned his back on Franz again and had started to take off his rings which he put beside his cigar case and his watch.

A minute later he came out into the kitchen to the washstand to brush his teeth. His foot shoved the basket with the eggs brusquely to one side.

She was at the cupboard putting away the first bowlful of eggs. She cried out in an oddly held-in, shrill voice: "My eggs!" then rushed to the basket to rescue it. "They hurt you that you had to kick them," she said bitterly.

Father ignored her. He had started to gargle into the slop pail. Again Peter had the feeling that he had not even heard her. . . .

The sullen, forbidding silence with which Father had moved around the flat on that first evening was to be permanent, Peter saw the next day and in the days that followed. Father spoke only to demand hot water for shaving or to announce at dinner: "This meat is tough. I don't eat muck like this!" Otherwise, he came and went, carefully dressed as usual, without a word or a glance for anybody. Even Franz had to content himself with a muttered "*Servus*" when he greeted him.

Peter learned to keep out of his way. Formerly he had always been sure of Father's warmth underneath his gruffness. He had even come to identify the gruffness with the kindliness it screened. Now he was no longer sure. The day after they had come back from Almzell, he had put a box of green hazelnuts on the window sill to get ripe. One of the nuts had fallen on the floor and Father had happened to step on it. Father had turned on him, his face a cold, impenetrable mask:

"If those nuts aren't gone from here instantly, I'll give you a taste of the strap."

If he had been angry, Peter would have felt less cowed. It was the dull-voiced sternness that frightened him. Father had threatened him with the strap before, but the threat had never seemed more than a figure of speech. Now Father was suddenly in earnest about it. He had an oppressive feeling that he had somehow lost his most powerful friend.

There was one advantage in the change that had come over Father: the tenseness at home made the opening day in the new school seem much less dreadful than before. Even the gloomy school building in the Ziegelgasse where he was to report was less oppressive than their flat. Then he found that he was in for another disappointment. The teacher in the office, who received them one by one and assigned them to the different classrooms, frowned when he failed to find his record. He asked to see his last report. At once his face folded into a knowing smile. He pointed to the conduct mark——

"Aha," he said. "Neubaugasse! You're going to school in the Neubaugasse, young man. We don't take boys with a 'two' in conduct here. They know how to deal with scamps like you there. The walk will do you good. Next—"

Peter stepped away from the heavy table with the green cloth on it. The teacher's playful harangue had made him flush. They would not have him in this school because he had drawn a few pictures in class last June. The two other boys who lived in the house, especially Karl Breitner whom he had always considered as somehow beneath him because Karl did not get good marks and had always been in the slow class in grammar school, looked at him with a superior smirk. He hurried out of the school office and through the courtyard with its gym apparatus out into the street. When he had got half a block away from the school, his pace slackened. He felt despondent and afraid. What would they say at home when he told them that he had to go to school in the Neubaugasse? All the boys in the house went to school in the

Ziegelgasse. He would have to tell the truth. Perhaps Father would get angry and beat him this time. . . .

The school in the Neubaugasse was newer but it also looked more severe. The very lamps in the corridors and the high, modern windows and double doors struck him as stern. He was sent to a classroom where a tall, hard-shouldered man of aggressively military bearing stood very erect beside his desk and talked in a clipped, staccato voice about the margins to be observed in exercise books. He was wearing a glittering pince-nez on his narrow-bridged nose. Every once in a while his hand picked up a bunch of keys and set them down again with a sharp metallic clatter to emphasize a point.

The teacher had taken no notice of him when he came in. Peter remained standing beside the door, wondering whether perhaps he should walk up to the teacher with the paper he had been given downstairs in the office, but he did not dare to interrupt him. When the teacher finally stopped, he beckoned him to approach. Peter said, "Good morning, sir," and held up the slip of paper toward the desk. The teacher did not take it.

"Name!" he demanded.

Peter repeated his name twice under the cool, expectant stare of the dull blue eyes behind the rimless pince-nez. The teacher gave no sign that he had heard but kept on looking. Peter shifted uneasily. He knew that he had done something wrong but he could not think what. He had spoken distinctly and he had said "*Herr Lehrer*" each time.

When he had stood there for what seemed to him many minutes, painfully conscious of both the teacher's stare and the eyes of the boys in their seats on his back, the teacher finally said:

"I can neither hear you nor see you!"

Agonized by his insistence, Peter tried again. He raised his head higher and tried to look the teacher straight in the eye, although he felt himself quailing before the monotonously stern gaze.

"My—"

"Stop!"

The teacher stepped down from the platform, seized his shoulders and forced them back until they hurt.

"Heels together! Stomach in! Has no one ever told you how to stand at attention? Now. . . ."

The teacher turned out to be strict, little short of a martinet, but not impossible to satisfy. Provided they came up to his exacting demands for military precision in everything from the lettering of drawings to the way they asked for a new copybook, he was fair and even allowed them to see that he was interested in them. He was a former naval officer who had been disqualified from active service by his eyes. He taught them arithmetic, mechanical drawing, and gymnastics.

During the second week of school, at the end of a drawing class, when Peter handed in his second drawing, Herr Lein said:

"I entered your marks from grammar school on my records yesterday. I shall expect you to be at the head of this class—in all subjects."

There was no relaxing of the sharply drawn features. Herr Lein's voice had remained aggressively level and severe, but Peter sensed his interest and he felt flattered and grateful.

Herr Lein's challenge became the sole element of zest in the drab, dispiriting monotony which lay before him each morning when he went to school. The teachers he had in his other subjects, though considerably less exacting than Herr Lein, could not arouse his enthusiasm and left him with a feeling of dull drudgery. Neither could he find any friends among the boys in the class.

There were still the two hours of choir practice every evening on which he had counted so much; but the choir only made him more conscious of what he had come to consider the disgrace of having to go to public school. Not only did the boys in the choir seem infinitely more intelligent and agreeable than the boys in school, but their matter-of-fact references to the exciting routine of the *Gymnasium* were constant reminders of what he had missed. And there was the equally bitter realization that Rudi was drawing farther and farther away from him.

Rudi had not been back the first evening Peter had gone to choir practice. The second afternoon, Peter found him in the garden on their favorite bench under the big mulberry tree with three other boys. They were all talking animatedly about their first day in the *Gymnasium*—the professors, the books, fraternities—all the painfully bright furnishings of that glamorous world in the white stone building in the Kandlgasse from which he was shut out. He had shaken hands with Rudi, but shyly, hesitantly. Rudi's hand had felt more pink, clean, and cool than ever, or perhaps it was the new corduroy suit Rudi wore and the flosslike way his brown hair was brushed over his forehead that made this seem a different Rudi: too precious for him to approach.

All through rehearsal, Peter's throat felt fuzzy with fear that Rudi might not make a move to walk home together as they had always done before.

But Rudi was waiting for him outside the music room. His relief made him inarticulate at first. He was glad that Rudi started to talk at once about his own summer in Hütteldorf, even though each new sentence seemed to raise a new barrier between them. Rudi had learned to swim; he had taken French lessons from the lady in the villa next to theirs; Rudi's father had bought him a stamp catalogue. . . . In not one of these interests, Peter saw at once, would he be able to follow Rudi. It cost money to go swimming in the winter and to collect stamps. And now that he himself had an Erector set with which he had thought to complement Rudi's set and build bridges and viaducts for Rudi's railroad, Rudi was no longer interested in his railroad. He did not even mention Mizzi's Erector set, but he did tell Rudi about the parcel and about Almzell and the quarry. As he talked about Almzell, he gathered confidence. But he did not take out the hazelnuts which he had brought for Rudi. The hazelnuts seemed suddenly trivial. He wished that he could have brought a snake instead, or a young doe, or some other startling present for Rudi.

The next day he brought along the pocketbook with the American coins, and for a few minutes he was exuberantly happy when not only Rudi but all the other boys envied him the coins. But it was also the day when Rudi showed him his books from the *Gymnasium*. The books were much larger than the ones Peter had in his school; their very appearance was impressive.

That evening he got Franz to lend him the Latin grammar he had used in his first year in the *Gymnasium*. Franz's book was old and worn, but it was the same text Rudi had shown him that afternoon. He started to study the first page with the same eagerness with which he would ordinarily have returned to the middle of an exciting story. After that, he studied every afternoon when he came home from school, before he even looked at his own homework. He was baffled by the difficult rules which were hard to understand, but he memorized them nevertheless. The vocabulary was easier. All he had to do was to memorize it. . . . He found when he asked Rudi after a week how far along they were in the Latin text—he asked casually for he felt reluctant to tell Rudi that he was studying by himself—that he was actually a page ahead of Rudi's class.

Then one day toward the end of October, Rudi and the other boys in Rudi's class started to talk about the translation of a difficult sentence they had been asked to do. Peter listened eagerly and during a lull in the argument proffered his version. It was greeted with a silence compounded about equally of surprise and resentment. One of the boys burst out into loud guffaws. Peter discovered that he had mispronounced one of the words. The others joined in the laughter. Rudi looked uncomfortable and vaguely apologetic. Peter felt as he did when *she* made him wear a pair of humiliatingly homemade pants.

After that, he concealed and even denied the fact that he was trying to keep up with them. He still opened Franz's worn Latin grammar every afternoon to study it, but he did so with a kind of desperation.

The incident had shown him how fast the gulf between him and the others was widening. He began to feel more and more left out when they talked. He also knew that he had lost Rudi. Another boy began to join Rudi and him on the way home from rehearsal, and the other boy and Rudi had so many things to talk about that he began to make excuses for going home by himself by way of the Kaiserstrasse. He could not bear to take second place in Rudi's eyes. .

Chapter Fifteen

THERE still remained the choir itself and Herr Granini. In his loneliness he turned to the rich, aristocratic beauty of the music they sang to satisfy an exacerbated craving for warmth and beauty. He became more sensitive to the mellow dignity of the Latin words of the liturgy, which seemed to change texture and meaning with each composer, from the poignant gravity of Schubert to the irrepressible gaiety of Haydn. He was thrilled by his sudden perception of each composition as a work of art to be gradually evoked from the printed page by the suave-voiced, smoldering-eyed Herr Granini. As long as they were singing—even though they were only rehearsing some difficult passage over and over again—he felt sheltered and secure. Rudi's friendship with the other boy and the drabness that waited for him at home had both faded into the distance.

The Sunday mornings had also become more precious to him. Merely climbing the narrow corkscrew staircase to a choir loft filled him with a sense of belonging and with happiness. He loved the discreet bustle and the friendly whispers while the musicians and the choir were crowding into their places, just as he loved the warm, gay talk in the coffeehouse afterward and the rollicking trip into the Innere Stadt for their second Mass.

He went home reluctantly from the Innere Stadt, for at home there waited the endless gray Sunday afternoon. After dinner when Poldi and Franz and Father had left, the living room closed in on him with dreary finality.

He was supposed to do his homework or at most to read. Because it was Sunday, *she* would not allow him to use any tools, such as the fretsaw he had recently found in the attic. There was only the monotonous droning of her sewing machine out in the kitchen and the creaking of her chair. He had no heart for schoolwork, and the books Poldi brought seemed either childish or unbearably dull.

His only escape was into the world of dreams. He imagined himself back in Almzell, going into the village with Karl or climbing the hill to Grandfather's quarry. Karl was lucky. He did not have to stay in a room all afternoon and go to church with *her* afterward. . . . Then he would remember the parcel from America. Invariably, he started to pull out the Erector set which he kept under the chest of drawers and study it curiously. Like the fairytale books and the sweaters, the Erector set had kept its quality of foreignness for him.

If Mizzi was really his mother, why didn't she come and rescue him? She was rich! The last photograph had shown her sitting in an automobile with the little boy and girl who were his brother and sister, Poldi said. Only rich people had automobiles. Why, then, did Mizzi leave him here with *her?*

In the end, his thoughts always came back to *her*. It was she who would not let him go anywhere, not even to the Verein to play with the other boys who were in the choir with him! As the paralyzing afternoon crawled on toward evening and the time when she would tell him to get ready to go to church, his resentment and his feeling of impotence congealed into solid hatred. He wanted to hurt her, to damn her with pain. He experienced a guilty stab of delight at a sudden vision of *her* writhing in the hands of torturers, the way he had seen martyrs pictured in the book she had. The realization that it was wrong to harbor such thoughts made him disown them virtuously as a temptation of the devil, but the troubling, voluptuous memory of her suffering remained and assuaged his bitterness.

It seemed to him that all the drabness that had settled on them like a hateful fog emanated from her. She was even in some obscure way, the nature of which he felt too dispirited to explore, responsible for what had happened to Father. With his mind he knew well enough that Father had been pensioned on account of his fingernails. But the conviction persisted nevertheless that it was really *she* who was to blame.

Often now on his way to the choir in the afternoon, he saw Father sitting in the *Weinstube* at the corner of the Westbahnstrasse. Father sat alone with a forgotten glass of wine in front of him, staring unseeingly out into the street. Only once out of all the times when Peter had tried to attract his attention had Father waved back to him. He looked as solid and aggressive and alert as he always had, but he did not notice anything.

It was the same way at home: Father went through the same meticulous motions of getting dressed to go out, of picking out a cane, of brushing his hat on the landing, but the motions lacked conviction. Peter sensed a listlessness behind the outer shell of these rituals, a despondency which was akin to his own feelings when he was alone with her. Formerly, whenever Father had come home, he had felt a delightful tingle as of something exciting about to happen. Even when Father had been lying down on the divan after dinner, he had been intensely and pleasantly aware of him. Father had somehow filled the room. Now it seemed to Peter as if Father had shrunk and were not there at all in spite of his red, frowning face on the divan. He almost wished sometimes that Father would get drunk again and be angry and shout as he had done before they had gone to Almzell, in the hope that in that way Father might swell to his former warmth and power and be as he had always been.

There was also the grim fact of their new poverty. They were poor now. Not really poor like people who lived in smelly, old houses in Ottakring, or like Frau Agnes who had taken the place of Frau Gerstecker and who came every Friday afternoon for a meal, but forced to consider every penny twice before they spent it. *She* reiterated it constantly: when he wore a hole in an already darned stocking, when he needed two heller to buy a sheet of drawing paper for school, or when he asked for butter on his bread to go with the plate of vegetables which was all he ever got for supper now. Since Father had been pensioned they rarely had anything but soup-meat for dinner during the week. If Father threatened to fly into a rage, or if Poldi complained: "Oh, Mother, soup-meat again!" she immediately flaunted her formula that was half a mumbled whine and half stubborn defiance: "With the money I get, I suppose I can buy you a chicken every day?"

Yet in the cupboard, there was the fluted, gold-rimmed cup in which she hid the housekeeping money, and which always tinkled with silver coins and whispered with banknotes when she reached inside. They could not be as poor as she said. He knew that Father gave her less money than before, but didn't Poldi and Franz also give her money on the first of every month? And Poldi had been having a much better job since September: he had heard *her* say so herself to Frau Werner.

He was angrily certain that she exaggerated their poverty, cherished it even, to assert herself against Father and punish Father, just as she was always punishing him, although he had not done anything. Like the time when he had asked her to let him go skating in the Verein! There was a skating rink in the garden, and all the boys in the choir skated before the rehearsal, and many came back to skate in the evening, too.

He had known that she would not let him buy skates with the money Aunt Wetti had given him, but he could have rented a pair at the Verein for only five heller an afternoon, and there were the American coins Mizzi had sent. She would not let him go. "Other boys have fathers and mothers," she said; "I have enough to do to make ends meet and put food on the table and pay the rent, without having you tear your clothes and wear out your shoes!"

He was sure that the reason she would not let him play with the other boys was not so much that he might tear his clothes, as that she did not want him to be as happy as other boys—just as he was convinced that she had registered him with the charity organization to humiliate him. There was a boy in school who wore a suit he had got from the charity league the Christmas before. The boy was scrofulous and stupid and a constant butt for the entire class. If he had to wear a charity suit he would be bracketed with that boy, for the suits were all alike—of rough green cloth and always much too large—and everybody in school and in the choir would know where it came from. He pleaded with her harder than he had ever pleaded before. She would not listen to him.

She took him to be measured for it on All Souls' Day. They spent the afternoon in the cemetery in Baumgarten. It was a gloomy day with heavy clouds hanging low over the bare trees, and with the cold, dank smell of the steaming loam on the new graves and of decaying plants stinging in one's nostrils. He had always liked All Souls' Day before because of the excitement of seeing so many people in the cemetery, and because of the long row of booths which sold all manner of artificial flowers and beaded wreaths and gaily-colored candles and paraffin tapers in beautiful red glasses. She had always let him buy half a dozen of the little colored candles to light on Frau Wimmer's grave, and there were all the candles and oil lights which the wind had blown out on graves here and there which he could relight. But most important of all, the day had been a sure presage of Christmas. This year the knowledge that after the cemetery she would take him to be measured for the suit would not let him be at peace. And she had refused to let him buy candles to light on Frau Wimmer's grave.

The day seemed to project its chilly hopelessness into the future and to engulf even Christmas in its gray gloom. . . .

They had been told to call for his suit and shoes at a restaurant in the Mariahilferstrasse a few days before Christmas. The charity organization which was giving away the suits had arranged a Christmas party in the ballroom which was crowded with a milling mass of mothers and boys. Only the front of the room, where a small group of ladies and two men were talking together beside a Christmas tree which reached nearly to the ceiling, had remained empty. Even when one of the two men stood on a chair and asked them to come forward and use the chairs up front, the crowd was reluctant to move up. But the furtive buzz of voices became louder, and a few mothers less shy than the others started a rush for the chairs. Peter wanted to hold back, to keep aloof from the crowd. Their eagerness and a certain shrill, breathless humility in their excitement revolted him. But *she* had taken his hand and was pulling him forward toward the empty chairs. He was relieved that they found seats where there were at least a few rows of people ahead of them.

The stout, moon-faced man now made a speech in which he urged them to be grateful to the ladies of the charity league. One of the ladies went to the piano and the other man got up and led them in singing two Christmas carols. The speech and the undisciplined singing made Peter uncomfortable. He was aching to get out of the room. At last, after still another speech, they were told to line up beside the long trestle tables stacked high with bundles behind the Christmas tree. As their names were called they were given the bundles that had their names on them. He hated the waiting in line only little less than having to kiss the ladies' hands when he was given his package.

They walked home through the Mariahilferstrasse where all the shop windows were bright with Christmas displays. She had taken the smaller package with the shoes and he was carrying the ungainly bundle which held the charity suit. The bundle tortured him. He would have liked to throw it away, to leave it behind the door in the dark entranceway of some house. He was sure that every person they passed knew that the bundle contained a charity suit.

The suit was a greenish-brown and much too large for him, just as he had dreaded. The shoes were made of rough, stiff leather and he could tell at a glance that no amount of shining would ever make them gleam like shoes that came from a store. She made him put on the suit the very next Sunday because it was warmer than the blue serge suit she had made for his first communion. It was the first time that he had ever been unwilling to go to the choir. He remained in mortal terror all morning that one of the boys might say something about the suit. The fact that nobody appeared to notice it did not lessen his humiliation; he slunk away from the rest as soon as they had finished singing their second Mass in the Innere Stadt and walked home by himself, still harrowed by shame.

The boys in the choir had been talking of nothing but Christmas and all the presents they hoped to get. He had listened disconsolately. There would not be any Christmas at home; they were not even going to have a Christmas tree. He knew, because he had looked in the attic where Father had formerly always hidden the tree before he trimmed it with Franz the night before Christmas Eve. Nor had there been any of the other signs of Christmas: neither Franz nor Poldi nor Father came home with mysterious-looking packages which they hid in the wardrobes.

Only on Christmas Eve itself, Poldi came home with a few small packages. She was busy with something in Franz's room, but there was none of the festive excitement that had always marked the evening in the past. He saw with dismay that Father was getting ready to go out. Poldi had seen it, too, for she came out into the living room to plead:

"You're coming back, Father, aren't you? You are not going out on Christmas Eve?"

Father finally muttered something about being back. They had to wait until ten o'clock before he came home.

Peter's fears turned into dismal certainty when Poldi rang the little bell in the living room. Father was standing by the mahogany chest with his back to the room. On the table was an artificial tree; it was much smaller than the Christmas trees they had always had before and not half so gay. There were only a few packages on the white damask cloth under the tree. He found two books for him from Franz, and a pair of gloves and a box of water colors from Poldi, but nothing from Father or from *her*. Father merely grunted when Franz gave him a box of cigars, and he did not sing when Franz started "Holy Night. . . ."

It seemed to him that the day climaxed the drab, dismal months since Father had changed.

Chapter Sixteen

He stood at the head of his class in February. Herr Lein even went so far as to hold him up as an example in a clipped, military little speech he made before handing out the report cards. But his triumph was short-lived. Father signed the report card without comment. Peter wondered whether he had even noticed the marks, although he appeared to examine them. Franz who would have said something nice was away for a whole week skiing with Baron von Ortner and another friend, and Poldi seemed to see only the three "twos" and said critically: "Why did you get the 'twos'? You ought to have nothing but 'ones'!" When his disappointment finally drove him to complain to *her* that nobody cared what marks he got, she bridled instantly: "I s'pose you expect me to bake cookies for you or go out and buy you candy just because you have a few 'ones'! I didn't do that even with my own children and I'm not going to start with you. Franz never had anything but 'ones' all the time he was in school. . . ."

Yet he had only wanted some sign that they appreciated his marks, and permission to go skating once a week at the Verein. And he knew that Franz had not always had good marks. He had seen two of Franz's old report cards one afternoon when Father was cleaning out the drawer of his desk: Franz had twice had a "three" in arithmetic. He had never had a "three."

That same evening Rudi and a group of boys in the choir were discussing their term marks. As always when they talked about anything to do with the *Gymnasium*, he listened with heavy-hearted, yearning intentness. Suddenly Rudi turned to him and asked about his marks. Stung by what he felt was merely an impulse to be kind to him, he made some evasive remark when he saw Rudi's eyes suddenly pleading with him. Rudi had made at least two unmistakable efforts since Christmas to be friendly again, but his pride had made him ignore Rudi's overtures.

"Did you flunk anything?" one boy asked.

With the eyes of all the boys expectantly on him now, Peter could not help boasting:

"I had the best marks in the class: only three 'twos.' "

The same boy who had made fun of his pronounciation of the Latin word in the fall sneered: "That doesn't mean anything! Anybody can get good marks in public school. If you were in the Gymnasium you wouldn't be at the head of the class. You'd probably have flunked Latin."

"How do you know?" Rudi challenged the boy.

"Because I know. He wouldn't get 'ones' in Latin and botany and algebra and all the other things. Public school is for morons and—riffraff. My brother says so," he concluded triumphantly.

His brother was Herr Laufer who often came to the Verein and whom they all knew by sight. He was a tall, tousle-haired man who was an engineer and who was always building new airplane models almost as big as real ones and who had actually been up in an airplane several times. The argument was conclusive. A minute later they had started to talk about a duel two sixth-year students in the *Gymnasium* were going to fight and they had forgotten about him. His report card had suddenly become meaningless. The hope he had secretly cherished that good marks would somehow disassociate him from the public school in the eyes of Rudi and the boys in the choir and bring him closer to them had been dashed.

He lost all interest in his studies. To cheat the boredom of the long hours in class he started to draw again; he was caught at it several times. His marks began to slip lower and lower until he was failing in four subjects. Herr Lein was friendly at first and admonished him privately; then he became exasperated. He flew into a rage with him at the slightest inattention in class and sent home one note after the other. Herr Lein's bullying and his own feeling of guilt made him only more obstinate. He did not answer questions even when he knew the answers and he handed in a blank sheet of paper when they had examinations. Herr Lein seemed a tyrant to him now, whom he had come to hate and dread only slightly less than he did *her*.

She had not shown the first few notes the school janitor had brought from Herr Lein to Father, but she had taken to nagging at him almost incessantly. He was not supposed to read any more until his marks improved. Poldi refused to bring him books and locked her own in a drawer so that he could not get at them. When the second note came, Father got out the thick belt with which he had threatened him so often before but which he had never used, and hit him twice across the legs. It was the first time Father had really hit him. The fact that Father, too, had turned against him hurt more than the physical pain and fanned his resentment of *her* as the cause of his unhappiness. He felt they were all lined up against him now, even Franz, although Franz had not scolded him.

They were taken by the school to see a movie about Africa. The film and the lecture that accompanied it gave direction to the idea of running away—an idea with which he had often toyed recently. He could think of nothing else after that. He had secretly joined a lending library in the Kaiserstrasse and he devoured all the books he could get about Africa. He had to read them on the sly, at odd moments when *she* was busy in the kitchen and could not catch him, not only because he had been forbidden to read, but because the library from which he borrowed the books was run by a socialist club. She had an almost superstitious horror of socialists, whom she classed with atheists and anarchists and on whom she blamed all public calamities, including the recent rise in the cost of bread. He had not forgotten how she had clutched his hand and hurried him away when they had accidentally run into a procession of socialists on the first of May, and how she had made a long detour to avoid seeing them again as if she had been afraid of some contamination. . . .

There was also an old five-volume history of exploration which Father had. He was free to read in that because the big tomes looked dull and harmless and because he could always claim that he was looking up some information for geography class. The text was not so interesting as the adventure stories he got from the library, but he was fascinated by the detailed descriptions of life in strange parts of the world and by the abundance of steel engravings which depicted everything from the interior of a Lapp hut to a human sacrifice among the Aztecs where a cruel-looking priest was cutting out the heart of a live victim with a flint knife.

The idea of running away, which had been only an absorbing

daydream at first that allowed him to cheat the monotony of school and the hours she made him spend beside her in church, came to possess him completely. It exhilarated him like a secret weapon held in reserve. It also allowed him to turn some of the drabbest aspects of the daily humdrum to exciting use. If he ran away, he would be on his own. He would have to be strong, wily, resourceful! He would have to know about everything and be able to do everything. The five volumes of Father's history of exploration were constantly stressing the practical difficulties of an explorer's life.

Even some of the subjects in school would prove to be useful. He applied himself with new zest to physics and botany and French, although he made no effort to improve his marks. But the most important thing was to make his body hardy and strong. He ran to and from school to improve his wind and he devised strenuous exercises to strengthen his arms and legs. The heroes of the adventure stories he had read were without exception stoically able to stand pain: he barked his shins deliberately against a chair once a day for a week. It was also important to do without sleep: he managed to stay awake one entire night by dint of pinching himself whenever sleep almost got the better of him; then he forced himself to wake up first at six, then at five. When he failed to wake up at five, he punished himself by barking both shins until the pain brought the tears to his eyes. From a boy in the choir he had borrowed a book on ju-jitsu. After that he got up regularly half an hour earlier every morning to do the exercises indicated at the end of the book.

His determination to become tough and strong drew him to a clique of boys in his class whom he had hitherto despised. They formed part of a gang which spent its afternoons in prowling through the streets and picking fights with rival gangs.

The boys in the gang were suspicious of him at first. In spite of his recent bad marks and Herr Lein's severity with him, they had not forgotten that he had stood at the head of the class in February. They wanted proof that he was not going to become Herr Lein's favorite again. Peter agreed to undergo a series of tests.

One afternoon when Herr Lein had left the room, Peter went up to the closet where the teacher kept his hat and coat, took out Herr Lein's derby and whitened the top with chalk. He had just time to run back to his desk before Herr Lein returned. He sat with taut nerves through the endless class, waiting for the inevitable explosion when Herr Lein saw his hat. If one of the boys who did not belong to the gang told on him, he might even be expelled from the school. . . .

Herr Lein did not fly into as much of a rage as Peter had feared: he seemed disappointed and hurt. The relief Peter felt when it became clear that in spite of the drastic punishment assigned the entire class—they were kept in for two hours and they had to write out one thousand times "Vandalism is the lowest form of depravity; I am a Vandal"—nobody dared to give him away for fear of reprisals from the gang, was tempered by an unexpected twinge of shame at having hurt Herr Lein. But the feat had earned him the respect of the gang. All he had to do now was to fight a boy in a rival gang.

He did not know the boy they had picked out for him to fight. He was from another class and turned out to be shorter than Peter, but stocky, with thick arms and shoulders, and lowering, shifty eyes. Peter fought down his apprehensions when the boy was pointed out to him by telling himself that the tricks he had learned from the book on ju-jitsu would offset the other boy's greater strength and experience.

It was easy enough to pick a fight with the boy by tripping him in the corridor. It was agreed that they would fight that afternoon, immediately after school.

The fight took place inside the hoarding around a demolished house in the Neubaugasse. The two rival gangs had declared a truce to watch the fight; they lined up in two hostile semicircles. When the two leaders finally lowered their caps, Peter dived for the other boy's knees in a tackle that was supposed to bring him to the ground. But he had not counted on the other boy's fists. The ju-jitsu tricks he had practiced so hard against imaginary opponents were of no use at all against the very real blows that landed on him everywhere. Bewildered by his helplessness, he succeeded in locking the other boy against him for a second.

They stood panting into each other's face, then the other boy suddenly pretended to relax, only to butt his head against Peter's nose. Peter lost his balance and went over backward with the other boy on top of him. They went on struggling on the ground, each of them trying to get a decisive hold. Again it was the other boy who was successful. He had got hold of Peter's arm and was twisting it up his back. Through the pain of his twisted arm Peter heard the boys in the rival gang shouting for his opponent to twist harder and the boys on his side calling to him not to give up. In a last desperate effort, he bit back his pain and wrenched himself free. The pain in his left arm filled him with savage fury. He hit out with all his might, determined to hurt the other boy as much as his arm hurt him. His second blow landed on the boy's nose and brought the blood trickling from it. Not only did his rage make him insensitive to the other boy's fists but it seemed to have improved his accuracy. His right fist landed three times in a row, the third time so hard that the other boy lost his balance and sat down on the ground. Peter saw triumphantly that the other boy got up slowly and seemed unwilling to go on with the fight. Just then the watchman appeared from his hut behind the house; they all rushed for their books and hurried over the fence.

Outside, on the sidewalk, the two gangs wrangled over the fight. His own gang insisted that he had won; the other gang claimed that it had been a draw. It was decided that the fight was to continue the following day. Elated with his triumph, Peter hurried home. He was already late and he had torn his pants. *She* would ask questions and scold. But he was in luck. It was washday and she was still down in the cellar when he got home. He was able to wash his face and brush his clothes, and even sew up the rent in his pants.

The next day the other boy was not in school. His staying away was taken as proof that he was afraid to fight. Peter was accepted as a full-fledged member of the gang. He made himself a whip such as the other boys had, by braiding a piece of lead wire in with several strands of rope. There were fights almost every afternoon, but he could rarely stay in them long. *She* was growing suspicious because he was coming home late from school. The only chance he had to be with the gang was before school in the morning and at noon, and on the two occasions when he played hooky from choir rehearsal.

The gang had made the choir seem tame and much less interesting. He would have stayed away from rehearsals more often, had it not been for the fear of being dropped. Herr Granini did not tolerate many absences. One boy had been dropped for that very reason and he had had written excuses from his father each time. And the choir was still too important to him to run such a risk, not only because he had lost none of his secret admiration for Herr Granini, but because it was the only link between him and Rudi and the other boys in the *Gymnasium*. More important still, he would have dreaded the prospect of the long summer without the daily excursions Herr Granini would again take them on.

They were already beginning to make trips into the country on Sundays. One Sunday, toward the end of June, they took a train to Melk to sing for High Mass in the monastery. The monks were jovial and made much of them. They were given a delicious dinner in the refectory and they had the run of the vast garden for the entire afternoon. They played soccer on the lawn and Rudi had insisted that he be on the same team with him. Although he tried hard to appear indifferent, Peter was flattered. Rudi also sat next to him in the refectory when they were called in for coffee and rolls.

It had been a beautiful day and Peter hated to leave. At home drabness would be waiting for him again. *She* would make him brush his clothes and get ready for school on Monday.

Sadness made him silent by the time the train drew into the Westbahnhof. In a few minutes now he would have to leave Herr Granini and Rudi and the rest of the boys. The streets would breathe the rich, mellow somnolence of Sunday evening, which always afflicted him with a feeling of depressing finality and unfulfillment, especially when he heard the gay talk and the laughter of people obviously hurrying toward some enchanting evening at a restaurant or theater.

But when they got off the train he saw at once that this was no ordinary Sunday evening. An oddly subdued excitement pervaded the station. People were crowding together in agitated little clusters, breathlessly talking to strangers as they swarmed from one group to the other. It could not be an accident—there were too many groups. Then he noticed that people were craning their necks to catch a glimpse of a newspaper someone was holding at the center of each group. He heard one man call something about an archduke.

It was the same way in front of the station. On the plaza, newsboys were hoarsely shouting, "Extra, extra!" They were still advertising their papers from sheer excitement, although a dozen hands were reaching out for the few rumpled copies they had left.

Herr Granini had sent several boys to try to get a paper. But they did not have to wait for one to get the news. A cabby shouted at the top of his lungs to Herr Granini: "The Archduke's been killed—Ferdinand!—his wife, too! Assassinated in Sarajevo!"

One of the boys had succeeded in getting a copy of the extra. It had a heavy black border and smelled of ink. They crowded around Herr Granini to read the huge headlines which said the same thing the cabby had shouted at them. The facts meant nothing to Peter, but Herr Granini's suddenly grave face when he said, "I guess it must be true," and the excitement of the people all around them infected him. All the way home to the Schottenfeldgasse, people were standing together and discussing the same news. The word "assassination" recurred like a refrain. . . .

His first thought when he awoke the following morning was fear that he had only dreamed about the assassination and the excitement the night before. Father's morning paper lying open on the living-room table reassured him; it had enormous black borders and pictures of the murdered archduke and of his wife. He could only glance at it because Father did not allow him to read the newspaper. In the kitchen Poldi and *she* were talking. He listened closely while he washed, hoping that something new might have happened in the streets while he had been asleep. But *she* was only saying glumly: "Only the dear God knows what all is going to happen. Troubles never come singly like that. Herr Pfeiffer said there was going to be a war when he brought the bread this morning. Things just couldn't go on like this forever! People thinking of nothing but having a good time instead of going to church. . . . God will stand just so much. . . ."

He could hardly wait to get out into the street. He was afraid that the exhilarating tension there had been about people the night before might have disappeared. But he saw at once that the same taut expectancy as of something momentous about to happen was still there. It was, if anything, stronger, more intense. It was in people's voices, in the nervous haste with which men unfolded their newspapers right outside the tobacconist's shop next door and in the petrified concentration with which they read. Even the way people walked seemed to him different.

About half the houses on the way to school were flying flags, but the flags were at half-mast. That must be because the Archduke was dead. In the stationer's window across the street from the school the pimply, redheaded clerk was draping black crepe around a large framed photograph of the Archduke. Several boys from Peter's class were in front of the window watching him. They were too busy arguing about a rumor that there was not going to be any school on Thursday, when the coffins were to arrive in Vienna, to annoy the clerk by tapping on the window and making faces at him as they ordinarily would have done. One boy whose uncle was a teacher was claiming heatedly that they were going to get the whole week off. . . .

In the end they were given the day of the funeral when the caskets were to be put on the train at the Westbahnhof. Franz had got up very early to go into the Innere Stadt to get inside the church where the requiem was to be held. Peter had asked him to take him along, but Franz had said that it was dangerous because of the huge crowds there would be everywhere. He had to content himself with going to the station with *her* in the afternoon.

There was already a swarming mass of people all along the Gürtel where the cortege was to pass. They could not get within a quarter of a mile of the Westbahnhof, but he could see that the whole station was hung with black cloth and that all the tall arc lights along the Gürtel were veiled with black crepe. He had never seen so many people before. They were everywhere, on balconies, leaning out of windows, crowded at attic windows, on the roofs. Boys had climbed most of the lampposts and the policemen did not even protest. *She* would not let him climb up on top of a wall near which they were waiting, but when suddenly an excited murmur ran through the crowd and her umbrella got caught in another woman's reticule, he slipped away from her. A man helped him up on the wall, where there was just room enough for him to squeeze in between two boys.

From the wall he could see all the way to the Mariahilferstrasse. It was thrilling to look out over the thousands of heads. The boy in back of him jostled him once so that he almost lost his balance. "If I fall," Peter thought, "I'll fall right on top of their heads. I'll have to walk on their shoulders until I find a hole in the crowd."

The music of some military band was becoming more distinct. Men were taking off their hats; a hush had fallen over the immense crowd. Then the first of the procession appeared in the Mariahilferstrasse. It was a drum corps whose sticks sounded strangely muffled on the crepe-covered drums. They were followed by grenadiers. Behind them came other infantry regiments, then hussars and cuirassiers, then more infantry. Peter recognized only a few of the resplendent uniforms. It seemed as if the procession of soldiers would continue all afternoon. At last, carriages began to appear, but they were only used to convey mounds of wreaths. He counted forty of them and then grew tired of counting. There were still more coming out of the Mariahilferstrasse and turning up the Gürtel toward the station.

Quite a distance away from the wall there was a sudden commotion. A woman had fainted. . . . He watched two men half carry and half lead her toward a tree. The crowd was opening a narrow lane for them which closed as soon as they had passed. A policeman's helmet bobbed up and down near the tree. The policeman was shoving people back and clearing a little space for the woman. A thermos bottle flashed in the sun. After that he could not see any longer what was happening. He felt tired and sat down on the wall. *She* was still standing beside the stout man with the flowing mustaches and the loud, checked suit; he could tell that it was she by the violets on her hat.

A sudden stir among the people on the wall made him climb back on his feet. This time it really was the hearse, drawn by sixteen shiny black horses with waving black plumes over their heads. One could see the silvery casket through the glass walls of the sumptuous hearse. Behind it, in a simple, somber carriage, rode the Emperor. Then came still another hearse, drawn by fewer horses than the first one—it held the Archduchess' casket, people whispered below him—and behind it, an inexhaustible line of carriages.

The hearses had stopped under a black marquee with the imperial arms in silver on it. It was hard to see what was happening because the marquee and the solidly massed soldiers cut off the view. Somebody said that the Emperor had already gone into the station. Here and there people were beginning to leave. Out of the corner of his eye he noticed that *she* was making her way to the wall. A minute later, she was poking at him with the tip of her umbrella. When he pretended not to be aware of it, she poked harder. He had to look down. She whispered with the same sibilant urgency she used in church: "Time to go home! You've seen all there is to see."

He hated to leave before the crowd had really started to disperse.

"Can't I stay a little longer? It isn't over yet."

"I've got to start supper, and you're coming home with me."

He got down and they began to thread their way through the crowd. He derived a vindictive pleasure from the difficulty she found in getting through. It was not until they got near the Westbahnstrasse that they no longer had to worm and twist their way between people and say "Pardon" at every step. The Westbahnstrasse was deserted. Not even the confectionery shop opposite the Verein was open. Their own house, when they walked through the entranceway, was quieter than he had ever seen it. Frau Frankl's dog barked behind her door on the second-floor landing as they went upstairs.

Something of the strangely hushed stillness that had lain over the huge crowd around the station like a spell seemed to be still in the streets the next morning. But at noon when he came out of school there was another extra. People were again crowding around each possessor of a copy to read. The excitement had come back into people's voices and it stayed. Every day now there were black headlines in Father's paper. On the hoardings appeared white posters with the imperial coat of arms and the word "Manifesto" at the top. Everybody was talking about something called an "ultimatum." Herr Lein explained that an ultimatum was very serious and that there might be a war.

The renewed excitement came as a godsend for him, for it coincided with the close of school. His report card showed an alarming number of "threes" and "fours." Worst of all, he had a "three" in conduct for having drawn a caricature of Herr Lein. But the newspapers with their big headlines had suddenly made his report card much less serious. Father scowled when he saw the marks, but he said no more than, "That's got to change next fall," and picked up his newspaper again. Only Poldi sounded really dangerous when she threatened to make him drop the choir, unless he got better marks in the fall.

He felt relieved, for he had expected some drastic punishment. The fall was still a long way off. . . .

A couple of days after the close of school, *she* sent him to the bakery in the Westbahnstrasse for yeast. He sauntered leisurely up the street. This was vacation. It was pleasant to take his time. But as he approached the Westbahnstrasse, he saw that people were hurrying in the direction of the church. People came rushing out of shops. There was already a crowd around the bulletin board outside the church. A florid-faced man shouted up to the masons on the scaffolding of the new apartment house that was going up:

"It's war, you fellows! We are going to fight."

"You sure?" one of the masons called down.

"Absolutely! It's war—we'll show those Serbs!"

The mason up on the scaffolding waved his trowel and cheered. Somebody near the florid-cheeked man laughed. People were jostling one another to get to the two posters which were still wet with paste. When Peter had squeezed his way to the front, he saw that one of the posters was headed "Mobilization" and the other "Manifesto." It was all he was able to read, for already people were crowding him away from the bulletin board. They, too, did no more than read those two words.

Exhilaration and a strange new kind of enthusiasm gained on the crowd which already extended out to the middle of the street. A man had climbed up on the iron fence in front of the parish house and was shouting something about going to the Emperor's Palace on the Ring. The suggestion was greeted with cheers. The jostling was invariably accompanied by laughter now. The masons who had come down from the new building across the street had linked arms and had started to sing.

He was swept along by the laughing, cheering crowd which started to move slowly down the street. Somebody started to sing the national anthem and in no time at all everybody was singing it. There were cheers for the Emperor, then for the minister whose name Peter had heard so frequently in people's mouths of late. They reached the Neubaugasse and more people were joining the procession constantly. The newcomers were greeted with cheers. Men were walking with their arms about each other and making jokes about the Serbs. It was even gayer than at the *Heurigen.* When they finally got to the Mariahilferstrasse, they had to slow up and stop, for the Mariahilferstrasse was already black with people. All traffic had been blocked. Then they moved forward again, around stalled, empty streetcars and carriages that had been forced to the curb. Once, a cab horse reared alarmingly between the shafts. . . .

He realized suddenly that he was almost at the Ring and that *she* would be waiting for the yeast. He hated to leave the exuberant crowd, but he fought his way out of the procession and up a side street. The sound of cheering and singing followed him all the way back into the Westbahnstrasse.

When he came to the bakery, the shop was closed.

Chapter Seventeen

THE locked door of the bakery in the Westbahnstrasse startled him, because now he would be unable to get the yeast and she would be sure to scold. It meant little more to him than that.

Yet, it seemed to him later, that he ought to have been struck by it as a portent of what the war was to mean to him, and to all those thousands singing and cheering themselves hoarse on their way to the Ring; and when afterward he sometimes spent half of a bitter-cold night standing in line for a loaf of black bread in front of the same locked door, he often remembered the moment and felt angrily that he had been somehow obtuse. But that was much later. Now and for many weeks to come, he was aware only of the boundless enthusiasm everywhere.

Within a few hours, spreading irresistibly from house to house like a gay contagion, flags began to billow and flutter in the warm July breeze. Beneath them, all of life seemed suddenly to have become richer and more gay. Voices sounded exuberant, people's steps were springier, and the orchestras on the coffeehouse terraces had taken on an oddly haunting brilliance in the way they played the familiar strains. It was as if the whole city had been caught up in a prolonged and unexpected holiday.

Every day now, there was something new that was exciting to hear or see. In the Mariahilferstrasse and on the Ring, there were the shiny, new, yellow military cars with generals and colonels being whisked importantly to and from the War Ministry. There were the ponderous new army trucks, and there were the shops which seemed to vie with each other in producing the largest variety of patriotic trinkets and jewelry. There were the new uniforms: gray and drab, when compared to the regimental trappings the soldiers had worn before, but fascinating too, because Franz said that the gray uniforms were to keep the enemy from seeing the soldiers distinctly at the front.

But most exciting of all were the railroad stations where the soldiers left. The stations and the trains were gaily festooned with garlands and flags, and there were always bands playing when a troop train pulled out. Poldi had taken him along to the Ostbahnhof one night when she and some other girls from her congregation went to distribute chocolate and cigarettes. The soldiers had been singing and laughing in the train, a band had played, and it had all been very gay, even though the women who had come to see the soldiers off had cried. He found himself wishing ardently that he could grow up soon, so that he could be a soldier, too.

Everywhere the men he knew were now in uniform: in the house, at the Verein, even in school. He had felt a little ashamed at first that Franz was still at home, until he heard Poldi explain to Fräulein Gisl that all the men in the War Ministry had been told that they were more important in Vienna than at the front. Still, he would have rather had Franz live in one of the barracks out on the Schmeltz—like Herr Prohaska, for instance, who was Franz's best friend since Baron Ortner had left. Baron Ortner was already in that half-mysterious region called "the front" and sent Franz postcards with amusing drawings of his quarters in a peasant hut.

It was exciting! There were drives for the Red Cross, with handsome girls dressed up in nurses' uniforms, giving away stick-buttons and collecting money. Poldi took part in all of them and came home at night full of stories about the big donations she had got. Poldi also brought home cartons of tobacco and empty envelopes, and allowed him to help her make cigarettes, which were to go to the soldiers at the front.

Even Father was much friendlier and discussed the war with Franz at every meal. The change in Father, Peter knew, was due chiefly to the fact that Father had been promised another job in the theater because the mobilization had left the Burgtheater short of men.

Only *she* brought a discordant note into the harmony that seemed to bind together everybody else. Once, when Poldi was talking about the war, *she* snapped:

"You go on as if war was a picnic. You'll find out! Many's the time my mother used to talk about the hard times they had in '66. And the old people when I was a little girl always used to tell how they had to drive all the cattle into the woods, not once but many times, and bury everything they had when the Moors came up from Italy. You'll see. . . ."

"Oh, that was a long time ago, Mother!" Poldi said impatiently. "You're always looking for the black side of everything—I'm going to the station with Gisl. It's our night with the Red Cross. So don't wait up for me. . . ."

In school, the teachers talked confidently of victory when they explained the war news every day. Belgrade had already fallen or was about to fall, and it was only a question of time until the Serbs would ask for peace; and in the north, the Germans, who were a strong military nation, would make short work of the Russians and the French. . . .

He minded school much less. Herr Lein was in the navy, and his place had been taken by an elderly man who was much less strict. There were frequent interruptions in the school routine, as when they were given three whole days off to collect old bronze and nickel and rubber in the neighborhood. They had been divided up into teams, and Peter had been astonished by the piles of handsome, almost new things people had got ready for them to take down to the waiting carts. It was like the time when they were sent to collect linen which was to be made into bandages, or later when they collected Christmas packages. . . . The excitement, and the fact that they got out an hour earlier each afternoon, made school seem much less dull. But most important of all, there were now the voice lessons at Herr Granini's apartment right after school to look forward to!

One day, just before school had opened again, Herr Granini had called him aside in the garden where he had been kicking a soccer ball around with two other boys.

"You aren't getting yourself overheated?" Herr Granini had asked. His curiously rich, vibrant, and always faintly husky voice which never failed to rouse in Peter a tingling sense of alertness was solicitous. The question was alone enough to make his heart beat a little faster, for he had heard Herr Granini ask it many times of the soloists when he was worried that they might be playing too hard. And now Herr Granini had put his arm around his shoulder, as he did only when he had something important to say to a boy.

"There's a singer in you somewhere, Peter," Herr Granini said. "Possibly a good one. I've been thinking we might have a try at bringing him to the surface. That'll take work! Do you think you'd be willing to work hard—I mean, at home by yourself and with me sometimes?"

Excitement had clutched at Peter's throat. He could only nod. Working with Herr Granini, he knew, meant spending whole hours at a time in the wonderful apartment in the Mariahilferstrasse, and it meant perhaps chocolate and cake every time he went, and then riding to rehearsal in a cab with Herr Granini afterward.

"All right, then. We'll start next Monday. Who knows, you may be our next alto soloist! Can you get to the Mariahilferstrasse by four from your school? And that reminds me: Franz says that you haven't been doing very well in school! That right?"

He nodded guiltily. His stubborn defiance of the teachers all last spring, the importance he had attached to belonging to the gang of rowdies in his class, even his daydreams about running away seemed suddenly childish. He was about to promise that he would study hard this year, when Herr Granini got ahead of him:

"That's all going to be different this year, isn't it? That's fine. I'll look for you on Monday, then."

After that, on three afternoons a week he went to Herr Granini's house. He went directly from school, making his way impatiently through the boys who always lingered on the sidewalk, jealous of every minute he might be made to waste. If, as sometimes happened, some of the boys in the gang tried to detain him by force to make him join in one of their brawls, he hit out with a viciousness that surprised even himself; just as he became beyond all reason exasperated when Nowak, the second soprano soloist with whom he shared the lessons and who had to come all the way from the *Gymnasium* in the Kandlgasse, was late in getting to the corner where they had agreed to meet. Once started, however, and as they approached Herr Granini's house, every other emotion in him gave way to joy.

Herr Granini, more often than not, was out when they first arrived. They would be received by the brusque-mannered housekeeper and taken into the drawing room to wait. He came to prize those five or fifteen minutes before Herr Granini arrived almost as much as any part of the afternoon. He was free to imagine that he was alone in the apartment, with untrammeled leisure to explore its treasures and to saturate himself with the mellow, deep-toned charm of the place. Nowak bothered him hardly at all, for Nowak had a passion for detective stories and lost no time in bringing out a dime novel from his pocket and settling down with it.

As he wandered a little furtively from the drawing room into the music room and out again, Peter found nearly always something that had escaped his attention before. One time it was the gold-bronze death mask of Beethoven on the wall; then it was the blue and white Chinese vase half hidden behind a door; another time, he was struck by the secretive gleam of the ebony top of one of the two grand pianos standing tail to tail; and still another time, he discovered that the long red velvet draperies at the windows were lined with a flowered yellow silk that was even more beautiful than the deep-red velvet outside.

He came to feel that each discovery formed a new and secret bond between him and this place, so that each time the door opened from the vestibule with the soft abruptness that could only mean Herr Granini, he experienced a little shock of guilt because he was sure that Herr Granini's watchful black eyes could not fail to see how passionately he had possessed himself of every sensation of sight and touch that lived in the rooms.

Herr Granini's arrival transformed the rooms. He came in swiftly, seriously, in his inevitable black mohair coat and loosely knotted black bow tie, stopped for a second to examine them from under his beetling brows as if he had forgotten that they were to come that day, then smiled as swiftly as he had frowned, and asked:

"Ready, boys?"

The lesson had begun. They hurried forward to follow him into the music room, so close behind his wide back and slightly forward-tilted head that Peter could see the strip of tawny neck between the lustrous black locks and the white collar. They took their places beside the piano. The very walls of the room, it seemed to Peter as he waited for Herr Granini's nod, had become charged with the dark, watchful fire in Herr Granini's eyes.

They usually started with a set of exercises meant to round out their tones and place their voices—"Out here!" Herr Granini said and flung his cupped hand far out in front of his own mouth—then went on to trying solo passages from the endless supply of masses and oratorios that appeared from the enormous bookcase that took up an entire wall. All through the lesson, whether they were singing mere exercises or intricately phrased solo parts, Peter remained glowingly conscious of the seriousness of what they were doing, because of the unremitting watchfulness in Herr Granini's eyes. They were, he felt, building something important together, even though Nowak and he were somehow only the instruments and it was really Herr Granini who did the building. Only rarely did he become aware of the music apart from Herr Granini until afterward, at home or in the street, when some melody would suddenly return and keep running through his head. The important thing would be to bring about the swift flicker of approval that could kindle Herr Granini's face; his worst dread was to provoke the nervous frown and the beetling of the dark brows if he faltered on a note or was guilty of a ragged release. He felt bad then even before Herr Granini stopped playing and said: "Let's start again!" Excuses, he felt, were out of place in this room; only perfection had a right in it.

But best of all he liked the few minutes at the end, when Herr Granini explained the music they were to study next, for from the music Herr Granini would go on to tell them fascinating anecdotes about the oddities of famous singers and musicians, which would often keep them laughing all through the *Jause* in the dining room. And sometimes Herr Granini would even show them some of the treasures of which Franz had spoken to him—as once, when Herr Granini brought out the baton which had been used by Haydn, or another time when he showed them the Mozart manuscript with the big coffee stain sprawling all over the last two sheets and the amusing note which began, *"Ferdl, Pferdl, edles Vieh!"* scribbled on the margin of the title page by Mozart himself.

He never failed to experience a little thrill at the calm familiarity with which Herr Granini spoke of the great composers, so different from the rapturous tone with which he had heard Poldi and her friends refer to them on one occasion when they had been talking about some opera. It made him feel almost as if he knew them, too; as if Herr Granini had drawn him into an intimate inner circle where even the humblest initiate was allowed to treat Haydn and Gluck and Beethoven with the calm assurance of a fellow aristocrat.

The hour and a half at the apartment went much too quickly for him. He wanted to put off the moment when Herr Granini started for the vestibule to get into his overcoat, for he always had the feeling that once they left the apartment, some magic tie between him and Herr Granini was broken and that he lost him to all the other boys. Yet, in other ways, he was glad to get to the Verein. The afternoons with Herr Granini had gained him a flattering amount of prestige. He was often made captain now when they played soccer in the afternoon, and allowed to pick a team, which had never happened before. And Rudi had made new overtures to be friends again—advances which he had repelled even more coldly than in the spring. But he had remained intensely aware of Rudi and cherished the one advantage the singing lessons gave him over Rudi and his new friends in the *Gymnasium*—an advantage, he dreamed hopefully, which might someday be the means of bridging the gap the *Gymnasium* had put between Rudi and him.

Chapter Eighteen

If the lessons were important because of Rudí, they began to matter even more as a refuge from home and from her. The war, which at first had promised to scatter the gloom that had weighed on him at home all last spring, had suddenly and treacherously turned into her ally. The drabness had come out of the corners again and hung in the living room and the kitchen and even in Franz's room, somehow grimmer and more hopeless than ever. Again he saw her as darkly responsible. She had moved, silently and stubbornly, within the narrow circle of her housekeeping chores, like a spider inexorably spinning the web of her gloomy predictions, until the early exhilaration of the war had somehow got caught in it and died. It had started with the food.

Food was becoming scarce. At least, some of it was: such commonplace staples as flour and sugar and lard, which had always been so inexpensive that he had not even liked to go to the store to fetch them for her. It puzzled him why it was not the delicacies in the windows of the expensive shops which had become hard to get, since he had always looked on them as rare and wonderfully desirable. He asked Franz, and Franz explained that it was because the army needed vast quantities of everything. For once, Franz's explanation explained without satisfying. It only left him with the impression that soldiers at the front became suddenly inhumanly hungry and devoured outrageous quantities of food.

One by one, the staples disappeared from the shelves and the Sold Out signs in the shopwindows multiplied. Things could still be had here and there, but the news that a tub of butter or a few sacks of flour had arrived at some store spread with such disheartening rapidity that by the time he reached the shop there was always a good-sized crowd already ahead of him.

He did not mind standing in line at first. People joked and laughed; it was almost like a game. Then the novelty wore off and he found the long hours of waiting not only monotonous, but exasperating, because of the uncertainty of getting anything when he finally got inside the store. More often than not, a clerk or the policeman who had kept the line in order would suddenly announce: "All sold out!" and he would have to go away empty-handed.

Their meals had been becoming steadily leaner, too. She used black flour for noodles and *Nockerl*, and even for thickening. They had meat only twice a week and she would give him only a small piece of gristle or of fat. When he complained, she would turn on him instantly: "You eat what you get and be glad you have something to put in your stomach. A child doesn't need a lot of meat."

It seemed to him that he was always hungry now, especially in the afternoon, and he had come to look forward to the trip to the Mariahilferstrasse more than ever because of the cocoa or chocolate and the cake. In spite of the SOLD OUT signs everywhere, there had been no change in Herr Granini's dining room.

He realized that that was due to the fact that Herr Granini was rich. Everybody knew that wealthy people had laid in vast supplies of everything. Even people in their own neighborhood who were not rich had done that. Karl Breitner boasted that his mother had two hundred pounds of white flour and a whole tub full of lard. It infuriated him to think how little *she* had stored away. He had looked one day when she was in the cellar and he had found only a ten-pound bag of flour, a little more than three pounds of sugar, and a pail of lard. It was no more than she had always kept on hand. Only with a small part of his mind was he willing to acknowledge that she had not had enough money to buy things ahead.

She herself lost no opportunity to remind them of it whenever Poldi or Franz complained about the meals. "If I had had the money other women had, I could bake cake now, too, and make *Apfelstrudel* every day."

But what surprised and secretly irritated him was Father's patience with the food. A year ago, Father's face would have darkened instantly if there had not been any meat; now he merely scowled a little, but he did not flare up. Father, of course—Peter knew—was not dependent on the meals at home; he had frankfurters and gravy for ten o'clock breakfast in some restaurant, and he ordered things to eat in the evening, too! Peter had seen him with a succulent-looking plate of smoked ham and grated horse-radish in front of him, one evening when he had passed the restaurant in the Kaiserstrasse on his way home from a late rehearsal.

But the real reason for Father's failure to protest, Peter realized, lay in his general good temper ever since he had been assured of another job in the theater. The change in Father no longer gladdened him. He saw it only as an exasperating inertness on Father's part, because his own daily disappointment at the dreary procession of vegetables ached for an outlet in one of Father's former rages.

He suddenly got his wish with jarring unexpectedness. It was going on toward the end of November. He came home from school one noon, hungry but already buoyed up by the prospect of the *Jause* at Herr Granini's that afternoon. Father was at the mahogany table that stood between the foot-ends of the two beds against the wall; he had flung back the green and brown tapestry cloth which usually hung down over the drawer, and he was taking out bundles of papers and thick, bulging envelopes and laying them on the red-gleaming table top. He seemed to be looking for something that he was unable to find. His back and shoulders looked preoccupied and he gave no sign that he had heard when she said for the second time: "The soup's on the table—don't blame me if it gets cold!"

Peter sat down at the table and waited impatiently for Father to come. She had gone back into the kitchen and was making a testy-sounding clatter with the pots and pans. Something about it caught Peter's attention: the noise she made was somehow less resentful and irritable than worried-sounding. He remembered suddenly her watchful glance at Father's back when she had brought in the soup and that her voice had been harsher than usual when she had said grace in the kitchen.

But perhaps it was only his imagination! After all, he always felt vaguely apprehensive when Father went into the drawer where he kept all their documents along with his own papers, simply because she had never allowed him to play under the mahogany table when he had been small and because he associated Father's going into the drawer with such important events as Franz's starting in the Ministry and with paying the rent every month.

Father finally came and sat down. Peter saw that he had left the drawer open and several bundles of papers out on the table; he had never known Father to leave the mahogany table before without first locking the drawer. He glanced cautiously at him and saw that his face was gathered in a frown. It was not an angry frown. Father looked rather as if he were trying very hard to recall something important that had slipped his mind.

When they had finished the soup, she brought in a dish of red cabbage and a plate of boiled potatoes. Father had not seemed to notice even that she had changed his plate. She shoved the bread and the bread knife closer to his elbow, and he gave a little start. Alertness crowded into his face.

"Where's the meat?" His voice sounded dangerously subdued.

She went back into the kitchen without answering. Peter could hear her folding a piece of old wrapping paper by the cupboard. The crackle of the paper had something desperate about it.

Father had speared a potato and put it on his plate. He looked preoccupied again and Peter wondered whether he had forgotten his own question. Then he reached for the cabbage, looked at it for a second, and set the dish down angrily.

"Where's the meat, I said!"

She came to the kitchen door.

"You got eyes to see with. I couldn't get any meat today."

Father pushed the table away from him so that the dishes and the silver on it clattered ominously. He went back to the open drawer of his desk. Peter was left alone at the table. After waiting for a minute to see whether she would come back to serve him, he went out into the kitchen and said: "I haven't anything to eat."

She turned on him irascibly. "You'll starve just because you have to wait for a minute." But she went into the living room and ladled out some cabbage on his plate and gave him a boiled potato. Then she went out into the kitchen again.

A few minutes later Poldi came home. From his place at the table, Peter could see her take off her hat and the new raincoat she was so proud of and lay them on the flat board top of her bed. Poldi started almost at once to tell her about some bazaar for the wounded soldiers that her congregation was organizing. Poldi's enthusiasm about the bazaar seemed to keep her from noticing that *she* remained grimly silent. Then Poldi came into the living room to get a book from the big chest of drawers, said "Hello" to Father, got no answer, and suddenly seemed to realize that something was wrong, for she went back into the kitchen and asked: "What's the matter? Anybody die?"

He listened carefully.

"What's the matter, Mother?"

"Don't ask me!" she said forbiddingly as she carried Poldi's plate to the kitchen cabinet where Poldi usually ate on weekdays.

"Well, I never saw such long faces! What, cabbage again? No, really, Mother!"

Poldi said no more after that. She had propped up a book behind her plate, Peter knew, and was reading while she ate.

A glum silence hung over the rest of the hour before he could leave for school. It took the lesson at Herr Granini's to free him from the shadow the meal hour at noon had thrown over him.

Poldi happened to be standing in front of the house talking to Fräulein Gisl when he came home from rehearsal. He had to stop and say hello to Fräulein Gisl who asked about the choir and the lessons, then Fräulein Gisl said good-by and he and Poldi went through the courtyard. On the way up the stairs, Poldi said:

"You aren't saying much about school. I hope you haven't forgotten about what I said last spring: you get bad marks again and it's good-by choir for you. By the way, how are you getting on?"

"All right, I guess."

"Don't say 'I guess.' I asked you how you were getting along."

"I said, all right."

"Well, just remember!"

They had reached their landing. The door of their apartment opened abruptly. Father came through it with such brusqueness that Peter did not have time to get out of the way and was knocked to one side. He looked after Father for a second, then he followed Poldi into the kitchen. On the floor beside the cupboard lay the pieces of a broken vegetable dish in a puddle of red cabbage. *She* was on the floor beside it, picking up the shards and putting them on a sheet of newspaper.

"Well!" Poldi gasped. "What's all this about? What happened, Mother?"

She went on doggedly picking out the shards from the mess of red cabbage.

"What happened?"

"You can see what happened as well as I can."

"But can't you tell me?"

She got up from the floor and took the newspaper with the broken pieces of porcelain to the ash can.

"Father got a letter from the Burgtheater," she said finally.

"Well, that's no reason why he has to throw things around!" Poldi burst out. . . .

Peter remembered Father's preoccupied air at noon: Father had not got the job in the theater! They had turned him down!

"Don't stand there like a statue!" *she* said acrimoniously. "Get me a pail of water."

He took the pail and went out on the landing to the water tap. A host of nightmarishly precise details of the year before when Father had come home drunk every night crowded in on him. Was it going to be like that again? A nauseating fear clutched him and would not be shaken off all evening in spite of his efforts to concentrate on his homework. And when she sent him to bed half an hour earlier than usual, he lay awake for a long time, listening for Father to come home. He heard Franz come in and Franz and Poldi talking in the kitchen. They were talking in an undertone but he knew from their voices that they were talking about Father. They talked for a long time. He finally fell asleep before Franz came in to go to bed.

Several times in the course of the next few weeks he was seized by sudden, anguishing conviction that they had all been plunged back into the time a year before when Poldi had gone to see the lady on the Gürtel. A paralyzing, fear-fed lethargy settled on him then. He felt that no time had passed in between, that nothing at all had changed.

Yet he knew that there was a change. Only the way they all avoided Father was the same. Franz had been eating dinner at a restaurant once or twice a week all fall when he was especially busy at the Ministry: now he was never home at noon. Poldi insisted on eating in the kitchen, so that he was always alone at the table with Father, except Sunday noon when Franz ate at home and *she* came and sat down, too.

They and Father reminded him of a vicious bull he had seen in

Almzell and of the family that owned him. At a safe distance from the animal, the peasants had discussed him with cool, almost patronizing detachment. But in back of their talk Peter had sensed a constant, obsessing fear that their bull might tear loose from the wall where he was chained and break out of the barn and go on a terrifying rampage. And when they had to go near him, he noticed that it was with elaborate precautions.

In the same way, their unspoken anxiety had created a tension that isolated Father, until it seemed to Peter that Father's least movement was fraught with menace. Yet there had been only one of the violent scenes late at night which he had dreaded most. It was not that Father drank less than the year before—he drank even more, for Peter saw him in the *Weinstube* at the corner of the Westbahnstrasse almost every time he passed there now—but Father did not seem to get drunk. In place of the dark, frightening outbursts of a year ago had come a permanent irascibility that searched her out with cold, hard-eyed vindictiveness.

There were other changes in Father: often now when Peter came home from school in the afternoon, the living-room door was still closed and she made him stay in the kitchen. Father was still lying on the divan taking his after-dinner nap, and sometimes it would be four o'clock before he finally came out into the kitchen to wash his face at the washstand and gargle. There were Father's fits of brooding abstraction when he seemed suddenly to forget what he was about to do. It happened most frequently when he was getting ready to go out after his nap. He would pick up one shoe, then set it down again, or interrupt lacing a shoe and sit for whole minutes on end staring straight ahead of him. Or Peter would see him by the chest of drawers about to put on his collar and tie, but picking up a brush or some other object instead and moving it from one place to another for no reason at all, only to move it back a minute later.

At moments like these Peter had the impression that Father was trying to recapture some idea that was desperately important and without which he was somehow lost. Something essential, deep-voiced, and powerful had gone out of Father, so that all his being seemed to live now in his irritable surface. Even Father's voice bore out that impression: it had become acrimonious and metallic, as if he felt it necessary to say things louder and more bitingly to assert himself.

But what astonished him most was the increasing amount of attention Father paid to her. Ever since they had come back from Almzell a year ago, Father had either bluntly ignored her or had at most lashed out at her in a few quick, angry words if he could not find some particular shirt or if she had not pressed some suit to his liking. Now he went out of his way to rail at her about going to church and about Pater Alfred. He watched when she got ready to go out and came into the kitchen to sneer: "Going to see that priest?" or if she came in from shopping: "Did you take him something to eat, your fat priest? Don't let him go short of anything! He needs his roast chicken every day. Any muck is good enough for me—but I'm going to put a stop to that!"

Peter wondered why she did not defend herself. She remained stubbornly silent, even when Father accused her of having been to see Pater Alfred in the middle of the day, when Peter knew that she had been at the market in the Burggasse, shopping and standing in line. It seemed to Peter that the more abusive Father became, the more submissively tight-lipped and even conciliating she grew. She managed somehow to have a piece of boiled beef for him every noon, and she was painstakingly intent on keeping Father's things in order. Unlike before, when these tasks had had a fixed but quite unnoticeable place in her daily routine, shining Father's shoes, pressing his clothes and getting his shirts back from the laundry now came before everything else. She even appeared to be defending Father, for on one or two occasions when Poldi said something against him, *she* bristled instantly: "You mind your own business! God has given me my cross to bear, and I'll do it without your help!"

Peter found the same baffling indulgence in what she said to Herr Gregor one evening when Herr Gregor stopped them in front of his shop. It was late. They had been standing in line for half a pound of sugar ever since supper, and they were coming home through the Kandlgasse. In front of Herr Gregor's shop two heavy drays were unloading boards on the sidewalk. The three apprentices whom Peter knew by sight were carrying the boards into the courtyard of the house next to the shop. Peter had been noticing for some time on his way to and from school that Herr Gregor was gradually turning the house next door into an addition to his shop.

Herr Gregor had come out into the street. "Well, hello, Frau Bartsch!" he said cheerfully. "However are you? Seems to me I never see you passing through the Kandlgasse any more!"

Peter had been half afraid that she was going to mumble a hasty "*Grüss Gott!*" and hurry on, as she usually did when Herr Gregor greeted her in the street, but something about his effusive, awkward friendliness and the eager tilt of his bony shoulders had made her stop. Peter felt flattered to be standing beside Herr Gregor who owned the big shop and who had all those men working for him; he wished that Karl Breitner, who had often boasted that he had been all through the shop because he knew one of the apprentices, could see him.

"It's this war," she said. "It's upset everything. Shops I used to go to for twenty years—now you have to run all over town to get a quarter of a pound of sugar."

"Yes, the war," Herr Gregor sympathized. "My wife tells me how hard it is to get things. Take it one way, I oughtn't to kick with my shop and all the war orders, but I'll be glad when it's over. Fellow I know—he's pretty high up: a major, and right in with all the generals because he's at headquarters—told me only yesterday that they didn't think it would last through the winter."

"Only God knows what He's got in store for us."

Herr Gregor shuffled uneasily as if he had something on his mind and did not know how to lead up to it. The taut skin over his bony face stretched and strained with his frown, and his big, knuckly hand reached for the sheaf of papers he had tucked under his left arm, only to hold the papers clumsily in front of his stomach.

"How's Ludwig these days?"

She shrugged. "A man like him, without anything to do . . ."

"Fellow that takes a glass now and then up in the Westbahnstrasse tells me Ludwig is after another job in the theater!"

She said dully: "He didn't get it. They turned him down on account of his nails. He got a letter from the Burgtheater two weeks ago."

"Now, that's a shame!" Herr Gregor's brown eyes looked distressed. "A shame, I call that! At a time like this when everybody else is hollering for men, to make a fuss over a little thing like that! What's he going to do?"

"Goodness only knows." She hunched her shoulders despondently. "It wouldn't be so bad if he could only leave drink alone. I've always said wine was going to be his downfall. Well, now it's come. It stands to reason, too: a man who's been used to working all his life and regular hours, with nothing to do all day except sit in a *Weinstube*. . . ."

"But why does it have to be just the theater? Why can't he take something else? Any shop would be tickled to death to have him: good cabinetmakers like Ludwig don't grow on every bush."

"He won't do it. You can't blame him after all those years in the theater. And there's his pension—if he takes a job somewhere, they'll cut off his pension right away. . . . I guess we'll just have to bear it."

Herr Gregor looked concerned. His tall, bony frame became more noticeable as his shoulders sagged unhappily. Suddenly, he straightened up; his brown eyes beamed at her. "I have an idea, Frau Bartsch, an idea! They don't have to know everything in the Burgtheater, now, do they? They are going to draft my foreman just as sure as anything next January. Ludwig won't mind working for me. I'd be tickled to death to have him around again. It'll be just like old times. You leave it to me, Frau Bartsch. We'll put one over on those fuss-budgets in the theater." His whole face shone with glee, just like a little boy's, Peter thought as he watched him, not without a certain amount of patronizing wonder at Herr Gregor's enthusiasm. "I'm going to talk to him right away—just as soon as I get this lumber inside the yard. I don't suppose you'd know where I could find him at this hour of the night, though," he checked himself.

"He's probably in some *Weinstube* somewhere, drinking. . . ."

Peter had been caught by Herr Gregor's buoyancy. He knew that he was not supposed to say anything when older people were talking, but his excitement got the better of him:

"I know where Father is. He's at Hofstedter's."

"Up on the corner?"

Peter nodded. He felt shy now that Herr Gregor was looking at him. Herr Gregor put one hand on his shoulder and shook him playfully. "And how's the youngest?" he said gaily. "Growing all the time. It won't be long now before he'll be ready to be a soldier!"

"He's growing fast enough. I don't know how to keep him in clothes from one week to the next."

Herr Gregor smiled at him and showed a large gold tooth in the upper right side of his mouth. His face looked even homelier when he smiled and each bony protuberance bulged more tight-skinned and irregular, but his homeliness had something warm, open, and helpless that drew one to him. "Herr Gregor's skin is too tight," Peter thought. "I like him."

"How would you like to come and learn cabinetmaking with me, in my shop?" Herr Gregor asked him. "Be a cabinetmaker like Father and me? There isn't a better trade. After you've finished school, I mean?"

Before he had even had time to answer, she said: "There's plenty of time to think of that yet. He's still got two more years in school." He was surprised at her curt tone. It might have been Poldi speaking who did not like anyone to suggest that he learn a trade. Poldi had more ambitious plans for him. The prospect of being an apprentice in Herr Gregor's shop looked pleasant, even exciting at the moment.

"How is his—how is Mizzi?" Herr Gregor asked now. "Do you hear from her often?"

"Oh, she!" she said. "She isn't one for writing letters, and with this war . . . the last letter we got came in August."

"Well, she's doing all right in America, isn't she? I hear she's married and has two children."

"Leave it to her to get along all right!" Her mouth set with grim disapproval. "She's riding around in an automobile and playing the grand lady the way she always has, leaving other people to clean up behind her."

"Well, as long as she's happy. I wonder if she's still as pretty as I remember her. My, she used to look pretty when I used to see her going out with you, all decked out on a Sunday morning, time I first started the shop here! Do you remember that time we were all out in Klosterneuburg together?"

Peter had felt an unexpected thrill of pleasure at hearing Herr Gregor talk about Mizzi. He wanted him to go on saying things about her, but *she* put an end to Herr Gregor's reminiscing:

"What's past is past. We aren't any of us getting any younger."

"Guess you are right, Frau Bartsch, but those were the good old days! Wonder whether it'll ever be the same again after this war. . . ." Herr Gregor remained silent for a second or so, then pulled himself together and smiled again: "Well, don't worry about Ludwig any more! Just leave everything to me. I'm going up to the Westbahnstrasse to have a little talk with him right away."

They said good-by and walked around the corner to their house. Peter felt elated. Herr Gregor was rich and friendly, and he was going to talk to Father and everything would be all right again—better even than before!

Father was up earlier than usual the next morning, and that seemed to Peter a good omen, even though he tried in vain to read in Father's face some sign that he had talked with Herr Gregor. At noon Father's face was still inscrutable, but Peter was sure that there was a new alertness in it, and Father did not even lie down for a nap but went out immediately after he had finished dinner. He was almost certain then that Father had talked with Herr Gregor. He wondered when Father would start working in the shop. Father would earn a lot of money and they would have meat at dinner and perhaps they would even have butter, and pastry again on fast days! His certainty that Father would be in Herr Gregor's shop was like a warm, happy, shimmering lining for the usually drab hours in the afternoon in school.

It was one of the days when he did not have a lesson with Herr Granini, and he came home directly from school. He went into Franz's room where he was now allowed to use the piano when he practiced the music he brought home from Herr Granini's. He knew little more than the scales, but it was sufficient to pick out the melody and give himself the pitch. He had gone through only the preliminary voice exercises when he heard a knock on the front door. He got up from the piano to look. It was Herr Gregor. *She* was bringing him into the living room.

He decided to stay where he was. If he went out into the living room, she might decide to send him to some store or other because she might not want him to hear what they were saying.

Herr Gregor had sat down nervously on the chair she had pulled out from the table, protesting that he had only a minute. Peter saw that he fidgeted uncomfortably, alternately picking up his hat from his knee and putting it down again.

"I thought I'd better come and tell you, Frau Bartsch. . . . I happened to pass by the place in the Westbahnstrasse and I saw that Ludwig was in there, so I thought I'd better take the chance and come up. . . ."

There followed an uncomfortable pause during which the tick-tock of the pendulum clock on the wall became very distinct. Herr Gregor's brown eyes, set so nearly flush with his thin, hemp-colored eyebrows that they struck Peter as lidless, were fixed on her in helpless appeal. He tugged at the corner of his overcoat which was draped over his knees until it slipped on the floor and exposed his wide-striped gray trousers underneath.

"Well, I . . . I guess I better tell you, Frau Bartsch," he said at last. "Ludwig won't do it. I guess he just doesn't like the idea of working for me. Still, you would have thought, the two of us having been boys together and all—it isn't really as if he'd be working for me—it'd be more like being partners, the way I saw it. I offered to make him foreman: he'd be in the shop, and I'd tend to things outside. I tried everything I could to get him to change his mind, but it wasn't any good. You know how Ludwig is once his mind is made up—a team of oxen couldn't budge him."

He stopped as if he expected her to say something. When she remained silent, he went on uneasily:

"Maybe a little later, Frau Bartsch. That's what I said to my wife last night. Ludwig always was a proud cuss—as touchy as an opera singer, you might say, from the time we were boys together. You know how he is. . . ."

"I didn't think anything was going to come of it," she said. "It was too good to be true. I suppose God knows what's best."

Herr Gregor got up and stood facing her awkwardly.

"I tried once and I'll try again, Frau Bartsch. Maybe after he's had a little time to get used to the idea . . . I'd give anything to have him in the shop with me. . . . Well, that's what I came to say, Frau Bartsch." But in the kitchen, on his way out, he turned and said: "If there's ever anything I can do, Frau Bartsch . . . I don't like to talk about it, but these are bad times for everybody, and my wife and I have more than we know what to do with. . . ."

She cut him short. "The children are all grown now, thank God, except the boy. We've managed to get along so far and God won't let us starve now."

"I just thought . . . for old times' sake . . . no offense meant, Frau Bartsch."

Peter could hear the front-door latch click into place. Herr Gregor was gone.

He went back to the piano and struck a few halfhearted chords so that she would not think he was idling and make him come into the other room. His mind as he sat staring at the music kept running over the scene in the living room as if determined to find some grain of hope which might still give the lie to what he had just heard. Yet he could not shake off the bleak certainty that it was no use. There was not going to be a sudden change as he had dreamed all day: he would have to go on being hungry most of the time, there was not going to be an end to the constant, treacherous, frightening tension at home. . . .

The dry, irritatingly familiar creaking of her chair in the kitchen stung him into a sudden rage. It was all her fault! She had somehow known that Father would not take Herr Gregor's offer. She had in some obscure, exasperating way influenced Father so that he had said "No" to Herr Gregor!

But even while his jaws clenched unconsciously and he shivered a little with the violence of his exasperation, he knew that she could not have had anything to do with it. His rebelliousness turned for an instant against Father: Why hadn't Father taken it! Herr Gregor had been so anxious for Father to be in his shop. . . . He could find no explanation. A sense of frustration gripped him and made him feel even more despondent than before. He felt suddenly confined and oppressed in Franz's room and very hungry.

It was almost dark. He looked at the little bronze clock on Franz's desk. It was still half an hour before he could go to rehearsal and at least two hours before she would give him supper. His hunger became suddenly unbearable. He closed the piano and went out into the kitchen.

She had lighted the lamp by the sewing machine and was sewing buttons on Franz's shirts.

"I'm hungry," he complained. "Can I have a slice of bread?"

She bit off a length of thread and started to thread a needle with it. "You had your piece when you came in from school. That's all you're going to get until supper."

"But I'm hungry."

"You'll wait until supper like other people."

"Other people can get something to eat," he said more irritably than he had ever dared to talk to her before.

She pushed back her chair and got up. Involuntarily he pulled away, afraid for a moment that she was going to hit him across the mouth with the back of her knuckly hand. But she twisted away from him to drop her sewing on her round, leather-upholstered chair and then headed for the cupboard with some angry, indeterminate purpose. Her grimly silent progress the whole length of the kitchen conjured up a new hope: sometimes when he had begged long enough she became irritated to the point where she went to the cupboard and thrust a piece of bread at him with the words: "Here, eat it all! You must think yours is the only stomach in this house!"

She opened the glass doors of the cupboard, but she reached up on the shelf above the breadbox for her pocketbook. His heart sank. She was going to send him to get something! She came back with the pocketbook and put a few coins on the corner of the kitchen cabinet. "Here," she said, "if you're so hungry: Frau Fuchs is selling two sacks of corn meal."

"But it's almost five o'clock! I have to go to rehearsal in fifteen minutes."

She had picked up her sewing and had sat down by the sewing machine again.

"They'll miss you, just because you aren't there this once!"

"Sure, they'll miss me!" He felt his voice becoming shrill with alarm. "I'm going to sing a solo on Sunday."

"Solo or no solo, you're going to get some corn meal if you want any supper."

He recognized the obstinacy in her voice and decided to plead with her: "But I've got to be at rehearsal! Herr Granini is very strict about rehearsals. Can't you come and take my place in half an hour?"

She jerked out the needle which was stuck in a seam.

"I've got to be here when Franz comes, if you must know. He's got to have his supper early. Otherwise, do you think I'd sit here arguing with you? I'd have gone myself long ago rather than ask you to do anything."

Her injustice stung him. He dug his nails into his palms until they hurt, to restrain his anger. "I stood in line for two hours yesterday for the butter!"

"I notice you eat it, too! If Herr Granini is so anxious to have you in the Verein all the time, why don't you go to him and ask him to feed you too?"

"All right, if I get kicked out of the choir, it'll be your fault! I'm going to tell everybody it's your fault!"

She half rose from her chair. "You wait until I tell Franz!"

"Tell him!" he defied her from the door. "I don't care. I'll tell him, too, that you made me miss rehearsal."

Hot, helpless rage made his eyes smart all the way down the stairs. He ran along blindly, aching to kick walls, boxes, people—anything to give vent to his anger—until he was nearly in the Burggasse. Then he slowed down to consider. Perhaps the line wasn't very long yet and he wouldn't be very late for rehearsal. Or perhaps there wasn't any sale, or Frau Fuchs was already sold out. . . .

But the line when he came to the enclosed market extended out into the street and around the corner. He saw Frau Herzig, who lived on the floor below them, standing fairly close to the entrance. He stopped to talk to her in the hope that she might let him slip into the line beside her. At once, several people in back of her grumbled. Frau Herzig made a helpless grimace. He had to go to the end of the line; it was halfway down the block around the corner.

He played for a minute with the idea of not staying and simply going to the Verein, but in the end he was afraid to leave. Frau Herzig might say something to her about it. He had a brief, hate-sharpened picture of *her*, sitting and sewing. The violence of his hatred made him shudder a little. . . .

The clock of St. Ulrich's down the street struck a quarter past five. A few people with blue paper bags were coming around the corner. The sale had started. Slowly the line moved nearer to the market. It struck him suddenly that this was the first time that he had known of people having to stand in line for corn meal. His own dislike for the yellow corn-meal pudding which she made from it made it seem bewildering that people should want corn meal badly enough to make it hard to get. He had a troubling feeling that it was part of the gloomy perverseness that clung to this particular afternoon that he should have to stand in line for nothing more than corn meal.

It was half past six before he finally got inside the big doors of the market and up to Frau Fuchs's stall. He got the smooth, blue paper bag and hurried out with it into the Burggasse. The rehearsal was usually over by a quarter to seven. If he ran all the way he might get there for a few minutes at the end. He decided to take the Ziegelgasse for fear of meeting Poldi in their own street: Poldi might not let him go to the Verein now for the few minutes left of rehearsal.

He was hot and out of breath when he reached the Verein. In the hall outside the music room he could hear laughter and voices and the scraping of chairs. The rehearsal was over. He hid the blue bag of corn meal hastily behind a stack of folding chairs in one corner and went inside. Several boys, Rudi Martin among them, were standing around Herr Granini, listening to something he was saying. The rest were putting on their coats and beginning to leave. Peter waited impatiently for the little group around Herr Granini to break up. He did not want to admit in front of the others that he had had to stand in line: neither Rudi, nor Nowak, nor any of the other boys, he was sure, ever had to stand in line. Their families had maids who did the shopping.

Herr Granini had seen him. A flicker of recognition kindled in his black eyes which had been hooded with listening. For a split second the dark gleaming eyes bored into him, so that he felt uncomfortably that all his thoughts had been laid bare. Then Herr Granini looked away and said something that made Rittmeyer laugh boisterously and the rest of them titter. They all talked at once for a minute, then one by one said good night and went. Only Nowak had stayed behind.

Herr Granini nodded to him and Peter went up to the music stand. The presence of Nowak embarrassed him so that he stammered a little as he explained about the corn meal.

Herr Granini listened earnestly.

"That's quite all right, Peter," he said softly—a little wearily, Peter thought. He felt relieved, yet not wholly relieved, for Herr Granini's eyes had remained serious. He turned to Nowak:

"I guess you won't need to go now that Peter's come."

Nowak grinned. "No, Herr Granini." Then Nowak said good night and went.

Herr Granini came around in front of the music stand and put one arm around his shoulder.

"I was just going to send Nowak to your house with a message. I won't be able to see you boys tomorrow afternoon." There was a little pause which somehow had the quality of a sigh and filled Peter with alarm. "I'm afraid we'll have to let the lessons go for a little while. We all have to do what we can to help win the war. I've offered my services and the War Ministry has given me a job, something to do with music. . . . I'll be able to get here for rehearsals all right, but I'm afraid my afternoons will be pretty busy. . . ."

Something of the disappointment akin to terror which made his heart go *boom* painfully, at long, desperate intervals, must have shown in his face, Peter knew, for Herr Granini's hand pressed down affectionately on his shoulder.

"It won't be for long. The war will probably be all over by Christmas—in a few more months anyway. Then we'll go on with the lessons and work twice as hard. In the meantime, I'll give you some music to study at home and if we work hard at rehearsals, it won't make so much difference. . . ."

"It won't make so much difference" kept dinning in Peter's ears. *But it did! It did! Herr Granini could not understand!* he told himself bitterly.

It was as if some bright court where he had been able to find refuge from home had suddenly been closed to him.

He wandered forlornly through the Kaiserstrasse. He felt bitter and crushed. Once when he stopped to look into the window of a toyshop where an electric train was busily rushing around the quivering track and an elaborate system of tiny signal lights blinked on and off, he had the feeling for the second time that afternoon that the day was doomed and that everything that had happened had been inescapably held in store for him. Involuntarily he started to search his memory for some offense which could have brought on this punishment. He remembered *her* threat of the Friday before: "That's right, sing on the day of our Lord's Passion! Sing on Friday, cry on Sunday! . . ." But this was Wednesday! Nothing at all had happened on Sunday. . . .

A desperate need to find some reason for what had happened obsessed him. But there was no reason. There was only the numbing fact that tomorrow he would not be able to go to Herr Granini's house—there was Father, and there was *she!*

Chapter Nineteen

THE next day in school he pondered despondently on what to do that afternoon in place of the lesson. He did not want to go home. From force of habit and because he did not know what else to do, he started for the Mariahilferstrasse. He forced himself to walk slowly to put off the moment when he would reach Herr Granini's house and when there would be nothing else left to do but to turn around and come back.

The day was cold and gray. It had been snowing while he had been in school and the sidewalks were covered with slush. By the time he reached Herr Granini's house, his feet were damp and cold. The familiar entranceway struck him as at once infinitely inviting and smugly indifferent to him. It seemed to him, as he walked yearningly back and forth in front of it, that it withdrew more and more into its own sheltered intimacy and that it was telling him to go away. He remembered the lovely rooms upstairs and felt shut out.

He decided suddenly to walk toward the Innere Stadt. There was more to see on the Ring.

He wandered past the big hotels by the Opera. In front of the Bristol, a foreign-looking man in a fur-trimmed overcoat was being obsequiously escorted from a *Fiaker* to the hotel entrance by the doorman. Peter caught a few words of the doorman's ingratiating talk. He was speaking French. The stout gentleman appeared hardly to be listening. His round face looked glossily aloof as if he were accustomed to such effusive attention. Only when he stepped into the revolving door, which the gold-braided doorman was holding for him, did he make some crisp, perfunctory remark which Peter was too far away to catch. Two pages were lugging heavy-looking leather bags with many stickers on them through the service entrance beside the revolving door. Several of the stickers said "Lausanne." That was Switzerland. . . . It must be wonderful, he found himself dreaming, to arrive at a big hotel like this, without knowing anyone in the city, and to leave again for some far foreign place whenever one felt like it. Someday, he would be like that gentleman: he would come to Vienna from Switzerland without letting anyone know that he was here. . . .

In back of the Opera, stagehands were unloading scenery from three ponderous vans. The scenery reminded him of Father—no, he was not going to think about Father! He was going to imagine that he belonged here amid the gay, studiously reserved elegance of the luxurious shops and hotels and coffeehouses.

The shops along the Kärntnerstrasse fascinated him. It was still three weeks until Christmas, but most of the window displays were already subtly exciting with intimations of Christmas. Little sprigs of mistletoe and spruce had been tied to cigarette cases, to the fur-lined gloves, lighters, thermos bottles, and to all the other gifts for soldiers in the trenches—for officers, rather, he corrected himself, since only rich people shopped in the Kärntnerstrasse.

He had almost reached the Stephansplatz. Before him rose the jagged bulk of St. Stephen's with its fantastically upthrusting steeple and its gigantic portals—all its recesses and niches and stonework tracery mysteriously deepened with shadow in the early dusk. For a second he played with the idea of going inside the cathedral. He had never been in it alone. No, not today! he decided.

He came to a florist's window and stopped to look at a long basket full of violets and at the two big bunches of red roses behind the snow-flecked window. A saleswoman was wrapping a bunch of mimosa very carefully in tissue paper for a woman in a blue governess' cape. The pretty little girl beside the governess was stretching on tiptoe to smell a vase of carnations on a shelf against the wall. The little girl wore a sailor hat tilted far back over her brown curls—and no stockings, he noticed with surprise, but short socks as if it had been summer.

He watched while the governess paid for the mimosa and then took the little girl's hand. The saleswoman smiled familiarly while she held the door for them. Perhaps, he speculated, they came here every day to buy flowers. Flowers must be terribly expensive at this time of year. . . . He tried to picture the place where they lived. It would be a fine house like Aunt Wetti's, with an elevator and a carpet on the stairs. He wondered suddenly what would happen if he were to call on Aunt Wetti: would she be nice to him and give him cake and candy like the last time, or would she be angry if he came alone? Then he remembered that he was wearing his old school clothes and the worn overcoat which *she* had cut down for him from one of Franz's, and he felt embarrassed at the mere thought of facing Aunt Wetti in them.

The governess and the little girl were standing on the edge of the sidewalk and the governess was hailing a cab. The little girl was chattering happily all the time. She looked pale and had large, gray, animated eyes. Her brown curls dipped forward over her cheek as she climbed into the cab. He felt a curious sense of loss when the cab drove away.

It was still light, but here and there lights were being turned on in the shops. He was suddenly tired of the Kärntnerstrasse and decided to walk over to the big square where Poldi went to church on Sundays and to her congregation. But he did not turn directly into the side street. On the corner was an art gallery and he paused to look at a picture in the window. The painting showed a bowl of fruit and a blue and white pitcher on a window sill. The little plaque on the frame said: CHARDIN. He liked the crisp interplay of color, but the picture itself bored him. It did not look hard to do. Then he saw the smaller canvas of St. Stephen's in the other window. The cathedral was mantled with a warm amber haze; its details were only sketchily indicated, yet the church looked immensely solid. Perhaps someday he might learn to paint like that, without apparently first drawing an outline with a pencil. Franz had said that he might be an artist someday. . . .

He turned down the side street. He felt uncomfortable in the narrow, dark street with the many sharp elbows where it abruptly changed direction. Unconsciously he quickened his pace to get to the end of it. Then, as he approached the square, the luminousness above it and an indistinct murmur preluding some agitation made him walk even faster. . . .

The vast square was crowded with booths of every description, all of them gaily lighted up with storm lanterns that hung from their roofs, and covered all over with spruce and fir branches; the aisles between the booths were murmurous with many voices and the excited squeaks of children—it was the Christmas market to which Poldi had brought him once when he had still been small and about which he had forgotten completely!

The sight filled him with festive excitement. Directly in front of him was a veritable forest of Christmas trees already fixed in wooden standards and ranged in long rows. The pungent scent of the trees pervaded the whole square and mingled with the fragrance of chocolate and candy that came from the booths. There was an endless variety of things to see. There were booths with toys and dolls, booths that sold nothing but ornaments for Christmas trees and lovely-colored candles, booths with boxes and boxes of glittering ice skates and beautiful sleds; there were mounds of figs and dates and blood oranges, of chocolates and marzipan. . . .

The magic concentration of all the fragrant, glittering enchantment of Christmas caught him up in its dreamlike spell. There was a reassuring promise in the abundance of wonderful things all around him that made him dismiss in a sudden burst of hope the thought that their Christmas at home might be as dreary as last year.

He had inspected only about half of the booths when the clock on the church tower struck the hour. He looked up in sudden alarm: it was five o'clock! The rehearsal would start in twenty minutes, and it took nearly three-quarters of an hour to walk to the Verein!

He ran until he had to slow down to get his breath, then he ran again. He was only a few minutes late for rehearsal.

The next afternoon when he pretended to go to Herr Granini's house for a lesson, he set out eagerly for the Innere Stadt. He followed the same route he had taken before, even to walking on the same side of the street and crossing at the same corners, from a superstitious fear that he might not recapture the same mood if he deviated in any important particular from what he had done last time.

But in spite of his precautions, the mood of his first trip eluded him. The shops in the Kärntnerstrasse seemed much less dazzling. There was no little girl in the flower shop; the saleswoman was monotonously tying sleeves of crinkly green tissue paper around tiny pots of four-leaf clover. Everything that had quickened him with a sense of delicious excitement the time before had become infected with drabness. Even the Christmas market succeeded only in reminding him of the dreary Christmas ahead of him at home. By half past three he felt that he had seen all there was to see. He decided to go to the Verein early and watch the skating in the garden.

The rink in the garden was already crowded. He saw at once that at least a dozen boys from the choir were on the ice. Rudi was among them, and Nowak. He reflected bitterly that Nowak did not have to hide the fact that the lessons had stopped from his parents; he could probably go home and get a good *Jause* and then come here and skate.

He sat down on a bench to watch. Rudi, he saw, had learned to do the figure eight backward; he had on new gray and red mittens and a cap to match them. A string of seven older boys were cracking the whip. . . .

Rudi had seen him and came toward the bench; he swerved to a graceful stop.

"Why don't you come and skate?" Rudi asked.

"I haven't any skates."

"I'll lend you mine. I've had enough anyhow."

Peter was aware of sounding rude:

"I don't like skating."

"You would, if you tried it. I know you would," Rudi urged. He had already sat down on the bench and was unlacing his shoes. The temptation to try Rudi's skates which were permanently fastened to a special pair of shoes, not just to be screwed on ordinary street shoes like some of the other boys', almost got the better of Peter. He stood up quickly.

"I turned my ankle in gym class this morning," he lied. "I'm going inside to read."

He walked away quickly from fear that Rudi might guess how much he really wanted to put on his skates. Even so he could not help seeing the puzzled expression in Rudi's eyes.

There was nobody in the long clubroom except two men, one of them in uniform, who were playing chess. He took down a few magazines from the rack and started to look at them, but he could not keep his eyes away from the window and the garden outside. More boys were arriving constantly on the rink; their flushed faces and the sound of their shouts and laughter made him miserable with deprivation. . . .

After that he could not spend the afternoons in the Verein either. He was at a loss for something to do. He tried the library of the Socialist club on the Gürtel where he had occasionally borrowed books ever since the spring. The reading room was bare and cheerless, and the worn books he took down from the shelves at random seemed all equally dull and the stories unreal. The time dragged unbearably. Yet anything was better than spending the afternoons at home now!

Chapter Twenty

FATHER was getting worse! He taunted her a dozen times a day about Pater Alfred in his new, hard, vindictive voice, until Pater Alfred became a black, troubling figure in their life, as real as if he had actually been there. Father had also taken to following her whenever she left the house. Even if she went only to the store to stand in line for flour, Father was always somewhere in the vicinity, watching. In church, he hovered near the entrance in the rear, his small grayish-blue eyes glittering behind his pince-nez in a rigidly focused stare which never left her. When she came toward the holy water stoup on her way out, he greeted her with a sarcastic: "Did you see him all right? Don't miss him, your fat priest!" And sometimes he even went up front to where she was kneeling, right in the middle of vespers, and whispered so hoarsely that all the people around them could hear: "Time to go home! I want my supper."

Peter felt humiliated when that happened. He tried to make out that he did not belong to her. He ignored her tug at his sleeve and waited until they had left, before he himself would get up. He came to listen for the menacing clatter of Father's walking stick in the aisle and he tried to warn her when he heard it and saw Father coming, but she would not budge. She prayed only more ardently, so that whole phrases always became audible just before Father spoke to her, and her shoulders hunched forward a little farther.

Father's relentless, harsh-voiced ferocity toward her made him uneasy. Once, at home, when she had talked back to Father, she had called him a "jealous old fool." Peter began to wonder about that. He knew what jealousy was! In some of the novels he had read, some man had been jealous of a woman, but always the woman had been young and beautiful. He looked at her tear-swollen eyes and at the frumpishly old-fashioned clothes she wore and wondered how Father could possibly be jealous. And when he himself had felt all sick inside the year before because Rudi had made friends with a lot of new boys from the *Gymnasium*, that had been jealousy too. But he had loved Rudi, whereas Father had never been anything but indifferent toward her as far back as he could remember.

Nothing fitted. There were discrepancies everywhere. The nearest clue to Father's sudden perverse interest in her lay somewhere between the words Father used. He knew that they were bad words. They had to do with that mysterious world of women and that whole blurred, dankly-intimate region of things she and other women talked about sometimes when she made him go into the other room. Not that he had ever minded being sent away—the snatches of talk he had overheard had always struck him as dull and faintly disgusting—any more than he minded Karl Breitner's recent boasting about some secret, superior knowledge he had acquired lately from the older boys in the house. Karl and the older boys huddled together secretively to talk and whisper, and then suddenly burst out into strident, artificial-sounding laughter which was always strangely tinged with obscenity.

But although up until now he had not minded being excluded from their hole-and-corner whisperings, now he became suddenly curious. Father's persistent dark hints about her and Pater Alfred tantalized him. He became obsessed with a violent curiosity about women.

For it was women who stood at the center of the mystery. A host of long-forgotten sights and phrases crowded into his consciousness. He remembered passing two women who had rouge on their cheeks in a narrow street in Ottakring, one evening when he had been delivering some Red Cross packages with Poldi, and Poldi saying: "Those are bad women—only the scum of mankind live in this street." He had barely paid attention to Poldi at the time, but now the picture of the two women came back to him. He knew what Poldi had meant: the two women had been prostitutes, but what was a "prostitute"? All women were shrouded in a peculiar aura of difference, now that he came to think of it. They wore skirts and corsets and frilly underthings—they had breasts! He remembered the woman he had seen suckling a baby one time when he had gone visiting with *her* in Almzell: the woman had sat on a low chair with her blouse unbuttoned and one side of it folded back so that he had seen one large, white breast. The woman had put salt on the pink-brown nipple and then the baby had pulled at it with its mouth. The memory of it made him shudder with an odd kind of loathing even now.

She and Poldi had breasts, too, and Fräulein Gisl and all the other women. You could tell from the bulge in their blouses. And they were different farther down, too. That was why they wore skirts and why he always had to go into Franz's room when they changed their dresses, and even when Poldi changed her stockings. They had softer legs than men, but that was not all—there was something else! What about their middle . . . ?

The question stayed to torture him. It became a black feverish pressure which pursued him even into his sleep. He had horrid, tantalizing nightmares in which he saw some big, fleshy, loathsome woman, who in the end always turned out to be *she*, who was always just about to take off the last of her clothes when he awoke, shivering and bathed in perspiration. Occasionally, just before he awoke, he caught a glimpse of some monstrous growth between the fleshy legs of this creature of his dream-frenzied imagination.

If only it had been summer! In the summer the girls out on the playground on the Gürtel sometimes rode on the swings and the wind caught their skirts and blew them up above their thighs. If he were able to watch them, he might get some idea. . . . But it was only January! It would be months before the girls would be playing again on the Gürtel, and he could not bear to wait. There was no hope of finding an answer anywhere except through Karl Breitner. . . .

He began to pump Karl on the way to school every morning, but Karl was evasive and patronizing about his superior knowledge. He saw that it would take careful maneuvering to get Karl to tell him things. For days he had to content himself with veiled bits of information which only exacerbated his curiosity. Then one morning Karl began to hint at some mysterious adventure he had had the night before.

"I bet you're just making it up," Peter goaded.

"I bet I'm not! But you wouldn't understand anyway—you're too young."

"I'm older than you are! I'll be thirteen in September, and you won't be until October."

"But you don't know things!"

"I do too!"

It went on like that until they were almost at the corner of the Ziegelgasse where Karl had to leave him. Karl suddenly capitulated:

"We went down into the cellar, with Trudi Wachter! We did things—things you wouldn't even know about. . . ."

A vague excitement in Peter at the mention of Trudi gathered precision and urgency and rose in his throat like some actual physical obstruction which threatened to choke him. Trudi—Trudi Wachter in the cellar with Karl and the other boys! He knew Trudi only from seeing her walking to and from school with other girls. She lived on the same landing as one of the boys on the front stairs, and she had reddish-blonde hair that was braided into two pigtails, and a pert face and she laughed a lot—that much he knew without ever having paid any attention to her, just as he knew that she was in the same grade in school as Karl and he, and that her father owned the leather-goods store in the Kaiserstrasse. But now that Karl's words had brought her so vividly before his mind, he was also aware of a certain daintiness about her which made it seem curiously shocking that she should have been in the cellar with Karl and the older boys. He had to know more!

"What things?"

"I won't tell you."

Terrified now that Karl might leave him with his ravening curiosity unsatisfied, he sneered:

"Girls—who'd ever want to take a girl into the cellar? Girls aren't any fun! Now, if it had been Frau Schreier . . ."

He could see that Karl was impressed. Karl was even on the defensive:

"I bet you haven't even seen a girl!"

"Maybe I haven't—I've seen a woman, though!"

"Where?"

"In Hütteldorf—in the woods," he lied, remembering a man and a woman he had once seen kissing under a tree. "When I was with my father—she was all naked."

"Were they doing it?"

He was baffled. Did Karl mean something besides kissing? He felt again up against one of the many blank walls that surrounded the mystery. If he made a mistake now, Karl would know that he had been lying and then Karl would not tell him all the things he knew!

"Sure," he said. "Of course, they were doing it. I saw everything."

"I don't believe it."

"You don't have to. Ask my father! What about Trudi?"

"Well, we looked at each other."

"How?"

"How do you suppose, stupid? She pulled up her dress. Kurt showed us the scar from his appendicitis operation last summer, and then he dared Trudi to show us if we showed her. We felt each other, too!"

The image of Trudi in the cellar haunted him. If only he could have been with Karl and the other boys in the cellar! He was racked by impossible daydreams in which he elaborated one scheme after the other for getting Trudi to come into the cellar, but when he saw her on the way to school or even if he only heard her laughter somewhere behind him, the consciousness of his guilty thoughts made him blush and tremble. Once, indeed, when he happened to see her alone in the Kandlgasse, he screwed up his courage to talk to her, but after the first few words he became tongue-tied and so wretched that he was glad to get away from her.

He felt thwarted and more than ever ravaged by the need to know. Then, finally, toward the end of January he found relief from his torment. For ten precious minutes one morning before school, Karl let him look at the illustrations in a medical book he had found hidden among his mother's things. The book had several photographs of a woman about to give birth to a baby. He devoured the photographs and the diagrams. His tension was relieved, but in its place had come a profound disgust for what he had seen. For weeks he was unable to look at her or at Poldi or any other woman without instantly being reminded of the book.

He knew now what Father meant when he called her a priest-slut: he meant that she and Pater Alfred did the things Karl was always talking about, the things married people did to have babies. But understanding what Father meant did not make it any easier for him to see why Father so obstinately accused her of things which were so obviously without any basis.

Yet Father was growing daily more extravagant in his accusations and more violent. He had even threatened to kill Pater Alfred, and one night he threatened to kill her as well. It happened on the night before Ash Wednesday. Franz had left half an hour before, all dressed up in the gay troubadour costume he had had hanging in his clothespress all week; he had gone to the big Mardi gras ball in the Konzerthaus, Peter knew. Poldi was at a charity bazaar her congregation was holding and would not be home until late, either. He was all alone with *her* in the flat when Father came home. Father was silent at first. Only his preoccupied, jerky motions as he took out his billfold and his watch and arranged them on the chest of drawers betrayed the imminence of an explosion. It started suddenly. For no apparent reason, Father went to the kitchen door and began to rail at her—or rather, he did not begin, he went on where he had left off that morning or that afternoon.

She took advantage of a lull in Father's abuse to motion him to go to bed.

He undressed in the dark in Franz's room and hurried into bed. But even pulling the blanket over his head did not shut out Father's voice. His very anxiety made him lift the blanket every few minutes to listen. Father's voice sounded like an overstretched, frayed cello string being plucked with maniacal disregard for the fact that it was near the breaking point. He felt a paradoxical impulse to warn Father about it. . . .

"I'll show you!" Father was saying. "I'll show you all that you can't make a fool of me. I'm going to put an end to it—right now!"

Peter could hear him fumble for something on top of the wardrobe. The key! Father was getting the key to his desk. A chair was being pushed roughly to one side.

"Dear Jesus," she was half praying and half scolding, "now what is he going to do?"

"I'll show you!" Father grated harshly. "The dynamite in the stove—that'll fix you and your fat priest! You thought you could pull the wool over my eyes, running to church——"

"Yes, he wants me, Pater Alfred does!" She sounded cajoling and out of breath with anxiety. "He wants an old wreck like me!"

Peter could hear him unlocking the drawer in the mahogany table.

"What are you going to do? I believe he's really gone crazy. . . ." There was the sound of a brief struggle. She gave a sharp, low cry of pain—Father must have hurt her.

Peter jumped out of bed and stood shivering on the floor. His ears strained for the slightest sound from the other room. What was Father going to do? Was dynamite like gunpowder? His fear became too strong to be borne alone: he tiptoed to the door into the living room and opened it cautiously. Father was taking out bundles of papers from the drawer and placing them methodically on top of the table.

"You better use the sense God has given you!" she warned. She was standing a few feet away from Father, pressing her right forearm where Father must have hurt her against her stomach with her left hand.

"The dynamite is all I need," Father said without stopping to take more and more papers out of the drawer. The grim obstinacy of his back completed Peter's alarm.

An impulse compounded equally of fear and of a sudden exhilarating image of himself as a hero, and of what Franz and Poldi would say when they heard that he had saved *her* life, made him open the door and venture out into the living room. The linoleum was very cold under his feet—the sensation heightened his feeling that he was a hero. But when he came up to Father his courage was all gone and the fear that Father might strike him made him put his hand on Father's arm.

"Please don't blow us up, Father!"

He was aware even as he said it that his voice sounded childishly pleading and pathetic as if he had been taking the part of a little boy in a play. He felt ashamed that he had let his fear betray him into such play acting.

Father had pulled his hand out of the drawer and stood looking at him uncomprehendingly for a second. Then his face darkened and his eyes snapped.

"You get back to bed before I get the strap and give you something you won't forget in a hurry!"

He drew away quickly. Father's anger was full-bodied and unmistakable. "Yes, Father," he said meekly and hurried back into Franz's room. He felt disappointed and irked by the failure of his trip into the other room. But after he had lain under the warm covers for a minute, his first irritation gave way to satisfaction: he had succeeded in making Father angry, really angry, the way Father had been angry formerly. While he had talked to him, Father's voice had not had that strange, taut, absent-minded quality. . . .

He listened to what was happening in the other room. Father was still at the desk, but now he was leaving it and going to the chest of drawers. A minute later the bed creaked as Father sat down on it: Father was taking off his shoes—Peter could hear them being set on the floor, first one, then the other. He had not failed after all! Father was going to bed. . . . He wondered whether she would tell Franz and Poldi about tonight.

His first thought when she woke him the next morning was of the dynamite. Father had dynamite in the drawer of the mahogany table! He saw that Franz was still asleep. The gay blue and yellow costume Franz had worn to the ball lay carelessly flung over a chair by the bookcase. A few bits of confetti clung here and there to the velvet. He wondered whether it was fun to go to a ball and dance all night with beautiful girls, as Franz said people did at a ball. . . .

As soon as he opened the door into the living room, his eyes went to the mahogany desk between the foot-ends of the two beds. It looked ordinary enough with the familiar tapestry cover hiding the drawer as usual, but the knowledge of its sinister content made him feel that its disarming familiarity was only a mask. He glanced at Father in bed: his face looked flushed and wore a frown. Then his eyes went to the stove. She had already started a fire. He remembered Father's threat to throw the dynamite into the stove—it had become an accomplice in menace.

All day his thoughts kept going back to the mahogany table. By evening he was determined to find out about the dynamite. . . .

He had to wait for a whole week before he found the opportunity he needed. In the meantime, Father had twice repeated his threat, although he had not again opened the drawer. On the afternoon of her next washday, Peter hurried home from school and down into the laundry to get the key to the flat. He pretended to listen very attentively to her injunction to come back in half an hour and help her carry the wash upstairs to the attic. He even forced himself to linger for a minute or two in the steam-filled laundry to put her off guard in case her suspicious eyes had noticed anything unusual about him. Once out of her sight, however, his impatience made him run up the stairs so fast that he was out of breath when he let himself into the flat.

He had half an hour. He locked the door from the inside and left the key in the lock to keep from being surprised. As an added precaution he closed the door between the living room and the kitchen. Then he glanced into Franz's room to make sure that no one was in the flat. Next he laid out his schoolbooks on the table to make it appear as if he were in the midst of doing his homework. He looked at the pendulum clock: it was twenty minutes to four. He had lots of time! The important thing was not to get scared.

He got the key off the top of the wardrobe and unlocked the drawer. Before him lay the bundles of papers and envelopes, all neatly held together by broad elastics and arranged in two rows which extended all the way to the rear of the drawer. In front was the little rosewood box which held Father's rings and tiepins and the thin watch, which Father never wore. Beside it was the brass knuckle-duster and the silver cigar case which Father used only rarely because it held but three cigars. It was the cigar case which was responsible for the faint tobacco odor which rose from the drawer.

He lifted up the first bundle of papers. There was nothing underneath it except a stout envelope. He poked the envelope—it contained more papers. One by one, he lifted up the bundles to look underneath. He did not know what the dynamite would look like; he supposed that it would be in the form of a cartridge. When he lifted off the next to last bundle, he was startled. Sticking out from between the covers of a thin blue booklet were the corners of a whole sheaf of banknotes. He examined them and saw that they were fifty kronen notes and that there were nine of them. For an instant the prospect of possessing one of the banknotes intoxicated him. With fifty kronen he would be able to buy a flashlight and perhaps even an air pistol such as one of the boys in school had, and to feast for weeks on cheese and sardines and chocolate. . . .

The violence of the temptation paralyzed him for an instant and made his limbs go soft with guilt. He thought suddenly that he could hear footsteps on the landing. His heart pounded as he stole out into the kitchen to listen. Everything was quiet on the stairs. He was quite safe.

He came back to the drawer and took out the two big manila envelopes from the right-hand corner. Beneath them was a small cardboard box. He raised the lid gingerly and saw a short yellowish stick, about the thickness of an ordinary candle. The fact that it was carefully bedded in cotton and that there were two revolver shells beside it made him sure that it was the dynamite. He touched the stick cautiously. It felt smooth and a little greasy.

He had originally planned to do no more than look at it. But supposing he took the dynamite! Wouldn't he be really doing them all a service if he were to take it and throw it away somewhere—not before he had cut off a tiny piece, though, and had lighted it to see what would happen?

But the thought of Father's fury if he found out that someone had been in the desk made him give up the plan as impossible. Father would find out that it had been he who had been in the drawer. There would be no telling what he would do to him. No, the thing to do was to get some other substance that looked just like the dynamite and substitute it in the box. He must start looking around for something that looked sufficiently like the stick. Perhaps if he could get a piece of rosin or even glue—that was it: glue! He must get hold of a tablet of yellow glue such as the paint store in the Neubaugasse had in the window. . . .

Delighted with his plan, he replaced the lid on the little box. He was about to put back the two manila envelopes on top of the box when he noticed that one of the envelopes bore his own name in Father's large handwriting.

He glanced at the clock. It was only twelve minutes to four. He still had lots of time. He folded back the flap and recognized the little sheaf of his report cards and the document from the District Poor Supervisor which she always took along in November when she got him certified for charity shoes. The mere sight of the red seal on it made him cringe with loathing. He went on quickly to the next paper, which turned out to be his vaccination certificate. Then came a smaller, faintly yellowed document which he did not remember ever having seen before. He slipped it out of the envelope.

It had to do with him all right! There was his name: *Peter Domanig*. His eyes went to the heading on top, above the large municipal seal. *Maternity Hospital*, it said, and below it, in smaller print: *Bureau of Foundlings and Orphans.*

He knew a premonitory tightening of his throat, a stringent stillness inside of him, an almost painful alertness.

Maternity Hospital! his brain echoed dully. Why *Bureau of Foundlings and Orphans . . .*

He saw that the paper was a certificate of dismissal from the hospital—his dismissal, or Mizzi's, for beneath his own name he read: MOTHER: *Maria Domanig . . .* That was as it should be; nothing new about that—but the next two lines puzzled and stunned him: FATHER: *Information refused*, and then: STATUS: *Illegitimate . . .*

—refused! Information refused! What did that mean? And *illegitimate . . .*

A swarm of baleful memories crowded into his brain: things that he had heard and read in books, things that Karl Breitner had said, her remarks about Mizzi—no one clear image, but a sudden crushing conviction that there was some scabrous taint on him—something to do with Mizzi and the words "information refused" and "illegitimate." . . .

There was little more, except for two separate notations written diagonally across the lower corner. He turned the paper to read them. The first in a fine, spidery hand said: *Not nursed by mother—lack of milk.* The second said: *Dismissed on ninth day.*

He looked over the paper once more, intently, as if his eyes meant to absorb the very print from it. He felt chilly and drained of all strength. Mechanically, he slipped the paper back into the envelope and put the envelope back in its exact place in the corner of the drawer, then he locked the drawer and put the key back on top of the wardrobe. He felt as if he were moving in a nightmare.

Instinctively he went to the lower end of the divan opposite the chest of drawers, where he had always played when he was small. He found that every word on the paper was as if seared into his brain. All of them started at once to torment him: *Bureau of Foundlings and Orphans—information refused—not nursed by mother—illegitimate—foundling . . .*

But how could he be a foundling? Or an orphan? Foundlings were babies found on doorsteps, in baskets, and nobody knew where they came from, whereas everybody knew that Mizzi was his mother. . . . And Mizzi was *her* sister and Aunt Wetti's sister—all the people in Almzell knew that and Herr Gregor knew it. . . . And why had he been born in a hospital—why hadn't he been born at home the way other children were? He suddenly remembered Father's occasional threats when he was still small and had not wanted to eat something: "If you don't eat what you're given, you'll go to the Foundling Home! They'll make you eat there all right!" But Father had only been joking, the way he might have said: "I'll get the belt!"

Someone was at the door. He got up to unlock it. She was on the landing with a basket of wash.

"I thought I told you to come and help me carry the wash upstairs!"

"I must have forgotten. . . ."

She went into the kitchen and peered suspiciously into the living room. "What do you have to lock yourself in for?"

"I was afraid all alone," he said automatically.

Her pinched lips showed that she was not satisfied with his explanation, but she said nothing more and went out on the landing to unlock the door to the attic. He carried her basket up the attic stairs, then made two trips into the cellar for the rest of the wash. Several times in the attic he had the impression that she was watching him surreptitiously. He felt utterly indifferent. He had a feeling that he had grown an envelope of numbness all around him through which not even her voice had power to penetrate.

When he was alone again back in the living room, ready and almost impatient to resume his brooding, he found that her interruption had worked a change in him. His earlier, passive confusion had given place to a sudden, rapidly growing anger with Mizzi, which absorbed every fiber of his consciousness.

Why had Mizzi not nursed him? Why?

Hundreds of disapproving remarks *she* had made about Mizzi rushed into his mind: Mizzi had wanted to play the grand lady! He remembered some conversation *she* had had with another woman in the courtyard about some woman in the house next door who had not wanted to nurse her baby for fear of spoiling her figure——

That was it! Mizzi had not wanted to nurse him! That was the reason, too, why he could not stand the sight or smell of milk now. . . . The scene on his first morning in Almzell flashed back into his mind and Lisl's warning: "But you won't get big like Franz if you don't drink milk. . . ." Lisl and Gretl and Karl, and Rudi Martin—all drank milk. That was why Karl in Almzell was so much stronger than he was—not that he was weak, he defended himself, but Karl was stronger.

And it was Mizzi's fault that he had been born in the Maternity Hospital and that that ugly paper was in the envelope in Father's drawer! And what about afterward? That must have been the time when he was with the peasants in Styria—Mizzi must have taken him there—foster parents they called people like that. . . .

His resentment flared into a consuming, tearing hatred of Mizzi that made him go rigid with passion. Mizzi was rich and she did not care what happened to him—if she were here now, he would hurt her, torture her until she cried for mercy. . . . An uncertain image of Mizzi rose before him against which he flung his rage. The image was built around one of the photographs in the plush-covered album where she was shown in profile, one hand resting on a high jardiniere, her head with its high hairdress bent slightly forward, the blouse sweeping out to a fold just over the waist, and the long skirt flaring back elegantly to trail on the floor—but along with the photograph there were the thousands of monstrous images of nude women which had peopled his brain during the past month, and the illustrations from the medical book Karl Breitner had shown him.

But even while he was thus punishing Mizzi, an element of doubt had entered his consciousness. He had suddenly remembered all the nice things he had heard about Mizzi: things Father had let fall from time to time, then the people in Almzell, and lately Herr Gregor. A certain hesitancy had crept into his spasms of rage against Mizzi. He was disconcerted to recognize in himself an almost prayerful yearning to be proved wrong about her. . . .

Chapter Twenty-One

He felt bewildered, desolate, crushed. There was nobody to whom he could turn—unless indeed he went to see Aunt Wetti. The idea seemed so daring at first that he only played with it fitfully, longingly, as with something impossible. He hardly knew Aunt Wetti; she might not even receive him if he came alone. But three days later his mind was made up: he was going to go and talk to Aunt Wetti!

It happened that on that particular day Herr Granini was going to take them to a composer's house after rehearsal to serenade the composer on his birthday. He used that as an excuse to put on his Sunday suit at noon before he went back to school. The Sunday suit was essential; he could not imagine himself going to Aunt Wetti's house in his patched school clothes.

It was snowing when he came out from school. He left his books at a grocery store and started out on the long walk to the Kolowat-Ring. He was tempted several times to hang on in back of some delivery wagon to get there quicker but the fear of soiling his hands and clothes kept him from it. When he crossed the square in front of the Karlskirche, his courage almost failed him. The problem of what reason to give Aunt Wetti for his visit loomed insuperable again, as if he had not gone over every detail a dozen times that morning.

The wide, quiet street looked even more reserved than when he had last seen it almost two years ago. The balconies which had been crowded with flowers and plants and had seemed so charming then were bare now, and the wrought-iron and stone railings stood out starkly against the façades and made them look severe. He found the house quite easily. Nothing was changed in the entranceway. Along the marble-paneled walls there were the same heavy, red ropes looped from one massive brass ring to the next; in the rear was the same gleaming oval glass cylinder with the gold and black elevator cage waiting sleepily inside it. His heart pounded a little as he started up the stairs. Perhaps Aunt Wetti's husband was home! He had only a dim picture of Herr von Garnhaft which dated from some early visit when he had been small and centered around Herr von Garnhaft's white beard which had made him look like a doctor. Well, suppose he was home! he told himself defiantly in front of Aunt Wetti's door; he would simply say that he had come to pay a visit. He pushed the bell.

Somebody opened the brass-grilled peephole in the door. He felt himself being inspected for what seemed a humiliatingly long time before the door was opened. He saw at once that it was the same maid who had been so scornful of them two years ago who was measuring him now. He asked:

"Is Frau von Garnhaft at home, please?"

The girl said neither "yes" nor "no." She kept on measuring him and insisting that he say something more. Annoyed by her supercilious silence, but also cowed by it because he was afraid that she might shut the door in his face, he added quickly:

"She is my aunt."

"Oh," she said. It sounded disappointed as if she would have enjoyed telling him to go away. She pulled the door open stiffly. "Frau von Garnhaft is entertaining. I'll tell her. . . ."

The announcement filled him with alarm. It had not even occurred to him that Aunt Wetti might have visitors. Through the door which he remembered as leading into the drawing room came the muffled sound of women's voices—voices that sounded warm, carefree, and instinct with a subtle self-complacence that made his errand seem as shabby as his old overcoat with its frayed buttonholes. He wondered how many women there were. The voices stopped abruptly—the maid must be telling Aunt Wetti about him. He suppressed an impulse to run away just as Aunt Wetti opened the door. She was wearing a robin's-egg blue dress with fluffy yellow lace edging the neck and the sleeves. She looked very tall.

His uncertainty made him scan her features intently. Her face, he saw, wore a faint flush as if she had just been laughing. Her lips were parted expectantly. He found even time during the brief moment while she stood framed in the door to reflect that she had the same kind of mouth that *she* had, but that Aunt Wetti's lips were fresh and gay and somehow self-assured. And he saw that the momentary hesitancy in Aunt Wetti's eyes had given way to a welcoming warmth.

"Why, Peter!" she said. "How are you, Peter?" Her dress whispered softly as she came toward him. Before he knew it, she had bent down to kiss him. The brief contact of her face, which felt warm and smooth against his, and the delicate scent of lilies-of-the-valley which came from her made him unaccountably happy. For a a moment he had an intoxicating illusion that he belonged here and that this happened every day. Then Aunt Wetti's eyes became troubled.

"Is anything the matter at home?" she asked quickly.

"Oh, no, Aunt Wetti."

She looked relieved. The warmth had come back into her eyes. "Then, you've just come to pay your aunt a visit? Why, how nice! Here, let me help you off with your coat. . . ."

She was actually glad to see him! He felt reassured. Aunt Wetti hung up his coat and reached for his hand, the way women always did, as if he had still been a little boy. He did not dare pull away from her and his mind was still on the frayed buttonholes in his coat. He spun the coat around on the hook with his free hand, so that only the lining showed.

Aunt Wetti was taking him into the drawing room. Two ladies watched them with expectant eyes. He was glad that there were only two of them.

"This is my nephew Peter who has come to see his aunt," Aunt Wetti introduced him. The plump lady with the caramel-colored hair and the cameo brooch, who was knitting on one of the thick socks women were making for the soldiers, disentangled her hand from the wool and held it out to him:

"How nice! How do you do, Peter?"

Her comfortably extended, pink hand threw him into a quandary. Was he supposed to kiss her hand the way he had seen rich children do in the Innere Stadt, or would it look like servility in him as when *she* made him kiss the hand of the Poor-Mother every time they went to see her? The hateful memory of the visits to the Poor-Mother made him decide against it. He took the plump lady's hand and bowed very formally. She smiled, and he took it as a sign that he had not blundered and took the other lady's hand much more boldly. The second lady was small, with a dainty figure and brisk brown eyes. Her eyes fastened on his feet:

"But the child's shoes are soaked! Mercy, did you walk?"

"Yes, *Gnädige Frau*," he said, embarrassed by her solicitude.

"In this weather? Why, you might catch a terrible cold! Are your feet wet?"

"No, they're quite dry. I like to walk."

"Just like Albert," the plump lady on the sofa said. "Albert came in the other night, too, soaked through and through. They'd been throwing snowballs of course. And the next day he had the most frightful cold—you better get something hot into him right away, Betty."

He wondered who Albert was and why the plump lady called Aunt Wetti "Betty." It must be fashionable to say "Betty." He decided that he liked the small lady much better than the other one on the sofa who simpered a little and sounded affected, but he was not wholly comfortable under the lively brown eyes of the small lady either, for he felt that she was shrewdly taking in everything about him. She would be sure to notice that his suit was getting too small for him and that his right stocking was darned at the knee and that his shoes were charity shoes. Fortunately, Aunt Wetti was talking to him:

"Have you had your *Jause* yet, Peter?"

"No, Aunt Wetti."

"Well, we'll have something for you in a minute," Aunt Wetti said, and left him alone in the room with the two ladies who promptly began to ask about school. He could see from their questions that they assumed as a matter of course that he was in the *Gymnasium*, just as a minute later they assumed that he had had money for carfare to Aunt Wetti's. When he told them that he lived in the Schottenfeldgasse, the plump lady gasped:

"And you walked all that distance! What is your mother up to, to let you do a thing like that?"

Aunt Wetti who had come back beside him said reproachfully: "You mustn't ever do that again, Peter!"

"Supposing your aunt told on you, you rascal?" the small lady threatened. "Then there'd be trouble! I bet you spent the carfare on candy, didn't you?"

He felt himself blushing because his false position made him increasingly ill at ease. The small lady interpreted it as a confession: "There, I knew it!" she said triumphantly.

He felt relieved when Aunt Wetti made a motion to take his hand again and said: "Come on, young man, your *Jause* is waiting."

Aunt Wetti stayed in the dining room until he had sat down before the steaming cup of coffee and the buttered rolls and the slice of enticing-looking cake.

"Eat slowly now, and if you would like anything else, Louise will get it for you," she said; then she left him.

The maid was busy by the sideboard, putting away cups and saucers. He wished that she would go away, but she seemed to him maliciously determined to hover by the sideboard and watch him out of the corner of her eye. Defiantly, he decided to act as if she did not even exist, or rather to prove her wrong if she was hoping to catch him out in the matter of table manners. He unfolded the napkin with a negligent flourish, the way Franz always did, and started to eat indifferently, as if he had buttered rolls every afternoon and as if coffee with whipped cream were nothing out of the ordinary for him either. The maid finally went. Her going left him free to enjoy all the wonderful things in front of him. The coffee was delicious, and the white roll was the first he had had since the lessons at Herr Granini's had stopped. Even in the coffeehouse where Herr Granini took them on Sundays, the rolls were made of black flour now. He squinted at the cake: it had layers of what looked like apricot jam, and a lovely yellow icing.

He became suddenly aware of the voices in the drawing room. Aunt Wetti had closed the connecting door so that he could not hear what they were saying, but they must be saying pleasant things, for he could also hear them laughing. Was he going to get a chance to talk to Aunt Wetti alone, or would he have to go away without being able to ask her the questions which had been burning in him for days now? It struck him that Aunt Wetti's friendliness had been a trifle glib and that there had been something watchful in her eyes. Perhaps Aunt Wetti would be in a hurry to get rid of him as soon as he had finished eating. There would be nothing for him to do but go. . . .

The voices in the other room had become louder and there was a sound of people moving about. Yes, they were going! He sat very erect, thinking that the two ladies might come in to say good-by, but the voices moved farther away. They must be in the vestibule now. . . . He finished the second roll hastily and reached for the cake. It was delicious cake with apricot jam, just as he had hoped, and lemon icing. He lingered over each mouthful as long as he dared. While he was watching the door through which he expected Aunt Wetti to come in, the maid had come up behind him so silently that he had not even heard her. She looked from the empty plate where the rolls had been to his nearly empty cup.

"I suppose you'd like more coffee?"

Her tone stung him. He said as haughtily as he could with his mouth full: "No, thank you."

The maid looked as if she were going to say something else. Just then Aunt Wetti came in from the drawing room.

"Well, did you get enough of everything? Did you have a second cup of coffee?"

"He said he didn't want one, *Gnädige Frau,*" the maid put in quickly.

"No, I didn't, Aunt Wetti." He tried to sound very firm for the benefit of the maid. "It was very good, thank you." He put down the napkin. Aunt Wetti waited for him by the door.

"Now you must tell me all about yourself," she said. Her hand smoothed over the collar of his blouse and stayed there as they went through the door, but she did not ask him to sit down beside her on the needlepoint sofa as she had done two years ago. He sat down very carefully on one of the fragile Biedermeier chairs opposite Aunt Wetti and waited for her to speak. He realized suddenly that it would be difficult to bring up the question he was aching to ask. Everything about the room felt strained and precarious.

She started to ask about home. He answered, "Fine," to everything, partly because all his attention was taken up by the problem of how to broach the subject of Mizzi and himself, and partly because an inexplicable feeling of loyalty to all of them in the Schottenfeldgasse made him unwilling to tell Aunt Wetti about Father and the scenes at night. Aunt Wetti asked about the choir and then the conversation came to a standstill. He became alarmed. Now that he was here, was he going to be afraid to ask what he had come to ask? He looked in despair at a marble-topped console on which there had been a bronze clock two years ago and which was bare now except for a slender vase with one rose in it.

Aunt Wetti had followed his glance. "Are you looking for the clock? We gave it to the boys when they came around collecting metal for the army. It's probably been cast into a gun by now. . . ."

Now that she spoke of it, the clock came back to him vividly. He remembered the finely wrought figures of shepherds and shepherdesses around a miniature mill, the wheel of which had spun around when the clock had struck the hour. It seemed incomprehensible to him that Aunt Wetti should have given away anything so delicate to be melted up with old doorknobs and brass hinges.

"The works too?"

Aunt Wetti was smiling. "Yes, the whole thing. It was always fast and much too noisy. It belonged to your uncle and he didn't care—and we had to give something, didn't we?"

But he was no longer thinking of the clock. "Your uncle"—that was Herr von Garnhaft. He felt a little disturbed by Aunt Wetti's referring to Herr von Garnhaft as his uncle.

"Is Herr—is Uncle well?"

"Yes, he's fine. You must come sometime when he is home. He'd be home now except that today is his day for playing chess. He is very busy, of course, with the war and everything. You must be sure and tell your Aunt Kathi that he's been using the nettle tea she told me about and that it's helped him a great deal. . . ."

"She doesn't know I came," he said guiltily.

"Then you came of your own accord. Isn't that nice!" But her eyes looked worried. "Tell me, is anything wrong? Is that why you came to see me?"

"No, Aunt Wetti."

He was furious with himself for not having taken advantage of the opening she had given him, but his courage had failed him again.

"I had a long letter from your mother two weeks ago," Aunt Wetti was saying. "Your little brother skipped a whole grade in school, and your little sister had the whooping cough—did you know that?"

He shook his head. The sudden mention of Mizzi made him feel a little giddy.

"Do you think of your little brother and sister often?"

"I . . . I guess so, Aunt Wetti," he stammered, but *why should I?* he thought angrily. A blurring wave of antagonism had been released in him by Aunt Wetti's question. Mizzi wrote Aunt Wetti long letters because Aunt Wetti lived in the Kolowat-Ring, but she only wrote him a few lines when she wrote to *her*. And there had been no letter since Christmas, he was certain. His bitterness gave him courage to burst out:

"Why am I a foundling, Aunt Wetti?"

He could see that she was startled. Instinctively, Aunt Wetti turned her head to see whether anyone had heard him. A number of emotions struggled in her face by the time she said:

"Who put an idea like that in your head? Has anyone at home said that?"

"Oh, no," he protested quickly. "A boy in the house said it."

"You mustn't listen to what bad boys say," she said almost sternly.

"But there was something else! I saw a paper—a long time ago," he added hastily, from fear that she might come to the Schottenfeldgasse and tell *her*. "It was when Father took out my vaccination certificate. This paper fell out—it said Bureau of Foundlings and Orphans!"

"That doesn't mean that you're a foundling. It merely happened that way. You'll understand when you are older."

He could see that Aunt Wetti was embarrassed and was trying to put him off. It made him only more determined to make her answer his question.

"But why did the Foundling Bureau make out that paper?"

"Now, Peter, you aren't even supposed to know about such things: a foundling is a child that hasn't any parents. You have a mother who loves you very much and who is worrying about you all the time."

"Then why does she leave me here all alone?"

"Because your mother is married and can't leave your little brother and sister now to come for you. That doesn't mean that she doesn't love you. . . ."

"Yes, but——"

"You mustn't ask so many questions, Peter. When you are older you will understand."

But he was not going to be stopped now. This might be the last chance he would ever have to ask Aunt Wetti about Mizzi and the paper. He avoided her eyes and plunged:

"The paper said I was illegitimate!"

"Peter, come here!" Aunt Wetti rose from the sofa and reached out for his hand to draw him down beside her. She took both his hands in hers and pressed them against the crinkly silk of her dress against her thigh. He was embarrassed by the warmth of her flesh under the silk and stiffened involuntarily.

"Do you realize that it was very bad of you to look at that paper in the first place?" she chided. "All right! But now that you did see it, I'll try and tell you about your mother. . . . Your mother, Peter, was a very beautiful girl and she wanted to be an actress. Then she met your father, who was studying to be an artist—now, you know what happens when a young man and a young woman fall in love, don't you? They want to get married. Your mother and father wanted to get married too, but they were both poor and both of them had to go on studying for their careers—and there were other difficulties: your father had to go back to England because his father wanted him to come back. That's why they didn't get married. But that's nothing for you to worry your head about. Lots of children have parents who didn't get married and they have grown up and become important people! That's what you must do, so that your mother and everybody else can be proud of you!"

Then, Father was not *his* father! Not once in the three days since he had looked at the paper had it even occurred to him to connect the word "illegitimate" with the information he had acquired from Karl Breitner about what men and women did to have a baby. He had thought only of Mizzi. Even now Mizzi was still uppermost in his mind, although the shadowy man whom Aunt Wetti had called his father usurped his attention for the moment. . . .

"Why did he have to go to England?"

Aunt Wetti misunderstood. "Because he depended on the money his own father sent him every month to study, and because it takes a long time before an artist can make enough money to support a family."

"I didn't mean that, Aunt Wetti. I mean, why did he have to go to *England?*"

"Because he was an Englishman. That was his country."

"Is that where he is now?"

"I suppose so. He may even be fighting for his own country the same way our soldiers are fighting for our country."

He sat quite still for a moment. Aunt Wetti's revelation had dazed him a little. This man who she said was his father was an enemy. He tried to picture him and immediately thought of the war posters depicting grim-looking, cruel-faced men in queer uniforms. The next moment, Aunt Wetti's voice asking, "Now are you satisfied?" brought back his anger with Mizzi with redoubled force. He made no effort to hide his resentment:

"Why can't Mizzi get me now?"

"You mustn't say 'Mizzi'—you must say 'my mother'!" Aunt Wetti had adopted a very grown-up tone. She had let go of his hands. "Now, I have told you why your mother can't come right now. In the meantime, you must be a good boy and not worry your head about things that don't matter. Will you promise me that?"

There was nothing for him to do but nod. But this forced acquiescence made it unbearable to remain sitting beside her any longer. Aunt Wetti was in league with Mizzi! She was defending her. He suddenly experienced a violent dislike for her elegant dress, for the comfortable luxury of the room, and even for the two friends who had been there and who had assumed so casually that he must have had money for carfare.

"I think I'll have to go now."

Aunt Wetti had got up, too.

"You haven't any carfare—wait!" Aunt Wetti left him alone in the room for a minute. She returned with some coins between her fingers. "There—and with the rest you can buy some candy." He could feel as he let them slide into his pocket that each coin was a whole krone. Aunt Wetti walked out into the vestibule with him. He had a feeling that she was anxious to get rid of him.

"Give my love—oh, I forgot! they don't know that you came—that's a secret between us."

Her smile left him unmoved. He felt bleakly detached as if Aunt Wetti were performing on a stage and he were watching her from the wings.

"Here, let's bundle you up warmly now," she said, and started to button the collar of his overcoat—and that, too, he felt, was false. Aunt Wetti's solicitude had selfish limits. She did not want to know about the times he went hungry and could not even get a slice of bread. This momentary concern for him was only part of the cushioned elegance, the circumspect polish of life here in the Kolowat-Ring. Aunt Wetti would have fussed just as much over "Albert"—whoever "Albert" was. It was at last as if every nerve in him bristled with irritation at Aunt Wetti's nearness; he found it hard to hold still when she kissed him good-by.

Then he was out on the landing. His relief at getting away was instantly succeeded by despondency. As he walked down the stair, the shiny elevator was slowly rising in the glass shaft. A slim lady was holding a small white dog in her arms and smiling over it at a stout man with a fur collar on his overcoat. A sudden reluctance to leave this atmosphere of matter-of-fact affluence, which was breathed by the very staircase and the handsome double doors on the landings, assailed him and sharpened his bitterness.

He stood in front of the house for a minute, undecided where to go. He did not want to go to rehearsal. That left him almost three hours to get through. He had the two kronen Aunt Wetti had given him—he might go to a coffeehouse and order coffee like a grown-up! But his churning emotions clamored for something more out of the ordinary and more exciting. Then he remembered the station where the wounded soldiers came in from the Russian front —he set out for the Ostbahnhof.

Theoretically he knew how to get from Aunt Wetti's to the Ostbahnhof. He had to take the Heugasse which started somewhere along here from the Ring and ran like the spoke of a wheel to the Gürtel, where it crossed quite near the station. But he was in a strange part of town and he had to ask his way twice before he got on the Heugasse.

It was already dark with the somber grayness of winter twilight, splotched and sickened by the cold light of the street lamps. The houses in the Heugasse looked bleak and unfriendly and gave him the impression of shouldering their neighbors sullenly. A cold wind was blowing from the direction of the Gürtel. But even though he shivered with the cold, he was unwilling to take one of the streetcars which passed every few minutes. Something in him welcomed the tearing gusts of wind and the cheerless street. It was as if some dark impulse were urging him forward toward some reckless adventure in which he could bury this feeling of being all alone. For he was alone! They at home were thinking only of what Father was going to do each day—Aunt Wetti sat in her fine apartment on the Kolowat-Ring and defended Mizzi, who did not want him—and there was the shadowy figure of the man in England Aunt Wetti had talked about, who did not want him either! But it was Mizzi who was responsible, he told himself fiercely, Mizzi who had not wanted to nurse him and who lived in luxury in America and did not care what became of him. . . .

He reached the station just as two more ambulances joined the long line of ambulances already waiting along one side of the building. He hurried up the steps. The big hall was fairly crowded with people, but it managed to look bare and empty somehow. In the far corner some soldiers with Red Cross brassards were taking stacks of empty stretchers out on the platform. By the time he had crossed the hall, the big gate on the platform had closed behind them and so had the door of the first-class waiting room from which they had come out. A drooping Red Cross flag hung over the entrance to the first-class waiting room. Once, the door opened briefly and he caught a glimpse of several nurses unpacking bandages on a white-enameled table and of a doctor eating an apple, apparently quite undisturbed by the sickly-sweet reek of disinfectant that came out of the room.

He wandered slowly around the station. There was really very little to see. The troop transport was not due for another twenty minutes. More to kill time than because he was hungry, he decided to buy a bar of chocolate at the newsstand. He was about to take out one of the two coins Aunt Wetti had given him when he noticed that a boy who was leaning against a pillar was watching him. The boy wore long trousers and was smoking a cigarette. There was an ungainly swelling on his left upper lip—it was Jerabek, from school!

He had never paid much attention to Jerabek in school, although he had always been uncomfortably aware of him. Jerabek sat in the rear of the class and spent most of his time paring his fingernails or polishing a rather valuable-looking cigarette case. If sometimes one of the teachers still bothered to become exasperated with him, Jerabek immediately sought refuge behind a cringing, propitiatory, yet subtly sneering smile. He was equally disliked by the boys, not only because of the ugly bulge on his lip and because he was considered a coward, but also because of a friend he had, a hulking locksmith apprentice who had once brutally beaten a boy who had molested Jerabek.

The sight of Jerabek leaning so casually against a pillar here at the Ostbahnhof startled Peter. He tried to appear unconcerned by Jerabek's stealthy, derisive watchfulness and stepped up to the newsstand. When he had got the bar of chocolate and his change, he was still uncertain what to do. All he knew was that Jerabek was a challenge and that he was drawn by him as by a magnet.

He sauntered with elaborate unconcern toward the pillar. The slippery, defensive grimace had already appeared in Jerabek's face. Peter felt encouraged. He said: "Hello."

"Hello . . ."

"You waiting for a train?"

Jerabek shrugged. "Sure. What you doing here?"

"I want to see the transport come in."

"What for?"

"To see the wounded soldiers."

The sneer which lifted the ugly swelling away from Jerabek's teeth became more pronounced, only this time the grimace was less defensive than superior.

"Who wants to see wounded soldiers?"

"I haven't ever seen any. Are you waiting for another train?"

"I'm here every day."

"Why?"

"Just because . . . Troop trains aren't any good!"

"What do you mean?"

"You going to stick around till the Budapest express comes in? It's due at six."

"I guess so—sure."

"Well, you'll see then."

"You mean, you carry bags and things for people?"

"You'll see."

Peter did not like to press him any further. He felt that he had made a little progress toward breaking down Jerabek's reserve but that their relationship was still extremely tentative. He unwrapped the chocolate and offered it to Jerabek whose crooked lip lifted scornfully. "I don't eat cheap chocolate like that!"

Suddenly ashamed of the chocolate, Peter wrapped the tinfoil around it again and put it into his pocket.

"What kind do you like?"

"All kinds, only it's got to be good."

"But that comes only in big bars—that's expensive."

Peter could make nothing of the smile Jerabek gave him. Jerabek's eyes had narrowed as if he were studying him.

"Not the way I get it, it's not expensive."

"You mean, you know somebody who works in a candy factory?"

"I don't have to." Jerabek pushed himself away from the pillar. "I'll show you."

"Where are you going?"

"You'll see."

Jerabek was starting out of the station.

"But I don't want to miss the transport. . . ."

"You won't miss it. Lots of time."

Jerabek was leading the way toward the Gürtel. When they came to a confectionery shop that Jerabek appeared to have been heading for, Jerabek stopped to light a cigarette. Through the window Peter could see that the shop was empty of customers. The saleswoman was sitting by the counter, crocheting.

"You go in and buy ten hellers' worth of gumdrops," Jerabek said. "Don't ask for them right away. Pretend you can't make up your mind."

"What are you going to do?"

"I'm coming in, too—just to look around."

The treacherous smile with which Jerabek mocked his own words worried Peter as they entered the shop. The woman had got up from her chair and had gone behind the counter.

He followed Jerabek's directions. But while he pretended to be unable to make up his mind, he remained acutely, fearfully aware of Jerabek. Jerabek had wandered away from him and was looking at the cakes under the glass counter which stood at right angles to the one where Peter and the woman were. On top of the glass counter, Peter noticed with a pang of alarm, were three stacks of chocolate bars. He asked for the gumdrops. The woman had to turn around to reach for a jar on the shelf against the wall. As soon as she had turned her back, Jerabek reached up for one of the big chocolate bars with an insolent leisureliness that made Peter feel as if he were seeing it all in a dream. There was only a split second between the time Jerabek shoved the chocolate into his pocket and the woman's turning around with the jar. Peter was sure that the woman had seen everything; he had to force himself not to run out of the shop as soon as he had paid for the gumdrops. His fear made him hate Jerabek for lingering in the shop and brazenly asking the price of some small cakes before he finally came away.

Once they were out on the sidewalk, Peter started to walk as fast as he could. He wanted to run. Jerabek's hand was gripping his coat.

"What's your hurry? Did you steal anything?"

It was said so loudly that Peter looked around in a panic to see whether anyone had heard. Jerabek's cold-blooded daring frightened him. It was not until they had crossed the open square in front of the station that he dared to ask:

"Did you really take it?"

"What, this?" Jerabek pulled out the chocolate and held it up so that all the cabbies standing at the top of the steps could see it. "What do you suppose I went there for?"

"Supposing somebody had seen you from the sidewalk?"

"I'd have seen them first! Have a piece?"

"No—I don't want any now." Fear of Jerabek's scorn kept him from admitting that the stolen chocolate filled him with a kind of horror. He was still hot and cold at once at the memory of what Jerabek had done, but he was also guiltily aware that he had somehow known that that was what Jerabek intended to do from the very moment they had started out of the station—aware also that there had been an excitement about it that he cherished.

The transport was already in the station. It was difficult to see much from the main hall, but he found that by pressing his nose against one of the windows in the third-class waiting room he could get a good view of the platform. He saw that the train was made up of baggage cars with huge red crosses painted on their sides. The doors of most of the cars had been rolled back and soldiers were lifting the wounded men out of the cars on stretchers and carrying them down the platform. The wounded men were all bundled up in gray blankets so that only their heads showed. Occasionally there was one who had his arms out of the blanket and was smoking a cigarette.

It was not half so gruesome as he had expected. He felt a little disappointed. The men on the stretchers looked ill and exhausted rather than wounded. Only a few fitted into the picture he had brought with him. One in particular whose head was completely swathed in bandages, except for a narrow slit where his eyes were, brought him up sharp with a sensation of horror.

He had been so absorbed that he had forgotten about Jerabek.

"You can see more outside where they load them," Jerabek said indifferently. "I'll show you."

He followed Jerabek out into the street and around to the dimly lighted side entrance where the ambulances were lined up. Several cabbies and one old woman were watching on the sidewalk. Presently two soldiers came out with a stretcher. They lifted it very gently into the first ambulance. Then two more soldiers arrived with a second stretcher. The doors of the ambulance were shut and it drove off. The next ambulance moved up to the door. A steady procession of stretchers passed across the sidewalk.

Peter saw now that the faces of the wounded men were mortally sunken. Thin as the unshaven faces were, the heads of the men seemed to press into the pillows with the weight of lead. Only occasionally one of the men rolled his eyes feebly.

One of the cabbies said:

"Frozen legs from the Carpathians, every one of them. The sawbones are going to have a field day—be more men without legs after this winter, than with them!"

The cabby's words gave a grizzly significance to the stillness of the men. Involuntarily, Peter started to look for the bulges in the gray blankets where the men's legs were. He was almost glad to see the soldier with the bandaged head again: he had one arm out of the blanket and his fingers picked at it. A cloud of disinfectant moved with him.

"Shrapnel!" the same cabby who had spoken before said knowingly.

Peter leaned forward to look at the next man. This one, too, had a bandaged head, but his mouth and nose were left free by the bandages and he was smoking a cigarette.

Jerabek said, "Time for the train."

"Already?"

"Sure. How much longer do you want to stand here!"

They went back into the station.

"We have to get tickets to go out on the platform," Jerabek said. "They're twenty heller. You give me the money and I'll get yours."

The gate to the platform was already open. Jerabek gave their tickets to the guard and they went outside. There was only a sparse sprinkling of people on the platform: several porters with their little baggage carts and a handful of men and women who were evidently meeting the train. Jerabek strolled up and down with an air of having been used to railroad platforms all his life. The big gong overhead rang three times. The brilliant light of a locomotive appeared in the distance, and presently the train blustered into the station and came to a stop.

Jerabek made no move toward the train. If he was going to carry bags, he looked strangely disinterested in the people who were getting off. A lot of young officers were crowding out of the train. In no time at all, the meager supply of porters was exhausted and officers and civilians alike were looking around for someone to carry their bags.

Jerabek sauntered closer to the train. He had taken only a couple of steps when a lieutenant asked him to carry his bag. Jerabek ignored him, but picked up the much smaller bag of another officer. While he was still watching Jerabek, Peter noticed that another lieutenant was waving to him and calling as well. Encouraged by the lieutenant's friendly grin, he overcame his reluctance and picked up the suitcase. He followed the young lieutenant into the station and out into the street to a cab. But he felt himself flushing when the officer held out a coin. He murmured hastily, "That's all right," and wanted to run off, but the lieutenant caught him by the arm and made him take the money. He felt humiliated by the tip. As long as he had carried the bag, he had been free to imagine that the officer was Franz or one of Franz's friends. Poldi would be furious if she knew. He did not look at the coin until he was back in the station. He saw that it was a whole krone.

He looked around for Jerabek. People were still coming in from the platform. A prosperous-looking civilian hailed him and practically bullied him into carrying his valise. It was heavy and Peter found that he had to carry it all the way across the square to the streetcar stop. He felt no reluctance about accepting the half-krone the man held out to him.

He realized suddenly that he had earned a krone and a half in less than ten minutes. Even after he counted off the twenty heller for the ticket to get out on the platform, he still had one krone and thirty heller left. Together with what Aunt Wetti had given him, he had almost enough to buy a flashlight—or he might buy all sorts of good things to eat for ten o'clock breakfast for at least a week.

Jerabek was waiting for him at the entrance to the station. He had a small package under one arm.

"How much'd you make?" Jerabek asked.

Peter told him.

Jerabek did not seem impressed. "I've got to take this junk to the Blindengasse." He weighed the package scornfully in his hand. "Candy! If it were cigarettes, I wouldn't bother."

With a shock, Peter realized what he meant. There was no boastfulness in Jerabek's voice, only the same lazy, sneering matter-of-factness with which he always talked. To keep from showing his alarm, Peter asked: "How much are you going to get for doing that?"

"Two kronen so far and I'll get another one at the other end."

"How do you know you will?"

"It's for a girl: they always shell out big when you bring them a package."

They took the same streetcar. Jerabek showed no inclination to talk, except once when Peter asked:

"Why didn't you go after the first-class carriages instead of the second-class ones?"

"Why should I? Only rich people ride first class. They don't give you anything. You might as well bother with the poor trash in the third class. It's the young officers who send parcels and letters—that's where the money is. Sometimes they ask you to take their bags home and that's even better!"

They did not talk again until they came to the Westbahnstrasse.

"I'll see you tomorrow at the station," Jerabek said.

"I can't come tomorrow." There was not enough time to explain about the choir. "I can go day after tomorrow. Are you going to be there then?"

"Maybe," Jerabek said.

Chapter Twenty-Two

He could not have explained the dark fascination Jerabek had for him. He knew that Jerabek was evil in a much more dangerous sense than any of the notorious bad boys in their neighborhood. Jerabek stole things and he did not even feel guilty. He was cold-blooded and treacherous, and he had remained evasive. After two weeks of spending every minute he could manage with him, Peter knew that he had come no closer to him than on their first night at the station. What was more, he was convinced that if Jerabek were ever caught in one of those guilty exploits he was forever staging for his benefit, Jerabek would not scruple for a moment about involving him and even shifting the blame on him somehow.

Yet he could not keep away from him. He had even taken to cutting choir rehearsals for his sake. Facing Herr Granini's grave, faintly puzzled eyes the next day, while he lied that he had had to stand in line at some store, filled him with the same defiant agitation as when he watched Jerabek steal something. His smoldering resentment of Mizzi was driving him, he realized dimly, to outrage all the things he secretly cherished, just as it was at the root of his craving for the feverish intoxication of danger which merely being with Jerabek always brought. And there was also the revolver Jerabek had——

Jerabek had shown it to him one night at the station. It was an old-fashioned revolver with a mother-of-pearl handle and five chambers. A piece of the mother-of-pearl inlay on one side was broken off, but the mechanism was menacingly intact. The sleek coldness of the gun in his hand made him quiver with excitement. With the revolver he would be able to defend himself against anybody! He would even be able to protect them at home if Father threatened again to throw the stick of dynamite into the stove—and if he decided to run away, he would have to have it!

Jerabek wanted thirty kronen for the gun. He started to hoard every heller he could earn at the Ostbahnhof. By the end of the second week he had saved twenty-one kronen. It was only a matter of days before he would possess the gun. Then Jerabek suddenly announced that he was not going to the Ostbahnhof any more. He did not give any reason, but the cynical glint in his eyes made it clear that he had done something that made it dangerous for him to go back. The new silver watch Jerabek had been polishing all morning at his desk suddenly assumed a sinister significance—had Jerabek opened a bag and stolen the watch, or had he perhaps stolen the whole bag? In that case he himself could not go back to the station either: he had been seen with Jerabek by any number of people! He said irritably:

"How do you expect me to get the money for the revolver if you spoiled it for me at the Ostbahnhof?"

They were standing in front of the bookshop opposite the school. Jerabek took out a cigarette and lighted it with a sophisticated flourish.

"There are other ways of making money," he said.

"How?"

"I'll show you. . . ."

Jerabek started up the Westbahnstrasse toward the Gürtel. He was heading for the Schmeltz. The huge parade ground stretched before them in a dreary, deserted expanse of mud and snow. They walked along the crumbling brick wall which inclosed what had once been a cemetery and now was only a romantic wilderness of lush grass and lilac and rose bushes during the summer. The ancient graves had long ago been emptied and the bones moved to a mass grave in another cemetery. The war had stopped the work of turning it into a park, just as it had interrupted the construction of some thirty apartment houses a few hundred yards beyond the cemetery. The houses had been left in various stages of completion, and only two of them were actually finished and occupied. All the rest were still inclosed with board fences. The houses had been rather ambitiously planned and promised to be even handsomer than the new houses on the Gürtel; they were grouped around little squares with parks in the center or ranged along wide streets that were obviously going to be landscaped.

Peter wondered why Jerabek had come out here. Jerabek walked past the two houses that were occupied—then that wasn't it! Jerabek didn't know anyone there. . . . Only when they came to the fence around one of the new houses that was nearly finished, did Jerabek show any signs of interest. Peter could see that he was looking for an easy place to get over the fence.

"Are you really going inside?"

"That's what we came for."

It was easy enough to climb over the fence. The ground inside was still littered with troughs and scaffolding. Jerabek tried the front door, which was locked, then went around to the back and examined the basement windows. He found a broken pane and reached through it to undo the latch. Once they were inside, Jerabek started up the stair to the first floor. Their steps echoed eerily in the empty house. Unconsciously, Peter had started to walk on tiptoe.

"What are you afraid of?" Jerabek scoffed.

"I'm not afraid. What are you going to do?"

"This!" Jerabek seized one of the shiny, new brass knobs on the wrought-iron banister and started to twist. "We're going to get a lot of these, then the doorknobs and the catches on the windows, and the faucets. Next time we'll bring some tools."

"What are you going to do with them?"

"Sell them."

Peter suddenly understood. The hardware stores were buying up metal scrap for the government, especially copper and brass. Apprehension gathered in his chest into a lump.

"But they're new! They'll know they're stolen!"

Jerabek's blemished lip lifted sardonically. "We've thought of that—we're going to age them first. Besides, you aren't going to sell them: Pfeiffer is."

"Who's Pfeiffer?"

"You'll see. Let's get going before it's too dark. All you do is twist. It's easy. . . ."

It was easy. In less than half an hour they had made a little pile of brass knobs on each floor. Up until this moment, Peter had been too busy unscrewing the occasionally stubborn knobs to allow him to think ahead, but now when Jerabek stopped him and said, "That's enough; get as many into your pockets as you can," he was beset by qualms. Unscrewing the knobs in the empty house had after all been no more than a dangerous game, but taking the knobs out of the house was different. He protested:

"I don't want to tear my pockets."

"You worry too much. I thought you wanted to make some money? I've got to have the money for the revolver by Saturday, or I'll sell it to another guy who wants it."

Only the thought of the revolver made him cram as many of the knobs into his overcoat pockets as he could. They got over the fence and away from the house without being seen; but he hated Jerabek for making him walk with his pockets sagging and bulging with the knobs. His fear that one of the pockets might really tear and all the knobs fall out on the sidewalk grew as they approached the Westbahnstrasse. He insisted on turning left on the Gürtel and taking the Seidengasse where it was darker and where there was less danger of running into anyone he knew. He had not wanted to ask Jerabek where he was going. He followed him sullenly into the Bandgasse to the entrance of a house across the street from a locksmith shop. Jerabek gave two shrill whistles.

After a few minutes an apprentice with a tool kit slung over his shoulder came out of the shop. It was the same apprentice who had beaten up the boy on Jerabek's account that time outside the school. He had a thick-featured face which wore a deceptively good-natured smirk. The smirk broadened when he joined them in the entranceway of the house. "What'd you get?" he asked Jerabek.

Jerabek pulled out one of the knobs. "All we could take," he said. "Next time we'll take some sacks."

The apprentice slipped the leather strap of the tool kit off his shoulder and set the wooden box on the ground. He took the knob and examined it. "Not bad. Lot of zinc in it, though. Let's have them in there. The boss is away; I'll be able to work on them right now."

When they had emptied their pockets into the took kit, the apprentice slung it over his shoulder and turned to Peter. "You going with Willie tomorrow? I'll pay you when you bring the rest of it. You going tomorrow?"

"I don't know whether I can tomorrow." Then he remembered the revolver and he said hastily: "Maybe I can on Saturday."

"That's fine. You try and make it tomorrow. Willie won't like it, if you don't come!" He gave Jerabek a broad wink and started back to the locksmith shop with a thickset, lazy swagger.

Jerabek came as far as the Westbahnstrasse. Peter hurried away from him at the corner.

. . . but he had to have the revolver, he had to have it! he kept telling himself all evening while he sat at the big table in the living room doing his homework. And he was not going out on the Schmeltz again with Jerabek—unless there was no other way of getting the money. But already in the back of his mind, darkly, tentatively, a way suggested itself: why shouldn't he take the ten kronen out of her china closet? She had never let him spend the money Aunt Wetti had given him. The money was his, wasn't it?

The more he thought about the crinkly blue banknotes tucked away in some cup or other in the china closet, the more insinuatingly and certainly he knew that he was going to take the money. He was going to get it either that night or the next. It would not be hard either, for he was sleeping in the kitchen now. Poldi had moved into Franz's room. Franz was no longer living at home.

The change was fairly recent. Franz had had a violent quarrel with Father one night about the way Father talked to *her*. The next day Franz had volunteered for active service. It was Poldi who had known first and had told *her*. She had gone around with red, swollen eyes for days and had accused Father at least once of sending Franz to his death. But Franz had not been allowed to leave his job in the ministry and go to the front. A few days later the scenes at home had started again. There had been another quarrel and Franz had moved into the Lerchenfelderstrasse to stay with Herr Schmidtmeyer. Franz had taken all his clothes, and he came home only for a few minutes at a time now, usually in the late afternoon when Father was out, to talk to her. Sometimes Peter did not see him for three or four days.

The fact that Franz was gone made it possible to get the money. All he had to do was to stay awake until she was asleep in the living room. . . . But Father came in later than usual and he kept on railing at her about Pater Alfred for what became an exasperating stretch of time. One o'clock struck, and then two o'clock. Once, Poldi called out from Franz's room that she wanted to sleep. Father finally stopped. After another interminable wait until he was sure that *she* was asleep as well, Peter crept out of the bed.

There was just enough light from the red vigil lamp she kept burning in front of the little statue of Saint Joseph in the corner by the sewing machine to find his way. He carried a chair to the cupboard and started to explore the inside of the many unused cups on the two top shelves. He found three twenty-kronen notes in one of the cups. It was her housekeeping money, for in the bottom of the cup was the aluminum medallion of the Virgin which she always kept with it. He could not take anything out of that; she would be sure to notice it right away. He had to find the little emergency fund she always kept somewhere! Then he found it: four ten-kronen notes in a glass pitcher. He took one of the bills, carefully put back the pitcher, and took back the chair to the kitchen cabinet. He felt tense and exhausted. He fell asleep almost instantly.

Jerabek showed no surprise the next morning in school when he told him that he had the money. But he had to wait until the afternoon before he could get the gun. Jerabek's indifference in handing it over at last, in the grimy doorway of the house where he lived, made the pearl-handled revolver seem much less desirable for a moment, somehow incomplete. He tried the trigger half a dozen times to see whether the gun still worked; each time, the hammer gave a sharp click and the drum spun without fail. Cartridges—

"What about cartridges?" he asked Jerabek. "What good's a gun without cartridges?"

Jerabek's habitual silence became lean, lurking, vicious.

"I can get you ammunition. I'm going to see a guy tomorrow. It's expensive."

"How much is it?"

"It depends. You go out on the Schmeltz and get fifty pounds of brass by tomorrow night and I'll have a dozen cartridges for you. Maybe more."

"Aren't you going out on the Schmeltz yourself?"

"I've got something more important on. I showed you how. You can bring the stuff around to Pfeiffer tomorrow night. Do you want the ammunition?"

"I don't know yet. . . . I'll let you know tomorrow. . . ."

Jerabek had started to saunter toward the Innere Stadt. Peter kept stubbornly by his side. He was not going back to the Schmeltz! The ammunition could wait! He would manage to get cartridges somehow—he didn't have to get them through Jerabek. The important thing was that he had the revolver. It felt reassuringly heavy and sinister in his overcoat pocket, and it filled him with a defiant sense of not caring what might happen now.

He was still walking beside Jerabek. They had not spoken since Jerabek had told him to get the brass fixtures. But when they came to the Mariahilferstrasse, Jerabek said:

"I'm going to the Esterhazy Bath. You can come, if you like."

Peter knew about the public baths where one could rent a complete bathroom by the hour or go into the Turkish bath which had steam rooms and lounges, but he had never been in one. She made him bathe at home Saturday night in the tin sitzbath, but she and Father and Franz and Poldi went to the public baths. Franz and Poldi went to the new Diana-Bad where Franz said there was a huge swimming pool with artificial waves and a gymnasium and even a restaurant. . . .

"I haven't any money."

"You don't need any."

"How do you get in, then?"

Jerabek shrugged. "There are ways. . . . There's always somebody I know going in about this time of day. I can get you in if you want to go."

Peter followed him uncertainly. The public baths were a part of the adult world which had always struck him as vaguely improper; they at once repelled and enticed him for that very reason. And he was curious to see how Jerabek would get in without paying.

The baths were housed in a long, low building with recessed statues all along the façade. Across the street from it stretched the high iron fence of the Esterhazy Park. Jerabek stopped in front of the doorway and boldly lighted a cigaret.

There was almost no traffic in the short street and very few passers-by. Only one woman had entered the baths while they had been standing there. Peter began to feel restless. He knew that the street was not really unfriendly, but the houses were unfamiliar and he felt ill at ease, partly because of the consciousness of the revolver in his pocket, and partly because they were waiting there without any apparent purpose. He was just about to leave Jerabek, when a plump, well-dressed, elderly man with a black brief case under his arm crossed the street and—there could be no doubt about it!—smiled and made exuberant little gestures of recognition to Jerabek. Instinctively, Peter drew away a little from Jerabek. It surprised him that Jerabek should know such a well-dressed, almost distinguished-looking man; he was even more surprised at the familiarity with which the man began to talk to Jerabek.

He was going to steal away from them, but the man noticed it and raised his voice:

". . . and who is this? A little friend of yours? Is he coming upstairs with us, too?"

There was a cloying intentness in the way the man was looking at him which embarrassed Peter. He was also annoyed by being referred to as Jerabek's "little friend" when he was a full two inches taller than Jerabek. He mumbled something about having to go home and started to walk away. The plump man hurried across the sidewalk and grasped his arm.

"Now, don't rush off like that," he simpered. "You aren't afraid of me, are you?" He gave a sirupy giggle.

Peter said hastily, "I have to go home," and tried to free his arm. But the man shifted his grip to Peter's elbow and started to walk alongside him.

"Is this the first time you've ever been here? Then you've never seen the Esterhazy Bath! Now, you'll like it. . . ."

Peter hardly heard what he was saying. He knew only that he disliked the man's smoothly shaven face with the yellow pouches under his eyes and that he had to get away from him, but he did not know how to make the man let go of his arm without being impolite.

They walked past several houses with the man still clinging to his arm and talking about the Bath. At the next doorway the man made him slow down and crowded him into the corner of the door. He was pressing against him, so that Peter could smell the sickening scent of pomade that came from his hair and see the large pores on his nose.

"Now, why don't you want to come upstairs with us? We'll all have a nice bath together and have lots of fun. And I'll pay for everything and perhaps give you a little present besides. Now, what do you say?"

Not only was the man pressing still closer against him, but his hand which had been fingering Peter's arm until then was now fumbling down over Peter's side—though, at least not the side where the revolver was!

The man's nearness, his warm, dank breath against his face, but most of all the man's hand suddenly filled him with panic. He braced himself against the wall and pushed out with both hands. . . .

He did not stop running until he was safe in the Mariahilferstrasse. Even then, he could not keep from turning around every few steps to see whether the man was not somewhere behind him. And he felt an ungovernable need every few seconds to take out his handkerchief and rub the portions of his face where he could still feel the man's clammy breath.

He realized dimly that the man had wanted to do something disgusting in the baths, something to do with the man's body and his own—*and Jerabek had known the man!* He knew suddenly at the very core of his being that he would never be able to look at Jerabek without revulsion again.

An overpowering need for the clean, astringent, familiar world of the Verein came over him, but it was too late to go to rehearsal now. It was after six o'clock. The realization plunged him down further into a turbulent loneliness. He felt that he was slinking along the street, rather than walking. Then he remembered the revolver in his pocket and with it the ten kronen he had taken from the cupboard. A sudden fear that they had found out about it already helped him to escape the memory of the man at the Bath.

He managed to steal upstairs into the attic to hide the gun under a rafter before he entered the flat.

She had not found out about the money yet! But his anxiety was not relieved. He quivered with apprehension every time she went near the cupboard. The experience in front of the Esterhazy Bath survived as a sinister increase of menace ahead of him, for he felt weakened and a sure target for catastrophe. When his sense of being trapped grew almost more than he could stand, he steeled himself against it by telling himself over and over: "I've got the revolver! I don't care what happens! I don't care——"

Chapter Twenty-Three

He awoke with a start of sheer fright the following morning when she dropped a spoon. Instantly, quiveringly alert, his ears assayed each sound to catch any variation in the familiar noises that marked her movements by the stove. No, she did not know yet! For now she was complaining to Poldi in her usual tone about the smallness of the sack of potatoes Aunt Resi had sent from Almzell. Reassured, he tried to go back to sleep until she made him get up. Once up, however, the minutes dragged unmercifully until it was time to go to school. He ran down the stairs with a sense of reprieve.

It was Saturday and there was no school after lunch. He noticed as soon as he came home at noon that there was an ominous quiet about her which centered on him. Her heavy watchfulness tore at his nerves. Yet he could not be sure whether it was the money he had taken that was responsible for it, or whether she had found out that the lessons at Herr Granini's had stopped, or whether she knew about his visit to Aunt Wetti. The important thing was not to give in to her mute pressure and to make her speak first. . . .

He had half feared, half hoped that she would charge him with whatever it was she was so obviously holding against him after Father got up from his nap after lunch and went out, but she preserved her stubborn, accusing silence all afternoon. Most alarming of all, she did not even object when he left ten minutes earlier than she usually allowed him to go to rehearsal.

He ran into Franz at the foot of the stairs.

"Where are you off to?" Franz asked.

"Rehearsal."

"Have you been behaving yourself?" Franz was trying to sound jocular, but the worried frown which creased the soft, blond skin of his forehead into three broad ridges and which he always wore now when he came home for the brief visits in the afternoon had not gone away. Franz misunderstood his hesitation and asked: "Is anything wrong?"

"No, nothing."

"Oh—well, don't sing too many sour notes." And Franz poked him in the ribs with exaggerated playfulness and started up the stairs.

An eagerness that was tinged with gratitude gained on him as he neared the Verein. The strain of the long afternoon with her, and the oppressive alternative now of going out on the Schmeltz to get the brass fixtures for Jerabek, made him impatient for the warm, safe world of the choir. It seemed incredible to him that he should ever have wanted to stay away from rehearsal to be with Jerabek—incredible and foolhardy, since he had run the risk of being dropped from the choir. Even the revolver at home in the attic no longer seemed worth that risk.

It was still a quarter of an hour until rehearsal. Seven or eight boys from the choir were scattered at different tables in the clubroom, playing checkers and dominoes, but most of them were still out in the garden. As always on Saturday, there were a good many men and more kept arriving all the time; they were joking and laughing and talking in little groups all over the room. Peter started to watch a game of chess. Then one of the new boys in the choir asked him to play checkers. The deference of the new boy flattered him and he sat down with him. They played one game, then started another. Rudi came in from the garden and stopped to say hello and to watch their game for a minute. Just as Rudi was about to drift away, another boy bumped into him. The boy said:

"Domanig, your cousin is looking for you! He's out in the garden."

Alarm paralyzed Peter's legs, then settled like an enormous weight on his stomach and throbbed in his head. She had told Franz! He got up fearfully and hurried to the door to stave off the peril of having to face Franz in the clubroom, in front of the other boys. Franz was already in the corridor, coming toward him with long, menacing strides. His eyes were stern. Franz drew him into the embrasure of the nearest window.

"Mother says that you took a ten-kronen banknote out of the cupboard—is that true?"

"Yes, but——"

He realized as soon as he had said it what that other thing in Franz's eyes had been: Franz had been hoping that there had been some mistake, that he would be able to deny it.

"Why did you do it?" Franz asked angrily.

Perhaps if I tell Franz about the revolver he'll understand, flashed through his mind. But the next instant the feeling that Franz was an antagonist, because he was bound to be on her side, stopped him.

"Why did you take the money? What did you do with it?" Franz shook him angrily. "Do you hear?"

"I spent it."

"On what?"

"I just spent it!" The shaking Franz had given him made him sound more defiant than he had meant to do.

"All right, we'll talk about that later. You wait right here!"

He watched Franz go into the clubroom and head for the group around Herr Granini. *Please, don't let him tell Herr Granini!* he prayed. But it was already too late: Herr Granini had seen Franz's signal and he was detaching himself from the group and walking to one side with Franz, where Peter could no longer see them. A number of boys came in from the garden and along the corridor. Peter pressed farther into the recess. In spite of the animated voices of the boys as they passed, he felt convinced that they knew all about him and Franz. Their animation sounded false; Franz had probably blurted out everything to some friend out in the garden.

Herr Granini came out into the corridor, alone. His shoulders were pitched forward with evident concern. Franz had stayed behind in the clubroom to talk to a lieutenant who carried his left arm in a neat, black sling. Herr Granini's smoldering black eyes were grave.

"Is it true that you have been taking money at home, as Franz says?"

"Yes, Herr Granini."

"But you know that it's wrong to steal!"

He nodded. The thrilling huskiness of Herr Granini's voice seemed infinitely priceless again. Hot anger with himself possessed him at the thought of ever having had anything to do with Jerabek.

"Why didn't you go to Franz—or you might have come to me if you needed the money for anything! Franz wants you to stop the choir. I'm sorry, Peter, but Franz insists on it. . . ."

The blow was so unexpected that he felt dazed. Searing flashes of grief stabbed at his eyeballs. He seemed for a moment to be somebody else, standing alongside of himself, surmising rather than experiencing his reactions to what Herr Granini had said. Even the sudden, scathing hatred of Franz seemed to be somebody else's.

Franz was approaching from the clubroom. Herr Granini said quickly, softly:

"So I'm afraid we'll have to say good-by for the present. Will you promise me not to do anything like that again, Peter?"

Again he nodded, but he found it impossible to think of anything but the ravaging fact that he would not be going upstairs to the music room in a few minutes, and that he would not be in the choir loft at the Lazarist Church tomorrow, nor in the coffeehouse afterward, nor riding into the Innere Stadt just before eleven to sing in the University Church.

He heard Franz say behind him, "Thanks, Granini. Sorry to bother you," and Herr Granini's "Good-by, Franz." Automatically, he followed Franz out of the Verein and down the Westbahnstrasse. Franz was striding along heavily—self-righteously, he thought once. Franz did not speak all the way home. When he opened the front door, Peter saw that she was putting two of Franz's shirts in a carton on top of the ironing board. Franz gave him a little shove toward the living room and followed on his heels. He did not close the door into the kitchen.

"I want to know what you did with the money! Did you buy this with it?" Franz had picked up the flashlight which Peter had bought with the money he had earned during the first two days at the Ostbahnhof. It had been lying on top of the chest of drawers where Peter had not noticed it. She must have gone through his things and have found it underneath the old copybooks!

"No," he said.

He saw Franz's hand come toward his face but he could not dodge the full force of the slap. He was knocked off balance and his cheek stung. He remained leaning with one hand on the divan and shouted:

"I didn't, I said!"

"Stand up! What did you do with the money?"

"I spent it." He stood sullenly poised, ready to duck if Franz struck him again.

"Spent it on what?"

"For *Wurst* and cheese! When I was hungry . . ." He was not going to tell about the revolver, no matter what happened! He was going to need it now! The mere thought of the revolver up in the attic gave him confidence and steeled him against Franz.

"Where did you get this flashlight?"

"A boy gave it to me."

"What boy?"

"A boy in school." If he mentioned the Ostbahnhof, Franz would would know that he had been lying about the lessons during the last three months and things would be even worse!

"What's his name?"

"Jerabek—Willie Jerabek."

Franz remained undecided for a moment. He was still holding the flashlight. He grasped it more tightly and said: "I'm going to find out about this, whether that's true or not. And I'm coming tomorrow and I'll be here every day—if Mother has the slightest complaint about you, you'll hear from me."

Then Franz went out into the kitchen and closed the door. Peter sat down on the divan and held his cheek which still burned from the slap. If Franz wanted to go to Jerabek, it wouldn't do him any good! Jerabek was much too clever for Franz. . . . He could hear Franz talking to her about the shirts in a voice that he was forcing to sound casual but which had overtones of excitement in it. Then Franz left.

Now she would start!

But he had to wait for almost twenty minutes before she finally opened the door. She came in holding the carpetbeater with which she had spanked him when he had still been a little boy. When he saw her with it, he stiffened with rage. She was not going to beat him with it!

She pointed with the carpetbeater to the tufted red rug in front of her bed.

"Now you're going to kneel down and ask our Heavenly Father for forgiveness for your sin!"

Her unconscious theatricality set up a hysterical diapason of jangled mirth and fury in him. But he had to obey. There was no escape. He went to the bed and knelt down.

"What am I supposed to say?" he asked, knowing that the question would anger her.

"You're going to say the Act of Contrition first!" When he would not start, she started in behind him: "*Oh, my God—I am heartily sorry*——"

He loathed her grim, pious singsong. There was nothing for it but to go on with the prayer. When he had finished with it, she began a rosary. Again he writhed under her stubbornly insistent voice which was forcing him to pray. His attention was taken up by his resentful uncertainty of what she was planning next, for she was moving around by the wardrobe where she kept her clothes. Then he knew: she was getting ready to go out. Her voice swelled and grew muffled as she moved about the room. When they came to the last "Amen" of the rosary, she was behind him again. "Now you're going to church and to confession," she said.

A kind of anesthesia dulled his consciousness after they got to church, numbed him to the humiliating experience of having to kneel beside her while they waited their turn at Pater Alfred's confessional and to her sibilant confidences when she told Pater Alfred about the ten kronen, no doubt!—numbed him even to the final humiliation of having to go to Pater Alfred of all people to confess.

He felt drained of emotion when they came out of church. Only the shame-throbbing memory of the last hour survived. He said, because it was what Pater Alfred had ordered him to do:

"I'm sorry I took the money."

She acknowledged it with sour, grim promptitude: "I forgive you all right. Whether God forgives you is another matter—He can see into your heart. You can't fool Him!"

She did not speak to him again, except once after supper when she came to the living-room door to say: "Time to shine your shoes—tomorrow is Palm Sunday!" The rest of the evening, her silence with its brooding watchfulness followed him about like a rancorous dog. He felt too numb to care. Even the thought that there still remained Poldi to be faced appeared to him only as one more irritation to be borne.

He was already in bed when Poldi came home. Before long, *her* querulous muttering in Franz's room and Poldi's blunt, challenging interruptions told him that she was telling Poldi about the ten kronen. A minute later Poldi came out into the kitchen and tugged the blanket away from his head.

"Don't pretend to be asleep, you!" Poldi said. "A thief in the family, that's all we've been needing. But we're going to talk some more about that tomorrow! And keep your hands outside the covers!"

Poldi had been angry, but there had been something reassuring about her very brusqueness. Poldi was going to take his part! Already, while they had been talking in the other room, the habitual antagonism between Poldi and her had come into play and Poldi had begun to minimize what he had done. Not that Poldi would be less severe with him, but Poldi would be open and blunt and not make him feel that there was something inherently wrong with him, as *she* always did! And Poldi was better than Franz! He realized suddenly that underneath Poldi's gruffness there was a greater affection for him than under Franz's engaging warmth. Poldi would never have told Herr Granini about the ten kronen—she would have been too proud to let an outsider know about something disagreeable at home; neither would Poldi have been so cruel as to make him stop the choir as Franz had done tonight!

He saw how right he had been about Poldi and Franz the very next morning. They were both in the kitchen with *her* when he came in from High Mass. They had stopped talking the moment he had come in. Franz refused to look at him and Poldi ordered him to go into Franz's room and close the door.

He realized with a sort of bleak merriment that they were holding a council of war. His pride would not let him open the door to listen, but every once in a while a word or a phrase was so loud that he could not help hearing it. Franz's voice was vibrant with indignation. It was a shock to realize that Franz was talking about him. Once Franz said something about sending him to reform school. Poldi said irritably: "Don't make such a fuss! You talk as if he were a criminal. . . ."

For a moment he had an eerie illusion that the muffled drama in the kitchen did not concern him at all, that he was caught up in a dreamlike web of unreality where nothing mattered because it had all happened a long time ago. Poldi's voice brought him back to reality again. *She* had obviously been saying something about Mizzi, for Poldi burst out:

"Oh, stop it, Mother! That's all a lot of nonsense."

She said: "You mark my words: no good can come . . ." He missed the rest, but the sound of her voice made him grit his teeth.

Chapter Twenty-Four

POLDI'S words became a lens through which he saw them. Poldi had said: "You talk as if he were a criminal. . . ." And that was precisely how they were treating him, *she* and Franz, he told himself bitterly—like a criminal! Franz never spoke to him now when he came home in the evening. He asked *her*: "Has Peter been behaving himself?" and even if she gave him a grudging acquittal, the menace of Franz's frown remained.

But at least Franz was home only for a few minutes in the early evening, whereas her tight-lipped determination to reform him pursued him every minute of the day and night. She made him get up an hour earlier and go to Mass with her. She insisted that he say his prayers out loud in the morning and at night as he had had to do when he had still been little. She went through his pockets and through his things in the drawer. He felt like a prisoner.

Worst of all were the evenings. It was Easter week and there was a mission in the church in the Lerchenfelderstrasse which he had loathed as far back as he could remember because of its ponderous Gothic gloom. Only a handful of old women were scattered through the high, black oak pews near the pulpit during the rosary and the interminable Holy Week prayers that preceded the sermon. The cavernous gloom of the apse with its half-circle of shadowy columns was rendered stealthy, almost malignant by the faint red flicker of the vigil light in front of the altar. An ancient, superannuated verger in the front pew was leading the rosary. His cracked voice and the monotonous responses of the old women formed a lugubrious island of sound on which the massive columns and the dark recesses appeared to frown. The old man droned on and on until at last a few electric lights near the pulpit lighted up and one of the missionaries came out of the sacristy and climbed the stone stair to the pulpit.

By Good Friday Peter felt his despondency close in on him like the black shaft of a well from which it was useless to try to escape. A black-bearded missionary was preaching about the Crucifixion and about dying. Occasionally, the missionary's harsh, foreign-sounding voice became a somber blur when he turned in another direction; then his words rose into staccato precision again, relentless and dreary with his sepulchral fervor. Even when Peter's thoughts carried him out of the church for a moment, he could not escape the swarthy-faced missionary's voice. He had a nightmarish sensation that the sermon would never end. He sought refuge in some daydream again, only to find in despair when he had come to the end of it that the missionary was still talking.

She had noticed that he was not listening and nudged him.

The hateful, soft jab of her elbow made him go rigid with anger. Then, suddenly, a hard, brilliant clarity invaded him like a revelation. He told himself: *I can't stand it any longer.* He said the words to himself simply, without bluster, as if he were repeating the formula of a long overdue truth.

But what was he going to do? He had to get away, that much was certain! The wooded hillside above Aunt Resi's house in Almzell rose before his eyes—no, he could not go to Almzell! He must go where nobody knew him, only where? It was still too cold to run away to the front where the soldiers were. If only it were spring. . . . But spring was still far away—he could not wait until then!

He suddenly thought of Mizzi: why shouldn't Mizzi help him! She was supposed to be his mother, wasn't she? The rancor he had felt against her ever since his visit to Aunt Wetti flowed eagerly into the new mold: he would force Mizzi to do something about him! He would write her a letter that would make her come and take him away—that was it: a letter! He would write it tonight!

A grim exultation possessed him from the moment he had decided to write the letter. With sardonic patience he waited for the missionary to end his sermon. All this would last only a few more weeks and then he would be free!

She seemed to sense the new strength in him which challenged her power, for on the way home she threatened: "You just wait! I'll tell Franz all right how you've been acting. . . ."

"Tell him," he defied her. "I don't care." He could see that she was baffled.

They had warmed-over lentils for supper. He hurried through the meager meal and barely noticed that he was still hungry in his impatience to get started on the letter. He took advantage of the few minutes while she was out on the landing to draw water for the dishes, to sneak into Franz's room and get a sheet of paper and an envelope out of the box of stationery Fräulein Gisl had given Poldi for Christmas. He also managed to get Mizzi's last letter from the top of the chest of drawers. As soon as he was sure that she was safely settled down by the sewing machine in the kitchen, he got out the sheet of writing paper and put it on top of the copybook. He wrote:

> Dearest Mother: [The two words had always made him uncomfortable in the past when he had had to write to Mizzi, but this time he hardly noticed them.]
>
> I am very unhappy. Father gets drunk every night. He says that he is going to put dynamite in the stove and blow us all up. Father has a stick of dynamite. I saw it. Franz made me stop the choir and he beats me. I never get enough to eat. If you don't come and get me, I'll run away and become a criminal like a boy I know. He steals things in stores and on Sundays he breaks into villas in Mödling. Please come right away. Your loving son,
>
> Peter

He felt elated when he had finished the letter. It gave him a malicious pleasure to calculate the effect of each sentence on the shadowy woman in America who was Mizzi.

He got out Mizzi's last letter and carefully copied the meaningless foreign words of the address on his own envelope. Then he slipped his letter inside it and sealed it. There remained only the problem of getting up in the attic for the half-krone which he had had left over after he had paid Jerabek for the revolver and which he had hidden with the revolver. She was watching him so closely now that it was difficult even to get into the attic. He managed to escape from church the next morning while she went up to the altar rail for communion; he ran home and got into the attic without Poldi's seeing him. On the way to school he stopped to get a stamp and mail the letter.

Once mailed, the letter assumed for him a wonderful but perilous life of its own. It had become a marvelously potent hand reaching out for Mizzi and capable of making all the intoxicating daydreams that jostled each other in his head come true. But its very power which made it so precious also made him see it beset by a thousand perils. Supposing it got lost and Mizzi never saw it? People were always talking about all the ships that were getting sunk; the only way he could be sure that Mizzi knew about him was to write again. He had just enough money left over from the half-krone to buy a postcard for abroad. He decided to wait at least a week before he sent it, to make sure that it would not be on the same boat as the letter.

But that evening Franz slapped him again for running out of church and for talking back to her. He forced himself to hold on to the postcard another two days, then he sent it. He wrote on it, remembering a recent headline about a suicide in the paper: "If you don't come for me right away, I'm going to hang myself!"

The consciousness of the letter and the postcard hardly ever left him. Over and over, his imagination tried to picture what Mizzi would do. She might come for him herself, or she might send somebody else—or she might even have him travel alone. He was sure that she would telegraph—perhaps she would telegraph Aunt Wetti to take him to her house in the Kolowat-Ring! He never entered the flat without looking hopefully for some sign of agitation in her which would mean that the telegram had come. Even in school, his chest tightened when the janitor came into the classroom: the janitor might be coming to summon him to the office, because the telegram from Mizzi had come and he had to go home and pack right away. . . .

A whole month went by like that. He had been to the post office twice and he had been assured that even though letters to America had to go by way of Sweden now, Mizzi should have received not only the letter but the postcard as well. But still the telegram failed to come. There could be no other explanation than that Mizzi did not care what happened to him. An utter hopelessness gained on him. Almost without realizing it, he began to wish darkly for some catastrophe, some cataclysmic happening which would punish them and put an end to his arid waiting!

So guiltily familiar was this craving, that his first glimpse of

Father lunging after her down the stairs from their landing when he came home from school one afternoon, froze him with a quaking, clammy knowledge that he was responsible for Father's clutching her big sewing scissors in his right hand, which jerked spasmodically in front of his stomach.

She was hugging the curved wall of the staircase in her headlong descent. Her hand slithered and skipped over the brown handrail as she tumbled past, and Peter had a hysterical sense of the ludicrousness of their silent chase. He saw the dry glitter in Father's eyes and that Father's pince-nez was about to jiggle loose from the red folds of skin at the base of his nose. He saw also that Father's lips moved with soundless imprecation just as hers had twitched in anguished prayer. . . .

When Father had clattered past him, Peter started running down the stairs after him without knowing why and without consciousness of the exact moment when he had stopped standing still and had started to run. She got down to the second-floor landing and skidded across it, stopping once for a second, with both hands clutched to the banister as if to say something scathing and obstinate to bring Father to his senses, before she plunged down the next stairs.

It occurred to Peter that it was part of the unreality in which they were all three caught up that she should be flinging herself down the stairs with such amazing sureness of foot that he had the impression she could not possibly stumble. His real fear as they got closer and closer to the bottom of the stairs was that someone might see them. He began to hope desperately that Father would stop on the ground floor and after a few violent words of abuse would turn around and go back upstairs. But Father did not stop. He ran out into the courtyard after her. Frau Schreier and Frau Herzig were standing in the entranceway, talking. He saw the startled look on Frau Schreier's face. She called: "What's the matter, Frau Bartsch?" just as he passed her. Then they were out on the sidewalk.

Karl Breitner and two other boys were in front of the house. Peter found himself hoping against hope that they would not notice the scissors in Father's hand. He also felt an irresistible temptation to slow down and pretend that he did not even know Father and her, but when they came to the corner of the Kandlgasse he was still running behind Father. He heard Karl and the two other boys close behind him, and he was agonizingly aware that several people had stopped to stare at her and Father.

He realized now that she was heading for Herr Gregor's shop. She had hesitated again at the corner as if she had decided not to run any farther, but when Father had shown no sign of slowing up and had been only a few feet away from her, she had lifted her chin with a desperate gasp and had started down the Kandlgasse. It was only a few houses to Herr Gregor's shop. A pile of office desks were stacked on the sidewalk. She ran around the desks and toward the shop door, but then continued to run on down the street. An instant later, Peter saw what had made her change her mind: two apprentices with a desk were blocking the entrance, and also, there was a policeman coming up the street. Both she and Father slowed up as they drew near the policeman who had put one hand on his saber. The policeman stepped between her and Father. He was a plump, elderly man whom Peter had often seen directing traffic in the Westbahnstrasse. He still had his hand on his saber hilt and asked:

"Here—what's all this?"

She was panting and a thin, reedy rattle came from her lips which she was trying in vain to press together. Father's face was bright red, but he seemed angry rather than out of breath. Father appeared hardly aware of the policeman; he glared at her and growled:

"I'll fix you and that black priest!"

"You better let me have those scissors," the policeman said good-naturedly. He reached for them and Father gave them to him with a baffled glance at his hand as if he had forgotten that he had been clutching the scissors all this time.

Karl Breitner and the two other boys had stopped a few yards away to watch. A woman and a man stared curiously from the other side of the street. The whole street seemed to Peter to be full of staring eyes.

"I think we'd better go to the station, Herr—Herr——"

"Bartsch," she supplied.

Father was still glaring at her.

"Come on, Herr Bartsch," the policeman said.

It was only now that Father seemed to understand. He drew himself up sharply, then lowered his head and glared at the policeman. "I have no business at the station! When I want something from the police, I'll come and ask for it."

"Sure, sure, Herr Bartsch. Only, we can't stand here. Come on, now." The policeman touched Father's elbow. Father jerked his arm away truculently, then started of his own accord down the Kandlgasse. He strode forward so angrily that he gave the impression of being on his way to lodge a complaint against the policeman, who was hard put to it to keep up with him.

She followed heavily behind the policeman. Peter saw that her eyes were red and that only the fear of adding to their disgrace kept her from crying. As it was, she wiped her eyes once or twice with the handkerchief she had managed to pull out of the pocket of her black apron. When they reached the entrance to the police station, she turned to him and whispered fiercely:

"You go home. No need for you to come in here!"

He turned away reluctantly. It would have been much easier to disappear into the police station than to go back up the Kandlgasse. He started to walk as fast as he could without actually running. Karl Breitner came up behind him.

"Are they going to lock him up?"

"Lock whom up?"

"Your father. He was trying to kill your mother—I saw it!"

"You're crazy!" He rushed away from Karl and the two other boys who had come up. Shame made him keep his eyes on the pavement all the way home. He pretended not to hear when Frau Schreier asked him in the entranceway: "What happened, Peter? Did they—"

Upstairs, the door to their flat stood wide open. He closed it and started to look around for some clue to what had happened before Father had picked up the scissors. But everything was in its place. Father's billfold and the pince-nez he used for reading lay side by side on top of the chest of drawers. The leather slippers were still at the foot of the divan. Father had evidently been about to go out. The entire flat seemed abnormally still and drained of familiarity.

He tried to cheat his uneasiness by getting out his schoolbooks. The picture of Father going into the police station kept intruding between him and the geometry exercise. He found that he had drawn two caricatures of the policeman on the margin of the textbook. He gave it up and went out into the kitchen to listen.

No one was coming. Would they, he worried, come home together—or would the policemen actually put Father in jail! The fact that Father's billfold was still on the chest of drawers and that Father was without all the other things he always carried in his pockets made him seem incomplete and at a humiliating disadvantage with the police; it also filled Peter with a curious sense of maturity toward Franz and Poldi, as if he had witnessed something shocking that had been preparing behind the scenes and which Poldi and Franz would always see only from the innocent outside.

She came up the stairs at last, and she came alone. As always when she was upset she sought refuge in her housekeeping chores. Now and again when she passed the living-room door, Peter saw her dab at her eyes with the obstinate gesture he knew so well. He could not contain his curiosity any longer.

"Isn't Father coming home?"

She dabbed at her eyes more fiercely. "You can see that he isn't home, can't you?"

"Are they keeping him at the police station?"

She grumbled forbiddingly: "You'll find out soon enough. I have enough troubles without your foolish questions."

He had to wait until Franz came home at six to find out any more. She wiped her eyes frequently while she told Franz. Out of her grudging, labored account, which seemed so chary that Peter had the feeling that she was withholding some significant truth, one fact emerged to torture him: Father had been taken somewhere *for observation.*

He did not know what the sinister phrase meant; nor did the next few days do anything to clarify it. All he knew was that Franz and Poldi were pale and silent, and that she had taken Father his reading pince-nez and his cigar case, and that she went to see him every afternoon at some hospital in Währing.

It was Karl Breitner who finally enlightened him. Father had already been gone for three whole days. Karl said: "I know where your Father is—they've got him in Währing. Frau Schreier told my mother. That's where they take crazy people."

He felt an impulse to hit Karl, but he realized suddenly that he had known for a long time that Father had been strange and that if it had been a question of anyone else, he would have said the same thing as Karl. But Father couldn't be crazy, not Father! Crazy people were sent to Steinhof, out beyond the cemetery in Baumgarten.

He avoided Karl after that. He remained hidden in the entry in the morning until he was sure that Karl and the other boys had left for school, then he hurried out through the courtyard and made a long detour to school. When she made him go on an errand in the middle of the day, he slunk in and out of the house in an agony of apprehension that some inquisitive woman in the house might stop him and ask about Father. He knew that Poldi and Franz suffered from the disgrace that attached to them now, too, for twice Poldi had warned: "If anybody asks you about Father, you say that he's sick and nothing more, do you hear?"

On the afternoon of the fifth day, *she* came home from Währing a whole hour later than on the previous days. She sat down by the sewing machine without taking off her hat and started to cry. Dry, hiccuping sobs racked her body like some grim disease. There seemed to be no connection between her swollen, tear-filled eyes and the choking grief that convulsed her. He felt frightened. Fear rather than pity made him ask: "What is it? What's happened, Mother?"

Another sob, more savage than any that had gone before, wrenched her shoulders.

"They've taken him to Steinhof!"

The words were as if torn from her. He tried to find something to say to console her, but everything he could think of sounded inadequate. He asked:

"Shall I call Frau Herzig?"

"Only God can help us now!" Her hand fumbled in the little drawer in the sewing machine where she always kept an old rosary. He went into the living room and listened. Her sobs came less frequently. Then his own shock at the realization that Father was in Steinhof made him forget about her.

Vaguely he knew what Steinhof was. It was the gilded cupola on top of the hill above the Baumgarten cemetery which one could see all the way across the Schmeltz—it was also the handsome, bisque-colored brick wall that ran for more than a mile along the road to Neuwaldegg—it was the place where crazy people were. That much he had always known without ever giving it a second thought. But now, suddenly, the mere thought of Steinhof set him quivering with shame and anxiety.

Would Father always have to stay in Steinhof now?

He listened desperately to Poldi and Franz when they came home, in the hope of learning something comforting. But their very efforts to console her showed him that there had been no exaggeration in her grief. Franz was to go and see the doctor the following morning. There was a vague promise of hope in that.

Franz and Poldi were both home the next day at noon. Franz looked serious but also more confident. The doctor had said that after some treatments Father would be all right again, but that in the meantime Father would have to stay in Steinhof.

"Well, he's not going to stay there!" Poldi exploded. "Did you ask about the sanitarium they have out there for private patients?"

"I didn't have time. I'll call from the office this afternoon. But the sanitarium is going to be expensive. . . ."

"I don't care. I won't have Father in the public asylum!"

"And where's the money to come from?" *she* challenged Poldi. "I haven't any. A sanitarium is for rich people, and not——"

"We can borrow the money from Aunt Wetti."

"Not while I am alive!" *She* braced herself darkly. "If God has sent us this trial, we'll bear it without Wetti's help."

"And leave Father where he is? Franz!"

"It mayn't be so expensive after all," Franz put in quickly. "We can settle all that later. Perhaps we won't need to borrow anything. There's Father's pension, and I can always get what I need from Schmidtmeyer."

They did not mention the sanitarium again while they ate lunch, but when Franz got ready to leave, Poldi said: "You'll be sure and find out today, Franz! And try to get them to transfer Father right away!"

That evening in bed, Peter could hear them talking in the living room. Father was already in the sanitarium and the bill was going to amount to more than three hundred kronen a month. She grumbled about going into debt. But Poldi refused to listen: "At least, he's in the sanitarium now where he gets decent care and good food. Gisl knows of a man who had a nervous breakdown and who was in the sanitarium and came out completely cured." But however often the word "sanitarium" appeared in Poldi's mouth, the glittering dome of Steinhof rose inexorably before Peter's eyes—and before theirs, he knew—whenever they thought of Father.

She went every afternoon to visit Father. On the fourth day she made him come along. They took the streetcar as far as the Baumgarten cemetery, then they walked up the road past the stonecutters' establishments and the gardeners, past the cemetery itself and up the hill to the big gate in the bisque-colored wall of Steinhof. She showed her pass to the two guards in the gatehouse and then they were out in a broad, sanded avenue. They were inside Steinhof! Avenues branched off in every direction and wound between trees and shrubberies to buildings half hidden among the trees. Peter had not been prepared for either the immensity or the parklike innocence of the place. But the innocence, he felt, was treacherous. The knowledge that the fine, new buildings held insane people, the barred windows everywhere, the weird sound of singing that came from one of the buildings made him afraid.

They waited in a glassed-in lounge while an attendant went to get Father. The lounge anywhere else would have been cheerful; there were a great many potted plants and bright wicker furniture and gay curtains. The bars on the windows hardly showed. . . .

Father came in from the hall by himself and Peter's worst fears were dispelled. He had half dreaded that Father might come in shackled to a guard and wearing some ugly uniform. But Father looked much as he always had. He wore his light-brown suit and he was freshly shaved. Only the consciousness of where they were made everything seem queer—that, and Father's apathy.

Father took the oranges, the cigars, and the newspapers she had brought him, and sat down beside them. But he did not talk. He answered curtly when she asked him some awkward-sounding question from time to time about his food or about his clothes. The rest of the time he sat glowering at the other side of the room or looking out through the windows on the left. He did not even mention Pater Alfred. Once he spoke to Peter in a tone he might have used years ago about grammar school and asked: "Have you been learning your lessons?" Then he sank back into his abstraction again.

It was torture to sit like this. Peter could not for a moment forget where they were. His ears strained to listen for shrieks and ravings in other parts of the building, and although everything remained peaceful, he was feverish with the need to get away.

Father shook hands with him, but not with her, when they went.

Then they were out in one of the broad avenues again. Other visitors were walking down toward the gatehouse ahead of them. . . .

After that, she sent him to Steinhof by himself every second day. On alternate days, she went herself. Franz and Poldi visited Father on Sundays and once or twice during the week.

He came to be familiar with the maze of avenues inside the walls. From other visitors with whom he climbed the hill from the streetcar line, he learned about the pavilions for the violent cases hidden deep in the park. He watched the little toylike trains on which food was carried to the various buildings from the central kitchen. He went into the marble church whose gilded dome it was one saw from the Schmeltz. And he became familiar with the dull, strained hours of sitting with Father in the lounge.

He tried to tell himself that Steinhof was not terrible at all, that it was really pleasant, especially the part where Father was. He had found some charmingly remote spots in the course of the strolls he took between the time he left Father and the closing hour when he had to get back to the gate. There were meadows with all kinds of spring flowers, and fir groves, and once he even saw a deer. . . . But his power to deceive himself about Steinhof failed him the moment he came out of the gate. He became aware then in the faces and the stooped shoulders of the visitors trudging down toward the streetcar of all the degrees of sadness and despondency which they had striven so hard to hide behind an artificial cheerfulness while they had been with their relatives inside the wall. It was just outside the wall, between the gate and the streetcar stop, that the full horror of the asylum—call it "sanitarium" as much as you like—resided.

Sometimes, partly to get away from the despondent faces in the streetcar and partly to save the money of the fare, he walked. It was a long walk across the meadows, past the truck gardens and the ancient windmill to the outer reaches of the Schmeltz, and then across the Schmeltz itself where soldiers were maneuvering in the network of trenches that had been dug. Without needing to turn around, he remained aware of the gilded cupola of Steinhof. Hideous, troubling memories of the asylum dogged him: the isolated pavilion with the special fence around it where the maniacs were kept and the obscene confusion of sounds that had come from the windows. One man had been declaiming poetry, another had laughed—a bloodless laugh that had had no beginning and no end—and still another had seemed to be arguing with an imaginary antagonist. And all the voices had had a curiously absent-minded timbre which had made them terrifying.

He began to dread the visits and especially the time he had to spend with Father in the lounge. After he had given Father the cigars and the newspaper he had brought, there was never anything to say. The minutes drew out endlessly as he sat there beside Father, hoping that he would send him away, and then feeling guilty because he was the one who was free to come and go while Father had to stay behind.

But more than anything, it was the knowledge that all the people in the house and in the neighborhood knew now where Father was that became unbearable. There was nothing to prevent him from going down into the courtyard now, or out into the street, on the afternoons when she went to see Father, yet he stayed in the flat. He was in constant terror that one of the boys might refer to Father. Once, when he did stop with Karl and another boy for a minute, the other boy had suddenly greeted some statement he had made about machine guns with: "You are crazy!"

He had gone hot all over and he had challenged the boy:

"Who is crazy?"

"You are! Sure you are," the boy had jeered, "just like your father. Everybody knows he's in Steinhof!"

He had thrown himself on the other boy then and had twisted his arm until he had taken it all back, but there had been no satisfaction in that; for when it was all over, there had still been a malicious gleam in the other boy's eyes.

And there was the time when Karl Breitner started to ask about Steinhof. Karl was only curious. Peter hated the questions, but there was no ground for anger with Karl. "What's it like out there?" Karl had started.

"It's nice! There's a big park and a little railroad that runs all over."

"Do you see the maniacs when you go in?"

"Of course you don't! They're in a separate building, way off by themselves. You don't think everybody out there is a maniac!"

"Does your father have to wear a strait jacket?"

"Why should he!" he had flared up. "He's just the same as he always was. He can do anything he likes."

"He must be a little funny—he ran after your mother with the scissors!"

"That doesn't mean anything. He was just mad about something."

"My father says your father is a dipsomaniac," Karl said.

"He is not!" The word was new to Peter, but the "maniac" part of it stung him. "He's only out there for a few weeks, that's all."

By sheer coincidence Poldi that evening asked:

"Has anybody in the house said anything about Father?"

He distrusted her question. "What should they say?"

"Have they?"

He saw a chance to find out about the word Karl had used. "Somebody said that Father was a dipsomaniac."

"Who?" Poldi's eyes were flashing. "Who said that?"

"Some boy did. . . ."

He heard Franz's chair scrape on the floor in his room, then Franz came already striding toward him. His forehead was white and taut. Franz slapped him hard, first on one side of his face, and then on the other.

"Don't let me hear you use that word again!"

Peter started to shout angrily: "I didn't say it!" but Poldi got ahead of him.

"You don't have to hit him for that!" Poldi protested. She was talking to Franz's back. Franz was already inside his room and slamming the door.

Since Father had been taken away, Franz had been living at home again, but he slept alone in his room. Peter had had to go on sleeping in the kitchen. Poldi used the divan in the living room.

"Father is not a dipsomaniac," Poldi was saying. "A dipsomaniac is a man who drinks so much that he goes out of his mind. Father did drink, but not like that! You ought to know that yourself."

His throat was still burning with rage at Franz. He managed to say: "Sure, I know."

"The doctor says that Father may have a tumor on the brain, but they don't know yet. That's a growth and that can happen to anybody. It's got nothing to do with insanity, and after they operate on Father, he'll be like any other normal person again. . . . And don't look so sulky just because Franz slapped you. He simply misunderstood. Is all your homework done for tomorrow?"

One thing stood out clearly in his mind after his resentment over the slaps had died down a little: Poldi and Franz were just as sensitive about what people might be saying as he was. And they were touchy also about Father's drinking, or Franz would not have flown into such a rage over that one word.

It was getting on toward the end of May. The parks were bright with flowers and blossoms again, but he was not cheered by them. It was almost seven weeks since he had sent the letter to Mizzi. There had been no sign from her that she had received it, until one day the postman brought a registered letter. It contained a bank draft—a larger one than usual; he could tell from the way Poldi and Franz talked about using it to pay the bill at the sanitarium for the whole summer—and it contained the usual enclosure on a separate sheet of paper for him.

He skipped impatiently over Mizzi's inquiries which always irritated him because they sounded as if they were addressed to a little boy. Toward the end of her note he found what he was looking for:

> I know, dear Peter, that it must be hard for you in Vienna with the war and everything. I wish I could come and get you this very instant, but your little brother has been very ill with scarlet fever and I can't leave him yet. I also thought of sending for you, but the steamship companies all say that it is very dangerous to travel now because of the submarines. But the war can't last much longer and just as soon as it's over, I'll come flying to my Peter and then we'll all be so happy together. . . .

Then she had got his letter! And she did not care what became of him! *Scarlet fever,* he thought jealously, *your little brother has been very ill with scarlet fever!* He had never been ill with anything! Illness suddenly seemed to him a luxury reserved for more fortunate children. . . . He was not going to wait until the war was over! He had given her her chance, and she had turned him down. Very well, he was going to run away. The very resolution no longer excited him. He felt a calm detachment from what he had to do. The only question was how and when. . . .

The next morning he hid his schoolbag in the cellar. He ran into Karl Breitner just outside the house.

"Where are your books?" Karl asked.

"I'm not going to school."

Karl misunderstood. "I wish my father was sick and I didn't have to go to school."

"They don't know I'm staying out."

"No? Where are you going?"

"Out on the Schmeltz to watch the soldiers. Maybe I'll go all the way to Hütteldorf."

"I'd rather go to Neuwaldegg and see the fortifications. They have big guns out there—would you go to Neuwaldegg if I come along?"

"I don't care."

Karl left his books behind the door of a house in the Kandlgasse and they started out across the Schmeltz. They watched a large group of soldiers deploy with fixed bayonets and practice charging a fortified hill which was defended by other soldiers with machine guns. Then they came to the truck gardens and the old windmill and they had only to continue past the cemetery to get to the meadows beyond and to the woods. There was no need to climb the hill to Steinhof, yet Peter found himself urging:

"Let's go up there. They're laying a new water main along the road, with huge pipes you can walk through."

He could not have said why he wanted Karl to come up with him to the wall of Steinhof. It was true that men were excavating along the road, but he knew that that was not the reason. When they came to the big gate in the bisque-colored wall, he started to point out the buildings and the tracks of the little railroad to Karl, and even as he did so he wondered: Why am I telling him all this?

Karl said: "Boy, I'd like to get inside there sometime! You think you could take me along when you go again?"

He suddenly knew that this was what he had been waiting for. He wanted to impress Karl with the size and the handsomeness of Steinhof to lessen the disgrace of Father's being there, as much as if he had said directly: "You see, it's really fascinating. It's not what people think. It's only a beautiful park with fine buildings. *It's really a privilege to be in Steinhof.*"

After Karl's tribute, he felt quite content to leave the wrought-iron gate. They walked as far as the first few villas in Neuwaldegg. There was not time to get to the fortifications. But they stopped to see whether there were any ripe cherries in a large orchard. The cherries were still green.

"This orchard isn't half as big as my grandmother's in the country," Karl boasted. "She's got hundreds of cherry trees. I wish I could be there now. I'm sick of school! What are you going to do about an excuse for this morning?"

"I'm not going to bother. I'm running away."

"You mean for good?"

He could see that Karl was impressed. "Certainly."

"When?"

Now that Karl's scepticism was goading him, he found it easy to make the decision.

"Tomorrow."

"Where are you going to go?"

"I'm going to the front where the soldiers are and then to Turkey and to Asia. I'm going all over."

"How'll you get to the front? They won't let you."

"That's easy. I'll go to the Ostbahnhof and stow away in an army transport like the boy who was in all the newspapers."

"If I went along, we could go to my grandmother's first and get a lot of food. I bet the cherries'll be ripe. . . . Then we could walk to Odenburg and get on a transport there. Odenburg is right on the main line and all the trains stop there for water."

Although he did not wholly trust Karl's enthusiasm, the prospect of not having to go alone tempted Peter. "How far is it from your grandmother's to Odenburg?"

"It isn't far at all. Only about ten kilometers and you can always get a ride on a wagon. There are farmers going to Odenburg all the time. You can look it up on the map: my grandmother lives in Zienau."

"But your grandmother would be suspicious. She'd write them that we were there. . . ."

"No, she wouldn't!" Karl sounded very sure of himself. "I can say that school is closed for a week because of measles, like last year, and that my mother sent us. . . ."

"And how are you going to get there? We can't get on a transport and get off at a small place like that. Besides, once I get on a transport, I don't want to get off again. I want to get as far away as I can."

Karl said eagerly: "I've got eleven kronen in my bank. I bet it's much easier to sneak into a transport at Odenburg than it's here at the Ostbahnhof. The station in Odenburg is all open; nobody would see us at night. How about me coming along?"

"All right."

"Then it's all settled?"

"I'm going whether you come or not. . . ."

Chapter Twenty-Five

"What else have you got in there?"

The police *Kommissar's* chair creaked as he leaned forward across the desk to poke Peter's rucksack with his stubby fingers. His bald, preposterously egg-shaped skull glistened under the electric droplight.

"Empty it!"

Peter reached down once more into the rucksack. His hand encountered the barrel of the revolver. He fumbled quickly for the bottle of blueberry brandy from which Karl and he had each taken a sip in the freight car when Karl had complained about being cold.

The plain-clothes man who had recognized them in the railroad station and had brought them here picked up the bottle. "And what's this?" he asked.

"It's blueberry cordial. . . ."

"You don't say!" He uncorked the bottle and smelled it. "Blueberry cordial it is. Regular little explorers, aren't they?" he said in mock amazement to the *Kommissar* and to the other policeman who was standing beside Karl, lazily puffing at a long porcelain pipe. "Come on!" the plain-clothes man suddenly bullied. "Let's see the rest of it!"

Peter stiffened under the exasperating closeness of the man's body. There was nothing for it now but to let them see the revolver. He took it out with a gust of defiance and laid it on top of the two gray sweaters from Mizzi. It soothed his quivering irritation to note the stern attentiveness that had spread over the *Kommissar's* jowly face.

The *Kommissar* reached for the gun. He pointed it toward the floor beside him and spun the drum several times to look through the chambers. Then he swiveled his chair back to face the desk. He held up the gun between his fingers. His elbows shifted ponderously for a proper purchase on the desk.

"You're getting off to a good start, aren't you? What was the gun for?"

"We were going to the front—that's why I took it."

"Where'd you get it?"

"I found it on the Schmeltz."

"When?"

"Two weeks ago."

"Why didn't you take it to the police?"

It was really laughable, Peter thought vindictively, how easy it was to fool these three men who were so sure they knew everything.

"I didn't know I was supposed to." Maliciously, he adopted the whine which had so infuriated him in Karl before, when Karl had answered their questions.

"What do you know about this revolver?" the *Kommissar* snapped at Karl.

"Nothing," Karl whined again. "I wasn't with him!"

Thank God that he had at least had sense enough not to tell Karl about Jerabek! They might have found out about the brass fixtures. . . . The thing to do was never to tell anyone any more than one absolutely had to!

The telegraph instrument on the little table beside the desk started to click fitfully. The *Kommissar* swiveled around to it and picked up the white paper ribbon. The room was silent except for the stuttering of the telegraph and the noisy breathing of the policeman with the pipe.

Peter looked away from him at the big wardrobe in the corner. Inside, on the partially open door, hung two sabers and two helmets. Next to the wardrobe stood a glass case with several shelves on which lay an incongruous assortment of knives, blackjacks, brass knuckles, and revolvers. They were all tagged and had evidently been taken off thugs. In the far corner was a telephone booth and another desk. Above it hung a pendulum clock—seventeen minutes to three! They had been here only ten minutes, then. It had seemed much longer.

The telegraph stopped with a final splutter.

"All right," the *Kommissar* said impatiently, "take them out in back."

The policeman said: "Come on, you."

Peter reached for his rucksack, but the plain-clothes man was pressing it down on the desk with his hand. "We'll keep that for you. You won't have to worry about it. We'll keep it safe for you until tomorrow—this morning, I mean. It ought to be a big day for you after your father gets here with the strap!"

His juicy chuckle infuriated Peter. He turned his back on him scornfully and went after Karl. The policeman led them down a narrow corridor with doors all along one side of it. When they came to the next to the last door, the policeman unlocked it and motioned them inside with his pipe. The room smelled strongly of carbolic acid. There were two wooden cots along the walls and a simple toilet in one corner. The window above one of the cots was barred. The only light in the room came from the wire-screened peephole in the door which was being locked now on the outside. The policeman's steps moved away in the corridor.

Karl's voice buckled with alarm: "This is a jail!"

"What did you think it was?"

"Are you going to lie down?" When Peter refused to answer, Karl sounded even more afraid than before: "Where are you going to sleep?"

"I don't care." Peter went to the cot by the window and moved the rolled-up blanket to the foot of the cot, then he lay down.

"Are we supposed to take off our clothes?"

"You haven't any nightshirt," he said coldly to discourage any more talk from Karl, but Karl still wanted to spill his tearfulness on him:

"My father is going to be mad. . . ."

Peter turned his face to the wall. The wooden cot felt hard and he was chilly, yet he felt unwilling to use the rough blanket at his feet. He realized that his reluctance came from *her* horror of vermin. A cock crowed and tore the gray stillness like a jagged knife. Peter felt cowed by the sudden assault of noise which had something brutal about it—were they really like criminals now, and would they have what the newspapers called a "police record" because they had been in jail? Several cocks crowed and his confidence returned. He didn't care! Only, Poldi would be furious. . . .

He heard Karl use the toilet and lie down on the other cot.

"Aren't you going to use the blanket?"

"No."

"I'm cold!"

He listened to Karl unfold his blanket. Karl had wanted his approval, just like a little boy. What a fool he had been not to go alone! Without Karl, he might have been at the front by now, or at least in Budapest. He ought to have known from Karl's enthusiasm that running away was only an adventure for him, bound to end like this, tearfully. Karl had never expected to get any farther than his grandmother's in Zienau!

He saw again the tame little village and the prim yellow-stuccoed house where Karl had taken him. He had disliked the village and the flat country from the beginning. . . .

Even their falling into the water had been Karl's fault. Karl had insisted on wrestling in the brook when they had gone wading on the second morning. It had been their wet clothes that had made Karl's grandmother ask why they hadn't brought along any clothes, so that it had been easy to guess where she was going when she had suddenly said that she had to see somebody in the village. She had been on her way to telegraph Karl's parents!

Of course, the transport hadn't been anybody's fault. . . . The transport had been heading in the direction of Budapest when they had climbed into the empty boxcar and it had had a lot of soldiers in the cars up front. Nobody could have told that after all the shifting back and forth of the train on the sidings they were moving in the wrong direction, so that they had ended up here in Leobersdorf, practically back in Vienna. But even that wouldn't have mattered if Karl hadn't kept on nagging about going into the railroad station and lying down on the benches, where the plainclothes man had caught them!

But next time they would not catch him! Next time he was going alone. In the meantime, he would have to face them at home again. No matter—he wasn't going to be home more than a few days! It was while he was still wondering whether Franz or she or Poldi would come for him in the morning that he fell asleep. . . .

A different policeman from the one who had locked them in came for them in the morning. The big room where they had been questioned the night before was full of people now. A different *Kommissar* sat behind the desk, and there were six or seven other policemen—then he saw Poldi: she was standing beside Frau Breitner who was sitting on one of the yellow benches outside the railing. The policeman went ahead of them to the little gate in the railing. Karl's mother was already on her feet. She rushed to Karl and hugged him.

Poldi took only one little step forward and stood there, tensely poised, the way she did in the Turnverein just before she took off for a jump. Her eyes flashed darkly as they did when she was either very angry or very moved and was trying to hide it. Poldi said:

"So there you are!"

Her voice was husky and strained into casualness. He still could not tell whether she was angry or not. But the spell which had frozen them for an instant had been broken. Poldi started to move forward and, without meaning to, he took a step toward her. The next moment he realized that with the few words Poldi had reasserted her authority over him and he was piqued at having given in so easily. He hardened himself against the familiar softness in his very muscles which had betrayed him.

Beside them, Frau Breitner was combing Karl's hair with a brown tortoise-shell comb and softly scolding Karl.

Poldi said impatiently: "Well, let's get your things and get out of here!"

She came after him through the little gate in the railing. His and Karl's things were spread out on the desk in the corner. Two policemen looked on with a grin while he put his belongings into the rucksack. The revolver, he saw, was not anywhere on the desk. Frau Breitner had joined them and was doing most of the packing for Karl. When they had got on their rucksacks, Poldi and Frau Breitner went up to the *Kommissar's* desk to thank him. The *Kommissar* pulled open the top drawer in his desk and took out the revolver. He did not seem to know whether it belonged to Karl or to him; at least, he looked first at Karl and then at him while he said: "I'm going to keep this. A revolver is nothing for boys like you to play with."

Then they were out in the street and presently sitting around a table in a coffeehouse, waiting for rolls and coffee. Although Poldi and Frau Breitner exchanged an occasional remark, there was a strain between them which had to do with Karl and him, Peter sensed. It was clear that each of them was blaming the other boy for their running away. It was the same after they got on the train. He and Karl sat facing each other by the window, but he knew that they were not supposed to talk. As if he would have wanted to! The mere sight of Karl's scared eyes filled him with scorn. If it hadn't been for Karl. . . .

Poldi did not say anything about his running away until they were in the streetcar in Vienna. Frau Breitner and Karl were sitting a few seats away.

"You couldn't think of anything better to do, could you? As if we hadn't enough to worry about with Father, without your having to run away!"

He had not prepared himself for this particular note of reproach. Poldi's voice was somehow drawing him into her confidence about Father. He felt guilty against his will. *I don't care!* he thought. *Next time nobody is going to catch me.*

Frau Schreier was polishing the brass bell push in the big doorway. She stopped when she saw them and sniggered:

"So you've brought back your two runaways?"

Poldi swept him hastily past Frau Schreier. Fortunately, there was no one out in the courtyard. They were about to start up their entry when Karl's mother hurried up behind them and called:

"Thanks for everything, Fräulein Poldi."

He wondered what Poldi had done that Frau Breitner had to thank her. Perhaps he would find out later—in the meantime, he had to face *her!*

It was less difficult than he had feared. Poldi opened the door into the flat and said: "Well, here we are."

She had been dusting the mirror over the washstand. She stopped for a minute with the dustcloth held over her stomach and looked at him with hooded eyes. Then she went on dusting again. He wondered whether it was only part of the strangeness everything about the flat had in his eyes, or whether she was really at a loss for something to say. He had a curious feeling that he no longer belonged here. He had taken off his cap and stood holding it in his hand. A sort of shyness constrained him. He did not know what to do next, until Poldi said:

"Don't stand there like a dummy! Get that silly rucksack off your back."

He took off his rucksack then and laid it on the chair by the sewing machine.

She had finally found her tongue. "First it's taking money, then it's running away and having to be brought back by the police—only God knows what's in store for us next."

"Nothing's in store for us," Poldi said testily.

"That's what you've been saying ever since—"

"Not now, Mother! You better get him into bed right away!"

"Into bed!" He was puzzled. Was that how they were going to punish him?

"The divan's made up for him."

"All right, in you get! And don't act as if this were the first time you'd ever been in this place!"

He went into the living room. A clean nightshirt was laid out on the divan. He took off his clothes and got under the covers. In the kitchen Poldi was saying: "I've got to have lunch right away, Mother. I have to get back to the office." Then Poldi went through the room with a quick, sidelong glance at him and stayed in Franz's room. He felt as if suspended in time and place. It was queer lying in bed like this, with the sun flooding the courtyard outside and the warm air coming in through the windows, billowing the lace curtains a little in front of the chest of drawers. He heard the voices of children down in the courtyard on their way back to school for the afternoon.

She came in with a steaming cup of tea and set it down on the corner of the big table. She noticed his glance at the tea:

"It won't bite you! It's nettle tea and you get it down while it's hot. All I need is to have you get sick because you have to run away and fall in the water!"

"All right, Mother!" Poldi called out. "He'll drink it."

While he sipped the hot tea, he reflected that there was a new authority in Poldi's voice which seemed determined to shield him from *her*. Then he wondered how they had found out about their falling into the water. He suddenly remembered how Karl's mother had thanked Poldi—that was it: Poldi must have gone to Zienau! . . .

She called Poldi to lunch out in the kitchen. A minute later she came to the divan with a plate of soup. Her serving him like this embarrassed him. He protested:

"I'm not sick. I'm all right."

She said gruffly: "You eat your soup. I'm not going to have you on my hands with pneumonia."

It was beef broth and much better than the thin soups they had been having. When he had finished it, she brought a plate with kale and boiled beef and potato dumplings. The large piece of meat and the fact that she had gone to the trouble of making dumplings which she knew he liked made the meal exceptional, festive. The realization troubled him. To fight off his momentary softness toward her, he told himself caustically: *I'm the prodigal son, until they're sure I'm not sick!*

Poldi came to the door of the living room with her hat already on. "You're to stay in bed and do what Mother says, do you hear?"

He finished eating and then slid down under the blanket. The divan felt cosy and familiar. He was suddenly drowsy. . . .

The sun still shone into the room when he awoke. The clock over the chest of drawers said half past four. The door to the kitchen was closed and he noticed that the plate was gone from the table. She must have come in while he was asleep. The purring of her sewing machine sounded discreet and pleasantly reassuring. He wondered whether she had not gone to Steinhof this afternoon because of him. Perhaps Franz had gone. . . .

The thought of Franz brought him up sharp. Was he, too, going to act as if he were sick, and wait with whatever he was going to do to him until afterward? But perhaps Franz was really going to send him to a reform school this time and that was why there had been so few recriminations—because it was all settled, and they felt a little guilty with the knowledge that he was going there.

His throat tickled and he had to cough. Almost at once her sewing machine stopped and he heard her push back her chair. She was moving around by the stove. A few minutes later she came in with another cup of tea. She set it down on the table and asked:

"Is your forehead hot?"

"No, it isn't."

Nevertheless, her hand reached out toward his forehead. It surprised him that her nearness irritated him hardly at all. Instead, an insinuating confidingness made him wait almost eagerly for the touch of her rough hand, made him feel just as he had felt when he had had an earache once when he had been very small and she had dripped warm oil into his ear with a spoon. Yet he could not help jerking his head a little when her fingers actually came down on his forehead. They stayed there for a little while, then the knuckly back of her hand felt his cheek. She did not say anything if he did have a fever, except:

"You drink your tea while it's hot!"

He hitched himself up on one elbow and started to sip the tea. She went back into the kitchen. When he had finished the tea, he lay back on the pillow and looked at the brass rings on the chest of drawers. It was pleasant to lie like this, absolved from all tension, his senses at peace in a cottony numbness. Even the thought of school in the morning seemed unimportant. It might have been the summer vacation years ago. . . .

He suddenly heard a step on the landing. It was only a quarter to five, early for Franz, yet it had to be he. Alarm crowded up in him. He heard the door being opened and Franz saying: "Hello, Mother." Franz did not ask whether he was home—that was understandable enough: Poldi had probably telephoned him. There was another minute while Franz told her about Father and then he came into the living room!

He struggled for an instant with the temptation to close his eyes and pretend that he was asleep, but the thought that that would be cowardly kept him from it. He braced himself and met Franz's eyes squarely. Franz, he saw, was not frowning at him, the way he had been doing ever since the night at the Verein. There was an unmistakable eagerness in the set of Franz's shoulders.

From sheer embarrassment at finding himself staring at Franz, he said:

"Hello, Franz."

He said it tentatively, shrinking in advance from the possibility that Franz might answer him coldly. But while Franz's "Hello!"

sounded preoccupied, it was not cold. Franz was still standing there. He said:

"So they caught you!"

Peter could not be sure, yet it had seemed as if there had been the briefest twinkle in Franz's blue eyes. Yes! There could no longer be any doubt about it: Franz was smiling. A hot surge of gratitude traveled through him.

"Yes. . . ."

"What on earth did you want in Zienau? That must be an awful hole. I was betting that you had at least gone to Almzell to look at the mountains. . . . Are you all right?"

"Yes, Franz." He looked away quickly because Franz's eyes made him feel suddenly foolish and hot again with happiness.

He was glad that Franz went on into his room.

Chapter Twenty-Six

THEIR attitude toward him had changed.

It was as if Franz without putting it into so many words admitted that they had been in the wrong. Franz's pale-golden eyebrows were always arched a trifle anxiously now when he greeted him or made some pointedly friendly remark, as if Franz felt penitent and afraid of a rebuff.

He no longer had to get up an hour earlier and go to church before school. On his second morning home, he was awakened by her grumbling: "As if it would hurt that boy to go to Mass in the morning. A boy—"

Poldi was by the washstand, brushing her hair.

"We've been all over that, Mother. He can go to church with you in the evening."

He was not waked again after that.

He had more freedom in other ways. Indeed, so marked was the watchful aloofness with which they surrounded him that he had the feeling at times of being only a visitor in the flat. Some intimate hold they had had over him was gone: he was no longer afraid of them. It was rather they now who seemed afraid, as if they had been frightened by his running away. The realization alternately flattered and embarrassed him, for he could not rid himself of the feeling that there was a certain impropriety in their sudden gingerly respect for him. In spite of his resolution to run away again at the first opportunity, the spectacle of this unexpected new state of things fascinated him. He told himself almost irritably while he pasted the map of Europe back in his school atlas: *Nobody said I had to go right away. I can go next week or the week after. . . .*

Going back to school had not been an ordeal at all. The boys in the class were under the impression that he had only been playing hooky and were full of admiration. He did not enlighten them. Sooner or later they would find out that he had run away and had been brought back, and then the teasing would start. Mostly to escape their bothersome questions he buried himself in schoolwork, but he was also aware of a sneaking sense of obligation to Poldi which prodded him to work. . . .

They had been having a special confirmation class twice a week ever since February. He had followed the instruction given them by a plump, young priest from St. Ulrich's without any interest because he had not felt that it concerned him. Confirmation was associated in his mind with rich godfathers and silver watches and a gay jaunt into the Prater afterward to ride on the merry-go-rounds all the rest of the day. There was no one they knew who would want to be his godfather and who had enough money to buy him a watch and hire a *Fiaker* for the whole day. Now, if they had been friendly with Aunt Wetti's husband, or even with Herr Gregor! . . . As it was, they were almost sure to put off his confirmation until the following year. Franz would probably be his godfather then, and everything about it would be cramped and shabby—not because Franz liked to do things that way, but because she would have her say about it. Only, it didn't matter what they planned for next year! He was going to be far away by that time. . . .

Thus the paper they were given by the young priest to get signed at home was no more than a dead-end formality.

He handed the slip to Franz. But instead of signing it at once where it said NOT TO BE CONFIRMED THIS YEAR, as Peter had expected him to do, Franz put the slip on top of his billfold on the desk. He said:

"I'll have it for you tomorrow."

He was puzzled. Were they going to have him confirmed this year after all? But if Franz was going to be his godfather, why hadn't he signed the thing right away? It could only mean that they were still undecided and wanted to talk about it some more—only, there had been a settled abruptness in the way Franz had taken the slip, as if he had been expecting it. Was Franz perhaps going to see Aunt Wetti's husband after all? He could not subdue his curiosity.

The following evening Franz called to him from his room.

"It's there on the desk."

The slip was folded now. He picked it up and was about to take it out into the living room, when Franz stopped him:

"Aren't you going to look at it?"

His first glance at the signature stunned him like a blow on the chest. Scrawled over the word GODFATHER, in an aristocratically jagged hand, was "Baron Heinrich von Ortner."

Baron Ortner! Pleasantly dizzying pictures flashed through his head.

"It isn't everybody that can have a baron for a godfather, and a war hero at that!" Franz joked.

He managed to say: "Thank you, Franz."

"You probably won't ride in a *Fiaker* but Heinrich has his car."

Through the tremulous golden haze of his elation Peter was aware that Franz was pleased with himself. He felt an impulse to say something to show his appreciation to Franz, but he felt awkward and shy. He said finally:

"Are you coming, too?"

Franz gave him a grin. "Well, if you want me to. I don't know whether I can get off. . . ."

"Sure, I want you to," he said lamely.

"Well, we'll see. . . . And you better take my gray suit around to the tailor tomorrow; he thinks he can cut it down for you. If Father weren't ill, you would have had a new suit; as it is, I'm afraid my old gray one'll have to do. Next year perhaps, when Father is better again. . . ."

He was to have Franz's gray suit, the nice one! And Herr Feiertag was bound to make it look all right, not funny so that people could tell—but why was Franz giving up one of his favorite suits? He said uncomfortably: "Thank you, Franz."

"Don't thank me. Poldi is the one who is going to pay for it. It was too tight around the shoulders for me anyway. . . ."

A host of warm, exciting questions licked at him as soon as he had left Franz's room and had put away the precious slip in his catechism. Was Baron Ortner going to take him to lunch afterward? Would he perhaps even take him to the Prater? And would he wear his two medals and come for him in the big yellow staff car in which he had seen him once just after he had come back from the hospital in Budapest?

Baron Ortner was a captain now and he limped and carried an elegant yellow cane. He had been wounded somewhere in Serbia and he was a war hero—no need for Franz to tell him that. The limp and the two medals were proof enough. That one time Baron Ortner had stopped out in front of the house, half a dozen boys had gathered right away, and even the grownups had stared discreetly. . . .

It remained unbelievable right up to the morning when he was to be confirmed. Baron Ortner was to call for him at nine. But by a quarter past eight his ears had begun to strain for every noise that sounded like an automobile out in the street. He sat carefully forward on the edge of the divan so as not to wrinkle the new trousers. Behind him, she was making the beds. He had half expected one of her tight-lipped sermons on the meaning of confirmation, but she did not say anything. Only once, when the minute hand on the pendulum clock had at last crawled to a quarter to nine and he was about to take the two narcissus blossoms he was to wear in his buttonhole out of the vase, she turned around quickly and said: "You leave those flowers alone! I didn't put them in water to have them all wilted by the time you go."

The sound of strange footsteps on the landing drew his whole being into one anguished point. There was a preliminary shuffling of feet on their mat, a knock. She had already gone to the door. A bass voice was saying:

"The *Herr Baron* sends his compliments—is the young gentleman ready?"

It was all right! His fingers proved exasperatingly clumsy while he dried the stalks of the narcissus blossoms with a piece of tissue paper and fastened them in his buttonhole. He picked up his prayerbook and hurried into the kitchen. The man who had brought the message was waiting by the sewing machine; he saluted smartly and grinned. Where his army duster stood open at the collar, Peter saw the two little stars of a corporal. . . .

He forced himself to hold still while she dipped her finger into the miniature holy water basin on the wall beside the door and with her scratchy thumb made the sign of the cross on his forehead. Then at last he and the chauffeur were going down the stairs.

The huge yellow staff car was waiting in front of the house, and Baron Ortner sat smilingly erect in the tonneau with that urbane, deprecatory ease of bearing which had always seemed to Peter the most enviable part of his elegance. Baron Ortner gave an exuberant little wave with the handle of his cane. He was not, Peter saw with a twinge of disappointment, wearing his uniform and his medals; but he could hardly, he consoled himself, have looked more distinguished than he did in the beautifully tailored, dark-blue suit with the little spray of lilies-of-the-valley in his buttonhole. And the car doors bore the imperial coat of arms——

"Well, here we are!" Baron Ortner called. He held out his hand as Peter climbed into the car. "All set?"

"Yes, Baron Ortner." He felt a little shy sitting there beside him in the deep leather seat, but he was also exultantly aware that the grocer across the street had come out to look and that a handful of children were pointing and staring, and that Frau Schreier was smirking at him from the entranceway. He pretended not to see any of them as the car swung away from the curb.

As if Baron Ortner had guessed what he had been thinking only a minute before, he said: "I got special permission to wear mufti today—all in your honor. Now we can do all the merry-go-rounds in the Prater." His dark eyes flickered mischievously and the exciting news that they were going on to the Prater afterward took on the added glow of an escapade.

They turned into the Burggasse and passed several *Fiakers* with their lanterns and the horses' harness all trimmed with flowers. Baron Ortner flicked his cane to point to the horses——

"Pity we haven't any horses to festoon. Perhaps we ought to hire a couple and hitch them up to this old tub and do things in style, what do you think? How about that team of Pinzgauer over there?" Peter looked at the two ponderous draft horses lumbering along with a dray, and then he really had to laugh. "I'm afraid you'll have to bear with me," Baron Ortner was saying; "this is my first experience as a godfather. Now let me see: which one of us gets slapped? Is it you or me?"

"I do. . . ."

"Good! What I mean is—" and after they had both laughed: "And I have my hand on your right shoulder to show the bishop that he'd better not go too far, isn't that it? Yes, of course! It all comes back to me: I got biffed an awful one when I was confirmed. Good thing I have my stick——"

And again Peter had to laugh, first at the comical way Baron Ortner had grasped his stick and then because he felt himself swept along by Baron Ortner's high spirits. It was a glorious day, he told himself exuberantly as they turned into the Kärntnerstrasse. Only a few pert wisps of cloud floated in the brilliant blue of the sky. It was not going to rain! And it was wonderful to ride beside Baron Ortner like this.

Flags were flying from all the buildings on the Stephansplatz. The whole square was caught up in an exhilarating holiday mood. Mounted policemen in gala uniform were directing the long line of *Fiakers* and cabs that were waiting to pull up in front of the cathedral. They were slowly moving forward like the rest when one of the policemen spotted their car, saluted solemnly from his horse, and motioned the chauffeur to pull out of the line. Two more policemen saluted them on the way. A *Fiaker* which had been about to drive up to the main portal was imperiously waved back.

A surge of pride swelled in Peter at the attention they had aroused. One of the flower girls on the sidewalk when they got out sketched a pert curtsy—"Violets, *Herr General?*" Baron Ortner gave him a broad wink, but this time his pride in Baron Ortner made him slow to smile. Baron Ortner's limp seemed to him immensely distinguished as they entered the cool Gothic portal.

A young priest sent them to join the line of boys and their godfathers which extended already halfway down the nave. Facing them was a line of girls all in white which was steadily growing longer, too. Priests kept shuttling back and forth across the nave to squeeze more candidates into the lines. The organ was softly playing in the shadowy choir loft. Slowly the ceremony got under way. The archbishop with his train of priests was coming down the line of boys and then he was actually in front of him. But not even during the few awed seconds while the archbishop touched his forehead and then his cheek, did he lose the proud consciousness of Baron Ortner behind him. He felt a sense of loss when it was all over and Baron Ortner took his hand from his shoulder.

Then they were out in the sunshine among the cajoling cries of the flower girls, the cracking of the cabbies' whips, the jostling crowd of girls and boys. Baron Ortner was saying:

"Well, we're relatives now, you and I! What'll we do next? Franz said he couldn't get off until noon. . . . Hungry?"

"Oh, no—I'm not."

Baron Ortner's eyes lighted up mischievously. "Tell you what: let's go and pry Franz loose from his desk! Half an hour more or less can't make much difference in the conduct of the war."

A minute later they were back in the yellow car and rolling over the Ring.

"Here, before I forget . . ."

The flat package Baron Ortner handed him made him feel shy again. "Shall I open it?"

"Of course, you've got to open it! I have to know whether you like it or not; otherwise we'll go and exchange it right away."

He undid the paper around the green leather case and after a moment of hesitation snapped open the lid. Before him on the shimmering silk lining lay a thin silver watch.

"I hope it's still running!" Baron Ortner joked.

Peter raised it gingerly to his ear. "Yes—it's wonderful!"

"Then you don't want to change it?"

He knew that Baron Ortner was teasing him, but some of his alarm at the mere idea of parting with the watch crept into his voice: "Oh, no! . . . It's beautiful." He fought down his jubilance and tried to sound dignified: "Thank you very much, Baron—"

Baron Ortner brushed away his thanks. "Someday we'll go together and pick out a chain—ah, here we are!"

The two sentries presented arms as they drove into the courtyard of the War Ministry. Baron Ortner was out of the car before the chauffeur. "Only be a minute," he promised and limped toward the dark entry on the right.

Peter lifted the leather case to his ear. The ticking was almost inaudible. Then he opened the case to look again at the watch. It felt delightfully thin in his hand—Franz's watch was at least half again as thick. He turned it around to look at the back and saw that his initials—P. D.—were at the center of the engraved pattern. The discovery enchanted him. That made the watch really his! He held it up to his ear once more, then put it back into the leather case and sat holding it with both hands.

His anticipation of the afternoon was like a glowing, golden haze in which he was floating. Only a small, unimportant part of his brain registered: So this is where Franz works! The courtyard was rather somber. Three high-ranking officers, one of them a general, were getting out of a staff car, but he no longer had any time to watch them, for Franz and Baron Ortner were coming out of the entryway. Franz was striding half a step ahead and carrying his hat in his hand, swinging by his side, the way he did when he felt especially happy.

"What's that you've got there?" Franz asked as soon as he had got into the car.

"It's a watch."

"No! Let's see. . . ."

Franz whistled.

"Boy, just the kind of watch I've always wanted! You are going to lend that to me now and then, aren't you? When I go out somewhere. . . ."

"Don't you do it, Peter! He'll probably pawn it."

"Your nerve! Sit there and accuse me—what about my ruby tiepin in Budapest? I hope you haven't forgotten already that you were going to leave me that in your will?"

Baron Ortner chuckled with a kind of guilty complacency. "Those were very special circumstances, Franz."

"I can imagine—in a ballet skirt!"

Peter knew that they were talking about some girl, about something that must have happened while Baron Ortner had been in the hospital in Budapest. Bright, tantalizing fragments of their banter floated across and round him and formed an enthralling picture of their enviable grown-up world. He was glad that they kept talking across him, yet subtly including him in their talk, and even appealing for his opinion every once in a while, as at the entrance to the Prater when Baron Ortner turned to him:

"How about Reicher's for lunch?"

He could only nod. He had never even heard of Reicher's before. It was, he discovered presently, a restaurant that was all but hidden in a thick grove of trees. A small orchestra was playing on the veranda of the glass pavilion from which waiters kept hurrying out with loaded trays. A waiter murmured: ". . . *Ehre, Herr Baron,*" and then they were at one of the gay little tables with the graceful wicker chairs, and the waiter was handing them the menus and Baron Ortner was saying:

"Well, Peter, what do we eat? Franz and I are all ears!"

"And stomach—don't forget that," Franz joked.

It was a wonderful meal, not only because the food was so delicious that he found himself constantly torn between lingering over each mouthful and hurrying on to the next, but also because the passionate gratitude he felt toward Baron Ortner and Franz had widened to embrace everything else about the garden—the orchestra on the veranda, the people at the other tables, even the gray cat which prowled from table to table with its comically arched back. For they had all contributed to the festive progression from moment to moment which had culminated in this exquisite sense of well-being now while he watched Baron Ortner and Franz sip their yellow liqueur and talk about some opera called *Tristan*, and while he himself was finishing the last of his second cherry tart.

Franz's voice deepened suddenly as it always did when he was about to laugh. "She looks like an elephant in a nightgown and she certainly sings like one!"

Baron Ortner smiled. "You and my mother agree on that. You ought to get together. . . ."

"No, thank you, Heinrich. We tried that once!" They both laughed at Franz's emphasis. It was some joke they had between them, something to do with Franz's visit in Hungary the year before.

Baron Ortner had flicked open his cigarette case and was taking out a cigarette. Watching the suave movements of his slim, tanned hands, Peter was suddenly seized by an overwhelming desire to be like him. He saw as if for the first time Baron Ortner's lean, fine-featured face, with its dark eyes and the smooth brown hair lying low over his tanned forehead, and wished that by some miracle he would grow to look like that. The next instant he felt that he had somehow been disloyal to Franz. But he did not want to be like Franz! Compared to Baron Ortner, Franz was soft, slow, vulnerable—innocent. Yes, that was it: Franz was innocent. It was precisely that warm eagerness Franz brought to everything that made being with him so much fun. Only, for himself he wanted the knowing elegance of Baron Ortner. If he stayed—

The ambitious daydream just about to take shape was broken off abruptly. Baron Ortner was speaking to him:

". . . time we started doing the Prater, Peter, isn't it? Where'll we start?"

"The Ferris wheel, of course," Franz said. "Now, while the view is good. Besides, there's a tradition for doing these things. First the *Riesenrad*, then the merry-go-rounds and all the rest of it until we've worked up to the scenic railway."

"All right, then, let's be off. . . ."

But until they were out among the shining-faced crowds that thronged the avenues between the merry-go-rounds, and until Baron Ortner was actually sitting beside him in the madly whirling gondola, smiling at him and calling to Franz who was in the gondola behind them, Peter had not really believed that Baron Ortner had been serious about the merry-go-rounds. Even after the first half-dozen rides, he was still afraid that presently Baron Ortner and Franz would say: "You ride alone this time; we've had enough." Then he saw how groundless his fear had been. Baron Ortner and Franz were vying with each other in trying everything, so that he reached the Trench Exposition which they had left until last with the feeling that not one of the boys and girls around them could have done the Prater more thoroughly than he. And there was still more to come, for when they had seen the Exposition, Baron Ortner asked:

"Peter, now what? The Kobenzl—no, that wouldn't be any fun for you! I'll tell you what: we'll go back to Reicher's for dinner and to the circus afterward! That satisfactory?"

He could only give a happy nod. There was no way of telling Baron Ortner either then or later, as the wonderful evening wore on, that the joy of just being with him and Franz was infinitely more important than even the pleasure of going back to Reicher's once more and of seeing the circus afterward. . . .

It was after eleven when the yellow staff car pulled up in front of their house and Baron Ortner leaned out of the car to ask:

"Well, did I do it all right? I hope I wasn't too much of a disappointment as a godfather?"

He had to struggle against the surge of gratitude which threatened to block his throat. "Yes . . . thank you, Baron Ortner. It was—wonderful!"

Chapter Twenty-Seven

"It was wonderful!" he repeated to himself the following morning and often during the next few weeks. For the memory of the day with Baron Ortner remained more vivid than the present, or rather it had the power of instantly, magically, transmuting the present until he was no longer with her in the flat or sitting in school, but with Baron Ortner in the Prater again.

She had put away the green leather case in Father's desk. But in the afternoon when she had gone to Steinhof, he was free to get down the key to the desk from the top of the wardrobe and look at the watch. The same exultant, half-incredulous glow he had felt that day with Baron Ortner came rushing back to him as soon as he held it again in his hand. The slim, cool watch was at once a deliciously tangible proof that for one whole day he had really belonged to the world of Baron Ortner, and an exciting promise—he did not know exactly of what; he only knew that it had to do with a future in which he had become like Baron Ortner, utterly sure of himself and incisive and elegant, yet friendly and smiling, so that he always left the desk after he had put back the watch pleasantly troubled by a host of elusive ambitions.

He had been in Steinhof only once since he had come back. He realized that her not making him go every second day any more was Poldi's doing, although not a single word had been said about it. Poldi obviously felt that the trips to Steinhof were bad for him, but there was—he was sure of it—still another reason for Poldi's orders to her: Poldi had sensed how thoroughly he disliked the trips to Steinhof.

Slowly, a little reluctantly, he was forced to the conclusion that their new considerateness of him was to be permanent. Poldi and Franz made a point of no longer discussing things behind closed doors, and they never asked about his schoolwork now or insisted on knowing what books he read. The unaccustomed elbowroom made him almost uncomfortable at times, as did his own growing sense of obligation toward them. For quite apart from their greater friendliness, all three of them—first Franz, by getting Baron Ortner to be his godfather, then *she*, and then Poldi—managed in the course of the few weeks before the close of school to tie him to them by some intimate bond, so that he felt put on his honor and somehow trapped.

She came home from Steinhof one afternoon and Peter could see at once that she had been crying. Her shoulders under the faded black satin blouse looked stricken and old. There was something listless about the way she emptied her black reticule by the sewing machine; her hands moved with a weary automatism as if she had lost faith in the life line of familiar things.

He realized that this was different from the time when her whole body had been racked by choking sobs because Father was to be taken to Steinhof. He had not been touched then by her sobs; he had even taken a certain satisfaction in seeing her brought to grief. But now he felt strangely moved by her silent tears. He asked:

"What is it? What's happened, Mother?"

She reached for a folded pillow slip on the sewing machine while tears continued to roll down over her cheeks.

"Was Father worse?"

She tried to wipe the tears from her cheeks—"He said: 'Kathi, you did this to me! You let them take me to Steinhof!' As if I hadn't stood everything . . . all these years . . ."

"But Father will be better again. The doctors said so—after they operate."

"It's all over now," she said hopelessly.

He felt helpless in the face of her grief. Her fingers pulled and picked at the pillow slip. Insincerely, and yet sincere in his desire to do something to comfort her, he said: "God will make him get better again."

He was able to gauge the full depth of her despair when she ignored his remark and failed to clutch at one of her pious formulas:

"After twenty years of being married to him—I'll hear those words until my dying day! If only the children don't hear about this . . ."

That evening when Poldi and Franz came home, he saw how determined she was not to let them guess what had caused her swollen eyes and the inflamed network of tiny veins in her cheeks. She let them infer that Father had been much worse, rather than tell them what Father had really said.

The consciousness of having seen her stripped of all her defenses and of sharing a secret with her which had to be kept from Poldi and Franz, left him with a confused sense of power and sympathy. It was the first time that he had ever thought of her as something other than an antagonist. Yet enough of his former resentment remained to make him annoyed that at the very moment when he was for the first time stronger than she, she should also have gained a hold on him that made it impossible to hurt her. Almost against his will, he offered to go to Steinhof the next afternoon in her place. . . .

Poldi's claim on his loyalty was much more agreeable.

Poldi's birthday fell only a few days before the close of school. Presents for her had been coming all morning, and there was quite a sizable array of packages when she came home at noon. The presents were mostly from her friends in the congregation, but there was one package that was not from a girl: the bunch of red roses that had been delivered along with it proved that it was from Herr Schmidtmeyer. He noticed that Poldi shoved it to one side and opened it last of all. It contained a black lacquer box which was filled with expensive chocolates. Once he had seen and smelled the chocolates, he could not keep his mind off the box. He knew that Poldi would offer him some after lunch, but he was not prepared for the abrupt gesture with which she lifted out the whole top tray and said:

"Here—and don't eat them all at once!"

Her brusque generosity left him breathless. Chocolates had become very rare even in the windows of the most fashionable confectionery shops, and since Poldi was sure to give away a lot more from what she had left, she had actually given him more than she would have herself. And the candy was bound to have a special significance since it had come from Herr Schmidtmeyer.

He had not been able to figure out whether Poldi liked Herr Schmidtmeyer or not. Herr Schmidtmeyer was plump and awkward and he was always knocking against furniture and then blushing furiously and apologizing. Everything about him was somehow ludicrous because of his self-effacing gentleness, so that even Franz and all his other friends were always making fun of him. On the other hand, he was not ugly, as Poldi had once said. His naïve, round face had a disconcerting dignity which made one feel suddenly guilty at the very moment one was about to laugh at him. And it was also true that Herr Schmidtmeyer was a brilliant musician who had composed a quartet which had been performed in the Konzerthaus last fall, and that he was already a full professor in the *Gymnasium*.

Herr Schmidtmeyer's attentions to Poldi dated from the time when Franz had gone to stay with him because of Father's scenes at night. Since then, Herr Schmidtmeyer had been sending Poldi tickets for the theater and the opera almost every week. Sometimes Poldi and Fräulein Gisl had used the tickets, but usually Poldi had given them to somebody else. Only once had she actually gone out with him and then it had been a large opera party and Franz had been along. Yet lately, even though Poldi had turned down all of Herr Schmidtmeyer's invitations point blank because Father was in Steinhof, she had been much less inclined to sniff scornfully when Franz teased her about him. Peter was almost certain that Poldi had not given him all those chocolates because she disliked Herr Schmidtmeyer. . . .

School closed and he got his final report. It was as bad as he had expected, but for once he was not worried about taking it home. Franz and Poldi must have known all along how bad his marks were going to be; the tacit understanding seemed to be to let bygones be bygones and that he was to make a new start next fall; and seen in that light, the report card was even a blessing, for his bad deportment mark had—quite inexplicably and contrary to all expectations—caused him to be transferred to the better school in the Ziegelgasse for next year.

The prospect of getting away from Jerabek and from the gloomy school in the Neubaugasse filled him with joy. If only now he could get away from the house in the Schottenfeldgasse as well, if only they moved somewhere else, as Poldi had recently hinted a number of times! For the certainty of seeing people who knew all about his running away and all about Father, every time he went in or out of the house, had come to torture him. That Poldi and Franz suffered from people's inquisitiveness about Father he knew without words.

His heart pounded with excitement when Poldi announced one noon that she had found an apartment. He realized that the airy calm with which Poldi spoke was aimed at overriding her inevitable opposition to anything new.

"It's one of the new houses on the Schmeltz," Poldi said. "I telephoned Franz about it. He's going to look at it this afternoon. There are three big rooms and a bath and a huge kitchen, and there's gas and electricity, so you won't have to bother with filling lamps any more. Just wait until you see the kitchen! It—"

"If you think you can get me away from here after all these years, you can think again!" she broke in ominously.

"And if you think I'm going to go on sleeping on a divan all my life, you're mistaken, too!"

"You can move if you like. There's nobody stopping you. I'm staying right here!"

The battle was on. It lasted all through lunch. But when he came home from Steinhof that afternoon, she put on one of her small, frumpy hats and put the paper with the address into her handbag. It was a full hour before the time they usually started for church. They found the house quite easily. It was one of the houses, facing on the square with the oval-shaped park, which had still been boarded up in the winter. He looked guiltily toward the street which led to the house Jerabek and he had broken into, and his first glance as they entered the house went to the brass fittings. They were all there! Everything about the house was shining and new. It had a handsome entranceway and the apartment was lovely. He could see that in spite of her grudging remarks to the janitor she was impressed by it, too.

Yet that evening and for a whole week the fight at home went on. Only, he realized with secret elation that for her it was a losing fight. The new authority Poldi had gained in the last few months was bound to carry the day. Poldi had had her way about how he was to be treated since he had run away and in the matter of having Father transferred to the sanitarium from the public asylum. And Poldi had been promoted again and held a man's job in the bank where she worked, a rather important job, it seemed. At any rate, Poldi was earning more money than Franz and was carrying the bulk of the household expenses now. But more important than any of these was the fact that *her* former tight-lipped assurance had somehow been cracked. And to weaken her still further in her battle against moving, Franz was on Poldi's side. Not that Franz argued about it: it was typical of Franz that he tried to cajole her with the prospect that on the Schmeltz she would be closer to Father in Steinhof and that there was a fine church within a few minutes' walk.

They moved on the last day of July. There were more arguments about the furniture. Poldi tried to have some pieces which she had long detested left behind. But *she* fought like a tigress over each piece—"That chest of drawers we had before you were born! If you're so grand . . ." In the end she consented to get rid of the old box bed in the kitchen and of a few other odds and ends, but the chest of drawers and the rickety chair by the sewing machine were loaded into the moving van.

He loved the new apartment. Even their familiar furniture took on something of the brightness of the new rooms, and Poldi was threatening to buy all sorts of new things. She had already bought a handsome desk and a bookcase and a modern couch for her own room, so that *she* was constantly making grim prophecies about Poldi's extravagance.

And he was proud of their house. The people he encountered on the staircase were much better dressed than their neighbors in the Schottenfeldgasse had been, and much more interesting. He discovered that the man above them owned the big machine shop which manufactured precision instruments for the army and which took up the entire basement of a house just beyond the square. And the lady in the apartment adjoining theirs had a daughter married in Holland and had only just returned from a visit to her.

The days began to pass pleasantly. He was free to go out and play soccer with some boys whom he had got to know. He was, in fact, free to go anywhere during the day, as long as he stood in line for her at the stores when she needed him. But even that was less of a burden than it had been. Such staples as flour and lard and sugar were regulated now by rationing cards; the lines in front of the stores were rarely very long.

Every second afternoon he went to see Father. He had taken to going regularly again ever since the afternoon when she had come home crying from Steinhof. He minded the trips much less, partly because the doctors were increasingly optimistic to Franz, and partly because Father seemed much better already. What was even more important: they did not have to sit in the oppressive lounge now that the weather was fine. They went for walks in the park, and except for occasional spells of boredom when Father decided to sit down on a bench to read the newspaper, he hardly minded the hours inside the walls of Steinhof.

The rest of the time he read. Poldi was bringing him books from the library again, and Franz had suddenly given him permission to read anything in his bookcase that interested him. Only occasionally he remembered the choir, and then he always brushed aside the thought of Herr Granini and the excursions and told himself that this was the happiest summer he had ever known. For there was not only his new freedom now, but also the constant possibility of seeing Baron Ortner. Several times already Baron Ortner had come to call for Franz and then he had always stopped for a few priceless minutes to talk to him.

A certain tentativeness adhered like a bloom to the long, lazy summer days. He was grateful for Franz's friendliness, but he was also conscious of a mutual uneasiness which had remained between them like a glass wall. But of Franz's good intentions there could be no doubt. Franz was always throwing out unexpected little suggestions of things for him to do. He would say: "There's a garden fete in the Augarten tomorrow. It's for the benefit of the Red Cross and all the army bigwigs'll be there. I can't go myself, but if you're interested, here's my ticket. . . ." Or he would say: "I passed by the new swimming pool in Ottakring today. It's open for boys every morning. Mother will give you the money, if you'd like to go. . . ."

It was in the same groping, deprecatory way that Franz said one evening: "I'm starting on my vacation Saturday. It's only up into the Wachau. How would you like to come along?"

For a moment he doubted his ears. Franz's vacations had always seemed so important and so glamorous, precisely because Franz went to some fascinating place far away from home, lived completely apart from anything connected with them, became almost a stranger.

Yet now Franz was offering to sacrifice that apartness which was the very essence of his vacation.

He asked, stupidly, he realized: "Who, I?"

"Heinrich has a shooting lodge up there. It's part of his estate up on the Danube. He offered it to me for the two weeks."

"Is Baron Ortner coming, too?"

"He may come up later. It all depends on whether he can get away." Franz stopped to grin at him for a second, then warned: "This won't be like going to Almzell, you know. It's only three hours or so on the train, and there aren't any high mountains. But there are woods and we'll be in the country. . . . Mother will get your things ready along with mine. . . ."

It was as simple as that. Saturday afternoon they were on the train, and by six they had arrived at the little station where the caretaker was waiting for them with a quaint wagonette with a tasseled white and yellow striped canvas top. The blunt-shouldered caretaker in the green *Loden* suit had raised his hat with a provincial flourish and seemed delighted to see Franz. That was understandable enough, for Franz had chuckled reminiscently when he had explained on the train:

"I should say I've been there before. Heinrich and I used to go there all the time during our last year in the *Gymnasium*. We imagined we could study better there—that's how we both almost flunked out and how I lost the scholarship I had."

And Franz had also explained about the hunting lodge:

"Heinrich happens to be very fond of it because his father used to stay there a lot. Heinrich's father liked to hunt and he wrote poetry and liked the solitude. When his father died, Heinrich got the lodge, although he was only about your age then. He didn't get the rest of the estate, of course, until he was twenty-one. . . ."

There was an "estate"—but was there a castle, too? Peter was consumed by curiosity as the wagonette drove through the summer-drowsy little town and turned through a gate into a private park. He had not liked to ask Franz, from a perverse desire to keep his anticipation deliciously intact. . . . Minutes more of driving through the dusky avenue, then he saw something shimmering white through the trees, red tiles on a roof—a long two-story building with turrets at the corners and a stone coat of arms set above an imposing double door! Not one of those ancient castles he had seen illustrated in books: but beyond all doubt a *Schloss!*

Franz gave him a quick smile as if he had guessed his joy. The caretaker was saying from his box up front:

"We've been airing the second story this week. But I don't think anybody will be coming this year. It's five years since the *Frau Baronin* came from Hungary, and when the *Herr Baron* comes, he always stays at the lodge." There was a note of grievance in his voice.

They passed the balustrades and the steps that led up to the massive double door, then the end of the building and a terraced lawn, and then they were in the dusk of trees again. Instead of the sanded avenue, there was only a simple forest road. Bushes brushed against the wagonette. They rode a long time like that, it seemed to Peter, before they stopped. For a moment he did not make out the dark, square lodge against the trees. It was much bigger than Franz had led him to expect. He got down eagerly to follow Franz. There was a long sitting room with a freestone fireplace, and antlers everywhere on the walls, and there were at least three other rooms. The beds in two of them were made up: he was going to have a room all to himself!

In the sitting room, the caretaker was telling Franz about the lamps and asking when his wife was to come in the morning to fix breakfast for them. Then the caretaker left, and they were alone in the lodge.

"Well, how do you like it?" Franz asked.

"It's beautiful, Franz."

"Let's get unpacked and then we'll go down to the inn. We could have had Frau Scheffl cook dinner for us, too, but I thought it would be more fun if we went to the inn at night. It's what Heinrich and I always did."

He loved the walk through the park down to the little town, and back again to the lodge with Franz. Already it was as if he were attached by a hundred bonds to everything he had seen since they had first driven through the iron gate, and lying in the unaccustomed bed that night and listening to the dark whispering of the trees, he felt a hot surge of gratitude to Franz. . . .

The next day was typical of all the rest. Franz called from his room and defied him to be the first to get dressed. It was only half past six, but the caretaker's wife was already there. They had breakfast in the big room where all the antlers were, and then they set off through the woods to climb one of the neighboring hills. They climbed a different one each day, until he felt that he knew the country for miles around almost as well as Franz did. For lunch they ate the sandwiches Frau Scheffl had fixed and afterward they lay in the grass and talked. On the way home, they nearly always sang and Franz taught him dozens of the gay student songs he had always wanted to know. When they did not sing, Franz talked about his student days, or about Herr Granini's parties or about Baron Ortner. They hardly ever mentioned home. In the evening there was the stroll through the park, and when they came back to the lodge, Franz lighted the lamps and they read until it was time to go to bed. It was an enchanted round.

But on the fifth day it rained. It was too wet to go tramping through the woods. They sat in the lodge until twelve, then Franz said:

"Let's go down to the inn and get something hot for lunch. We can't sit indoors all day. And on the way back, we might ask Herr Scheffl to show you the inside of the *Schloss*. You've been wanting to see it. . . ."

The caretaker was eager to show off the castle. He hurried ahead of them from room to room to pull up blinds and push open shutters. The rooms had an air of waiting to be waked from sleep. Dust covers lay over most of the furniture, rugs were rolled up against the walls, dust bags hid the chandeliers. Only the pictures in the stately gold frames had been allowed to go unshrouded and looked slyly alert.

Ballroom, little salon, blue salon, library—Peter tore himself reluctantly from each room. The gracious, faintly outmoded, and yet somehow imperturble elegance of everything made him want to linger for hours yet when they reached the conservatory in the rear. . . .

"Well, now you have seen it," Franz said when they were out again in the park; "different from our little apartment on the Schmeltz, isn't it?"

"It's beautiful."

"You ought to see their place in Hungary!"

"Is it nicer than this? It couldn't be, Franz!"

"I don't know whether it's nicer or not, but it's huge. The castle here would just about fit into one wing of it. And the estate is so big that you have to ride all day to get from one end to the other."

"Baron Ortner must be awfully rich!"

Franz grinned. "Well, he isn't exactly poor. The place in Hungary doesn't belong to Heinrich, of course—that belongs to his uncle, the one I said was a general."

"But you said that Baron Ortner's mother was there all the time?"

"There—I should say she was! She runs it, too!"

"But why doesn't she ever stay here?" It seemed inconceivable to him that anyone should prefer even a huge estate in Hungary to the mellow charm of the *Schloss* he had just seen. If he had had the chance, he would be here all the time! Of course, Baron Ortner and his mother were different: everybody knew that people like that spent the winter in Vienna and went to the opera and to balls, but now, during the summer . . .

"Well, for one thing," Franz was saying, "the estate in Hungary is where she grew up; and for another, I don't think she ever liked it here. One of the few times Heinrich's mother ever condescended to speak to me, she told me that she felt 'cramped' up here in the woods. I imagine what she really meant was that all this was on too humble a scale for her. You'd have to understand about those Hungarian aristocrats and their enormous estates: they're not only very wealthy, but very haughty, too, and Heinrich's mother's family has one of those old titles you see mentioned in history books. Heinrich told me one time what a to-do there was when his mother fell in love with a poor little Austrian baron and insisted on marrying him. Well, when Heinrich's father died, his mother simply reverted to type and became the great Hungarian lady again."

The corners of Franz's eyes crinkled with secret amusement at something. Peter urged:

"What, Franz?"

"I was just thinking of all the trouble she went to last year when I was visiting there to put me in my place. It's always irritated her that Heinrich should have a mere nobody like me for a friend."

"What did she do?"

Franz chuckled. "Everything—everything she could think of. For instance, she'd put me next to the tutor for dinner, with a stone-deaf old countess on the other side, because she thought that would humiliate me."

"Whose tutor, Franz?"

"Heinrich has a younger sister, haven't I told you? . . . Well, being next to the tutor didn't distress me in the least because he was an extremely interesting Dane who had been all over the world. And as for the old aunt, the one who was deaf, she and I got along like a house afire! She'd shout some question at me and I'd write out the answer on a scratch-pad she always carried with her, but most of her questions didn't call for an answer anyway—they were really caustic remarks about somebody at the table she disliked, made at the top of her lungs. She was a holy terror, that old countess!"

"What else did she do?"

"Heinrich's mother? Well, she'd always start to talk in French when I came into a room and when Heinrich wasn't there; at least, she did until she found out that I knew enough French to follow a conversation anyway! After that, she tried English and that was funny, too, because she didn't know it very well herself and her foreign cousins had to ask her to say everything three or four times."

"But didn't you mind?"

"I?" Franz raised his eyebrows and laughed. "No, I enjoyed it enormously!"

Even though he could not help laughing, Peter felt suddenly critical of Franz. He knew with a defiant tightening in his jaw that in Franz's place he could not have borne being snubbed. The more he thought about it, the more humiliating it seemed. Yes, he would have been twice as haughty as Baron Ortner's mother, and he would have left at once. Yet Franz talked about it as if it had been a huge joke.

For a minute he nursed a guilty feeling of superiority over Franz, then the feeling became blurred by his eagerness to find out more about the estate. He listened greedily to Franz's deep, warm voice.

Before his eyes there arose a picture of an enormous house with so many rooms that you lost your way in the corridors; a house dominated by an imperious, haughty woman who was Baron Ortner's mother; of guests who were first cousins and second cousins and who came from every part of Europe—"because a family like that has relatives everywhere, even in the countries we're at war with now"; of servants and peasants in picturesque Hungarian costumes dancing at some kind of feast on the lawn. . . . But subtly threading through the picture, like a constantly shifting, exotic focus which left a trail of color everywhere, was the figure of Baron Ortner's sister. Her name was Bianca, he found—a strange, foreign-sounding name at first, a name which was Italian, Franz said, so that he was reminded of Herr Granini and all sorts of dreamy things, but a name too which somehow fitted the dark, self-willed girl who rode horses bareback and hunted like a man.

Once Franz had spoken of her, he waited impatiently for her name to reoccur in Franz's talk. For a long while he was left wondering how old she was, for he did not like to ask; then he discovered that she was sixteen. *Only three years older than I!* he told himself exultantly. It puzzled him a little how hard he found himself thinking of Bianca and straining to see her with his mind's eye. His questions became at once warier and more bold. Franz did not seem to notice it; he talked of her indulgently, humorously, yet with a lingering tenderness that was a little like his own.

More even than Baron Ortner, Bianca brought him close to Franz. Their tramps through the woods, the hours they spent lying on the grass, the evenings in the lodge—every minute now shimmered with the joyful possibility that Franz might speak of Hungary again or that he himself might think of some innocent-sounding question which would not, however, deceive Franz. Something in Franz's eyes showed that he was aware of his tremulous delight when they were talking of anything even remotely connected with her. And in the place of the awkward, slightly distrustful reserve which had been between them when they had first arrived, there had come a shy, new intimacy of whose delicate balance they were both aware and which they were equally careful not to disturb.

In a way, Peter told himself on their next to last day at the lodge, *this is nicer than it's ever been before. Franz treats me like an adult now. . . .*

Then their last day had come. They were having lunch at the inn. The caretaker had already taken their things to the station and had checked them there. Franz suddenly faced him across the table and asked:

"Have you ever thought what you would like to be? This is going to be your last year in school. Next year you'll be fourteen."

The question took him by surprise. It was the first time that Franz had mentioned school in the entire two weeks.

He said: "No . . . I don't know, Franz."

"Well, you're always drawing. You ought to pick something where you can use your talent for that. Perhaps—have you ever thought of becoming an artist? You know, your father was one!"

Franz had spoken lightly, but there was an overearnest insistence in his eyes that made Peter shrink. Why did Franz have to have that guilty air of raking up a mystery? Did he think he didn't know, or that he cared! But all the same the memory of the day when he had opened Father's desk and of the visit to Aunt Wetti made him wince. More to keep Franz from saying anything further about "your father" in that probing, queasy tone than because he really meant it, he said:

"I want to do something that has to do with machines."

"I guess that's drawing of a kind, of course." Franz sounded a little disappointed and not quite convinced. "In that case, you'll have to go to a technical school. The thing for you to do will be to transfer to the *Realschule* next year. But you'll have to have exceptionally good marks for that. Even so, you'll probably lose a year. Not that that matters so much; a lot of boys lose a year along the way because they've been sick. . . . Of course, the chances are that by next summer the war'll be over and then your mother'll come and take you to America where the schools are quite different anyway."

The prospect of Mizzi coming for him, now that he had found Bianca and Baron Ortner, irritated him.

"I don't want to go to America."

"You'll want to go all right when Mizzi comes. Just think of all the interesting things you're going to see!"

"You wouldn't go to America!"

"But that's quite different. There is no reason for me to go. All my friends are here and I have some sort of a career ahead of me, while you have your mother in America and your little brother and sister, and a stepfather who sounds extremely nice. And your family is well off. They'll be able to give you a good education, which we can't. You see how cramped we are for every heller with Father sick—besides, I should think you'd have had enough of the food we've been eating all winter. In America there'll be lots to eat. Just think of it: cakes and tarts and all the butter you want!"

There! Peter all but said it out loud. Of course, Franz would not go! He knew precisely how Franz felt about America: it was a new country and rough and there were all sorts of fascinating things, especially machines, but it was nothing like Vienna, and the only people who ever went there were engineers and poor people from the provinces who hoped to get rich. No, he wanted to stay, now that everything had changed!

Franz was talking about school again:

"You'll have new teachers in the Ziegelgasse. There's no reason why you shouldn't turn over a new leaf."

He said, "Yes, Franz," and realized that he sounded merely polite. The contrast between the way he had sounded and his sudden knowledge that he was going to work so hard that it would take Franz's breath away exhilarated him. He realized that his restlessness during the last few days whenever he had thought of Bianca and of Baron Ortner had merely been another form of the passionate desire to excel which seized him now. He was suddenly impatient to get back to Vienna and to the new school—Franz had no idea of what he could do!

Chapter Twenty-Eight

It was a long walk from where they were living now to the Ziegelgasse. He had to leave the house in the morning at an hour when other boys were just getting up, and at noon there was only enough time to bolt his lunch before he had to start back again to school. Yet he did not mind the distance; it became part of the challenge the new school in the Ziegelgasse represented to him.

He had been put into the fastest section of his year. The thirty boys in the class came mostly from within a few blocks of the school, from what had been his own neighborhood before they had moved, but apart from two of the boys he did not know any of them. They were tradesmen's sons or their fathers were skilled craftsmen or minor executives, and they all bore an unmistakable stamp of coming from just such comfortable, easygoing, middle-class homes. They looked well fed, confident, and at ease in school. It was this last which struck him most after the two years in the fractious, teacher-hating atmosphere in the other school. These boys were almost without exception eager to get good marks; they talked already about the various technical and commercial schools to which they expected to be admitted the following year.

There were several cliques in the class. One group—the largest, and the one which included the most prosperous boys—was usually clustered around the window in the rear from which one had a full view of the windows of the girls' school next door. The boys talked knowingly about the theater and about the latest musical comedies; they smoked and read novels of the sort Poldi would have taken away from him at once; and they generally affected an airy sophistication which reached a climax every afternoon at four when they flirted with the girls on the way home from school. Another group was made up of half a dozen soccer enthusiasts who either discussed the games their own team was going to play or wrangled endlessly over the comparative merits of the professional teams. Four other boys were inseparable because of their passion for airplanes and the little models they made. . . .

Drawn though he felt to each one of the groups, he stayed away from them all and kept to his desk during the breaks between classes, partly from a feeling of newness, but mostly from fear of becoming involved and thus jeopardizing his plans.

He had thrown himself into work from the very first day. Each task was a hulking antagonist to be assaulted and overcome. He had worked so little in the past year and he had been in such a slow class that he was far behind in nearly everything. It was not going to be easy to catch up. And there was the suspicion with which the teachers looked on him because he had been expelled from the other school: it was going to be even harder to overcome that.

But the handicaps only stiffened his determination. He spent hours on even the simplest exercises because he realized that nothing short of absolute perfection was going to satisfy him. He memorized everything, and he got into the habit of carrying an open book or lists of dates or French verbs to study on the way to school across the Schmeltz.

Little by little, he saw the vigilance in the teachers' eyes give way to something like interest. A few of them even began to encourage him. He liked almost all the teachers they had in class. Unlike the testy old men and the young substitutes he had been used to in the Neubaugasse, these men were even-tempered and friendly but alert. It was fun to fight their prejudice against him and to give the lie to the marks from the other school. But above all, it was the man they had for drawing and French whom he was most anxious to convince.

Herr Heitvogt was like no other teacher he had ever known. He was a big man, inches taller even than Franz and at least twice as heavy, but the impressiveness of his great bulk was rendered curiously appealing and intimate by the eager forward tilt of his lively, round face and the grotesque thickness of his spectacles. He was nearly blind. To correct their drawings he had to bend down until his nose almost touched the drawing board. If any boy had chosen to read a novel quite openly on his desk, Herr Heitvogt would not have detected it—yet no one did.

It surprised Peter at first. His first impression of Herr Heitvogt had been that here was an easy mark for all the schoolboy pranks he remembered from the other school. Then he became aware of the pleasant expectancy that always stole over the room when Herr Heitvogt came in. Arguments that had seemed important only a minute ago dwindled and died even before the class began, and presently Peter saw the reason for it: Herr Heitvogt was interesting! At almost any time he might start to talk about Paris or Italy or about the war—familiarly, seriously, enthrallingly—as if they had been adults like himself. But even when they were only translating sentences from the French and Herr Heitvogt sat silently listening at his desk, his presence there gave an exciting sense of completeness to the room and to the minutes as they passed. It was more like being with Herr Granini just before a choir rehearsal again than being in school.

He discovered that Herr Heitvogt had lived in Paris for many years and that he had been an artist before his eyes became so weak that he could no longer paint. It astonished him how much all the boys knew about him; but what surprised him even more was the informality with which boys—and not only the ones who got good marks—went up to Herr Heitvogt's desk before or after class and talked to him. He watched them enviously and wondered how long it would be before he would feel free to go up and talk to him like that. It was still another incentive for him to work.

By the end of October he ranked somewhere in the upper half of the class. But there were at least ten boys still ahead of him. Stubbornly he redoubled his efforts to get nearer to the top. Then something happened that encouraged him even more than good marks: Herr Heitvogt singled him out for a special assignment in drawing class.

They had been making drawings of chrysanthemums, which they were to tint with water color afterward. Peter had just finished his drawing and he was about to get out his water-color box when Herr Heitvogt got to him. Herr Heitvogt picked up his drawing board and as usual held it within a few inches of his eyes. When he put it down, he said:

"Don't color this, Domanig. I want you to try something different. Get a new sheet of paper and try painting the chrysanthemum without making a drawing first. Just take a fine brush and use it like a pencil for the outlines. . . ."

Herr Heitvogt had already turned to the next boy. Hastily Peter got out a fresh sheet and set to work. If he could finish the sketch before the end of class, he would be able to go up to Herr Heitvogt and show it to him. He worked along feverishly. But the bell rang before he had done much more than sketch in the flower and paint three or four petals in front and on one side. He felt angry with himself for muffing an opportunity to get closer to Herr Heitvogt; now it might be weeks before he might have another chance. . . . He was about to go to the sink to wash out his brushes, when Herr Heitvogt came to his table and pulled up a chair. Herr Heitvogt had tilted up the sketch to examine it.

"Not bad," he said. "The shape is there, and you saw that the tips of the petals are paler than the rest. But now look at this—" Herr Heitvogt had taken out a pencil and was pointing to one of the lower petals on the chrysanthemum in the vase—"what color is that?"

"It's brown."

"Look again!"

Peter hesitated. "I guess it's really orange there. . . ."

"Certainly it's orange, and there's a good deal of red in it—that's because you have a warm shadow there. You missed that, and you haven't got the highlights—here—and here! Those petals are nearly white—can you see? But not bad for a first try." Herr Heitvogt slipped his pencil back into his breast pocket. He seemed to have said all he was going to say, but just when Peter thought that he was about to slide back his chair and get up, Herr Heitvogt turned to him once more and asked:

"Do you like to draw?"

The momentousness which lay hidden somewhere in Herr Heitvogt's question disconcerted him. The gleaming slabs of crystal in Herr Heitvogt's spectacles, through which his eyes looked alarmingly small and helpless but also very kindly and alive, had become monitors warning him that they would shrewdly assay whatever he answered now.

He felt again as he had done when Franz had talked so seriously about his drawing: a little embarrassed and guilty somehow. How could he explain, he wondered uneasily, how he felt about drawing when he had never even stopped to think about it. In the past, when he had drawn caricatures, it had always been because some stress in him had been relieved by what his hand and the pencil had done. It had been as natural at those times as the urge to sing or whistle when he was gay. But "like it"! He knew what he liked: soccer, for instance, and playing with any kind of machine. . . . Yet Franz and now Herr Heitvogt obviously saw something important in the ease with which he drew. Perhaps that was all Herr Heitvogt meant when he asked whether he liked to draw. He said:

"Yes, I think I do."

"Has anyone been helping you at home—been giving you lessons, I mean?"

"No, Herr Heitvogt."

"I have been watching your work. You should have lessons now. I am here on three afternoons a week with the rationing commission next door. I could just as well give you some lessons then. Would you like that?"

He saw only the distinction it would give him in the eyes of the other boys to be taught all alone by Herr Heitvogt after school. Even the other teachers might hear of it. He said quickly:

"Yes, I—"

"Good. You will have to bring me a written consent from home. We'll see how it works out. . . ."

That evening at supper he told Poldi and Franz. Franz, especially, seemed pleased; he sat down immediately after supper to write Herr Heitvogt a note.

The lessons started the very next day. After the last class in the afternoon, Herr Heitvogt took him to the drafting room and made him sit at one of the tables up front. He brought a new pad of drawing paper out of the supplies closet and put it on the table for him, then his eyes wandered undecidedly over the plaster casts on the shelf along the wall. In one of the corners up front stood a cast of a life-size male figure—Herr Heitvogt pointed to it.

"Do you know that? That's the 'David' of Michelangelo. You won't be able to do much with it at first, but try it anyway. Draw it just as you see it from here. I'll be back after a while to see how you are getting along."

Then he was alone in the big room. Through the closed door came the muffled voices of the last of the boys hurrying out through the corridors. The gas lamps overhead purred lazily. He picked up his pencil and looked at the cast. The white plaster of Paris figure had taken on an air of bland arrogance which seemed to defy him to penetrate its complexity. The longer he looked, the more difficult it appeared to him to draw.

He found himself reaching for the eraser after almost every line. This, he realized suddenly, was not only different, but infinitely more difficult than letting his hand run on in the little caricatures he had always thought of as drawing before. Even the pencil no longer felt natural between his fingers and seemed to have developed a perverse will of its own which was set on foiling him. What he finally got down on paper after an hour of work was a labored, wooden drawing which looked as if he had done it years ago, when he was still in grammar school. Yet when he tried to improve a line here and there, he seemed only to be making it worse.

He was about to rip off the sheet and start all over again when Herr Heitvogt opened the door.

"Well, how are you getting on?"

"It's not good. . . ."

"We'll have a look at it. Bring up that other chair."

Peter watched him anxiously. He had expected a look of disappointment to appear in his face, but Herr Heitvogt only said: "M'hmm!" and looked quite cheerful.

"A little harder than drawing a chrysanthemum, isn't it?"

"Yes, sir."

"All right, now let's see—in the first place, you've drawn the head too large. Look at the statue again! . . . Now, the way to take care of that is to measure—do you know how that is done?"

"With the pencil?"

"That's it. Let me see you measure the distance from the top of the head to the point of the chin."

Peter held out his pencil in front of him and closed his left eye, the way Franz had shown him once.

"Accurately, now! Stretch your arm out all the way so that the perspective won't change when you measure some other part. Got it? Now measure the whole height of the figure—if your pencil isn't long enough, you simply use something else! Here—" Herr Heitvogt folded a sheet of paper into a narrow strip and handed it to him—"Now try it!"

Peter measured again.

"All right. Now, here is what you do next—" Herr Heitvogt drew a long vertical line on the side of the sheet, then took the strip of paper from Peter and after he had measured some part of the statue with it, rapidly marked off each measurement on the vertical line. . . . "There you are! Here's the top of the head, and this line marks the level of the right foot; here's the point of the chin, this shows you where the left elbow comes, and so on all the way down. To get the width and thickness, you do exactly the same thing. Do you understand?"

Peter nodded. This part of it looked delightfully easy now.

"Now let me show you something else." Herr Heitvogt's pencil traced over the lower part of the drawing. "Your man looks as if he were standing with his weight equally distributed on both legs. Look at the statue again!"

"He's standing on his right leg more."

"Your drawing doesn't show that. Do you know what's wrong?"

Peter looked hard at the statue, then at his drawing again.

"All right, stand up! Now stand just like 'David' out there—that's it! Put your hands against your hips—lower down, so that you can feel what's happening. Now stand up straight—now like the statue again! Notice anything?"

"This hip moves out. . . ."

"Of course it does. That's your haunch bone and it's part of the pelvis. When you throw all your weight on your right leg, the pelvis shifts over the right leg to support the upper part of your body. Like this——"

Herr Heitvogt bent over the drawing again and drew a bulge on the left side of the figure. On the opposite side he flattened the hip and the thigh. Then Herr Heitvogt sketched in the skeleton between the hips. "There, that's the pelvic girdle, and that's how it looks when a man stands in this particular position. You have to know what goes on under the skin if the outside is going to look like anything. Wait——"

Herr Heitvogt went up to the cupboard behind his desk, and

after peering into it for a second or two, came back with a thick book. He leafed through it until he found a plate showing the human skeleton. "There you are. Here's the pelvis, and these are the haunch bones. The thighbones fit into these cavities! Take this book home and study this whole part of the skeleton. Make a few drawings of it until you've got the shape of it clearly in your head. Then on Monday we'll try the statue again." Herr Heitvogt got up, and added with a smile: "Rome wasn't built in a day. You'll find it much easier next time!"

But it was far from easy either the next time or at any time after that. No sooner had he mastered one difficulty than Herr Heitvogt opened his eyes to half a dozen new ones. The bland, innocuous-looking statue was like a maze of mirrors through which he groped his way arduously, with Herr Heitvogt always just beyond and the reflection of his own awkwardness mocking him on every side.

There were the three weeks he spent studying the neck alone. Herr Heitkopf had called his attention to the diagonal bulge that ran across the throat of the statue:

"What you've drawn there looks like a wen. It doesn't mean anything. That bulge is caused by an important muscle: the sterno-mastoid. You'll have to study it. . . ."

Another time, Herr Heitvogt nodded approvingly. "M'hmm. Well, now I'd like you to begin to watch out for form. The neck up there on the statue is round, isn't it? But your drawing is all in outline like the silhouettes the man in the Prater snips out of black paper and pastes on a white card for you—very nice, but that isn't drawing. Start by watching carefully where the light falls and how much shadow there is, and then shade accordingly. Don't overdo it, though! Always act as if you were just a little afraid of wearing out your pencil. A great painter in Paris used to say that the reason the old painters were such fine draftsmen was that pencils were very expensive then and they couldn't afford to use them up too fast. The fewer lines you can get your picture with, the better. Try it now. . . ."

After the neck, Herr Heitvogt had set him to studying the shoulders, then the arms. He got used to spending hours at home with the thick anatomy book Herr Heitvogt had lent him. To save him carrying the book back and forth, Herr Heitvogt had produced still another book for him to use during the lessons. It was a French text on anatomy. On the inside of the cover Peter had found written *Theodor Heitvogt—33, rue Vavin, Paris.* Looking now and again at the writing, he found himself wondering what the rue Vavin in Paris was like, and all the other streets which occasionally cropped up in Herr Heitvogt's conversation.

For Herr Heitvogt often talked about Paris. Some point that needed explaining would remind him of an incident in the art school in Paris or of some painter there whom he had known. Sometimes when he was in no hurry to get back downstairs to the rationing commission, Herr Heitvogt would go on to tell him about parks and about excursions on the Seine to a place called Suresnes, about the good wine he had drunk at the sidewalk tables of little restaurants, and about dancing in the streets on the Fourteenth of July, but above all about the wonderful light for painting which seemed to be there even when it rained.

Listening to him, Peter had a feeling as if Paris were only a few miles away, not much farther than St. Pölten, certainly not as far as Linz or Salzburg. It was hard to believe afterward that they were at war with France. And when, as sometimes happened on the way home, his eye was struck by a war-loan poster, he had the feeling that the poster was untrustworthy and forged. For either Herr Heitvogt was right, or the newspapers and posters were—there was no question in his mind that both the newspapers and the posters were wrong.

One Sunday morning Herr Heitvogt took him to the museum. It was the first time he had ever been inside the impressive building he had so often passed on his way into the Innere Stadt. The magnificence of the marble staircase that rose from the lobby and of the resplendent baroque corridors left him breathless. For a long time he found it hard to focus his eyes on any one picture—the vastness of the rooms and the profusion of pictures distracted him. But he listened intently when Herr Heitvogt talked. He was determined to remember everything, although he was not always certain that he understood what Herr Heitvogt meant. Sometimes, though, it was delightfully clear, as when Herr Heitvogt called his attention to the simplicity of Breughel's drawing, and said:

"But you have to know a great deal before you can leave out as much as Breughel did, and make one line do the work of six. That kind of simpleness is only for the very great masters. . . ." And he felt that he had at least an inkling of what Herr Heitvogt meant by the "pure color" of a whole roomful of pictures which Herr Heitvogt referred to as "the Italian primitives."

The longer he looked, the more interested he became. And he had seen only a few rooms! There seemed to be dozens and dozens of them. He was delighted when Herr Heitvogt said:

"I'm going to give you a card tomorrow, so that they will let you in alone next time. You ought to come here every week. I'll try and come with you occasionally to explain some things, but the important thing for you is just to see the pictures. That way you'll learn to look, and nothing is more important to a painter than to look. . . ."

He walked home exultantly. The pictures had stimulated him. He would go every Sunday now. He might want to become a painter after all!

Chapter Twenty-Nine

ON THE last day of school before the Christmas vacation Herr Heitvogt handed him a large, thin book and said:

"This is a volume of reproductions of famous drawings and etchings. Handle it carefully, but don't be afraid to look at it. That's what it's for."

That evening while he sat looking at the book, he became suddenly aware that *she* had stolen up behind him to peer over his shoulder. Involuntarily, he gave a little start. She came around swiftly to the side of the table, her hands reaching out for the book.

"What's that you're so interested in? It can't be anything good, or—"

She started to tug softly at the book. He had to let go for fear that it might tear, but his exasperation made his voice sound shrill in his own ears:

"Look out! That's Herr Heitvogt's book. If you ruin it, it'll be your fault!"

She had already started to turn the large leaves.

"I won't ruin it! I just want to see. . . ."

She came to the etching of Bathsheba. At once her mouth set with grim complacency.

"We'll see whether Franz thinks you ought to be looking at things like that!"

It was the first open conflict with her since spring. For a moment longer his old irritation grated and twitched through him; then the certainty of what Franz would say, and the something ridiculous about her stubbornly self-righteous march with the book into Franz's room made his anger melt away. As often in the last few months, a mood of indulgent amusement came into its place.

The following morning Franz called to him from his room. Franz was just putting on his overcoat. He nodded toward the desk:

"There's your book. Did Herr Heitvogt lend that to you?"

"Yes, I'm supposed to study it over Christmas."

Franz' eyes fixed him earnestly, intently:

"Mother simply didn't understand. . . ."

The room was suddenly murmurous with Franz's unspoken plea not to exploit this petty triumph over her. But there was also something else which made an uncomfortable tension between Franz and him: Franz was dubious about some of those drawings in the book and did not quite know how to begin.

Peter waited uncertainly. But if Franz had intended to say anything about those pictures, he evidently thought better of it. He leaned over his desk to pick up his gloves.

"Well, see you later," he said a little awkwardly and went out.

It was still another defeat for her. Increasingly Franz and Poldi had been siding with him and against her. She had had to yield about letting him stay at home in the evening when she went to vespers, about High Mass on Sundays, about a dozen breaches in the wall with which she had always hemmed him in before. As long as he could appeal to Poldi or Franz on the score of his studies, he was almost certain of their support.

But she fought doggedly against every new concession, especially—he had been aware of it for some time—where anything connected with the drawing lessons was concerned. He had noticed the wide, sullen circle she described around the table in the living room when he was drawing there, and once, while she was dusting, he happened to see her pick up the thick anatomy book as if it were filled with contamination. He sensed that behind her lowering disapproval she was thinking of Mizzi and of what in this mood she would certainly have called "Mizzi's downfall," that she saw a dangerous parallel between his drawing and Mizzi's ambition to be an actress, and that finally she was darkly grinding on the fact that the shadowy figure who was somehow his father had been a painter.

The setbacks, Peter realized, hurt all the more since they had been scored on the larger wound of her defeat over Father. The coming operation hung over her like a sword. It was not so much the operation that worried her—although she missed no opportunity to prophesy glumly: "As if God would have sealed up our heads so carefully, if he had meant the doctors to go in there with a knife!"—as it was Father's persistent refusal to let her bring a priest and receive the sacraments. The operation had been put off twice already and was set now for some time after Christmas. She saw these delays as partial answers to her prayers and prayed all the harder, but she also did not conceal her dread and horror at the thought that Father might "really go under the knife without making his peace with God."

Looking at her now and again, when she came home from visiting Father or when he was kneeling beside her in church, and seeing the despondency in her shoulders and the desperate fervor of her knuckly hands and of her lips, he was moved by a swift pang of sympathy for her. But those moments were rare. Ordinarily he was too aware that without Poldi and Franz he would still have been exposed to all her former oppression not to be callous to her anxiety.

He was glad that Poldi and Franz were pleased over his marks. When he had shown them his report card he had almost persuaded himself that he had worked so hard chiefly for them. But he knew that pleasing them had really only been a by-product of something else. What alternately drove and lured him to work with a kind of exhilarating frenzy was the consciousness of Baron Ortner and Bianca, which stayed with him even when he had not consciously thought of them for days. He was certain that each new success in school was bringing him nearer to some as yet intangible but infinitely promising goal.

He had seen Baron Ortner only once since the summer and that had been months ago, in September. He knew that he was still at the barracks in Baden. Now and again, Franz dropped some hint that showed that he had spent an evening with Baron Ortner, but those meager bits of information were never enough to satisfy his curiosity. Yet he could not bring himself to ask the questions that burned on the tip of his tongue; it seemed impossible to recapture that warm intimacy with Franz that had made it so easy to ask him things while they had been in the country. To do that, he felt that he would have to be alone again with Franz and, above all, away from home—so that he was pleasantly startled when Franz came out into the living room on the afternoon of Christmas Eve and asked:

"Do you want to come for a walk? I'm going out to Schönbrunn."

It was Sunday and a gray afternoon, but already the indefinable expectancy of Christmas Eve hung everywhere in the more than usually hushed Sunday streets. The dingy remnants of the snowfall earlier in the week looked much less dismal than they had that morning. The low-hanging sky conspired with the indrawn, slyly secretive and knowing air of the houses to create the illusion that they were moving within a strangely small, friendly space; the city seemed to have shrunk to the immediate neighborhood of the street through which they walked.

They got on the streetcar in the Hütteldorferstrasse and rode as far as the reservoir, alongside of which the street ran down to Schönbrunn. Peter could not remember ever having been here before in the winter. Schönbrunn—the botanical garden, the zoo, the long, clipped avenues, the Palace itself—had always been associated with hot summer afternoons. It was part of the uniqueness of the walk that Franz should have thought of coming here today.

They walked briskly down the sloping street. At the foot of it, still quite a distance away, the two tall monoliths with the golden eagles perched on top towered a little bleakly above the square in front of the black and gold grill gates. Still farther back, where the ground rose again, the vast horseshoe-shaped bulk of the Palace appeared so indistinct in the gray light as to melt into the sky.

Neither Franz nor he had said anything since they had got off the streetcar. There seemed to be no need to talk. Just being with Franz like this had thrown him back into the mood of those weeks in the country again.

They neared the foot of the hill and walked past the long stretch of tangled hedge which Peter could remember from his earliest trip to Schönbrunn. During the summer the hedge was so high and so dense that it had always been impossible to see inside. He noticed now that the wilderness of trees and undergrowth inside was as unkempt as the hedge itself. Great piles of dead wood stuck out of the snow. It was evidently a large estate since there was no sign of any building to be seen even through the bare trees.

He broke the silence to ask:

"Who owns this, Franz?"

"That? That belongs to an English nobleman, to the Duke of Cumberland."

The information, the word "English" especially, irritated him for no reason he could discern. A corner of his mind that lay usually dormant—though menacingly so, like a lazily potent, coiled animal—became darkly alert and argumentative.

"Now it belongs to him? In spite of the war?"

"Of course!" Franz sounded amused and a little like a teacher. "You don't go taking things like that away from people just because you're at war with their country. This estate has probably been in their family for hundreds of years. The war isn't going to last forever, you know. Besides, some of our people have estates in England, too."

"But this is all run to seed," he carped, trying to find an excuse for his irritation in the neglected state of the park. "It doesn't look as if anybody had cared anything about it for years."

Franz already appeared to be thinking of something else. His tone dismissed the park: "Maybe the Duke of Cumberland likes it that way."

Peter's annoyance still gnawed at him when they crossed the open square to the grill gates. It suddenly took the form of vexation with anything foreign that resembled Schönbrunn. He remembered the description of Versailles Herr Heitvogt had given them in class——

"Is it true, Franz, that Versailles is older than Schönbrunn?"

"Yes, I think it is by a few years."

"Did you like Versailles better?"

"No, I wouldn't say that. Versailles is harder, colder—it makes you think of an etching. But the two are really quite different—you've seen pictures of it!"

"But is it as nice?"

"It isn't to me, but it's very beautiful. A Parisian would probably feel the same way about Schönbrunn."

"Herr Heitvogt says that people lie around on the lawns. . . ."

"That's quite true. The park at Versailles is more like our Prater that way, but that's because France is a republic and the palace is just a museum now. If they still had a king, the gardens would be kept up more—it must have been magnificent under Louis the Fourteenth. . . ."

He felt satisfied. His eyes swept proudly over the honey-colored façade with its rows on rows of high windows flanked by charmingly fragile-looking green shutters.

Franz tilted his chin toward the long guard-shelter under the arcade in the right wing. The guard was drawn up at attention.

"Look, the Kaiser is in residence. He must be going to spend Christmas out here."

They walked through one of the arched passageways under the Palace, past several tall guardsmen with their shining sabers and resplendent uniforms, and came out on the terrace on the other side. The park lay before them, gray and a little wistful and deserted. The big carp pond with its rearing granite sea monsters in the center and along the rim had been drained and looked asleep. The trees along the avenues which were trimmed to form straight walls of green during the summer presented only a nostalgically regular and somehow loyal tracery of black and brown against the leaden sky. For some reason it felt warmer here than it had in the street.

They took the avenue to the zoo and walked by the empty cages. Only the polar bears were outside. When they came to the elephant house Franz looked at his watch. He seemed reassured. They went on to the botanical garden. It was pleasant to walk like this. A dreamlike sense of fulfillment gained on Peter as he moved along beside Franz through the silent avenues. They came to the big hothouse which rose even above the tallest trees. Electric lights were on inside and one could see the great palms which nearly touched the ceiling, and here and there splotches of color from some tropical growth. He was hoping that Franz would suggest that they go inside, and Franz appeared to be considering it until he looked again at his watch.

"I'm afraid there isn't time." A sudden eagerness had come into Franz's walk. After they had gone another fifty yards, Franz explained: "I have to meet somebody at the Hietzinger gate. . . ."

Then, that was the reason why Franz had come here today! But whom did he want to meet just here? It was at best an eccentric meeting place, although he was glad that Franz had chosen it. Ordinarily, Franz always met his friends at some coffeehouse in the Innere Stadt. . . .

They had got about halfway to the Hietzinger gate when Franz suddenly pulled him behind a tree. It was at the very moment when Peter himself had caught sight of a lady coming toward them, but still a considerable distance away. He looked at Franz and saw that his eyes were shining mischievously.

"Did you see that lady? That's Heinrich's sister. We're going to play a joke on her. You go up and give her this book—" Franz brought out a flat little parcel from his overcoat pocket—"and say, Franz sends his apologies but he couldn't come. All right?"

That was Bianca! It was unbelievable somehow. A poignantly sweet terror seized him at the thought of going up to her by himself.

"I . . . I . . ."

"It's just a joke," Franz urged.

"But I don't know what to say. I—"

"Don't be silly! Haven't you ever talked to a girl? You simply ask, 'Baroness Bianca?' and introduce yourself, and then you tell her that I couldn't come and give her the book. By that time I'll show myself anyway. Go on, before she gets too close!" Franz gave him a little shove out into the avenue.

The lady had come alarmingly nearer while they had been hiding behind the tree. She was wearing a brown fur jacket and a black astrakhan toque. Her hands were in a small black muff that matched the toque. He noticed that her tan skirt was much shorter than the skirts Poldi wore; it came just a little below her knees. He was still too far away to make out her face, which was partially hidden by the collar of the jacket. He forced himself to walk on steadily.

This was Bianca!

She was taller than he had pictured her. And she walked with a graceful, brittle determination that added further to his shyness. Then he saw her face. He had no longer time to find out whether she was beautiful or not; he was aware only of the large, dark eyes which had a disconcerting calmness and of the lovely color the cold had brought to her cheeks. She was almost on top of him now.

He fought back his shyness and took off his cap. "Baroness Bianca?"

She listened attentively. The dark eyes traveled over him in astonishment, quickly and frankly, then met him so fully that he stumbled over what he was supposed to say. She took the book from him and said, "Oh!"

For a fraction of a second he was afraid that the joke had succeeded too well. He did not know what to do next. Then she appeared to sense that something was wrong and looked past him down the avenue. Franz came out from behind a tree and called gaily, "Hello!"

Now that Franz was hurrying up to them, some of the tension Peter had felt with her was gone. He felt a nervous desire to laugh and he half expected her to laugh, too, but her dark brown eyes were still grave, only much softer than before. She gave him a quick smile, before she said to Franz:

"Franz, you are a pig!"

Franz laughed and bent to kiss her hand, which she was gravely holding out to him.

"This is Peter," Franz said.

"We've already met, thank you." Her voice would have sounded petulant if, like her eyes, it had not held that engrossing note of graveness. "How are you, Peter? I have heard a lot about you from Heinrich and from your good-for-nothing cousin here—let's not talk to him, shall we?"

But she hooked her hand through Franz's arm with a determined, faintly possessive little gesture, even while she said it. They started up the avenue in the direction from which she had come. A little self-consciously, Peter measured his step to hers.

"I'm the one who almost couldn't come," Bianca said. "Steffi insisted on coming along. She has a nose like a hound, *cette femme!*"

Franz laughed. "How is Steffi?"

"Simply unbearable! She has two Pekes now and she insists on bringing them to the table and feeding them. One of them looks just like Maxl—you should see her face when I tell her that! Simply livid . . ."

Now that she was talking to Franz, he felt free to examine her more closely. He took in the fur-edged overshoes, trim and precise like her step, the gay tweed skirt which folded and unfolded over her knees, the unconsciously tense crook of the arm next to him, which held the little astrakhan muff so that it seemed as much a part of her grave eagerness as the lovely line of her chin, twisted now toward Franz as she questioned: ". . . but is it? I don't believe you, Franz!" In the end, Peter knew, it was her voice that thrilled him most. It had a fuzzy, exotic timbre that was haunting. Probably, he told himself, because she must have spoken Hungarian in Hungary. The words were crisp and clear, yet they lingered in the air as if they had been sung.

Franz was gay, in a chaffing mood, but underneath his gaiety there was a subtle excitement that troubled Peter when he became suddenly aware of it. He felt embarrassed, as once—a long time ago when he was still small—when Franz had taken him swimming and they had undressed in the same cabin. He forced his attention away from Franz. They were walking more slowly now. He gave himself up to enjoying Bianca's nearness until she suddenly turned to him.

"Is it true that you want to go into the army?"

Franz must have told her about his running away. There was only one answer possible now. "Yes," he said.

"Or are you just tired of lessons?"

She had said "lessons," and not "school," reminding him of the tutor Franz had told him about and making him feel that she was on his side. He wondered what her lessons with the tutor "who had been all over the world" were like; she must be studying very difficult things. . . .

Franz said: "He's been working very hard lately."

"Horrid, isn't it?" she asked.

"No . . . I don't mind this year."

"Well, I do! I hate studying!" She turned back to Franz: "André Kohut is going to do *Egmont* this Thursday—did you see? I can't wait to see him again. . . ."

They were almost at the Hietzinger gate. With a little pang of alarm Peter measured the distance that still remained. She would probably leave them at the gate! He had an impulse to reach out and touch the silky brown fur of her jacket to add that sensation, too, to the store he was gathering greedily with his eyes and ears.

Just outside the gate Franz and Bianca stopped.

"Let's go to the confectioner's over there and have some hot chocolate," Franz proposed.

"What time is it, Franz?"

"Only half past four."

"Oh, I can't! Mama is having a lot of people in to tea—all the old dodoes for miles around! Such a bore!"

They went across the little square to the corner where two taxis were parked. She held out her hand:

"Good-by, Peter. You must get Franz to bring you again."

For a brief second her warm, firm hand which had a surprisingly strong grip held his. He saw only now that she had a beautiful mouth. Then Franz kissed her hand and she said, already from inside the taxi: "Thursday night, don't forget!" Then the taxi pulled away, and he and Franz were standing alone on the curb.

"We might as well walk back through the park," Franz said. "We can get back to the Palace before five. Well, how do you like Bianca?"

The question embarrassed him. His happiness warned him to be on his guard. "I like her," he said.

"You don't sound very enthusiastic."

"Oh, but—I mean, I like her very much." He felt he had to defend himself quickly against any more questions from Franz. "She doesn't look as if she rode wild horses like you said!"

"No?" Franz suddenly gave the impression of exultantly breasting a storm. He laughed happily. "You ought to see her!"

"I thought she was in Hungary most of the time?"

"Not during the winter."

"Do you see her often, Franz?" he ventured after a little while.

"Not as often as I'd like to." Franz's chuckle seemed to take him into his confidence. "But I usually manage to see her at least once a week in the Burgtheater. They have a box for Thursday nights."

"But I thought Baron Ortner's mother—"

"That's right!" Everything he said seemed to make Franz grin. "Only, fortunately, 'Mama' doesn't go to the theater much. Bianca usually comes with the tutor or with her mother's companion, and they are both good friends of mine."

He remembered then that several times recently Franz had put on his full-dress suit in the evening when he had gone out. It occurred to him with the belated impact of something that had been staring him in the face: *Franz is in love with Bianca!*

But why, then, had Franz brought him along? Everybody knew that lovers wanted to be alone. If he had been in Franz's place he would certainly have wanted to be alone with Bianca. . . . Was it only because Franz was like that: naïvely without duplicity and kindhearted and wanting everybody to be happy because he was? Yes, that was it. Franz had simply acted on impulse when he had asked him to come along, but how wonderful that it should have happened!

They walked through the rapidly darkening avenue without speaking now. More even than on the way to Schönbrunn there was no need to talk. Their silence was a rich woof between them, Peter felt, which glowed with the warm consciousness of Bianca.

The outlines of the Palace were completely swallowed up in darkness when they got back to it, but long rows of the tall windows on the upper floors gleamed softly where the lights had been turned on. In the passageways under the palace, clusters of lamps had also been lighted. The guardsmen with their drawn sabers stood as motionless as before, but they looked friendlier somehow.

They were about to start up the wide avenue toward the outer gate when a little church bell began to ring slowly from the direction where the left wing formed a shadowy angle with the main façade. They had both stopped to look. Light streamed out from an arched door as someone opened it to go inside.

"That's the chapel. Wait a minute. . . ."

Franz went back to one of the guardsmen and talked to him. He looked a little excited when he returned.

"There's a vesper service. It's open to the public. Let's go in. . . ."

The chapel was small, gay, exquisite with its white and gold moldings and its crystal chandeliers, like a rare china vase holding a slender sheaf of flowers on a sun-washed window sill. A charming simplicity, something toylike almost in its intimacy, breathed from the plain altar and the two short rows of pews. An oblong section of the wall up front on the right was glassed in and through the panes one could see two tiny rooms, not unlike two adjoining boxes in the theater, which contained several red brocade chairs with the imperial monogram embroidered on their backs. The lowest row of panes all along the glass partition had been raised so that the two boxes had a curious, knowing air of expectancy. The candles on the altar were already lighted and the organ in the low choir loft in the rear was playing softly. Around them in the pews were some sixty or seventy people, most of them elderly and wearing dark clothes, and all of them with something indefinably austere and a little self-important in their bearing, who obviously belonged to the staff of the Palace.

Irresistibly, as he waited for the service to begin, Peter's thoughts strayed to Bianca again. The memory of the walk along the avenue to the Hietzinger gate stole in and out between the words when he tried to pray, until only his consciousness of Bianca was left.

Franz nudged him discreetly. "Look, the Kaiser!"

It was true. Exactly in the middle of the farther box, his hands clasped and resting on the ledge below the glass partition, there was the familiar light-blue uniform coat and the white-bearded face of the Emperor. The brief row of medals on his chest just showed above the ledge. In the nearer box two ladies with elegant hats were just kneeling down—archduchesses probably, Peter told himself. He wondered which ones they were.

He kept watching the two boxes out of the corner of his eye. It surprised him that he did not feel more excited. On the few occasions when he had seen the Kaiser before, it had always been from a considerable distance; there had been bands and soldiers in dazzling uniforms and crowds of people jostling each other just for a glimpse. Yet now he was so close that he could see the wrinkles around the Kaiser's eyes and the bony ridges on his skull. He realized with a pleasant tremor of alarm at his boldness that he had only to raise his voice and that then the Emperor and the two ladies in the other box could not help hearing what he said.

The Kaiser's head was bowed. He seemed absorbed in prayer. He looked a kindly old man, just as the stories he had read in grammar school had always depicted him. But he looked also very tired and oddly defenseless without the glittering guards and soldiers around him. No doubt, he was praying so hard because he was harassed by all the worries of the war. People said that the Kaiser had not wanted the war. . . . A surge of loyalty welled up in Peter and included not only the lonely-looking old man but the chapel and the Palace outside and the avenue where Bianca and Franz and he had walked.

The service began. It was like any other vespers—benediction, litany, benediction—only marvelously rich somehow because of his mood. A sweet poignancy held him like a shining mesh from which he did not want to escape. It seemed to him that everything had worked together that afternoon to lift him to this pinnacle of joy. He would always remember how Bianca had looked when she had turned to walk across the street at the Hietzinger gate, the sound of the voices around him now making the responses to the litany, the particular fragrance of the incense here.

He looked up toward the glass partition again. The Kaiser had put on a pair of spectacles which rode far down on his nose and he was reading in a prayerbook. He did not join in the responses, but the two ladies in the other box did. They also sang when the organ modulated into "Silent Night" after the final benediction. During the last stanza the Kaiser slowly took off his spectacles and put them into a silver case he picked up from the ledge. The priest followed the two altar boys out into the sacristy. The Kaiser knelt for a minute longer, then crossed himself and put his hands on the ledge to help himself up. He held himself very erect for a moment before his shoulders sagged again as he turned around. A small door opened in the rear of the tiny room and he was gone. Another minute and the two ladies in the other box left too. The organ dwindled from pianissimo into a faintly rheumatic echo. People in the pews around them began to leave. Franz glanced at him and got up. . . .

It had begun to snow while they had been inside.

"We were in luck," Franz said. "That's the private chapel where the Kaiser hears Mass every morning when he's at Schönbrunn. It's only open to the public a few times a year. Aren't you glad we went in?"

"Yes, Franz."

"You mayn't get many more chances like this. The Kaiser is getting very old." Franz sounded concerned; then his voice became brisk. "We better hurry or Mother'll scold. We were supposed to be home early today."

The hurry forced on him by Franz's lengthened stride found no counterpart of eagerness inside him. Except for the fact that he was hungry, he was reluctant to face the gloomy Christmas that would be waiting for them at home.

The table was already laid in the living room. Poldi was hanging some candy on the small potted Christmas tree on Father's desk. As soon as Franz and he had washed, *she* brought in the soup, then commandingly and a little bumptiously she stationed herself in the middle of the room and began to say grace.

Ordinarily, Poldi and Franz avoided saying the Angelus with her before meals, or if they did happen to be in the room and joined in, they always did so in a deprecatory murmur, finishing usually a sentence or two ahead of her; but tonight, as if in deference to some special authority conferred on her by the combination of Christmas and Father's illness, their voices were not only clearer and very grave, but strangely docile and waiting on hers. She wiped her eyes several times as she prayed. At the end of the Angelus, her back stiffened woodenly to warn them that there was still something else—she said: "And now we'll say three Hail Mary's for Father!"

The consciousness of Father in Steinhof weighed on them throughout supper, although Franz was trying hard to sound cheerful. It would have been even more depressing, Peter realized, had it not been for the feeling that he had already had his Christmas. The happiness he had known at Schönbrunn was like a solid treasure which he could touch and which made him immune to sadness now.

They had baked fish as they always did on Christmas Eve, and she had made *Apfelstrudel*, even though she had had to use black, gritty flour for the crust and there had not been enough sugar for it either, so that it was only a dreary mockery of the *Apfelstrudel* he remembered from before the war. And there was a bowl of the special compote of prunes and dried pears and quince which also belonged to Christmas Eve. He realized that she must have been saving up sugar and lard for weeks to give them all this.

Poldi lighted the tiny tree. There was not even a semblance of the mysteriously closed doors of former years. But, then, why should there be, he chided himself impatiently; he was grown up now and he knew as well as anyone that there could be no presents, with Poldi and Franz needing every krone to meet Father's sanitarium bills. But his heart pounded a little all the same when Poldi called to him to come and when he saw a number of packages under the tree. As usual, most of them were for Poldi and

Franz. But there was also one for him! It was from Franz. He opened it and found a handsome gym suit from the big athletic goods store in the Kaiserstrasse. The present puzzled him—they needed only sneakers for gym class in school, and his were still quite good!—until he opened the envelope Poldi handed him and saw the membership card to the gymnastics club to which Poldi had always belonged until this year.

It had clearly been Poldi's idea to send him to the Turnverein. He was touched that Poldi, who was so passionately fond of everything connected with the club and who could no longer go herself, should have thought of this. He thanked Franz first and then tried to turn to her. She would not listen to his thanks.

"The dues for this month are already paid. Afterward, I'll give you the money on the first of every month, and you'll get the streetcar fare on the days when there is class. The boys' class is Tuesday and Thursday evening, I think—it tells you on the back of the card. . . ."

Chapter Thirty

He had not expected that anything could possibly add to the happiness he had brought home with him from Schönbrunn, yet the prospect of the Turnverein did. He knew one boy who belonged to it; he was a boy named Meissl, who had attracted his attention by the playful ease with which he executed even the most difficult exercises in gym class, but who was also conspicuous because he was one of the leaders of the fashionable group which always gathered by the rear window to discuss girls and plays. But Meissl was in all probability the only boy in school who was a member of the Turnverein; the boys there, Peter knew, came mostly from the *Gymnasium* and the *Realschule.*

He waited impatiently for Tuesday afternoon. The Turnverein was on a side street off the Mariahilferstrasse, not very far from Herr Granini's house and the Ring. The front of the building looked unimpressive and even drab, but there was a handsome entrance above which hung a white flag with the navy-blue insignia of the club. He waited until he had seen a considerable number of boys disappear behind the wide glass doors before he got up courage enough to go in, too.

The locker room downstairs was boisterous with laughter and talk and slammed locker doors. He saw at once that a great many of the boys were much older and bigger than he; their talk made it clear that they were already in the last year or two of the *Gymnasium* or the *Realschule.* He felt a thrill at his nearness to these older boys. He realized that the fact that it was still vacation accounted for some of their exuberance, but there was something else besides—then he saw the eagerness with which they trooped out through the wide tunnel that led into the gymnasium and he sensed that the explanation lay out there. He dawdled a little longer over his sneakers, then he ventured out, too.

The gymnasium was so huge that for a moment he felt utterly lost. Groups of boys had moved out some of the apparatus from the walls and were practicing on it. Because all the other boys seemed to be doing something, he went to the climbing ropes in one corner and started to pull himself up hand over hand. But after he had gone once to the top of the scaffolding and come down again, his arms were exhausted and he was again at a loss for something to do. He sauntered over to a high horizontal bar to watch. A redheaded boy was going through a series of dizzying gyrations that reminded Peter of the circus and made him catch his breath. Another boy took the redheaded boy's place and it was then that Peter noticed Meissl among the little group waiting their turn.

Meissl had seen him too and grinned. He looked singularly self-confident among these older boys, some of whom were a whole head taller than he. It was not until one of the big boys boosted Meissl up to the high bar that Peter saw the reason for Meissl's smiling self-assurance. Everything that the older boys had done on the bar, Meissl now did, too, but the very slimness of his body gave the stunts an elegance they had not had before.

Meissl finished a giant swing and let himself drop on the mat. His handsome face was still flushed from the exertion and he was a little out of breath.

"Hello," he said. "How long have you been here?"

"I'm just starting today."

"What team did they put you in?"

"The twelfth—is that bad?"

"Well, you've got to start somewhere. There are still three teams behind that. Up to the ninth, they're really all beginners' teams. . . ." Meissl did not sound superior so much as anxious to explain. "They move you up pretty fast until you get into the tenth; after that it gets hard: you have to pass the same tests they give in the men's division and the head instructor gives the tests himself. I'm in the fifth team now; I'm trying to make the fourth before the exhibition in May. There's only one team in the men's division that's better than our first."

Meissl's enthusiasm infected him. He glanced around at the confusion of boys. "How do I know which is my team?"

"Oh, that's not until after the setting-up exercises. Everybody does those together with the head instructor. That's Herr Graan over there—see the man with the Olympic shield on his jersey? That's the head instructor. He was on the Olympics team in 1912. You'll hear the whistle in a couple of minutes. See you some more!"

Peter strolled away. He did not want Meissl to think that he was going to cling to him like a burr just because Meissl had been friendly. But he felt warmed by Meissl's interest and no longer as strange among the many boys as before.

He suddenly saw several boys he knew, two who had been in grammar school with him and one from the choir. He turned away hastily. He did not want to be reminded of the choir and perhaps be asked questions about the evening when Franz had talked to Herr Granini. He was still wondering how many other boys there were from the choir when a whistle blew.

Lines began to form, extending down the whole length of the gymnasium. At the far end of the hall, four boys were letting down a platform which had been folded against the wall. Peter went to the end of one of the lines and waited with the rest. The man with the Olympic insignia had got on the platform up front. Presently his voice rang out:

"All right—hands above the head and jump—one, two! One, two . . ." A piano somewhere up in the gallery had struck up a gay tune.

The instructor stopped them and outlined another exercise, then another and still another, each one more difficult than the last. Peter began to understand why Meissl always appeared politely bored by their gym class in school. His own muscles were shrilly protesting against the unaccustomed strain. Yet it was exhilarating to twist and strain in unison like this, even though there was a wide gulf between the smooth perfection of the boys up front and his own limping determination not to give up, as he saw a few younger boys around him do. He felt a sense of triumph when it was all over and they were dismissed to their teams.

He found his team. The instructor was rolling one of the standards for high jumping into place. While Peter was still waiting to report to him, someone touched his arm. Rudi!

He saw at a glance that Rudi was much heavier; his arms and

shoulders had thickened into a pink fleshiness that reminded Peter of the plump-muscled torso of the baker he had once watched kneading dough in the Seidengasse. Only Rudi's soft brown hair and the girlishly placid eyes under the long eyebrows were exactly the same.

"I saw you before, when we were lining up," Rudi said. His voice had changed and sounded leathery and all wrong. "Did you just start today?"

"Yes."

"This your team? I'm in eleven, over there—I'll see you in the locker room afterward!"

Rudi did not run across the floor to his team as other boys were doing; he walked with the peculiar deliberation Peter remembered so well. A multitude of uneasy memories stirred in him as he watched Rudi a moment longer to see where he was going; he did not know whether he was glad over Rudi's promise to see him in the locker room or not.

The jumping began. There were eleven boys in the team and the wait between jumps gave him time to look around. Meissl's team was working on the flying rings, doing intricate, stuntlike exercises that were engrossing to watch. He realized that to look at Rudi just after he had been watching Meissl was unfair, yet something drove him to measure Rudi Martin as it were through Meissl's eyes. He had a feeling of hardening himself against the suggestion of soft awkwardness which still survived in the way Rudi raised himself on the parallel bars across the way and swung to a handstand, then let himself down on one elbow——

Out in the locker room afterward, Rudi Martin came while he was struggling with the damp knot in the string of his sneaker.

"Oh, here you are," Rudi said. "My locker is over there, in the next to last row. You'll probably be ready before I am. . . ."

Nothing in Rudi's voice indicated that they had not seen each other only last week or even just yesterday. Yet actually it was almost a year, Peter told himself irritably. For a minute or so he toyed with the idea of not stopping at Rudi's locker at all. Only a certain curiosity and a faintly sardonic feeling that he must at least meet Rudi's politeness with equal politeness made him go finally.

Rudi was putting on his coat. His brown corduroy suit looked new. As he watched Rudi button the Norfolk jacket over his tie,

Peter reflected that it was the same pink, placid daintiness about Rudi which had formerly kept his hands from ever getting dirty when they had played in the garden at the Verein, which also kept his clothes looking so new. He himself was hard on clothes—she always reminded him of it as if it were some vicious flaw in his make-up when she found a hole in his pants or a small rent in a coat. The memory of it and something about Rudi's soft, angular motions were responsible for the subtle antagonism he had to overcome in addressing Rudi now. He asked:

"Have you been in the Turnverein long?"

"I started last fall, just as soon as I was thirteen. Why didn't you come before?"

He did not want to explain that his membership had been a Christmas present. He said instead, trying to sound very casual:

"How is the choir?"

"All right, I guess. I'm not in it any more. I can't spare the time every evening with all the homework I have to do." Rudi sounded pompous and a little smug.

Peter watched while Rudi put his gym suit in a brown leather satchel. No doubt Rudi took his gym suit home to be washed every time he used it! In the satchel were two books, carefully covered with the gray oilcloth Peter remembered from grammar school.

They started up the stairs.

"Do you have so much homework this year?"

"Of course. It gets harder every year, and I'm taking lessons in Greek besides. I have to, because I'm going to be a philologist."

"What's that?"

"It's a scholar who makes a study of languages," Rudi said importantly. "It's fascinating. All modern European languages are related because they come from the same language originally. You can trace our words right back through Latin and Greek and Old High German to the parent language. That's why the dead languages are so important, and Greek is one of the basic ones. Our Latin professor says you can't start too early with Greek. Then afterward, I'm going to study Gothic and Sanskrit and maybe Oriental languages, too—it all depends whether I decide to specialize in European or Oriental languages."

Exasperation gathered in Peter as he listened to him. It was not as formerly when Rudi had eagerly invited him to share some new enthusiasm. Now Rudi was not enthusiastic at all—he was pompous and proprietary about his languages, as if they were some fabulous villa in Hütteldorf he was condescendingly telling some outsider about, over the garden wall.

Without meaning to, he blurted out:

"I'm taking lessons, too—in drawing. I'm going to be a painter. My father is one."

A raw sensation of panic seized him as soon as the words were out. Now, why did he have to say that! It was the first time any mention of *that* had ever passed his lips—he had not even thought of it since that last day in the country with Franz, when Franz had said: "You know, your father was one!" He felt himself flushing painfully. His discomfort turned into anger with Rudi: it was Rudi who had goaded him into saying it!

"I thought your father worked in the Burgtheater?"

He stiffened defiantly. "That isn't my real father—that's only my uncle."

They were approaching the Mariahilferstrasse. More to keep Rudi from pursuing the dangerous subject than because he was interested, he asked:

"Are you trying to get into the gymnastics exhibition in May?"

"I'm not interested in that. The only reason I come to the Turnverein is to build up my body—a scholar has to have a sound body—and for that, the setting-up exercises are much more important than the other stuff."

"Yes, but working on the apparatus is the most fun and that's what gives you muscles."

"That's only a popular superstition. It doesn't really make you strong. I have a book by a famous Swedish authority and he proves that all that stuff about working with dumbbells is old-fashioned. He has statistics that show that acrobats are just as susceptible to disease germs as anybody else. The important thing is to harden the skin. I do a special set of exercises every morning by an open window and then I take an ice-cold shower. That hardens the skin. I'll lend you the book if you like—are you taking the streetcar?"

"No," Peter lied. "I'm going to walk."

"Oh—well, I'll see you Thursday, then."

"Yes, Thursday. . . ."

But to himself, Peter stormed as he hurried away: *No, not on Thursday nor any other day! He was through with Rudi! Rudi had become just as patronizing as some of the other boys in the* Gymnasium *and—yes, that was it: stodgy!*

The bitterness Rudi had aroused in him had thrown a shadow over the whole evening in the Turnverein. It did not lift until he started to think of Meissl. Compared to Meissl, who was Rudi anyway? Meissl was in the fifth team and even the older boys treated him with respect; Meissl would have had a right to be condescending to him since he was only a beginner, but Meissl hadn't been.

Although he realized it only vaguely at first, it was really Baron Ortner and Bianca who were behind the growing attraction which Meissl began to hold for him. There was much about Meissl that reminded him of Baron Ortner. He had the same dark eyes, smooth forehead, and dark hair which he parted in the identical spot over his left eye; he even spoke in the same pleasant, unhurried, and slightly playful voice which made one listen even though one was too far away to hear what he was saying. And as if the resemblance to Baron Ortner were not already enough, there was Meissl's constant, lithe-muscled disregard of danger to make him seem even more directly akin to Bianca. Just being with him brought Peter an exciting illusion of being also somehow nearer to Bianca.

He was doubly attentive to Meissl now when they had gym class in school. He took pride in the modesty with which Meissl went through the exercises, which seemed so childishly easy after what he had seen him do in the Turnverein. The secret of what Meissl could do was between the two of them, referred to only by an occasional wink just before Meissl took his turn at the parallel bars or at some other apparatus.

Meissl had taken to coming over to his desk during recess. Peter was also aware that he was trying to draw him into the group by the rear window, and although he was rather bored by the boys' constant boastful talk about all the girls they knew, he stayed. He borrowed a novel from one of the boys, simply because he knew that Meissl had read the book and because it would be something new to talk with Meissl about. He found out that Meissl's mother was a widow and that they lived in the Neubaugasse, not far from the Turnverein. He began to wish that Meissl lived somewhere near the Gürtel instead, so that they would have had the same way to school and there would have been more chance to get to know him better. Almost the only opportunity for seeing him now was in school or when they both happened to be early for the Turnverein and could talk for a little while before Meissl joined the older boys.

He met him like that one evening toward the end of January. Meissl was carrying a book which looked like a novel. While they were killing time in the lobby, Peter reached out for the book:

"Mind if I look at it?"

"Of course not. I swiped it from my aunt. She always buys all the new ones. It isn't very interesting."

Peter leafed through it. It did not look very interesting. He was about to hand it back to Meissl when several folded sheets of theme paper caught his attention. The outside sheet was covered with conjugations of French verbs which they had not even studied yet in school.

"This isn't yours, is it?"

"Yes, they're mine. I'm taking private lessons. I've just come from one. Here—" Meissl unfolded the sheets and showed him a French theme which was heavily scored with corrections—"I had all this to do for today."

"But you have a good mark in French anyway; why do you have to take lessons?"

"Oh, it isn't for school. I'm getting ready for an examination I have to take in May. I'm going to cadet school next year."

"I didn't know you could get into cadet school from just a public school!"

"You can't, usually. You are supposed to have three years of *Gymnasium* or *Realschule*, but they make exceptions if you have a lot of pull. You have to pass a special examination and you have to be in perfect physical condition, of course. The examination is the only thing I'm afraid of."

"Are you so keen on being an officer?"

"I wouldn't want to be anything else. Besides, you have a wonderful time in the cadet school. I know three boys there now. You have regular army orderlies to wait on you in the mess, and fencing and all kinds of sports, and maneuvers in the summer—they had them in Styria last year—and you get marvelous food. . . ."

As he listened to Meissl's enthusiasm, an idea began to take shape in Peter. He had often passed the cadet school in Baumgarten on the way to see Father, and once or twice he had seen the cadets marching through the streets, in their light-blue capes and their plumed shakos. The memory of it suddenly became vivid before his eyes. If he could get into the cadet school—

"Is it a hard examination?"

"Sure, it's hard. They don't take just anybody. There's history and French and algebra and some other stuff. French is the hardest: you have to write an essay."

"Do you think I could get in?"

Meissl hesitated. "I don't know. You have to have a lot of pull. It's easy for me because my father was an officer and I have all the officers in his regiment to back me—you have to have some high-ranking officer to sponsor you."

"How high-ranking?"

"Oh, at least a colonel. That's what the commandant of the school told my mother last year."

Already Peter's thoughts had reached out toward Baron Ortner. Baron Ortner could get somebody, and even Franz might know some important officer in the War Ministry. . . .

"Suppose I can get somebody?"

'You mean, you are going to try to get in?" Meissl's face had become eager. "You know, we could study together! You'd have a hard time with French, though; I've been taking lessons for over a year."

"I can do it!" he said in a burst of self-confidence. But the next instant doubt assailed him again: "Do you have to be the son of an officer to get in?"

"No, you don't. I know, because one of the boys who's there now isn't, either. I'll tell you what: I'll bring you an application blank tomorrow. I have an extra one. It tells you everything you have to do. . . ."

It was as if by great good fortune a door had suddenly been flung open where there had been nothing but sheer wall before. It he could really get into the cadet school, if he became an officer, he would automatically belong to the world of Bianca and of Baron Ortner. He would also at a single stroke wipe out the handicap with which not going to the *Gymnasium* had saddled him as against Rudi and Rudi's friends. Everybody knew that you could go far in the army if you were ambitious. He felt himself tense with power when he thought of it.

He hurried home jubilantly, impatient to tell Franz. In his eagerness he barely noticed that she was crying as she worked by the kitchen stove. Franz was in his room looking through some papers which he recognized as one of the bundles of documents from Father's desk.

Franz listened absently while he repeated what Meissl had said. A scowl gathered on his forehead toward the end. He said:

"I'll have to think that over. There's your mother to consider, too. What you don't realize is that you have to serve in the army for three years after you get your commission if you go to a cadet school. You saw what Mizzi said in that last letter that was sent on to us by the man in Sweden: she's planning to come for you just as soon as the war is over."

"But if I want to be an officer? You are my guardian now. . . ."

"I may be your guardian, but Mizzi is still your mother. You'll feel differently about everything a few years from now. You may not even want to be in the army then. Anyhow, it's not something we can decide from one day to the next."

"But could you ask Baron Ortner?"

"Yes, I can ask him. I suppose it might be possible for Mizzi to get you released from serving the three years by paying some sort of tuition for the time you'd spent in the cadet school. We'd have to find out about that. In any case, we'll have to write to her about it first."

"But a letter through that man in Sweden takes two months! It would be too late by the time her letter comes!"

As if he had not even heard, Franz looked up suddenly and said: "Do you know that Father is going to be operated on?"

Chapter Thirty-One

It was as if Franz had suddenly thrown the switch of a circuit ominously installed months ago but still unused after all this time, so that Peter had nearly ceased to believe in its menace.

For just an instant the picture of Father impatiently jiggling his pince-nez into place on his nose and unfolding the newspaper with his dry, peremptory air of standing no nonsense rose sharply before him, then it escaped him again. He realized guiltily that for some time now he had been growing more and more callous toward Father, somehow less than aware of him even when he had been with him in the wicker-furnished lounge of the sanitarium, and that right now the tantalizing thought of the cadet school kept him from feeling as sorry as he ought. Repentant, he tried to lash himself into a semblance of the concern he had read in Franz's eyes, but the proper emotion eluded him somehow.

Even when he went with her the following afternoon to see Father, it did not help. Father had been moved to the hospital pavilion. He lay in the prim, white bed with an air of having already asserted his customary authority over these new surroundings. His powerful arms were loosely stretched by his side and gave the impression that he might swing himself out of the bed at any moment and that he had only provisionally consented to stay there at all. His mustaches were meticulously brushed and his voice was as deep in pitch as usual.

Seeing Father like this made it harder than ever to believe in the seriousness of the operation. The feeling gained on Peter that Franz had exaggerated somehow. Nothing at all was changed about Father, nor about the relation between Father and her. After a few perfunctory inquiries, a cramped, awkward, testy silence settled around the bed. Boredom expanded each minute like a rubber balloon until it finally burst, then there was another balloon. . . . He was glad when she made him go home by himself after half an hour.

He knew why she had sent him away. She was going to make one final attempt to get Father to see a priest. That had been the reason why they had stopped in the asylum church first and the reason for the two big candles she had lighted in front of the statue of Saint Joseph. He had sensed her nudging, nagging assaults on Father's own stubbornness through the silence up there in the room.

He did not expect her to succeed, but when she and Franz came home together, he could see at once that Father had given in. She looked relaxed and almost indecently complacent. The grim resignation in her face had to do only with her habitual distrust of doctors and hospitals. He could almost visualize what had happened: Franz must have kidded Father into it, must have made light of the whole thing in that irresistible, cajoling way of his, until Father had consented at last. He felt vaguely resentful as he thought of it and full of fear all of a sudden, as if Father had been tricked into giving away his strength and had laid himself open to disaster. He waited for a whole hour before he asked her what had happened.

Her mouth set virtuously. "He's at least made his peace with God. His first confession in twenty-six years, since the day we were married! . . . That nice young priest Franz brought from the Verein is going to give him communion tomorrow morning and the last sacrament—and you are going to get up and go to Mass and pray for Father!"

It seemed queer to go to school as usual the next morning. The operation was to take place at nine o'clock. When he came home at noon, Franz was already there, nervously pacing up and down in his room. He said:

"Father isn't out of the ether yet. I telephoned just a minute ago. We'd better go out and get something to eat."

Franz picked a restaurant in the Kaiserstrasse. Toward the end of the lunch Franz said suddenly:

"We have to pray very hard for Father!"

His voice sounded soft and desperate. It was, Peter told himself as he looked hastily down on his plate, the sort of evidence Franz's soft-hearted, ingenuous nature was bound to give sooner or later of his distress over Father, but it was a remark which Poldi would never have made.

He did not see Poldi all day. She had gone straight from her office to relieve her. She came home a little after six and started to cook. Her eyes were swollen and tears rolled slowly down over her cheeks. As soon as she had washed the dishes, she got ready to leave again. He had been unable to get any information about Father from her, and when he had suggested that he come along to Steinhof, she had turned him down gruffly with a dark: "There's nothing you can do out there—you better say a few prayers for Father right here. . . ."

Neither Franz nor she had returned from Steinhof when Poldi woke him in the morning. He could tell from Poldi's face that Father was at least no worse, but her expression was too forbidding to risk asking questions. But he felt too restless to go to school. He protested:

"If Father is sick, I want to be with him, too!"

"You are going to school and not make things more difficult than they are already! Father is still unconscious. Maybe tomorrow, if Father is better. . . ."

Sitting in class through the endless forenoon, with his thoughts weaving back and forth between himself and Steinhof, he discovered a new, quite unsuspected facet to what had at first seemed only an inexcusable callousness toward Father. The day before while he had been with Franz, he had become aware of a secret exhilaration over his own detachment from the crisis because it had made him feel so much stronger than Franz; now the same feeling of strength suddenly turned into an urge to make things easier for Franz and for all of them by doing his share and if possible more than his share of sitting up with Father or whatever else there was to do in Steinhof. It annoyed him to think that Poldi had been trying to shield him from what she no doubt considered a morbid experience for him—he resolved to insist on going to Steinhof at noon.

It was a letdown to find all three of them at home when he opened the door. He had a sick feeling of having landed in a dead-end street. Franz came hurrying out into the kitchen with an air of hushing him on the threshold of a sickroom. There was a desperate pause, then Franz said solemnly, warningly:

"Father passed away at a quarter to ten!"

Franz stared at him for a moment with his blue eyes oddly veiled and dulled, as if he were searching for something in his face.

Peter followed him into the living room. She was sitting in the chair by the sewing machine. Her black marketing bag was on the floor beside the chair—Peter had never known her not to set it down in the kitchen when she came in. Franz went up to her and said:

"It's all for the best, Mother. We must think that Father might have been sick all the rest of his life if he had lived. We did everything we could. Father is with God now."

She sobbed: "If only—"

He felt wretchedly at a loss for something to do. It was easier after Poldi sent him out to a restaurant to bring some food. *She* got up from her chair by the sewing machine the moment Poldi started to set the table, and she went out into the kitchen to serve out the soup and the veal stew he had brought from the restaurant. But she refused to come to the table and eat. When Poldi urged her, "You've got to eat something, Mother!" she lowered: "You let me alone! I've got my soup out here. . . ."

He was glad that Poldi and Franz were so busy with all the arrangements for the funeral that they had to delegate a long list of errands to him. As he hurried from the printer where he had to order the funeral announcements to the post office to send the telegrams Franz had written out, and from there to the florist in the Westbahnstrasse, he could not help reflecting that apart from the misty and only distantly troubling fact that Father was dead, this was the most exciting thing that had ever happened at home. He was allowed to sit up until nearly twelve o'clock to help Poldi address the announcements.

He had a curious dream that night. . . .

He dreamed of something that had happened years ago, when he was still so small that Father had invariably carried him pickaback in the evening on the way home from some outing. . . . They were all on an excursion to the woods somewhere behind Mödling, and it was one of those ineffably gay and wonderful days when Father laughed and joked with everybody but most of all with Franz, and when even she seemed to be happy. They had had a picnic lunch on a meadow at the far edge of which blackberry brambles grew down into a ravine. Butterflies flicked capriciously from flower to flower through the lazy, sun-quivering air. The summer day had a golden quality of stretching out endlessly. . . . And then, later, Father and he were alone on a heavily shaded path and there was the cyclamen between the roots of an old tree! Father was bending over and gently parting the leaves with the tip of his walking stick to show him the three pink, spiral-petaled blossoms and the one which had not opened yet. The joy of the discovery came back to him. He felt himself flooded with affection for Father in his dream—then everything changed suddenly: it was winter and he was drearily alone with Father on the road just below Steinhof. He had half climbed up on Father's back and Father was shaking himself feebly and saying: "You are too big for that now!" And then it was Father who was suddenly on his back and Father had something horrible the matter with his head and was holding a huge pile of funeral announcements under one arm. Peter felt himself staggering under the desperate weight. It seemed frightfully important for Father and him to get down to the Baumgarten cemetery in time for somebody's funeral. . . .

The oppressive dream haunted him even after he had been awake and up for hours. It made him alternately dread and rush forward to meet the moment of seeing Father's body.

He went out to the cemetery church with Poldi that afternoon. Father was laid out in one of the side chapels. The coffin rested on an impressive catafalque, on both sides of which burned six candles. Several wreaths had already arrived and were banked against the foot of the catafalque. There was the one Poldi had sent him to order at the florist's yesterday and two others. He glanced furtively down at the gold lettering on the black streamers. One of the wreaths was from Herr and Frau Gregor, but the other one had been sent by somebody who only identified himself as "a friend."

He finally looked at Father. He wore the black suit she had taken out to Steinhof yesterday afternoon and his hands were folded on his chest over her silver crucifix. The entire top of Father's head was tightly swathed in a very white bandage.

He breathed easier. The lingering horror of his dream had left him a prey to a hundred terrifying speculations as to what had happened to Father's head. The austere white bandage reassured him. It only made Father look more distinguished, and it gave an exotic plausibility to Father's lying here in a coffin between the two rows of too-quietly burning candles. The face was a waxen yellow as he had feared. . . .

Now that he had seen Father he felt devoid of all emotion again. The forbiddingly aloof figure in the coffin bore no relation at all to the joyful reality of Father in the first part of his dream.

He noticed that Poldi had bent down to rearrange the three wreaths. He saw her frown suddenly at the one with the mysterious legend *From a friend* and pick it up brusquely and place it at the far side of the catafalque where it could hardly be seen. Poldi's resentment of the innocent wreath spelled itself out in his head: the wreath must have been sent by the lady he had seen with Father that time, the same lady Poldi had been so angry about.

The longer he thought about it, the more certain he became that he was right. But how could the lady have heard so soon about Father, since Poldi was not likely to have sent her one of the printed announcements? She might of course have seen the notice in the newspaper, but that would hardly have given her time enough to get the wreath made and sent out here. The Gregors' wreath was quite different, because Franz had stopped in to see Herr Gregor yesterday afternoon. . . . She must have been very fond of Father, he went on thinking, to have sent the wreath so promptly. Or perhaps she had even brought it herself! But would she also dare to come to the funeral, since she must know how Poldi felt?

He could no longer conceal from himself that he was actually looking forward to the funeral. The realization shocked him even more than his lack of grief over Father's death. He reproached himself for it, yet the harder he tried to prod himself into some feeling of sorrow, the more sluggish his emotions seemed. . . .

They rode out to the cemetery in a *Fiaker* Franz had hired for the afternoon. Her face was completely hidden behind the long black veil which made even her handkerchief look dark when she reached up under it to wipe her eyes. Poldi, he decided, looked rather handsome in her new mourning clothes; her warm, energetic, oval face was held up defiantly as if she were angry with the gray sky. Franz's black-gloved hand brushed nervously around and around the crown of his top hat which he was holding in his lap.

They had come early so as to have some time alone before people began to arrive. A large number of wreaths had been piled in a great mound at the foot of the catafalque. The sight of them filled him with pride. Even the heavy scent of the hothouse flowers, which had always seemed so loathsome at other funerals before, was welcome to him now. He calculated proudly that there would not be room for even a third of the wreaths on the hearse and that there would have to be one of the special flower wagons with four glossy black angels at the corners for the rest.

Franz and Poldi had been called out of the chapel by the undertaker who was whispering to them just outside the door. A fly buzzed noisily over the lower end of the coffin. *She* beat at it with one hand and caused two of the candles to flicker violently, but she had not taken her eyes from Father's face while she was doing it. She reached up once under her veil and slowly wiped her eyes; then with the same fluid, almost somnambulistic sort of gesture which he had often observed in her in church, she bent over the coffin and started to do something with Father's hands. When she moved away, he saw that she had twined her rosary with the mother-of-pearl beads around Father's fingers.

Somebody else besides Poldi and Franz had come back into the chapel. Herr Gregor was wringing Franz's hand. Herr Gregor's other hand was stiffly holding a shiny top hat like a present against his chest. His long, gawky body was bent apologetically toward Franz. Frau Gregor, who had been murmuring to Poldi, jostled Herr Gregor and for a minute took possession of Franz; then, stoutly impetuous, prosperously rustling with silk, she came hurrying up to *her*. Frau Gregor's sympathy loosened some control in her and made her choke with sobs. Herr and Frau Gregor stood unhappily by the coffin until Fräulein Gisl and another girl came up; then they moved away toward the black-hung wall.

More and more people began to arrive: friends of Father's from the theater, people from the house in the Schottenfeldgasse, Herr Schmidtmeyer with a huge bouquet, tradespeople from their former neighborhood, and some people who had apparently known Father and her years ago and whom he had never seen before.

With a thrill of pride he saw Baron Ortner stop for a minute beside Franz, then limp up to the coffin and with infinite courtliness bend over and kiss her hand. Baron Ortner remained gravely at attention in front of the coffin for some seconds, one hand elegantly resting on his saber hilt, before he came over to him. There was an exciting intimacy in his "Hello, Peter." With a twinge of disappointment, Peter saw that he was not going to stay beside him; he moved away and stood between—of all people!—Frau Fuchs who ran the vegetable stall in the Burggasse and one of the men from the theater.

There was a discreet stir on the other side of the catafalque. Two of the undertaker's men came up along the far wall and stood beside the coffin lid. The undertaker whispered something to Franz, who nodded slowly. . . . Aunt Wetti, in a very elegant black costume and with only the merest wisp of a veil hanging down over her eyes—Peter noticed irritably—and Uncle von Garnhaft arrived only just in time to join all the other people who had started to file past the coffin once more.

Alarm spread all through him in a chilling rush. Now there were only a few minutes left! He looked guiltily at Father's face. It seemed less forbidding than the day before, but also infinitely more aloof. Father's thin-lipped, resolute mouth had softened somewhat, as it had done formerly toward the end of Father's naps on the divan. It had always been a sign of good humor then, at least half a promise that Father would take him along on a walk, but now it was as meaningless as the white bandage around Father's head.

The two men with the coffin lid had come up to the catafalque. She started to sob. Franz and Aunt Wetti were murmuring on each side of her, trying to comfort her. Poldi stood by, with her elbows tensely crooked. . . .

The memory of the time when Father had shown him the cyclamen in the woods came suddenly back to him. He clutched at it eagerly. It was, he knew, only a poor substitute for the sorrow he could not make himself feel, but its poignancy gave him at least an illusion of sharing in Poldi's and Franz's grief. He clung to it while he watched the men close the coffin, all during the service in church, and afterward as he walked beside Poldi in the slow procession behind the hearse up to the newly dug grave.

Just as before, in the chapel, time had at moments seemed to stand still, so events now followed each other with stealthy rapidity. The undertaker's men rolled the coffin out of the hearse and brought it to the iron frame which had been placed over the grave. There was a brief pause while the men got ready to work the winches on which the heavy canvas straps under the coffin were wound. Then the coffin sank slowly and disappeared.

Her shoulders jerked under her black veil. Franz was holding her hard by the arm because she was leaning out too far over the grave. Already the undertaker had placed the cast-iron urn with dirt on the corner of the iron frame. She took the little shovel from him blindly and described three shaky crosses with it as she dribbled down the dirt. Poldi took the shovel next, then Franz, and then the undertaker handed it to him. The crumbs of earth made a dry clatter on the coffin below. One by one, people came up to the urn, then turned around awkwardly to say good-by to her and to Franz before they started down the avenue.

Baron Ortner came away from the grave and motioned him to come to one side.

"Franz says that you want to go to cadet school. . . ."

"Yes, a boy told me about it."

"Well, I think we can arrange that easily enough. When will you need the letter?"

"The application blank said April first."

"Fine. Just tell Franz exactly what you need. I'll see to it that my uncle writes the letter in time. All right?"

Baron Ortner gave him a quick grin and held out his hand. Then he limped back to Franz to say good-by. A minute later he was gone.

Only a few people were still left. The gravediggers were starting to fill in the grave. The funeral was over—and not only over, but because of Baron Ortner already far in the past. He minded hardly at all when Aunt Wetti insisted on kissing him before she went. Nothing mattered, nothing at all, now that Baron Ortner had made it practically a certainty that he would be in the cadet school next fall.

But on the way home, and later that evening, he felt guilty again. The gentleness with which Poldi and Franz treated her, the grave softness in their voices when they spoke to each other or to him, brought back the feeling that he had been inexcusably callous ever since Franz had first told him about the operation. As he watched them more closely, however, he became reassured. There was now, and he recognized that there had been all along, a certain reservation in their grief. Their sadness was tempered by an unavowed but almost tangible relief. It was as if an ugly shadow had been lifted from the apartment. When Franz stopped by the sewing machine, where she had sat down after supper, and said softly: "It's much better this way, Mother. Father is happy now," he was only voicing something that had been in all their minds, that Father was now safely and honorably dead and that they no longer had to tremble with secret fear that Father might have to spend the rest of his life in Steinhof.

A strange peace had come into the house. As the days slid by in a sort of limpid hush, Peter observed that when Poldi or Franz or she were driven by some inner need to speak of Father, they always spoke of him as he had been long ago, before he had been pensioned by the theater and before he had been ill. The whole period in between was as if it had never been.

He watched with a certain astonishment the tacit conspiracy in which they were all engaged. Seemingly trivial remarks became important elements in this vivid new image of Father they were so busy creating in their minds. One day when Franz had gone into the attic to unpack some books and on coming down had complained that his best leather suitcase had begun to crack, she had promptly taken the blame: "Father always said that leather ought to be saddle-soaped once a year. I forgot all about it this fall with all the worry. . . ." Another time, when Poldi and Franz were talking about the money they still owed for Father's operation, she had come to the living-room door to admonish them somberly: "Father always hated debts worse than poison. The first thing he would have done if he were still alive would be to get those doctors paid, and not order a tombstone for show. . . ."

In no uncertain way she had appointed herself the custodian of Father's memory, and its oracle and interpreter as well. It was as if now that Father was dead, she had completely subordinated herself to him. She would not allow anything that had belonged to Father to be touched. Once, when Poldi wanted to take Father's wardrobe for her own clothes and had protested: "What's the use of keeping all of Father's clothes, Mother? Why don't you give them to somebody? There's a nice old man who sweeps the rooms in our congregation—" *she* had been up in arms immediately: "That wardrobe stays just as it's always been. Father's things aren't going to be touched by you or by anybody else, not as long as I'm alive. When I'm gone, you can do what you like!" And when Poldi had objected: "That's just being morbid, Mother!" she had justified herself glibly: "Morbid or not! Those clothes are going to come in mighty handy for him—" Peter noted not without surprise that he no longer minded the special inflection with which she always referred to him—"with everything going up all the time. Maybe you can go to the store and buy him new clothes every year. I know I can't."

And while he exulted secretly in the knowledge that by next year he would be in the cadet school and would not need Father's clothes, he yet felt indulgent toward her stubborn duplicity, since it was so closely connected with the strange new peace that had settled in the apartment. For it was precisely this sense of peace which made him feel so free to give himself up to his dreams of the cadet school next year and to the exhilarating task of getting ready for the examinations in May.

Chapter Thirty-Two

He did not lose any time in reporting to Meissl what Baron Ortner had said.

"But do you really think," Meissl asked, "that you can catch up in French? I told my tutor about it and she said it couldn't be done. At least, she said that it'd be very difficult. . . ."

His happiness resumed its course with a rush. *If that was all!* . . . He boasted:

"Just wait and see whether I don't!"

He had already found an advanced French grammar and a number of French novels among Franz's books. He set himself a goal of learning at least twenty-five new words each day and mastering all the forms of some irregular verb. Memorizing the words was the easiest part; he could do that from little slips of paper on the way to and from school. And with the rest, working together with Meissl helped. They would go over the corrections the tutor had made on Meissl's paper and memorize those; then they would both do the assignment the tutor had given Meissl for the following week.

He enjoyed going to Meissl's house every Saturday afternoon. Meissl's mother was well-to-do. There was a maid and an oil painting of Meissl's father in full-dress major's uniform and a grand piano on which Meissl's mother sometimes played while they were working in Meissl's room. At four o'clock Frau Meissl tapped on the door to tell them that *Jause* was waiting for them. They sat around a small, inlaid coffee table and had coffee and rolls. Frau Meissl usually teased them about working so hard. She was vivacious and pretty, but Peter never felt wholly at ease with her. There was a crispness about everything she said and did which disconcerted him and which he attributed to the fact that she was from Germany and a Protestant. Yet the subtly foreign atmosphere at Meissl's house also stimulated him; he thought he saw some connection between it and the brisk military life which awaited him in the cadet school, and he always worked especially hard when he came home from an afternoon in the Neubaugasse.

He came to grudge the time he had to put on homework from school, unless the subject was one in which he was going to be examined in May. And there were also the drawing lessons which took away three afternoons each week. It was not long before Herr Heitvogt noticed that his work for the drawing lessons had fallen off. He was forced to explain about the cadet school, and he saw immediately that he had been right in fearing that Herr Heitvogt would be disappointed. Herr Heitvogt was angry as well. His usually friendly eyes grew hard behind the thick glasses as he sneered: "Cadet school! Is it the uniform or the easy life? As if we hadn't enough fools who can strut on the Ring and bellow at the soldiers on the Schmeltz! I suppose you want to stop the lessons altogether now?"

Peter felt trapped in the bristling pause. He protested hastily: "No, Herr Heitvogt, I don't." He had already decided to manage to satisfy Herr Heitvogt somehow and study for the examination, too.

He worked harder again until Herr Heitvogt showed signs of having forgiven him. A few weeks after the outburst over the cadet school, Herr Heitvogt examined a drawing of a head he had just finished and said:

"Well, now you can do a reasonable likeness of a figure or a head. But that's not drawing, of course. A camera can do that much better than you. What you must learn now is to catch the inner rhythm of a figure, and plaster models are no good for that. I want you to do a lot of little sketches of people working, getting on a streetcar, coming downstairs—anything at all. Don't try to get a likeness: I don't want to see who it is, but what the person is doing. . . ."

It was an easy assignment because he liked to do the quick little drawings and because they made hardly any demand on his time. He could always get half a dozen good sketches just by sitting in the gallery at the Turnverein for a few minutes before the setting-up exercises started. There was an abundance of material in the streetcar and even in church; but most productive of all were the otherwise hateful mornings when he had to get up early to stand in line for food. Once, just before Easter, one of the casual sketches he made like that had an unexpected success.

He had been standing in line for potatoes since four o'clock. It was cold and wet, and nearly everybody had brought a piece of board or a few burlap sacks to stand on. It was very doubtful whether there would still be any potatoes left by the time the rear half of the line got up to the stall. The uncertainty had made people irritable and their ill-humor had fastened on an officious policeman who had never been on duty in the market before. When the morose April dawn finally turned into light, Peter started a caricature of the policeman. A man who was standing behind Peter became interested and kept chuckling as he watched. As soon as the sketch was done, the man insisted on showing it around. He kept exclaiming gleefully: "Isn't that good? You know, I'd like to have that!" He suddenly pulled out his pocketbook. "I'll give you half a krone for it—" The man pressed the money on him.

At the end of the next lesson, Peter told Herr Heitvogt about the caricature. Herr Heitvogt beamed.

"There you are! Your first success as an artist and a real sale—and you want to be an officer! . . ."

But while the incident of the caricature flattered his pride, it did little to reconcile him to standing in line. The war, which had long ago palled as a topic of conversation between people because the monotonous reports of victories on the Russian and Italian fronts still failed to bring about the end of the war, had become sharply insistent again in the greater hardships every day. Ever since February, and in spite of the rationing cards, food had not only become desperately hard to get, but it was increasingly vitiated by substitutes. Bread, which had only been black before because of the wheat chaff and oatmeal used in it, was made entirely of corn meal now. It was as gritty as a sand pie and made many people sick. The new vegetable fat of which they got altogether half a pound a week looked like butter, but had no taste at all. Instead of sugar there was saccharine. It seemed to him as if everything they ate was tainted with the sickly sweet taste that went with corn meal and turnips and saccharine. Of late a new kind of potato had made its appearance in the markets. The newspapers explained that it was an American delicacy called "yams." The yams, too, had the same sweet taste as everything else. He could not imagine how anyone could possibly consider them a delicacy.

He was hungry nearly all of the time. But even the perpetual gnawing at the pit of his stomach became somehow part of the excitingly rigorous discipline he had imposed on himself. By August he would be in the cadet school and then he would get plenty of food, and delicious food at that! And it was only a few more months until then. Already the bushes and trees in the parks were turning green.

He had never been so conscious of spring before. He watched the trees along the Gürtel turn luxuriant with brilliant new foliage, and the different flowers come into bloom, with a deep, eager joy. Meissl and he had taken to spending a great deal of time in the parks. They took along their books and worked until they grew weary of the long lists of history dates and of French verbs; then they wandered along the sanded paths and talked about the cadet school and the endless, fascinating details of an officer's life.

One Sunday morning while they were strolling like that on the Ring, just outside the Volksgarten gate, Peter suddenly noticed the choir approaching through the park. Herr Granini was walking in front with Professor Wessely and several other men; behind them came the familiar, cheerfully straggling groups of boys. It was the first time that Peter had seen Herr Granini or the choir since Franz had had him expelled. He was startled by the sudden tightening in his chest. He turned his back hastily on the gate and pretended to be fascinated by the medals of an artillery captain on the other side of the Ring.

Fortunately, Meissl had not noticed anything. Meissl studied the artillery captain in all seriousness for a second and said scornfully:

"He's only a reservist. Just look how he carries himself—you can always tell a civilian in uniform."

The choir had gone past. Peter breathed freely again. It had been a narrow escape. He hastened to agree with Meissl's disdain for the reserve officer, who in spite of all his medals was farther from the enviable status of a professional officer than they would be just as soon as they had been admitted to the cadet school. . . .

During the last week before the examination, they studied every evening at Meissl's house. Meissl's tutor came and worked with them on French. Afternoons they crammed history and algebra.

They were both letting their schoolwork slide so as to have every available minute for a final review.

The examination was held in a large lecture room in the polytechnical institute just off the Ring. There were several hundred boys. The examination took all morning and lasted until five in the afternoon. They spent the rest of the day checking their answers, but except for history and algebra it was hard to tell whether they had passed or not. The uncertainty kept them on tenterhooks for the next two weeks.

Then, one Saturday morning, Peter breathlessly opened the long, blue envelope which had come addressed to him. It contained a curt notice to present himself for the medical examination on the tenth of July. He rushed to school and found Meissl waiting for him outside. Meissl waved a blue envelope when they were still half a block apart. . . .

Chapter Thirty-Three

If the months since Meissl had first mentioned the cadet school to him had been not unlike scaling a formidable but challenging mountainside, the weeks which now followed were like a deliciously drawn-out halt within very reach of the summit, before climbing the last, almost playfully easy crag. For there could be no longer any doubt of his getting into the cadet school now. The medical examination would be no more than a formality since he was healthy enough, and as for the board of admissions before which he was to appear on the same day, there the letter with the three impressive army seals from Baron Ortner's uncle was certain to smooth his path.

There was all of a sudden time and space enough for everything. Almost from an excess of leisure he applied himself to drawing again. But infinitely more engrossing was the opportunity to be around machinery which had suddenly offered itself. Herr Geiger, the man who owned the big machine shop in the next block, still lived in the apartment above theirs. One evening just after the examination, Frau Geiger had asked him to take over to the shop a telegram which had come for Herr Geiger. It was late and except for Herr Geiger who was hunched over a litter of blueprints on a tall desk there had only been three mechanics still at work. Herr Geiger had allowed him to stay and look around.

The shop had proved even more fascinating than he had imagined. There had been long rows of machines which loomed like gleaming monsters where they receded into the shadows toward the rear of the shop, and there had been the equally enthralling skill of the three mechanics under the glare of the powerful droplights over their machines. After a while Herr Geiger himself had left his desk and had thrown on the power at a brightly polished, new precision lathe. So intense was his concentration as he worked that Peter did not think that he was even aware of him watching on one side.

Once, however, Herr Geiger looked up briefly from measuring the small cylinder into which he was cutting a spiral groove and explained:

"This little socket has to be correct within one ten-thousandth of an inch. If it's more than that off, it's egg-shaped anyway."

Only Herr Geiger's grin showed that the remark was meant for a joke. Silence settled again around the machine as he resumed his work. He measured again and again before he seemed satisfied. Then, almost visibly, he relaxed. He was about to shut off the lathe when he asked: "Ever see how one of these works?" But his explanation turned out to be no more than a rough outline of the intricate mechanism of the lathe. When he had finished, Peter wanted to know more. His curiosity made him ask for permission to come back the following day.

He spent the next evening and nearly every evening after that in the shop. He came to love the soapy smell of the lubricants which hung around the machines, the isolated glare of the droplights where the mechanics worked, but above all the atmosphere of austere and yet friendly concentration which gave the shop something of the hush of a church. There was an uncompromising element in the mechanics' passion for precision which appealed to him and made him feel singularly at home with Herr Geiger and the three men. He observed the almost mystic communion which existed between all of them and the machines and tools with which they worked. This quality which seemed to him like a sixth sense that set the four men apart from ordinary men, Herr Geiger almost put into words one evening when Peter had been allowed to file the burrs off a casting. After a while Herr Geiger had come over to the vise to see how he was getting along. He felt the surface on which Peter had been filing and said: "Well, that's even enough. Almost level . . . Filing's not so easy as it looks! You can always tell a born mechanic from a mucker by the way he files. Most people seesaw all over the place, even if they've spent half their lives in a machine shop and call themselves mechanics. I guess it's something you are born with."

The implication that he was one of the elect thrilled him for several days. Gradually, Herr Geiger showed him how to operate all of the machines, and one day he was actually allowed to run the precision lathe. He also discovered that what kept Herr Geiger and the three mechanics so busy in the evenings was a new type of gun sight which they had nearly perfected to the point where it would replace the gun sights Herr Geiger's shop was manufacturing during the day. . . .

He was vaguely troubled now and again by the pleasure he got out of being in the shop. Next year, in the cadet school, there would not be any chance to be around machines. But when that thought crossed his mind he quickly put himself off with a bold dream in which he saw himself as a combination of officer and engineer in some army arsenal or in one of the new factories where airplanes were built. The surge of self-confidence which had lifted him ever since the examination made nothing seem beyond his power now. He would be an officer but he would also be a mechanic and an engineer—perhaps he would even manage to draw and to paint besides! All that would come later on; right now the cadet school came first!

He was doubly sure of it when he was with Meissl again. They were spending as much time as ever in the parks, but now their talk often wandered to other subjects besides the military life of which they would so soon be a part. It seemed to Peter as if they were only really getting to know each other now that they no longer had to study and had endless leisure to talk. Thus it was only lately, for instance, that he had become conscious of a subtle and sometimes baffling difference between Meissl's way of looking at things and his own. The difference had to do with the fact that Meissl was a Protestant.

Deliberately he steered their talks around to religion to find out what Meissl believed and what the services in a Protestant church were like. Meissl was quite ready to tell him what he wanted to know, but it was clear that the subject held no interest for him. Unless Peter kept on asking questions, the conversation quickly drifted on to something else. There were only a few exceptions, such as the time when Meissl suddenly showed a lurid curiosity about the lives of priests and nuns, and said: "But the priests and the nuns sleep together, don't they? I read about it in a book. Besides, I know a man who's actually seen the tunnel between a monastery and a women's convent next door!"

He was astonished by his own vehemence in denying the charge and other similar ones that Meissl made. It seemed strange to him that after the past year, when he had been more than ever bored with going to church and had even had doubts about the existence of God, he should be so ready to defend the Church. He was aware that on those occasions he was always thinking of the May-devotions in the lovely chapel at the Verein, with the little altar banked with lilac and peonies, the choir grouped around the small organ in the rear and singing the *Tantum Ergo* and then the *Stella Maris* at the end. . . .

It struck him that precisely there lay the crux of the difference between Meissl and himself: Meissl had no such secret corners of warmth and joy inside him as this luminous memory of the chapel in the Verein. But neither—Peter noticed—did Meissl have to contend with that paralyzing sense of mingled awe and guilt which he himself had always known and which he also associated with religion and church. In a sense, he had always been afraid, whereas Meissl was not afraid.

It was especially so when it came to girls. Meissl was easily the most successful of the eight or nine boys in class who made it a point of honor to flirt with the girls from the school next door. Meissl's poise gave him an insinuating, dashing ease which made the other boys appear raucous and fresh. And the girls made no secret of the fact that they preferred him to all the rest. There was one girl in particular with whom Meissl's banter always took on a note of familiarity that made Peter curious about her. She was dark and pretty and in some indefinable way much more grown-up than the other girls, who either giggled a great deal or affected every theatrical extreme of seriousness. When he asked Meissl about her one day in the park, Meissl spoke quite calmly of kissing her and let it appear that there had been much more than that. He did not boast; his tone implied that it was the most natural thing in the world for him to do.

To that extent at least, Peter envied him, for when he himself had flirted with one of the girls he had always felt too self-conscious to enjoy himself very much. On the one hand, the nearness of some girl or other had sent his mind racing ahead to all sorts of guilty possibilities, so that he had become embarrassed and tongue-tied; and on the other hand, there was always the memory of that precious half-hour with Bianca in Schönbrunn, and compared to Bianca these girls were hopelessly callow and dull.

The entire spring as he looked back on it had been filled with Bianca for him. It was not so much that he had actually thought of her so often as that he had rarely been without the consciousness of something wonderful and exciting just ahead.

He had waited in vain for Franz to mention Bianca again. He was not even sure whether Franz saw her any more, for Franz had stopped coming home on Thursday afternoons to put on his full-dress suit since Father's death. It rather looked as if Franz had felt obliged by his mourning to give up going to the Burgtheater on Thursday night.

Then, just a few days before his medical examination, Peter happened to pick up a novel on Franz's desk. A blue theater-ticket stub fell out. It had been for the last Thursday in June. He noticed that it was for the Gentlemen's Parterre—the big box directly in back of the orchestra seats where one was admitted in ordinary street clothes but had to stand. He could almost visualize how Franz had salved his conscience about going to the theater so soon after Father's death by telling himself that standing in the Gentlemen's Parterre was almost like not being in the theater at all. . . . Bianca was still in Vienna then! He started to look eagerly through other books. He found three more stubs, the earliest dating from a Thursday in May, less than four months after Father's death. He put the stubs back carefully into the books, but the mere sight of them had brought Bianca excitingly close and had left him with a pleasantly guilty feeling of sharing a secret with Franz.

It seemed to him an unmistakable, happy omen that Franz should choose the very novel in which he had discovered the first stub to take along to the cadet school on the morning of the examination. The book in Franz's hand—when he came out into the living room to ask: "Ready?"—took on the rich assurance of a talisman. Now nothing could possibly go wrong! He answered, "Ready!" with all the confidence the radiant July morning had already aroused in him.

Chapter Thirty-Four

THEY were to be at the cadet school at nine. It was barely half past eight when their streetcar passed the reservoir and the street alongside it which sloped down to Schönbrunn.

The sly exuberance of the July morning was everywhere. One by one, the familiar stops of Breitensee slid past. The streetcar was pleasantly empty and the sun played hide-and-seek over the polished woodwork of the seats, over the blue sticker announcing the third war loan on the window just opposite, over the Panama hat of the man reading the newspaper.

It was the streetcar line Peter had always liked best. As far back as he could remember he had ridden on it with Father on Sunday outings to Hütteldorf, and the many landmarks along the way still had their old power to make him tingle with anticipation. They were in Baumgarten now. He watched for the tall iron fence which inclosed the cadet-school grounds.

One other boy and a lady got off at the school and entered the wide grille gate. Franz and he followed a few steps behind them up the drive which swept in a stately loop around an oval-shaped lawn. An intricate scrollwork of flower beds in the center of the lawn enlaced a weather-blackened bronze monument commemorating some famous battle. It occurred to Peter that this would be only the first of many times that he would pass the monument on his way to the imposing building which rose beyond the lawn and stretched far to the right and the left.

A young officer came out through the middle one of the three arched doors and briskly returned the salute of the two sentries, just as Franz and he started up the steps. The lady and the other boy had stopped uncertainly in the vaulted hall beyond the door: there was no one in the porter's lodge on the right. Franz smiled at the lady, and after hesitating himself for a moment, walked boldly forward into the huge glass-domed rotunda with the imperial double eagle inlaid in gold and black on the mosaic floor. For a minute there was no sign of life anywhere in the building; then a sergeant with a sheaf of papers appeared from the corridor on the left and directed Franz down the opposite corridor.

They had no difficulty in finding the infirmary. The door of the waiting room stood wide open; some twelve or fifteen boys and their parents were already in the room. Meissl and his mother had not yet come. Franz glanced toward a group of vacant chairs between the windows and said: "Shall we go over there?"

A number of eyes were watching them as they crossed the room, but Peter was pleasantly aware that the scrutiny was prompted by nothing more than an innocent and well-bred curiosity. He thought he recognized two of the boys from the written examination in May. Several others interested him because they bore certain indefinable but unmistakable traces of coming from the provinces—it showed chiefly in the angular, somewhat defiant constraint with which they sat and in the blunt watchfulness of their eyes. But all of the boys, and their parents as well, were affected by the tension that hung over the room. Occasionally some boy whispered briefly with his mother; apart from that there was hardly any conversation. The only exception were two fathers, both of them officers, who now and again exchanged a few remarks.

Franz's eyes also rested for a second on the two officers, then brushed discreetly over the other people in the room. A sort of holiday gaiety clung to Franz. He was wearing his light-gray mohair suit with the darker pin stripe, which in itself suggested long summer evenings when Franz came boldly striding down the street with an air that his day in the ministry had been a lark and that the evening was going to be better still. Franz said:

"Well, there don't seem to be very many of you. This oughtn't to take long. . . . Scared?"

"No, I'm not scared," Peter said quickly and wondered whether the not unpleasant tenseness he felt might be described as being scared.

Five boys and their parents arrived nearly all in one bunch, and then Meissl at last. Peter got up and managed to catch his eye. It was part of the strained atmosphere that even Meissl seemed a little distant and strange at first. Only when Peter had introduced Frau Meissl and Franz, and when Frau Meissl had taken his chair, and Meissl and he had moved into the embrasure of the window, did Meissl seem again like himself.

The window opened on a vast parade ground, beyond which were still other buildings. Meissl pointed out the armory, the building which housed the mess hall, two dormitories. Some fifteen cadets came marching out of the dormitory on the right, swung rhythmically and with easy precision along the path to the armory, and finally disappeared inside the tall doorway. They were the only cadets Peter had seen around the school. Meissl claimed to know for sure that most of the cadets were away on an excursion for the day. The stillness between the buildings seemed to bear him out. They turned their backs on the window and started to examine the other boys. They counted twenty-nine boys in all.

"But is that all there are going to be?" Peter asked.

"Sure. I told you they'd weed them out with the written examination. That's what it's for."

Meissl's mother and Franz were talking together with that pleasant, zestful familiarity Peter had observed before when Franz talked with strangers anywhere. Twice Frau Meissl smiled at something Franz said and each time her smile lingered as if she were certain that presently Franz was going to say something amusing again.

One more boy arrived just as the clock on the square tower of the armory struck nine o'clock. The measured peals had the effect of a lid suddenly clamped down on the room. People sat even more stiffly. Even Franz and Frau Meissl were watching the white door through which a white-coated orderly had twice come out on some errands that had taken him out into the corridor.

Five long minutes went by, then the orderly came out and read off the names of ten boys. Meissl's was among them. They disappeared behind the orderly into the dispensary. There was another wait, nearly a quarter of an hour this time, before the orderly reappeared. Peter's name was second on the list.

The dispensary turned out to be a long, white room that was

flooded with sunlight from the cheerfully open windows on the left. Peter felt reassured. The absence of anything more formidable than a few slender glass cabinets between the desks where orderlies were taking down the murmured remarks of the doctors gave an impression of good-natured, almost casual routine. Meissl was already waiting his turn in front of the doctor who was examining chests. The only sinister figure was a short, wizened surgeon major who sat on a low, white-enameled stool beside the desk nearest the door. He did not wear a smock like the other doctors and his stethoscope hung crookedly around the collar of his uniform. Each boy came to him last of all. It was clear that the final decision rested with him.

They were told to take off their clothes and leave them on a row of chairs along the wall. An orderly came and took them to a partition at the far end of the room where they had to line up. They were called behind the partition two at a time. A doctor made Peter sit down in a dentist's chair and examined his teeth. Another doctor tested his eyes and his ears. There was no hitch. He was given a folded card and told to report to the doctors outside.

Meissl, he saw while he stood on the scales to be weighed, was already getting dressed. There was a rather long wait in front of the doctor who examined chests, but it went fast after that. The only scare came from the wizened surgeon major at the end. The boy just ahead of Peter was tall and thin and his shoulder blades stuck out sharply from his back. The surgeon major made the boy lean down toward him and pulled down the skin beneath his eyes, then dictated to the orderly at the desk: "Undernourished, underdeveloped—unfit." His voice was flat and as expressionless as his eyes. The boy was swallowing hard. A large tear had formed under his left eye.

Peter's alarm left no room for sympathy with the boy. He found himself repeating without being able to stop: *My arms aren't as thin as that boy's. . . .* Involuntarily, he pulled back his shoulders as far as they would go when he stepped up to the little doctor who sat crouched on the white-enameled stool. An impatient glint showed in the doctor's eyes. He said dryly: "You are not on parade. Stand the way you usually stand!"

He hastened to let his shoulders sag, but they still felt taut. The surgeon major glanced at his card, then raised the black cup of his stethoscope and clapped it to Peter's chest. He had to breathe deeply, exhale, cough. It was what all the other boys had been asked to do, but when the doctor made him lean forward and started to pull down the skin underneath his eyes, his apprehension sharpened into panic. The surgeon major dictated:

"Undernourished—but we can fix that—fit."

Relief rushed through him in all directions at once. He hurried to get into his clothes to tell Meissl and Franz, but when he finally was about to open the door into the waiting room, he remembered how unexcited Meissl had looked and he forced himself to appear casual, too.

Franz looked up brightly: "All right?"

Both the question and his own nod had a happy superfluousness. Frau Meissl was smiling. She said half to Franz and half to him:

"We'll have to celebrate this somehow!"

"Why, of course!" Franz agreed.

Meissl straightened up a little impatiently beside his mother's chair. They went back to the window again.

"One boy got turned down because he was color-blind," Meissl said. "He just left."

Peter told him about the tall boy who was still inside.

"They oughtn't to have applied in the first place. The application blank said you had to be in perfect condition. They've already started to call boys in to the board of admissions," Meissl went on; "it's very formal—you'll see."

A minute later Peter saw. An adjutant came in from the corridor, looked pleasantly around the room for a second, then read the name of a boy from the pink medical record card in his hand. His tone was conversational, smilingly deprecatory as if he meant to apologize for interrupting people's talk. Almost all the parents were chatting with their neighbors now, and several boys had started to talk with each other, too.

The boys who returned from their interview with the board of admissions looked solemn and shyly self-important—almost, Peter thought, like the boys had looked after the first communion outside the Schottenfeld Church. Meissl and he decided that they were being sent for in the same order in which they had been examined in the infirmary. There were still five boys ahead of Meissl.

Franz and Frau Meissl were still talking together, but Meissl and he found hardly anything to say. It was as if in the long talks they had had about this very day they had exhausted every subject they might have talked about now.

Meissl was called. Peter was left alone by the window. Franz turned around to him once to say: "Cheer up, it'll be your turn soon." Then he and Frau Meissl went on talking about the war again; but Peter noticed that in spite of what he had come to think of as her Protestant self-assurance, Frau Meissl's eyes strayed frequently toward the corridor.

Meissl was gone only a short time. His face when he returned had the same excited glow as when he had successfully completed some difficult exercise on the horizontal bar. Frau Meissl excused herself to Franz:

"We promised to go to my sister's for lunch. She lives all the way in Ober Sankt Veit. . . ." She was already holding out her hand to Franz.

Meissl said lightly, a little glibly, Peter thought:

"It's just like my cousin said. They ask a few questions, that's all. There's a captain who has the German Iron Cross. . . . I'll start for your house at half past three sharp. . . ."

When they were gone, Franz said:

"I like your friend. He looks like a very manly boy. Frau Meissl thought we might all go to Kummer's tonight and then to a theater somewhere—better not say too much about going to the theater before Mother, though! Would you like that?"

"Yes, thank you, Franz." He felt a little embarrassed by Franz's generosity. To hide his emotion, he started to tell him what the surgeon major had said.

Franz grinned. "You bet, you'll get fed all right in this place. I'll envy you. I'll be the one who'll be undernourished! You better save me a couple of rolls and things once in a while and slip them to me when I come to visit you. . . ."

Still another boy and his father left. The crowd in the room had considerably thinned out. Only about half of the people who had been there in the beginning were still left. Franz looked at his watch and frowned.

"I wish those high muck-a-mucks would hurry up a little. It's five to twelve. I only took the morning off. . . ."

A tremor of alarm at Franz's disrespect made him look around quickly to see whether anyone had heard. No one had. An even more pressing fear rose from what Franz had said: supposing they were told to go home at noon and to come back after lunch, or perhaps some other day! He could not bear to think of such a delay. . . .

The clock on the armory tower struck noon. Somewhere off in the distance church bells started to ring. At last, the boy who had been just ahead of the tall boy who had been turned down by the surgeon major was called. He told Franz.

Franz smiled encouragingly. "Well, you won't have anything to worry about. The letter from Heinrich's uncle will make things easy enough. Short of an archduke, you could hardly have got anybody more powerful to recommend you. Just speak up clearly when they ask you anything. . . ."

The adjutant returned and called out his name.

They went the whole length of the corridor back to the rotunda at the entrance, then down the corridor beyond it until they came to tall double doors with massively wrought silver handles very high up. The adjutant reached up to one of the handles and pressed it down. The door was immediately pulled open from the inside by a soldier who stood at attention as they walked in. But Peter had barely got beyond the threshold before he had to stop abruptly because the adjutant had stopped. The adjutant gave him a slight nod, then walked away along the wall on the right.

It was clear that he was no longer supposed to follow the adjutant, that he was suddenly on his own in the lofty-ceilinged room. On the wall facing him hung a gigantic painting of some battle scene; it covered nearly the entire wall, and its heavy gold frame at the bottom ran within three feet of the floor. Across the short side of the room—it seemed a considerable distance from where he was standing—stretched a preposterously long solemn desk with several officers sitting behind it. Peter had only a confused impression of the officers. The desk stood out much more clearly. It was divided into five even panels by a delicate gilt molding. On the wall behind the officers hung a full-length portrait of the Emperor in gala infantry uniform. A red carpet with the imperial monogram woven in the center covered the floor. The drowsily brilliant noonday sun flooded in through a number of windows on the right. . . .

His hesitatiton had lasted only for a fraction of a second, but the entire room was as if etched on his brain. He realized that he was expected to walk up to the officers at the long desk, and that it was meant to be something of a test. Meissl and he had often talked of just such a possibility as this: *They wanted to see how you behaved!*

He stepped up on the rug and started toward the long table. He was aware that the major who was sitting next to the stout brigadier general in the center was frankly studying him. The brigadier general must be the commandant! He had thin, gray hair and a jowly, red face which yet gave the impression of being stubborn and firm. He was talking to the colonel on his right—earnestly, a little pompously, as men talked in a coffeehouse. Beyond the colonel was the captain with the black-and-white ribbon of the German Iron Cross. He was lean and large-boned and bald. He sat facing straight out into the room, looking at once very alive and alert but also as if at the moment he were thinking of something very far from the room. He suddenly flicked out a black leather cigarette case, his whole body moving with the gesture, and took out a cigarette. . . . The last chair at the opposite end of the table was empty. A little distance away from that end of the table, directly under a window, was an ordinary-sized desk at which the adjutant was sitting.

Peter stopped when he was within arm's length of the table and faced the commandant. He felt very conscious of the way he was standing. Meissl, speaking of this very moment, had said repeatedly: "The important thing is not to look like a rookie who expects a dressing-down. The idea is to stand at attention and still look relaxed—the way an officer would look talking to a lady on the Ring." He tried to stand just like that: shoulders back, yet not too far back. He noticed out of the corner of one eye that the captain with the Iron Cross was looking at him now, too.

The adjutant got up from his desk with a gray folder in his hand and walked over to the major. He laid the folder on the table by the major's elbow and announced quietly:

"Peter Domanig. . . ."

The commandant finished a sentence to which the colonel on his right nodded a grave assent, and then took the folder which the major was holding out to him. He glanced at the name on the outside and looked up. His eyes were blunt and formidable.

"Peter Domanig?"

"Yes, your excellency."

The commandant looked at him for a second longer. "M'hmm," he said approvingly. He opened the folder and took out the letter from Baron Ortner's uncle. Peter recognized it at once, although it was no longer in the sealed envelope now, by its heavy, official, stationery. While the commandant was reading the letter, the colonel sat gently tapping the table with his pince-nez. He looked more like a teacher than an officer; his shoulders appeared bony and brittle under his uniform coat and his face was sallow as if he were rarely out of doors. Because he was aware that the colonel was scrutinizing him, Peter kept his eyes on the commandant who was still reading the letter.

An inexplicable frown had appeared between the commandant's eyes. *It couldn't be that there was anything wrong with the letter!*

The captain with the Iron Cross asked in a placid voice:

"Why do you wish to become an officer?"

This was the question for which he had come prepared. He started eagerly:

"I—"

He did not get any further. The commandant's hand sketched a dry little gesture which at once halted him and begged the captain's pardon for the interruption.

"What is your connection with General Count Arany?"

Although he was alarmed by the subtly hostile brusqueness that had come into the commandant's voice, the very mention of Baron Ortner's uncle gave him confidence to answer clearly. When he had finished, the commandant said:

"I see."

He said it negligently, as if the information no longer interested him. It seemed to Peter that the commandant had become much less friendly than before. He put down the letter and picked up the application blank. Peter wondered whether he was still expected to answer the captain's question, but the captain was leaning back in his chair and appeared to be waiting for the commandant to say something more.

The commandant abruptly put the application blank down on the table between the colonel and himself and pointed to something on the inside sheet. There was an exchange of ominously indistinct murmurs between him and the colonel. The major on the other side of the commandant had leaned forward to listen. Peter caught a syllable now and again, and then—starkly, inescapably—the word "illegitimate."

A hot flush rushed to his skin everywhere and stayed there like a blistering sheath, inside which he felt rigid and bleakly isolated with sudden fear.

The commandant looked up. "Who came with you this morning?"

He had to swallow twice to be able to speak at all.

"My cousin, your excellency—he is also my guardian."

"Oh, yes. Ask your guardian to come in here—alone, please!"

The hot sheath of shame which felt like something outside his body moved with him toward the door. A curious numbness blunted his eyes and ears. The soldier pulled open the door. Then he was out in the corridor....

He felt afraid to think, to let himself sound the danger behind this order to summon Franz. But the effort not to think was a nearly unbearable strain. It was like holding his breath under water too long, like the time when he had tried to swim under the platform with the cabins on it in the swimming pool and he had lost his way among the piles.

They simply wanted to see Franz about something, that was all, he told himself twice in a row to down his sick fear as he approached the infirmary. *Nothing so very unusual about that!* But he was wretchedly aware of people's eyes as he entered the waiting room and sharply glad that Meissl and his mother had already left. Franz looked up with an air of "Well, that was quick!" but he did not say it.

He whispered quickly:

"They want to see you, Franz."

He was grateful that Franz got up immediately, looking only a little puzzled and appearing already to have discarded the idea that anything very serious could be wrong.

"I suppose we forgot to fill in something on the blank," Franz said out in the corridor. "Where is it?"

"It's down this way. . . ."

"Here?"

Nothing could still the sick quivering at the pit of his stomach, but Franz's cheerful confidence as he knocked on the tall double doors at least had the effect of making him disown his fear hopefully. Franz would straighten everything out!

The door closed behind Franz. To keep down his fear, he tried to picture to himself how Franz would act. He could almost hear Franz introducing himself: "Franz Bartsch, second lieutenant in the reserves. . . ."

The seconds piled up heavily. He did not dare take his eyes from the door. Would Franz come to call him back in, or would they send the adjutant? He was conscious of a continual effort to keep from thinking of the word he had heard the commandant whisper to the colonel, much as he would have jerked back and walked cautiously around a series of hot stoves in a dark room.

He took two quick steps toward the door when Franz came out—then he stopped. Franz's forehead and his cheekbones showed the pale pink splotches Franz got when he was very angry and was holding himself in.

Franz did not look at him.

"We better go now," Franz said.

Chapter Thirty-Five

Then it was all over!

A tumultuous surge of thoughts reared and strained in the desperate emptiness which sucked at him but would not be caught and put into words. Panorama-like the whole past year rose up suddenly before him in jeering reproof. First, there had been the confirmation—that had started it all—then the trip with Franz, then Bianca, and finally this dream of the cadet school—all too wonderful somehow to be really true. He knew suddenly that he had had a secret dread all along that it would all come to nothing. The feeling that he had been led on deliberately up to this particular moment crushed him and filled him with a fierce, groping rage. . . .

If I had not wanted it all so much, he thought dully, *I should have got in. Like Meissl . . . Meissl didn't care! Meissl had wanted to get in all right, but not the way I wanted to. For Meissl it was only another school. For me it would have been what Meissl's mother and his father—even though his father is dead—are to him. I should have been like other boys.*

Instead of that, he had been humiliated in front of those officers because he was *illegitimate.* The word burned into his brain. And Franz had been ashamed too—that was what those angry splotches in his cheeks meant.

Decent! decent! he lashed out angrily; that was Poldi's favorite word. He had been decent all year—Poldi and Franz had shown that they thought so, too—and this was what had come of it! A troubled notion that for him everything beautiful and desirable was filled with treachery left him feeling hollow with discouragement. The next instant he rebelled again, but his blindly flashing anger groped in vain for something to fasten on.

They passed between the two sentries and went down the steps. Everything lay hot and still in the midday sun. The monogramlike flower beds around the monument on the lawn, he noticed with a sense of stilted unreality, were planted with coleus and dwarf begonia.

When they got down to the gate, Franz turned left along the wrought-iron fence instead of crossing over to the streetcar stop. He strode along with jerky, oblivious strides. In spite of his own self-absorption, Peter was aware that Franz was struggling for something comforting to say and did not know how to begin. When they reached the corner of the fence, Franz said:

"I'm going to write to Heinrich this afternoon. Perhaps I'd better telegraph. . . ."

Franz's promise to write or even telegraph to Baron Ortner seemed utterly without importance, on the mere margin of things. He had to struggle against a leaden sense of futility and against his shame to ask:

"Was it because of my father, because Mizzi—"

"It's only because your father is a foreigner and because we're at war with England."

"The commandant said I was illegitimate!"

His voice sounded brash and violent in his own ears. He realized also that he had sounded as if it were Franz's fault. Yet he did not feel like taking any of it back. The fierce, dark pressure which had been coming and going inside him ever since they had walked down the cadet-school steps had at least become permanent with his speaking of the words, so that some of its menace was gone and he had the feeling that he could control it now because he was one with it.

Franz sounded alarmed:

"You mustn't think of it like that! It would have been exactly the same if your father—they couldn't have taken you when they knew your father was English. I had to tell them that. . . ."

Franz was slowing down solicitously and was matching his steps to his. "It isn't as if anybody attached any importance nowadays to the other thing," Franz went on. "Just think how lucky you are to have a healthy body. You might have been born with a clubfoot or a hunchback or even with bad eyes like some people. . . . If anything, it's an advantage; everybody knows how many children who were born like that turned out to be famous people. Look at Leonardo da Vinci and—well, dozens of them. All you have to do is read history!"

Where was it that he had heard that same argument before? Of course, Aunt Wetti that time! Only, it did not anger him now. It was almost as if Franz were speaking to somebody else and not to him at all. And at least, Franz was sincere and was not trying to whitewash Mizzi, the way Aunt Wetti had done. . . .

"Anyhow," Franz said more confidently now, "the cadet school isn't the only school in the world. I've always thought that you ought to go to an art school, and if you don't want to do that, there are all sorts of technical schools. We can find out about them right away. . . ."

Yes, of course, he could go to some drab school or other—like making oneself believe that the gritty maize bread was as good as the rolls before the war, or that the cardboard shoes in the windows of shoe stores now were as good as real shoes! Franz did not even suspect what the cadet school had meant to him! A sudden realization that the world of Bianca and Baron Ortner—of Meissl even—had retreated forever from his grasp settled on him with dull finality.

"I'm not going to any more schools. I'm going to be a machinist."

The statement bulged out and lay there heavy and immovable like his previous outburst. In the pause which followed, Franz seemed to be weighing each word.

"You'll feel differently in a few days. I'll wire Heinrich first thing after lunch. We'll see what he thinks first. . . ."

They walked along silently until they came to the corner of the reservoir where the street led down to Schönbrunn. Franz suddenly reached to his back pocket and brought out his pocketbook.

"Look, I've got to get back to the office. I'm late already. But why don't you spend the afternoon out here in Schönbrunn? There's a little restaurant just before you get down to the square: you can have lunch there! I'll tell Mother that you won't be home."

Franz held out a five-kronen note to him.

For a moment he was tempted. He saw himself eating alone in the restaurant, then walking along the avenue where they had met Bianca that day—then the whole picture he thus had of himself struck him as melodramatic and cheap.

Without taking his eyes off the letter box just beside Franz he said:

"No, I'll come home with you."

They waited for the streetcar without speaking again.

The dull hopelessness which had succeeded to his first feeling of despair lasted on into the afternoon. He was aware that his growing animosity against all the officers at the long table that morning screened his reluctance to think about the cause of his having been turned down. Only once, just as he got up from the mockingly festive lunch she had somehow managed to get together, the thought which he had been pressing back like a coiled spring escaped him and pointed with shattering, naked directness to the shapeless, faceless figure who was his father. A flame of cold, white hatred seared through him. *It was his fault!* "Your father was studying to be an artist. . . . It takes a long time before an artist can make enough money to support a family. . . . That's why they didn't get married. . . ." Aunt Wetti had said! For a moment, the impulse to go and see Aunt Wetti and shout at her all the hatred he felt roared in his ears like lust, then a paralyzing sense of futility seized him again. What would be the use of that?

Instead he felt himself harden with the resolve: *No more schools! No more of anything that savored even faintly of the daintily artificial and elegant world which had shut him out!*

He had a sudden image of himself pulling one of those heavy handcarts he had often seen apprentices pull—that was what he wanted: to forget all the soft things utterly and assert himself with his bare hands—the muscles in his forearms tightened involuntarily with the imaginary strain of lifting an anvil—as he had once tried to do in Herr Geiger's shop—without help from anyone else!

When half past three came, he forced himself to go out and meet Meissl. It was better to face Meissl in the street than to wait for him to come to the house. He met him just beyond the Gürtel. Meissl looked so eager and pleased with himself that his whole being stiffened with jealousy and dislike. Meissl asked when he was still half the length of a house away:

"Well?"

"I didn't get in."

"What! Why?"

"It was something about my father being a foreigner."

"But my mother has the evening all planned for us. It was all arranged with your cousin. He was going to come, too—then you won't come?"

"No, I can't." He hated the awkward pause. He added stiffly: "I've got to go somewhere. See you tomorrow." He walked away quickly.

It was even harder the next day in school. He had to repeat what it had already cost him so much to say to Meissl to several other boys. As through a mist he saw the boys crowding around Meissl to hear about the medical examination and the cadet school Already a shyness had set in between Meissl and himself, so that they avoided each other as if by some elaborate agreement. Nor was Herr Heitvogt's open satisfaction anything but a burning goad.

"The best thing that could have happened to you," Herr Heitvogt said loudly enough for several other boys around them to hear. "I hope that's the last of all this nonsense about the cadet school."

That much he said in the morning when he stopped for a minute beside Peter's desk. But that afternoon at the end of the drawing lesson he spoke again.

"We'll have to get busy and see about getting you into an art school now. It's a little late for applying, but I have some connections there and I think we can still get you a scholarship."

He realized impatiently how settled it all was in Herr Heitvogt's mind. Herr Heitvogt, too, and all his passion for drawing belonged to the world from which he felt already separated as by a chasm across which he still had to talk. He felt almost cynical in his concern not to hurt Herr Heitvogt's feelings.

"I don't think, Herr Heitvogt, I want to go to an art school."

"Oh?"

"I'm going to be a machinist."

"A machinist!" Anger thickened in Herr Heitvogt's face. "First you want to play soldier, and now you are going to be a machinist! Don't you know that you have a talent for one special thing and that happens to be drawing, or do I have to write it all out on the blackboard for you? Just exactly why did you think I bothered with you?"

In spite of his elaborate calm of only a minute ago, Peter felt himself squirm. He had not expected it to be so difficult as this.

"I'm sorry, Herr Heitvogt, for all the bother—"

"Sorry! You've got nothing to be sorry about. When God gives you a talent for something, all you've got to do is be thankful and use that talent. Do you realize that people put in years of drudgery to get what comes to you much too easily, I guess? Have you any idea of what I wouldn't give to be in your place and have my eyes back and be able to draw again?"

For just an instant Peter had a fleeting impression that the reason why Herr Heitvogt had taken such an interest in him was because Herr Heitvogt had seen him as a continuation of himself, because in Herr Heitvogt's eyes he was doing what Herr Heitvogt wanted so passionately to do himself but was no longer able to do.

"I'm sorry," he said again.

"You better talk this over with your cousin and take the summer to think about it before you do something you may be sorry for after a while." He walked out of the room without saying good night, which was something he had never done before.

That evening Franz asked:

"Did Herr Heitvogt speak to you?"

He knew then that Franz had been to see Herr Heitvogt.

"Yes."

"Well?"

"I don't want to go to art school."

"You mean you still want to be an apprentice?"

"Yes."

"Now look, don't you think that you're being just a little foolish to throw away something you've got, as Herr Heitvogt says? If you're really so set on being apprenticed somewhere—it wouldn't be exactly my idea of a rosy life, if I could go to school instead!—then, why not at least be apprenticed to an engraver or a lithographer, someplace where you could use your drawing?"

He realized from Franz's tone how unreasonable he must seem to Franz, and how hopeless it was to try to explain the loathing he felt—the hatred almost—for anything as prissy and sheltered as some engraver's shop or some art school which would only travesty the cadet school for him and remind him of the interview with the officers. Equally impossible to make Franz understand this violent need for hardship he felt, this craving to use his whole body, and not just his fingers, in some brutal labor that would at once dull him like a drug and also be like hitting out at something he hated but could not name to himself because he did not want to think about it. . . .

It was in back of all his refusals as the rest of the week crept by. Day after day, Franz came home with some new idea of something for him to do. One day it would be a marine engineers school in Trieste—"A man told me about it in the office today. It's a first-class engineering school that's run by the navy. You'd get good food there, and when you graduate you are a practical engineer. . . ." Another time it was a *Realschule* connected with some monastery in Kalksburg, then a technological institute somewhere else.

He could not but be aware of all the trouble to which Franz went, just as he was secretly touched by Poldi's concern and by *hers*. It was almost as if he had just been seriously ill and they thought it necessary to humor him for fear that he might have a relapse. The consciousness of it made him uncomfortable at times, as when *she* failed to wake him to come with her and stand in line. The second time it happened he rebelled brusquely, but it was much less easy to rebel against Poldi's much less obvious concern. Poldi had been much angrier about what had happened at the cadet school than Franz. She was silent and watchful with him, but he sensed that she had secret, insistent talks about him with Franz. If she rarely added anything to Franz's latest suggestion for the following year, it was only because she was convinced that sooner or later he would give in and agree to go back to school. . . .

On Sunday, Baron Ortner came. Franz came upstairs half an hour before lunch and said:

"Heinrich is downstairs. He wants to see you. I'll be down in a minute. . . ."

Baron Ortner was sitting in his car. He held out his hand and grinned. "Well, how's the passionate soldier today?"

It was strange, this final test of what had happened to him. The very elegance of Baron Ortner's gloved hand resting lightly on the steering wheel, the handsome crease in his uniform sleeve, even the distinguished modulation of his voice—everything about Baron Ortner was as if separated from Peter by a perfectly transparent but inexorable glass wall. The live, warm bond between them had been cut. He obeyed with a feeling of lending himself to a game of make-believe when Baron Ortner asked him to get into the car.

"Franz told me all about Tuesday," Baron Ortner began. "You mustn't take it too seriously. In fact, you mustn't pay any attention to it at all. There happens to be a lot more behind all this than meets the eye, and none of it had anything to do with you. The fact is that the commandant and my uncle were together in the same regiment once and my uncle happened to be promoted ahead of the other man. There's an old grudge there and your commandant simply saw a chance to do my uncle in the eye by taking advantage of a technicality. There was also some other business at maneuvers one time when my uncle was one of the judges—I forget all the details and they aren't important anyway. My uncle explained it all to me over the telephone. He hit the ceiling when I told him what had happened, and he has a Magyar temper, if you know what that is!"

Baron Ortner chuckled and under the spell of his laughing eyes Peter found himself compelled to smile. It would have been boorish not to smile. Yet he had remained untouched by anything Baron Ortner had said. Was Baron Ortner trumping all this up, he wondered coldly, merely to make him feel better? No, he wasn't. It suddenly came back to him how the commandant had scowled while he was reading the letter. Yes, that was probably quite true. *But if there had not been that other thing—the technicality, as Baron Ortner called it—nothing could have gone wrong!*

"Now here is what we are going to do," Baron Ortner said. "Tomorrow morning, you and I'll run into the ministry and we'll see the man who is in charge of the military schools. I'll have my uncle's authority behind me and we'll make things hum, just see if we don't! You can go to your cadet school in Baumgarten if you still want to—though personally I shouldn't advise it, because the commandant would probably find ways to make things difficult for you. But why not go to the cavalry cadet school instead? What's wrong with that? Or the artillery school, since Franz says that you're so interested in machinery anyway? Now, how does that sound to you?"

He felt uncomfortable in the face of Baron Ortner's eagerness.

"I don't think I want to go to cadet school any more, Baron Ortner."

"But you can't mean that, after all the work you've put in! You mustn't let the spitefulness of a jealous old dodo stand in your way."

He had the same feeling he had already had with Franz of owing an explanation and of being unable to put the truth into words for fear of leaving himself unbearably naked and ashamed. But in spite of himself, the very thing he was trying so hard to keep under burst out.

"They said I wasn't fit to be an officer."

"Who said that?"

"They implied it."

"That's nonsense. Look here, let's talk man to man. In my regiment there was at least one officer who could have been said to suffer from the same disqualification as yours, if anybody had been stupid enough to look at it that way. There are plenty of others in the army, you can take my word for it, although I don't happen to know them. And as for your father being a foreigner—"

Franz came out of the house.

"Well, how are you two getting along?"

"We are still negotiating," Baron Ortner said gaily. "How about it, Peter, do we go to the ministry tomorrow?"

It was easier now that Franz was there, since he had only to repeat what he had already said to Franz. He saw that they were both looking at him expectantly, Baron Ortner leaning back against his corner of the car and Franz beside him with his hands resting on the car door.

"I really don't want to go any more."

Franz looked nettled.

"But look at all the trouble Heinrich has taken on your account. He came especially from Innsbruck because of you, and he's probably used up one of his leaves to be able to come at all."

He said guiltily: "I'm sorry, Baron Ortner. Thank you very much." He started to get out of the car, but Baron Ortner reached out and put his hand on his arm.

"Here, wait a minute. Let's forget about the cadet school. What are you planning to do instead?"

"I'd like to learn to be a machinist."

"How?"

"As an apprentice, in a shop."

"So Franz told me—but can't you do that much better in some technical school?"

"I want to learn it practically, sort of from the ground up."

"You see!" Franz said. "You can't do anything with him."

This time no one stopped him from getting out of the car. When he had walked around the front end and came to stand beside Franz to say good-by, Baron Ortner gave him a broad grin. "I suppose there is always time to change your mind," he said lightly. "You've got all summer to do that. In any case, Franz will let me know how you get along."

He walked away quickly from them into the house. He had to bite back the sudden raw ache that went with the knowledge that he had cut himself off—finally, irremediably now—from the sort of future he had pictured so confidently for himself only a week ago. At least, it was done now.

But he was not yet through for the day. During lunch Franz started again:

"What about Herr Geiger upstairs? Have you thought about that at all? If you must be in some shop, why not his? I thought you liked Herr Geiger, and you'll be near home. . . ."

Another aspect of the dark urge inside him became more clear. He did not want to be near home! He wanted to wrench himself free completely, get away from everything familiar, from Herr Geiger, too.

"I want to be in a shop where they work with heavy machines."

She spoke up suddenly:

"Heavy machines! Do you think you're so strong? And who's going to buy you all the clothes you're going to tear working around with rusty old iron all the time? And if you get sick—"

"Nonsense, Mother," Poldi broke in. "He isn't going to tear any clothes and he isn't going to get sick!"

She misunderstood what Poldi meant. "You don't need to tell me! As if I hadn't seen those boys with their handcarts, loaded up until they can hardly pull them, out in every kind of weather!"

"That's only the locksmith apprentices; I'm going to be in a shop, inside."

"All the same, have you ever thought of the sort of people you are going to be with in a place like that?" Franz asked. "Those people are rough. Supposing you come up against some ruffian who kicks you around? We won't be there to help you."

"I can do my work and I won't have to be kicked around."

"Well, we'll see. At any rate, I'm going to stop in at the Verein tonight and talk to Huber. He's an engineer and he knows more about these things than either you or I."

He had won the long argument. . . .

The following morning before he left for his office, Franz said:

"Huber told me about an order which runs an apprentice home and a placement agency for apprentices. They know the different masters and also what conditions in the various shops are. You are still serious about wanting to be an apprentice?"

"Yes."

"All right, we'll see what the Brothers at the agency have to say. I'll meet you on the Gürtel at four."

Chapter Thirty-Six

THE apprentice home was in Margareten. Its interior, and especially the reception room to which they were taken by the Brother Porter, had the replete, dark-woodwork silence which Peter had always associated with religious houses. The fact that the building faced on a side street so that only a meager light came in through the recessed windows, and the memory of the locked outer door which had had to be unlatched from the inside gave him a feeling of being shut in.

The "Brother Albert" whom the other Brother had gone to fetch came in. He was a lumpishly built man with a bloated face and shaggy eyebrows, who, in spite of the womanish black-cloth cassock and the initial impression of softness he gave, had something trenchant and active about him, something bullying also in his knowingness and his lack of ceremony.

Franz explained why they had come. Brother Albert asked for his report card and Peter handed it to him. Brother Albert studied it.

"And you want to be a machinist?"

"Yes, Brother Albert."

"That's an unusual thing for a boy with your marks to want to be."

Was the same argument going to start all over again!

"The worst of it is," Franz said reproachfully, "that he has a real talent for drawing. His drawing teacher in school thought enough of it to give him lessons outside of class all year. But he refuses to make use of it now."

Brother Albert appeared to have listened only to the first few words.

"That puts a different complexion on things. The Siemens Electric people want an apprentice for their drafting room. There isn't a better place in the city to learn machine design, and you'll be with a first-class firm." Brother Albert's manner announced that it was all settled to his complete satisfaction.

"I'm not very good at that kind of drawing. I can't letter well."

"You have a 'one' here on your report card for mechanical drawing!"

"That's only because I did every drawing over several times. It always takes me a long time."

"I'm sure that's something you can learn, lettering and all that."

The man was really not important enough to let himself become exasperated by his stupid harping on that apprenticeship in a drafting room! After today, he would probably never see him again. If he did not want to get him a job in a machine shop, he would simply find one for himself!

He said firmly:

"I'd rather be in a shop where I can work on machines."

For the first time, Brother Albert appeared actually to take notice of him. He thrust his head forward to emphasize what he was saying.

"Apprentices nowadays have to do a good many things they didn't have to do before the war. There is a shortage of helpers. The kind of boys we send into machine shops are sturdy country boys who are used to hard work. I'm not saying that you're weak, but you're pretty tall for your age and you don't look husky enough for that kind of shop."

"But I'm willing to work."

"That's commendable, but I think that you ought to find something that you're better adapted to. I was apprenticed to a coppersmith once and I know what I'm talking about."

"That's exactly what we've been trying to tell him," Franz said. "There's a man we know who makes gun sights for the army and who would be glad to take him, but he doesn't want to go there for some reason."

Brother Albert gave an ungainly jerk. "We can't always do what we like. Wait a minute, though—I have an idea. Will you come into my office?"

The office was another somber room across the hall. It contained one old-fashioned desk above which hung a carved wooden crucifix, a filing cabinet and a safe. Brother Albert went to the desk and opened a black ledgerlike book. He turned the leaves until he found what he was looking for; his hand brushed caressingly over the lower half of one page.

"Straka and Sons," he read. "Ever hear of them?"

Peter shook his head.

"Well, it's biggest hardware house in the country. You can get your fill of machinery there. They sell everything from American harvesters to portable smithies for the army, and they have their own iron works in Styria and a factory in Upper Austria. Herr Straka is a fine Christian gentleman; we've been sending boys to him and before that to his father ever since the Home first started, thirty-five years ago. It'd be something for you to get in with a firm like that! One of our boys got to be their representative in Hungary and Rumania before the war and today he has his own exporting house—I talked to him just the other day. You better look that over carefully before you decide on something else!"

Franz asked:

"Well, what do you think?"

Peter felt undecided. His first reaction had been one of scorn at the mere idea of going into a hardware shop, but the mention of an iron works and the something like awe in Brother Albert's voice in speaking of the firm had aroused his curiosity. In any case, it did not look as if he would get a place in a machine shop here—he might as well look at the other thing.

"Yes, I think so."

"That's fine," Brother Albert said. "I'll find out whether we can see Herr Straka this afternoon." He went to the telephone booth in the corner behind them.

Franz said tentatively:

"There won't be any harm in looking it over. If you don't like it, you won't have to take it. But Brother Albert knows more about these things than we do."

They could hear Brother Albert's voice at the telephone. He sounded obsequious. When he came out of the booth, his voice was pompous again. "Herr Straka will see us at half past five. That gives us three-quarters of an hour. You'll be able to see something of the store, and I'll also have time to show you over the Home."

Franz looked taken aback. "Do all the apprentices you place have to stay here?"

"No, indeed. They don't have to. We place a good many hundreds of boys every year that we couldn't take even if we wanted to—we have only room for eighty-six boys. But Herr Straka's boys have always stayed with us. The reason for that is that Herr Straka has always preferred to take promising boys from the orphan asylums and they wouldn't have any other place to stay. Herr Straka is one of the most generous patrons of our Home," Brother Albert said unctuously. He turned from Franz to him: "The firm takes only two apprentices each year and the other boy has already been engaged. He was the top boy at the orphanage in Mauer. . . . If you come with me now, I'll show you around."

They followed him through a gloomy corridor with a coffee-colored statue of Saint Joseph at the end into a cheerless dining hall. Long, ungainly tables adjoined each other around the walls; except for another statue of Saint Aloysius in one corner and a large picture of the Good Shepherd up front, the room was entirely bare. Then came another, smaller room with a number of bookcases and a few tables and chairs. Brother Albert said proudly: "This is our recreation room. The boys can come here to read in the evenings and on Sunday afternoons. . . ." They went upstairs and saw two dormitories with beds sticking out like teeth from the long walls, square beds with rust-colored counterpanes. . . .

The garden downstairs was equally drab. A few flower beds surrounded a grotto of the Virgin of Lourdes; there were four or five lilac bushes, some stone benches, primly sanded paths. . . . High walls closed in two of the sides. Across the rear stretched another building to which Brother Albert was taking them now to show them the kitchen and the chapel. . . .

It was all spotlessly clean and orderly and depressing.

When they were back in the reception room again, Brother Albert excused himself to get his hat, but just as he was about to leave the room, he suddenly faced Peter and asked:

"Tell me something: don't you ever smile?"

Embarrassment drove him to force a grin, but the muscles around his mouth felt taut and sick with the grimace. Anger at the bullying of the shaggy-browed man in the black cassock gathered in him.

"That's better," Brother Albert approved. "You won't make a good impression with Herr Straka if you don't try to look a little more cheerful."

He avoided Franz's eyes after Brother Albert had left. He knew without looking that Franz was worried about him again. A few seconds went by before Franz said reproachfully:

"After all, you don't have to do this! It was all your own idea!"

Then Brother Albert returned and they started out. . . .

The store was about ten minutes' walk from the Home. It occupied the entire angle where the Margaretenstrasse and another street met in a point. They passed a long row of show windows, rather neglected-looking and filled with dusty blacksmith supplies, then a wide carriage entrance through which Peter caught a glimpse of a cobblestoned courtyard in which two drays full of wagon springs were being unloaded by laborers, then came five very large show windows, and finally the entrance to the store itself.

The store ran clear through the block down to the lower street where there was another entrance. It gave the impression of a wide, massive tunnel in which many people clustered together at the counters, milled around and moved to some other spot with engrossing purposefulness to a steady drone of voices and an occasional clangor of iron and steel. Electric lights glowed over the standing desks which were scattered at irregular intervals down the ponderous length of the counters on each side. Down near the middle of the store there was a brighter region where two large skylights allowed the sunlight to filter in. Directly under one of the skylights was a glass cage with two desks and some filing cabinets. In front of the wicket in the cage a number of customers and clerks were waiting to have invoices and other papers checked over by the curly-haired, rather dandyishly dressed man inside. After the glass cage came an iron-plated door which led out into the courtyard, Peter saw, and beyond the door was a cashier's cage in which a woman was taking the money for what appeared to be the smaller purchases.

He had only a confused impression of what he saw. There were too many people jostling each other between the counters, too many laborers lugging heavy steel springs and carrying sharp-cornered cases and rolls of sheet iron to avoid, too many things going on all at once to see anything very clearly. Only one thing was quite clear: this was no store where one went for a pennyworth of nails or for a new lid for the stove. Everything here was handled in quantity and in bulk.

He watched a clerk lift a bundle of sledgehammer heads up on a scale—the deft ease with which the clerk swung the heavy hammers up from the floor filled him with a sudden desire to be able to do that, too. Another clerk barely glanced at a piece of steel a mechanic handed him before he said expertly: "Fifteen-sixteenth, high speed steel. . . ." "Right the first time," the mechanic agreed; "what I want. . . ." Listening to the snatches of absorbingly technical talk, which occasionally crackled with a crisp, humorous familiarity that argued a long acquaintance between the customers and the clerks, Peter became aware of an insinuating urge to become part of this vibrant, grown-up world where no one would know about him at all and where he would be so busy as not to have time to think of anything that had happened before. . . .

Brother Albert led them out through the iron-plated door into the courtyard. Vast storerooms surrounded the yard. Tiers of shelves that were reinforced with iron girders held enormous quantities of things. One whole building was entirely given over to axles and carriage springs; another held nothing but endless packages of screws and rivets on its rows and rows of shelves.

"You see," Brother Albert said with a twisted, reminiscent smile that made Peter like him for a second as they came out from the storeroom, "I know my way around this place. I used to come here thirty years ago when I was still an apprentice myself. This part of the store hasn't changed very much. It's an old firm: Herr Straka's great-grandfather founded it around eighteen hundred and twenty, I believe."

"It's a big store," Franz agreed.

"Oh, this isn't all of it. I'll show you one of the warehouses now."

They went out into the Margaretenstrasse. A street ran down at a right angle to the store. Brother Albert pointed to the corner house across the street:

"That's where the offices are. The whole row of houses up to where all those drays are parked is used for warehouses now. But that's the main one up there. We'll just have time to look in for a minute."

When they came up to the drays, Peter saw that the inside of the warehouse yard was already crowded with drays. Loading platforms and galleries with derricks projecting over them ran clear around the huge yard. The buildings through which Brother Albert led them hurriedly were filled with unbelievable quantities of sheet iron, machinery still in crates, bundles of horseshoes piled into formidable stacks, frowning masses of steel bars and tire iron leaning against the walls. Yet even so, it appeared that they had not seen all there was to see.

"There's another warehouse over in the next street," Brother Albert said, "and there's a new one in Hernals. And there are the stables and the garage—the firm has its own fleet of drays and trucks! . . . I think we had better go down to the office now. Herr Straka is a very busy man!"

The offices on the second floor of the house on the corner offered a striking contrast to the old-fashioned store and the rough warehouses below. They were bright, astringently modern, new. An expansive leisureliness seemed to circulate with the very air stirred by the handsome electric fans in the spacious rooms, so that Peter had the impression that the cool, measured activity up here was like a calm Sunday morning commentary on the blustering weekday exertion he had seen downstairs.

Herr Straka's own office when they were taken to it by a secretary turned out to have the studiedly subdued luxury of a rather severe drawing room. An oil painting of an elderly man with a domineering, ruddy face and several water-color sketches of factories hung on the walls. Five brightly polished steel cubes of diminishing sizes were ranged in a row in front of the inkstand on the imposing golden-oak desk. Two of the windows overlooked the store across the street; through the windows on the right came the occasional rumble of a dray lumbering down from the warehouse.

Herr Straka had come forward to greet Brother Albert and exchange a few polite remarks with Franz. He was a large, plump-faced man who spoke in a deliberate voice and moved with an air of quiet authority. He was much younger than Brother Albert's awed-voiced references to him had led Peter to expect—he could not be more than five or six years older than Franz—and he was elegantly dressed. The light-brown suit of some very thin cloth was impeccably fitted over his wide, plump shoulders; his shoes were immaculate; he wore a beautiful green tie. Watching him uncertainly, narrowly, Peter decided that he had that commanding air of conscious refinement he had so often observed in men on the Ring. It was not the same elegance as Baron Ortner's, of course—Herr Straka had a circumspect, patrician gravity which differed radically from the dashing assurance of Baron Ortner—but it was elegance nevertheless.

There was also—and this was really most important of all, it struck him suddenly—a momentous implication for him in the connection between the soft-mannered, yet so anxiously deferred-to person of Herr Straka up here and the uncouth, crusty, but powerful conglomeration of store and warehouses below: the promise of power in all those staggering quantities of iron and steel he had just seen was as if drawn to a fine point in the person of Herr Straka, into a suave spearhead which could easily approach and penetrate the haughty armor of the world of the Ring and the Innere Stadt. People like the officers and the commandant at the cadet school, like the boys in the *Gymnasium*, like Aunt Wetti and her two friends, might sneer at the store but they would not be able to ignore Herr Straka himself.

If I become like Herr Straka, he thought with a little thrill at the clarity of his calculation, *powerful and elegant, I'll be able to get even with all of them!* He was suddenly sure that he wanted to be an apprentice here. . . .

Herr Straka had asked Brother Albert and Franz to sit down. Herr Straka himself had walked around behind his desk and was looking over the report card Brother Albert had handed him.

"Will your marks be as good for this term?"

"Yes, Herr Straka."

"And you would like to learn the hardware business?"

"Yes, Herr Straka." He remembered what Brother Albert had said about smiling, but he could not get himself to smile.

"We make a point of engaging only young men who have made a good record in school," Herr Straka said slowly, "but your marks are somewhat out of the ordinary. Were you thinking of being in the office rather than downstairs?"

"No, I should like to be downstairs."

"I see." Herr Straka still seemed a little dubious. "Our apprentices are usually a little sturdier than you and you may find the work too hard. On the other hand, there is only one way to learn this business and that is in the store. Once you have done that, there is no limit to how far you can go. In any case, there is a trial period of one month before the articles of apprenticeship are signed; that should give you time to find out whether you like it here or not." He turned to Franz: "We have been in the habit of paying for room and board for our apprentices at the Home. Our experience in having boys stay there has been very satisfactory."

That made it definite, then, that he was to stay at the Home.

"When does your school close?"

"It stops on Saturday."

"The other young man who has already been engaged will start on Monday. It would perhaps be easier for both of you if you started at the same time." Herr Straka looked inquiringly from him to Franz.

Franz caught his eye. He nodded quickly, and Franz said:

"I can't see any reason why not, if you think that's best."

Herr Straka spoke to him again: "The older apprentices will help you get acquainted with the store. You won't have any difficulty there. And if there is ever anything that you wish to see me about, I shall always be here."

It was the end of the interview. Herr Straka rose and saw them to the door.

Brother Albert walked with them as far as the Gürtel and explained what he had to bring with him to the Home on Sunday afternoon. As soon as Brother Albert had left, Franz said cheerfully:

"Well, this looks a whole lot better than a machine shop to me. You'll at least be with intelligent people, and you heard what Herr Straka said about feeling free to go and see him if anything gets too difficult for you. And as far as the Apprentice Home is concerned, I don't think Herr Straka will insist on your staying there if you don't like it. You might get more to eat there than you do at home; you saw all those sacks of potatoes in the kitchen. . . ."

On the whole, Franz seemed rather pleased with the result of their two interviews. But Poldi's anger that evening knew no bounds.

"A hardware shop!" Poldi blazed. "Why didn't you pick a linen draper's while you were about it!"

"What's wrong with that boy's learning an honest trade, I'd like to know?" *she* asked from the kitchen door. "You and your grand ideas! Your father was—"

"Oh, Mother!"

He saw that in her anger Poldi was on the verge of tears. He was suddenly moved by her ambition for him, *but he could not do anything else now! This was what he had to do!*

"And what about his mother?" Poldi flashed.

She had already turned to go back into the kitchen. She came back to the door. "Yes, we are going to worry about his mother," she jeered. "A fine lot his mother cared what happened to him when she boarded him out with the peasants in Styria. If it had been up to her, he'd be herding cows and cleaning out pigsties."

"But he's not in Styria now, and we are responsible for him!"

A flurry of new thoughts and emotions stirred uneasily in him as he watched them facing each other in stubborn, silent conflict across the room. The suspicion slid suddenly into focus for him that Poldi, although she hardly ever spoke of Mizzi, had always had the thought of Mizzi in the back of her mind where he was concerned, had been measuring every decision involving him against some standard that was Mizzi's somehow, as if she had been secretly afraid that Mizzi might not approve. It occurred to him that perhaps Poldi had once admired Mizzi in much the same way that he had admired Baron Ortner during the past year. It astonished him that he should never have thought of that until now. . . .

It was obvious that *she* was still thinking of Mizzi, too. He could almost feel her grim satisfaction in humbling Mizzi by having him want to become anything as drab as a clerk in a store. . . . It irritated him to find himself thrown on her side and ranged against Poldi, yet he could not free himself from her words: *What had Mizzi ever cared what happened to him!* But his thoughts did not stay on Mizzi for long. Mizzi was unimportant! Behind Mizzi, behind the scene at the cadet school, there was the man who was his father——

For just one instant the faceless, elusive figure became solid enough for his hatred to fasten on, then Poldi looked at him again with her angry eyes.

"A counterjumper!" she said fiercely.

He did not answer her. Again he felt a twinge of remorse. But how, he asked himself helplessly, how could he explain to Poldi this dark need to plunge into darkness and work furiously, to dull himself and get as far away from Bianca and Baron Ortner and all those other things as he could, this craving to get close to iron and to the promise of power he had sensed in the store, power and—yes, that was it: REVENGE!

PART II

Chapter Thirty-Seven

IT WAS only a dream and he knew that he was dreaming, but he could not get himself awake. His dream had shrunk the daytime world to a small, inexorable space in which everything was horribly foreordained and confining with jagged reality.

And now, still in his dream, he was suddenly aware that the sloping skylight across the middle of the store had become glumly darkened by snow. He knew that the snow lay at least a foot thick and looked stodgily beveled around the edges of the skylight like an eiderdown. He knew it although he was down below, in the store itself. . . .

He was supposed to be sweeping behind the counter where Herr Meier's standing desk joined onto the side of the cashier's cage. It was always hateful to sweep in that particular spot because the floor boards were so worn that splinters kept peeling off and catching in the broom, but now—grotesquely—there was also the long, shiny saber hanging from his side and getting in the way of the broom. Whenever he tried pushing the saber out of the way, it banged against his shin or his knee. Herr Meier stood looking on with his small cantankerous eyes and testily pursed mouth. Behind him, Frau Redlich had briskly swept out her cashier's cage with the little whisk broom she kept hanging behind her high stool and now she, too, had come to watch.

Herr Meier pointed to a scrap of paper that had got caught under a splinter and rasped: "And there, too!"

He struggled with the obstinate splinter which pinned the scrap of paper down like a spring—he had to push the saber out of his way again and again. Then a new menace was added to his already crushing sense of constraint: across the short aisle which led to the iron-plated door out into the courtyard, Herr Kropfl was sliding back the glass door of the bookkeeper's cage and was coming to watch, too. Herr Kropfl with his bland pink and white face and dandyish mustache and his curly black hair was lowering sneeringly. As if to justify himself to Herr Kropfl's glistening eyes, Herr Meier pointed to the bottom shelf under the counter where a bunch of bolts stuck out irregularly and said: "And what about down there—don't forget that!"

He tried desperately to get under the bolts. The saber was still swinging forward and had to be pushed to one side. The three pairs of eyes were watching malevolently. The strain became unbearable. He woke up. . . .

His fingers wandered cautiously over the rough linen sheet and found the square bedpost. From somewhere behind him came a trumpeting snore——

The Apprentice Home, of course! He was in the Apprentice Home!

He opened his eyes the merest slit and instantly closed them again: it was still dark. From the row of open windows on the other side of the room came sullen, sharp-edged waves of cold air which smelled of snow. In the next bed, Hacker tossed over on his side with the peculiar violence Hacker brought to everything.

Why the saber? Why had he dreamed of the saber?

Of course, the Emperor's funeral today! It was that article about the funeral he had read in yesterday's paper which had said that the cadet corps would march in the cortege. His mind veered away sharply from the thought of the cadet school. Instead, he told himself: Only half a day in the store today! And no commercial school tonight!

From the curtained-off partition where Brother Kajetan slept at the end of the dormitory there came a scraping noise as of a shoe being picked up from the floor. Time to get up already! Alarm and the sudden consciousness of how tired he still was made him clutch at oblivion again.

Almost instantly the leaden-languorous tissue of another dream enveloped him. This time he was down in the cellar, looking among the many shelves crammed with locks for a ten-inch mortise lock. All the wrappers in the ten-inch shelf said, *For Right-Hand Door,* and Herr Benesch had expressly sent him for a lock for a left-hand door. Besides, he had stupidly forgotten to ask whether the door opened out or in—it made all the difference! Then Herr Benesch was suddenly beside him, asking impatiently: "What's keeping you so long?" Herr Benesch reached into the shelf and picked up the first lock on top and held it out for him to see: it was plainly marked, *For Left-Hand Door.*

"There!" Herr Benesch said good-naturedly. "Lots of them. You just don't know how to look—rafts of them."

Then Herr Benesch was gone and he was again alone in the cellar. He did not want to go upstairs. He wanted to stay down here where it was warm—WARM——

Brother Kajetan's bell clanged mercilessly and was only a few yards away.

"Praised be Jesus Christ—everybody up!"

The brassy clangor of the bell mounted to a climax as Brother Kajetan went past. Peter dug his head into the pillow and slipped down a little farther under the blanket to drown out the noise. He hated the bell and the blatant cheerfulness of Brother Kajetan's singsong. It was safe to wait until Brother Kajetan returned from the other dormitory where the older boys were; by then, however, one had to be out of bed, or Brother Kajetan would jump at the chance of pitching one out on the floor with that nasty trick he had.

Still through the haze of sleep he listened to the bell grow louder again. When he judged Brother Kajetan to be almost at the foot of his bed, he jerked his legs hastily out on the floor. On the bed facing him, Hacker was running one hand through his bushy, tow-colored hair.

"Praised be Jesus Christ—now, then, everybody up!"

"Bastard!" Hacker said.

Brother Kajetan came back and looked sharply from Hacker to him. "What was that? What was that you said?"

Hacker yawned elaborately and reached for his shirt. "I didn't say anything. You say anything, Peter?"

Peter shook his head dully.

"Well, just mind your manners!" Brother Kajetan warned, with all the boisterous good nature he usually affected gone from his face.

"Bastard!" Hacker said once more as soon as Brother Kajetan had turned his back.

Now, what had been the use of that? Peter thought irritably, still annoyed with Hacker for prying him out of the somnolent stupor which usually dulled him to the shivery morning routine. But Hacker always had to show off how strong or how clever or daring he was, just as now he was stretching with his torso naked down to the waist as if he were not even aware of the cold.

Peter left him and started up the aisle. Other boys were hurrying out from the short aisles between the beds and making for the washroom. In the hall between the two dormitories, Otto, he noticed, was finickingly brushing his coat and vest in front of his locker. Otto was already fully dressed. His hair was neatly plastered down over his forehead, and his shiny face with the two high-colored pink splotches just below his cheekbones looked exaggeratedly clean. Otto's sly, docile neatness suddenly exasperated him: he must actually be getting up now even before the bell!

The washroom was crowded. Every washbasin around the square, white-tiled room was already taken. He went to a bowl where there was only one other boy ahead of him and waited sleepily. There was no other noise in the room except the rush of water from the taps and the splashing in the basins and an indistinct shuffling of feet. The faces of the boys who came away from the bowls, although reddened by the cold water, were still heavy with sleep.

He saw that Hacker who had only just arrived had already got possession of a basin by shouldering aside a puny boy who was apprenticed in some leather-goods shop. The small boy went away without protest, and Hacker started to run the cold water over his head and to splash it over his chest. It was just like Hacker, Peter reflected dully, to use his second-year status and his size to bully the smaller boy. It was what Hacker had done to Otto and him in the store until they had learned the ropes.

Brother Kajetan appeared in the door.

"Now, then, lively, you boys—five minutes to five!"

Peter got to the basin. He brushed his teeth hurriedly and sloshed some water over his face and neck. There was no use trying to wash one's ears with the wartime soap which would not foam and with the cold water; tonight would be time enough. He hurried back to the dormitory to put on his vest and coat.

"Don't they ever close the windows even in the winter?"

"What do you want the windows closed for?" Hacker jeered. "You aren't cold, are you? Look at all those radiators going full blast!"

It was a stale joke to refer to the big radiators along the wall below the windows—not even the third-year apprentices had ever known them to be warm.

"I don't see why we have to get up at half past four in the winter, too! Summer was bad enough. . . ."

"Good for you, my boy!" Hacker mimicked the unctuous sententiousness of Brother Norbert downstairs. "It's all done for a purpose—yes, indeed, a great purpose! We're thinking of your immortal soul: we keep you nice and tired so's you won't masturbate so much——" He ended up with a leering guffaw.

Peter turned away quickly and busied himself with the bedclothes which had to be pulled up to air before they went downstairs. Hacker never failed to give that kind of a twist to every subject sooner or later! Just when you had about convinced yourself that Hacker wasn't so bad after all, he always brought you up sharp with some nasty jolt that made you distrust him again. It had been even worse in the beginning when the jolts had taken a cruder form. . . .

He remembered during his first week when Otto and he had helped Hacker unpack some cases of rivets, how Hacker had tossed the ten-pound packages so hard at him that it had been difficult to catch them and keep from getting hit in the head or the groin. And there had been the time when Hacker had pulled out a ladder from under him so that he had cracked his shin and had limped for a week. There had been no end to Hacker's playfulness. Still, lately, ever since his fight with Hacker and even though he had done no more than bloody Hacker's nose before Hacker had punished him so much that he had had to give up, it had been almost easy to get along with him, Peter reflected gratefully as they started downstairs.

They were nearly the last to enter the dining hall. The other boys stood already waiting alongside the tables for Brother Norbert's signal to kneel down. The peculiar sodden hush which always preceded morning prayers lay over the room.

Brother Norbert stood beside his *prie-dieu* in front of the statue of Saint Aloysius and looked like a statue himself. His leathery-skinned face with its wry Slavic features was stonily impassive and turned toward the picture of the Good Shepherd on the wall, but his beetling eyes swept over them every few minutes and sternly registered every boy who was late. Later on, when he would ladle out the coffee, Brother Norbert would remember again and would send the late ones away with only half a cup. Two more boys arrived and hurried to their places. Brother Norbert reached into the slit in the side of his cassock and jingled the bunch of keys he carried hanging from a chain under it. A third-year hurried to his table up front. Brother Norbert slid his black skullcap off his tonsure, held it in his hand for a second, and then tinkled the little silver bell he had on his *prie-dieu.*

They knelt down.

He usually managed to drowse right through the prayers, but today, in spite of the weariness he felt, Peter remained wide-awake. He noticed a boy on the other side of the room lose his balance and topple over forward; the boy caught himself on hastily outstretched hands and righted himself sheepishly. Several other boys' heads drooped lower and lower and were jerked upright again. *I wish they'd give us something decent to eat instead!* he thought angrily and wished that the trip to chapel were over and he could at least get the watery coffee they were given for breakfast.

The prayers came to an end. The boys around him got up listlessly and knocked the dust off their trousers. The ones nearest the door paired up and filed out into the corridor. Without thinking, Peter fell into line beside the Bosnian boy who sat next to him at the table. They filed out through the corridor and the drafty cloister into the church.

The black hangings and the black vestments of the priest at the altar reminded him of the Emperor's funeral again. He wondered whether Poldi would go to see it in the afternoon. Perhaps if he could catch Brother Norbert in an amiable mood, he might get permission to spend the afternoon at home. . . . The Mass dragged on endlessly. Around him, several boys were half-asleep again. He jogged the elbow of the boy on his right when it was time to get up for the Gospel, and again for the Consecration—if Brother Norbert caught you asleep in church, you went without breakfast altogether. There were more prayers for the dead Emperor, and then it was over at last. They filed back through the cloister into the dining hall.

The stacks of thick porcelain cups were already on the big serving table up front. Two boys brought in the pot with the coffee and hoisted it up on the table. The third-year boys began to line up. Brother Norbert shoved his skullcap a little farther back on his head and pulled up the sleeve of his cassock. Otto and another boy came in from the corridor with the basket of bread and set it beside the pot. Brother Norbert picked up the ladle. . . .

Peter watched Otto and the other boy hurry past him on their way back into the kitchen. His dislike of Otto flared up again:

now Otto would swill the good coffee the Brothers drank and fill himself up with bread. Only Brother Norbert's favorites were assigned to bring in the food from the kitchen, and it had only taken Otto one month to insinuate himself into Brother Norbert's good graces, just as he had known how to ingratiate himself with Herr Meier and Frau Redlich and with Herr Kropfl in the store. It was a knack Otto had, Peter reflected scornfully as he moved closer to the serving table.

His turn to pick up one of the chipped, heavy cups. Brother Norbert swung away the ladle when the cup was little more than half full, then handed him one of the smallest slices of bread. Peter refused to see the queasily reproachful look with which Brother Norbert tried to fix him. He cupped the crumbly corn bread carefully in his hand so as not to lose any crumbs on the way to the table.

The coffee tasted of charred wood and saccharine, but at least it was still hot. He tried to eat the bread slowly, but his hunger was too much for him and he devoured it in two mouthfuls. Beside him, the chubby Bosnian boy was rolling some of his bread into pellets and saying: "In my country we feed slop like this to the pigs, then we eat the pigs. . . ." Nobody answered him. It was easy for him to talk, Peter thought irritably, with a fat parcel from Bosnia every week! He did not have to depend on the meals they got at the Home!

Brother Norbert tinkled his silly little bell and they got up to take the cups back to the serving table. Then they trooped upstairs to the dormitories. Peter hurried through making his bed. Always after breakfast he could hardly wait to get out of the Home. Besides, Hacker had insisted from the very beginning that they start out for the store as soon as they had made their beds; it was one of the few regulations Hacker had imposed on Otto and him which Peter actually liked. He watched Hacker throw his bed together and lower the wooden lid and the brown cover down over it. Otto was already waiting for them downstairs, wearing his innocent "you-see-how-I-love-to-do-everything-I'm-told" expression even for Hacker. They waited by the door while the Brother Porter fumbled with his bunch of keys for a minute before he found the right one, then they walked out into the street.

Today, out of sheer capriciousness, Hacker forced them to take the long way around. Hacker paused on the sidewalk to sniff in the snow-wet air with noisy exuberance and to puff out his chest——

"Let's go by way of the Gürtel. We've got lots of time."

"It's cold!" Otto protested.

"What of it? Wait'll it really gets to be winter—this is just perfect for me."

Peter had kept silent. There was not the slightest use in protesting, once Hacker had taken it into his head to show off. It only goaded him on further to try to argue him out of it. And even if they let Hacker go by himself and they themselves took the shorter way, they would still not have gained anything: they could not get into the store until Hacker got the keys from the yardmaster in the Kohlgasse, and it would be just like Hacker to keep them waiting out in the cold for half an hour to punish them.

They set out for the Gürtel.

It had snowed only a few inches during the night, but the air was heavy with the threat of more snow. The white-crested tracery of the trees on the Gürtel brought no joy to Peter as it had always done formerly; he noticed instead that out in the road the early drays from the Ostbahnhof had already made soggy, yellow ruts which were fast turning into slush. He walked along carefully so as not to get his shoes soaked again before he had even started the day. The last soles the shoemaker had put on were of some thick, puffy leather that soaked up the water like a sponge. Beside him, Hacker was pretending that he had on skis and was scuffing the snow with the square tips of his new army brogans which he had wangled somewhere on his daily rounds to the railroad-freight stations.

"Nordbahnhof today," Hacker announced. "Guy I know there has promised me half a bushel of apples."

"How about bringing us some?" Otto said insinuatingly.

"Fat chance! You stuff yourself out in the kitchen anyway. No, sir, those apples are going to stay right in the dispatcher's office where I can bake half a dozen every day on the stove. Boy, are they going to taste good! Why don't you ask old Fat-Ass out in the kitchen if you want some apples?" he goaded Otto.

Otto did not answer. He should have known better in the first place, Peter thought indifferently, than to ask Hacker for anything. Hacker might give you an apple or a piece of bread if he wanted you to do some unwelcome errand in his place, but he would never give you anything because you asked him for it.

"After tomorrow one of you is going to the Westbahnhof every day," Hacker said importantly. "I talked it over with Herr Brandt. I can't get around to all the stations in the winter—and if the clerk at the freight-collect window asks you for a file or a padlock or something, you better take it to him because he's a friend of mine. Besides, if you don't, he can fix it so's the drays can't get the freight when they come and then you'll get the blame. Herr Brandt knows all about it. . . ."

Then, that was how Hacker always got apples and even shoes on his trips to the freight stations! Peter remembered suddenly the time when he had caught Hacker stowing away a rather expensive bitbrace under his overcoat before he started out from the store. Hacker was covering up in case Otto or he got onto anything at the Westbahnhof. . . . He did not want the job, he went on thinking. The freight station at the Westbahnhof meant trudging through the slush for half a mile before one got to it, and there was nothing to be had to eat there or Hacker would not have given up that particular station. But he would probably draw the assignment whether he wanted it or not, because Herr Meier would see to it that Otto could stay in the store where it was warm. . . .

A streetcar came gliding across the Gürtel just as they reached the Margaretenstrasse. Without any warning, Hacker took a few quick steps and swung himself expertly up on the rear platform. "So long, chumps!" he called back derisively.

In spite of his head start Hacker kept them waiting for a quarter of an hour outside the store. When he finally came out of the office building across the street, his swagger made it clear that he had either been flirting with Herr Brandt's maid or that he had been given some hot coffee and things to eat. Probably both. Peter was not interested. His only thought was to get inside where it would be warm. But he could see that Hacker was annoyed because neither Otto nor he had asked and given him a chance to boast.

They went in through the big carriage gate, which Hacker slammed shut again. In the courtyard the huge tarpaulins over the hundreds of cases of screws and nails and rivets which the laborers had unloaded yesterday afternoon were white with snow. It seemed already warmer in the narrow corridor which led from the courtyard, past the locked cellar door and the stairway to the attic, to the iron-plated door into the store. Hacker flipped the keys up and down on the key ring a few times before he found the keys for the two Yale locks. The store was dark and dankly cold. The gray skylight let in hardly any light at all. A few mice scampered away from the open space between the cashier's cage on the left and the glassed-in bookkeeper's cage on the right.

Hacker made immediately for the glass cage. He turned on the light over Herr Kropfl's desk and lighted the gas heater in the corner. Then he settled himself comfortably in Herr Kropfl's chair and watched condescendingly while they warmed their hands over the shining copper grate.

For a minute or so Hacker was content to lounge in the softly squeaking swivel chair, then he looked up importantly at the clock over the safe:

"Half past! You guys better get busy with the stove."

"Wait'll we get warm!" Otto's voice hovered between stodgy truculence and a whine.

"You've got no business in here in the first place. Supposing somebody comes in!"

Stubbornly they stayed on. They both knew why Hacker wanted them out of the cage. As soon as they were busy with the big stove, Hacker would try all the drawers in Herr Kropfl's desk in the hope of finding some cigarettes or some candy there.

A trifle too obviously indifferent to them now, Hacker arranged the two stacks of invoice books in front of him and started to exchange the carbons. There were two sets of books, each used on alternate days while the other set was being checked by Herr Kropfl. Collecting the thirty-four books each evening from the clerks and distributing the second set in the morning was one of the few chores Hacker had still left. Riedl, the other second-year apprentice who had started in a few days before Hacker in the store, no longer had any set chores at all.

Hacker turned around threateningly:

"Go on, get out of here!"

This time they went.

Peter switched on the lights over the middle of the store. In spite of their powerful glare, the far ends of the aisle and the counters still lay in darkness. They got busy with the big cast-iron stove across the aisle from Frau Redlich's cage. It was Otto's turn to take out the ashes and get the coal. The stove each morning was one chore Otto could not escape! Peter waited scornfully while Otto went behind Herr Meier's desk to put on a pair of old leather mittens so as not to soil his hands. When Otto had finally shaken down the ashes, Peter started the fire with the paper they had swept up the night before and some old crates. It always took a long time for the big stove to get even warm. Otto came back with the empty ashpan and started back out into the courtyard with the coal scuttle.

Hacker suddenly pushed up the window in the glass cage—

"Hey, come here! Get a load of this!" Hacker held up a flat white cardboard box which he had taken out of the center drawer of the desk. "What do you guess is in it?"

"How should I know?"

After another second to savor his supense, Hacker lifted off the lid. In the box, loosely stretched over a cardboard yoke, were two scalloped black-and-pink silk garters.

"Boy, isn't that something!"

Uncomfortable because Hacker was prying among Herr Kropfl's things and because there was something vaguely indecent about the crinkly woman's garters with their showy pink rosettes, he asked—stupidly, he realized:

"Whose are they?"

"Whose do you think! He's got them for some dame, of course. I bet she's hot stuff too! I wouldn't mind—" Otto was out in the corridor. "Beat it!" Hacker commanded hastily and slipped the box back into the drawer.

Otto put down the scuttle by the stove and went behind Herr Meier's desk to return the leather mittens. Hacker came out of the cage with the stack of invoice books and started to distribute them on the standing desks. He stopped once by the stove to whisper hoarsely: "I bet he's going to put them on for her. I wish I could be there in his place! Boy, black silk stockings and nice fat—"

He pretended to be busy with the drafts on the stove. The hot, sultry picture Hacker loved to call up of some woman clad in nothing but long black silk stockings made him uneasy again. He realized that this time it repelled him not only because of the lubricity with which Hacker's tone had surrounded it, but also because the picture was associated with Herr Kropfl. Ever since the day in October when Hacker had first forced him to realize what the salve

Herr Kropfl was always ordering from the pharmacy was really for, he had been unable to think of Herr Kropfl without a feeling of instant angry nausea. He felt relieved when the electric buzzer from the carriage gate tore his thoughts away from Herr Kropfl.

The buzzer clamored a second time. That would be Herr Meier—he was the only one who ever came as early as this. Otto was already bustling out into the courtyard to let him in.

He put on more coal. The stove was at last getting warm.

Herr Meier came in from the corridor. He was a small, angular man with stubborn shoulders and an absurdly puppetlike jerkiness about his walk. The bristly gray hair which ended in a point over his forehead and his turned-up overcoat collar made his sharp-featured face look even more like a bird's than usual. His "Good morning" was uttered with a grumpy insistence peculiar to his biting voice. He went immediately behind Frau Redlich's cage to his own desk and took out a bunch of keys and a number of papers and envelopes from various pockets. Then he went up the aisle toward the Margaretenstrasse and turned behind Herr Lehnert's counter into the carriage-fittings storeroom, where the lockers were.

When he came out again he had on his patched green smock and was adjusting the black wool wristlets he had been wearing since it had got cold. He looked captiously up at the clock inside Herr Kropfl's cage:

"Isn't it about time for you to start opening up? And when you get through, I want you in here. Those eight cases of rivets have to be unpacked before noon!"

Otto had already gone to the cashier's desk to pick up the keys for the shutters with that ingratiating pink-cheeked eagerness he always exhibited for Herr Meier's benefit, but Herr Meier checked him with a jerk of his head:

"You, Otto—I want you to take this bill of lading to Herr Brandt right away!"

Irritation licked up in Peter's throat. This was the third morning in a row that Herr Meier had found some errand for Otto just when Otto was supposed to help with the shutters. Now he would again have to struggle with them alone!

While he tried to gain a few extra moments of heat by the stove by pretending that it was not burning as it should, he watched Herr Meier derisively. Herr Meier was fussing with the key to his desk.

Nobody else ever bothered to lock his desk. But, then, Herr Meier had a mania for locking up things. There was the stupid little closet off the corridor where he kept the small screws on the pretext that the little packages might get broken or mixed up—but in reality because it made him feel important, as Herr Trost had once said. If things had gone his way, Herr Meier would no doubt have had locks on the big storerooms where the nails and screws and rivets were kept as well! As it was, Peter reflected acidly, and as if his ridiculous overlordship over his own department did not give him enough to fuss about, he also had to use the fact that he had been in the store for thirty-five years to set himself up as custodian of all the moth-eaten traditions of the store!

It was a quarter to seven.

He picked up the keys from Frau Redlich's desk and got the stick for pushing up the shutters. As always when he had his choice, he took the Margaretenstrasse side first. He went out through the courtyard and turned right outside the carriage gate to walk toward the farthest one of the small shutters, almost down at the Point where the Margaretenstrasse and the Brauhausgasse met. There were eleven of the small shutters and they were easy enough, even though several had broken springs and would not roll up without a struggle. But it was the five big ones around the entrance that he had come to hate. All five of them had something wrong with the drum on top where the corrugated sheets rolled up, and one could raise them only a few inches at a time. It seemed to Peter as he unlocked the first one that the early weeks in the store when he had taken pride in pushing up the shutters were ineffably far away.

He got them up one by one. Then he unlocked the one over the entrance and paused to look up toward the warehouse yard in the Kohlgasse. No sign of Otto yet! A number of drays were already lined up in front of the yard. Two girls from the office got off the streetcar down at the Point, also Herr Trost who lived all the way in Hernals. Herr Benesch came striding along from the direction of the Gürtel.

He pushed up the shutter far enough to duck under it, then pulled it down again from the inside, as they were supposed to do until it was time to open up. He went down the length of the store to the entrance on the Brauhausgasse and unlocked the door and the shutter there, and got outside. He went again down toward the Point to take the small shutters first.

He had barely got the first one up, when a young woman who had been standing on the opposite curb crossed the street and was clearly coming toward him. She wore a gray winter coat which was only loosely buttoned at her throat and a bright-red felt hat with a large rhinestone ski across the ribbon in front. Something about the hat especially gave the impression that she had dressed without much care, as for some pressing errand from which she expected to return home at once. The next instant her close-set gray eyes and the willful tilt of her chin made him remember her: she was the girl from the Kenyongasse to whom Herr Kropfl had sent him once with a package and a note.

The girl asked abruptly:

"Has Herr Kropfl come in yet?"

"No, he hasn't. . . ."

"Will you give this letter to him when he comes?"

He took the cream-colored envelope gingerly because his hands were wet from the shutters. The girl's eyes followed his hand as he slid the letter into his pocket.

"You won't forget?"

"I won't forget."

Still she hesitated.

"It's very important!" But as soon as the words were out, she seemed ashamed of her anxiety. She added quickly: "I just wanted to be sure. . . . Well, thanks very much."

She walked away briskly, but again Peter had an impression that her jauntiness was put on. He wondered for a minute why she had not mailed the letter in the first place, instead of waiting for him or for Otto out in the street; then the recalcitrant shutters took up all his attention again and he forgot about her.

His hands were purple by the time he had coaxed up the last shutter. Otto still was not back from the warehouse yard. Frau Redlich had come and was arranging her stool in the cashier's cage, and bending over to put away her rubbers in one corner with a soft swishing of her gray skirt against the little door of the cage. Herr Meier was clawing at some papers on his desk. . . .

He went out into the corridor to unlock the attic and the cellar door and then the storerooms off the courtyard. Five of the laborers were already busy with the big shipment of rivets and nails and were getting ready to cart the heavy cases into the store on the two-handled warehouse trucks.

It still lacked three minutes to seven when he came back into the store. Herr Breitkopf and several other clerks were warming their hands by the stove and discussing the crowded streetcars with Frau Redlich across the aisle. For a minute, the temptation to join them and get warm almost got the better of him. But the risk of standing by the stove was too great—Herr Meier would only make him go to work unpacking rivets right away. He went to the Brauhausgasse entrance and waited for a minute before he rolled up the shutter. A few mechanics came trooping in. Then he pushed up the shutter at the upper entrance and hurried behind Herr Lehnert's counter into the carriage-fittings room to take off his overcoat. Most of the clerks were still crowded around the lockers. They sounded unusually gay. The half-holiday for the afternoon made their voices as sprightly as on a Saturday night.

He waited for Herr Lehnert to finish talking to Herr Götz. Herr Lehnert had charge of all the carriage-building and blacksmith supplies, the department Peter liked best, not only because the complicated technical knowledge involved in carriage building had fascinated him from the first, but because of Herr Lehnert himself.... Herr Götz finally went away. He went up to Herr Lehnert and asked:

"Is there anything I can do?"

"Do?" Herr Lehnert looked amused. "You can clean up the storeroom in here. That'll keep you busy for a couple of weeks!" But they both knew that he was only joking. There was no time for putting the storerooms in order now, when they were so busy in the store. "Well, let's see," Herr Lehnert said; "there are a couple of orders of axles and springs I have to get together. You can help me with that. You might go out to the warehouse and wait for me; I'll be along in a couple of minutes."

Peter remembered the letter for Herr Kropfl. He looked cautiously down toward the glass cage. Herr Meier was not around. Herr Kropfl had come and was just pulling out the chair from his desk and getting ready to sit down.

He went down to the glass cage and waited until Herr Kropfl saw him and raised the window:

"Well?"

"A lady asked me to give you this. . . ."

"What lady?"

"From the Kenyongasse."

At once, Herr Kropfl's black eyes were glitteringly alert. He reached for the letter and threw it on his desk——

"How did she come to give it to you?"

"I was pushing up the shutters. You weren't here yet."

It irritated him to be made to sound as if he were apologizing. Herr Kropfl was again using that trick he had of putting him in the wrong although he had actually done him a favor. But it was not safe to go away from the window until Herr Kropfl told him to go. He waited while Herr Kropfl moved the invoice books Hacker had left on the blotter.

"Well, what are you waiting for? Haven't you anything to do?"

"Yes, I have to help Herr Lehnert."

"Get going, then."

He managed to slip out into the corridor without Herr Meier's seeing him. He made straight for the warehouse at the far end of the yard. Once inside it, he felt safe, as he always did out here. He went into the farthest room where the heavy springs were and sat down on a ladder to wait.

It was colder here than in the store, but he did not mind. Perhaps Herr Lehnert would have enough for him to do to keep him busy all morning and he would not have to help Otto at all. He speculated hopefully that if Gustl, the senior apprentice who was assigned permanently to Herr Lehnert's department, were really called up by the army in January, then perhaps Herr Lehnert would pick him to take Gustl's place. . . .

Someone was coming. He listened for the faint limp which Herr Lehnert had got in the war, before he risked going into the outer room.

"Oh, here you are. . . ." Herr Lehnert flicked over some papers he had brought. "We might as well take the axles first. . . ."

Herr Lehnert climbed up the ladder to the upper shelves. For a few minutes Peter was busy taking the axles Herr Lehnert handed down. They shifted several times to other sections of the rack. Herr Lehnert worked along swiftly, pleasantly. Once he stopped to read off an item out loud: "Two sets of twenty-eight-pound axles for phaetons, roller bearings, brass caps—here's a bird that doesn't seem to know there's a war on. He'll have to take iron caps and like them."

"Aren't twenty-eight-pound axles heavy for a phaeton anyway?"

"A little heavy, all right. And he's going to spring his phaetons with two-inch, five-blade springs—must be one of those old-timers who believes in wearing suspenders and a belt."

They worked in silence again until Peter had leaned the last of sixteen dray axles against the counter. Herr Lehnert got down from the ladder to check the three lots.

"The dray axles go to Vorarlberg. I'll leave you the order blanks so you won't make a mistake. When we get through, you might skip up to the office and see whether they've made out the shipping tags. And you better paint the address on every fourth axle in case the tags get torn off."

Herr Lehnert came and sat on the edge of the counter to roll a cigarette.

"Well, what are you going to do with yourself this afternoon?"

"Nothing—stay at the Home, I guess."

"Do you like the Apprentice Home so much?"

"No, but they won't let us go home except on the first Sunday of the month. Are you going to the funeral?"

"I don't know yet. I promised my youngster to rig up a swing for him. Depends on what the weather is like."

"Is it true that the Kaiser was poisoned?"

Herr Lehnert grinned. He had a homely, likable face with intelligent eyes. "You don't want to believe all you hear. You always get a lot of rumors like that when there's a war. When a man gets to be eighty-six like the Kaiser, he doesn't have to be poisoned to die."

"But that story about the reservoir was true. . . ."

"Well, maybe. The chances are that it was only some lunatic the police picked up. Things are bad enough without all those scare stories. I saw this morning that a good half of the trees on the Galitzinberg are gone; they'll be starting in on the parks next."

"Half?"

"The whole side of the mountain over toward Neuwaldegg is bare. Nothing left but stumps. I guess the police can't stop it either: people go out there during the night. After all, what are the poor people in Ottakring going to do if they can't get any coal? . . .

Well, let's get at those springs. You can get out some of the eight-blade ones for the drays. Fourteen pairs of these, and then the three-inch ones. . . ."

Peter set to work. He liked to handle the springs. They were slippery with oil and the eight-blade ones weighed sixty pounds, yet if one knew how, one could slide them out with one hand, then flip them neatly off the top of the pile and catch hold of them with the other hand to lift them down on the floor. It always gave him a pleasant sense of power to work with the springs, for along with his pride in his sheer physical skill with them now, there also went the feeling that he already knew more about axles and springs than most of the ordinary clerks. Someday he would be able to talk as authoritatively as Herr Lehnert to the blacksmiths and carriage makers who came to the store!

He had just set down number eleven on the floor, when he was startled by Herr Meier's voice—

"I thought I told you that I wanted you inside?"

"I was helping Herr Lehnert. . . ."

Herr Lehnert appeared from behind the rack. "Yes?" he asked.

Herr Meier shrank visibly. His truculence became cautious:

"You going to need him much longer?"

"About twenty minutes. After that, I guess I can get along without him."

"I've got to get those rivets unpacked. There's another carload of nails coming in!" Herr Meier turned away from Herr Lehnert; he sounded bossy again: "As soon as you get through out here, you come inside. I don't want to have to look for you again!"

Peter went back to the springs. He would have to help Otto now! He reflected dully that even Herr Lehnert, who was infinitely more important in the store, allowed Herr Meier to impose on him. Something in Herr Meier's voice always sufficed to remind Herr Lehnert that he had been in the store only nine years and that he had served his apprenticeship in the provinces, while Herr Meier had still known Herr Straka's father. . . . Not that Herr Lehnert could not quite easily have asserted himself if he had wanted to, but Herr Lehnert was at once too good-natured and thought Herr Meier too unimportant to bother. If Peter had needed any proof of it, there were Herr Lehnert's remarks when he had finished with the springs. Herr Lehnert asked:

"Got all of them now?"

"Yes, I'm taking them up front."

"All right, that's good enough. You better report to Meier, or I'll have the old buzzard on my neck again. You can tie on the tags later, if you get through inside before twelve. . . ."

There was nothing for it now but to report to Herr Meier.

The store was nearly as crowded as on an ordinary day. Only the absence of the customary sprinkling of merchants and blacksmiths from the country marked a difference. The country people had evidently figured that the store would be closed all day. Herr Benesch had not even bothered to put on his smock; neither had Herr Breitkopf, who was packing mail orders as usual down by the lower entrance.

He threaded his way through the customers in front of Herr Meier's desk, and went down to where Otto was leisurely unpacking the six cases of rivets leaning against the counter. Otto was taking out each package as if it contained butter or glass, with that knack he had for making each job last a maximum of time. He pointed to the packages already out on the counter:

"They go down into the cellar."

"And what are you going to do?"

Otto deliberately raised his voice for Herr Meier to hear:

"Herr Meier said I had to get the cases unpacked!"

At once Herr Meier left his customers. "You start taking those rivets downstairs. I need to get those cases out of the way. When Otto gets through unpacking, he's going to help you take them down." He bustled back to his customers.

Peter loaded up his left arm. The rivets came in ten-pound packages. You piled five of them in the crook of your left arm and held the top package with your right hand so that they would not topple off. Getting through the crowded aisle and around Frau Redlich's cage was always the worst; then came the corridor and the winding cellar stairs and then the long walk in the cellar to the rivet shelves.

After the first few trips the rankling stupor which the monotonous drudgery for Herr Meier always induced in him made his mind go fuzzily blank. Only his left arm, which went through the familiar process of getting tired, then aching with weariness, and at last becoming so numb that he had to support it with his right hand, still served to remind him of his irritation with Otto.

The hands of the clock in Herr Kropfl's cage crept sluggishly forward a few minutes between trips. At half past nine, nearly an hour later than usual, Herr Straka made his round of the store. He still had on his overcoat and he had evidently come in straight from the automobile which brought him every morning and noon from the beautiful old house in Hietzing where Peter had been sent on an errand once. As usual, Herr Straka came slowly down the aisle, his eyes gravely observant but friendly, stopping now and again to talk to a clerk or to some customer he knew.

It irked Peter that Herr Straka should again see him at nothing more important than carrying rivets out of the store. Once or twice, especially in the beginning when he had still been allowed to work more or less regularly for Herr Lehnert, Herr Straka had stopped to inquire what he was doing, whom an order was for. But what was there to ask about the stupid rivets he was loading on his arm? Herr Straka returned his greeting and passed on. A minute later, he had stepped into the glass cage and stood talking to Herr Kropfl who had got to his feet with unctuous alacrity.

The contrast between the flashy, would-be elegance of Herr Kropfl—with his pretentious seal ring and his wavy black hair—and the quiet dignity of Herr Straka awakened his antagonism for Herr Kropfl again. He remembered what Herr Trost had once said about Herr Straka's serving a full-term apprenticeship in the store—Herr Kropfl had served his apprenticeship in the office across the street! An office boy, that was what he had been, and head bookkeeper was all he really was now—an outsider, who knew things only from the pictures in the catalogue and who could not have told a piece of cast iron from a piece of chromium steel and who had usurped Herr Emmerich's place as manager since Herr Emmerich had been called into the army.

He was still chewing on his dislike of Herr Kropfl, and of Frau Redlich and Herr Meier who formed Herr Kropfl's clique, when Herr Benesch called after him down the cellar stairs. Herr Benesch made sure that they were not being overheard——

"Has Meier unpacked any hobnails yet?"

"I haven't seen any."

"Well, keep an eye out for them. He's got two cases coming in—I saw the invoice yesterday. Watch where he hides them and grab a couple of packages if you can. I need them for a customer. I may be able to get some bacon. . . ." Herr Benesch hurried off.

Peter continued on down the cellar stairs. If he could get the hobnails for Herr Benesch, Herr Benesch would perhaps give him a piece of country bread and a slice of bacon again. He looked surreptitiously over the markings on the four new cases Otto was starting to unpack, but they all contained rivets. Herr Meier had probably already hidden the two cases somewhere. He would have to look around when they were closing up!

Half an hour dragged by monotonously. Otto was still smugly taking his time over the unpacking. One by one, the clerks disappeared to eat their ten o'clock breakfasts. His own hunger, which was usually no more than a familiar dull prodding that had to be ignored, became suddenly rebellious and unbearable. He went into the carriage-fittings room to get a drink of water and saw Herr Dornbirn standing by his locker, biting into a sandwich of bread and cheese. The sight of the sandwich tortured him for some minutes in spite of all the water he had drunk; then he forced himself to forget his hunger again.

At half past ten, Herr Breitkopf called to him from the counter across the aisle:

"Hop up to the attic and get me half a dozen balls of heavy twine."

"Herr Meier said I wasn't supposed to stop——"

"Never mind that. I need the twine. And see whether there isn't some hemp string still around somewhere. This paper twine's no good at all. . . ."

He was glad enough to get away from the rivets for a little while. It was cold in the attic, but at least it was a change. He climbed over the tangle of rafters to the rolls of wrapping paper. The wartime paper twine was easy enough to find; he took half a dozen balls off the cord on which they were strung. Then he looked under the rafters and behind the rolls of wrapping paper and finally found one ball of hemp string. It would probably be the last one Herr Breitkopf would get for tying up his parcels until the end of the war! As he made his way out from behind the rolls of paper, his eyes fell on a stack of old magazines.

He picked up a copy to look at it. It was from the spring of 1914. The back cover was taken up entirely by a gay advertisement of cocoa. Inside the magazine were pictures of Ostende and other

Belgian seaside resorts, pictures of the book fair at Leipzig, more pictures of the English king and queen at a place called Balmoral, and a whole series of views of Spanish cathedrals. And all through it, there were advertisements of chocolate and liqueurs and of imported cloths—all the things that had disappeared since the war. A description of a dinner party in the middle of a story caught his attention and he read on, fascinated by the tantalizing description of food, until he heard someone on the stairs. He hastily put down the magazine, then on second thought he picked up a whole sheaf of them and put them under a rafter—he would get them at noon and take them along to read at the Apprentice Home!

Otto had at last finished unpacking. But Otto made only four trips into the cellar before Frau Redlich sent him out for change. Ordinarily, Otto could not have taken more than ten minutes for that, but today when all the banks were closed he would probably manage to kill half an hour before he came back. It looked as if he would have to take all the rest of the rivets down into the cellar by himself. Then, unexpectedly, there came a break. Herr Meier himself stopped him with a gruff toss of his head:

"Herr Kropfl wants you to go somewhere. . . ."

He went to the glass cage. Herr Kropfl looked up from a letter he was sealing:

"You're going to the Blindengasse. The address is on the letter here. . . ." He shoved out a small package and the letter, and then slipped a two-kronen note from his billfold. "It's a quarter to eleven—that gives you ample time to get back in time to sweep up. And another thing: in the future, if anyone gives you a letter for me out in the street, you are going to ask them to put it into the mail instead. That clear?"

"You mean the lady this morning?"

"That's the lady I mean! Now get a move on!"

He got his coat and went out into the Margaretenstrasse. It had cleared up a little and the flags over the house fronts fluttered feebly in the wind. At the Point, where the Brauhausgasse forked off, Hacker jumped neatly off a streetcar which was still going at full speed.

"Where you going?" Hacker asked.

"Blindengasse, for Kropfl."

"What's in that?" Hacker had already taken the package from

him and was shaking it close to his ear. "That's one of the boxes of candy he got from Schmidt's. Who's it for?"

Peter took out the letter, but held it out of Hacker's reach.

"Greta Wagner. . . ."

"That's a new one. I wonder whether he's going to put those garters on for her—what's she like?"

"How should I know? Otto always runs his errands for him."

"Well, I bet she's hot! Bet you anything he's getting a little whoring lined up for this afternoon." Hacker pretended to let the package drop into the slush and then tossed it to him. "By the way, you've got to lock up for me this noon. I have some business I've got to tend to."

"Whyn't you ask Otto for a change? I don't want to miss lunch on account of you."

"You won't be late," Hacker cajoled. "All you've got to do is take the keys over to Herr Brandt's and make sure that the lights are out."

Hacker's overcoat pockets were bulging with something. Peter asked: "How about a couple of apples, then?"

Hacker took out an apple and tossed it to him. "That's all I can spare. Be sure the lights are out. . . ."

He was still eating the apple when he got on the streetcar. A woman and a child immediately began to watch his mouth with that envious, resentful look that came into people's eyes nowadays when they saw somebody eating. Peter stopped guiltily. At the next stop when some people got off, he crowded his way farther into the streetcar to get away from the child who was still staring at him.

What Hacker had said about Herr Kropfl and his own memory of the girl with the rhinestone ski this morning came back to trouble him. Why had Herr Kropfl been so emphatic about ordering him not to take any more letters from her? He must be expecting another one—and the letter must have been important to the girl or she would not have waited out in the street. Yet Herr Kropfl was not sending him to her now, but to some other girl, and with some kind of present at that. He found that his dislike of Herr Kropfl had come to include the girl to whom he was taking the candy now.

He looked around critically when he had rung the bell at the apartment in the Blindengasse. An elderly man in a worn knitted jacket opened the door and asked him into a narrow hall which smelled of stale pipe smoke. A girl came rushing from the living room at the end of the hall. She was small, pert, not pretty at all, and theatrical in her attempts to give herself the airs of a grand lady. There was an excited jump in her voice when she asked him to wait. The man in the knitted jacket lighted a stubby pipe and started to talk about the weather. After some minutes the girl returned, still licking the flap of an envelope. The flap of the envelope was irritatingly moist when he took it from her. Between the finger tips of her other hand she held out some coins—"This is for you. . . ."

He pretended not to see her hand. "No, thanks."

"Go on, take it—it's for you!"

"No, thank you. Herr Kropfl wouldn't want me to——" He backed away hurriedly and got out of the door. He hated to take money on these amorous errands Herr Kropfl usually sent Otto on, fortunately. But on the streetcar he scolded himself for not taking it anyway: with the money he could have bought an apple perhaps, or one of those licorice sticks that lasted for hours. Yet he knew that he could not have taken the money.

The same repugnance cost him another black mark with Herr Kropfl twenty minutes later. Herr Kropfl took the letter from the girl and waved away the money that remained over from the carfare:

"You can keep that."

"Thank you, I'd rather not."

At once, Herr Kropfl's eyes sucked fast to him; his over-red lips parted menacingly beneath his black mustache: "When you are given anything, you'll take it, do you hear?"

Luckily, Herr Brandt was that very moment rolling back the door of the glass cage and Herr Kropfl looked around. Peter left the money on the ledge of the window and hurried away. It was time to sweep up. Down by the Brauhausgasse entrance, Otto had already begun. He got the sprinkling can and sprinkled the upper half of the aisle and behind the counters.

Herr Straka came in from the office across the street to check the cash with Frau Redlich. When Peter started to sweep, Herr Straka and Frau Redlich were already at the cash register across the aisle from Frau Redlich's cage, reading off the totals for the day. There were still a number of customers in the store. It was five minutes to twelve. He would never get to the Apprentice Home in time for lunch!

By the time he had swept down to the open space under the skylight, Herr Straka had finished counting the money and had already put it into the little steel box in which he always took it back to the office to the big safe. Herr Kropfl had come out from the glass cage and stood talking to Herr Straka. Herr Meier was craning his head to hear.

Peter swept around them carefully so as not to raise any dust. Herr Kropfl's eyes suddenly flashed around to him——

"I suppose you can't wait for a few minutes!"

"And hasn't anyone told you to sprinkle the floor first?" Frau Redlich promptly asked.

He felt himself go red with annoyance: he did not mind the other two, but he hated to be put in the wrong in front of Herr Straka—and unfairly at that, for only two days ago he had been scolded by them for not sweeping up before closing time. It was Herr Kropfl's fault that he had not been able to start earlier; Herr Kropfl was merely punishing him for refusing his tip!

He leaned the broom against the counter and got the stick for the shutters. Otto had already taken the keys and was piously making it appear that he was waiting for him. They closed the entrances and then the shutters. When they had finished, Herr Straka had gone and Frau Redlich was getting ready to leave. Most of the clerks had disappeared into the carriage-fittings room to wash up.

Otto locked his share of the storerooms and then started to get his coat. Peter decided to make at least an attempt to get him to wait: if they were both late for lunch, Brother Norbert would believe that they had been kept at the store. He said:

"There isn't anybody to take the keys to Herr Brandt. . . ."

Otto shrugged. "That's Hacker's job."

"Hacker had to go somewhere."

"Nobody asked me to lock up."

"You might at least wait for me!"

"Why should I? I've got to be there to take in the food from the kitchen."

He let Otto go rather than argue any more, and locked the rest of the storerooms. When he came to the attic, he remembered the magazines and got them down. Then he went into the store and finished sweeping.

One by one, the clerks went out through the iron-plated door. Only Herr Meier was still lingering by his desk. As always at closing time, Herr Meier seemed unable to tear himself away from the store. Peter put on his coat and waited another ten minutes before Herr Meier finally came to wash up. It was a quarter to one when he took the keys across the street to Herr Brandt. . . .

At the Home, Brother Norbert was already serving seconds to his favorites. Peter saw with relief that there were still three slices of bread left. He got one, and a ladleful of turnips, and one potato. He was still eating when Brother Norbert tinkled his bell for an announcement.

"All those," Brother Norbert was saying with an air of announcing a great treat, "all those who wish to go into the Innere Stadt with Brother Kajetan to watch the funeral procession will report in the vestibule at half past one."

At least, it was not a compulsory excursion like the ones they had had to go on during the summer on Sunday afternoons. He had loathed marching through the streets, two by two, like boys from an orphanage. But the announcement had revived his hope of getting permission to go home for the afternoon. He asked Brother Norbert when he returned his plate:

"May I go home for the afternoon?"

Brother Norbert wrinkled his wry forehead. "Any special reason?"

"No."

"Our rule is that no one can go home except on the first Sunday of the month. You have not been so assiduous in the performance of your duties here to entitle you to any special privileges!"

Brother Norbert looked as if he wanted him to go on pleading so that he could preach some more. His eyes went hard, Peter saw as he turned away. It had been worth trying anyway. . . .

About twenty boys gathered in the hall to go with Brother Kajetan. Otto was one of them. When they had left, the dining hall settled into the same dreary, paper-rustling silence as on a Sunday afternoon. Boys sat at the tables by the windows to read; a few went out into the library. Brother Norbert jingled his keys a few times, then sat down at his tilted desk up front and opened what looked like one of the illustrated Saints' Lives of which there was a whole shelf full out in the library.

He went out into the half-dark corridor off the hall to get the magazines he had brought from the store. When he had taken them out of his locker, he decided to take along a book in which to hide the magazines. Brother Norbert would be sure to make the rounds several times in the course of the afternoon to see what every boy was doing; he might object to the magazines. He picked up the large bookkeeping text from the night school, to which he had to go twice a week, with a vague idea of doing his homework. He put the book back again; he was not going to spoil his afternoon! Beneath the schoolbooks there was a thick catalogue from the store and half a dozen others from different firms; they dated from the time when he had brought home a new catalogue every night to memorize all the intricate lore the clerks had at their finger tips. He chose the one from the lock company because of its size and went into the dining hall.

He hunted for the story he had started in the attic. He finished it; then he read another, and still another. It was the first time since he had come to the Apprentice Home in July that he had felt like reading a story through to the end. Hitherto, on Sunday afternoons and in the evenings when he had sat in the dining hall with a book, it had always been to study some catalogue or some engineering yearbook Herr Lehnert had let him take from the store; on the few occasions when he had been tempted to pick up a novel in the library, he had always lost interest after the first few pages and had put it down in disgust. The sharp reality of his life in the store and here in the Home had been like a cynical lens under which the stories had appeared hollow and false.

But these stories from the spring of 1914 seduced him like a drug. It was the innocent prewar opulence and complacency they breathed in every paragraph which enthralled him and made him hunt for every new evidence of it. Everything about the magazines spoke of that same scandalous, legendary abundance of things: the advertisements of caviar and candy and of luxurious soaps, the pictures of foreign countries which suggested a freedom of movement that seemed incredible now, even the articles on the woman's page—he spent a long time reading the cooking recipes and tried to imagine the reckless quantities of butter and eggs required for each dish.

It had grown dark. When Brother Norbert switched on the lights, he realized that it was nearly time for vespers and how hungry he was. The magazines with their thick prewar paper irritated him suddenly. He looked at an advertisement by an English railroad, and thought: *I needn't be here at all! Mizzi is in America and my Father is English—I'm really on the wrong side! They must have lots of food in England and in France, or they wouldn't talk about starving us out. . . .*

No telling how long the war would still last! People had stopped saying: "It can't be much longer. It'll be over by Christmas, you'll see!" A weary hopelessness had set in. People went on dully from day to day and no longer talked about the war at all. . . .

No, he was not going to quit the store as Poldi was always urging him to do! Only a month more until Christmas, and then only six months more before there would be new apprentices and he would be like Hacker with none of the heavy chores and free to work for Herr Lehnert, and after that he would have a chance to show Herr Straka all he could do. The important thing was to get through the winter and to keep clear of Herr Kropfl——

The picture of a white porcelain bottle of hair lotion in an advertisement suddenly brought Herr Kropfl before his eyes with odious vividness, not only because the hair lotion made him think of Herr Kropfl's dandified airs, but also because the white porcelain bottle reminded him of the small white jar in which the pharmacist had handed him the salve Herr Kropfl had sent him for. Twice, once in August and once during the last week in October, Herr Kropfl had made him go to the pharmacy with his prescription. The last time, Hacker had seen him come back and had said: "Know what that stuff is he's always sending for—mercuric ointment, wasn't it? Well, it's for syphilis! All right, ask Gustl, if you don't believe me. . . ."

He had asked Gustl and others, too. Even Herr Lehnert, after stalling—"What do you want to know about things like that for?"—had admitted that mercuric ointment was for some sort of loathsome disease. Since then, he had never been able to look at Herr Kropfl's smooth-skinned face without an immediate impression of all manner of corruption lurking under his smooth skin.

He suddenly remembered the rhinestone ski on the red hat of the girl that morning, then the other girl to whom he had taken the candy. Herr Kropfl was probably somewhere with her now, perhaps in one of those equivocal little hotels Hacker was always talking about, and she had no idea how tainted he was. A sense of outrage mingled with his revulsion and also revived the incident when his dislike of Herr Kropfl had taken root: it had been during his very first month in the store when Herr Kropfl had made out his sick-benefit card and had looked at his birth certificate—" 'Father: information refused!' M'hm!" Herr Kropfl had said, and had enveloped him with a slimy, ignominiously enslaving look. . . .

He still writhed when he thought of it. Herr Kropfl had made no reference to it since; he had probably even forgotten about it. And he himself would have disliked Herr Kropfl just as much, he told himself, even if someone else had made out the sick-benefit card, since he had somehow disliked Herr Kropfl from the very first day.

But he did not want to think about him! . . .

He closed the magazine and looked away from it at the windows. It was almost dark outside. The boys who had gone with Brother Kajetan were not back yet. He wondered whether Poldi had gone to see the funeral. Franz certainly would have gone, if he had been here. . . . He felt suddenly guilty for not having thought of Franz before. Franz might be at the front by now! He had said in his last letter from Graz, two weeks ago, that he expected to be sent to the Italian front; he had sounded gay about it, but perhaps that had been put on. He remembered when Franz had been called up in September: Franz had made light of that too—"At least, I'll get something decent to eat for a change!"—but that had been mostly for *her* benefit. Franz had not really been eager to go. It was no longer as it had been in 1914 and in 1915 when all of Franz's friends had hardly been able to wait to get to the front. Still, it would be true that even at the front Franz would get good things to eat—everybody knew that the army was well fed!

He felt torturingly hungry again. . . .

He must remember to get the hobnails Herr Benesch wanted for his customer! Perhaps Herr Benesch could really get some bacon and some country bread. He must watch very carefully tomorrow to see where Herr Meier was hiding the nails. . . .

Chapter Thirty-Eight

He discovered Herr Meier's cache quite by accident, and after he had nearly given up hope of ever finding it among the hundreds of deep compartments up and down the racks out in the storeroom.

Nearly all the clerks had hiding places for articles that had become rare and therefore valuable beyond their actual price in the store, since customers from the provinces were only too glad to bring in presents of food to get the saws and nails and files which the war had made so hard to get. Only the week before, Peter had seen Herr Brandt and Herr Lehnert divide a whole smoked ham which some country blacksmith had brought them for saving him a few sets of steel tires and some axles and springs. . . .

The two cases of hobnails Herr Benesch had asked him to be on the lookout for had completely disappeared. They were not locked in the little closet off the corridor—he had made sure of that. On the third morning after the funeral, he was carrying bolts into the cellar. He had about filled up the bin for eight-inch bolts, and he did not know where Herr Meier wanted the remaining packages put. Herr Meier had taken advantage of a lull in the store to get together some big order out in the storeroom—at least, that was what he had said when he had taken Otto away from carrying bolts.

Peter found them working with suspicious secrecy behind the last partitioned stand where the big nails were kept. Otto was up on a ladder and just bending down to take a bundle of small packages from Herr Meier's outstretched hands. The small packages did not belong in that bin. They must be the hobnails! If he had needed any further proof, Herr Meier's annoyance promptly furnished it:

"What do you want here? I thought I told you to get on with those bolts?" Herr Meier had moved close to the ladder so as to screen the pile of small packages in one of the lower shelves.

"The bin downstairs is all filled up. I don't know where to put the rest of the bolts."

"I'll be down in a minute. Put them on the floor until I get there!"

Otto was looking down from the ladder with smug innocence. Herr Meier in a final attempt to convince him that he had not seen anything out of the ordinary, grumbled irascibly:

"Does one have to show you everything? You are smart enough when it comes to talking back!"

Peter went back to carrying bolts. A few minutes later, Otto joined him. Herr Meier was back in the store. Then Otto was sent on an errand by Frau Redlich, and Herr Meier was caught in the rush that always came around eleven o'clock. It was a good time to tell Herr Benesch about the nails. . . .

Herr Benesch came at once. "Where are they?"

"Back in the last rack."

"All right, you skip back there and get half a dozen packages. I'll stay here by the door. If anybody comes, I'll turn on the lights."

The ladder which Otto had been standing on had been moved into another aisle. Peter got it and climbed up. The front of the bin had been crammed full of large packages of four-inch nails. It took him several precious minutes to shift enough of the packages into the adjoining compartments to get to the rear of the bin. Twice Herr Benesch called to him to hurry. His fingers finally found the small packages. They contained hobnails all right. He took them out one by one. Herr Benesch came dangerously far away from the entrance——

"Haven't you found them yet?"

"I've got them."

"How many?"

"Six, you said."

"Better get a few more while you're at it."

He reached for three more packages. At least, Herr Benesch had gone back to his post to watch. He put the big packages back in front; then he returned the ladder to the exact spot where he had found it.

Herr Benesch beamed when he saw the packages. He shoved four of them into the pockets of his smock and picked up the rest so that they hardly showed under his big hands. They both got safely out of the storeroom. . . .

Two whole days went by. The customer who had promised Herr

Benesch the food had not come, although Herr Benesch had sent him a telegram. Then, just before noon of the third day, Peter saw that Herr Meier had found out about the nails. He was spluttering with rage as he told Frau Redlich about the raid on his cache. A minute later, he accused Herr Trost of taking the nails. Herr Trost became angry and started to shout. Herr Kropfl came out of the glass cage.

It was time to lock up for lunch. Peter got the keys from the hook behind Frau Redlich's desk. Herr Meier was complaining to Herr Kropfl:

"I've had customers waiting for those nails for three months! I needed every package. . . ."

As he walked away with the keys, Peter reflected gleefully that Herr Meier would never suspect Herr Benesch, since Herr Benesch had not made Herr Trost's mistake of showing any interest in the nails. And as long as Herr Benesch was safe, he was safe. . . . But a minute later, he realized that he had exulted too early. Herr Kropfl and Herr Meier fell abruptly silent when he returned to hang up the keys. Herr Meier fixed him with an ugly glare——

"Did you take those hobnails?"

"What hobnails?"

"Don't act so innocent!" Herr Kropfl bullied.

"The nails you saw me put away in the storeroom! You were the only one who came out there!"

"I saw you working out there, but I thought you were getting an order together—I don't know anything about any nails!"

"If I ever catch you stealing anything—"

Herr Kropfl's voice coiled like a whip:

"We don't want any thieves in this store!"

Anger at their accusation boiled up in him. Herr Benesch had as much right to sell the nails as Herr Meier: everybody was raiding everybody else's cache! What right had they to call him a thief—

"I didn't steal any nails! I've never taken anything!"

"You better not!" Herr Kropfl warned.

It was clear that his own outburst had startled them. It accounted for the nasty inflection with which Herr Kropfl was covering his retreat.

They let him go, but he knew that they had not relinquished their suspicion, any more than he could keep his resentment from flaring up every time he went even near Frau Redlich's cage. His need to do something to get even with them grew as the afternoon wore on. He began to watch for a chance to get two or three minutes alone in the storeroom. The chance came when Herr Straka came in at closing time to check the cash. Otto was still busy sweeping his half of the store, and Herr Meier never stirred away from his desk while Herr Straka was by Frau Redlich's cage.

It happened to be his turn to lock up the storerooms. He pulled down the shutter over the entrance of the nail storeroom from the inside to make it look as if it had already been locked. Then he groped his way to the rear in the dark. He found the ladder with the aid of a match. It was difficult to work in the dark, but the very risk he was running gave him a tense, frozen calm. He cleared a hole among the big packages in front and lighted another match to see whether the hobnails were still in back. They were—but so were two vicious-looking steel traps which had been carefully placed to clamp shut on any hand that reached for the nails. He moved the traps grimly to one side. Then he took out nine packages and tumbled them as far back in the adjoining shelf as they would go.

His heart pounded furiously when he lowered the shutter from the outside. Only when he had finished locking up in the yard, did his sense of triumph get the better of his belated fear—

That would teach them to call him a thief! Now they had nine packages less to trade in for delicacies from the country. . . . He tried to picture Herr Meier's rage when he discovered the new raid on his cache. This time they would be forced to assume that someone else had taken the nails, since their pompous conceit would never allow them to believe that he would have dared to go back to the rack after the scene they had made at noon! For an instant he shuddered again at the risk he had run—if he had had the electric light on, if he had not had to use a match, his hand would be mangled now and he would have been caught! But he had not been caught! . . .

All that evening the satisfaction of having got even with Herr Kropfl lulled him into a pleasant conviction that the incident was closed. For it was of Herr Kropfl he thought whenever his mind went back to the scene in front of Frau Redlich's cage. The two others did not matter so much. If one looked at it fairly, Herr Meier had actually had a reason for being suspicious—whereas Herr

Kropfl had acted gratuitously and had fairly jumped at the chance to accuse him of things. Still, now that he had vindicated himself, he could afford to forget about Herr Kropfl again. All he needed to do was to keep away from him and give the glass cage as wide a berth as possible.

But the very next morning all his easy confidence was swamped by a dismal realization that some perverse fate seemed determined to thrust him against Herr Kropfl. The girl with the rhinestone ski on her hat was back! She was waiting across the street when Otto and he went out into the Brauhausgasse to open up. This time she did not cross the street; evidently, she did not want Otto to hear. She beckoned to him twice, the second time so imperiously that he could no longer ignore her signal and went over to her.

Her close-set gray eyes merely shifted their focus when she attempted a smile as he came up. He noticed again how singularly without expression her eyes were; they had an opaque bluntness which made them look isolated in her sultry, full-blooded face. It struck him that there was some direct connection between their sluggishly unmanageable stare and the impulsive movements of her shoulders and arms.

She twisted a thick envelope out of the pocket of her coat. "I hate to bother you again—will you give this to Herr Kropfl?"

"Herr Kropfl said I wasn't to take any more letters."

"But you must take this! I've been waiting for you. It's important—it's a matter of life and death!"

Her intensity frightened, then irritated him. Why did she have to pick on him? Why didn't she go to Otto? Otto had made dozens of trips for Herr Kropfl to her house, while he had gone only once. . . .

"You will take it, won't you?" She thrust the letter at him with fierce, almost childlike insistence.

"I'll get bawled out if I do. I can't!"

"It's only this once. This is the last time! It's terribly important—please!"

He felt himself weakening. She sensed it and pushed the letter into his hand.

"Please!"

"All right," he agreed uncertainly.

Immediately her brief spell of meekness was superseded by roughshod assurance again. "You know where I live in the Kenyongasse—number 15—for the answer?"

"But if there isn't any answer?"

"There has got to be!"

"I mean, suppose Herr Kropfl sends it through the mail, or some other way?"

"Oh. . . ." The possibility seemed not even to have occurred to her. "But you can come and tell me! I mean at noon, when you go home for lunch. I have to know what he says—you'll come?"

The desperation in her voice softened him to the highhanded way in which she was disposing of his time.

"I'll try."

"Right after twelve!" She turned away without even thanking him. He noticed that this time she did not bother to appear breezy and offhand when she walked away. . . .

He waited until Herr Kropfl had settled down at his desk with his usual pompousness, and until there were already a number of customers in the store, before he went up to the window in the glass cage.

Annoyance in Herr Kropfl always showed itself in a viscous, enveloping glance that was a warning. "It seems to me I told you not to take any more letters!"

"I didn't want to take it. She—"

"I guess I'll have to teach you what's meant by obeying orders!" The letter which Peter was still holding through the wicket in the glass cage had been turned into exasperating evidence that he had done something wrong. He stiffened truculently:

"I said I didn't want to take it! She made me—she said it was a matter of life and death!"

Herr Kropfl's eyes flicked from right to left to see whether anybody had overheard it. "Give me that——" Herr Kropfl ripped the letter out of his hand and immediately tore it into four pieces. "What else did she say?"

"She said that I was to bring the answer to the Kenyongasse at noon."

"You are not going anywhere at noon unless you are sent there!" Somebody had come up behind Peter: it was Herr Lehnert with a customer. . . . "And you are going to learn to do what you are told without back talk!"

Anger at Herr Kropfl's shifty treacherousness which had made him out to be in the wrong in front of Herr Lehnert and the customer kept gnawing at him all morning. He also kept thinking of Herr Kropfl's alarm when he had quoted what the girl had said. Herr Kropfl had been afraid!

Hacker stopped him out in the corridor—"What was Kropfl beefing about?"

He told Hacker about the letter. Hacker whistled. "I bet he's got her in trouble!"

"You mean the disease?"

"Don't be a sap. I bet he's given her a baby! Did she say anything else—you going to see her this noon?"

"I don't know. . . ."

But he did know. He realized that he had already decided to go, first to spite Herr Kropfl, and then because of a vague sense of pity for the girl, and lastly from curiosity. It would mean that he would be late for lunch. He might not get anything to eat at all. When he thought of that, he had to tell himself quickly that he had given her his word and would have to go now.

He watched closely to see whether Herr Kropfl was perhaps sending Otto with an answer. But Otto stayed in the store. There was little likelihood that Herr Kropfl was sending anyone else. At noon when Herr Kropfl left for lunch, Peter followed him out through the yard to see which way he would turn in front of the store. Herr Kropfl headed for the Ring and he was walking with Herr Dornbirn as he did every noon. Herr Kropfl was not going to see the girl, then!

He realized from his dully throbbing excitement how irresistible his curiosity had become. It had even subdued his hunger, so that the gnawing emptiness in the pit of his stomach had become one with his need to see the girl. He came to the Gumpendorferstrasse and started up the long incline of the Gürtel. The big, cube-shaped clock which dominated the intersection at the Mariahilferstrasse drew nearer and nearer. . . .

It occurred to him suddenly how strange and even foreign the whole section around the Mariahilferstrasse had become for him. It was as if the once so familiar neighborhood had died some time ago—he could not say exactly when—so that its hollow, brittle continuance was like that of dead flowers some people preserved under glass. Reality lay back there between the Apprentice Home and the store. Yet the sight of the Lazarist Church where he had so often sung with the choir awakened a quick surge of nostalgia in him; but when he actually rounded the corner of the garden behind the Church to turn into the Kenyongasse, the garden wall seemed oddly foreign again even though he remembered the pattern of the bricks.

The apartment house in the Kenyongasse had an air of sedate middle-class prosperity. There were coco-fiber runners on the stairs. . . . He found that everything about the girl was of interest to him. He glanced at the directory in the entranceway and saw that she was staying with a family which had a different name from hers—she must be renting a room!—then he went upstairs.

She opened the door herself. Her eyes nudged him briefly like a horse nuzzling for sugar. "In here . . ."

He followed her into a rather large room off the vestibule. It struck him how much the room was like her. Rather handsome if somewhat heavy and uncompromising furniture, which she had primped unskillfully with all manner of ruffles and cushions and throws. He noticed the canary-yellow pouf in front of the sofa, on which she had evidently been lolling among the fatuously bright-colored cushions, the pretentious leather writing set and the crowded bric-a-brac on the little desk, the mirror-paneled door of the wardrobe which gaped a little and allowed one a glimpse of an untidy, bulging confusion of clothes.

She shut the door into the vestibule, and he experienced an uneasy thrill at finding himself all alone with her. She looked much bigger in the red dirndl dress she was wearing now than she had done that morning in her winter coat.

She demanded a little hoarsely: "Where is it?"

"He didn't give me any letter."

"Did he put it in the mail?"

"I don't know."

"What did he say? Tell me!"

"Well, he didn't say anything. He just bawled me out for taking your letter——"

"Then he didn't answer!"

He did not want to tell her about the four pieces into which Herr Kropfl had torn her letter. Her turbulent closeness disconcerted him. He said hopefully:

"He may put it in the mail this afternoon. . . ."

'No, he won't! He's just going to do like he did with all my other letters!"

Again it was her face and her throat, rather than her eyes, which were stormy. She wrenched her body around violently and marched to the sofa. A cushion tumbled down from the top of the pile. She flung it passionately to one side, threw herself down on top of an open magazine, and kicked the canary-yellow pouf so that it rolled toward him. He bent down to stop it, and set it down beside the desk.

"The swine!" she said. "The dirty dog! The swine!"

She crouched rather than sat on the sofa, with the back of her neck angrily pressed against the wall. He felt more uneasy even than when she had been standing so close to him. All sorts of things about her appearance suddenly struck him as wrong. The mere fact that she should be wearing a summer dress with a low-cut neck and with short sleeves which showed her disturbingly full, white arms was bizarre! And her dress was of silk, a loud red silk with some outlandish flowered design—nobody ever wore a dirndl dress made of anything but gingham, any more than they would think of wearing silk stockings with it and high-heeled patent leather shoes as she was doing! But what disturbed him most was that her tight-fitting bodice was stretched so taut by her bulging breasts that untidy white ovals of underwear gaped between the buttons. . . .

More to ease his tension than because he had any faith in his suggestion, he said: "Maybe if you wrote to him at his house . . ."

She started at the sound of his voice. Then, immediately, she was all fierce concentration again:

"Do you think I haven't tried that? I even went to see his mother. Do you know what she said? She said: 'Don't come to me—I don't know what's been going on between Ernst and you—you'll have to settle it with him. . . .' That's the kind of mother he has! But I'll show him! He can't treat me like some servant girl he picked up in the park!"

The words came from her with a savage rush. A vindictive thrill at the prospect of what she might do to Herr Kropfl blotted out his embarrassment over her brazen frankness. She did not seem to care how much he knew, and she was taking it for granted that he was on her side!

She had seized one of the cushions and was convulsively pumping it up and down on the sofa. One of the buttons on her bodice burst open so that a long slit of white underwear lay exposed. . . . He looked away hastily and around the room. He discovered a big trunk under the Paisley throw in the corner, then some schoolbooks in the bottom of the wardrobe. He recognized the binding of one of the exercise books used in the commercial schools—then she had been in school down here! For he was certain that she was from the provinces somewhere, perhaps from Moravia: her flat, harsh way of pronouncing words and the garish dirndl dress were almost proof of it. . . . His eyes went to the two windows and found—lying between the double panes of one of them—several wax-paper packages which he was certain contained food. One package was undoubtedly a stick of *Wurst;* the other looked like bread. A violent craving for food took hold of him. If only she would offer him something to eat! He must get to the Apprentice Home!

Again she started out of her knotted self-absorption and pounded the sofa with her fist. But she did not speak.

She did not look or act as if she were going to have a baby! Neither did she look like a girl who would jump off a bridge. . . . He had always imagined those girls who jumped into the Danube as broken and dissolved in tears—she was rather like a tangle of wrath and violence which could not make up its mind as to exactly where to strike. Awkwardly, he waited again for her to speak. When he could not stand waiting any longer, he ventured:

"Are you going home?"

"What?"

"I mean, are you going home?"

"How can I go home! You don't know my father—my father is one of the aldermen in Olmütz!" she burst out incongruously.

"But if Herr Kropfl won't answer you?"

Her heavy cheeks and her throat became flushed and desperate. "He's going to answer me! I'll go to his house and to the store, and make a *scene!*" She made the word sound like some mystic cataclysm which would not only crush Herr Kropfl but engulf the house and the store. "He can't do this to me—I'll show him—I'll kill him, and then I'll kill myself!"

The outburst sounded at once ludicrous and fierce and naïve, as if she had just painfully remembered the words from some lurid account she had read as a child. She had been shouting. Someone was coming along the hall outside—a big, solid woman pushed open the door.

"What is all this, Minna?" the woman demanded. "What's going on in here?"

Peter found himself retreating from her glance. She had the same sort of blunt, gray eyes as the girl.

"Nothing, Aunt Marie."

The woman gave him another distrustful look. "Well, lunch is ready!" she said. She left the door pointedly wide open when she went out.

He said quickly:

"I think I'd better go. . . ."

The girl looked up distractedly. "You'd better go now. . . ." she said.

"If there's anything I can do . . ."

"There isn't anything!"

He had to let himself out of the apartment door. This time, in the vestibule of the apartment, he was certain about the odor of roast pork. The ravaging fragrance stuck in his nostrils and expanded into more and more imperious visions of delicious brown crackling the farther he moved away from the house, and made him feel dizzy with longing for the meal to which the girl and the big woman would presently sit down—which they had perhaps already started to eat.

His hunger throbbed with what might have happened if the girl had not been so callously self-absorbed: she might even have asked him to stay for lunch! But at the very least she might have offered him a slice of bread! He was almost sure now that the big package in the window had been bread. And there had been Wurst. . . .

When he was far enough down the Gürtel to make out the big clock, he saw that it was ten minutes to one. The boys would nearly have finished eating at the Home. There was not even any use in hurrying any more. Irritably, he recalled that the girl had not even thanked him once. . . .

She continued to be as vivid as if he were still with her in her room. Her sultry violence—the brash, naked whiteness of her full arms and throat—but most of all the straining buttons on her dress gave an astringent quality to his sympathy for her. It was not so much, he realized, that he was sorry for her as that he felt increasingly angry with Herr Kropfl. He remembered the candy Herr Kropfl had sent to the other girl, the crinkly black-and-pink garters in his desk, the loathsome prescription he sent to the drugstore for. . . .

His thoughts veered to the girl again. There had been a point when her angry crouch had given way to a despairing listlessness: her arms had been limp by her sides, and her knees had parted until her thighs had been clearly outlined under the thin dress. She had been completely oblivious of him. The memory of his embarrassment suggested to him now that Poldi would never have sat like that. But then Poldi would never have been in such a room, waiting for a letter——

But Mizzi! Had Mizzi been angry like that? Was that how it had been—?

He retreated in alarm, in a panic almost, from this new aspect of things. It was as if his body suddenly harbored myriads of splintery, glasslike chips, each one of them reflecting Herr Kropfl and somehow Mizzi, too. No matter which way he turned, it was at the peril of lacerating his flesh on the implacably imbedded splinters. Only the thought of the girl was really safe. As long as he thought of her, he could think of Herr Kropfl, too. He was still thinking of her when he entered the Apprentice Home. . . .

The other boys had already taken back their plates to the serving table. The bread and the soup were all gone. There had been potato soup for the first time in a month. He tried not to think about the potatoes while he gulped down the insipid, watery turnips Brother Norbert had dribbled out on his plate. . . .

He felt all that afternoon, as he watched Herr Kropfl sleekly sitting at his desk or sliding back the glass door of the cage to come out and talk to some customer in his insinuating voice, like an author watching his own play and patiently waiting for the foreknown catastrophe. Every new counterjumper elegance in Herr Kropfl only made the outcome more sure. There was a voluptuous sense of power in the knowledge that presently the girl would strike.

But three days went by and nothing happened at all. His certainty began to drain away. In its place had come a feeling of being irresistibly driven into a conflict that was bound to come. He knew that Herr Kropfl had become aware of his exasperation from the way Herr Kropfl's antagonism moved out and tried to beat him down.

One morning when he went to Frau Redlich for carfare to the Westbahnhof, Herr Kropfl was standing by the desk. He jeered:

"Carfare—to the Westbahnhof! The walk will do you good. And see to it that you don't take all day!"

Herr Kropfl had a way of raising his black eyebrows that heightened the impression of his sinuous and yet infinitely muscled glossiness. For one long moment Peter drove home his resentment into the supercilious black eyes.

Hacker had always got carfare to the Westbahnhof; he himself had got it for errands that hadn't been half so far and when the weather had been good. By the time he would get to the freight station, his shoes would be soaked. But he forced himself to keep his anger from breaking loose. Here, beside Frau Redlich's desk, Herr Kropfl had the upper hand—the time had not yet come! . . .

When he had finished at the Westbahnhof, he angrily thought of the girl's threats. What was she waiting for? Had she lost her nerve, or was she ill? He felt he had to know and the Kenyongasse was only a few blocks out of the way. He went.

The big woman whom the girl had called Aunt Marie met him in the door. "What do you want?"

"Fräulein Gabish—"

"She isn't here! She's gone to her parents in Olmütz—and you can tell that Herr Kropfl of yours that if I ever lay eyes on him, he's going to get a piece of my mind he won't forget in a hurry!"

"He didn't send me."

"You can tell him anyway!" But she relented somewhat.

"I only came to ask how Fräulein Gabish was—is she all right?"

"All right!" the woman scoffed. "As all right as a girl in her condition can expect to be!" It was clear that she had said much more than she had meant to say. "Was there anything else?"

"No, thank you. I just wanted to know."

"Well, now you know——" She slammed the door.

Then the girl had lost her nerve! She had slunk off to Olmütz—where her father was an alderman!—without doing anything. Just like a silly little girl, all of whose threats had amounted to nothing more than a petulant stamping of feet. Or perhaps the woman had been afraid of what she might do and had made her go, had packed her off home. . . .

At any rate, Herr Kropfl had got away with it!

The realization choked him with wrath. Herr Kropfl was free now to go after that other girl, after any number of other girls, in spite of that disease! He pictured him secretly gloating over his easy escape, indulging more than ever now in his smug affectations of refinement, arrogantly secure in his glass cage!

And there was nothing he could do! Herr Kropfl was too powerful.

His impotence festered in him like a thorn. It was responsible for the feeling he had all the rest of that day that he was pushing recklessly forward over a single narrow plank which stretched over a dark abyss. Somewhere along the plank Herr Kropfl and he were going to meet. He was as certain of it as if it had all happened before.

He knew that the moment had come when Herr Kropfl shoved out the sinister little envelope with the prescription through the wicket the following noon. Herr Kropfl had slipped a banknote out of his wallet and had put it on top of the envelope.

"Well, what are you waiting for?"

"I'm not going to the pharmacy!"

The words had come from him without any previous thought. They seemed to be leading him, and all he had to do was to follow behind. He had the satisfaction of seeing a sallow flush creep over Herr Kropfl's cheeks.

"Just let me hear that again——"

"I'm not going for that kind of medicine any more."

"You aren't going for what kind of medicine any more?"

Herr Kropfl had got out of his chair. He leaned menacingly forward over the desk.

"That mercuric salve for—"

"Listen, you—" it was a hiss rather than a shout, but it was meant to drown him out—"when I send you somewhere, you are going to go!"

Herr Meier appeared as from nowhere, fatefully drawn by Herr Kropfl's rage. "What's that? What's that?"

"The young gentleman refuses to go on errands now!"

It was Herr Meier's turn to look as if he could not believe his ears. His cantankerous mouth twitched fretfully——

"Well, that's all we need—to have our apprentices tell us what they'll do and won't do! Why don't you send him up to Herr Straka right away?"

There followed a curious, shifting pause. Herr Meier was baffled by it and looked vainly at Herr Kropfl for a clue. But Peter suddenly knew why Herr Kropfl was not going to send him to Herr Straka: Herr Kropfl was afraid! Afraid of what he might say . . . Herr Kropfl had hastily slid the prescription and the money off the ledge down to his desk; his eyes remained evasively hooded for a long moment, and when he looked up, it was not at Herr Meier but at him.

"I didn't say I wouldn't go on an errand. I only—"

"Silence! You speak when you are spoken to!" Herr Meier glared as if daring him to say anything more; then he turned back to Herr Kropfl: "I still don't see why you don't send him to Herr Straka!"

Herr Kropfl shrugged one shoulder. He had already slipped into the role of the indulgent young executive who had been an apprentice himself once and who was willing to overlook things. For just one moment, Peter realized, he had held Herr Kropfl in the hollow of his hand, and now the moment was already gone. He read the concentrated venom in the depths of the black eyes.

"Next time I will."

It had been said with just the right inflection of forbearance and threat. Herr Kropfl had regained his detestable, velvety poise. His white bookkeeper's hand stretched fastidiously to pick up a blotter to announce that for him the incident was closed.

Herr Meier jogged Peter's arm—

"You come with me! I have a little job that'll teach you to talk back when you're told to do something. In there—in the washroom!"

Peter saw that several customers had begun to watch. Up until this moment he had been wholly unconscious of the people close enough to the glass cage to overhear. It had been as if Herr Kropfl and he had been locked in a lonely struggle, with only Herr Meier buzzing around them like an exasperating fly.

He hurried toward the carriage-fittings room to put as much space as possible between himself and Herr Meier, who came charging after him, in and out among the clerks. Even so, the knowing grin of a master wheelright flicked him on the raw. Herr Lehnert looked up from an invoice he was making out and frowned.

Once safely inside the storeroom, he slowed down defiantly. Herr Meier came up and made as if to push him again. He twisted away from his hand and went into the narrow cubbyhole where the four washbasins were. Again, Herr Meier came so close that Peter had to endure his breath on his cheek.

"I want all that cleaned up. There's the brush; you know where Rohan keeps the polish for the taps. I want everything spick and span! And under there, too, under the bowls and in the shelves—this place is getting to look like a pigsty. . . . And when you're through in here, I'll have something else for you to do! . . ."

At least, Herr Meier went after that. He wiped his cheek where he had felt Herr Meier's breath. Then he looked angrily at the row of basins and taps, each one encrusted with grime and the yellow sand which came out of the tins still labeled "Mechanic's Soap," although there was not even a trace of soap in the gritty sand.

Cleaning the washroom was one of old Rohan's chores. But Rohan, who did little besides sweeping the courtyard and the sidewalks, had lately excused himself from cleaning in here because of the rheumatism in his hands. It was perfectly true that the washroom was filthy, as Herr Meier had said; yet Herr Meier would not have dared to order one of the other helpers to clean up in here—they would have refused! Nor had an apprentice ever been asked to do Rohan's chores—he thought for a minute of going across the street to Herr Straka to protest, then decided against it because it smacked too much of what Otto might have done, and because in the end nothing would be gained. Herr Meier and Herr Kropfl would always have the upper hand. . . .

He soaked the smelly scrubbing brush and went to work on the first basin. Once he had started to scrub, he minded less. He vented his anger on the stubborn grime. When all the bowls and spigots were clean, he started to clear out the moldy accumulation of filth on the floor under the bowls and from the bottom shelves on the opposite wall. He was nearly through when Herr Meier came in to inspect.

"That's the way it's always going to look from now on! What about under there?"

"I'm doing that now."

"All right. Just so it gets done! Then you're going to get the oil and the mop and go over the floor in here."

Oiling the floors was another of Rohan's jobs. It was more disagreeable than cleaning the bowls because of the acrid stench of the oil and because of the splinters that constantly peeled off the boards and caught in the mop. But what exasperated him most was that when he had not only done the floor in the washroom but—of his own accord—all the aisles in the storeroom as well, Herr Meier came up with still another task.

"Tonight, when you've swept up and after everybody's gone, I also want you to oil the floor out there in the store!"

"It takes an hour to do the whole store—I'll miss supper if I'm late at the Apprentice Home!"

Herr Meier's shoulders pitched forward spitefully. "Still talking back! I'll knock that out of you yet. A few minutes aren't going to make any difference at the Home—that floor's got to have overnight to dry! . . ."

For a week Herr Meier kept venting his spleen on him like that. But that could be borne. The important thing was that Herr Kropfl was holding aloof, seemed actually to be avoiding him. Then, suddenly, a moment came when he knew that Herr Kropfl was no longer afraid. Little by little, so blandly as to be almost imperceptible, Herr Kropfl began to join Herr Meier in harassing him with chores. Only, Herr Kropfl's was a more vicious slant: Herr Kropfl was out to make things so unbearable that he would have to quit the store.

It started with nothing more tangible than a silken interest in some errand on which he was being sent. To anyone listening, Herr Kropfl's inquiries had an almost caressing purr. Then, presently, the errands became a weapon in Herr Kropfl's hands. Herr Kropfl made him walk no matter how far he had to go. He waited until just before noon to send him out again so that he had to go without lunch. He made him fetch things that had always been called for by one of the drays—long, awkward steel bars with which he could not have got on a streetcar even if he had had the fare. Then, again, he professed a sudden concern that some package might be too heavy for him, and made him take one of the four-wheeled handcarts the helpers used around the warehouse yard, and made him drag the heavy cart halfway across town to pick up a few gears or a single roll of wire which he could have easily carried under his arm. . . . And always now there were Herr Kropfl's jeers—"Peter can do that! You'd like that little jaunt out to Ottakring, wouldn't you?"—and the habit Herr Kropfl had lately formed of seizing his sleeve and twisting it until he pinched the skin on his arm.

He felt bewildered and trapped. There was only a spurious comfort in the observation he had made recently that even Herr Meier and Frau Redlich were puzzled by Herr Kropfl's viciousness, that they drew back and subtly disassociated themselves from Herr Kropfl's orders to him. There was no reliance to be placed in that. He knew that the moment he rebelled, they would side with Herr Kropfl again, would tell Herr Straka that it was he who had been at fault. He came to hate the feeling that he must hold on doggedly, beyond his strength and against relentless odds, and that he could not quit now since that was what Herr Kropfl wanted him to do. . . .

Not even the short Christmas Day at home with Poldi and *her* was any respite from gloom. Franz had been wounded on the Italian front. There was the telegram on Father's desk and the letter Franz's captain had sent. And while it did not seem to be a dangerous wound—the captain's letter said that the bullet had only touched the right lung—Poldi and she were worried and glum.

They had a stew and a few pieces of candy Poldi had managed to buy and the regular sandy wartime bread. It was the first year when *she* had not even been able to save enough flour to make a few cookies or a loaf of white bread. There was the miniature Christmas tree from the florist, and the two neckties and the book and the pair of wool gloves Poldi had bought for him. When he tried on the gloves, Poldi frowned.

"And I want you to wear those in the store. Look how chapped your hands are! Tell me, haven't you had enough yet?"

It was the same angry question Poldi flung at him every time he came home. He pretended not to have heard. But he was moved by her concern, even while he grimaced secretly at Poldi's belief that he could really wear such gloves as these while he worked. The gloves would have been in tatters in less than a day.

He could not forget the store. In the afternoon while he tried to read the novel Poldi had given him, the thought of the next day hung over him like a cloud. He could not read, and he nearly forgot to take the book along when he set out for the Apprentice Home at five. . . .

Yet, all unexpectedly, there came a rift in the seemingly impenetrable gloom that made up his life between the Apprentice Home and the store. It was not that Herr Kropfl had fallen seriously ill, as he often hoped; neither did the Home suddenly get vast supplies of food, as he occasionally dreamed. And yet, it was like a belated Christmas for him——

It happened a few days before the end of the old year. Otto and he were summoned to the office across the street. The tall girl who was Herr Straka's secretary told them what they were to do—they were to take one of the handcarts and collect six sacks of apples which were to be taken out to Herr Straka's house. The apples were waiting at a dairyman's, a few blocks from the store.

It was still early afternoon, and nobody ever inquired very closely about the time spent on an errand to Herr Straka's house. From that standpoint alone, the errand was a treat. And there was the hope which the mere mention of apples had immediately raised in his mind. He found that Otto shared it, too. As they approached the dairyman's, Otto said cautiously:

"I wonder whether we could get into those sacks?"

They found they could.

As soon as they had got far enough beyond the Gürtel to feel safe, they pulled into a side street and opened two of the sacks. It was a feast! They ate as many apples as they could and crammed their pockets with more to eat on the way. Otto agreed that they ought to draw out the errand as long as possible; for once, Peter found himself almost liking him.

Just to be in Hietzing among the winter-stilled gardens and the placid, friendly villas was fun. The snow was suddenly exhilarating again. The leisurely streets made one feel free. . . .

They stopped once more to finish the apples in their pockets and to make sure that the sacks they had opened looked just like the other four. Then they pulled into the driveway beside Herr Straka's house.

A stout, elderly cook and two maids were in the big kitchen, which still smelled enticingly of recently cooked food. One of the maids, a pink-cheeked, rather pretty girl with mischievous eyes, unlocked the outside door into the cellar for them.

Otto and he started to take the apples down in the two fruit baskets the girl had found for them under the cellar stairs. They took their time. It was pleasant to linger over this job, pleasant and somehow exciting to see all the food stored in the cellar. Whole cases of eggs, long shelves of preserves, a huge bin still half-full of potatoes, and behind a wire-screened partition all sorts of still more precious things. Partly because the apples had stilled his hunger, and partly because it was Herr Straka who owned all this priceless food, he felt none of the angry envy that always rose in him at even the faintest evidence of hoarded food somewhere else. He was even glad the food was here. It was proper somehow that Herr Straka should have an abundance of things—a promise that justified his hardships in the store.

It turned out that there was another part to their errand. The girl with the pink cheeks informed them of it when they returned the keys. They were supposed to take a chair back with them to an upholsterer's in the Mariahilferstrasse. They were to come around to the front door and to wipe their shoes carefully on the mat!

They would have done so in any case. There was something so charming and innocent about the patrician intimacy of even the front hall that Peter felt as if he were trespassing. There came a drawing room, in which he had only time to take in the ebony grand piano with the soft, red throw over its lower end and a delicate eggshell-colored bowl of mimosa farther up front. Then came a much larger drawing room with a towering Christmas tree between its two French windows. Beyond it was a dining room. . . .

Rapidly, while the girl pointed out the chair they were to take and showed them the two tiny holes burned in the upholstery, he looked around the room. He saw the exquisite little white marble figure of a nymph on a slim pedestal beside the door, the charmingly recessed windows behind the draperies, the paintings, the wide tapestry on the wall. . . .

When he stooped over to pick up the front legs of the chair, the micrometer and the pencil he carried in his breast pocket slipped out and fell on the rug. He picked up the pencil and let the micrometer lie; he even managed to kick it a little to one side where it could not be seen. When they got out to the cart with the chair, he said quickly:

"I've lost my micrometer. It must have dropped out of my pocket inside. . . ."

The maid was just closing the front door. He explained why he had come back.

The micrometer was still where he had kicked it, under a chair. He pretended to keep on searching for it until the girl's eyes suddenly bubbled with suppressed laughter.

"You sure you dropped it in here?"

He had not counted on this. She thought he had come back because he wanted to flirt. She must be at least nineteen, and she was making fun of him! Hacker would have known what to do!

"Certainly!" He tried to sound at once bold and sly, and he attempted a knowing wink. It did not come off. He could feel himself blush.

The girl looked still more amused, but at the same time something uncomfortably tender and lingering had come into her eyes.

"It's about so big——" he said hastily. "It's made of brass."

Unaccountably, after her mocking disbelief of only a minute ago, she began to hunt for it now on the rug. She was no longer watching him, but because of his awareness of her now, he was unable to get another look at all the beautiful things around the room, as he had hoped.

"Here it is! . . . What's it for?"

He showed her how it worked. Once their fingers touched—she giggled a little and he felt crowded by her closeness and that troubling air of expectancy she had. When he had put away the micrometer, he was at a loss for something to say. He looked helplessly at the tall Christmas tree and away from it at the Venetian mirror in which he only saw her again.

"It's beautiful in here. . . ."

Her red lips twitched as if she were about to laugh. She was not interested in the room and she was clearly waiting for him to say something else. Just then, from beyond the dining room, someone called. Her eyes flickered mischievously—"Don't go away!"

She left him alone in the room.

It was even better now than he had hoped. He looked around him with happy deliberateness; then he went as close to the big tapestry over the console table as he dared.

The tapestry hung in the shadow, on the wall away from the windows, and its subdued colors blended into such close-knit harmony that he had difficulty at first in making out what it was supposed to represent. Then his eyes grew accustomed to the elusive interplay of the soft tones. It was a boar hunt! Oddly-foliaged, golden-leaved trees trailed off in stately confusion through a ravine and up a gentle rise into a serene blue sky. In the right foreground, among the ferns, a vicious-tusked boar had just gored a dog which was running off yelping into the woods. One knight had already thrown his spear, which had overshot the boar and stuck quivering in the ground. Grooms and drivers were hallooing among the trees, closing in on the boar. The dogs had been caught at the precise moment where they were torn between rage and fear. From the left, the hero was boldly approaching with his spear held ready to strike. . . .

Everything was caught up in one eternal moment of suspense. One could afford to pause and notice the birds in the trees, the enchanting flowers growing between the gnarled roots of a tree, the two grooms who were dressing a slain boar in the ravine, three other grooms carrying still another vanquished boar on a pole out of the forest on the left. . . . Far off, in the upper left-hand corner of the tapestry, there was a castle from which a gay cavalcade was just setting out, evidently to welcome the hunters home. A proud lady riding sidesaddle, the gorgeous train of her gown sweeping nearly down to the ground, was in front. She carried a falcon perched high on her gloved hand and she seemed wonderfully at ease on the prancing horse. Behind her came other ladies and knights. Everything in that corner was sunny and gay. . . .

The stately reticence of the tapestry which had at first made it so hard to read, now made the whole scene seem enormously real and intense. It was a world that was closed in, and singularly self-sufficient. The lady with the falcon suddenly reminded him of

Bianca. . . . By some magic of the moment, which he did not even wonder at, his memory of Bianca blended into the harmony of the tapestry, fused with his consciousness of the beautiful room behind him, and became the final seal on the happiness he felt. It was as if he had been completely lifted out of the oppressive world of the store into a larger world that was yet more intimate and infinitely reassuring. Hope had come back to him, and a sudden confidence in the future. . . . He let his eyes revel once more in the luminous greens, the wonderful amber of the leaves, the exquisite blues.

He was so absorbed by his happiness that he was startled by the sound of voices in the hall. Someone was closing the front door. A little boy, still bundled up in a ski suit, was skipping into the room and pulling at the hand of his governess. But ahead of them even—he saw with dismay—was Frau Straka! She must have seen him looking at the tapestry!

The little boy was staring at him with the engrossed look little children had. Frau Straka was smiling. It was the first time he had ever seen her as close as this. She wore a burgundy-colored tailored suit which must have come from abroad—where else could one get such beautiful wool as this!—and she had evidently been out for a walk with the little boy and the governess. Her cheeks were still glowing from the cold. He realized that she had a lovely skin but that she was really not beautiful at all—attractive rather and likable, with an engaging plumpness that resembled Herr Straka's somewhat because she too was tall; but where Herr Straka's bearing was measured and grave, hers was vivacious and gay. He watched the light, quick motions with which she was already tugging at the fingers of her gloves while he hastened to explain:

"We came for the chair and I dropped my micrometer in here—I came back to look for it. . . ."

"Come on, Wolfi!" the governess was saying.

"Mama!" the little boy squealed. He was still staring with large-eyed absorption.

"Go with *Fräulein*, Wolfi! I'm coming in a minute."

The little boy trotted off. Frau Straka turned back to him. Her smile was so friendly that he felt sharply grateful to her for not destroying the happiness in him.

"Do you like it?" she asked. "You were looking at the tapestry, weren't you?"

"Yes—it's beautiful."

Frau Straka came and stood beside him as naturally as if he had been a guest. Again he had an overwhelming, joyful awareness of the innocence of this room.

"It's a Gobelin," she said. "My grandfather brought it from France. Could you tell what it represents?"

"It's some kind of hunt. . . ."'

"Yes, a boar hunt—" She looked as if she were going to say something more, but to his disappointment, she did not go on. She was looking at him, taking in his grimy clothes and hands. He saw the pointed concern in her brown eyes—was she going to scold him now for coming in here with hands that looked as if they had not been washed, although they had, ask perhaps whether he had touched anything!

"*Gnädige Frau*—"

"I am coming—*Fräulein*, will you see that the young men get some hot cocoa before they leave? They must be cold!"

She gave him another smile and then she was gone.

It was again the pink-cheeked girl who waited on them at the bright, white table in the kitchen. There was a warm fragrance of cocoa and of freshly made buns. The girl brought their cocoa and a plate with four buns. When he reached for one, she winked.

"You're a smart one!" she said.

A few minutes later, she came back to ask:

"Do you want another bun?"

It pleased him that she paid no attention to Otto at all, and this time he winked back. For once, he had beaten Otto at his own game and without resorting to Otto's tactics of crawling for sympathy. Quite the contrary! The girl was clearly admiring him for what she considered to be his boldness and for having got himself asked to have cocoa and buns.

But he did not think of her on the way back. He thought of Frau Straka and the little boy and of the beautiful tapestry. . . .

It had been a little thing. Altogether their trip had barely taken more than two hours; yet it had filled him with a warmth that lasted for days. And even after his memory of it had shrunk somewhat and he was hungry again, it still survived in the form of a stubborn determination to outlast Herr Kropfl's malice and the winter in the Apprentice Home and in the store.

Chapter Thirty-Nine

It was after New Year's that his hands began to crack. Ugly fissures opened across the back of each hand and especially across his knuckles where the flesh had been puffily swollen for weeks. His right hand was the worst. On it two bone-deep gashes stretched from the middle finger clear over to the last knuckle and bled almost constantly. But the smaller cracks were rapidly widening too. It was impossible to wash the oil and grime out of them after work; they were painful at even the slightest touch, and the cold water from the taps burned on them like salt.

He watched the festering sores with helpless and oddly detached alarm. It seemed to him at times as if his hands were no longer a part of him. He felt ashamed of them and kept them out of sight as much as he could. Only in the morning and evening, and at certain moments during the day when he had inadvertently brushed up against something, the sudden pain made them again sharply his own.

He did not know which he dreaded most: night, after he had gingerly slipped his hands under the blanket and they itched so unbearably that he felt he had to claw and tear at them with his nails—or morning, when he was forced to break the scabs that had formed over the fissures during the night. Sometimes, too, he was torn out of his sleep by an agonizing twinge because the back of his hand had scraped against the blanket. He lay then with his hands softly writhing for some position that would cheat the ache, first outside the cover and then under it again, until he finally found the blind side of the pain and fell asleep.

There was nothing he could do to protect his hands. Once, on a long errand, he had put on the gloves Poldi had given him, only to find afterward that the wool had stuck fast to the wounds, so that he had to tear the gloves loose. And it was constantly growing colder as January went on. Herr Lehnert and Herr Meier and old

Rohan out in the yard all agreed that it was the coldest winter in years. And quite apart from Herr Kropfl's malice, there were more chores and more errands than ever before. Five laborers from the warehouse yard and Herr Götz and two other clerks had been called up by the army on the first. Herr Benesch was ill with the flu. They became more shorthanded in the store with every day.

Toward the end of January Otto got sick. He complained one morning of a stitch in his side and was promptly sent to the doctor by Frau Redlich, who was all clucking solicitude. Otto did not appear again in the store all the rest of that day. He had been put to bed in the dispensary, which was the only really warm room in the Apprentice Home. He did not appear to Peter to be sick at all: the pink splotches in his cheeks, which gave him such a look of sly innocence, were as bright as before. But four days later an ambulance came and suddenly took him away to the Lazarist Hospital. He had pneumonia.

It meant that he had to push up all the iron shutters in the morning by himself, and that now all the chores fell on him!

It infuriated him to listen to Herr Meier's and Frau Redlich's exaggerated concern. They had both gone to the hospital the very first evening that Otto was there. And they had enlisted not only Herr Kropfl's sympathy for Otto, which was to be expected, but Herr Straka's as well. Herr Straka inquired every morning now how Otto was, and Frau Straka had actually been to see Otto in the hospital.

It seemed unfair that it should have been Otto who had got sick instead of himself—Otto, who had been so elaborately shielded by Herr Meier from ever doing any hard work and who had always gone around prudently muffled up, pulling on gloves, even though he had to go no farther than up to the corner to the bank. Now Otto would be able to loaf in the hospital for weeks! But what he grudged Otto most was the good food. . . .

Their meals at the Home had become torturingly scant. The watery mess of turnips which Brother Norbert always ladled out of the big pot with as much ceremony as if it had been a delicious meat stew had become their staple diet at noon and at night. They had not had potatoes again since Christmas Eve. Once a week, for Sunday dinner, they were given a finger-sized sliver of boiled gristle, which Brother Norbert still referred to as "meat." The barley soup which they had every noon one could only eat if one pretended not to see the fat, white quarter-inch grubs which floated among the barley grains. When he had first noticed the stiff, wormlike shapes, Peter had been unable to touch the soup. But after several days of sitting hungrily by and watching other boys empty their plates and even argue that weevils were "natural" and no more nauseating than the barley itself, he had finally succumbed to his hunger, and after queasily pushing the barley and the larvae to one side had spooned out the liquid part of the soup. But the hateful sight of the white larvae stayed with him all afternoon and filled him with loathing even when his hunger made him think of the next meal.

They could not even count on the small slice of crumbly corn bread which they had hitherto had with every meal. There had already been days when they had had only one slice of bread all day, and then came a week when there was no bread at all. The shortage of flour was city-wide. Hungry mobs had overturned an army truck with bread in Floridsdorf and one in Hernals. There were rumors of a general strike, of food riots in Graz, of a change in the ministry. But the talk seemed singularly remote, just like the news from the fighting fronts which nobody bothered to read any more. It had no bearing on the hunger which gnawed at him all the time.

Not even the clerks in the store could get presents of food any longer from the country blacksmiths and merchants for saving them nails and screws and tools which had become hard to get. The heavy snow made it impossible for the country tradesmen to drive into town; they had to come by train, and on the trains government inspectors confiscated any food people attempted to bring. It had made all the clerks short-tempered and cross. Even Herr Lehnert was inclined to be testy and much less friendly.

There had lately, just before Otto got sick, been several afternoons when he had been allowed to work for Herr Lehnert again. He had almost convinced himself that Herr Kropfl's malice had worn off its edge. Then Otto's sickness had shown him how mistaken he had been. For some perverse, slippery reason which he tried in vain to capture and dissect, Otto's illness had made not only Frau Redlich and Herr Meier more harsh with him, but it had also sharpened Herr Kropfl's vindictiveness. It was almost as if in some obscure way they held him responsible that Otto had pneumonia.

A new note appeared in Herr Kropfl's jeers when he sent him out on some particularly grueling errand. Instead of pinching the sleeve of his coat, Herr Kropfl now fingered his arm and sneered: "You are good and tough, aren't you? You won't get sick—of course not! Not like Otto, are you? Here's another little jaunt since you're going out to Meidling anyway. . . ." And Herr Kropfl would manage to add some extra errand that took him far out of the way with some heavy package on his shoulder or under his arm.

He found that even the hardest days in December seemed mild now in comparison. The muscles in his arms and shoulders ached almost perpetually from the heavy packages he carried first in the crook of his arm, then on his shoulder, then on his arm again. His feet had become frostbitten, too, from trudging through the streets in soggy shoes.

A feeling of weary despair had settled on him when he came back to work one Saturday after lunch. He had spent the entire morning carrying cast-iron grates down the cellar stairs. Herr Kropfl had seen the grates in the corridor where they had been unloaded the night before and had ordered him to get them out of the way. There had been two tons of grates in all. He had barely got half of them down into the cellar. He started on the weary trips again.

At half past three Herr Kropfl came out of the iron-plated door and crooked his index finger in the loathsomely cynical way Peter had come to dread.

"Come here—I have a little job for you!"

Herr Herold was standing by the glass cage.

"Can't we get one of our trucks to go out there?" Herr Herold said. "It'll be dark before he even gets to Floridsdorf!"

"The trucks are all busy at the Westbahnhof. He won't mind if he gets back a little late—will you?" Herr Kropfl fleered, and slid his treacherous hand under his arm. He waited stonily. Herr Kropfl gave his muscle a hard, final squeeze. "All right, here's the address all written out for you. You'll take one of the handcarts and sprint out to Floridsdorf—because they close at six! They're going to give you four rolls of steel wire. That's all you've got to get. It'll just make a nice little outing for you."

Herr Herold came after him to the lockers.

"It wasn't my idea," he said. "They called up from Floridsdorf and said they couldn't deliver the wire any more tonight and Benzler's need it for a rush army order. They're coming for it first thing Monday morning. You better take my old leather gloves! They'll keep your hands warm at least. You know where they are, out in the storeroom in the desk."

He found one of the linen rags which Herr Lehnert brought from home to wipe the grease off his hands. The rag was still clean and he tore it into two strips which he taped around his hands before he slipped them into the tattered, fur-lined gloves Herr Herold always used when he had to handle axles or springs. Then he went up to the warehouse yard to get the four-wheeled cart.

It was a mile to the Ring, another mile around the Ring to the Danube Canal, say another mile from there to the Prater, two miles more to the Danube and across the bridge, then Floridsdorf. How far he would still have to go in Floridsdorf he did not know. He resolved not to ask until he got across the bridge. If he thought of the entire distance he felt immediately crushed by the sheer outrageousness of the job. The only way to think of it was in stages: The Ringstrasse first, then the Danube Canal. . . .

The gloves kept his hands warm and the sores itched only occasionally. He tried to use his right hand as little as he could by keeping the tongue of the cart tucked under his arm. As long as the Margaretenstrasse ran level or sloped uphill, the tongue obeyed quite easily. It was only when he went downhill that the tongue jerked capriciously from side to side so that he had to hold it with his hand. The same thing was true of the canvas loop by which he pulled the cart. It tended to slip off his shoulder when he was going downhill so that he had to hold it up with his other hand.

When he came to the Ring he had a moment of indecision. By cutting across the Innere Stadt he could save some time, yet he felt reluctant to go that way with the cart. The narrow streets were uneven and they might not be free from snow; the Ring would be much easier to travel on. But he knew that the real reason for his reluctance lay somewhere else. The nearness of the Innere Stadt had made him strangely alert. Supposing someone he knew saw him dragging the cart: one of Poldi's friends, or some boy from the choir, or Bianca! The fear was always in the back of his mind when some errand with an unwieldy parcel forced him to go into the Innere Stadt or to some part of the city where he was likely to run into someone he knew.

It struck him suddenly how much his slow progress with the cart amidst the heavy traffic of carriages and automobiles along the Ring made him feel exposed and as if he had to travel along a height. Without realizing it, the impression had grown on him in the last few months that the whole world of the store and the Home was down in the depths, on a lower level of the city almost. He puzzled for a while over the fact that the store and the Home did not really lie so much lower than many other parts of the city; he was finally driven to the realization that his impression had to do less with the location of the Home and the store, than with the hardships of the last two months and above all with his feud with Herr Kropfl. But he did not want to think about him!

He pulled the cart across the bridge over the Danube Canal, and the long stretch of the Praterstrasse down to the Prater lay ahead of him. People were already hurrying home from offices and shops. The street lights had been turned on. It seemed colder here; yet the snow was slushy underfoot so that his feet felt wet again and cold. At the Praterstern he saw an empty dray turn in from the Nordbahnhof. He hooked onto it by holding onto the rear end of the dray with his left hand and pulling the cart behind him with his right. It made his hands ache but he felt that he was saving his strength. He was in luck. The driver let him hang on and the dray went all the way down to the Danube and across the long bridge. An icy wind cut across the bridge and across the bleak flats on the other side. But he was in Floridsdorf.

He stopped a policeman to ask his way. The factory appeared to be quite close, but it was twenty minutes to six and out here the streets had not been cleared of snow so that it was hard work to pull the cart. And he found that the policeman's directions had failed to give him any idea of the distances involved. A block out here was as long as half a dozen city blocks. He became alarmed at the thought of not getting to the factory by six and tried to run. When he slowed up to get his breath, the wind made him shiver with cold. He told himself that at the factory he would have a chance to get warm and broke again into a run.

When he finally reached the factory gate, workmen were already coming out from grimy brick buildings in the rear. The clock in the gatekeeper's lodge said four minutes after six. He asked for the shipping room and had a moment of absurd relief when the gatekeeper showed him the four rolls of wire leaning against the wall.

"They brought them out to me when you didn't show up by closing time. Kind of thought you'd be late!"

The four rolls of wire looked much heavier than Herr Kropfl had led him to expect. His mind dully registered the fact as he went to the cast-iron stove in the corner to get warm. Behind him the gatekeeper lighted a second match and sucked noisily on his long-stemmed pipe.

"You've come quite a ways. Thought maybe you people had changed your mind. Whyn't you take off your gloves?"

Peter attempted to take off the gloves, but the fur lining had become stuck to the sores in spite of the bandages. The heat of the stove made his hands itch furiously. He moved them farther away from the stove.

"I can't," he said. "I got frostbite on my hands. There are a couple of cracks that bleed and the gloves stick."

"Know what the best thing is for frozen hands?" the old man asked. "Urine! Yes, sir! An old peddler in Salzburg told me about that one time. Only thing that helps. At night before you go to bed you piss on them and wrap your hands up good in a linen rag. One time when my—"

Peter had stopped listening to him. He had gone over to the rickety desk to sign the receipt and pick up the invoice for the wire. The four rolls, he saw, weighed three hundred and some odd pounds. Herr Kropfl must have known—he had lied deliberately. But there was nothing he could do about that now, and the prospect of the three hundred pounds he would have to pull on the cart only made him restless to get started. It was already twenty minutes after six. He buttoned up his coat.

"You got a long trip ahead of you," the old man sympathized. "It's always a long way home. Horses are just the opposite. They always know when they're heading for home and you've got a job holding them to a walk. I know from the time I drove a dray. . . ."

The cart did not seem too hard to pull at first. He moved fairly fast, thinking only of getting to the top of the Danube bridge. It had got much colder even in the few minutes he had spent in the gatekeeper's warm shack. The icy wind which tore across the open lots had an impersonal and stupid viciousness. He set his teeth and plodded on until he came within sight of the long rise which led up to the bridge. He had begun to sweat in spite of the cold and he could no longer ignore the throbbing pain in his side. He went more slowly the rest of the way to the foot of the slope and the pain in his side died down. It was quite dark except for the sparse street lamps and there was little traffic along the wide, desolate road.

Then he started the climb.

The first few yards showed him that the pavement was covered with ice. He had to put his feet down sideways and brace himself with every step. When he had pulled the cart less than a third of the way to the top, he was panting for breath; but it was impossible to stop here on the slope without first losing a dozen precious yards in backing the rear wheels of the cart into the bank of snow which the snowplows had left along the curb. He picked the fourth arc lamp ahead of him for a goal where he would allow himself a rest, and toiled on toward that. It seemed to him that the cart was no longer a thing separate from him. It was obstinate and treacherous, constantly threatening to roll back down the slope the moment he stopped to pull, a dead weight which he had to tug up step by step, but which he had to get to the top. Sometimes when his strength failed momentarily, his next tug succeeded merely in twisting the front wheels over to the right, and tears of exasperation gathered in his eyes before he got the cart rolling again.

He reached the fourth lamp and jammed the left rear wheel against the curb. He folded back the tongue and went to sit down on the cart. His lungs were the only sensation there seemed to be room for in his brain—that, and the pain in his side which rose and fell with each breath. He realized in a weary flash of thought that he was not even strong enough to feel any hatred for Herr Kropfl now. He shivered with each prolonged squall of wind and tried to ignore his shivering, just as he tried to keep himself from thinking of the remainder of the slope up to the top of the bridge. He thought instead that it must be after seven now and that ordinarily he would be going from the store to the Home and would have dinner soon. It seemed lucky to him that he felt hardly hungry at all. A dray went by but it was going too fast for him to catch up with it. He followed it with his eyes until it got to the top of the bridge. Then he was unable to rest any more. He hooked the canvas loop over his shoulder and started up again.

Once his foot slipped on a cobblestone and he fell in spite of his precautions and the cart dragged him back for several yards before he could regain control of it. It seemed to him during the last hundred yards that he was no longer pulling the cart with his left shoulder and his legs, but with his grinding teeth which had become the source of the desperate spurts of energy by which he yanked and tugged at the strap. He finally reached the top.

The asphalt pavement on the bridge made it almost easy to pull the cart. The only difficulty now was that he was shivering violently and that his temples had suddenly started to throb. This time he did not dare to stop. The wind which blew through the steel framework of the bridge was too ruthless and too cold. And by the time he had reached the halfway pier, the throbbing in his temples at least had abated somewhat. Slowly, with the smooth pavement, a little confidence returned to him. He reached the far end and started down the ramp where the cart ran of its own momentum. All he had to do was to run with it and keep from slipping on the cobblestones. Down at the bottom the road became level again, stayed level for quite a while, then the long incline up to the Prater began.

His muscles cried out at the renewed strain, even though the slope was not half so steep as the one up to the bridge. He argued with them as he would have with a child: "I can't stop now! I've got to get back to the store! Two more blocks and then I'll take a rest—just up to that new building there!"

Right now it was his shoulder that bothered him most, where the canvas loop cut into the bone. He shifted the strap to find a spot that would not feel so raw. It puzzled him how the seat of irritation and pain flitted from one part of his body to another. His soggily cold feet and his hands which burned fitfully no longer bothered him at all. Only the grueling weariness in his legs and in his back where he bent forward to pull seemed permanent.

A brewery dray came up from behind. It had two powerful draft horses hitched to it and it was loaded with empty kegs. He watched it out of the corner of his eye, instantly alert. The important thing was to keep the driver from noticing him! As soon as the dray had rumbled past, he swung the cart sharply in behind it and hooked on. The driver could not see him over the kegs.

He almost sobbed with relief. The dray was pulling him and the cart! Five long blocks went safely by. His hands started to hurt from holding on, but he drugged himself to the pain with the hope that perhaps the dray would go as far as the Prater and perhaps all the way up to the Danube Canal. Then suddenly the dray slowed down. The driver must have noticed the extra load! He let go quickly of the short piece of chain that hung from the dray, but he kept close behind it to keep from being seen. When it went faster again, he went faster too, and after thirty or forty yards he risked hanging on to the chain once more. Three blocks, and again the dray slowed down. This time it came almost to a complete stop. The driver shook the tip of his whip far out to one side and Peter could hear him curse. He waited for quite a while before he felt it safe to hook on again. The driver was an unseen antagonist who was determined to keep him from hanging on. Peter could visualize him perfectly: he would be loath to get out of the warm blankets he had no doubt wrapped around his legs, and he was trying to scare him away without actually having to get down. If he did get off the dray, he would be in a rage. It was a risky game, but he had to take the chance. Once more the driver attempted the same maneuver and Peter survived his bluff. But the third time, the driver outwitted him—he pulled over to the curb and really stopped so that Peter was forced to stop too, then he suddenly whipped up his horses and got such a lead that Peter could not catch up.

The long haul up to the Danube Canal passed in a weary stupor in which he was unaware of anything but the next lamppost or street corner which he had set himself for a goal. A moving van which was parked by the curb and which forced him to turn a few extra yards out into the street sent him into a dull rage. Then, at last, the Ring! The hardest part was behind him now, but he felt so worn that he could hardly move his leg forward for the next step. An automobile narrowly missed him because he had turned out into the middle of the street for some parked cabs and had not bothered to pull back over to the side. He measured the close escape with a wry kind of detachment. He found that he did not care, any more than he cared now whether he might be seen by someone he knew. He passed two theaters which glowed with the discreet warmth of performances going on inside. It was half past nine.

His temples had started their throbbing again. He realized that he had forgotten about them too. . . .

There was only the piece of Margaretenstrasse now. He slipped twice because he no longer put his feet down sideways to brace himself. The effort was too great. . . . Then, at last, the store! He went across the street to get the keys from Herr Brandt's maid and pulled the cart into the yard. It was odd to walk without having to pull the cart. He could not straighten his back without pain. And he was not hungry at all. . . . One of the young Brothers opened the door for him at the Home and questioned him suspiciously about being so late. The other boys had already gone up to bed. He went upstairs and had to undergo another examination by Brother Kajetan, who threatened to check up on him at the store.

He still had on the gloves. He went out into the washroom where he could see to take them off. The linen rags underneath were clotted with blood. He made one attempt to soak off the bandage on his left hand, but the cold water smarted unbearably and he went to bed with the bandages still on. His last thought before he sank dizzily down into an abyss of sleep was of the ordeal in the morning when he would have to tear them off. . . .

But the ruthless clangor of Brother Kajetan's bell—*there must be some mistake! Had he slept at all?*—awakened him not so much to the pain in his hands as to a torturing hunger which seemed to have been waiting for him to wake. It was hunger in a form he had not yet known: savage, cold, relentless, and sly. The naked winter morning with its raw, gray dawn and the familiar shoving and splashing in the washroom became brassy and violent with it. After the mockery of breakfast, the dreary Sunday forenoon turned into an endless corridor down which he sought to escape. But time itself was in league with his hunger, had become monstrously static and an antagonist not to be cheated or overcome. It was his hunger which goaded him into suddenly wanting to visit Otto, after he had devoured the exasperating mess of turnips at noon. He got permission from Brother Norbert to go.

It was with Otto just as he had known it would be. Otto looked pink-cheeked and thoroughly happy in the neat white bed. It was wonderfully warm in the entire ward. Otto lay with his bare arms luxuriously outside the covers, and the two men playing cards down near the end of the room sat on a bed in nothing more than thin linen dressing gowns. There was only a trace of the usual hospital smell of disinfectant. Everything about the white ward was modern and new, with great windows and shining white enamel everywhere. Envy clutched at him as he sat down on the edge of Otto's bed. He had a resentful impression that Otto had fooled even the doctors with those bright pink splotches in his cheeks and with that conveniently alarming fact that his parents had died of tuberculosis. If Otto had really had pneumonia, it had been calculated somehow! As if to bear out his impression, Otto started to boast:

"We had chicken today, and chicken soup with rice. We get chicken soup every day and white rolls in the morning, and I get all the milk I want."

On Otto's night-table there was a basket of fruit and several illustrated magazines and a new book. Peter forced himself to look away from the apples and the figs in the basket.

"Did Frau Straka really come herself?"

"She's been here twice! And yesterday she sent a maid with the basket of fruit and the magazines. And Herr Straka's mother came on Friday and brought me a box of cookies—look!" Otto twisted over on his side and pulled open the drawer of the night-table. He took out a square tin and lifted off the lid for Peter to see. "They're from Switzerland!" He closed the tin again and somewhat hastily put it back in the drawer and pushed the drawer shut. "And I got a big bar of chocolate and a bag of caramels from Herr Meier. Herr Meier comes every other day—oh, lots of people, Brother Norbert and Brother Kajetan from the Home, and Brother Martin from the orphanage where I was. Do you know what's going to happen when I get out of the hospital—" Otto paused to savor the suspense—"I'm going to stay out at the orphanage for a month, maybe two months, Brother Martin said, until I get my strength back. It's all arranged; Brother Martin has already spoken to Herr Straka."

Then Otto would not be back in the store until winter was nearly over! He would have to go on doing all the work by himself, while Otto was being pampered and spoiled. But there was still worse to come.

"And after I'm well, I'm not going to be downstairs any more. I'm going to be in the office. Herr Straka said so to Frau Redlich!"

Otto looked at him as if he expected him to share in his triumph. For just a moment Otto's eyes shed their blatant innocence and they became openly triumphant and smug. Peter nodded dully and looked away. He thought bitterly of the cookies, which Otto was not even hungry enough to eat. Probably Otto could afford to save the chocolate and the caramels, too, since he had chicken at noon and white rolls! If Otto had been as hungry as he, he would have devoured everything now, at once! He suddenly knew what had made him come to see Otto just today—his very hunger had driven him to the one place where there still was food, as if to torture him with his very nearness to it now. Some powerful, dark purpose in his hunger stirred under his despondency. He felt suddenly bewildered and on the edge of an extremity. He looked away from Otto at the row of beds on the window side of the room.

One of the beds across the aisle was very still. The man in it might have been asleep, or even dead, if there had not been a portentous air of tension about the bed. Twice a Sister had gone and leaned briefly over the man's face, which Peter could not see from where he sat. Something horrible was wrong with the man's stomach—it protruded grotesquely upward from his inert body and lifted the blanket in an obscene mound. A mixture of horror and embarrassment kept him from asking Otto about the man; he asked Otto instead about the groans that came every few seconds from behind the high linen screen that had been placed around the last bed at the end of the ward.

"Oh, he!" Otto said. "That's nothing *now!* You ought to have heard him last night when they brought him in. They had to amputate his leg—way up here!—it was gangrened. He's just coming out of the ether. They all sound like that after the operating room. See that boy over there, in the fourth bed from the end? He had a ruptured appendix when they brought him in——"

And Otto went on talking about other cases in the ward, with that peculiar callous and faintly lewd knowingness with which Peter had heard women discuss some woman's ailment with *her* when he had still been small. Otto appeared to have the same indecently intimate knowledge of what ailed the occupant of every bed. He finally got to the man across the aisle——

"He came in last night. The ambulance picked him up in the street. He ate a whole loaf of bread when it was still hot and it's made his stomach swell up like that."

"But can't they do anything?"

"I guess not. He's all blown up with gas. The Sister said he wasn't going to live through the night. . . ."

His eyes returned again and again to the grotesque mound. The other cases had seemed remote, but the consciousness of the bloated stomach which he could see by merely turning his head filled him not so much with pity as with alarm. It was, he realized, because he himself could so easily be in the man's place. He knew with terrifying certainty that if he had a loaf of hot bread now, he would not be able to wait until it got cold!

An elderly Sister came with a tray on which were several glasses of milk. She smirked at Peter and addressed Otto in a kind of baby talk. "We have a visitor, I see! Isn't that nice? Here's our milk. . . ."

Peter observed how deftly, cravenly, Otto played up to the Sister's mawkish solicitude. He got up and shifted uneasily.

"You don't have to go yet!" Otto protested at once. "It's only the *Jause*. I always get a glass of milk for my *Jause*. Visitors' hour isn't over until five. They ring a bell. . . ."

Otto had started to sip the milk. In spite of his hunger, the sight of the moist, white ring which appeared on Otto's upper lip revolted him. He had to force himself to wait a little longer before he said good-by.

As he passed the bed of the man with the distended stomach, he tried to get a glimpse of his face—it was gray and utterly inert.

The street was bleak and menacing after the bright warmth of the hospital. He happened to glance up into the Kenyongasse. The house where he had gone to see the girl reminded him sharply of Herr Kropfl. He walked down to the intersection of the Gürtel and the Mariahilferstrasse. It was only a little after four. He did not have to be back at the Home until five. Perhaps he could even manage to miss vespers, in the dreary church. He crossed the Gürtel and started out along the Mariahilferstrasse, chiefly because it led to Schönbrunn and reminded him of the time when he had gone there with Franz to meet Bianca, but also because it led away from the store and the Apprentice Home.

It was nearly dark again, but it was not very cold. His shoes were still wet from the night before and he could feel the water seeping in through the spongy leather. He came to the open-air market where he had often stood in line for potatoes during the previous year. The booths were all boarded up and the snow lay thick and wet in the avenues between. Something drew him to walk around among the blind, desolate booths. The chances were, he found himself thinking, that even if he managed to break into one of the booths he would not find anything to eat. Nothing but turnips and beets. . . . Almost without being aware of it, he had started to scuff his feet deliberately through the slush. *If he could catch pneumonia, he would be taken to the hospital, too, and get chicken and chicken soup with rice!*

Now that his motive for seeking the wet snow had become clear to him, he accepted it. It should be easy to catch pneumonia after the night before—his throat had been raw all day. He unbuttoned his overcoat and then his coat. It was almost pleasant to give himself up to the wet and the cold like this. . . . He stayed until he heard some church clock strike five o'clock; then he started slowly toward the Apprentice Home. Once, the image of the monstrously pregnant-looking man in the hospital gripped him and made him start to button up his overcoat before he knew what he was doing. He grimaced defiantly and pulled open his coat again. Already he was quite sure of it, he could feel a constriction in his chest—"You can't breathe and you get a pain in your side," Otto had said. It would be only a matter of days—tomorrow morning perhaps! . . .

Monday went by, then Tuesday. His throat was raw, but there was no pain in his side. There was not even a decent cough. There were only the now desperately sensitive gashes across his hands, and the burning itch in his feet, and the terrible weariness still in his back and arms from Saturday night.

But there was one satisfaction to be derived from the trip to Floridsdorf: Herr Brandt had heard from the maid how late he had got back and had been scandalized and had evidently said something about it to Herr Kropfl, and Brother Katejan had really called up the store. Peter did not know whether Brother Kajetan had spoken to Herr Straka himself or only to one of the girls in the office across the street. At any rate, Herr Kropfl acted a little guilty about Saturday night. Peter could tell from the way Herr Kropfl stopped him in front of Frau Redlich on Monday afternoon and jeered: "Well, I see you are still all in one piece. The little jaunt to Floridsdorf didn't hurt you then, did it?" Also, Herr Kropfl made a point of not sending him anywhere during the first two days of the week. Twice, Peter noticed, when there was an errand to be run, Herr Kropfl telephoned Herr Brandt for one of his men—presumably to annoy Herr Brandt.

But on Wednesday Herr Kropfl called him to the glass cage again.

"I want you to run out to Baumgarten with this parcel here. Ask for Herr Stetter. Here's the invoice. Herr Stetter is going to give you cash—four hundred and sixteen kronen. Be careful of the money now—have you got a strong pocket?"

Herr Kropfl had spoken softly, with that insinuating, husky-voiced quality which was only there when he talked to Herr Straka or to some customer.

"Can you carry that all right?"

The package was fairly heavy. It contained two short, thick bronze bars, but the bars weighed after all only sixty pounds. Herr Kropfl had often made him carry much heavier parcels than that, without worrying whether they were heavy for him or not. As if to top off his puzzling solicitude, Herr Kropfl went himself to Frau Redlich's desk and said:

"Peter is going out to Baumgarten. Will you give him the carfare?"

It was the first time in over a month that Herr Kropfl had let him have carfare for an errand.

The factory in Baumgarten was not very far from the streetcar stop. He had to wait in a grimy little office for Herr Stetter, who appeared to be exceedingly busy out in the shop among the machines. When he came into the office at last, he took only time enough to glance at the invoice and to count out the money from a safe. A mechanic had already come in to summon him back again into the shop. Herr Stetter hastily scrawled his name over the invoice and handed it back to him.

It was only out in the street that he realized that the invoice ought to have stayed at the factory and that Herr Stetter had evidently mistaken it for a shipping voucher, or he would not have signed it and handed it back to him. He decided against going back with it. It was of no importance anyway. Few people with machine shops to run had time to bother with bookkeeping nowadays. Herr Stetter had been much too interested in getting the bronze ingots to care about the invoice. He would simply hand it to Herr Kropfl along with the money and explain what had happened.

When he got back to the store, Herr Kropfl was in conference with Herr Straka in the office across the street. An hour went by and Herr Kropfl still had not come downstairs. At half past four Herr Lehnert asked him to go on an errand to Fünfhaus. He still had the money in his pocket. He did not want to leave it on Herr Kropfl's desk, and on the other hand he did not want to take it with him to Fünfhaus. He did not quite know what to do. It was rare for an invoice to be settled in cash like this. He finally decided to leave the money with Frau Redlich. He kept the invoice, intending to give it to Herr Kropfl later on.

When he came back from Fünfhaus, Herr Kropfl scowled impatiently:

"Where have you been all this time?"

"Herr Lehnert sent me to Fünfhaus. You were upstairs in the office. . . ."

"Where's the money?"

"I gave it to Frau Redlich. I didn't want to take it with me. . . ."

Herr Kropfl glared. Without meaning to, Peter shrank from his venomous look. He watched Herr Kropfl fling back the door of the cage. From where he stood he could just hear a phrase now and again as Herr Kropfl asked Frau Redlich for the money. He was aware that Herr Kropfl's voice sounded more than ordinarily unctuous. He was saying something about the bronze ingots and about sending the money directly to somebody in Favoriten.

When Herr Kropfl came back into the glass cage, he had the money and he put it rather ostentatiously on top of a bill of lading which he pulled out from among some other papers in the wire basket beside the adding machine. The bill of lading, Peter had just time to see, showed only the weight of the bronze and no price at all. There was the faintest flush around Herr Kropfl's eyes. His look when he turned back to Peter was hard and yet somehow concerned with seeming plausibly matter-of-fact.

"Next time you are sent somewhere to collect money, you bring the money to me and not to somebody else. Is that clear? Now get busy!"

While he got out the broom and the sprinkler to start sweeping, he reflected angrily that he had been a fool to build any hopes on Herr Kropfl's friendliness that afternoon. Herr Kropfl had merely forgotten for a few minutes, or he had play-acted the suave executive again, or he had deemed the errand especially important. . . . At any rate, he was right back again where he had started from! He himself had spoiled it all by leaving the money with Frau Redlich. . . .

The following morning, Hacker claimed some important errand and asked him to change the carbons in the invoice books. When he had nearly finished transferring the carbons, Peter suddenly remembered that the invoice for the bronze bars had been made out by Herr Kropfl in one of the clerks' books. He still had the invoice folded in his pocket. He took it out to look at the serial number—it had come from Herr Neubauer's book. But when he hunted for the duplicate of the invoice in the book, he discovered that that particular duplicate sheet had been torn out. Suddenly alert, he went through the wastepaper basket under the desk. The duplicate sheet was in it! It was crumpled up, and it was blank. Herr Kropfl had evidently wanted no record of the invoice. Something had been wrong about the whole transaction! Herr Kropfl's wheedling affability, the carfare, Herr Kropfl's anger over the money—everything became suddenly quite clear. Feverishly now—it was getting late, and Hacker or Herr Meier might come in at any moment—he looked through the papers in the wire basket beside the adding machine. He found the pink bill of lading—it was made out by the Army Arsenal in Favoriten and it bore Herr Kropfl's notation: *Enter for credit.* That meant that the store would pay for the bronze and that Herr Kropfl was going to keep the money! . . . Hurriedly he copied off the number of the bill of lading and the date. Then he smoothed out the blank duplicate invoice and carefully put it away in his pocket with the original one.

It was as if Herr Kropfl had sensed his suspicion the moment he entered the store—or perhaps it was only that he was still nettled from the previous afternoon—for all that day Herr Kropfl pursued him with backbreaking chores. First it was a trip to Meidling for some heavy locks, then an errand to Hernals with the cart to get file handles. The wooden handles were not heavy at all, but they came packed in clumsy burlap sacks which kept tumbling off the cart, so that he had to stop every few hundred yards to go back and pick up one of the sacks. And in the evening Herr Kropfl made him oil the floor, although it was the middle of the week.

Friday was even worse. His hands had become mere lumps of pain. The stitch in his side which he had been waiting for had not appeared. He felt alternately limp with despair and convulsed with fury when he thought of the next hour and the next. He knew that he was near the breaking point. On Saturday afternoon the moment came at last. . . .

He recognized it instantly when Herr Kropfl called him to Frau Redlich's desk. It was during the brief lull in the store which often came at about three on Saturday afternoons. Herr Kropfl was standing idly beside Frau Redlich's cage. Peter had been about to take an empty packing case out into the yard. Herr Kropfl made him set down the case and hold up his hands.

"Higher! We want to see them!" Herr Kropfl snapped. He jerked Peter's right wrist forward and twisted the hand for Frau Redlich to see. "Look at that! Ever seen anything as disgusting as that?"

Frau Redlich looked at it primly, disapprovingly.

"I suppose you don't believe in water and soap! Just when exactly was it you washed your hands last? About Christmas? That's what those sores are from, all the dirt you haven't washed off for months——" Herr Kropfl pushed his wrist away with exaggerated loathing and pretended to rub the tips of his fingers clean with his thumb. "God knows what filthy skin disease you've got! You're going to go in there in the washroom and scrub that dirt off your hands now, at once! I want to see them when you get through, and they had better be clean!"

Peter picked up the empty packing case and took it out into the yard. He avoided looking at Herr Kropfl on his way back to the washroom. He knew that it would be impossible to get his hands really clean, but he tried harder than he ever had before. By using his finger tips he could rub the gritty mechanics' soap over the spots between the sores, but as always he could not get the grimy lubricating oil out of the pores in his skin. The frost-sores across his knuckles had started to bleed just from scrubbing around them. He did not dare to touch the sores themselves, and it was precisely the ugly cracks which made his hands look so grimy. It seemed to him that the cold water which had turned his hands all red had only made them look dirtier.

Herr Kropfl was still lounging by Frau Redlich's cage, watching Herr Meier sort out some tiny packages of screws.

"Well?"

Peter held up his hands.

"Turn them over! You call that clean?"

Herr Meier craned his head to look. For once, Peter thought he read a note of concern in Herr Meier's eyes when he saw the sores. He addressed himself to Herr Meier.

"I can't wash them any more than that! They are frozen and they start to bleed."

Herr Kropfl stepped between him and Herr Meier's eyes.

"I can see I'll have to show you how to wash your hands. Come on!"

He twisted away from Herr Kropfl's hand, which had reached out to grasp his arm. He walked dully ahead of Herr Kropfl up the store. It was just like the time when Herr Meier had ordered him into the washroom to clean the washbowls; except that Herr Meier had crowded clumsily after him, full of stupid righteousness, and that Herr Kropfl now was allowing him to get half the length of Herr Lehnert's counter ahead of him. He even had a fitful illusion when he got to the lockers and entered the narrow passage to the washbasins that he had left Herr Kropfl behind him for good, that Herr Kropfl had been detained by some customer or clerk at the last moment and would not be able to come in here after all. Then his ears caught the discreet, catlike tread. He did not so much brace himself as retreat farther into his body, so that everything around him became abnormally still.

Herr Kropfl pulled off his crackling linen cuffs and stacked them one inside the other on the corner of the farthest basin. Then he slipped off his dandyishly creased blue coat, hung it on a nail, and stood there in his gleaming white shirt sleeves.

"Now!" he said. "Turn on the water. Lots of it!"

Through the stillness which clung to him like a numbing envelope Peter measured him warily. When Herr Kropfl kept at a distance, he himself was almost as tall as Herr Kropfl. But he knew that if Herr Kropfl moved in close, stood right up against him, he was at least three inches taller. And he was powerful. He remembered the vicious grip when Herr Kropfl had seized his arm in the past. It annoyed him to see how thick Herr Kropfl's arms appeared under the white shirt.

The bowl was nearly full.

"All right! Start in!"

He turned off the tap and scooped a handful of soap out of the container. He rubbed the gritty paste over his hands. He knew that the one thing he must avoid was to have Herr Kropfl touch him. The dark knowledge made him careless of the pain as he scrubbed over the sores. The sticky paste had turned pink on the back of each hand. *No matter! If anything happened between himself and Herr Kropfl now, Herr Straka would only hear Herr Kropfl's side of it and he would be thrown out of the store!*

"Harder!" Herr Kropfl ordered. "Get your hands in the water!" He took Peter's left elbow and shoved it into the bowl so that the water splashed up into Peter's face. "Like this! Now scrub!"

It was a relief to have Herr Kropfl let go of his elbow so quickly. There was even an advantage in having his hands down in the cold water; he could pretend to be rubbing much harder than he actually was.

For a minute Herr Kropfl appeared to be content just to watch him; then he straightened up and looked around the shelves. He took something out of one of the shelves. It was the filthy scrubbing brush which Rohan used for cleaning the bowls. Herr Kropfl brandished it in the air. With his left hand he seized Peter's wrist and forced it back into the bowl——

"This is what we need!"

Peter drew in his breath with a sob at the first tearing contact of the brush. His right arm jerked with furious strength but he could not get it free. Herr Kropfl's arm was locked over his and Herr Kropfl was leaning against him with all his weight to keep him clamped against the edge of the marble washstand. He clenched his hand in the water and tried to keep it twisted away from the brush. As he struggled his eyes fell on Herr Kropfl's full, smooth-shaven chin and the moist, red lips which were parted with almost lascivious eagerness. He suddenly remembered the loathsome disease which lurked under the smooth skin and dug his shoulder into Herr

Kropfl's chest. But again Herr Kropfl captured his arm, and then his wrist, and forced his hand back into the water.

Almost cravenly now he lent himself to the pain. The brush scraped backward and forward over his knuckles. The water in the bowl had turned red. The torn flesh on his hand shrieked with each new stroke of the brush. Yet he had a feeling of waiting almost voluptuously for his hatred to reach the point where he would forget about Herr Straka and everything else. Perversely also, he seemed to himself to be waiting for Herr Kropfl to get his fill.

Herr Kropfl let go of his hand.

"Now the other one!" he said. His voice sounded naked and oddly high-pitched. "Give it here!"

"No—"

"Give it here!"

Herr Kropfl had reached across his body after his left hand. Peter turned abruptly. The mere fact of being suddenly chest to chest with Herr Kropfl finally made him forget about Herr Straka. He jammed his body into Herr Kropfl just as Herr Kropfl tried to slip behind him again. He stepped quickly away.

"Come here, you!"

Leaning in the corner behind Peter were several old axles, some samples of steel, a rusty crowbar. They had always been there. Peter reached for them now. He felt the back of his hand scrape against the wall as his fingers closed around the crowbar. Herr Kropfl had hesitated for one priceless second when he had heard the jangling of the steel bars. It was long enough for Peter to take another step back and to get the crowbar clear of the shelf. The bar seemed intoxicatingly without weight once he got it up to his shoulder. He was still lifting it higher, exultantly, his eyes fixed on Herr Kropfl's white-sleeved arm on which he was going to bring it down. Then—too late—he heard the shuffling lurch behind him. Two hands were already clutching his arm. He recognized the stubborn, leathery strength in the two hands before he heard Herr Meier's voice croaking hoarsely: "Here! Here!"

A sob labored out of his lungs. Herr Meier was hanging onto his arm with all his strength. The cramped, narrow space did not allow him to twist away from Herr Meier without turning his back to Herr Kropfl. Herr Kropfl was swiftly coming in.

"Put down that bar— I said, put it down!"

Herr Kropfl got his hands on the bar and twisted it out of Peter's hand. He flung the crowbar behind him on the floor.

"So you wouldn't mind doing a little killing, too!" Herr Kropfl's hand came up hard and struck Peter across the mouth. "Bastard brat!"

When Peter lunged toward him, Herr Meier swung him around against the shelves and kept him pinioned there. He had to look on while Herr Kropfl lifted his coat off the nail and picked up his cuffs. Herr Meier kept pressing him against the shelves with his bony, jerky strength even after Herr Kropfl was already past the lockers, and then he let go of his arms, only to block the narrow passage. He was panting from his exertion and his voice was a reedy croak——

"What kind of goings-on do you call that! Next thing you'll be picking up a knife! Fine thing when an apprentice—"

In spite of the clammy bewilderment that had mingled with his rage ever since Herr Meier had kept him from swinging the crowbar, Peter somehow found time to note that Herr Meier was not half so incensed as he ought to have been, that Herr Meier was actually reasoning with him as if he were still afraid of what he might do. It was also clear that Herr Meier was tacitly admitting that Herr Kropfl had gone too far. He must have been suspicious of what Herr Kropfl might do, and have stolen in after them so quietly, that they had not heard him. . . .

Herr Meier looked at the water in the basin and pursed his lips: "Let out that water there."

Peter tugged out the plug. Some of the sandy paste still stuck to his fingers and he washed it off. When he was through, Herr Meier said:

"You come with me. Frau Redlich is going to bandage your hands."

Peter followed him out into the store. Herr Kropfl was not in the glass cage. Herr Meier stopped in front of Frau Redlich's desk and demanded grumpily:

"Do you have any more of those bandages? His hands are a sight!"

Frau Redlich moved with frightened alacrity. She shoved open the side door of her cage and bent down under the desk for the first-aid kit. When she straightened up, she gasped:

"Goodness! Why don't you take better care of your hands? If you wore gloves when you go out; your hands wouldn't look like that." She fumbled with the top of a small jar of vaseline. "Here—rub this all over.... And tomorrow—Monday morning anyway, you are going to the doctor! Now hold them up—that one first—"

Peter obeyed her mechanically; Herr Meier had gone around in back of her cage and was watching from his desk.

"Now the other one—"

"I don't need anything on this one."

"You let me bandage it! It's a wonder you haven't got blood poisoning already—why don't you say something when you have something the matter with you? You are old enough...."

Neither she nor Herr Meier asked where he was going when he started out through the iron-plated door. He stopped for a second in the corridor, undecided where to go. He needed to be alone! He decided on the cellar.

At the extreme end of the cast-iron cellar there was a low, dungeonlike recess where outsize furnace grates and all sorts of broken gear lay piled on the floor. It was a corner he had always hated to enter in the past, because of the large number of rats which seemed to thrive in the moldy shelves. No one would be likely to look for him down here!

One odiously plump rat waited brazenly until he had come down all four of the steps, before it finally turned and disappeared inside a shelf. He found a small packing case and set it in the middle of the floor under the one electric bulb. Then he kicked a pile of rusty brake shoes and listened to the hateful slithering noise of the rats behind the shelves. Everything remained quiet after that and he sat down on the packing case.

He sat there for a very long time. His body was cravenly, almost extravagantly grateful for the chance to rest. It had gone limp and it dissociated itself in advance from the sick fire which raged in him against Herr Kropfl. A hundred different ways of killing Herr Kropfl licked like flames out of his incandescent rage, but there was really no debate between his body and this fiery hatred which rushed heedlessly on: his body merely remained stolidly determined not to move or be moved.

There were really three of him. There was his body which was so belligerently conscious of the luxury of stretching his legs and of resting his white-bandaged hands on his thighs, aware also of the damp edge of the box on which he sat and of the moldy, sour stench that came from behind the shelves, and listening for the sly, skittering rustling of the rats; then there was the scalding memory of his humiliation and the frenziedly writhing hatred of Herr Kropfl that went with it; and lastly, there was a small, thin, exasperatingly colorless voice which was foreign and new. He could not tell where it came from at all. It spoke only at long intervals and then with a laconic, implacable authority which made him listen for it almost against his will. It remained irresponsible, cruel, new.

"I'll climb up on the platform over the courtyard," his hatred marshaled imperiously. "The stack of sheet metal is still leaning against the steel upright. Herr Kropfl comes out into the courtyard every half-hour or so. All I have to do is tilt up a dozen of the sheets and when he comes shove them over on him. It'll crush him into a pulp!"

"And then what?" the new voice wanted to know.

"Then I'll dash around behind the stovepipes under the rafters where the roof slopes down to the eaves to the place where I got away from Hacker that time, where I found the hole into the attic. I'll hurry back through the attic and come down the stairs. Herr Lehnert asked me to get some wrapping paper anyway—I'll simply bring down a roll of that!"

"They'll still know you did it. Herr Meier and Frau Redlich will know at once!"

"Nobody'll be able to prove anything!"

"They'll still know!"

"I don't care!"

But he did care. He could tell by his rage at his own helplessness and by the final wave of despondency which engulfed him.

In a sudden paroxysm of rage he picked up one of the rusty grates at his feet and hurled it on the pile of brake shoes in the corner so that it shivered into a dozen pieces, then another and still another, until he was exhausted. He felt horribly drained.

There was nothing he could do now except leave the store and give up in disgrace——

The light bulb overhead suddenly went out. Someone had turned off the switch at the head of the stairs. From force of habit he started to get up and shout, but his throat was too weary to obey and he sank back indifferently and stared into the dark.

The dark was even welcome and warm. His hands no longer smarted in the lazy stupor which washed over and around him like a sluggish sea. The ravaging fire inside him appeared at last to have worn itself out. His hatred had become an insurmountable wall which he could not scale; which there was not even any need to scale. . . .

After a long while the light went on again. Instinctively he listened for footsteps. No one was coming toward the part of the cellar where he was. . . . The thin, garish light of the bulb had not brought him out of the torpor into which he had sunk, but it had made him conscious of it. He felt completely nerveless and gutted and dry, as if he had been dead for a very long time. He also had a feeling of being indescribably and necessarily alone at the bottom of an abyss.

For a long time now the fiendish little voice had not troubled him at all. He was certain that it had died too. It was with a shock that he heard it again.

"Bastard brat!"

It was as if a fine, long, infinitely cruel needle had been jabbed through his bowels.

"Bastard brat!" the voice stabbed again.

He winced as if Herr Kropfl's pampered white hand had again struck across his mouth. But he could suddenly see what the voice meant. For the first time, the hateful compulsion which had always brought him up against Herr Kropfl became clear to him. There had always been that association between Herr Kropfl and his father in his mind.

If I had him here now I'd kill him——

A savage picture of torturing a figure which vaguely resembled Herr Kropfl convulsed him. It was the suave glibness of the figure which was exactly like Herr Kropfl's, that he must mangle and crush. But the passion which bent him as if he were a steel rod was without heat. He became even cooler.

I'm going to find him and I'll make him pay—like nobody ever paid before—England—I'll get to England—and I'm not going to give up the store!

Herr Kropfl had suddenly become unimportant. The way to get

Herr Kropfl was not by a head-on attack. That was stupid. He remembered the invoice and the blank duplicate. No use sending that to Herr Straka now. Herr Kropfl would somehow talk himself out of it. What he needed was more evidence, more false invoices to prove Herr Kropfl a thief and send him to jail, and that meant lulling him in false security, throwing him off his guard! Yes, he would even manage to get into Herr Kropfl's confidence, pretend that he did not bear a grudge for this afternoon and that he had reformed: *I'll be as subtle as a snake and as hard as iron!* His hand closed almost affectionately over one of the rusty grates—*Only not as stupid and brittle as cast iron; I'll be as supple as steel!*

He felt almost frightened by his ruthless clarity. And he was aware that the little voice and his hatred and even his body spoke as one. For just one moment his mind traveled back to the morning at the cadet school—his blustering rage on that day seemed feeble and childish now.

The fat rat had come out of the shelf and sat watching him. He realized that he must have been looking at it for quite a long time. It did not make him shudder now. Almost playfully he threw a grate at it without trying to hit it. It amused him to see it scurrying back into the shelf.

He stood up, suddenly impatient with himself for sitting there for so long. The leadenness had not so much gone out of his body as become something to be taken coolly into account and to be got rid of. As if to prove to himself that he could get the better of it, he flexed his arms and kicked one leg out to the side as they had done in gym class in school. He felt lean and hard and stripped to the bone—

I'm going to be so hard that nothing is ever going to hurt me again. And I'm going to get him if it takes me ten such winters as this! Only it isn't going to take me that long. I'll get to England! And I'm going to look at Herr Kropfl now when I go up in the store as if I felt thoroughly repentant for everything. I'll look him right in the eye and he'll never guess. . . .

The first thing he thought of the next morning when Brother Kajetan's bell clanged by his bed was the two hours after he had gone upstairs from the cellar. He thought of them even before he remembered his hands and the scene in the washroom with Herr Meier hanging onto his arm. It had all gone so smoothly that his strength had not even been tried, that he had had a feeling of being braced for something that never came off. Herr Kropfl had stayed in the glass cage all evening until Herr Straka had come down from the office to check the cash. There had been no need—no opportunity even—to meet his eyes. And Herr Meier and Frau Redlich had watched him with almost cloying solicitude. All he had had to do was to sweep. Herr Meier had made Hacker pull down the shutters outside, and Frau Redlich had given him the jar of vaseline and a new roll of bandages to take to the Apprentice Home. And now he had a whole day to get ready for next week. It was the Sunday when they were allowed to go home. He put on the new bandage after they came back from church, and after breakfast he set out for the Schmeltz.

She was alone in the apartment. Poldi had gone to the office. It was the second Sunday in a row that Poldi had had to work.

She had some hot coffee waiting for him as she always did when he came home, and he sat down at the kitchen table to drink it and eat the slice of bread and the jam she brought. She was fussing with some pots and pans on the stove. When he asked about Franz, she did not interrupt her fussing, but he could tell that she was relieved about Franz although her habitual pessimism would not let her admit as much. Franz, it seemed, was allowed to be up for two hours every afternoon and his wound had almost healed.

"But then he's all right," he said.

"All right!" she scoffed. "With a piece of iron in his lung!"

"But they've taken it out."

"They can take it out all they want to! The body's never the same after you go into it with a knife. . . ."

"Is he coming home?"

"Home! They're sending him to some convalescent home—to strangers!—as if his own mother didn't know better how to take care of him!"

"But he'll get good food there probably."

She retreated into a grim silence.

"If God doesn't stop this war soon, I don't know what's going to become of all of us. People falling down on the sidewalk from hunger and everybody sick from the things they are putting in the bread now . . . As if they hadn't killed enough soldiers already!" She came to take away his cup. "What did you do to your hands?"

"It's nothing. Just frostbite."

"You let me see!"

"You can't see. The bandage sticks. I can't take it off!"

It was true that in spite of the vaseline he had gingerly smeared over the sores, the bandages were again sticking to his hands and that the blood was showing through in two or three places.

He went into the living room and picked up Franz's newspaper which still came every morning. He did not usually look at the paper, but this morning he felt a luxurious desire to relax and to do the unusual thing.

He had been reading for about ten minutes, vaguely aware of her muffled comings and goings in the kitchen, when she came in with an old porcelain bowl of hot water in which floated some herbs. He recognized the stale, haylike smell.

"*Käspappeln*," she said. "You put your hands in this. *Käspappeln* are the best thing for frozen hands. They ought to be boiled in milk, but water is better than nothing. . . ." She had spread a towel on a chair and now set the bowl on it.

He saw the steam rising from the bowl. "That's hot!"

She dipped her finger into the bowl.

"That's not hot. It's got to be warm. You put them in!"

She waited until he had put his hands into the yellow brew before she went back into the kitchen. He had tilted the newspaper up against the back of the chair behind the bowl and tried to keep on reading.

After a few minutes she came back in to look; then she brought a small pot of hot water and poured that into the bowl. After a while the bandages soaked off. It was pleasant to sit in a warm room like this and keep his hands in the soupy liquid with the little sprigs of herbs sticking to his wrists. He looked out through the window; it was gray and forbidding outside. He could no longer read. The tepid vapor which rose from the herbs made him feel sleepy and oddly relaxed. When she came in with more hot water, he rebelled:

"That's enough. I'd like to lie down."

For a moment she looked as if she were going to object. But she set the hot water on the stove and went into Franz's room. A minute later she came back.

"I made up the divan, if you want to lie down. Wait until I dry your hands." She brought some clean old linen rags. It astonished him again how gentle her knuckly, rough hands could be. "Now I'm going to get some salve. You sit still. What I ought to have is tallow—sheep tallow is best of all—with this war you can't get anything any more! But I have some zinc salve, at least. That's healing, too. . . ." She picked up the porcelain bowl and started for the kitchen, for the drawer in the cupboard where she kept all her herbs and salves.

He got up from the chair. He felt so drowsy that he could hardly bear to stand up.

"Not now! After I get up!"

Somewhat to his surprise, she let him go.

He went into Franz's room and took off his clothes. It was blissful to slide between the crisp sheets. He had barely stretched out his legs before he sank down into sleep.

When he awoke it was dark. Through the crack under the door he could see that the light was turned on in the living room. He heard Poldi say something he could not make out, out in the kitchen probably. It must have been Poldi's voice that had awakened him. He must have slept right through the entire day. His hands, he noticed, were loosely wrapped in soft old linen rags—she had evidently come in while he had been asleep and had rubbed on some salve.

He heard Poldi ask: "What's the matter with him?"

"How should I know! He's been sleeping all day. He was all worn out, I guess! It's just a wonder he doesn't cough."

"You mean, he didn't even get up for lunch?"

"Well, if he needs the sleep! I'm fixing something for him now. . . ."

It felt luxurious to lie like this and listen to their voices. Then he was startled. Poldi was opening the door. The light streamed in in a widening swath. He sat up quickly. "I'm all right. Hello."

"Hello—what's the matter with you?"

"Nothing. I was just sleepy."

Poldi snapped on the light switch.

As he tugged involuntarily at the blanket, the linen rags came off his right hand. He was not fast enough in pulling them back over the sores.

"You call that nothing!"

"It's just the salve that makes them look like that. It's nothing. I'm getting up."

"All right, we'll talk about that later!"

He listened to Poldi out in the kitchen, while he dressed:

"Mother! Did you see those hands?"

"Sure, I saw them. Do you think I'm blind? I told him what it'd be like working in a shop like that."

"Well, it's got to stop! There's going to be an end to this!"

"You can talk to him. I've done all the talking I'm going to do. You won't any of you listen to me."

"Well, he's going to listen this time!"

He went out into the living room with some trepidation of what was bound to come. To put off the moment, he asked Poldi about her bank, about Franz, about Fräulein Gisl. But when they had finished eating, it came——

"I'm going to see your Herr Straka first thing tomorrow morning. You're going to quit that store."

It was funny, he noted, how patient his very determination made him with Poldi's wrath.

"I don't want to quit the store," he said very quietly.

"You are going to leave it—I'll see to that!"

"If you think that this is anything, you ought to see the hands of the men in the railroad yards! It's just a few sores. They'll go away in a week. Besides, I'm going to the doctor tomorrow morning anyway."

"You've probably got blood poisoning already! If you think I'm going to stand by while you lose your hands, you've got another guess coming!"

"I don't get blood poisoning. If I did, I'd have got it months ago."

"I'm just telling you what I'm going to do. You've seen the last of that store!"

He could see that Poldi would not be managed easily. He took a long, soft breath and forced himself to sound calm.

"Franz is the one who signed the articles of apprenticeship. He's my guardian, and he's the only one who can say what I have to do."

"Franz isn't here, and I'm going in his place."

"All right, and I'm not going to have a woman come and make a scene over me as if I were a little boy."

"We'll see about that!"

He suddenly saw all his plans for the future put into jeopardy. "You're not going anywhere and I'm not quitting the store. But if you still want to go, you've seen the last of me. There's no police that'll bring me back this time!"

They faced each other in one of those mute struggles he remembered so well. For a moment he thought that Poldi was going to slap him in her exasperation.

"I could just shake you and shake you——" she said. She flung back her chair. "All right, I'm going to telegraph Franz. He'll be ready to travel in a few weeks. We'll just see what Franz has to say!"

She had come in from the kitchen to get the last of the dishes.

"I told you from the beginning what it'd be like, him being an apprentice in a place like that. I haven't seen those boys with their carts for nothing all my life. . . ."

For once Poldi did not even say, "Oh, Mother!"

It was half past five. He had to be back at the Apprentice Home by six. He let her bandage his hands before he put on his coat.

Poldi had put twenty kronen instead of the usual ten on Father's desk. When he hesitated in front of the money, Poldi said angrily: "I want you to get your shoes resoled first thing! And with leather—not those paper soles!"

He was sorry that they parted like this. Down in the street he reflected ruefully that Poldi must have had a hard week at the office and that she must have been tired from working on Sunday too. But it was a struggle that he had had to win!

Chapter Forty

It amazed him how much easier things became for him almost at once. It was as if with his resolution some potent virtue had entered into him, which not only hardened him to the outside so that he felt more than competent to deal with it—for that, after all, was only to be expected; that was what he had resolved!—but what struck him was that this strange new potency seemed to have power even to shape external circumstances to his hand.

There appeared to be a flattering fatality about the way events now seemed bent on favoring him. He came to look for them, to expect them almost, and there revived in him an old childish illusion from the time when he had still been small that he was marked out and watched over by a lucky star. Once, in Hernals, when he was walking behind an army commissary wagon just as a whole carton of caramels tumbled out and after he had filled all his pockets with the caramels he had picked out of the snow, he actually put this feeling into words. *I'm lucky now,* he thought. *Before, if a hundred wagons had driven by, nothing would have fallen out of any of them. I was soft and everything always went wrong. Hate is more powerful than the other thing!*

Not that there was any less work at the store. Otto came out of the hospital, only to go directly to his orphanage in Mödling to be pampered for another two months. He was still alone with all the chores. But he had learned to stall and to sidestep the more back-breaking jobs. It came about naturally enough. On the Monday morning when he was to go to the sick-benefit doctor about his hands, he had waked up with a sharp pain in his back and side. He decided to mention it. The doctor muttered something about "pleurisy," taped up his whole side, and ordered him to stay in bed for three days. During those three days in the Apprentice Home his hands improved hardly at all, but the pain in his side went away and he was glad. He had no desire for illness now; he was eager to get back to the store. But the touch of pleurisy had had its advantages: Herr Meier and Frau Redlich were suddenly all concern. He noted a little sardonically that as long as he had been well and had worked desperately they had had no liking for him, whereas now when they thought of him as delicate he approached something of Otto's status in their eyes.

Herr Meier himself had shown him how to make things easier for himself. On his first morning back in the store, Herr Meier had ordered Hacker to help him with the shutters. After that, when a shutter was hard to raise he had only to go to Herr Meier and say that he could not get it up, and Hacker or even one of the third-year apprentices was made to help. He no longer had to go anywhere with the handcart—Frau Redlich saw to that. And he was given carfare by Frau Redlich for even short errands when he could quite easily have walked. When he worked for Herr Meier now, he worked as Otto had always done: neatly, showily, and without straining himself. Where before he had carried five and six packages of rivets or nails on each trip to the cellar, he now carried four. Yet Herr Meier's gruff friendliness became more pronounced every day.

There had been a still more important advantage in the few days of pleurisy. Frau Redlich had made him go across the street to report to Herr Straka when he came back. He saw at once that there had been no need for the faint trepidation with which he always entered Herr Straka's office. Herr Straka was gravely solicitous and very friendly. He wanted to know about the pain in his side, whether he wore heavy enough underwear and gloves, and he dismissed him with a warning not to do anything that went beyond his strength. . . . He felt when he came out of Herr Straka's office that the interview had been sheer gain: Herr Straka was more aware of him than before.

He had not lied when he had assured Herr Straka that he wore gloves. He wore the pair Poldi had given him for Christmas or a cheap pair he had bought for work, and he kept the bandages on his hands when he worked. He was careful not to get any more dirt into the sores. He realized now that his neglect of his hands had been of a piece with his dark wish that Sunday afternoon when he had deliberately sloshed through the wet snow to catch pneumonia! The frame of mind seemed foreign to him now.

Sometimes, in his almost continual contact now with Frau Redlich and Herr Meier, he had a feeling of duplicity which made him uncomfortable. He had to tell himself quickly that to feel guilty toward them was weakness. . . . It was different with Herr Kropfl. There he felt coldly relentless. Herr Kropfl was steering clear of him now—too clear, if he was to get the evidence he wanted! Such orders as Herr Kropfl gave to him were given as if he were a stranger. He executed them with minute attention. Gradually, he had the satisfaction of seeing Herr Kropfl relax ever so little. . . .

Without consciously thinking back to the terrible afternoon in the cellar, he yet derived from it a grim poise. He felt hard and alert, and he used himself shrewdly like a tool. His body had suddenly become important. Not only did he take care of his hands, but he used every means to eke out the starvation fare at the Apprentice Home.

When he took his shoes to the cobbler as Poldi had ordered, the cobbler complained about the difficulty of getting not only leather but tacks and hobnails. The cobbler offered to pay eight kronen for every package of hobnails he could bring. He remembered the hobnails he had hidden from Herr Meier. He waited for a morning when he was alone in the store and went into the storeroom to look. The hobnails were still in the bin where he had thrown them. He smuggled out one package that noon and took it to the cobbler. For six kronen, he found, he could get a small plate of meat stew with potatoes and even a slice of bread in a little restaurant off the Gürtel. The next day he took another package to the cobbler. That way he got one good meal a day for nearly two weeks. . . .

But he was careful to pay for the hobnails. He pretended to buy drills for some boy in the Apprentice Home, then he carefully saved the receipted bill. It cost him a struggle to part with the money which would have bought three extra lunches, but if he was to convict Herr Kropfl of stealing, he could not afford to be caught himself in even the most trifling dishonesty. There was always the danger that the cobbler might know somebody else from the store and mention the nails. Besides that, his very hatred for Herr Kropfl had brought into play a proud consciousness of his own loyalty to Herr Straka.

The experience with the cobbler had made him alert to other opportunities, and bolder. He spent his mornings before the store opened prowling through the storerooms in search of caches. Sometimes he was successful and he got a dozen saw files or a few packages of nails or screws, which he hid away in turn until he had a chance to wait on some customer from the country who had brought in half a loaf of bread or a small piece of bacon. It was not much, but three or four times a month he knew a few hours when he was free from hunger. What was important, he no longer felt helpless.

Spring finally came and with it another change for the better. Franz had been sent for convalescence to Vorarlberg, close to the Swiss border. There was apparently plenty of food so far away from the big cities, and Franz had begun to send parcels of flour and lard and potatoes. At first, Peter had managed to run home now and then to snatch something to eat between errands. Then, in the last week of April, Franz himself came to report to the army doctors.

Franz did not look as if he had been wounded. He looked handsome and rugged in his lieutenant's uniform when he got off at the Westbahnhof, and he had brought a whole suitcase full of flour and bacon and even some butter. He explained gaily how he had made friends with the farmers in the village where he had been staying and how he had got more supplies than he had been able to bring with him. For a week, Franz called on all his friends and went to the theater every night. He also listened to Poldi's complaints about the store. But Franz also listened to him. He said finally:

"All right, if you insist on keeping on at the store, that's your affair. But you must come and live at home where Mother can take care of your hands—I'll insist on that! Now that Mother has some flour and lard ahead, you'll certainly get more to eat here than you do at the Apprentice Home."

The following afternoon Franz went to see Herr Straka. Herr Straka made no objection at all. And Herr Straka had been very pleasant and had praised his work, Franz told him hurriedly when he dropped into the store for a minute afterward.

Two days later he packed his belongings in the bleak dormitory and went to live at home. . . .

It was an enormous improvement. He could sleep until six, and even a quarter past six, instead of being roused by Brother Kajetan's bell at half past four. There was food! Franz had been declared still unfit for active service and had gone back to Vorarlberg for another six weeks. And Franz was again sending flour and potatoes in the stout wooden boxes Peter sent up to him for the purpose, for ordinary parcels were sure to be broken open and plundered long before they got to the city.

Then there was the matter of money. Herr Straka had paid ninety kronen a month for him at the Apprentice Home. But when he opened his pay envelope on the first, he saw that Herr Straka had raised the amount to one hundred and fifty kronen. He gave a hundred and twenty kronen to her and kept the rest for himself. For the first time he had some money of his own to spend. There were not only the thirty kronen from his salary, but the pocket money Poldi still insisted on giving him although he had tried to persuade her that he no longer needed it, and anywhere from fifty to a hundred kronen he could count on from customers for saving things for them that were hard to get or even for just waiting on them when all the clerks were busy.

At first nearly all of the money went into food. He could not resist the temptation to buy jam or apples or an extra meal in the little restaurant off the Gürtel whenever he had a chance. The hours between meals were long and the habit of dreaming of food, bred in him by the bitter winter, was too much for him. Then, gradually, he took confidence from her increasing stock of supplies and he was able to force himself to save and to start thinking about English lessons again.

It was the catalogue of an American lock company—one day he had happened to glance at it—which had suddenly aroused him to the need to know English if he wanted to carry out his plan. Then, just after Easter, he noticed a self-study course in English displayed in the window of a bookshop in the Kärntnerstrasse. He bought the first two lessons at once and threw himself into the task. On the streetcar, in the cellar between trips downstairs, whenever he had a few minutes alone, he took out the folded booklets and memorized. It was a zeal that had nothing in common with the way he had crammed French for the cadet school the year before. This time there would be no examination and no reward; neither were there any set limits to the amount he would have to learn. He would have to know it all to speak this language, which was ever so much more difficult than French, *when the time came to start!* Coldly, efficiently, he addressed himself to each new list of words. But he soon saw that it would be impossible to go very far without a teacher to help. . . .

He heard about the language classes at a labor club in Ottakring. He went there one night, only to find that the classes were only for adults and for boys over sixteen. It seemed ridiculous to wait for a year when he wanted to start studying now, right away. . . . There was the Berlitz School in the Innere Stadt, but the beginners' class started at eight o'clock; he usually did not get home from the store until after eight. He saw that he would have to take private lessons if he was to study at all.

Toward the middle of June he found what he was looking for. An American woman was advertising lessons in the newspaper.

"English lessons—" the advertisment read— "Frau Susan Hobbs-Pechlar . . . afternoon or evening, by arrangement."

It seemed exactly what he wanted. But the address in Hietzing and something about the crisp wording of the notice made him apprehensive about the price and whether the "American lady" would consent to teach a mere apprentice.

He managed to get away early from the store one evening and he hurried home to scrub and put on his Sunday suit. By skipping supper he was able to get to Hietzing before eight. It was as he had feared: the address was that of a handsome villa in the fashionable section just above Schönbrunn. A taxi was waiting in front of the charming wrought-iron gate. He could not imagine why anybody living in a villa like this would have to give lessons at all. At any rate, the lessons would be far beyond anything he would be able to pay. A distinguished-looking man with an attaché case under his arm came out of the front door while he was still hesitating on the path. It was fortunate, for he had been about to lose heart.

The lady who had let the man out had stopped in the door and was eying him curiously, and now he had to go on. The woman was tall, rather heavy, and her dark hair was dressed with such exotic plainness that her face appeared strikingly set in expression. Not severe—waiting rather, and thickly attentive. A face, he felt, to which you had to prove things, yourself most of all, and he was not encouraged. He mentioned the notice in the newspaper and saw the surprise in her eyes. But she invited him into the house and made him sit down. He noticed that her face became animated when she talked and that he had been deceived about its immobility—it was simply a different rhythm he was not accustomed to—and that there was only a faint trace of something foreign in her voice.

He explained that he wanted to take lessons because his mother was in America and because he was supposed to join her after the war. He had had no intention of saying so much but his uneasiness about the cost of the lessons forced him to talk, just as it made him add defensively that he could only come late in the evening or on Sundays. He saw that the lady was watching him. It seemed to him also that she was amused. When she had heard him out she proposed that he come two evenings a week from nine to ten and Sunday mornings at ten. But there was still the matter of price. It was she herself who helped him out. The lessons would be eight kronen each. . . . It was terribly high and yet he had a feeling that she was charging less than she usually charged. It would take all the money he had, and he was not even sure whether he would always be able to get the money. But he plunged. He had already decided that he wanted the lessons from her, here in this subtly foreign living room in Hietzing, or not at all. He felt extraordinarily happy when she addressed some question in English to him and the first lesson began. . . .

He came away from the villa that evening with a feeling that a large interim of time had elapsed. Frau Hobbs-Pechlar had given him the title of a textbook he was to get. He bought it the following noon and that evening started to work. He put all his pride into mastering not only the few pages she had assigned, but doing several pages ahead. He was impatient for Sunday morning to come. The second trip to Hietzing was exhilarating when he compared it to the first. This time Frau Hobbs-Pechlar welcomed him with a friendly smile. She insisted on speaking English to him from the moment he entered the villa except at the end of the lesson when she asked him about his work. He learned that she herself had been born in a large town called Philadelphia, and that she had lived in Vienna for twenty years. . . .

The lessons became an event, a joyful break in the routine of the store. He dressed carefully for them, as he would have if he had gone to the theater, and he was wretched when he had to be late.

He paid for them twice a month and sometimes he was hard put to it to raise the money—he had to go to Poldi to pay for them on time. But he would sooner have gone without food, as he often did when he was tempted to buy something to eat in the afternoon, than to have dropped them now.

He was careful not to let Frau Hobbs-Pechlar see too much of his hands. The proud flesh which had formed over the sores in April and May, and had deluded him into thinking that the ugly fissures were healing at last, had all had to come away. New flesh and skin were growing ever so slowly into its place. The process of healing seemed exasperatingly delayed, and the sores still itched for hours at a time. He resolved never to let anything happen to his hands again. It was July before the tender new skin joined over the last wound spot.

After that—as if it had been a good omen to have his hands sound and intact again—the whole month turned out to be lucky. On the fifteenth, two new apprentices started in the store. Practically overnight he was relieved of all the heavier chores. Then, on the last day of July, Hacker ran off with nearly ten thousand kronen which he had collected at the freight stations. He never came back. The police reported that Hacker had got on the train for Innsbruck and had been seen in Linz, but that was as close as they came to catching him. He got Hacker's job of going around to the railroads. It not only removed him from Herr Kropfl's authority and put him under Herr Brandt whom he liked, but it also brought him into almost daily contact with Herr Straka.

As soon as the store was opened now in the morning, he reported to Herr Brandt at the warehouse yard and then started out on his round. There were seven freight stations in all and they were widely scattered over the city. He had to make anywhere from three to half a dozen separate stops at each station: to clear incoming freight bills and pay storage charges, to arrange for empty cars for outgoing shipments, to dicker with dispatchers and yardmasters to get cars shunted to the proper platforms for loading and unloading.

Hacker had never covered more than four stations in a day. He soon discovered the reason. Hacker had loafed in dispatchers' offices and had taken his time between stations. He made it a matter of pride to get around to all of them before evening. It made it easier for Herr Brandt to draw up more efficient schedules for the drays and to handle shipping, and it was only five weeks before Herr Brandt praised him to Herr Straka. It meant, of course, that he could not waste even a minute. He worked out a closely timed routine for himself for each station, and he learned to jump on and off moving streetcars to save time on the way. Even so, he found time to study for his next English lesson on the streetcar or as he waited his turn in some office. And he enjoyed the freedom of movement his efficiency had procured for him. He did not have to report back to the store at the end of the morning, but he could go home directly for lunch and then start out again for a station. Sometimes there was not even time to get back to the store in the evening. He merely telephoned Herr Brandt and was allowed to go home with the freight bills and even the money. Herr Brandt and Herr Straka were trusting him in spite of the recent experience with Hacker. It was *she* who became alarmed at the large sums he carried around in his pockets, and grumbled about it to Franz.

For Franz was back home again. He had been declared still unfit for service at the front, and he had been detailed to his old job in the Ministry of War. But he remained in uniform and they realized that it was only temporary. By November, at the latest, Franz was scheduled to be called into active service again. In the meantime, Franz was enjoying the respite he had. He joked about the months at the Italian front and he made light of his wound and of *her* solicitude. She was feeding him all she could, and Peter noticed with half an eye that their supplies of flour and lard were shrinking steadily. But he refused to be worried by it. For the present, at least, there was enough to eat, or almost enough. And it was fun to have Franz at home, for ever since August Franz seemed to have some special, secret cause for the high spirits with which he was fairly brimming over these days.

One Sunday morning, Peter confirmed his suspicion about the reason for them. He was setting out for his lesson with Frau Hobbs-Pechlar and Franz rode out to Schönbrunn with him. He asked cautiously:

"Have you been seeing anything of Baron Ortner?"

Franz's eyes jumped. He smiled. A new kind of happiness lay over his face——

"No, but I'm going to see Bianca in a few minutes! Any message you want me to give her? She's been asking for you. . . ."

"I thought she was in Hungary?"

"Not this summer!" Franz said exultantly, and his happiness made it clear that he had something to do with Bianca's being in Vienna at this time of year. "All right, I'll tell her that you want to be remembered, shall I?" And at once his eyes became softly veiled with some joyous, secretive expectancy.

When Franz got off at the Reservoir and as he watched the eager stride with which Franz set out for Schönbrunn, he himself became as if spun in a web of joy at the thought that Bianca was only a few blocks away. Though, oddly enough, he had no desire to see her now. "Later," he told himself, "when I am somebody!" For the moment, it was enough that Franz would see her and would bring back something of her in his face. For he found in the course of the next few days and weeks that the mere fact of Bianca's being in the city had revived that festive, wordless bond which Bianca had once before created between Franz and him.

The late summer which had been merely pleasant suddenly quickened with joy. Each new day appeared plump and golden like a sun-warmed fruit shoved within his reach. He remembered the winter when the days had been monstrous, dreary labyrinths and he had stumbled between endless walls of weariness and despair. Now he was facing an open road and he knew his goal, and though Bianca and Franz had not been responsible for that, they were yet in some deliciously obscure way involved in it. . . .

And then, suddenly, in October, Franz changed. Between one morning and the next, Franz had become brooding and very still. *She* tried to hide her concern over Franz, but her grimness said as plainly as words: "I always knew no good was going to come of that!" Franz had had some sort of interview with Bianca's mother and had been forbidden to see Bianca again. . . .

Franz's last month at home became a gloomy funnel which narrowed inexorably to its final issue at the Südbahnhof. Poldi and he went to see Franz off. It was not cheerful on the platform beside the sinister length of the grimy train. Nobody bothered to festoon troop trains with flowers and little flags any more. There was little one could think of to say. Franz tried to sound lighthearted, but they knew that his gaiety was put on. . . .

Chapter Forty-One

THE peculiarly apprehensive gloom waited not only at home. It hung over the whole city this time. The short season of fruit in the markets was gone. Already the green vegetables had disappeared from the stalls and from the grocers' racks. The promises that this autumn the war would surely end had not been kept. Something apathetic and haggard crept into people's faces as the early evenings sank down over the streets. There was no lift in the news of a big offensive launched against Italy. Peter was aware of it only because *she* prayed harder and looked more gaunt every day because of Franz. Not even the declaration of war by the United States had power to shock people any more. America was far away and the shortage of bread was there on the spot, between the baker and one's useless ration card.

Herr Lehnert said, "Well, one more can hardly make any difference!" on the December morning when the news came through.

But when Herr Dornbirn tended to make light of it—"I don't see what difference they'll make anyway. Look at how little they've been able to do against Germany since April! It's just American bluff"—Herr Lehnert had been quick to warn:

"I wouldn't be too sure of that. It's a rich country and they have lots of men and machines. Germany may have bit off more than she can chew. . . ."

But for the moment at least it looked as if Herr Dornbirn had been right. Except for the disappearance of the gay little flags from American-made bicycles and motorcycles, there was no difference. The only important fact was that a week's ration of bread was just enough to eat at one sitting and that there were no potatoes and no flour or fat. There were only turnips and beets again and jam made of beets. At home, their store of flour had dwindled to something under ten pounds and she was hoarding it jealously, using only a spoonful at a time for thickening.

Yet this new winter was immeasurably easier for him to bear. He came to feel like a bystander who kept telling himself coolly that sooner or later the war must end. He did not wish for defeat, but the war seemed to him now like a game that had turned into a brawl with both the timekeeper and the umpire lost. Exhaustion alone could stop it now, and the signs of exhaustion were on every hand.

His feeling of withdrawal, of disloyal detachment almost, was due at least partly to his lessons with Frau Hobbs-Pechlar. She had given him a book to read called *Huckleberry Finn*. There were words in it the dictionary did not even list, and during the lessons she talked to him about American customs, about a holiday named "Independence Day" and the firecrackers that were set off, about her own home. He learned about Philadelphia and the Quakers who had settled there, about the West and the South and the Civil War. It tended to make him look on Vienna from the outside.

There was still time to study on his rounds, though less than before. The streetcars had become scarcer—it was said that they were laid up in the carbarns for lack of repairs—and the cars that ran were usually crowded to overflowing. He learned to stand on the bumper behind, to hang onto the platform railing with one hand and with only one foot on the step. Often, especially at noon and at night, he clung with other men to the platform steps on the wrong side of the car. When a streetcar going in the opposite direction went by, they had to press together hurriedly to keep from being torn off by a similar cluster on the other car. There were accidents. He saw one man fall under the wheels. But the element of danger exhilarated him; it made him feel cool and competent.

It had become harder to get results at the freight stations, too. The railroad yards were jammed with freight cars waiting to be shunted to the loading platforms, to the shops for repairs, to the sidings where outgoing trains were made up. There were not enough yard engines and not enough men. The superintendents and the dispatchers were ill-humored and had to be handled with care. He cajoled them and got what he wanted most of the time. With some of them he had made friends: others needed things from the store. It would have been easy enough to take them the things they wanted without anyone's being the wiser in the store, but he made a point of always getting Herr Brandt's consent. His strategy worked. Herr Brandt spoke to Herr Straka about his work. He found out about it on Christmas Eve——

There was a custom on Christmas Eve that directly after the store had closed all the employees gathered in the office across the street to wish Herr Straka a Merry Christmas and to receive the important December pay envelope with the Christmas bonus from Herr Straka himself. They filled not only the secretary's room and the big bookkeeping room, but the waiting room and the hall beyond. There were jokes and a pleasant sense of expectancy. Herr Kropfl had gone in first and had stayed a pompous minute or two, but after that it went fast. Frau Redlich had gone in and come out, then the girls from the office, and then Herr Brandt, and then the clerks in strict order of seniority. Herr Meier had been first, just as the two new apprentices would be last. Behind them, the laborers and the draymen were again lined up according to seniority.

The ritual had meant nothing to Peter the year before, but this time he waited impatiently for his turn. It finally came——

Herr Straka was standing behind his desk. On it was the long cardboard box with the pay envelopes. Herr Straka returned his greeting, looked gravely at him for a second and asked about his health.

"I'm feeling fine, Herr Straka."

"Are you wearing warm underwear?"

"Yes, Herr Straka."

"You haven't had any more pains in your side?"

"No, I'm taking better care of myself this year."

"That's fine. . . ." Herr Straka paused significantly. "Herr Brandt has several times lately spoken of your efficiency in clearing freight. You are showing ability and I have been aware of your willingness to take pains. A firm like ours, especially in times like these, depends on the interest every employee takes in his work."

"I've tried to get around as fast as I can. . . ."

"Yes, I know." Herr Straka reached for the front envelope in the box, but he did not hand it to him yet. "I am aware, of course, that the work you are asked to do is harder than in ordinary times. Therefore, if your work continues to be as satisfactory as it has been, I shall be inclined to shorten your apprenticeship by half a year. We shall see during the coming year. . . . A merry Christmas to you!" Herr Straka handed him the pay envelope and shook his hand.

He came away from the office jubilantly. Nobody since Herr Emmerich—whose place as manager Herr Kropfl had temporarily usurped—had ever finished his apprenticeship in two and a half years. Another year and he would be a clerk—he had Herr Straka's word for it! When he opened the envelope another surge of gratitude to Herr Straka welled up in him: he had been given a raise of thirty kronen a month, and, according to Herr Straka's notation on the little slip, a hundred kronen for Christmas besides! He counted the banknotes feverishly—it was all there: a hundred and thirty kronen more for this month than he had any right to expect.

He knew of a grocer who traded in bootlegged food. The grocer had two pounds of white flour left, for which he asked an outrageous twelve kronen a pound. A pound of brown sugar was ten kronen more. He hurried home with the precious parcel under his arm. She had enough vegetable fat—now they could have a cake!

He hovered over her the following morning while she mixed the batter for the cake, and for him at least—in spite of the thick anxiety at home over Franz—this Christmas was gay. He had mentioned the bonus he had got, but he said nothing about the raise. He needed the thirty kronen extra for his lessons with Frau Hobbs-Pechlar. There was little money to be earned now. The clerks hid the things they wanted to save for their special customers much more carefully than ever before; it was next to impossible to find their caches. It was true that he was able to save around two kronen each day out of the carfare he got—the women conductors rarely could get through the packed streetcars to collect all the fares, and he had learned to chart his rounds so as to put the transfer tickets to maximum use—but even with the most rigid economies he was nearly always short when the time to pay for his lessons came on the first, and he hated to ask Poldi for money any more.

The temptation to spend whatever money he had on food was always there. For, once again, unbelievably, the food situation had taken another turn for the worse. For three weeks in January there was no bread at all. More and more people went into the country every week end in the hope of buying a few pounds of grain or potatoes or a few ounces of lard. They took along jewelry, pieces of silk, leather—whatever they had—to induce the farmers to part with a little food. The lucky ones had relatives in the country and got things from them. But when they had got their grain or corn, their foraging expedition was still far from complete: they still had to get past the special inspectors in the railroad stations who confiscated all food. Women hid food under their clothes and even sewed it in the lining of their coats. Men preferred to get off the train at some rural station close enough to the city limits to allow them to hike to the nearest streetcar terminus before night. There was a rabid demand for handmills with which to grind maize and grain. The mills were made of cast iron; they were crudely finished and even dangerous to use because the burrs had not been filed off and pieces of iron would be ground into the grain or corn, but even so they could never keep enough of them in the store.

He himself bought one of the handmills and carefully filed off the burrs. He had been promised all the corn he could carry and some bacon and wheat by a country blacksmith who needed horseshoe nails and colters and rasps. He got everything together at last and wrote that he was coming, and he got Poldi to come along. They started out before daybreak one Sunday morning for the Nordbahnhof. The train was cold in spite of the hordes of people that had crowded into the cars. They were stalled twice to let troop trains pass. It was eleven o'clock before they reached Gmünd and they still had a four-mile walk through the snow ahead of them to the village where the blacksmith lived. But they had been prepared for that. It was crisp and clear, and he even enjoyed the trek which was colored by his anticipation of proving to Poldi how important he was and with what deference he was treated by men three times his age. The blacksmith had been lavish in his promises, if he would only get him the colters and the rasps.

Other people had set out with them along the country road. They straggled out before them and behind and unconsciously made the uneven procession into a race. He took pride in holding Poldi back—no need for them to hurry at all! They were expected. They would not have to canvass from farm to farm.

They got to the farmhouse while the blacksmith and his family were still at their midday meal. Poldi and he both caught a glimpse of food-laden plates on a square, rustic table, before a buxom woman pulled a little girl away from a half-open door and slammed the door from the inside. The fragrance of potato dumplings and boiled ham hocks was unmistakable even out in the stone-paved hall where the blacksmith was welcoming them. When the door behind him was shut so emphatically, the blacksmith hastily ushered them into an unused Sunday parlor on the opposite side of the hall. His lips were still shiny with grease.

The blacksmith displayed the same peasant heartiness he had shown in the store, but he seemed to be evading any talk of their proposed trade. It seemed ungracious to press the matter in the face of his pretended indifference—ungracious and unwise. Peter realized suddenly how much he was at the mercy of the blacksmith here, just as this same peasant had been at his mercy in the store. And he could see how the blacksmith was exploiting the fact. Slowly, against the man's resistance, he worked the talk around to the things he had brought. He took out the colters and listened to the man's quibbling about the size, although the colters were exactly the size he had been so anxious to get. There was little to object to on the score of the nails and the rasps; they were everywhere desperately in demand. He read Poldi's irritation and distaste in her face, for the blacksmith in his deceptively lumbering, stolidly sly way was now pretending to be out of food——

"There are so many of you city folks every week, the whole village is cleaned out. And the government inspectors are after us all the time. We can hardly keep enough to keep the stock alive."

Sharp now, because of his anger with the man, Peter decided to drop all diplomacy——

"There are lots of blacksmiths who need rasps and the colters and nails. A man offered to bring me a sack of potatoes for half a dozen colters only last week. I came to you only because I thought we'd made a deal. You were the one that promised all that bacon and corn."

The blacksmith professed to be upset. "I'm sure sorry you came all the way up here. I can let you have a little corn, but it's still on the cob. We haven't had time to shell it yet. If you want that—"

Poldi said:

"I have three packages of pipe tobacco!"

In spite of his caution, his thick peasant features betrayed his greed.

"Tobacco. Well, now, I'd sure like to have that." He hesitated for a moment and then said brightly as if he had only just now thought of it: "You folks must be hungry after that walk. I'll see whether the wife still has some soup."

When he had left them, Poldi said abruptly:

"Let's go away. We can try somewhere else. I don't want their soup."

"No, not after coming this far. He promised me all those things!"

The blacksmith returned.

"The wife says she's got a little soup left in the pot. She's heating it up for you now—if you don't mind some plain country soup. Sure is a shame we haven't anything better to offer you folks." He had spoken glibly with that insolent mock deference which had been in his manner from the first. His eyes flicked over them shrewdly to see how they were taking it.

They had to take it, all right! Peter thought hotly. What else were they going to do? They were hungry and even a plate of hot soup was too good to refuse. Though Poldi still looked as if she wanted to go away. He himself forced her to stay by following the blacksmith out into the stone-paved hall to the door through which he had seen the food on the big table before.

The blacksmith's wife had not even bothered to change the blue-checked tablecloth with its fresh gravy stains. She merely brushed her red hands over her starched new apron and said: "I hope you city folks don't mind about the cloth. Soap's hard to get!" Her husband's sly deference appeared as open insolence in her. She brought in two plates of soup and cut off a slice of the delicious-looking country bread for Poldi and for him, then she immediately took the loaf out into the kitchen with her. The plump little girl who had peered out at them in the hall and a loutish-looking boy of about twelve had come into the room and stood beside the porcelain stove, watching them eat. The blacksmith had sat down on one of the heavy oak chairs by the window and was noisily drawing on a red-tasseled pipe. No doubt he was watching them, too. It was just as Poldi had implied: they were being treated as if they had been beggars, but Peter no longer cared. The soup was good, and so was the bread. It was only when he came to the bottom of his plate that his resentment rose again. There was not going to be any more! The woman had come back from the kitchen and stood there, buxom and sleek and insolent. "Sure are sorry things are like they are. If only you folks had come two weeks ago when we killed the pig! But the government inspector's been here since and the government just leaves us folks barely enough to live ourselves. . . ."

The blacksmith took them out to the barn. In a corner lay a big pile of unshelled cobs. He pushed a few cobs toward the pile with his foot. "It's like I said. We've been that busy without any help we haven't got around to shelling this yet. If you'd like to sit down—" He pointed to two milking stools.

"How about the bacon you told me about? How much do we get of that?"

"Well, I'll have to see the wife about the bacon. . . ."

He went and came back with a small slab, not much more than a pound. He stood his ground stolidly against the angry unbelief in Peter's eyes. "It's all I could get from the wife. We've only got a little left ourselves."

"What about some potatoes, then?"

"There isn't a potato on the farm except what we need for the pigs. You city folks don't know how the government measures everything out for us. I thought maybe you'd like some winter pears——" He went to a chaff bin and raked through the chaff with his hand to show them the shriveled pears.

They were trapped. The blacksmith knew it, too; it accounted for the taunting patience with which he was waiting for them to decide. Without giving him another glance, Peter kicked angrily at the milking stool.

"I guess we'll have to take the corn."

The blacksmith grinned. He was all sly good humor now. He brought two winnowing pans and showed them how to shell the corn. Presently the squealing of a pig gave him an excuse to get out of helping them with the corn.

They went on alone, doggedly prying the stubborn kernels off the cobs. It was cold in the barn with the big doors open to give them light. The sun, Peter saw, had disappeared from the gray sky. His fingers were getting sore, and Poldi's, he knew, must be raw from the cold and from the unaccustomed chore. By three o'clock they had filled only half of each rucksack. They still had to cover the four miles back to the station and the train left at half past four. They filled the rucksacks with ears of corn. The blacksmith came back smoking the tobacco Poldi had brought. As if to mock them, he kept on urging them to take some of the pears. Poldi finally put a few on top of the corn, and he filled up the pockets of his overcoat. . . .

The walk back over the lonely country road drew out endlessly. It was gray and cold. Poldi and he spoke only once. When they had covered about two miles, Poldi suddenly fell back and stopped.

"I can't walk that fast!"

The shrill protest in Poldi's voice chilled him with alarm. He came back hurriedly and led her to a stone fence on which they could prop up their rucksacks and rest. He did not dare to look at Poldi's face. He knew that her forehead and the skin all around her eyes were flushed, and he could hear her efforts to stifle her gasps for breath.

Slowly, as he stared out over the bleak winter landscape, there dawned on him the full significance of Poldi's outcry on the road. He had failed with the blacksmith, after all his vaunted shrewdness the day before, and to wipe out his humiliation he had tried to impress Poldi with his strength. It was quite true that his rucksack was much heavier than hers. But also—and this was at least as important as the other—he had taken it for granted that Poldi was as strong as he. Poldi was the athlete who had done giant swings at the exhibition in Schönbrunn, and she had taken over when Father had died—had in fact been the real head of the family ever since. He realized that it had never occurred to him that Poldi might break. "I suppose," he told himself caustically, "you've never seen Poldi's frilly white underthings on *her* ironing board to know that she was after all only a girl and wouldn't be as strong as an apprentice in a hardware store!"

He melted with a rush of solicitude for her. She was getting rested and it was all right now to look. Of course, she must be wretched with her thin-soled city shoes trying to walk fast over the icy, rutted road, and she must be horribly cold in spite of the ski socks and the silk muffler she had knotted in front of her throat, and he himself knew how the hard corncobs cut into one's back——

Poldi seemed to sense his new attitude to her. She tugged at the shoulder straps of her rucksack and said quickly:

"Well, shall we go?"

"I'm going to take your rucksack the rest of the way. I can put it on top of mine quite easily. Let me have it——"

"No."

"Then, let's carry it between us. We can each take a strap."

"You've got enough to carry. I'm all right now!"

There was nothing he could do. Poldi had already started across the ditch to the road. But he was careful this time not to walk too fast. If they missed their train, there was another one at seven. They would simply have to wait. He kept watching her out of the corner of his eyes and every few hundred yards he insisted on taking a rest. He felt oddly warmed by this new emotion of having to look out for her. Only when they were within sight of the station, his earlier rage with the blacksmith came back. He had let himself be tricked like an innocent little boy! After this, the farmers could bring their potatoes and bacon to the city and he was going to deal with them there where the advantage was his! Only, the peasants were stubborn and sly and they knew that they had the upper hand now. It was just as Franz had once said: the peasants were getting even with the city at last and they relished their triumphs like the blacksmith today.

He remembered the letter Franz had written after a brief furlough in January: Franz had gone to Almzell for two days and he had been enthusiastic over the big things Aunt Resi and Karl were doing with the farm. Karl especially. It appeared that Karl was driving the five Russian prisoners that had been sent on Aunt Resi's farm just as Grandfather might have done, and that they were making so much money out of the food they were raising that they had paid off all the mortgages Karl's father had saddled on the farm. Except for a tract of timber and a quarry which Aunt Resi had sold in the lean days before the war, the farm was as intact as it had been in Grandfather's day. As he thought of it now, Peter was moved by alternate pride because it was Grandfather's farm that his cousin Karl was pulling together again, and by resentment against Karl who was no doubt just like the peasant who had tricked him today. Karl, too, would manage to look sheepish and sly as he held out dozens of sacks of potatoes and wheat and goodness knew how much cheese from the government inspectors, only to sell it off later in the black market. No wonder Aunt Resi could pay off all the mortgages now. And they had never sent them a pound of anything to eat all through the war! . . .

They had not missed their train after all. It was more than an hour late. The cars were as crowded as they had been in the morning and still more uncomfortable because of the full rucksacks everywhere on the floor between people's legs. One hour before they were supposed to be in Vienna, the train broke down. There came a two hours' wait. It became colder and colder in the cars. Then they were told to get out to walk to another train that was waiting up ahead.

Once again his solicitude for Poldi asserted itself. He tried to help her while they stumbled along the embankment through the snow. . . . And when they finally got to Vienna at half past ten, he made no attempt to evade the government inspectors in the station by getting off on the wrong side of the train and walking across the dozens of tracks to the freight station and out through an unguarded side gate as he had planned. Poldi was too exhausted to be made to walk over the tracks! If the food inspectors in the station wanted to confiscate their corn, after all they had been through—well, if they dared, he would give them a fight!

They were hardly molested at all. An inspector poked their rucksacks and let them pass. . . .

It was after midnight when they got their feet into the hot baths *she* had had waiting for them since eight o'clock. They ate and Poldi went to bed without another word. He realized then how intently he had been waiting for Poldi to say something more, even if it was only to reproach him for the day.

But it was only during the following weeks that he became fully aware of how completely his relation with Poldi had changed. He realized how conscious he was of her as a woman now and that Poldi resented this consciousness in him. Neither Poldi nor he spoke of the foraging expedition again. . . .

Chapter Forty-Two

SLOWLY, reluctantly, the winter gave way to spring. The forsythia in the parks turned golden at last. Primroses and snowdrops in the woods behind Hütteldorf—the trees suddenly spilling bright green—and now this laughing, frolicking sun and full-blown peonies!

You overcame the days and weeks as you would carve your way out of a jungle. But the jungle was no longer your master now. You cut a path, a determined path, and you were no longer at the mercy of anything. You could look back at what you had accomplished, and you felt strong and proud. . . .

The thought wove pleasantly through his mind as he stood before the mirror in Franz's room on Whitsunday morning. He buttoned the new shirt *she* had made over for him from one of Father's, and with a sudden urge to celebrate he reached into Franz's dresser to borrow the dark-blue tie he had always wanted to wear.

He thought of the winter once more when he sat in the coffeehouse in the Kaiserstrasse. He had taken to coming here Sunday mornings when she believed him in church. It was simpler like this. It made her think that he had gone to Mass and it avoided disputes. Usually he had had breakfast at home first, but this time he had left without anything. Necessarily. She had already thrown out hints all through Holy Week about performing his Easter duty, and last night she had started again——

"Tomorrow's Pentecost. I hope you haven't forgotten it! If you're so independent now that you don't need God's blessing any more, you can at least go and offer up communion for Franz. He needs God's help!"

God's blessing! he thought indulgently. *If I had waited for God's help, I'd still be under Herr Kropfl's thumb. You've got to fend for yourself and hit hard, then maybe God is willing to help. . . .*

The waiter brought his coffee on a silver tray, and a morning paper. He put the pellets of saccharine into the cup and started to sip the wartime brew. It was bitter and thin. But, at least, the handsome porcelain cup felt as lovely as always here in his hand, and the damask napkins and the luxuriously upholstered seats were as elegant as before the war. He watched an elderly gentleman with a goatee and gold-rimmed spectacles come in through the revolving door, and the headwaiter step forward discreetly to welcome him: "Good morning, *Herr Hofrat*. Beautiful morning, isn't it?" Everything here was as it must have been before the war, except that the girl in the black dress behind the serving table with its tiers of crystal and silver would not have been tolerated then. He was sure that the old headwaiter suffered from having to have a woman in the place.

Yes, he had come a long way! Only seven more months before he finished his apprenticeship. There was no need for Herr Straka to speak of his promise again—Herr Straka's satisfaction with him lay behind the more frequent commissions with which he had lately entrusted him and behind the new twenty-kronen raise he had got on the first. If only Herr Benesch would get him the drills for the locksmith in Linz, there would be forty kronen net profit in that. . . .

The chubby apprentice waiter took away the tray with the empty cup and deftly slid another tray with two fresh glasses of water into its place. The *Herr Hofrat* in the corner of the two plate-glass windows was reading the *Neue Freie Presse*. Several other men, including the stout man who usually played chess with the *Herr Hofrat* later in the morning, were reading too. The coffeehouse was filled with a comfortable, lazy hush in which only the waiters were alert. He himself had not looked at the paper. Nor did he open the Tauchnitz edition of the Dickens novel he had brought along. He did not feel like studying today. Fortunately, Frau Hobbs-Pechlar had suggested on Thursday that perhaps he might not want to come today and he had taken the hint. No, no books today! He felt too expansive and restless with that sense of voluptuous tension which had been growing in him for weeks. His eyes went back to the girl in the black dress. She was bony and she had hardly any breasts, yet the fever gripped him nevertheless.

Passionate daydreams floated before his eyes, but almost immediately the bony girl by the serving table had been superseded in them by the pink-cheeked maid in Herr Straka's house. He saw the curve of Herta's throat and the torturing glow of her flesh in the V of her dress as it had first dizzied him when Herr Straka had sent him on an errand to Hietzing in March. There had been other errands since and nearly always Herta had happened to be in the kitchen with the cook and the other maid to trouble him with the sight of her body, and even more with her impudently laughing eyes which still mocked him about the time, more than a year ago, when she had thought that he wanted to flirt and had not known how.

But it had not only been Herta who had troubled him. There had lately been torture for him in every woman he saw. It was in a way like the period when he had still been in school and he had found no peace until Karl Breitner had finally shown him the medical book with the photographs and the diagrams. Only, that had been childish and bore no comparison to this imperious need which devoured his body now. It seemed as if everything that had happened in the last few weeks had conspired to bend his thoughts to that one thing: Herr Dornbirn boasting about some Hungarian girl he had taken to a hotel; the woman he had seen fixing her garter; the girls in the office and the women everywhere. Hence the dreams and their inevitable conclusion for which he had come to loathe himself.

Tonight! he resolved, *just as soon as it gets dark, I'm going down to the Gürtel where the prostitutes are!*

He suddenly felt a need to get out into the street and walk. In the window corner the *Herr Hofrat* was talking over his newspaper to the stout man who sat at the next table.

"Four years!" the imperial counselor was saying. "The country is exhausted. If the Allies really want peace, then why won't they listen to the Emperor's proposals?"

The other, obviously in awe of the *Hofrat* and proud of his coffeehouse acquaintance with him, ventured deferentially:

"But Germany is winning on the western front, isn't she?"

"Of course she is winning. One victory after the other. Russia is out of the war and now Rumania—but where does it get us! If only the old emperor had never agreed to that alliance with Germany. The Prussians are using us to butter their bread. They don't want peace. I shouldn't put it beyond them to use their secret channels abroad to quash any possibility of a hearing for our peace proposals!" His inflection made it clear that it was just possible that he might have had some information to that effect, and the stout man at the other table nodded appreciatively. . . .

Peter tapped one of the glasses with his fingernail. The headwaiter came and he paid. It was lovely out in the Mariahilferstrasse and lovelier still on the Ring. Along the Stadtpark the flowering lilac bushes crowded exuberantly between the bars and over the top of the fence. In just another week the chestnut trees would be in full bloom. He tried to walk along calmly and to forget his obsession, but the sight of a handsome woman in an attractive, thin, summer dress set his blood coursing wildly again. Almost mechanically, ruthlessly, he started to size up every woman he passed in the hope that she might be a prostitute and wink at him, although he knew that it was unlikely that one would venture out so early—especially here on the Ring. The worst of it was that his need made him feel so ungovernably bold and shy at once. He turned into the Volksgarten and saw two girls who smiled back at him, but at the last minute his nerve left him and he did not talk to them. Besides, what was the use of nice girls who only wanted to giggle and flirt! No, tonight! . . .

But that evening his courage failed him just as it had done on Friday night. He waited in an agony of impatience for dusk to fall. To kill time he rode back and forth over the Gürtel in the elevated steamcar line. At the point where the viaduct curved out toward Meidling one could just catch a glimpse from the train of the windows of a scabrous three-story house where some of the prostitutes lived. The second time he rode by, he was sure that he had seen a woman in a pink wrapper behind one of the windows and his imagination leaped to fever pitch. He got out at the next station and took the next train back. There was no one behind the window, nor the next time he rode past. Then, at last, it was dark enough to get off the train and to start down the Gürtel.

The women were already out. They stood in the shadowy doorways where the viaduct rounded the corner and they were under the trees on the Gürtel. It seemed to him as if there were hundreds of them, all watching him, so that he had to appear knowing and unconcerned. Yet he realized that there were hardly a dozen in all. Before he was aware of it, he had again started to walk fast. He had passed the corner and he had not turned in! He told himself that it did not matter, that there was time to spare now that he was here, and that it was only a question of deciding which one. He came back more slowly, but when two of the women left a doorway and headed across the street toward the Gürtel, he glanced away hastily and felt himself blush.

To make up for his cowardice he forced himself to walk close by the second doorway where a single woman was waiting for him. The woman took a step forward and invited him upstairs. Her voice sounded harsh and something about her stale dowdiness nauseated him. All his fears of the diseases he had read about in the book Franz had lent him and the loathsome memory of Herr Kropfl and his salve assailed him again. It was as if the little envelope Herr Leopold had bought for him at the pharmacy was not in his pocket at all. He said, "Later!" and walked away quickly until he was past the houses again. Then he lashed at himself for losing his nerve. He walked around the block in the hope that some other single prostitute would come along and accost him. But where there had seemed to be hundreds before, he saw only the same pair he had evaded once. He followed them for a while toward the Mariahilferstrasse, but they stayed together and would not split up. It was getting late. He had to go home. Exasperated with himself, he jumped on a fast-moving streetcar and promised himself that the next night he was not going to fail.

The following noon he was still berating himself for his squeamishness. Looked at coldly in the mocking noonday sun, his cowardice appeared all the more exasperating because of the drab lubricity of the neighborhood around the viaduct. What else had it been but fear that had kept him from going upstairs with the woman and getting it over with! His sense of frustration worked on him to the point where he swore to himself not to go home that night until—afterward!

It happened to be his afternoon for going to Herr Straka's house. For several weeks now, every other day, he had fetched the gallon can of milk from the dairy in the Kohlgasse, and had taken it out to

Hietzing. It was an errand Herr Straka himself had asked him to do. The little dairy which kept six milk cows in an old-fashioned stable in the rear of the yard was an anachronism which had turned out to be a blessing for Herr Straka's family. Some ancient friendship between the dairyman and Herr Straka's father had made the dairyman furnish Herr Straka with milk in spite of the strict rationing. But lately, people in the neighborhood had begun to grumble at the dairyman; they had even threatened to take the can of milk away from his daughter when she set out for Hietzing to deliver it. It had become necessary to go and get the milk. . . . He would have resented the errand if he had not had the feeling that it brought him closer to Herr Straka than even the most important errands connected with the store. And more recently, since Herr and Frau Straka had moved out to their summer place in Hinterbrühl, there had been the additional incentive of finding Herta alone, for she had been left behind in Hietzing to cook Herr Straka's lunches and to guard the house.

As usual, he started to walk faster as he drew near the house. He experienced a stab of disappointment when he saw the wide-open front door—it looked as if someone in authority had just gone inside and had deliberately thrown open the doors to let the sun stream into the hall. Perhaps Frau Straka had suddenly come into town. . . . He went around to the kitchen and rang. After a minute, Herta came from somewhere in the front part of the house and he knew another twinge of disappointment. She always wore some frivolous white lace apron over her black maid's dress, which itself sat so pertly on her troubling body—"brazen," he called it secretly—that it had become part of the excitement she possessed for him, but today she had on a shapeless blue apron which completely hid her dress. She made a face when she let him in. "You could have come through the front, now that nobody's here, instead of making me chase through the whole house!"

"Nobody's here?"

"Of course not. Whom did you expect? I've been dusting pictures in the drawing room—don't I look a sight?"

She reached up with both hands to her head to tighten the knot in her kerchief, only to decide abruptly to pull the kerchief off altogether and fling it on a chair.

"Not as much of a sight as I'd like to see you!" he said meaningly. The memory of his failure the night before and her blue apron which hid so much of her body made him feel bold.

"You aren't likely to!" Her round, brown eyes laughed at him. "You wouldn't know what to do about it anyway!"

"Oh, no?"

The sweet, poignant dilatoriness had again entered their banter. He watched her get two porcelain jars and start to pour the milk into them on the white kitchen table. The sight of her firm arms and the rich smell of the milk, which he had come to associate with the white enamel in Herr Straka's kitchen and with her, emboldened him still further: "Just see whether I don't!" He stepped behind her and put his arms around her waist. She giggled—

"Look out! You're going to make me spill the milk. Let go of me!"

"You don't really want me to."

"No, I'm talking for my health!"

He had been about to take away his arms, when she wriggled her head so that her hair tickled his nostrils. A new rush of daring made his mouth brush clumsily over her hair and her cheek as he sought for her lips. He realized exultantly that she had actually twisted her head toward him and that her full lips had pressed against his mouth and stayed there——

"That's enough!" She twisted away from him. "Your nerve!"

Still excited and a little tremulous from his unexpected triumph, he went and sat down on a chair on the other side of the table. He thought it safest to retreat behind the barbed banter that had become customary between them. He started to tease her about the soldier she was going to marry:

"When's the corporal coming?"

She pouted. "He didn't get his furlough. He's always into trouble!"

"Poor girl—now she's going to cry her eyes out! Do you really mind?"

"Certainly I mind. Do you think a girl likes to sit home all the time? I can't go out by myself! I like to go to the Prater and shows and things once in a while. . . ."

"I could take you!"

She did not even deign to answer. Of course, she would want somebody older. Still, she had said herself that she was only going to be twenty-two in October—six years, that wasn't so much! All the same, it had evidently been a mistake to propose it. To regain his composure, he asked brashly:

"Got any cake?"

She came back from the sink where she had rinsed the can and clapped the lid on noisily. She was still nettled.

"No cake."

"Any pudding?"

"No pudding, either! Herr Straka wasn't here for lunch today—if you want to, you can come and see what I'm doing. . . ."

He was usually only too happy to catch even a brief glimpse of the inside of the house beyond the kitchen. But today he had no eyes for the cool elegance of the two drawing rooms. She was working in the front one where a short stepladder was standing below one of the pictures. She went out into the hall first to close the door, then she came back and got up on the ladder.

"Hand me that cloth! No, the red one!"

She started to rub softly over the gilt frame. "Like this!" she said. "I have to go over all of them. This one's easy because it's got a smooth frame. It's my favorite picture anyway. Isn't she pretty? Fancy wearing all those jewels!"

"You've got pretty legs!"

"You were supposed to look at the picture!"

"I'd rather look at you."

"You're much too young to be thinking of that all the time. You're hardly out of your diapers. There, hand me that little bottle and the cloth. Careful, you don't—"

There was a sudden ring of the doorbell.

She scrambled down hurriedly. "Quick! Frau Straka—" She led him through the other drawing room into the hall behind the kitchen, to a little room in the back. "In there—"

It was evidently her room. It was small, but cheerful and briskly tidy. The muslin-curtained window looked out on the garden. On the dresser stood a framed photograph of a soldier. He glanced at it and then sat down on a chintz-covered chair in the corner to wait. Herta was gone for a considerable length of time, but when she came for him, she was smiling.

"All right, you can come out. It was only a friend of Frau Straka's with a book I have to send out to Hinterbrühl. It sounded just like the *Gnädige Frau*—she rings just like that. And I didn't even have the chain on the door. . . ."

"Did you put it on now?"

"What do you think? One scare like that's enough for one day! Am I stupid—" she burst out with a laugh—"it couldn't have been the *Gnädige Frau!* She's having a garden party this afternoon! All that worry for nothing."

"This is a nice room. . . ."

"It's the cook's. I stay in here during the summer. Come on now!"

He stretched out his legs comfortably. "I like it here."

"So do I! That's why you're going out of here. Think I want to lose my place if anybody catches you in my room?"

"You just said there wasn't any danger of anybody coming. Herr Straka's busy in the office—is that the dashing hero?"

She spun around to the dresser.

"You would see that! Isn't he handsome?" But she pulled open a drawer and slipped the photograph inside.

"Has he been in this room?"

"None of your business. Hurry up now! I want to get finished in there with the pictures." She came and tugged at his arm. "Get up now!"

He let himself be pulled to his feet, then finding himself so intoxicatingly close to her body, he encircled her waist and tried to kiss her again. "No—" She was strong and her hands pushed against him, yet he was blissfully aware that she could have pushed much harder. In the end, she again turned her mouth toward him.

"That's enough!" Her struggle this time was more determined. To free herself, she finally arched her back and pushed away from him so hard that she landed sitting on the edge of the bed. He slipped down beside her before she could get up and put his arm around her waist. She was suddenly laughing. "You learn fast, don't you? I bet this is the first time you've ever kissed a girl!"

Her unexpected laugh, he realized with a tremor, had again given her the upper hand. To gain time, he said:

"You look much prettier without this ugly apron."

"I've got to wear something when I'm dusting—here, let go! . . ." She shook off his arm and untied her apron strings. She had to stand up to get it off altogether. She turned coquettishly: "There! Is that better?"

"Much!" He had to sound very firm to keep his voice from quaking. Herta in the black serge dress with its narrow white collar, but without the familiar tiny white apron, looked disturbingly undressed. "Don't put it on again!" He seized her hand and pulled her toward him so that she had to sit down on the bed. "You know, you're pretty!"

"Do you really think so?"

"Of course!" He was happy that she was content to sit beside him and let his hand caress her cheek and throat. "This isn't the same dress you wore the other day. The other one had little buttons . . ."

Her hand touched the front of her dress. "This one has too, only you don't see them."

"Where?"

"Look out, you'll wrinkle my collar—I just put it on fresh this noon!" But when he had taken away his hand, in instant retreat before her annoyance, she smiled indulgently and undid the fastening at her collar, then hooked it together again—"It's a hook and eye, silly!"

"Let me see——"

She kept her hand watchfully close while he unhooked the fastening; when he undid the next one and tried to slide his hand down to her breast, she clutched his wrist—"No, you don't!" But he was voluptuously conscious that as he bent over to kiss her, her hand—even though it continued to clutch his wrist—allowed his fingers to slide farther and farther down over her flesh. Her breath was coming as fast as his own and felt hot on his cheek. He knew a fierce urge to caress her leg, to feel the naked flesh of her thigh, but the gesture seemed so enormous that he was afraid of it. In a blind rush of somehow indulging his passion, he undid the next hook and eye down her dress. She let him, only to quiver with a sudden sharp intake of breath——

"What are you trying to do—you're tearing my dress! . . ." Her hands had come up to the hook and eye, but instead of fastening it, she abruptly unhooked the one beneath it, and the next one, and the next——

"You're bad! you're bad!"

Mingled terror and joy paralyzed him at the sight of her naked shoulders and of her crinkly, rustling linen petticoat. But already she had let her dress fall around her feet. ". . . Bad!" she said again and threw her arms around him blindly to draw him close. Clumsily, then ecstatically, he devoured her with his joy. . . .

Afterward, as they lay on the bed side by side, he remembered his fear and at the same time, incongruously, he noticed how absurdly fine the three rebellious little hairs were that grew just above her ear. He laughed.

"Why are you laughing?"

"I don't know—I'm just happy, I guess."

"Are you happy? You're sure you weren't laughing at me?"

"Oh, no! I guess it was at myself. You know, I was afraid of you."

"Silly!" He was surprised again at how light her hand was when it brushed over the back of his head. "Are you going to take me to the Prater this Sunday?"

"I'll take you anywhere!"

His gratitude to Herta filled him with a softly throbbing glow which was at one with his joy. It was still singing inside him when he kissed her good-by and started away from the house. Only once, when he was nearly back at the store, the gray thought of Mizzi rose to trouble him. He thrust it away indignantly: This was entirely different! Besides, he had taken care. . . . He chose to think of Poldi instead: would Poldi be able to tell? He had a feeling that all women must sense that he was subtly dangerous to them now, and that he knew something so intimate about them that it also made him their brother somehow.

That evening as he passed the viaduct, he knew a rush of pity for the men who had to go to prostitutes. . . .

Chapter Forty-Three

He could not quite explain what it was Herta had done for him. When he was away from her, especially at moments when he was suddenly carried away by a gust of desire, his imagination would endow her with every kind of romantic attribute; but when he was with her again, all those extravagances of his anticipation appeared trivial and unnecessary. Her laugh which was waiting behind her red mouth and her robust impulsiveness mocked explanation, filled him with the same instant delight as the healthy animal scent of her body when they lay on her narrow bed in the evening and looked out at the moon through the lilac bush outside her window.

He did not try to tell her all that she meant to him. She had a way of interrupting with a throaty burst of laughter—"What nonsense you talk! But I like it. I like to hear you talk. . . ."—so that he felt exasperatingly conscious of being only sixteen and quickly fell to kissing her again. Yet the feeling that she had given him more than she knew persisted. Where he had prided himself before on his armor of hardness, he now felt full and solid. Bringing off his daily round of the railroads in record time was no longer a matter of triumph so much as play for his excess of energy. The store had become what he had thought it to be in the beginning: an exciting place for testing his strength and for building his future. . . .

He saw her at least every other day and sometimes oftener. Sundays they usually went to the Prater. She loved the operettas in the open-air theater, and the scenic railway and the merry-go-rounds afterward, and because she liked them and the excitement of being out with a girl was still new to him, he liked them, too. Then in the evening they would go back to Herr Straka's house and she would fix supper. She would be firm about that and fight him off if his kisses became too importunate. It was part of her sense of orderliness which had cowed him at first and had added to his pride of possession—an orderliness which went with the natural comelines she had and which even in moments of criticism when he got bored with riding in merry-go-rounds made whatever she did seem right to him.

He had had to resort to subterfuge at home to account for his Sundays and for the evenings when he came home late. Poldi and she were both suspicious. Fortunately, an apprentice with whom he had recently made friends was willing to help. He had the boy call for him on two successive Sundays right after lunch and he had made a great show of going on excursions into the country with him. It robbed them of any objection, although it did not do away with their fears. But even their suspicion pleased him because it added spice to the hours with Herta.

He was conscious that his new sense of completeness drove him into contradictory attitudes toward other people. At times, it made him proud of feeling so self-sufficient; then, again, it betrayed him into an exuberance that made him go out to others as he had not done before. He got to know the clerks in the store and the laborers and customers more intimately. He found it natural to laugh at their jokes. There was suddenly an excess of warmth in him that nudged him into doing things that puzzled him when he thought of them afterward. It was in one of those moods that he went one evening to commercial school. . . .

As usual, the several hundred apprentices who attended the school were lingering until the very last moment in the little square out in front. It was the second week in July and there were only three more sessions before the summer recess. He drifted off by himself to look for the group from his class. When he found them, he saw that they were gathered around two boys who were having an argument. Only one of the two was from the commercial school. He was an apprentice in a bank, rather well set-up and inclined to be noisily self-important, whom Peter had never cared for much. The other boy was from the trade school for engravers' apprentices around the corner. His name was Armbruster and Peter knew him much better, not only because he came occasionally to the store, but because he had been in Peter's class in the Ziegelgasse during their last year of school. He was a thin boy with a desperately honest face who even in school had shown a stubbornly passionate interest in grown-up affairs. One incident especially had stuck in Peter's mind. One day in literature class Armbruster had asked the teacher for permission to recite a long poem he had memorized from a newspaper, to the class. It had turned out to be an endless ballad about some obscure act of heroism by a soldier on the Balkan front. Armbruster's awkward patriotic fervor had made the whole class uncomfortable.

As he listened to the argument, Peter saw that Armbruster's earnestness was again making him into a laughingstock. He was arguing that the Socialists had a right to strike, and that labor ought even to be represented on the war council because labor was bearing the brunt of the war. The more heated Armbruster grew, the more supercilious the bank apprentice became. He was showing off. Nobody was interested in the argument except as an excuse to laugh at Armbruster.

It was hard to see how the argument had got started at all. Ordinarily, the small group of engravers kept to themselves on the other side of the square. Armbruster all by himself was at a disadvantage here. The boys in the circle kept egging him on. Then suddenly, the bank apprentice was angry, too. Armbruster had called him a "banker's pimp." Without warning, the bank apprentice hit Armbruster on the nose and drew blood. Armbruster did not even stand a chance. The other boy was heavier and he knew how to box. He kept deliberately punching at Armbruster's nose which was bleeding profusely now. Armbruster had to retreat to wipe off the blood which was trickling down over his mouth and chin. The bank apprentice sneered:

"Got enough?"

It was apparent that Armbruster was fighting against his will—just as it had been clear before that his "banker's pimp" had been meant less as an insult than as a vehement attempt to convince the other boy that he also belonged to the "laboring class"—but that now he had started, he intended to go on. He wiped his nose once more with the back of his hand and stepped forward.

For no reason, except that he felt suddenly irritated by the other boy's swaggering, Peter stepped forward, too, and with his elbow pushed Armbruster to one side.

The bank apprentice looked undecided and half lowered his arms. "What—" It seemed only fair to Peter not to give him any more warning than he had given Armbruster. His fist landed hard on the boy's mouth. The bank apprentice forgot his boxing tricks and came in with a rush, flailing wildly with his fists. Peter caught him in the stomach and landed another blow on his teeth that sent him back.

"Got enough?" he mimicked, while the bank apprentice rubbed the back of his hand gingerly over his swollen lips.

He felt elated by his quick success. This was different from the days when he had gone out of his way to avoid fights! Handling sixty-pound axles gave you fists that could jar. He was the one now who could make himself feared, at least by pampered office boys like this!

The school janitor called down from the steps:

"Can't you boys hear the bell? We're not going to have any fighting here. If you want to fight, go out to Ottakring!"

They trooped slowly into the building. The bank apprentice kept stubbornly alongside. "Who said anything to you?" he asked.

"Nobody. You didn't have to keep on hitting him in the nose."

It was all that was said. They drifted into the classroom to their seats. The professor started his lecture on commercial law. Peter listened with only half an ear; he was still thinking pleasantly about the brief fight. He had forgotten about Armbruster who had no doubt gone to his own school around the corner, but he could not help looking across at the bank apprentice every now and then. He did not feel in the least angry with him any more—he even felt that he liked him now. By the end of the second hour in bookkeeping his elation had worn off and he was thinking about Herta instead. He waited after class to see whether the bank apprentice wanted to continue to fight, but the boy walked past him with two of his friends without a word. He started home himself and it was only then that he noticed that Armbruster had been waiting for him out in the middle of the square.

Armbruster looked sheepish and the wings of his nose were still red.

"Thanks a lot. I wasn't afraid of him. It's only my nose—it starts bleeding right away."

"That's all right," Peter cut him short. "He had no right to hit you like that."

"Are you walking over to the Gürtel?"

"I can. It doesn't make any difference. I live on the Schmeltz."

"I live in the Poutongasse," Armbruster said eagerly. "Right by the Schmeltz. Do you always walk home this way? Funny, I never saw you before. . . ."

There was something subtly deferential and flattering in the way Armbruster had fallen in step with him, but also something irksome about his eager assumption that he was a friend about whom he had simply not known before. Peter responded guardedly. But even so he was aware of sounding friendlier than he really meant to do, because he did not have the heart to disappoint Armbruster's confiding warmth. He learned that he was apprenticed to a firm of engravers and silversmiths, that his father was a brakeman, that he went twice a week to the Socialist club in Ottakring. When Peter was about to leave him to turn off into his own street, Armbruster said eagerly:

"Maybe we could go rowing on the Danube this Sunday? Do you like rowing? I know a place where it's only two kronen for three hours for a boat."

He could not help sounding a trifle superior:

"I can't. I've got a girl and we always go to the Prater for the afternoon. Not for the merry-go-rounds, of course—we take in an operetta, then walk around."

"Oh, you like music, then! Do you ever go to the opera? I saw *Faust* last week. Maybe we could go to the opera sometime. . . ."

Although he felt little desire to see Armbruster again, he finally agreed to meet him on Friday night.

They met on Friday, and again the following week. And they walked home together from the last few evenings of school. It was inevitable, Peter came to see. Gradually his indifference gave way to a reluctant respect for Armbruster and finally even to a liking for him. He went upstairs and saw the little flat where Armbruster's family lived. They were very poor. There was an older sister who worked in a factory, and Armbruster's mother, a small, shriveled woman, who sewed on soldiers' overcoats for some army contractor all day long. Armbruster's father came home from the railroad, looking worn-out and grim with the same arrestingly dogged honesty that Armbruster had. It was easy to see how Armbruster had come by his passion for Socialism—his father was vindictive against the war profiteers, the church, the government bureaucracy, against all the rich. It was also clear that Armbruster's family had centered all their pride in him and that they were making sacrifices for his expensive apprenticeship. . . .

He saw the meticulous drawings of chalices and goblets and salvers Armbruster had made for his trade school. The intricate designs were lovingly traced in colored inks. It was the sort of delicate, painstaking drawing he himself had never been able to do and he could be sincere in his admiration of it. But he could not help thinking how hopelessly out of place the ambitious designs for sumptuous gold and silver vessels seemed in the humble room. . . . Then there was Armbruster's violin: Armbruster had taken lessons once and he still liked to play. He scratched through a few airs from an operetta Peter had seen with Herta at the Raimund Theater, but he was quick to explain that he played them only because his skill did not go beyond the simple melodies and that he did not care for operettas. He stood in line for a fourth-gallery seat at the Opera once a week. In the end, Peter was forced to pretend not to care for music at all to conceal his real reason for not wanting to go with him. The opera to Peter meant beautiful music to be heard in the no doubt excitingly luxurious interior of the Opera when one was beautifully dressed—*I'll go when I have clothes like Herr Straka,* he thought, *and then I'm not going up into the fourth gallery. I'm going to have an orchestra seat!* But he listened to Armbruster's enthusiasm about the last opera he had heard, just as he listened to his accounts of what had been said at the last meeting of the Socialist club in Ottakring.

Before he knew it his friendship with Armbruster had become a fact, although he could not help wondering about it at times. It was the first friendship he had formed in the two years since he had been in the store. Somehow he had not felt the need for a friend, or rather he had felt isolated with his ambition and complete because of it. And Armbruster fitted in no way into his plans. Quite the contrary. It was even hard to find the time to see him once or twice a week. There were the English lessons, which he was determined not to neglect, and there was Herta whom he wanted to see.

I must be ruthless with my time—I'm getting soft! he warned himself one evening after he had stayed out too late with Armbruster to do his studying in the English book; yet in the next breath he thought: *I'm the strong one now! He comes to me, just as I used to go to Rudi Martin, and to Meissl afterward.* And he felt a curious sense of obligation not to hurt Armbruster. Yet the very next time they were out walking across the Schmeltz and as he listened to Armbruster's defiant hopefulness for the future of what Armbruster called "the oppressed," he was again conscious of drawing apart—*I'm not oppressed! What am I doing here with him? I belong to the other side. I don't need unions and the Socialists!*

For he had lately made new strides in the store. It had been the custom for one of the older girls in the office to go every morning to the big bank in the Innere Stadt to deposit checks and cash and sometimes to draw out large amounts, but there had been an alarming number of hold-ups of bank messengers in July and Herr Straka suddenly turned the job over to him. There was a heavy cowhide attaché case which had always been used for going to the bank. After his first trip with the conspicuous yellow case, he had asked Herr Straka to let him stuff the bundles of banknotes into his pockets instead. It was only what he had been doing right along with the money he collected at the railroads. Herr Straka had been dubious about it at first, but when he had explained that the attaché case only called attention to him, and that it would be easier for him to get away with the money in his pockets in case he were attacked, Herr Straka had let him have his way. When three weeks had gone by without his losing any of the money out of his pockets as Herr Straka had feared, the leather case had not been mentioned again.

Other errands had come up that had increased Herr Straka's respect for him. All summer long there had been an acute shortage of freight cars on the two lines that went into Hungary. Since the fall of Russia and of Rumania all the available cars had been transferred to the railroads that supplied the army on the Italian front. Herr Brandt had sixteen carloads of farm machinery for one customer alone which had been waiting for over a month to be shipped to Hungary. Every time Peter had gone to the freight superintendent at the Ostbahnhof he had been told that there weren't any cars. Herr Brandt had finally taken him upstairs to Herr Straka after another negative report. "I need the space," Herr Brandt had complained; "that stuff's been in the way for weeks. Maybe we'd better cancel the order entirely."

Herr Straka had studied the invoices. "They're among our oldest customers. We can't do that." Herr Straka had turned to him: "Have you seen the station chief?"

Peter explained that the freight superintendent and even the chief dispatcher had more to do with assigning the cars than the gold-braided station chief who was nominally their superior.

Herr Straka deliberated for a moment. "Perhaps," he suggested, "a present of some sort? Of course, it should not come officially from the firm. . . ."

He knew what Herr Straka meant. The box of cigars on Herr Straka's desk was an example of the sort of present that was going the rounds nowadays. Just as the small country merchants brought in little packages of food to get a set of springs or a few hundred pounds of steel, so in Herr Straka's circle the owners of factories brought him boxes of fine cigars, sent whole hams and cases of eggs, to get what they needed. The pantry in Herr Straka's house was abundant proof of that.

He went once more to the superintendent's office at the Ostbahnhof and sounded him. The man was in a cantankerous humor.

"I've told you there aren't any cars. Do you expect me to shake them out of my sleeve? Rolling stock doesn't last forever, tell your boss! I've got seven hundred cars laid up in the sheds waiting to be repaired if I can ever get more than a handful of men to work on them. Tell your boss to go to the army if he's so anxious to ship his stuff—they have the cars!" And because the superintendent was just exasperated enough, he let him copy down the name of the official in the War Ministry who was in charge of transportation. "Much good that'll do you," he added cynically; "they'll throw you out on your ear there, if you pester them!"

He went to the War Ministry.

He remembered how he had come here once before with Baron Ortner to get Franz and how awesome the ancient gray courtyard had seemed. This time he had business here; he was no longer an intruder, even though the freight superintendent had not sounded very encouraging.

He asked his way from a sergeant at an information desk and found an anteroom where a dozen important-looking men with brief cases and portfolios were already waiting. He was aware of a few patronizingly raised eyebrows at his appearance in the room. They were businessmen and manufacturers, and they talked easily, freely about raw materials, replacements of machinery, and the stock market, but he noticed that they were singularly reticent about the shipping problem which was the reason why they were here.

The adjutant made him wait until long after all the other men had disappeared one by one through the impressive double doors and had come out again. After that, there was some urgent official business, it appeared, to which the "*Herr Generalmajor*" had to attend. Forty minutes went by. Two more businessmen arrived, pompously introduced themselves to the adjutant, and were admitted before him. It lacked only a few minutes to noon when the adjutant finally said:

"All right, you may go in."

The major general turned out to be a massive-chested man with bristling gray hair, a flat and forbiddingly expressionless face, heavy-lidded eyes. He kept Peter standing in front of the ponderous desk while he hunted testily through the papers on the desk and in the top drawers for what proved to be nothing more important than a cloth penwiper. The trivial exhibition quieted the misgivings Peter had had on entering the imposing room. He realized that the general's uniform with the row of medals across the chest awed him only slightly, compared to the time when he had still been panting to get into the cadet school; it even irritated him subtly and made him more determined to get what he had come for. And because he was still kept waiting, he had time to reflect that Herta had had much to do with the coolly calculating confidence with which he was able now to face older men such as this one. *He wouldn't look so important without his uniform,* he thought; *Herta would probably laugh at him. And I don't care who he is—all I want is the cars!*

The major general had wiped both pens and had put them back on the sprawling silver inkstand. He raised his sleepy eyelids briefly.

"Yes?"

He stated his errand. But while he mentioned the firm in the very beginning as he had done to the adjutant outside, he was careful to let it appear that he had been sent to the ministry by the superintendent at the freight station; he did not want to commit Herr Straka to anything that Herr Straka could not easily disown in case he made a blunder of some sort. The adjutant himself had given him the clue to his strategy: if he was to be treated like a callow boy who could safely be ignored, then that gave him all the freedom of action he would need. As long as he appeared stupid enough, he could be as forward as he liked. . . .

The major general was tapping the edge of the desk impatiently with his forefinger. It was clear that he was about to interrupt and end the interview. Now was the time——

"The Hungarian gentleman is desperately anxious to get this shipment; he is willing to do anything; he gave cigars to people in the store just to get everything ready for shipping right away; he even offered one to me. . . ."

"Oh, really!" The major general's sleepy eyelids went up and his gray eyes looked alert. There was also an unmistakable trace of irritation around his mouth at the thought that a foolish clerk in a store should have had a chance to get such a rare article as cigars. It was exactly the reaction Peter had been hoping for.

"Yes, Havana-Cubas they were."

"Ah, and I suppose he had a whole cigar case full?"

"Oh, yes! He had a whole box full. I saw them myself."

Peevishly, the major general's hand went to a bronze ash tray with two cigar stumps in it and moved it a fraction of an inch. "Those Hungarians have everything!" he complained. He had entirely shed his official brusqueness; he might have been talking to a colleague in the coffee house.

"I believe they can get cigars in through Rumania now. . . ."

"Well, the next time you see that Croesus again you might tell him to give a few to an overworked officer, if he is handing them out so freely. . . ." It had been said lightly, as something so very unlikely and altogether too-good-to-be-true that he could afford to play with the idea for a moment. And, as if to mark the end of the frivolous interlude and to dispel any false impression about what he had just said, he added sternly: "You will tell your Herr Straka that at the moment the freight cars are quite out of the question.

Later perhaps. . . . We would like to facilitate shipments to Hungary all we can, especially of farm machinery. But at the moment, quite out of the question! Good day."

Nothing could have sounded more discouraging, but Peter left the gray building exultantly. There had been that minute or so when the major general had let himself go. . . .

He caught Herr Straka the moment he returned to his office from lunch. Herr Straka listened and frowned.

"Von Pötzl?"

"Yes, Herr Straka."

"You should not have gone to such an important official without my knowledge. You might have done the firm considerable harm. We depend on the army for everything."

"I made a point of it, Herr Straka, that I hadn't been sent by you and that I had just blundered into the War Ministry because of what I'd heard at the freight station."

"How can you be sure that von Pötzl meant what you thought he meant? If we were to offend him, we would be worse off than before. When I spoke of a present this morning, I thought of a few cigars perhaps or something from downstairs for one of the dispatchers at the station. But an army official, that is quite another matter. I think I had better go to the War Ministry myself."

Peter could already see his near-triumph slipping from his hand. He had always prided himself on using a minimum of words in reporting to Herr Straka, but this time he forgot about being terse in his anxiety to make Herr Straka see how scrupulously he had managed things. He explained about the fictitious dispenser of cigars he had conjured up for the major general—fictitious, because the Hungarian merchant had long ago left for Hungary again, and because the cigars he had handed out freely enough downstairs had not been Havana-Cubas, but cheaper ones—and he stressed the fact that in his role of a mere apprentice he could safely make advances that would not involve the firm. "That was why the *Herr Generalmajor* talked so freely to me, because he felt that nothing he said to me could—well—commit him in any way!"

He had the satisfaction of seeing Herr Straka at least partly convinced.

"And when do you think you ought to go back?"

"I think it would be all right in a couple of days. . . ."

"I shall have to think this over very carefully. At any rate, I shall consult some firms who supply the army and who deal with von Pötzl constantly. We'll see on Thursday morning. . . ."

He could think of little else during the next two days. If Herr Straka decided to go himself, then he would lose all credit for obtaining the cars. His initial step of boldly going to the War Ministry would even count against him, because Herr Straka would return to his original unfavorable impression that he had overreached himself. And Herr Straka would probably get the cars: he would deal with the major general as one man of the world with another, confidently, suavely, and it would all be easy and quite simple! It was only because new restrictions everywhere followed one another so rapidly, and because every day called for new improvisations to get around the restrictions in order to get business done at all, that Herr Straka had not already known about this particular avenue.

But on Thursday morning, Herr Straka went to the big safe and took out a box of cigars.

"I hesitate to do this. . . . And you had better wrap the box."

"I thought of taking the brief case this time. There were quite a number of people in the waiting room on Tuesday. I'll put some cardboard into the brief case, so that it'll look exactly the same after I've taken the cigars out."

Herr Straka suddenly grinned. "All right, and remember that the firm is not to be involved. . . ."

Once again he had to submit to a long wait in the outer room. But he had the satisfaction of being recognized by the major general:

"You again! I thought I was explicit enough the other day."

"I only came to deliver this——" He unbuckled the brief case and took out the parcel. "The gentleman I spoke of sent this with his compliments."

"Oh! . . ." The major general took the parcel with precisely the air of a man gruffly accepting a birthday gift from a friend and handed to him by a messenger. He picked up a paperknife and slit the string, then folded back the lid of the box and sniffed the cigars. "Quite fresh! Very nice of the gentleman—very nice, indeed." He pulled out a drawer and put the box inside, paper and all. "Now let me see: your shipment was for Hungary, as I recall?"

"Debrecen."

"Debrecen, Debrecen—" He had picked up a sheaf of papers which he rapidly glanced at and discarded one by one, until he came to a sheet he had evidently been looking for. "Well, it just happens that we have to make up a number of trains to evacuate matériel from Rumania. I think we might be able to spare the necessary cars for our Hungarian neighbor—that will be on Monday. You will have to arrange about loading at the station. How many cars?"

"Sixteen."

"Sixteen—" He had already pushed the buzzer on his desk. To the adjutant he said: "Take this young man, will you, Lieutenant, and have a release for sixteen cars made out for—what was your firm again—?"

"Straka and Sons!"

"—for Straka and Sons, on one of the Rumanian trains we've scheduled for Monday." His voice was blandly bureaucratic again: "You will receive the necessary vouchers outside. Good day."

Herr Straka's astonishment—"Then you really got them!"—showed him the full extent of his success. He could sense Herr Straka's reluctant acceptance of a state of affairs in which an apprentice with a box of cigars, however priceless cigars might be nowadays, could obtain a result which had defied the time-honored, dignified channels of business procedure. But he also knew that Herr Straka had been forced to admit his preposterous value as a go-between. He had scored heavily.

He went twice more to the War Ministry when they were unable to get cars; the major general remembered him, and the adjutant no longer made him wait quite so long. And Herr Straka had got into the habit of sending him to other government offices—for export permits, for supplies of nickel and copper and charcoal for customers and for their own two factories, to dispatch payment on army accounts so that the constant rise in prices would not wipe out the firm's profits before the bills were paid.

It was always the same: the desperate tug between army orders and the shortage of raw materials, the delays in overworked government offices, and the accessibility of officials to discreet presents—provided there could be no imputation to their honesty and above all their dignity. Where a bribe would have been turned down frigidly and might have hurt the firm that dared offer it, a box of cigars presented with just the right shade of casualness became an amenity that could be answered by another amenity. . . .

But Herr Straka's greatest tribute to his new role came in September: he was sent to the steel mill in Styria to spy. It was Herr Lehnert who had originally been slated to go, but Herr Lehnert had developed a boil on his neck, such as many people were getting nowadays from the poor food, and he was barely able to drag himself around the store. One evening, Herr Straka entrusted him with the exciting job.

On the face of it, his mission was to take a set of blueprints and army specifications to Styria and to find out from the manager of the mill whether the drop hammers could forge the extra-heavy axles and how soon delivery could be made. There were certain modifications in the weight of the axles which would be permissible provided other compensatory features in the quality of the steel made up for it; the modifications did not show on the blueprints and had been arrived at verbally when Herr Straka had negotiated the contract with the army engineers. To that extent the assignment was important, but simple enough; but there was more to it. . . . There were rumors of another strike, such as there had been in January, at all the steel mills in Styria. There had already been food riots in Graz. The manager of the mill had reported that this time his men were threatening to join the strike, although they had stuck to their jobs in January and had not walked out. What he was to find out—"discreetly!" Herr Straka warned. "Perhaps you can sound out some of the men"—was what had caused the men to change their attitude, and also what had caused production in the mill to drop off since July.

He took the train for Styria the next morning, got there in the evening and went to the hotel where Herr Straka had told him to go, and early the following morning reported to the manager of the mill. It required less than half an hour to go over the blueprints and to deliver the instructions with which he had been charged. He was told to come back at three for the reply. It gave him the chance he needed to wander through the shops and to talk to the men. . . .

It was even easier than he had thought. The mill employed barely two hundred men and was run with the same old-fashioned, patriarchal informality as the store. Except for the Styrian dialect of the men he felt completely at home. The men, he found, agreed on a number of things: they were proudly loyal to Herr Straka, whom they saw two or three times a year; they had all of them the same complaint about the failure of the new harvest to increase the quantity of bread they were allowed; they were as weary of the war as people in Vienna were; and they were going to join the proposed strike not so much because of the shortage of food as because of their dissatisfaction with the manager. The manager—as Peter had seen himself—was a devoted, capable man who was proud of his long record with the mill and harassed by the sudden falling off of production in June. It appeared that in July the manager had added an extra hour to the working day of the men. "You can't work a twelve-hour day with nothing in your belly," one of the men complained. "I've worked here for twenty-four years and I've never held with all of these newfangled ideas about strikes. Strikes are for hoodlums who don't want to work anyway. But now with no more food than in the winter and an extra hour of work every day . . ."

It was all he needed to know.

He was through at the manager's office by half past four and he was free to spend the rest of the afternoon and all of the following day as he liked, since Herr Straka had told him to look on the Saturday as a vacation in case he finished all the business on the first day, and to stay over until Sunday morning if he wished. He played with the idea of spending the day in Graz, which was only twenty miles away. But his elation over his success and the opportunity of impressing Herr Straka with his efficiency would not let him rest; he found that by traveling all night he could be back in Vienna and in Herr Straka's office at ten the next morning, two whole days before Herr Straka would be expecting him. He took the night train. . . .

But there was still another reason for his eagerness to get back: he did not want to miss the Sunday afternoon with Herta. There were only two more weeks left before Herr Straka's family would move back into town, thus putting an end to the long, lazy evenings in Herta's room and to the wonderful suppers Herta had fixed for them. But more threatening than that, Herta's corporal had been wounded and was to get his furlough at last. And if he had been the one who had teased Herta about her corporal in the beginning, it was Herta now who mentioned the soldier with exasperating frequency and even held the corporal over him as a club.

For he had lately come to rebel against Herta's insistence on going to the Prater every Sunday afternoon. After the first few Sundays, the insipid musical comedies and the childish excitements of the amusement park had begun to pall on him. They had even quarreled about it recently, and although he had always given in to her in the end, he had found himself becoming critical of her in other ways. Then the threat of the corporal's furlough, and the added threat that Herta might marry him, had whetted his passion all over again. He felt that each evening with Herta now might be his last—for while he had come to know that Herta was free from any superficial prudishness, he also knew she could be inflexible about what she considered proper and decorous, and she had already said: "Do you think that after I'm married or really engaged, I'm ever going to see you again!" in a tone that had left no room for doubt.

She said it again this very Sunday afternoon when he had hurried back from Styria.

He came to wait with quivering suspense for the special delivery letter by which they had agreed that she was to let him know that the corporal had arrived.

And then, unexpectedly, it was not the corporal who arrived and forced him away from Herta—but Franz!

Chapter Forty-Four

FRANZ had been wounded—seriously, this time. Shell shock!

. . . one knew by now what that meant. It was not for nothing that one had seen dozens of soldiers with that horrible helpless tremor that seemed to infect their very bones, that convulsive twitching of the head and limbs that was like a major protest over and above the sickeningly exposed quivering of the flesh.

Poldi and *she* rushed out to Baden the moment the curt official notice told them where Franz was. They came home in the evening equally mute and shut up in their separate fears. A big shell had exploded close to Franz—the wound which a shell fragment had made on Franz's head was not dangerous, the doctor had said—but Franz had known them for only a few minutes at a time!

It was impossible to find out any more than that from Poldi or from her. He had to wait until Sunday when he could go and see for himself. Herta pouted at his proposed neglect. He refused to take her along. . . .

He realized guiltily, the moment he laid eyes on Franz, how selfish his own worst fears had been from the relief he felt: Franz did not shake! He was alarmingly tense and his eyes burned with feverish wakefulness, but he did not shake. He was by himself in a friendly room in the resort hotel which had been turned into an officers' hospital, and his window looked out on four ancient trees which rustled lazily in the autumn stillness, but the window—was it only chance?—was barred. Franz's taut restlessness and the fact that Franz had recognized him at once, intimately, with an air of having seen him only half an hour ago, prodded his new alarm. Nothing was as he had pictured it. There were moments when Franz was disconcertingly, nakedly clear about everything and even asked about the store. Only, the starkly preoccupied tenseness never relaxed.

Something monstrous seemed to terrify Franz. Yet apparently his anxiety had no connection with bursting shells or the front: he did not even seem aware of the heavy white bandage on his head. What he wanted to know was whether his dress suit was pressed, whether the tailor had brought it back. He seemed to have an obsession about a shiny place on one sleeve and about moth holes in the suit—also about what time it was! Every few minutes Franz would pull his wrist watch from under the pillow to look, then start to strap it on his wrist, only to take it off and place it carefully beside him under the pillow where he could reach it instantly.

"What about the dress shirts? Did Mother send them out?"

"Yes, of course, Franz."

"Are they back?"

"They're all in your dresser, all ready for you to put on."

Again the watch. Franz was clasping it so tightly that Peter was afraid his white-knuckled fingers would make the case spring apart.

"What is it, Franz? That's a new watch, isn't it? Let me see it!"

Franz seized his elbow with a fierce grip and pulled him closer: "What time is it?"

"Twenty after three . . ."

"I have to watch for four o'clock!"

"But it isn't anywhere near four yet, Franz."

For a little while Franz lay back on his pillow. Only the fixed stare of his dilated pale-blue eyes spoke of the furious activity which must be going on in his head. When Franz spoke again his voice was wary, almost sly.

"Have you seen Bianca?"

Peter was at a loss. Bianca! Now what was he going to say? Poldi had warned him especially that he must not say anything to excite Franz, and so had the nurse who brought him to the room. He decided to lie—

"Yes, Franz."

"When?" Franz had clutched his wrist with that desperate strength he had in his long fingers now. "Does she know I'm here? Is she coming to see me?"

"She's coming just as soon as the doctors will let her come," he lied again. He felt guilty because of the avidity with which Franz was hanging on his words. . . . "But you must get better first. You wouldn't want her to come until you can take her walking out in the garden, would you?"

"She's going to come?"

"Of course she is."

Again Franz lay quiet for a few minutes. Then a terrible anxiety made him start from the pillow. He had already jerked the watch out from under the pillow——

"At four they start!" Franz whispered. "Every day!"

"Who, Franz?"

". . . radio waves!" Terror sharpened Franz's features. He was again pressing the watch crystal so tightly with his thumb that Peter expected it to break.

"All right," he acquiesced. "We'll both watch. Let me hold it."

With a childlike accent that cut Peter to the heart, Franz pleaded:

"You won't leave me! You're going to stay?"

"Of course I'll stay. We'll fight them together."

Franz had let him have the watch. His bandaged head was pressed far down into the pillow as he stared up at the ceiling. He seemed to be listening. . . . As deftly as he could, Peter spun the hands of the watch forward to a quarter past four. He was just in time. Franz was already groping under the pillow, reaching toward him——

"What time? Let me have my watch! . . ."

"But it's already after four. Look!" He tried to sound very gay. "You see, nothing happened at all!"

"You don't know—they're after me all the time—it's Steinhof! They turn on the waves, radio waves—I have to be ready for them."

Instantly the glistening golden cupola of the asylum church flashed before Peter's eyes. A remnant of the secret terror with which he himself had always watched the sun play on the shining metal dome beyond the Schmeltz came wide-awake. He had to fight down a panicky consciousness of the similarity between Franz with his bandaged head here in this barred room and Father in Steinhof. *So that was it!* Franz was scared of *that*, had been scared of it for a long time. He remembered how Franz had flown into a rage that time when he had quoted Karl Breitner who had called Father a—what was it?—a dipsomaniac! But, on the other hand,

Franz had certainly not been worried by anything like that since Father died. What had brought all that back?

Hastily, to hide his thoughts, he said:

"Nonsense, Franz! Steinhof's on the other side of Vienna. They can't get you here. It's thirty miles. They can't send this far. I know all about machines. . . ."

Perspiration had broken out on Franz's forehead where the bandage had left a narrow strip of skin exposed above the eyes. Franz was breathing hard and yet carefully as if to propitiate the enemy that was all around.

"Don't go!"

"I won't. I wouldn't think of it," Peter tried to joke. He cast around frenziedly for something to distract Franz. He mentioned Baron Ortner and saw instantly that that was a mistake: Franz frowned. There was no time to think out the explanation for that. He told Franz that Herr Straka had asked about him and saw that he was talking to deaf ears. The only thing that remained was the dress suit Franz had been so anxious about before——

"Your dress suit is all ready, Franz."

It worked!

"How about the shiny place?"

"There isn't any shiny place. It's as good as new. You'll look grand in it. . . ."

But now Franz had lost interest in the suit. What else was there to say?

Suddenly Franz sat up and threw off the blanket—"I've got to get away from here!"

For a moment Peter thought of running out into the corridor to call the nurse who had looked in through the door several times. But he was also afraid to leave Franz. He tried to humor him:

"You mean because of the waves?"

"I've got to get away!"

"But look—look at your watch! It's long after four. It's all right now."

"Are you sure?"

"Of course! You must lie down or the nurse will bawl me out."

Slowly Franz let himself be persuaded. When Peter had folded the blanket over him, Franz seized his hand and held onto it with that fearfully strong and yet childlike grip that was itself a desperate plea—

"You won't leave me alone?"

A fierce anger rose in Peter against the war. He thought hotly: *They oughtn't to take people like Franz! He's not hard enough for war. It oughtn't to be allowed.*

For minutes now Franz had been lying quietly, except that Peter could feel the muscles of his fingers tighten and relax and tighten again over his own hand, as if they were speaking almost. He took comfort from seeing Franz suddenly remember something he had said——

"You're sure Bianca is going to come?"

"Dead sure."

"Do you remember the time we were in Schönbrunn?"

"Of course, and we walked to the Hietzinger gate——"

"The *Frau Baronin* won't let her come! And her uncle, the general!" Franz had again gripped his wrist. "You know, they want to put me out of the way! They don't like me. They want to put me out in Steinhof! You won't let them, will you?" The next instant, Franz had thrown off his blanket again. "I have to get up. There's a dress parade for the general. . . ."

He let Franz talk and tried only to calm him from time to time. Over and over, the fear of Bianca's mother showed its head; it had taken the place of that earlier dread of Steinhof.

Once, as he sat there beside Franz's bed, Peter thought of Herta waiting for him. *Herta will be angry,* he thought. But he hated to leave Franz, even when the nurse came into the room and nodded meaningly. . . .

One thing was clear to him on the long ride back on the electric train: whatever the shell explosion had done to Franz, the fear in Franz now had been there long before, ever since Franz had returned to the front almost a year ago. Bianca's mother was involved, and Steinhof. The head wound must have made Franz think of Father—else why was he in such terror of Steinhof?

He felt proud of figuring it all out. But when he got home he was careful not to let Poldi or her see what he thought. He mentioned only casually how Franz had fretted for Bianca, in the hope that Poldi might then be more likely to decide that it would be good for Franz to let Bianca know and ask her to come. He saw that his suggestion met with a resistance in Poldi that was at least as fierce as *her* silent resentment of Bianca had been all along.

He ate his supper and hurried out to Hietzing. Herta was peevish and he could not shake off the shadow of his afternoon with Franz. The evening was spoiled. They went to a movie and when they got back to Herr Straka's house, Herta stopped him in the door: "It's late. I'm tired." He realized that she was trying to punish him for the wasted afternoon. He minded hardly at all. . . .

If he had felt vaguely uncomfortable and even disingenuous somehow when he had first mentioned Bianca at home, the role played by his own desire to see Bianca again became clearer to him during the week. He was irresistibly driven to speak of Bianca again. A bitter argument with both Poldi and *her* was the result. He saw that he had if anything underestimated the depth of their bitterness against her. According to *her*, especially, it was all Bianca's fault. Bianca in her mere tone of voice became a seductress who had led Franz astray. And however preposterous her view might appear to him, he was forced to admit that in one respect at least she knew more than he: it appeared that when Bianca's mother had forbidden Franz to see Bianca again last fall, Bianca's mother had bluntly referred to Father's having died in Steinhof! It was useless for him to argue that Bianca could not be held responsible for what her mother had said, and that seeing Bianca would help Franz get well. . . .

His second trip to Baden the following Sunday afternoon only confirmed him in his view. Franz was better precisely because all his fears now centered in Bianca herself. His obsession with Steinhof and the watch had yielded to a much less terrifying if equally consuming and pitiful dread that Bianca might not come. It was true that Franz tried several times to tear the bandage from his head, but that was because at moments Franz had a feverish notion that Bianca might come presently and because he did not want her to see him with the bandage on. Peter felt reassured. Within the framework of Franz's fear, everything Franz said or wanted to do sounded logical and sane enough. But he saw also that Franz's desperate insistence on seeing Bianca had created a new problem for him. Franz wanted to know where he had seen Bianca and when. He wanted every detail. . . .

The lie he had told so lightly the week before had to be elaborated, buttressed, acted out—or Franz would lose faith in him and then the harm would be greater than before. For Franz was looking on him now as an ally against Poldi and *her*. He said with breathless urgency: "You mustn't tell Mother anything—or Poldi! They won't let her come and see me—I must see her, right away! We've always been close, you and I, haven't we? You know, there's a major who is after Bianca all the time, a big landowner down there in Hungary who wants to marry her!"

He promised Franz everything. . . .

But the problem—he saw—his problem, had become much more acute. It would not always be possible to stall Franz off. How was he to get in touch with Bianca and what was he to say? She was probably still on the estate in Hungary. . . . And supposing he did get her address from one of the letters which must be somewhere in Franz's desk, what was to assure him that she would even be willing to come? She might have changed toward Franz in spite of the number of times she had apparently gone out with him last fall: there was that rich major Franz was so worried about. . . . The longer he thought about it, the more presumptuous Franz's passion appeared. Yet he was aware of a happy tremor of excitement every time he returned to the enthralling task of planning the letter he was going to write. Only, he told himself, not yet! After Franz was better—perhaps in a week!

At home, between Poldi and *her*, Bianca played a more sinister role. They had made the mistake of letting Franz see how much they disapproved of her. As a result, for days now, Franz had barely spoken to them when they had gone to visit him. Once, Franz had been so excited that the nurse had even sent *her* away. *She* was so upset that even the fact that Franz was not delirious any more was no comfort to her. And because they knew that he was on Franz's side, their antagonism to Bianca extended to him.

It was a gloomy week. The only cheerful note was Wednesday noon when Peter found that Baron Ortner had called. Baron Ortner had been to see Franz; he was in town for a few days and he had promised to call again. Peter had missed him by only a few minutes—he made a point of hurrying home for lunch to catch him the next time he came.

He got home early like that on Friday noon and immediately saw the basket of oranges—evidently from some expensive shop which could still obtain oranges—and the smaller cardboard box. It looked as if Baron Ortner had called again, but something about her bristling silence and about the hostile isolation in which the basket and the cardboard box sat on the very edge of Father's desk in the living room disconcerted him. He asked:

"Was Baron Ortner here?"

She went on ladling out soup hostilely.

"Is there any bad news? Anything about Franz?"

"What more do you want to happen to Franz? Hasn't there been enough?"

"Well, who was it? Was it Herr Schmidtmeyer?"

"It was that girl, if you must know! Coming in here like her ladyship and wanting a written slip so's she can go and upset him some more. I don't need her oranges and eggs!"

"Did you give it to her?"

"Over my dead body! She's done enough harm."

It was all, he knew, he would get out of her.

What had Bianca looked like? How had she sounded? What had she worn?

The question pursued him all through the afternoon. He found it hard to concentrate on the springs and axles he was getting together for a customer; the consciousness of Bianca clung to him like a sweet, vibrant haze. And then, unbelievably, in the very midst of the store, among the blacksmiths and mechanics in the crowded aisle in front of Herr Lehnert's desk, he saw for himself—

Herr Lehnert had come out into the storeroom after him:

"A young lady inside to talk to you—since when have you been palling around with girls like that?"

Poldi! was his first thought. But Herr Lehnert would have taken Poldi in his stride; he would not have had this faintly awed, fatuous air. . . .

She was standing a little away from the counter—cool, slim, elegant, but above all arresting because of the intense aliveness one felt—in a little island of space the men had made for her by withdrawing ever so little and surreptitiously eying her. He was proud of the tribute to her, but it increased his awkwardness. And he had not counted on being now so much taller than she; it made him feel gangling and exasperatingly immature. But she was already holding out her hand with that same enthrallingly grave eagerness he remembered from Schönbrunn, and her dark eyes engrossed him so that he forgot about Herr Lehnert and the men who were watching, and worried instead about his hands which were bound to be oily from handling the springs——

"Hello, Peter! I had to see you about Franz. Is there any place where we can talk?"

It was a challenge to the helpless paralysis which still kept him rooted to the spot.

"Yes, of course. . . . We can go out into the courtyard or out into the street, if you don't mind that."

"Let's go outside."

He turned his customer over to Herr Lehnert, then held the door for her out into the street. He had not bothered to get a hat.

"So this is where you work. It's big, isn't it?"

"Those are the warehouses up there. . . ." He felt proud of the long line of drays in the Kohlgasse because she seemed impressed. "There are two more warehouses over in the next street."

"Do you still like it here?"

"Yes, I do."

They had walked nearly the length of the block.

"How is he?"

He had been expecting the question, yet her intensity startled him. It also lifted him on such a swell of joy that he was afraid his happiness might show in his voice. *He was bound to see her again!*

"I think he was much better last Sunday."

"He is very sick, isn't he? Tell me!"

"Well, I don't know. The doctor says the wound on his head is healing all right, and he isn't delirious any more."

"I was at your house this morning. His mother hates me! She won't let me go and see Franz. I must see him!"

"Perhaps Baron Ortner—"

"Heinrich won't take me, either! Besides, he's going back to Innsbruck tomorrow morning—has Franz asked for me?"

He felt extravagantly happy to be able to say something that she wanted to hear.

"Yes, he has."

"What did he say?"

"Well, he spoke of you all the time."

"Did he?" Her dark eyes fastened on him as if she wanted to make certain that he wasn't lying. "Frau Bartsch said that he didn't want to see me. That isn't true, is it?"

"No! Franz even wanted to tear off his bandage last Sunday and get up from bed because he thought you might be coming. I had a hard time."

"Really? Look, you must take me with you when you go again! You will, won't you? Can you go tomorrow?"

"I can't tomorrow. Besides, Poldi will be there tomorrow. I'm going on Sunday. . . ."

"What time?"

"About two o'clock."

They arranged—or rather, she proposed and he agreed happily—to meet at the electric train station in Baden. She turned down his offer to find her a cab.

"I'll walk. You won't fail me, will you?" Again she held out her hand and he thrilled to its quick, firm pressure that was like a boy's and yet like a caress. "And you mustn't say anything at home!"

He watched exultantly as she walked away toward the Innere Stadt. *She was beautiful! How lucky that Franz was ill and that things had turned out the way they had.* He found it difficult to keep his mind on the complicated carriage fittings the customer from Moravia wanted in the store. . . .

By Sunday his anticipation was shot through with worry that she might not show up. He dressed more carefully than he ever remembered doing before and he got to Baden forty minutes ahead of time. She herself was ten minutes early. She wore a charming beige suit, and her appearance was made even gayer by the festive confectioner's cartons in her hands. Her eagerness when she saw him pierced him with a happiness that was like a stab. The sweetness became more diffuse but it did not leave him as he walked beside her through the Sunday-mellow town and listened to her deliciously exotic voice:

"You must say I'm a cousin or they won't let me in. I tried Thursday afternoon. . . ."

They got by the white-coated orderly downstairs, but they had not reckoned with the Sister at the little desk on Franz's floor. The Sister was unyielding:

"Only members of the immediate family!" She sounded unnecessarily defiant, so that Peter was almost certain that Poldi had spoken to her. "Sorry—doctor's orders!" she said.

He feared for a moment that Bianca would flare up. Her dark eyes flashed dangerously. "But I brought all these things!"

"I shall be glad to take them in to Lieutenant Bartsch—or the young man can take them in now."

They drew away from her into a glassed-in bay. Bianca undid the strings of the confectionery cartons from her hand. She jerked impatiently at the gay silk ribbons so that he had an impression that she was crying with her fingers instead of with her eyes.

"I'll wait for you outside."

"But I may have to stay. Franz may want me to stay for quite a while."

"It doesn't matter. I'll get some papers. I'll wait."

He did not dare tell Franz that Bianca was just outside. Franz's excitement at the bare mention that the cakes and the chocolates in the little cardboard boxes were from Bianca frightened him. Franz had snatched at the little boxes and had instantly sat up in his bed——

"Where is she? Is Bianca here?"

He had to pretend that Bianca had brought the things to him at the store. And he had to try to calm Franz by assuring him that Bianca would come herself just as soon as the doctors would let her come, as soon as Franz was even a little better. . . . It was hard to get Franz to lie quietly. He insisted on untying the soft silk ribbons on each of the cardboard boxes in turn, over and over again, to look inside, tie up each box with infinite care, only to reopen it a minute later. Again Peter had the impression that Franz was like a child. Nor could he quench Franz's need to know how Bianca had looked in the store and what she had said. Once, Franz's anxiety about Bianca's mother reared its head.

"Does her mother know?"

"What's it matter?" he tried to joke. "Since Bianca is going to come. You aren't in love with her mother—the dragon!"

Franz smiled for the first time. For a second or two the childlike happiness that could transfigure Franz's face was back in his eyes.

"You are sure Bianca said she would come here?"

"Of course she did. It's only a matter of a few weeks—just as soon as your wound is all healed."

It went on and on. The same question tortured by the still lingering fear into a dozen shapes. Yet Peter was certain that the presents from Bianca had done more good than harm. The flimsy ribbons on the confectioner's boxes were a life line for Franz. He stayed until four, alternately torn by the thought of Bianca waiting for him outside and by Franz's need for him here. It struck him once how curiously their roles were reversed from the time they had been at Baron Ortner's hunting lodge: now it was Franz who hung on every shred of information about her, received it gratefully, wanted more.

He left at a few minutes after four.

Bianca was waiting for him in the park. It looked as if she had not once glanced at the papers beside her on the bench. She ignored them when she got up and started toward him with her resolute, eager—aristocratic, he thought it, because it somehow reminded him of her hunting and riding on the vast estate Franz had described—and yet infinitely feminine stride.

"How is he?"

"Much better. He wasn't delirious at all."

"You aren't just saying that?"

"No. It was because of the cakes—" he wanted to say "because of you," but he felt suddenly shy—"that he was so much better."

"And you told him that I'd sent them?"

He described how Franz had held on to each cardboard box. She brightened up.

"Did he know I was downstairs?"

"I didn't dare tell him that. He would have been too excited. He would have wanted to come downstairs."

She seemed content. They had walked out of the park which surrounded the old resort hotel toward the station. When they came to a coffeehouse, Peter took his courage in both hands and asked her inside.

She gave him one of those grave, enveloping glances which were like a smile.

"You're sweet! I can't—I have to call on a girl I knew in boarding school. Mama doesn't know that Franz is in Baden. I got Heinrich not to tell her. You might come with me as far as the house if you like—there's a taxi."

He felt thrilled riding down the esplanade in the open taxi with her. She made him take down her telephone number and promise to call her if Franz got worse. The house where she was going came much too soon. She got out in front of a ponderous grille gate that looked as if it had not been opened for a long time.

"I'd ask you to come inside but there's only my friend and her grandmother who's a terrible bore. You'll telephone?"

"Yes."

"Next Sunday, then. Good-by . . ."

While the taxi turned around, he watched her walk up the short avenue of plane trees to the hulking old villa. He waited until she had stepped through the door. It seemed out of keeping not to ride back to the station in state, although his jubilance would have made him prefer to walk. The memory of her presence dictated his mood even on the train. It was as if she were sitting beside him still. The other passengers struck him as suddenly unforgivably gross, and when a woman's elbow touched him accidentally, he shrank as if he had been defiled. He wanted imperiously to be alone to steep himself further in the joyous sensations Bianca had left with him; yet at the same time he wanted people to notice the distinction Bianca's eyes had conferred on him and which must be visible to everyone.

It was not a mood to meet Herta with; yet for that very reason, perversely, he clung to it. Herta was explosive over his neglect. They had already quarreled on the very evening before Bianca had so miraculously appeared in the store. They had been in the little hotel Herr Benesch had told him about and where he had taken Herta for the second time since Herr Straka's family had moved back into town. Herta's wrathful flouncing amid the equivocal, overstuffed elegance of the hotel room had rekindled his passion then, and they had made it up.

This time he did not even bother to excuse himself for spoiling her Sunday afternoon. It infuriated her. He was conscious of an irresistible desire to provoke her wrath. It was, he told himself, the fault of her wrists! He had noticed at once when he had met her on the Gürtel how raw and red they were when he compared them to Bianca's slender wrists. In an instant, all of Herta had become summed up in her pink-cheeked plumpness which now fairly shrieked at him. He found himself critical of her hat, of the long kid gloves which Frau Straka had probably passed on to her and which seemed so out of place on her hands, but most of all of her insistence to go to still another operetta. He sat through it in truculent scorn. When they came out of the theater, he headed deliberately for the little hotel.

She rebelled:

"What do you want to go that way for?"

"I thought we might—"

"I'm not going there any more!"

"Why?"

"I'm not that kind of a girl, that's why! I'm not going to a hotel like that at night."

"You didn't mind on Thursday."

"It wasn't as late as this."

Although somewhat to his own surprise he felt not the least desire for her, knew in fact that he would have felt it to be a desecration of his afternoon with Bianca to have come close to Herta again, yet he sulked. He realized vaguely that his very sense of duplicity toward Herta made him feel now that he owed it to her to pretend to feel hurt. They did not speak until they got off the streetcar in Hietzing a few blocks from Herr Straka's house; then she suddenly stopped under a street lamp to open her pocketbook and to pull out a postcard which she thrust at him.

"There! Maybe you thought Hans wasn't coming! Maybe you thought I was just fooling. Read it! He's coming on Tuesday!"

"I believe you."

"And what's more there's been a man who's been after me to go out with him for weeks! You needn't think I have to sit around every Sunday afternoon and wait for you!"

"It isn't my fault if my cousin is sick. I had to go and see him, didn't I?"

"You could have taken me along!"

"Well, if Hans is going to be here, I wouldn't be able to see you anyway. . . ."

"You might have, if you had acted differently!"

A poignant alarm at the danger spelled out by Herta's reproach to the whole exquisite fabric of his feelings for Bianca exploded deliciously into a vast sense of relief—of something escaped.

They both ignored the sheltered nook between the bushes along the driveway where, ever since Herr Straka's family and the other servants had moved back into the house, they had always lingered over their good-bys. . . .

But he could not, in spite of Bianca, keep from feeling uncomfortable when he had to go to Herr Straka's house during the week. Herta's reproachful anger only showed him how far from irreparable the rift between them was. She managed to sting him in a dozen ways with the still so live memory of her flesh. She even goaded him with the pointed absence of the little packages of things to eat, which she had always smuggled into his pockets before. He had to get at least a block away from Herr Straka's house before he could recapture the feeling of joy in the sacrifices he was making for Bianca's sake. But once he was by himself, it was easy to persuade himself that giving up Herta was a necessary tribute to the purity of his love, a guarantee of his intoxicating selflessness where Bianca was concerned, of a piece with his willingness to see Bianca in love with Franz.

The weeks became mere intervals between Sunday and Sunday when he could see Bianca again. The weekdays were endless and dull. He clutched at every chance at home to talk about Franz, since even *her* open hostility to Bianca was preferable to not being able to talk about her at all. Her resentment of Bianca had grown. Franz was so much better that they could no longer keep her from visiting Franz. He argued that it was wholly due to Bianca that Franz was so much improved; she had another explanation for it and one that pleased her enormously: Franz had become very devout!

Franz not only went to early Mass every day, but he had made Poldi buy him a copy of the *Imitation of Christ* and then a Latin breviary such as the priests carried around. The religious books lay prominently, almost ostentatiously, on his night-table along with a rosary. Between one week and the next, a humorless, stubborn-fibered earnestness had taken possession of Franz.

Peter felt more alarmed by it than he had been by the delirious ravings about Steinhof. Why this inexplicable, gloomy piety now that Bianca had come? Franz should have been carefree and glad! Yet Bianca was somehow connected with it—else, why did *she* at home have that righteous smugness which had finally even let her use the eggs Bianca had brought and which *she* had hitherto kept in a bowl in the cupboard as if they had been faintly poisonous.

He asked for an afternoon off at the store and went out to Baden during the week in the hope of solving the mystery. Franz was in his new room in the convalescent wing, reading still another of the black devotional books. It was impossible at first to get Franz to talk about anything but the *Confessions of St. Augustine!* Franz was full of it and full of his dreary religious intensity. He even wanted him to take the *Confessions* along and to read them at once. . . . There was no question about it: something abstracted, otherworldly, priggish had come into Franz. *What good is this kind of recovery*—Peter found himself worrying—*if Franz is going to be so changed, if he has forgotten to joke and to laugh!*

When he cautiously steered the talk around to Bianca, he found still more cause for alarm: Franz was absurdly, bizarrely fixed on the idea that he was in honor bound to marry Bianca, that he owed it to her and to God. He sounded as if it were some doleful duty and as if all the obstacles that had worried him so before were no longer of any account. As he listened to Franz's dark hints at some unspeakable sin, Peter was torn by anger at Franz's bigoted arrogance which disposed of Bianca as if she needed not to be considered at all, and by a grimly amused curiosity as to what the sin really was that worried Franz—likely, nothing more serious than that Franz imagined that he had compromised Bianca somehow! But when, in the same breath, he suddenly thought of himself in Herta's room, he hastily shied away from the picture he had evoked. He found it unbearable suddenly to stay any longer with Franz, and he was aware all the rest of the week of a subtle impatience with Franz which he had to fight off to prove to himself that it was not prompted by jealousy. It was even more difficult to shake off his worry that Bianca might get tired of Franz. . . .

He felt only partially reassured when Bianca lightly dismissed Franz's religiousness the following Sunday afternoon:

"It's just an aftereffect of the shock. It's a regular phase. I asked our doctor about it. It doesn't hurt me if Franz prays. . . ."

He had been waiting for Bianca in the garden. It was he now who waited while she was inside. He himself spent only a few minutes with Franz when he first came—as soon as Bianca arrived, he always made some excuse to leave. He was not sure whether Franz knew that he waited for Bianca afterward, and the probability that Bianca had not spoken of it to Franz added a deliciously possessive tang to the lonely wait. It was the second Sunday in October and the leaves were falling fast. There was a stealthy chill in the air that made one feel restless rather than cold. When Bianca finally came to the bench where she had waited for him that first Sunday afternoon—their bench, he felt—she said briskly:

"Let's walk fast, shall we?"

They started up the esplanade toward the center of town. He noticed all over again, at a new pitch of joy, how boldly and freely she strode along so that her beauty made all the other women appear mincing and stale. It was only after a minute or two that he became aware of the preoccupation, the faint note of urgency, in the way she held her shoulders and had raised her chin. She said suddenly:

"You know, Peter, that I'm going to marry Franz?"

In spite of the number of times he had dreamed—hopelessly, it had always seemed—of just such an event, her announcement caught him off guard.

"But your mother! I thought—"

"Mama will have to accept it, whether she likes it or not. I'm of age—at least, I'm going to be next spring."

"But if she doesn't like Franz?"

"Mama is just being stuffy! The family made the same kind of fuss when she married Papa, but she went through with it all the same—just as I am going to marry Franz!" Her tone showed him she already considered that aspect of the matter as closed. Something else seemed to trouble her much more. She sounded curiously humble and uncertain after her outburst of only a minute ago: "Do you think Franz's mother will ever like me? She hates me, doesn't she? And Poldi does too!"

His very shame for *her* exasperating hostility to Bianca made him try to excuse her:

"No, it isn't that; it's just that she's worried about Franz—she is afraid that he might get worse again because of—well, your family. . . ."

"Franz is very much attached to his mother, isn't he? Especially now that he's so devout. He might listen to her."

"Oh, but he won't! . . ." He realized that he had protested too ardently, but she did not appear to have noticed it.

"But if his mother goes on not liking me?"

"She can't. You're much too—too wonderful, for her to keep on."

She had noticed this time. He went rigid with fear that she might take offence. Her eyes lingered on him with their enthralling attentiveness. She smiled:

"That's nice."

Something was sealed between them by her glance—a pact which at once brought him wonderfully close to her but also put him on his honor somehow.

"There's something else: you know, Franz said something the other day about becoming a priest!"

"He won't. He—" it was exquisitely difficult to get out the words— "Franz loves you terribly." A guilty exaltation at his daring turned into a poignant sense of sacrifice at having kept himself out of it this time.

Bianca had stopped. Her hand touched his arm——

"You are sweet!"

They were within a few short blocks of the house of Bianca's friend. She had already taken her hand away from his arm. "You'll do all you can—at home, I mean?"

"Yes."

He could barely trust his voice. The ravishing artificiality which spun them in like a caressing web made even his own voice an intruder and strange. Only Bianca's eyes and her faintly parted lips and the graceful tenseness of her shoulders belonged at the center of things.

As he walked back to the station he puzzled about it. It was odd that all the easy assurance with women he had gained from Herta should leave him so completely the moment Bianca looked at him, that he should feel as tremulous and excited as if the summer with Herta had never been. And it was odder still that he was happy to have it that way. Bianca's "You are sweet!" kept trembling in his ears. He suddenly thought of himself in the store—"hard, ruthless, calculating!" Those were the qualities he had wanted for himself.

Once again, he went over each moment of their walk. *It's all I need,* he thought happily. *Franz can marry Bianca. I even want him to, since Bianca is in love with him. I'll always have this afternoon. If I can see her from time to time, that'll be enough.*

He found himself almost inviting a test, and as if his fervor had a sinister power to provoke the event, the test came with jagged promptitude. Within two days, Poldi brought home the news that Franz was being sent home from the hospital. There was going to be an end to the precious moments with Bianca on Sunday afternoons, and little hope of seeing her at any other time, since Franz had been advised to go into the country right away.

It came as something of a shock, because Franz's dismissal from the hospital was so obviously premature. Only a week ago, when Poldi had asked, the doctor had said that Franz would not be well enough to leave before Christmas at the very earliest. There were all the hourly proofs that Franz was still far from well: the morbid piety, the tense restlessness which would not let Franz sit still without his picking up a pair of scissors and cutting endless fringes in any scrap of paper that happened to be lying around, the stern injunction Poldi had given him not to say anything to excite Franz, the veronal Franz had to take, the overmeticulous way in which he packed and repacked his suitcases and tested each strap a dozen times.

He was going to Vorarlberg, to the little town on the Swiss border where he had recuperated from the wound in his chest. It was a place of which the doctor had approved. . . . There were oddly disturbing implications in what the doctor had said to Franz: it seemed that there had suddenly been an unprecedented number of shell-shock cases among the officers on the Italian front and that the hospital in Baden was crowded to capacity. The doctor had warned: "Get as far away from Vienna as you can. Things aren't going so well. Vienna is going to be no place for you in the next few months. . . ."

Chapter Forty-Five

BIANCA had taken up his awareness to the point where he had barely noticed the changes that had been going on. Now he was suddenly forced to notice them, and not only because of what Franz's doctor had said—the news was suddenly everywhere that the Emperor had appealed to President Wilson for an armistice.

Not that the news in itself created any stir. People in the streets had reached a state of weariness from which nothing could rouse them any more. The headlines in the papers were dully passed from mouth to mouth, like bits of floating wreckage by drowning men who found each new piece of wood too frail.

Two Italian planes appeared over the city early one afternoon and even they aroused only a brief interest. They were the first enemy planes after four years of war and they looked handsome and fragile and oddly unreal hovering in the sky. Only a few people gathered at street corners to watch them and to wait for the bombs. Instead, the black spots which dropped reluctantly away from the planes turned into lazily spiraling plumes of leaflets which looked as if they would hang for hours in the air and then land somewhere miles away. . . .

He saw two of the leaflets which had come down over the Ostbahnhof and looked at them curiously. They were printed on cheap paper; they were phrased in a stilted, outlandish idiom; there were two spelling mistakes. One noticed that. The dispatcher who had picked them up pushed them across his desk—"You can have them. Now they are trying that . . ."

The message itself held no interest. It was even silly. "Throw off the yoke of the army!" it said. It wasn't that way at all! The army were Franz and the men from the store. They had all been trying to win the war. He remembered the exhilaration of the first two years—how far away all that seemed!—and the way people had brought their jewelry and had given all the brass fittings off their doors, until everything that had once been bronze and nickel and silver and gold was of gray iron now. After all, they had defeated the Russians and the Rumanians and the Serbs—though one had to make an effort to remember that, since it seemed to have made no difference at all. The hunger and the cold had gone on for years, the lack of soap and the clothes made of paper fiber like the twine they used in the store, the eternal maize bread and the jam made of beets! If there was anger, it was certainly not directed against the army—the sullen resentment one felt had to do with the farmers who were getting rich and the hoarders and profiteers. . . .

And yet, in spite of the indifference to the appeal for an armistice and to the Italian planes, the weight of despondency had grown greater somehow. More and more, when he rode on the streetcars, Peter was aware of the number of crippled men and especially of the shell-shock cases whose twitching heads and hands made them into so many manikin clocks ticking off the time of fear. It was as if all the maimed and exhausted had come out of their hiding places at once to assert themselves, to take over the city with their reproach. Twice in one day, Peter saw women collapse in the street. "Undernourished—what can you expect?" an elderly man had said in the Burggasse, had shrugged and passed on.

There were other signs of the new callousness bred by despair. The streetcars were so crowded at noon and at night that people fought to hang onto the platform steps on the wrong side of the cars. There were no longer any jokes prompted by the common risk of being brushed off. Where only a few months ago people had helped each other to hold on, they now pushed each other off. The indignant cry: "Where are your manners, there? Watch out!" brought no apology in reply; it was the man or the woman making the protest who was left behind. The thick, ruthless silence that separated people though they touched each other's hands was everywhere.

Only in the coffeehouses on Sunday mornings—he had taken to going to different ones each time—could one hear the proposed armistice discussed. The *Herr Hofrat* in the Mariahilferstrasse talked earnestly about something called "Wilson's Fourteen Points."

"If the Germans want to go on fighting, that's their business," the *Hofrat* said. "We can't! The country is exhausted, bled white. Wilson is offering us an honorable way out. Wilson—"

But the *Hofrat* was glumly silent the Sunday after Wilson's reply had been printed on every front page. Another man held the floor.

"Settle with our minorities!" the man stormed. "What does Wilson think we've been doing ever since '48? How does he think the country's held together all this time? If the Czechs want autonomy, let them have it. Good riddance, I say."

"It's not so easy," another man warned. "Our industry is all tied up in Bohemia. It's Austrian capital that's invested there."

"Anyway, there's your great man! That's how much faith one can put in his Fourteen Points."

Even the corpulent, puffy-cheeked man who had always truckled to the white-bearded *Hofrat* turned on him.

"Wilson is just using the Fourteen Points as propaganda to divide us internally. He doesn't intend to give us a separate armistice. We are forced to go on fighting, as I see it!"

"And how are you going to fight with nothing to fight with?" the *Hofrat* challenged the men. "At least, Wilson—"

The discussion was still going when Peter had to leave for his English lesson. . . .

And then, suddenly, there was no longer any room for discussion or for weighing Wilson's sincerity. News—alarming news—was pouring in from the Italian front. It did not appear in the newspapers—it was brought much more directly and frighteningly by the irregular hordes of soldiers that arrived in the stations on every train from the south.

The soldiers had given up. The Italians were rushing into the Tyrol. And in Bohemia the Czech riots were multiplying hourly.

The following morning the newspapers appeared with a mourning border and the stark announcement that the Emperor had sued for an unconditional armistice.

The soldiers kept flooding in from the south. They rode on the roofs of cars and were crowded into the locomotive cabs. They looked disorderly, unshaven, wild. Outside the Westbahnhof several thousands of them formed a grotesque outdoor market that spread clear down to the intersection of the Gürtel and the Mariahilferstrasse. They were selling their guns, and extra pairs of shoes, medals, puttees, cigarettes. It seemed that a number of them had helped themselves to the company stores when the Italians came. One heard rumors of sergeants who had got away with big amounts of regimental cash.

The soldiers were everywhere. It was strange to see so many of them without bayonets and belts, and without discipline. They no longer saluted officers, and more and more frequently one saw evidence of a more active hatred of rank. One morning while he was riding into the Innere Stadt to the bank, Peter watched two soldiers enter the streetcar. The two soldiers were noisy and quarrelsome; they pushed their way through the crowd and they kept on smoking after they were in the car. People had begun to watch them uneasily. In a corner sat an officer with black glasses and a row of medals on his chest. His head was thrust forward and up with the attentive, wooden jauntiness of the blind. The two soldiers spotted him and immediately shouldered their way through the car. One of them said with mock deference:

"Morning, *Herr Leutnant.*"

The lieutenant saluted gravely and smiled.

"The war's over!" the other soldier barked. "Haven't you heard? No more ribbons—" and he reached out for the medals on the officer's tunic.

A stout market woman who sat next to the officer slapped at the soldier's hand. "Can't you see he's blind?" she said angrily. "You ought to be ashamed of yourself!"

"Blind or not, let him take off his medals!"

Slowly the officer groped and lumbered to his feet. It was clear that he also had an artificial leg. His face was set as if he were facing a firing squad. He stood very erect.

". . . and only one leg!" The stout woman had shoved her basket off her lap and had pushed herself angrily up from her seat. "Can't you see that? You get away from here now or I'll show you a thing or two—attacking a blind man with a wooden leg. Hoodlums, that's what you are!"

Exclamations of "Shame!" came from other parts of the car.

The soldier who had been going to rip off the officer's medals muttered sullenly: "Well, let him take off the gold braid. There are no more officers now. We've had enough of that. . . ." But they beat a retreat and got off at the next stop.

It did not always end as innocently as that. Within a week the officers appeared without their insignia, and only the cut of their uniforms showed that they had been officers once.

Waiting—everybody seemed to be waiting. The whole city seemed coiled in sullen suspense. It seemed a miracle somehow that the streetcars still ran and that the stores opened at all. Then the news of the signing of the armistice, and suddenly a new cry was heard —just as the soldiers had blamed the officers for the rout on the Italian front, so now the cry changed to getting rid of the Emperor.

The talk ran sluggishly in the suburbs—bitterly, heatedly, in the tumultuous gatherings that collected at all hours along the Ring. As if by a magnet the soldiers and the thousands of men from the factories that had shut down with the armistice were drawn to the Ring. More and more in these groups one began to notice foreign-faced, passionate men who insinuated themselves into the discussion to speak of Russia and to preach the overthrow of the government. And the police, which formerly would have dispersed such gatherings as these, made only perfunctory efforts to break them up.

Armbruster was exultant at the proposed change in government. Peter had seen little of him while Franz had been sick, but now they were again thrown together during the two evenings of school each week.

"The people are going to run things now," Armbruster exulted; "you'll see!"

Peter went with him to a mass meeting of the Socialists. The meeting was in Floridsdorf where the munitions workers had struck in 1917, and again in June. A huge crowd was gathered outside the arsenal. There was the usual sprinkling of unkempt soldiers in uniforms. People were saying that over a hundred thousand soldiers from the provinces slept in railroad stations and in churches and parks.

A burly laborer who spoke from the top of a dray had a hard time making himself heard. Smaller groups were heatedly debating around the fringes of the crowd. The man on the dray spoke of the mismanagement of the war by the capitalists and the monarchy, and of the rights of labor. There were sporadic shouts of approval, but there was nothing new in what he said and the crowd soon wearied of him. A band of soldiers hoisted a soldier up on the dray. The soldier railed against the officers and the clergy in a thin, shrill voice. He was soon hoarse. "But we are going to change all that!" he shouted in a final attempt to match the violence of his gestures with his voice. There was raucous approval from the soldiers in the crowd. Another man attempted to speak from the dray and was barely listened to. The little groups on the fringes asserted themselves and the meeting broke up into groups, some large, some small. Again, as he listened with Armbruster, Peter noticed the half-dozen men with foreign voices who spoke of Russia and of dividing everything equally. There was something alarming about their cold, calculated passionateness as opposed to the fumbling, heated sincerity of the other men. In one group a man objected to one of the foreigners:

"We don't need all that here. Where do you come from anyway? We can handle our own affairs. Live and let live, is my motto."

"And I suppose the profiteers believe in that, too!" another man promptly jeered. "Just go and ask them for a loaf of bread when your children are hungry—or the Kaiser! He isn't hungry, I bet!"

The same contradictory charges against the Emperor which one heard on the Ring could also be heard here. One man accused the Empress of having betrayed the country in 1916 by secretly negotiating with her Bourbon cousin for peace—another accused the Emperor of callousness for not having tried to make peace before 1918.

"The people are the state!" one of the foreign men preached. "Everybody is entitled to a share of the common wealth. . . ."

"This is the revolution!" Armbruster triumphed on the way home.

"Do you think they'll do anything?" Peter asked. "What about the army and the police?"

"There is no more army, can't you see? The soldiers are fed up with the government, and the police are on our side, too. The Kaiser has got to abdicate!"

The next day in the store Peter had his doubts about it, and about the significance of the meetings and the bold talk of the Socialists. The time-honored hierarchy in the store had not been impaired; everything was as it had always been; it was impossible to imagine any of the clerks or helpers revolting against Herr Straka or even wanting to.

It was true that there had been changes in the store since the collapse, but the changes involved only the customers. For since the first day when the soldiers had appeared in the stations, prices had climbed fantastically. It was, everyone knew, because the value of the krone had tumbled abroad. Where formerly new stickers had been pasted over the original prices in the prewar catalogue every two or three months, it was impossible now to fix the price of any one article for more than a day. One simply went each morning to the glass cage, where Herr Kropfl had formerly been, and asked what percentage to add to the last price pasted in the catalogues: fifty per cent plus fifteen per cent plus three per cent. . . . It was like a game almost, for their new customers didn't mind in the least.

There had been an abrupt falling off in the familiar customers that had always crowded the store, a complete disappearance of the country blacksmiths and merchants since the defeat. Only now, after a week, a few neighborhood locksmiths and carpenters drifted back to buy a lock or a package of nails for some immediate repair. Yet the clerks were as busy as they had always been, for ever since early October there had been increasing numbers of foreign merchants who wanted to buy unheard of quantities of every kind of tool and machinery for Rumania and Poland and Serbia. Only for a day or two had the foreign merchants in their expensive clothes been absent from the store, apparently to sit in the coffeehouses on the Ring and size up the shape of things. With the signing of the armistice they were back to pile up even larger orders than before. The question now was only one of shipping the goods, for the freight stations were still so jammed with trains from the front that it was next to impossible to get freight moved.

There had even been pleasant changes due to the abrupt end of the war. Herr Emmerich, who was the real manager of the store, was back from the army and installed in the glass cage. Herr Kropfl was across the street in the office with the bookkeepers where he belonged. Herr Emmerich was serious and capable, and he had clearly accepted Herr Straka's rather than Herr Kropfl's estimate of Peter. It was pleasant now to go to the glass cage with Herr Emmerich behind the window to check the bills. . . . Then there was the Rumanian merchant who had become Peter's customer: the Rumanian spoke hardly any German at all, but he spoke English and Herr Lehnert had—dubiously, at first—turned the Rumanian over to him. The American catalogues Peter had studied and the conversations with Frau Hobbs-Pechlar proved valuable now. The Rumanian made him a present of two hundred kronen after the first order was complete, and of three hundred kronen after the second one. And the Rumanian wanted a good many things of which they were out in the store: he had the chance of finding the files and nails and drills, buying them for the Rumanian, and making a profit on his own.

Something detached and even patronizing crept into his attitude toward the turgid, sluggish suspense from his contact with the Rumanian and the other foreign merchants. The feeling that he was really no part of Vienna because his father was English and because Mizzi was in America reasserted itself in him. And there was added to it the memory of his last afternoon with Bianca—still so vivid, that thinking about it he could watch two soldiers slugging each other viciously on the Gürtel over a tin of sardines without really seeing them—the memory of what Bianca had said, and of his intoxicating renunciation of Bianca for the sake of Franz (who was weak!) to make him feel strong with a crystalline hardness which he felt singled him out from the common herd.

"What—" he asked himself scornfully—"do I care about all these meetings and about the Socialists? Socialism is for the weak!"

And yet, when he listened again to one of the bitter diatribes about the hardships of the last three years and the iniquities of the war profiteers, his own anger was quick to rise in sympathy. He felt at one then with the murmuring crowd. It was that way one evening when he was late for commercial school—

He had been kept by a customer and he was nearly half an hour late. He had expected all the windows of the school to be lighted as usual and the little square in front to be deserted, but when he arrived the boys were still out in the square, milling around belligerently. On the school steps, Armbruster was making a speech. He was not being derided by the commercial apprentices this time, though his impassioned sincerity frequently tripped up his speech. There were even cheers. It appeared that there was to be a mass meeting of all the apprentices in the city on Saturday to protest against the long hours they had to work and against having to attend trade school at night. For the present there was to be a strike against the trade schools.

When Armbruster was through, three boys from the commercial school attempted a harangue. There was nothing to add to what Armbruster had said and they ended with lamely violent shouts that nobody was to go into the school. The excitement showed signs of frazzling out. Someone suggested that they break the windows. A few boys picked up handfuls of sand in the little park in the center of the square and started to throw the small pebbles at the windows with disappointing harmlessness. One by one, the classrooms went dark. The director of the school came out on the steps; he was a quiet, reasonable man who taught commercial law and he was listened to respectfully. He urged them to forget about the strike and to make a more peaceful appeal to the guilds to abolish the night schools. He sounded friendly and sympathetic; yet they suddenly had a feeling of treachery: in the far corner of the square four policemen had appeared, triumphantly led by the school janitor.

Catcalls greeted the police. The four policemen had spread out and were attempting to herd them into the school. They were paternal at first—"Now, then, you boys: into your school where you belong . . ." But when the taunting continued from the two crowds that had oozed away from them on either side, they became irritable and pushed roughly at the boys they could get their hands on. Some twenty boys trooped into the school. Armbruster had stuck to his post on the steps and was shouting: "Don't go in!" At once, one of the policemen went for Armbruster and seized him and another boy and pulled them to one side. The gesture had its effect. All along the steps, the apprentices pulled cautiously back, only to surge closer again when the three other policemen conferred briefly with the director in the doorway. One of the policemen came to the edge of the top step.

"All right, if you don't want to go to school, that's your business. Your masters'll probably know what to do about that. But you aren't going to stay here. Clear the square——"

And now the four policemen—the one who had seized Armbruster and the other boy was still holding on to them and pushing them before him—proceeded to drive them away from the steps. The jeers had become more insulting, but each boy was also more careful to keep out of reach, for another one of the policemen had collared a boy and showed no signs of letting him go. Armbruster was calling back hoarsely:

"Don't go in. Strike!"

But the crowd was drawing back ignominiously into the streets on either side of the school. At the last minute the policeman who had barked at them from the steps seized a straggler, apparently for no other reason except to have also somebody to arrest.

Peter was with some twenty boys who had retreated to the little park. The same policeman who had just arrested the boy came toward them menacingly.

"Out of there, you young good-for-nothings, or I'll take you all to the station!"

Anger at the bullying of the policeman, who was probably meek enough in dealing with the hundreds of ugly-tempered gatherings along the Gürtel, suddenly seized Peter. There was no telling what might happen to Armbruster—Armbruster might forfeit his two and a half years of apprenticeship!

His anger turned against the apprentices shouting bravely from the safe distance of the side streets down by the school. In just a few minutes they would begin to scatter, and Armbruster and the others would have to pay. Armbruster's half-baked idea of a strike—how had Armbruster come to think of that anyway?—would come to nothing, just like that Socialist meeting in Floridsdorf the other night. That meeting had gone to pieces because it had been—inefficient, that was it—and because the speakers hadn't even had loud enough voices to make themselves heard. But thanks to Herr Granini, *he* had a voice! He had only to pitch it—"out here," as Herr Granini used to say—and it carried. He took a quick breath:

"On the Gürtel! Meet on the Gürtel—everybody!"

The jeering down around the school wavered and stopped. He had been heard. The policeman came after him. He edged away and repeated his shout. The other boys in the park who had been puzzled at first took up the cry. He felt so exhilarated that when the policeman came after them, he joined in the taunts: "You've got to catch us first, flatfoot!"

They met the apprentices down by the school. Questions overwhelmed them at once. "What's going on at the Gürtel? Let's break the windows first!"

The questions had been addressed to all the boys who had been with him in the park. Several of them turned uncertainly to him. He said quickly:

"We're going on the Gürtel where we can talk things over and not be bothered by the police."

It astonished him how eagerly the few words were taken up, and presently shouted back from the fringes of the crowd. They marched in noisy, straggling disorder down the Wiedner Hauptstrasse. The boys from the park had stayed close to him, Peter noticed, and others had clustered around them, so that he was no longer at the end but nearly in the middle of the procession. One boy asked him almost deferentially:

"What are you going to do?"

"Get the boys they arrested out of jail."

Like wildfire the word was passed up and down the line. But the shouting that accompanied it filled Peter with misgivings. The boys were turning the whole thing into a lark. At the first obstacle they would falter again, if their rowdy swaggering did not all go up in smoke before they reached even the Gürtel. The Gürtel was the first place that had come into his mind when he had thought only of holding the crowd together. He turned to the boys around him: "Get them to stop at the corner there!" He shouted: "Stop at the corner!"

Reluctantly, the mob of apprentices slowed down.

He looked around hastily for some doorstep from which he could make himself heard. But another boy had got ahead of him and had climbed part way up a lamppost to shout: "We're going to the police station to get them out! We'll show those cops——" There were cheers. Jealousy mingled with Peter's scorn for the easy enthusiasm of the crowd. If they went to the police station, they would only make a lot of noise and run again in the end. If only he had some of the tough blacksmith and machinist's apprentices—that was it: the machinists' trade school! He took a quick breath:

"We'll get the machinists out first! Their school's only three blocks! Then we'll go to the police——"

The cheers which greeted his suggestion were twice as full-bodied as before. It was clear that the crowd preferred making an uproar outside another school to tackling the police. Whether he wanted to or not, he found himself shoved to the head of the new procession. He also noticed that a number of boys from his own class were trying to get close to him as they marched down the side street toward the machinists' school.

It was even easier than he had hoped. They crowded into the hallway and up the stairs and set up a rhythmic chant of "Everybody out—strike—everybody out!" Doors along the corridors opened uncertainly, then were flung wide open. Either the instructors were dismissing their classes or the machinists were simply walking out—it did not matter which, Peter thought happily. The main thing was that they came trooping down the stairs, looking excited and already belligerent. He knew the majority of them from the store. There was a band of eleven from a big shop with whom he was particularly friendly, and who had been foremost in his mind when he had felt the sudden contempt for the unreliability of the commercial apprentices. The eleven were bound together by a brawling solidarity that made them a powerful ally. He managed to get them to one side and to explain hurriedly about Armbruster and the police.

The clamor around them in the hallway and outside the school had become deafening. His own name was being called, first by a few scattered voices, then in chorus. A flush of pride and a panicking fear which seemed to hollow his bones assailed him simultaneously. One of the machinists was nudging him——"Hey, they are calling you!"

He fought down his panic and remembered to pitch his voice. His hatred of Herr Kropfl had come alive and scalded through his words while he repeated what Armbruster had said about the hardships of going to school at night and the long hours they had to work. A long-forgotten resentment against the police, who had kept order—sometimes bullyingly—when he had stood in line for potatoes or lard, made him lash out against the police.

He had to stop once to take a breath and after a moment of complete silence, applause rushed into the vacuum and surged all around him like the sea. He held out his hands—far out from his body so that he felt like a statue of himself—and the tumult subsided with flattering promptitude. More even than the shouting, the instant silence gave him an illusion of having suddenly grown to twice his size, so that he could get the crowd below him to do anything. More to test his power than because he had really said all he had meant to say, he shouted with all his might:

"To the police station!"

Instantly, the cry was taken up by the nearly six hundred apprentices. They faced toward the Wiedner Hauptstrasse. A minute later they were marching up the street, an impressive procession now because of the machinists, Peter felt exultantly. Along the Wiedner Hauptstrasse, people stopped to watch with that vindictive approval people now had in their faces for any disorder that promised excitement. Five ragged-looking soldiers who had been loitering on the sidewalk came out into the street to ask:

"What's it all about?"

One of the machinists explained about Armbruster and the strike.

"That's the ticket," the soldier who seemed to be their leader approved. "Show those flatfoot bastards they can't do as they like. We'll just come along. . . ." Before they reached the police station, the five soldiers had attracted several more soldiers to their side.

Seven policemen had come out of the station to drive them back from the door, and while the machinist apprentices gave ground slowly, they had to fall back when the policemen swished at their legs with the flat sides of their sabers. Up until now the soldiers had merely been looking on. Two of them suddenly closed in on one of the policemen.

"Who you trying to hit with that toy saber?" one of them growled.

"Where were you when the shooting was going on?" the other one asked.

Three other soldiers were crowding another policeman back. All of the policemen retreated precipitately toward the door of the station. The soldiers and the apprentices surged after them. The police sergeant made a sign for silence, but the crowd of boys roared only louder in response. Peter and the machinists finally succeeded in getting enough quiet for the sergeant to be heard.

"The street has to be cleared and at once!" he called in an attempt to assert his customary authority. "What do you boys want anyway?"

Peter stepped forward. "We want the apprentices you locked up. They didn't do anything——"

Already shouts of, "You know damn well what we want!" were drowning Peter out.

The sergeant made another attempt to look imposing, but failed, because he could hardly make himself heard. "I'll report to the Inspector. Meanwhile, you clear the street—or else!"

"Or else, what?" one soldier asked.

The sergeant's already flushed face turned purple with rage. He went inside the station, leaving the other policemen with their drawn sabers to guard the door. Five minutes passed without the sergeant's coming back. One of the soldiers said:

"They're up to some dirty work. Let's storm the damn place!"

The crowd, which had been milling around restlessly and had never stopped shouting, pressed forward. One of the policemen went hastily into the station. The sergeant returned and signaled for silence again. He got it this time.

"The Inspector wants to see a few of you. Just a few, I said!"

Some twenty boys immediately around Peter moved forward with him. He hastily picked the biggest ones: "You . . . and you . . . and—"

"That's enough," the sergeant snapped. They filed between the policemen through the door, but when the sergeant put out his arm to bar the last boy Peter had picked, the five soldiers who had joined them first crowded up to the door. "What do you want?" the sergeant rasped.

"Why, I'm just going to see that nothing happens to my little brother there," the leader of the soldiers mocked. He was pointing to one of the machinists who was half a head taller than he.

They were taken into the Inspector's office, the soldiers following closely behind. Beside the Inspector's desk, the sergeant looked important again. The Inspector scowled. He opened a folder to show that he intended to make them wait. One of the soldiers noisily struck a match to light a cigarette.

"There will be no smoking in here!"

"Sorry, *Herr Inspektor*," the soldier said with mock humility. "I didn't know we were in church." The soldiers laughed boisterously.

The Inspector glared. He turned to Peter and the other apprentices:

"What is all this?"

"You arrested some boys who didn't do any more than anybody else. . . ."

"There's room for you in the lockup, too!"

The soldier who had lighted the cigarette and had kept on smoking all this time, started to whistle the national anthem.

"Quiet, you! While you are in here you will show the proper respect for authority. You should be ashamed, wearing your country's uniform!"

The other soldier went: "T'ch, t'ch."

"We can't have riots in the streets—a fine how-do-you-do if we were to let children dictate to us what to do!"

The oldest of the machinist apprentices bridled sullenly:

"What do you mean 'children'! In a couple of months we'd have been in the army; we wouldn't have been children then!"

"That's telling him," one of the soldiers approved.

"Nobody was rioting," Peter said firmly. "We were simply not going inside the school."

"So you don't want to go to school any more now?"

"How would you like to work twelve hours a day and then go to school?"

"That is not for me to decide. You'll have to see your masters about that. And now—"

"What about the boys you locked up?" Peter insisted.

One of the soldiers cleared his throat.

The Inspector hesitated. "And if I were to let them go this time, are you boys going to behave yourselves?"

"We weren't looking for any trouble. . . ."

"All right, we'll let them go this once." The Inspector picked up a pen: "Your name and address!"

Alarm crowded up in Peter's throat. Supposing Herr Straka heard about this!

"What do we have to give our names for?"

"A record is kept of everybody who has business with the police," the Inspector announced dryly. "Your name—"

Peter swallowed to get rid of the grizzly tickling in his throat. He was caught! He was about to say "Pet—," when the soldier with the cigarette came forward to the Inspector's desk.

"None of that! We know your tricks."

All five of the soldiers had come up to the desk. The Inspector glared at them and threw down his pen. "Get out! And see that the street is cleared within two minutes!"

"Sure, sure, *Herr Inspektor*," one of the soldiers mocked.

"Take care of your health," another one said. . . .

A tumultuous acclaim welcomed them outside. A minute later Armbruster and the other boys who had been arrested came out through the station door and were immediately lifted up on some boys' shoulders. And while Peter was still watching Armbruster swaying uncertainly and just as he reflected tartly that at least one of the boys with Armbruster had done nothing more heroic than to have stupidly let himself be caught, he was himself seized by the machinists and hoisted over their heads. Out of the noise around and below him, his name was shouted at him with flattering regularity . . .

He looked around for Armbruster when the triumphant parade finally broke up on the Wiedner Hauptstrasse. The boys were scattering rapidly. Armbruster stood talking to a slender, stoop-shouldered man in the shadow of a doorway. It was the same man

Peter had noticed once near the steps of the school, and once again when they had marched on the police station, and whom he had put down as merely another bystander drawn by the excitement. Peter wondered about the half-secretive familiarity with which Armbruster was talking to him now. He decided to wait until Armbruster was through, but Armbruster had seen him and had stepped forward eagerly. "There he is," he said. "This is Comrade Bistron. . . ."

Peter felt uncomfortable. "Comrade—" and not "Herr" Bistron! He knew that the Bolsheviks in Russia were supposed to address each other that way, but to hear the word here on the Gürtel was disconcerting.

The man held out his hand with an air of knowing all about him: "Glad to know you, Comrade Domanig." His face was sallow, and his eyes when he raised his drooping eyelids were hot and piercing, almost like some priest's. "You did a first-rate job tonight—really first-rate," he repeated and turned back to Armbruster:

"You should have got their names right away. Once a boy has been brought into the limelight, he is important to you, whether he is interested in the strike or not! You must contact them as soon as possible and make sure that they will be at the mass meeting on Saturday. Another point: letting the demonstration outside the school go on after you had attained your objective was a mistake. A crowd must be kept occupied or you lose your hold on it. Fortunately, our comrade here saved the day. As it turned out, even your mistake was all to the good: a few martyrs help to cement a crowd. You should have a very solid section on Saturday. . . ."

The didactic tone of the stranger and the proprietary way in which he spoke of what had happened nettled Peter. Who was this Comrade Bistron anyway? Probably one of the foreign agitators, to judge by his accent and the wide-brimmed, foreign-looking hat. The next instant and in spite of his antagonism toward the man, a flush of pleasure stole over Peter.

"You are going to speak at the mass meeting, of course, Comrade Domanig! Your tactics tonight were excellent, especially getting the soldiers to come with you. Now, tomorrow . . ." It appeared that they were to meet him the following night at some coffeehouse to discuss the meeting on Saturday.

"Who is that?" he asked Armbruster as soon as they were by themselves.

"That's Leo Bistron! If you knew anything about Socialism, you'd know who he was. He's from the Central Committee in Zurich. He was one of the speakers at the Party Congress in 1913. My father heard him speak. . . . He was exiled to Siberia when he was only sixteen!"

"Then he's a Bolshevik?"

"You talk like a bloody capitalist—he's a Marxian Socialist. The priests and the capitalists are trying to make everyone out a Bolshevist that wants to get rid of the Kaiser and the whole rotten government!"

"But why's he bothering with us?"

"With us! Do you think the apprentices aren't important? There are over seventy thousand apprentices. You'll see next Saturday! Did you know that they struck in Ottakring and in Hernals tonight, too? And tomorrow night they're going to strike in Floridsdorf! We'll hear all about it from him tomorrow. You don't know how lucky we are to have a famous man like him help us to get organized. . . ."

He found it hard that night to go to sleep. Dreams in which he saw himself swaying vast multitudes of apprentices and soldiers in Ottakring alternated with pictures of himself manipulating great uprisings from behind the scenes, like Leo Bistron—but not like Bistron either, since he was constantly proving that he was superior to him.

The exaltation of the dreams still held him in the morning when he woke, and after he got to the store. He was almost sorry that they had agreed—even Otto in the office—not to mention the strike to anybody in the store, so as to get out half an hour early on school nights. He would have liked Herr Lehnert and the other clerks to know how important he was!

But Otto had talked——

It was his first angry thought when he was summoned to Herr Straka's office at three and found all the other apprentices already waiting in the switchboard room, looking scared. Only Otto appeared unconcerned and kept on ostentatiously running the mimeographing machine.

Herr Kropfl opened the door from Herr Straka's office and stood looking at them with glossy, catlike zest.

"All right, inside, all of you! You too, Otto!"

The two youngest apprentices, who had been nudged by the second-year boys to go in first, stopped timidly just inside the door, along the edge of the rug which extended forward from Herr Straka's desk. Otto, who had come in last, was at the other end of the line. Hans—the youngest apprentice—shrank a little away from Peter, so that he was left standing by himself. But it was not the isolation from the others so much as his unaccustomed distance from Herr Straka's desk which marked for him the oppressiveness in the room.

Herr Straka had got up from his chair. He looked somber and concerned. His frown repulsed Peter when he attempted once to meet his eyes. Even the formal, dark-blue suit which Herr Straka had not worn before lunch affected Peter as vaguely menacing.

Herr Kropfl had struck a stance by the front corner of the desk. His eyes glittered. "Now tell us where you all were last night! Speak up!"

One of the second-year boys said: "We went to school. . . ."

"Then you were in school last night?"

"Well, there wasn't any——"

"Oh, there wasn't any school? In that case, why didn't you come back to the store where you belonged?"

"We didn't think it was worth while any more," Otto said. "It was after seven."

Peter waited tensely for Herr Kropfl to pounce. So far Herr Kropfl had pointedly avoided him and had forced one of the others to speak. He wondered how much Herr Kropfl and Herr Straka knew. It did not sound as if Otto had talked after all; yet Herr Kropfl was clearly working up to some climax. . . .

"And why didn't you come back right away if you saw there wasn't going to be any school?"

Otto again: "We couldn't tell at first whether there was going to be or not, so we waited."

Herr Kropfl came closer to them. "So you couldn't tell! What about you, Peter?"

Here it was—the moment he had unconsciously been steeling himself for! He realized that ever since Herr Kropfl had first opened the door from Herr Straka's office, he had sensed the old animosity in Herr Kropfl which he had been at such pains to conciliate during the past year and a half. He looked past Herr Kropfl and addressed himself to Herr Straka:

"I was busy with a customer until ten minutes to seven. I was half an hour late for school."

Herr Straka looked serious and ever so faintly uncomfortable, as if he disapproved of Herr Kropfl's theatrical sneers. But he did not say anything.

"Oh, you have an excuse? Maybe you're going to tell us that you weren't there at all?"

"I didn't say that, but it was too late to come back to the store."

"I see. Perhaps you could tell us why there wasn't any school yesterday. . . ."

"There was a strike."

"A strike—you don't say! Did the teachers strike?"

Somebody must have talked! They knew all about it—*careful! oh, careful!*

"Some of the boys were . . ."

"Oh, the boys were striking! You didn't have anything to do with that, by any chance?"

"I didn't get there until after seven."

"And after you got there?"

"Well, I stayed around like everybody else."

"You bet you did! We've heard all about your triumphs. You're even in the newspapers, did you know that? Oh, you didn't?" Herr Kropfl took two catlike steps toward Herr Straka's desk and picked up a newspaper. He came and thrust it at him: "Here, read this!"

An icy foreboding tightened around his chest as he took the paper. It was the *Arbeiter Zeitung*—the radical Socialist paper! What had up until this moment been no more than an apprehensive wariness of Herr Kropfl turned into a panicky sensation of being trapped. Herr Straka would certainly never have seen this particular paper—he took the *Reichspost*, to which Franz subscribed, and he read the *Neue Freie Presse*, which all important people had to read. . . . Peter remembered suddenly that once on an errand to Herr Kropfl's house he had seen Herr Kropfl's father, the janitor, reading the *Arbeiter Zeitung*—Herr Kropfl had brought the paper! But there was no time left to think about that now. In the lower left-hand corner of the page a short article had been circled with red pencil. It was headed: APPRENTICES STRIKE!

With a shock as sudden as if he had unexpectedly come up against a mirror, he saw his own name in the first paragraph. It was all he could see of the article. A helpless rage possessed him. *Who? Who?* How could the paper have got hold of his name? He had not given it to the police. . . . Then he remembered—the foreigner last night, Bistron—"once a boy has been brought into the limelight. . . ." But again he did not have time to dwell on this new treachery which had conspired with Herr Kropfl. Herr Kropfl was prodding:

"Out loud! We want to hear all about it."

He read awkwardly:

" 'Strikes among the apprentices against the unfair night trade schools broke out simultaneously last night in Hernals, Ottakring, and Margareten. Notable was the strike in Margareten, directed by two brilliant young leaders, Georg Armbruster and Peter Domanig, who succeeded in calling out three schools. . . .' "

He tried to stop, but Herr Kropfl would not let him: "Go on, there's more. We don't want to miss any of it! You weren't so bashful last night!"

He forced himself to read:

" 'A mass meeting of all the apprentices in the city has been called for Saturday in Ottakring to protest against the tyrannous working conditions which hark back to the Dark Ages. A provisory committee has been named, consisting of—' " and once more he had to read his name.

Herr Kropfl snatched the paper away from him. He tossed it into the wastepaper basket, and picked up another newspaper from the desk——

"Now I'm going to read you what a responsible newspaper thinks of the likes of you. Listen carefully:

" 'YOUNG TERRORISTS BREAK WINDOWS, DEFY POLICE—Last night showed to what new depths of moral degradation our country has sunk when minors terrorized entire districts and defied the police. Under the guise of protesting against attendance of trade schools, gangs of apprentices took to looting and the wanton destruction of property in the best tradition of Russian anarchy. Our future looks indeed dark unless an immediate stop can be put to such unprincipled lawlessness among minors. Nothing less than a reign of utter anarchy will be in store for us! . . .' "

Herr Kropfl paused theatrically.

"But there is going to be no anarchy in this firm. We are going to put a stop to it right here!"

If I get fired on account of him, Peter thought, *there is going to be more broken than a few windows in Ottakring!*

Herr Kropfl came closer to him. "So you're a brilliant young leader——"

His hand partly parried the slap. He took an angry step forward so that his sleeve touched Herr Kropfl's chest. His cheeks felt on fire with humiliation at having been slapped in front of Herr Straka and the other apprentices. *He wouldn't have dared do that nowadays if we had been alone,* he thought furiously; *he wouldn't have dared do it in front of Herr Straka either if he hadn't first made me out a Bolshevik! He even wants me to hit back!*

The realization that Herr Kropfl was trying to provoke him to some act that he could call insubordination sufficed to check his rage. He had to act quickly if he did not want to lose everything he had worked for these last two and a half years! Herr Straka had placed one hand on his desk when Herr Kropfl had struck him; Peter was almost certain that he was about to voice his distaste for the proceedings and that Herr Straka felt that Herr Kropfl had gone too far. He stepped up quickly to Herr Straka's desk.

"I'm sorry, Herr Straka, about yesterday. I didn't realize how important it was."

"You mean, you didn't think we'd hear about it!" Herr Kropfl sneered.

"If you don't mind, Herr Kropfl?"

At last, but unmistakably, Herr Straka had asserted himself. The silence which had followed, while not exactly friendly, seemed at least to shut Herr Kropfl out. Peter went on:

"The police arrested some boys who hadn't done anything and I guess I was carried away. I did help to get them released, but I had nothing to do with the strike. It had started before I got there. And I'm not a radical. . . ."

Herr Straka waited for long seconds before he spoke. "I am glad that you at least realize that you did wrong. Nevertheless, this is a disappointment. You are the senior apprentice and I expected something better from you. Your work has been so conscientious in other respects that I am inclined to believe that you were carried away by some thoughtless rowdyism. I hope that in the future—"

Then, there was to be a future! He was safe. Even though Herr Straka's tone was making it clear how serious an offense he considered the strike. Herr Straka was talking to all six of them now.

" I believe this firm has always taken more than an ordinary interest in the welfare of its apprentices. If you had any complaints to make, I have always been here in the office. . . ."

He was safe! He might not be made a clerk at New Year's now, but at least he was not going to be fired. Herr Kropfl had failed! And Herr Kropfl was aware of it; he said viciously:

"And just remember, this is a respectable firm. We want no radicals here. From now on, you are all on probation. And that goes double for you—brilliant young leader! Now get back to your jobs! . . ."

It was not until nearly an hour later, after he had waited on several customers and when he was at last by himself in the warehouse checking over a shipment of axles, that he was free to think about the monstrous vitality of Herr Kropfl's venom. What a fool he had been to lay himself open to Herr Kropfl's malice like that. . . . It was all to do over now, the difficult task of proving not only his ability but his loyalty to Herr Straka, and all because of one half-hour of childish glory. What did he care about a lot of howling apprentices and about Armbruster's Socialist rant! Let the Socialists try to deal with a treacherous enemy like Herr Kropfl before they talked about oppression. . . .

He did not go to the coffeehouse in the Neustiftgasse where he was supposed to meet Armbruster and Bistron that evening.

At noon, the following day, Bistron was waiting for him on the sidewalk. His blue ulster looked shabby in the daylight and the wide-brimmed hat more foreign than ever. Just to be seen with him would look suspicious—Peter made an angry sign with his head and went on to the next corner. When Bistron came, Peter led the way down the narrow side street.

"Where were you last night?" Bistron asked. "We waited until half past ten. A meeting like that has to be planned carefully."

"I'm not going to be at the meeting."

He saw Bistron looking at him sharply, and the very shrewdness of the glance reminded him of Bistron's attempt to jockey him into a position from which there had almost been no retreat. He waited for some remonstrance, but Bistron pointed instead to a small red poster on a billboard.

"Did you notice the posters? We pasted up five thousand since last night. It's going to be a monster rally. You are down as one of the speakers."

"I'm not speaking anywhere."

"What's happened?" Bistron's lean face was as watchful as a rat's peering out from a shelf in the cellar.

"Nothing, except that I was practically fired yesterday! You had no business putting my name in the paper!"

"People have to know their leaders."

"Even if it costs me my job!"

"There is a bigger job waiting for you. There will be a permanent central committee for the youth section as soon as the republic is established. You have talent——"

"I'm not interested. I don't want my name in any more papers!"

Bistron spoke slowly: "It's people like you who lose revolutions. But this one is won already. Perhaps you will change your mind in the next few days when you see what is happening. . . ."

"Don't count on it, and don't bother waiting!" He walked away.

But he saw that evening that he was not yet through with Bistron. Armbruster was outside the store at seven.

"I saw Bistron," Armbruster began.

"So did I."

"You can't mean what you said!"

"Did he think I was kidding?"

"But we need you! You ought to hear what Bistron said to me about the way you handled everything, and he doesn't praise much—he's seen hundreds of demonstrations. Can't you see that we've practically won our strike? Next week we'll send a delegation to the guild chamber. They've got to meet our demands, or we'll call a strike in the shops. But it's much more than that: we've got to fight the Church and the aristocracy and the capitalists, or they'll try to get control of the republic!"

"All right, you do it! . . ." But it was more difficult to put Armbruster off than Bistron. He was forced to explain about Herr Kropfl. Only, Armbruster could not understand:

"That's unimportant, a private grudge like that, when you've got a chance to fight for the new order. It's selfish. It's people like you who lose revolutions!"

"That's a tag you've got from Bistron. You must think it's witty. . . ."

They parted angrily.

But he continued the argument with himself all the way home. The charge of disloyalty Armbruster had flung at him rankled. It did not help to tell himself that Armbruster was a fanatic and so warped by the dreary poverty of his parents as to be without personal ambition, and therefore incapable of understanding what his own career in the store meant to him—or of understanding the consuming need that had reasserted itself in him to vanquish Herr Kropfl. He was still justifying himself when he sat down at the kitchen table to eat his supper and without much interest picked up a letter from Franz.

Franz wrote that he had his old room back with his friends in Vorarlberg, that he would try to send some flour, that he was worried about them because of the reports of riots in Vienna. . . .

He had read inattentively and he was about to lay down the letter without finishing it, when Bianca's name riveted his attention. His eyes rushed over the words. Franz told—with that implacable sincerity which seemed to be an aftereffect of his illness, just as his exaggerated devoutness was, and which even assumed that Poldi and *she* would share his concern over Bianca—that Bianca and her mother had gone to Hungary to look after the estate, because they had received reports of marauding bands of soldiers in the neighborhood. . . .

He had a picture of Bianca coolly defying a horde of soldiers. He discarded it instantly as too romantic—after all, Franz had more than once spoken of the large number of servants and tenants on the estate—but there remained nevertheless a zestful glow which surrounded his resolution to have nothing more to do with Armbruster or the strike. Bianca had seen him in the store, had sanctioned his being there by her mere presence in front of Herr Lehnert's counter that time! She would approve of his having got Armbruster off, but not of seeing him permanently on the side of the—rabble!

He had an almost physical sense of being ranged with Bianca and Herr Straka against the mob. . . .

Chapter Forty-Six

THE disdain he had formed for the fractious gatherings which obstructed the sidewalks, for the sullenly aimless soldiers, and for the blaring Communist posters on the billboards, extended even to the larger events reported by the newspapers. He noted indifferently that the Czechs had proclaimed their independence, then the Hungarians, and then the Croats; that Germany also was suing for an armistice and that the German Kaiser had fled to Holland; that the Italians had occupied Innsbruck; and finally, on the eleventh of November, that their own Emperor had abdicated and that the Republic was to be proclaimed the following afternoon by a National Assembly.

He did not even feel any desire to go into the Innere Stadt to witness the proclamation. Only Herr Lehnert's remark that it was a "historic event," and the rumor that the Communists were going to attempt to seize control of the government by storming the Parliament, but most of all the silent, irresistible suction produced by the masses of people heading for the Ring even before lunch, made him decide to go after all.

Their own store had closed at noon. Most of the smaller stores had not opened at all. The streets looked drained and frowning. The streetcar he was on got stalled half a dozen blocks from the Ring by the dark throng of people which packed the Burggasse. There were, he could see, hundreds of clumsily manufactured red Communist flags and a smaller number of red and gold Socialist banners. A double chain of policemen blocked the approach to the Ring. He saw that it would be useless, even if he got past the police, to attempt to cover the quarter mile down to the Parliament building over the Ringstrasse. He fought his way back through the crowd and took the back streets to the rear of the Parliament. There, too, the crowd was so dense as to be nearly impenetrable. But he succeeded, by following behind a squad of policemen who were trying to keep open a passage, in working his way up to one of the stone lions at the base of the long ramp that led up to the building.

He was closer now, but it was impossible to see anything but the heads of the crowd for some twenty-five feet around him. The massive pedestal of the stone lion cut off his view of the front of the building. Two soldiers had somehow managed to get up on the smooth eight-foot pedestal and sat in enviable comfort between the front feet of the lion. Occasionally people in the crowd called up to them to ask whether anything was happening and they reported some minor commotion in front of the Parliament where a huge contingent of police, it appeared, was desperately trying to keep the crowd from pressing any closer. But nothing of any importance was happening.

It was only two o'clock, but the overhung sky made it seem as if it were already evening. It started to drizzle—a dreary, persistent November rain. A few people spread out newspapers and tried to hold them over their heads, only to provoke immediate protests from their neighbors whose eyes were in danger of being brushed by the papers. But it was less the actual physical annoyance of the damp papers than impatience with a personal finickiness that seemed out of keeping with the mood of the occasion which colored the protests—"You aren't made of sugar, are you? . . . Probably a profiteer that he has to be so careful with his new hat!"

Only the two soldiers up on the pedestal were comfortably sheltered from the drizzle and noisily, callously cheerful. They had crawled under the belly of the stone lion from where they continued to make their sarcastic reports of what was going on in the distance. One of them was rolling a cigarette. . . . Peter suddenly remembered the five cigarettes a customer had given him that morning and which were still in his pocket. He worked his way up to the corner of the pedestal and called to the soldiers. One of them stuck his head over the edge to look. When he saw the cigarettes, he got his friend and they each stretched down an arm. Immediately there were protests from the people around Peter. There was not room enough to brace his knees against the granite without kicking people. He slipped once and knocked his head against the granite but the soldiers kept on tugging and he got up beside them.

The two soldiers crawled back under the lion. Peter crouched down beside them and handed them the five cigarettes.

"Oh, Egyptian cigarettes!" the soldier nearest him said appreciatively. Each lighted one with a much-worn fuse lighter such as the soldiers had used in the trenches. Then they started to tease him.

"This isn't going to be such a healthy place when the bullets start flying. What are you going to do then?"

"I'm not scared."

"That's what they all say!"

"I can tell you right now what you're going to do——"

They guffawed over their joke, but after that they let him alone and turned their caustic humor on individuals in the crowd below.

From where he sat, half-crouched under the chest of the lion, he commanded a view over the Ring and the entire square on his side of the Parliament building. He had not realized that the crowd was so enormous. The red Communist flags on the Ring looked bedraggled and the wet cardboard signs were curling away from the laths to which they had been nailed. Immediately in front of the Parliament some thousands—he could not guess how many—of Socialists were massed, obviously to keep the Communists from getting any closer. The heavy silk banners of the Socialists had withstood the rain better and still looked imposing and respectable.

It occurred to him suddenly as ironic that the Socialists whom he had always heard abused as lawless and seditious should now form the bulwark against a much greater menace. For it was clear that even the thousands of policemen swarming in front of the Parliament would be unable to stem the pressure of the crowd which filled the Ring.

The silence, now that he could look out over the heads of the crowd, had something appalling about it. It was at once heavy with a feeling of already knowing the worst, and yet pregnant with fear, and expectant. There was none of the friendly murmurousness Peter remembered from the funeral cortege of the Archduke in 1914. Each person seemed isolated. Occasionally some rumor was passed along, as now when someone at the foot of the pedestal said anxiously: "They say there are machine guns on the roof of the Parliament!"

"Can you see the machine guns?" a man called up to the soldiers.

"Can't see anything," one of them said, and immediately added: "You won't need to see them—you'll hear them."

There was a commotion on the Ring, quite a distance away. A shot could be heard, then a whole volley of shots, all of them sounding faint and unreal as if they had been fired by toy pistols. It was impossible to make out what was happening. Only the jerky agitation of a number of red Communist flags and placards showed that there was some sort of scuffle. Two or three minutes, and the commotion subsided.

A whole hour went by and still nothing had happened. Once or twice a rumor came traveling down from in front of the Parliament that the members of the National Assembly were coming out on the balcony, of which Peter could only see the near corner, but it was always a false rumor.

It had stopped raining. Occasionally the silence was broken by an irritable: "Well, then don't push like that! Where do you expect to go anyway?"

Then, at last, something appeared really about to happen. The policemen in front of the Parliament, Peter saw, were trying to push the crowd back from the ramp. It was a wholly useless endeavor on the part of the policemen, but it proved that there must be some truth this time in the renewed rumor: "They're coming out!" A profound silence hollowed like a receding wave from in front of the balcony. Everywhere people were straining their ears to listen. It was impossible to hear anything, except once when Peter caught part of a word. A few minutes went by; then there were cheers from the Socialists who were waving their banners; then silence again, but broken this time by confused shouts from the Communists which traveled up and down the Ring and grew steadily in volume. It was impossible to tell whether the proclamation had been read in full or had merely been interrupted. The Socialists in front of the balcony seemed still to be listening. But farther up the Ring the confusion grew more turbulent. Shots were heard. Many shots this time. The two soldiers had got to their feet.

"It's started," one of them said. "This is going to be good!"

There was fighting now in front of the balcony. The shooting was suddenly closer, but the center of the conflict seemed to be on the far side of the Parliament. . . .

The crowd around the pedestal and all over the square had at first pressed forward. It was a futile attempt on the part of each individual to see what was happening, and the result was only that people were jammed still more tightly against each other. Shrill protests could be heard—"Look out, my arm! . . . My hat . . ." And then, suddenly, there was a steady staccato clatter from the roof of the Parliament—or so it seemed. Someone shouted: "The machine guns! . . ." In an instant, the cry was taken up by a hundred voices. In less than a second, the crowd had faced about, away from the Ring and Parliament, each man and woman frantically twisting and shoving to get away.

Panic!

With a tremor, Peter realized it. He looked up at the Parliament building and saw that what one of the soldiers had called down to the crowd—"It's only the shutters!"—was true. It was the steel shutters over the windows which were causing the clatter. He felt ashamed of his own moment of panic and moistened his lips to shout: "It's only the shutters!" He shouted it a dozen times without even the faintest effect. And as if to give him the lie there was a *ping* against the stone lion; one of the soldiers grasped his leg—he realized that they had ducked under the lion—and said:

"Hey, get down here!"

He got down beside them. The two of them were callously joking about the frightened crowd and discussing the bad marksmanship of the men fighting on the Ring. Listening to them, Peter caught some of their scornful detachment. Already the shooting had diminished in volume. A large troop of mounted policemen was slowly fighting its way up from the far side of the Parliament. The policemen on the ramp had driven back the Communists some ten or fifteen paces.

One of the soldiers said: "It's all over."

And it was all over, Peter realized scornfully, except for the innocent crowd in the square behind them which was still frenziedly struggling away from the Parliament. The Communist *Putsch* had certainly failed. On the Ring the mounted policemen were already dispersing both the Communists and the Socialists into the side streets. Six of the policemen on horseback were driving a part of the people from the Ring into the square with drawn sabers. About half the square was clear now of people. One of the policemen stopped by their pedestal.

"Down from there!" he commanded.

"Who says so?" one of the soldiers taunted.

But the policeman looked ugly. The second soldier said indifferently:

"There's nothing more to see anyway. Let's beat it."

Peter had got down ahead of them. He did not dare risk another encounter with the police. Several trampled hats and bits of torn clothing lay scattered on the pavement. Halfway toward the retreating crowd he passed a policeman bending over a woman who had been mauled in the crush and who was still unconscious.

He got out into the Lerchenfelderstrasse. There were no streetcars. Ahead of him and behind him people were straggling homeward. Sheer weariness seemed to keep chance groups together by a strange kind of cohesion. There was barely any talking. One man said:

"Well, now we have a Republic. I wonder when we'll get something to eat?"

The man's remark did not bring any reply.

Then, this is the Revolution! Peter thought impatiently as he started to cut across the Schmeltz. It was incredible that this could be all there was to it. He realized that up until now, as long as he had been walking through the Thalienstrasse in the midst of other people, he had still been secretly waiting for some staggering, cataclysmic happening somewhere behind them which would be commensurate with the picture he had always had of a revolution, and that he had still been giving the afternoon a chance to manifest itself as a "historic event." Herr Lehnert must have been wrong in calling it that in the first place.

He regretted now that he had gone at all, instead of using the afternoon to study for his next English lesson. He might have read two or three more chapters in the book about that American steelman, Carnegie. All told, what he had seen had amounted to nothing more than one of those mass meetings in Favoriten, except that there had been more people. Even the Communist *Putsch* had been a ridiculous fizzle. If the Communists had really hoped to storm the Parliament, they had been inexcusably stupid—if he had been their leader he would not have let them mass on the Ring where both the police and the Socialists were expecting them: he would have sent the bulk of them around to the rear of the building, and without flags and placards and red buttons on their lapels, to mingle with the harmless crowd who had merely come to look, and from there have caught the police in the rear. It would have been easy that way to carry the building!

He felt irritated by the thought that on account of the Proclamation—which nobody had heard anyway—the store was not open. It was just five o'clock, when they were always busiest. At least, if he could be in the store now, he would be busy winning back some of the good will he had lost through Herr Kropfl. Herr Emmerich had been friendly again just before noon, for the first time since that scene in Herr Straka's office. Perhaps Herr Straka might have had some errand for him. Or perhaps the Rumanian merchant might have come into the store with another order and he could have earned another present. . . .

He felt restless and not in the mood to go home and study English. He had come to the row of wire-glass windows of Herr Geiger's machine shop and he saw that several lights were on inside. He had met Herr Geiger now and then in the street or in the staircase, but he had not been in the shop since the days before the cadet school. He followed a sudden impulse and went down the few steps to the shop door.

Herr Geiger was alone in the shop. He got down from the high stool in front of his drafting table and raised his green eye shield.

"Oh, it's you," he said. "I thought it was my wife coming to get me for supper. . . . Well, it's a long time since you've been in here! Didn't you go to hear the Proclamation?"

"I've just come from there."

"How was it? Anything exciting happen?"

"Nothing. There was a little shooting and then the police cleared the Ring."

"That's just about what I figured it would amount to. I was too busy anyway."

"Am I interrupting you?"

"Just bills—" Herr Geiger riffled through a sheaf of papers on the tilted drafting desk—"just figuring out all I owe people. You don't want to buy a machine shop, by any chance?"

It was only now that Peter noticed that the machines which stretched away in dark rows toward the rear had all been covered with paper or sacking and that the drive belts were disconnected.

"Are you closing down?"

Herr Geiger shrugged. "Have to. The war's over. All those cases there—see them?—twenty-six of them, all full of gun sights, have just been turned back to me. I don't know what they expect me to do with them. Two months' output! I guess I'm just stuck with them."

"Can't you sell them to somebody?" Peter had remembered the Rumanian and all the other foreign merchants who seemed to buy nearly anything made of iron.

"I wouldn't know to whom. We certainly don't need them any more. Just so much junk now! Same thing with all those screw machines I had to have built to turn out army orders. Talk about war profits—I'll be lucky if I still have a single lathe and a drill press left after I've settled for everything. This is the kind of gun I'm going to make now——"

Herr Geiger reached up to the shelf over his desk and lifted down a puzzlingly encased piece of machinery of some sort.

"What is it?"

"A spray gun. You spray paint with it instead of laying it on with a brush. Works just like one of those atomizers women use, except that it's a little more complicated. Here's your tank for the paint—this is the nozzle and the mechanism for adjusting the spray—here's the pressure chamber! It's an idea I was working on just when the war came. I've got it so now that it'll really do a job—makes a surface as smooth as enamel. This particular one is a small model for painting china and small surfaces; the bigger ones will do for anything: furniture, houses, ships. With one of these, one man will be able to do the work of a dozen painters. . . ."

"Are you going to start making them right away?"

"As soon as I can get rid of this junk in here and find a smaller shop. Now the war's over, rents won't stay frozen much longer. My landlord's been after me already. . . . What do you think of my gadget?"

"It looks good! . . ."

But it was not of the spray gun that he was thinking after he left Herr Geiger, but of the specialized machinery that had become useless and of the canceled war orders. Herr Geiger was obviously right about the uselessness now of gun sights and of his own machinery, but what about all the other war orders and the huge supplies of material left on the hands of the manufacturers? What about all those cases of three-inch nails they had shipped to the man in Penzing, who had been making shell cases? They had no three-inch nails in the store and the Rumanian was avid for them. If he could get them for the Rumanian, there would be a handsome commission for him. Not just a present: he would ask for a commission! And there were all the other manufacturers with supplies on their hands—he might be able to find files and drills and padlocks, and all the other things the merchants from Galicia and Poland wanted. He might even, after he had made a little money, buy things on his own account and then dictate the price he wanted. It would be weeks, perhaps months even, before the steel mills would start producing again. . . .

Bold dreams in which he saw himself already triumphantly indifferent to Herr Kropfl's malice, and even independent of the store and of Herr Straka, made him impatient for the store to open the next day. He chafed until Herr Brandt sent him out to the freight stations. As soon as he had finished his business at the railroads—there was still half an hour left before noon—he hurried out to Penzing.

The ladder factory was as deserted as Herr Geiger's shop had been the evening before. Only a desolate few elderly joiners were at work in one corner making stepladders, working by hand amidst the silent bandsaws and planing machines.

Peter found the owner only too eager to sell the nails.

"Sure, I want to sell them! What am I going to do with fourteen hundred pounds of three-inch nails? I don't use that many nails in twenty years making ladders. Who sent you—Herr Straka? Your store want to buy them?"

"No, but I know a man who wants nails."

"Well, bring him on. The sooner, the better. I'll sell them for just what they cost me. Hinges, too—I've got enough hinges to pave all of Penzing! And six hundred shell cases out there—I don't suppose anybody'll want those: they're just good for firewood now. . . ."

He decided to do without lunch so as not to lose any time in getting in touch with the Rumanian. He hurried into the Innere Stadt to the hotel on the Neuen Markt where the merchant was staying.

The Rumanian was in, but he was in the dining room. It was annoying. Peter had entered the hotel boldly enough, but the dining room was another matter. It was crowded with important-looking men and bristling with haughtily officious waiters. He could not go in there even in his Sunday suit which he had expressly put on to go and see the owner of the factory: compared to the men he could see beyond the palm-fronded entrance, he would look hopelessly shabby. He hesitated for a minute between sending in a note and going away altogether to come back in the evening; then on a sudden defiant impulse he decided to brazen out the stares of the waiters. Fortunately, the Rumanian was by himself at a table.

The Rumanian in his precisely creased, double-breasted blue serge jacket and pin-stripe trousers, subtly foreign tie and shirt collar, and the more obvious touches of outlandish elegance such as his gray spats and the silver bracelet of his wrist watch, seemed to see nothing unusual in his coming into the dining room. He asked him to sit down at the table with him. And he not only still wanted to buy nails, but he was in an encouraging hurry to conclude the transaction.

"You have a bill of sale?"

"No. I wanted to find out first whether you still wanted them."

"That is a pity. We could have settled the matter immediately. You have had lunch?"

It was exhilarating and a little frightening to listen to the Rumanian calmly ordering the expensive lunch for him. It was even more exciting to taste the roast veal and to sip the wine the waiter had poured, and to be carrying on a conversation—however haltingly—in English.

The Rumanian had spent two years in America—as a partner in an export house, it appeared—and he spoke of the gigantic American industries and factories. The breath of vast foreign enterprises intoxicated Peter and emboldened him to look around the restaurant. He still felt a troubling impropriety in his being here at all. A group of four men at a near-by table reassured him: all four of them shared in the same flashy elegance, and they spoke and ate with a brash unceremoniousness which jarred against the decorum of the very walls and the furniture. And there were, Peter saw now, a good many others like them. War profiteers, obviously!

"After all," he told himself, "I'm no more out of place than they are. In the old days they wouldn't even have been allowed in here. It's only my suit, because it's old and because the sleeves have grown too short, that gives them an advantage. But as soon as I have swung a few deals like this one, I'm going to order a good suit. I'm going to get one of the kind Herr Straka wears, or those distinguished-looking men over there who are probably the sort of people who have always come here. . . ."

The waiter had brought a pancake folded over currant jelly. The Rumanian was waiting for him to finish it.

"Where is this factory?"

"Just this side of Baumgarten."

"And how far is that?"

"About as far as Schönbrunn."

"And it would not be possible for you to bring me a bill of sale and the bill of lading here to the hotel?"

"I don't think the man who has the nails would want to do it that way. He is—well, old-fashioned."

"I see. Then I shall have to go with you tomorrow."

He realized that the Rumanian had been willing to buy the nails without even checking the contents of the cases, and that he considered it a nuisance to have to go to Penzing at all. But there was no other difficulty. The Rumanian had offered to pay him a ten-percent commission and an additional five per cent for taking care of the shipping. . . .

Three days later when Peter returned to the hotel to deliver the bill of lading, he left the Rumanian with a thin but exhilaratingly stiff bundle of new fifty-kronen notes in his pocket. He had made twelve hundred kronen—nearly four times his whole month's salary, twice as much as Poldi earned in a month—and all in a few trips to Penzing! And this was only the beginning; the Rumanian wanted more nails and he still wanted the saw files and the drills and the padlocks. . . .

There were, now that he was alive to the supplies left on the hands of manufacturers who had been working on war orders—supplies which had been assigned to them by the army and which were still impossible to get—nearly endless opportunities for profit. More and more merchants like the Rumanian appeared in the store to buy in unheard-of quantities, paying the huge sums at Herr Emmerich's window in the glass cage out of thick billfolds crammed with foreign banknotes without as much as a quiver, asking over and over for the things that were unobtainable. It was like that, that he overheard a merchant from Croatia ask Herr Benesch for hacksaw blades; he drew Herr Benesch aside to tell him that he knew where he could get forty dozen. Herr Benesch and he bought the blades together and resold them to the merchant. It took less than an hour. They divided a forty-per-cent profit.

From the same machine shop where Peter had got the blades, he was able to buy the files a Polish merchant wanted. He borrowed two thousand kronen from Herr Benesch, and together with his own savings he had enough to buy half the files the machine shop had on hand.

He had been told to meet the Pole at a coffeehouse on the Ringstrasse. The idea of entering the coffeehouse with the two small, but ungainly cases of files which he had brought in a taxi appalled him at first. But when the taxi driver and he took the cases through the revolving door, he realized that the coffeehouse was so swarming with people that nobody even noticed them. A waiter came up with raised eyebrows, but another waiter who apparently had been promised a sizable tip by the Polish merchant immediately hurried up to the first waiter to whisper something. The cases were left by an umbrella stand beside the door.

The Pole had not come yet. Peter looked around for an empty table. There was none. He finally asked a man who sat busily scribbling figures in a notebook for permission to sit down at his table; the man barely raised his head from the notebook and grunted as if irritated by the formality. There was, indeed, a brash, thick-skinned disregard of propriety about the whole atmosphere of this coffeehouse. Men walked around freely between the tables, jostled each other, talked shrilly and all at the same time without bothering to lower their voices. They were nearly all foreigners, Peter noticed; swarthy men from the Balkans and from Poland, with many Jews among them. Snatches of talk in some Slavic tongue assailed his ears along with shreds and tatters of grotesquely broken German. A feverish alertness sharpened the bewildering confusion of voices. The talk and the brief, vehement arguments were almost solely about foreign currency and about stocks and bonds. He heard one bearded man quote a price on "ten thousand lire," saw the other man sneer and argue, yet presently saw the two of them side by side between two tables exchanging money from large billfolds.

Because the Polish merchant still had not shown up and because all the talk about foreign currency had aroused his interest, he picked up a paper and turned to the financial page. The small print and the condensed jargon of the notations baffled him for a minute; then he succeeded in solving the puzzling arrangement of the columns. The Swiss franc had risen from eight kronen the previous day to eight and one-half kronen, and the American dollar had gone up three kronen. . . . He figured rapidly. At that rate all the money he had earned so miraculously in the last two weeks had already lost one-fifth of its value—or would have lost it, if he had not used it all to buy the files for the Pole. He had known that Herr Straka and Herr Emmerich watched the foreign currency quotations, but he had been too intoxicated by what he had considered his windfalls to have even thought of the decreasing value of the krone. He had been too innocent—*until now!* he assured himself.

When the Pole finally came and, after hastily examining the two cases of files, prepared to count out the money, Peter checked him.

"I'd rather have it in dollars."

The Pole gave him a quick look, then said equably:

"I don't have dollars. I can give it to you in Italian lire. That's just as good."

"No, it isn't. The Italian lira has been dropping pretty fast. How about Swiss francs?"

"All right, if you insist. I guess I've got enough francs to pay you. . . ." The Pole turned over the bill of sale Peter had brought with him and started to figure on the back. "That makes 236 francs—correct? I figured it at the rate of thirteen kronen."

"Oh, but the rate is eight-fifty! That's the official rate."

"Oh, the official rate!" The Polish merchant grimaced derisively. "Wait a minute——" He got up and signaled to a man who at once came hurrying to their table—"What's the price of francs, Swiss?"

"Fourteen. How many do you want?"

"Not right now. . . ."

Peter suspected some sort of connivance. The Pole realized it.

"All right, you ask somebody yourself. They all deal in currency here. Ask that Jew over there. . . ."

Peter went.

"Fourteen," the Jew said.

"Well?" the Pole greeted him when he came back. "You can see now what the rate is when you buy them! The government rate means nothing. Do you want francs, or kronen?"

"I'll take it in kronen. . . ."

He had decided that much as he wanted the stable Swiss currency, he could equally well keep his capital from losing value by immediately buying more goods with it the following morning. But he was annoyed with the Pole and the currency speculators for having it in their power to cut his capital into half the moment he wanted to turn it into foreign money.

Instead of taking the next lot of files along with him when he went to meet the Polish merchant two evenings later, he went to the coffeehouse empty-handed. It was the Pole this time who twitched with annoyance.

"No files? Couldn't you get any more?"

"I can get them. But I wanted some sort of understanding about the price first."

The Pole was watching him warily. "Of course, if the files have gone up a little, that doesn't matter. One has to expect that. . . ."

Peter stated the new price into which he had figured the speculators' rate of exchange on the franc.

"But that is fantastic! That is sixty per cent higher than two days ago!"

"No, it isn't. It's exactly the same price as before if you figure it in Swiss francs."

The Pole frowned for a few seconds. "All right, I'll take them. You learn fast, don't you? . . ."

Oh, yes, he was learning fast! Peter mentally answered the tart question nearly five weeks later, while he was sitting by himself in a restaurant in the Mariahilferstrasse, luxuriously finishing a second portion of omelet. It was only a few days before Christmas. All through December he had been coming to this restaurant or to another for dinner. . . . Fast enough, he went on thinking, to wonder now at his innocence during those first few weeks of trading when he had considered the Rumanian openhanded for paying him ten-per-cent commission, and extravagantly kind for treating him to lunch. Fast enough, to know now that the foreign merchants were making from three to five-hundred-per-cent profit in overnight transactions, and that no matter how much one charged them in kronen they were still buying at less than prewar prices because of the constant devaluation of the krone, to say nothing of the fabulous prices they charged in the Balkans. Yes, he understood now about currency, and why since the end of November in the store Herr Emmerich had also insisted that the foreign merchants pay for their purchases in Swiss francs or at least in Italian lire. He understood so well that he himself had twelve hundred Swiss francs at home in the drawer, rather than sixteen thousand kronen. Not that that was all of his capital, he reminded himself pleasantly—there were the two dozen portable smithies he and Herr Benesch had bought together, and the two hundred pounds of bronze ingots he owned outright and which he would probably sell to the Italian tomorrow. The Italians, it appeared, were as short of tools and hardware as the Balkans. . . . Another three months like this last one and he could laugh at being made a clerk or not being made one this Christmas—though, lately, Herr Straka had been promisingly friendly. . . .

Herr Straka had, in fact, after an initial period of mistrust immediately following the strike in November, been multiplying important assignments for him. He had even been sent on another mission out of town—to Passau this time—to check the inventory of a small stove factory Herr Straka had taken over recently. But it had never been the same as before when he was with Herr Straka. The shadow of those humiliating ten minutes in the office still clouded Herr Straka's manner, and made him reserved and distant when he gave him directions for some errand now. There was no way of being sure whether Herr Straka was not merely admitting his efficiency, without really thinking him qualified in some intangible particular—in some half-mystic sense of reliability, which Herr Meier with his forty years' service stood for—to be a clerk. Peter had found it increasingly necessary to steel himself for a disappointment. He told himself again on the morning of the twenty-fourth: *I don't care whether I get to be a clerk now, or not! I can wait until July if I have to. I don't care in the least. . . .*

But that evening while he waited his turn in the outer office to go in and wish Herr Straka a merry Christmas and to receive his Christmas bonus, he was nonetheless racked by suspense and queasy with apprehension.

Herr Straka's deliberateness did not promise well.

"It has been the custom of the firm," Herr Straka was at last saying, "to present a silver watch to each apprentice on completion of his apprenticeship. But a watch nowadays seems somewhat less important than other things. I passed Gerngross' yesterday and saw some suits in the windows that looked quite well made—you might go and look at them and then draw the money from Frau Redlich. Herr Kropfl will see to it that your papers are properly made out to the Guild Chamber and to the Merchants Guild. Congratulations. . . ." Herr Straka held out his hand.

Peter tried to thank him connectedly. Herr Straka heard him out.

"I am sure that you will continue to do as well as you have in the past. You will, of course, stay in the store now. I am putting you with Herr Lehnert for the present as his assistant. That will give you an opportunity to master that particular department. Later on we may shift you to some other department—the important thing for you now is to get a general experience in the store. Then, after a few years, I may send you out with one of our representatives. There is every reason to assume that our trade with the Balkan countries will be as extensive as before the war. Your future with this firm will depend entirely on the interest you take in your work—a merry Christmas to you!"

He could not help blurting out to the switchboard girl with whom he had often flirted:

"I'm a clerk."

"Fancy!" she mocked. "Why, *Herr Domanig!* Congratulations."

The laborers from the store and the warehouses, who were still waiting to see Herr Straka, heard her and came up to congratulate him. Across the street, Herr Emmerich hurried out of the glass cage with a smile to shake hands. Then Frau Redlich and Herr Meier. . . . Some of the clerks were still left in the locker room. He saw that Herr Lehnert, like Herr Emmerich, had also known beforehand. The other clerks mobbed him, until his embarrassment at so much attention made him fight his way out of the locker room with his hat and coat, and hurry out into the street, to escape both their friendly pummeling and their noisy congratulations.

He had not thought that his clerkship would after all mean so much to him. He was a clerk now! And after only two and a half years. . . . He had the right to open his own store—or he could become general manager some day like Herr Emmerich, or a representative of the firm like the stout man who lived in Budapest and who was almost as important as Herr Emmerich. . . .

He waited until he was on the Gürtel before his curiosity made him open his pay envelope: a renewed flutter of gratitude to Herr Straka assailed him. His salary was nine hundred kronen—as much as Herr Benesch had been getting—and in addition there was a Christmas bonus of two hundred kronen. He marveled at the scrupulousness of Herr Straka's generosity. Not only might Herr Straka have made him serve another half-year, but Herr Straka was giving him a bonus over and above the big salary and the suit as an apprenticeship present. He realized that the very fact that he was making so much more money than the salary out of his private trading, only made him more alert to Herr Straka's action. That was the way to be, he thought almost piously; of course, it was true that Herr Straka was getting to be one of the richest men in the country—as Herr Lehnert had said several times—and that Herr Straka was buying more and more houses in the neighborhood for warehouses, taking over factories even, but Herr Straka was also sharing his profits with the employees and paying twice as big salaries as other firms. . . .

He started to think about breaking the news at home. It was a pity that Franz was still in Vorarlberg; it took Franz to lend sparkle to an occasion like this. . . . He walked hastily up and down the Mariahilferstrasse, scanning the shop windows in search of fine enough Christmas presents for Poldi and for her. He found a pair of real wool gaiters, which had only been imported from Switzerland that very week, for *her* to wear on her way to Mass on the cold mornings; and he got a handsome alligator-skin pocketbook for Poldi which he thought she would like. Then, still in the mood for shopping, he tried several confectionery shops in the Innere Stadt in a vain attempt to get some candy. He finally succeeded in getting two bars of Swiss chocolate on the Stephansplatz by dint of much winking and letting the confectioner see that he did not care what the price was. . . .

He hurried home with his treasures, but once there and alone with *her* in the apartment, he found it hard to begin. He decided that a roundabout opening would be less awkward. He tried to sound casual:

"Do you think Franz would mind if I borrowed one of his dress shirts?"

"What do you need a dress shirt for?"

"For the Merchants Guild ball on New Year's Eve."

"You need to think about balls at your age. You better think about going to church once in a while—you aren't going to any balls while you're in my house!"

"But I've got to go. Every new clerk has to go and stand treat to the older clerks. It's a tradition." He caught the sharp look she gave him. "I'm a clerk—aren't you proud?"

She was silent for a long minute. "If at least your mother could know it—so far away . . ." She dabbed at her eyes with the corner of her apron. "Goodness knows what's happened to her and those children with this war . . ."

But he did not care to think about Mizzi. It would open a compartment in his mind which he had kept closed for a long time now.

"Oh, my mother . . . Who cares whether she knows!"

"She'd care, all right! One's own child, after all these years . . ."

At least, *she* was proud of him; he could tell by her gruffness. But Poldi, when she came home, put a damper on his elation.

"I hope you don't expect me to be delirious with joy," Poldi said frostily. "Now you're a counterjumper. If you think that's something to be proud of—you could be in your last year of the *Realschule!*"

"Much good that would do me now!" he scoffed back. "Maybe you haven't noticed how all those boys from the *Realschule* and even with a degree from the university are starving to death right and left? I earn more in a week than most of them do in a month."

"Yes, and they're still gentlemen and you're only a counterjumper!"

He gave it up after that. They had supper, and then Poldi lighted the tiny Christmas tree from the florist, and for a few minutes while they exchanged presents and talked about Franz the room was warm and friendly. Then another argument started. Poldi had picked up his pay envelope which he had left for *her* on the kitchen table——

"What's this?"

"It's six hundred kronen. It's the money for Mother."

"Well, you aren't going to pay that. You can give Mother three hundred kronen if you want to, and that's all!"

"But I'm making nine hundred kronen. And Franz is still sick, and he's only getting his army pay—I'd like to know why I can't pay my share toward things?"

"Because Franz and I are still capable of supporting the family, thank you! . . ."

He knew then that he had offended Poldi by parading how much money, and especially how much more than Franz, he was making. His triumph seemed no longer so complete. . . .

But after Christmas, back in the store, everything served to reassure him about his new importance. He could linger by the lockers now with the other clerks at noon and in the evening and join freely in their discussions and jokes. He was "Herr Domanig," and Herr Meier was the first to growl at one of the second-year apprentices who forgot and called him "Peter." He was no longer accountable to anyone but Herr Lehnert for his actions, and after New Year's when Herr Lehnert became laid up with the flu—the disease which people said had come from the battlefields—he was in entire charge of the carriage-building department. He had two of the new clerks who had just come out of the army and were still in uniform under him, and three helpers, and it was up to him to decide how the springs and axles were to be stored in the huge new racks the carpenters were still working on in the new warehouse next to the office building. He worked harder than he ever had as an apprentice from sheer joy in his new position in the store. Even the trading he was doing on his own in the evenings, although it was constantly increasing in scope since his discovery that it was possible to buy vast supplies of tools and material from the army arsenals which were being closed, had sunk into secondary importance.

There was only one shadow over his satisfaction—Herr Kropfl!

Herr Kropfl was missing no opportunity to belittle his promotion. He was taking malicious delight in still calling him "Peter" and in pretending to have forgotten that he was no longer an apprentice. Moreover, Herr Kropfl had deliberately put off making out the papers to register him as clerk with the Guild Chamber. Twice when Peter had gone to the office to remind him of it, Herr Kropfl had struck a pose in front of the girls and had sneered: "You seem to be in an awful hurry for those papers. You wouldn't be thinking of leaving us by any chance, would you, Peter? Maybe tomorrow, if I haven't anything better to do . . ." In the end, Peter had had to appeal to Herr Straka. But being thus forced to make out the papers had only increased Herr Kropfl's venom. It was in one of those sarcastically playful moods that Herr Kropfl came after him to the new warehouse one day just before noon, when the three helpers had already started for lunch, and tried to hand him an envelope——

"Here, Peter, a little errand. Drop in at Czermak's on your way home and ask them to check this invoice."

"I'm not an apprentice any more. I'm not running any more errands."

"Oh? Perhaps you'd like me to tell Herr Straka that you refuse to deliver an important document to a customer who's waiting for it, although it's right on your way? But we won't have to do that—here!"

Peter dropped the wagon spring he had been holding. He went closer to Herr Kropfl. A slow voluptuousness filled him as he measured himself against him. It was no longer as it had been two years ago: besides being every bit as tall as Herr Kropfl, he had put on weight since last summer. He knew suddenly with an overwhelming certainty that he would no longer be satisfied with merely presenting the evidence of Herr Kropfl's thieving to Herr Straka—it was no longer enough! . . . He looked slowly from the soft cleft in Herr Kropfl's chin to the full lips and then into the glittering black eyes——

"It's just as much on your way home as it is on mine. You can take it yourself—Kropfl!"

He knew so precisely what was coming that he waited for each new detail with sardonic patience. The dark flush had crept up to Herr Kropfl's cheekbones, his eyes glistened secretively beneath the treacherously lowered eyelids. When his hand shot out with that catlike abruptness, Peter stepped in and blocked it with his body, while his own hand slapped hard against Herr Kropfl's cheek. *That's the third time somebody gets slapped,* he thought coolly. He had meant to go on enjoying his exquisitely pleasurable detachment, but the contact with Herr Kropfl's body brought his hatred surging over him like a blinding wash. . . .

They had seized each other and were wrestling rather than using their fists. He realized once more—with a tiny margin of his consciousness that was left free to wonder—how much stronger Herr Kropfl was than his pampered hands led one to believe. Only, it did not matter! He succeeded in backing Herr Kropfl against a case of axles, jarring him hard against the edge of the case, then Herr Kropfl kicked out with one leg, got partially free, and Peter felt the signet ring brush over his cheek. He knew rather than felt that the ring had cut his cheek. The memory of the showy ring he had seen so often enraged him. He smashed his fist into the soft face, hit again, until Herr Kropfl got away to one side. Twice Herr Kropfl dodged away, then they closed once more. Herr Kropfl was beginning to pant. He drew away suddenly when they both bumped into a row of truck springs tilted up against the wall, took another step backward and kicked over the heavy springs so that Peter had to jump to keep his feet from being crushed. . . .

He stepped over the springs and reached Herr Kropfl. They landed on the floor, struggling for a hold on each other. Herr Kropfl brought up one knee—an infuriating pain, through which Peter hit out savagely four times, ten times, he could not have told how often, until Herr Kropfl lay back limply on the floor. Kneeling over him, panting himself now, Peter asked: "Got enough?"

Herr Kropfl raised his head from the floor to nod.

"Just remember—"

The ring tore over his cheek just below his eye. He could feel it this time. He seized Herr Kropfl's wrist, then his shoulder and slammed him back against the floor so that his head landed with a dull thud. Herr Kropfl's eyes were suddenly wide open and terrified——

"Don't! . . ."

I could kill him now, Peter thought. *Just one more crack like the last one on the floor . . .* He shuddered suddenly. The afternoon in the cellar, when for one moment Herr Kropfl and the picture of his father had blurred into one, had come back to him. A convulsing mixture of loathing and terror made him let go abruptly of Herr Kropfl's coat.

He got up and started to knock the dust from his clothes; then he took out his handkerchief to wipe the blood from his face.

Herr Kropfl had raised himself on one elbow. With his free hand he felt the back of his head.

"You all right?" Peter asked. "Want me to call somebody?"

Herr Kropfl sat up, and shook his head.

Peter went. . . .

Chapter Forty-Seven

A WONDERFUL freedom came to him from the fight. It was as if some sinister, crouching menace which had been much greater than Herr Kropfl had been driven forever out of all the dark corners in the store. He felt almost grateful to Herr Kropfl for giving him this exuberant sense of release, and when some of the clerks tried to congratulate him on his triumph, he was abrupt and evaded their questions from a feeling that there had been something too important for talk in what had happened out in the warehouse.

He waited a little uneasily for what Herr Straka was going to say. Herr Meier was the one who had known about it first; Herr Meier had seen Herr Kropfl come out of the warehouse after the fight. Herr Meier and Frau Redlich had been scandalized. Two days went by and Herr Straka still had not sent for him. On the third day, Peter had to go to Herr Straka with some plans for the shelves of the new warehouse for carriage fittings across the street. Herr Straka was distant and reserved. When they had discussed the proposed arrangement of the shelves, Herr Straka pushed away the plans:

"What occasioned your disgraceful exhibition with Herr Kropfl?"

"I don't like Herr Kropfl, Herr Straka."

Herr Straka frowned. "I did not know that there were any members of our staff who did not like each other, so that they have to settle their differences with their fists. There is enough lawlessness in the streets. . . ."

It was all that was said. Peter did not mention the six forged invoices he had collected in the last two years. He thought: *I'm not a stool pigeon. I've settled my account with him. Kropfl can't steal now with Herr Emmerich over him. What good would it do?*

Two days later, Herr Straka was still cool in his manner toward him, but on Monday when he said, "Good morning," Herr Straka smiled. . . .

It seemed to him as if he had never really liked the store up until now. Even the musty bottom shelves in the storerooms and the worn treads of the cellar stairs became included in his affection. He had been toying with a plan to set up for himself as a commission merchant or of going into partnership with a Swiss merchant whom he had recently got to know, but now the idea of leaving the store seemed suddenly unbearable. He found that even the familiar, trivial talk of the clerks in front of the lockers every morning and evening had taken on a new charm, even though their talk lately had been of nothing but the forthcoming election and the election did not interest him.

He ran into Armbruster one evening, and Armbruster after the first few minutes of uneasiness was as full of election talk as the clerks. Peter could not help taunting:

"I thought the republic was going to make everything perfect—now it's the election! I don't see that things have got any better."

"That's because the Socialists haven't had a chance yet. Just wait until after the election when we really get control of the government! So far the priests and the capitalists have managed to keep their hands on everything and to keep on intriguing—or perhaps you don't know that they're plotting day and night to bring back the Habsburgs?"

"I thought it was the officers and the aristocracy who wanted the monarchy?"

"They're all in it together. They would like things to stay the way they've always been so's they can hold on to all their privileges. The priests are the worst: they're scared to death of losing all those big estates the Church has been holding! But we're going to confiscate them all the same—just wait until February!"

They were sitting in a small restaurant to which Peter had asked him to have some of the smoked sausage and potatoes which the restaurant procured twice a week from some farmer in the country. Armbruster had come in reluctantly, bristling with disapproval of the black-market practices of the restaurant, but once seated at the table and with the steaming food before him, his hunger had got the better of his qualms and he had even consented to a second portion. But Peter felt uncomfortably that Armbruster's lingering resentment of his desertion in November had not been softened by the gesture—Armbruster, and for that matter he himself for one ironic moment, looked on the food as an attempt to corrupt him.

Armbruster became suddenly restive at the distance between them. His blunt eyes focused awkwardly and pleaded.

"Can't you see what they're up to? They don't want the workingman to have any say in things. They'd like to keep us down and keep on starving us the way they did during the war."

"They didn't starve us; that was the fault of the war and of the blockade. There wasn't any food for anybody."

"I suppose the priests and the rich people went hungry as we did?"

"Well, a lot of them did."

"Where? You show them to me! And what about all the corruption that was going on: the black market and the profiteers and all the rest of it? I suppose they didn't exist either! All those Jews who came as refugees in 1915 with nothing but lice to their name and now they own half the stores in the city—and the farmers who got rich out of the war—and the currency speculators now, and the aristocrats who're smuggling all their jewelry out of the country as fast as they can! They don't any of them give a damn about the country—they're just looking out for themselves, the way they always have. That's the kind of people you're defending!"

"I'm not defending them. I was as hungry as anybody."

"If I had my way," Armbruster glowered, "I'd hang every last one of them. I'd take away all the money they made out of the war while the poor people were dying in the trenches or starving. And that goes for your boss, too!"

"Herr Straka isn't a profiteer."

"No? Maybe he isn't selling things to Poland and every place just as fast as he can? That's our national wealth that's going, in case you don't know it! He's taking advantage of all this currency manipulation like all the rest!"

"That's not true!"

"And you say you aren't defending them! You act pretty prosperous yourself these days!"

The simple meal to which he had invited Armbruster had become a weapon for Armbruster to use against him. It irritated Peter that Armbruster could make him feel on the defensive. He said hotly:

"I served my apprenticeship. I'm a merchant and I've earned the right to make some money. I like to eat once in a while!"

"You'd rather be on the side of the exploiters. But it isn't going to last much longer. We're going to put a stop to all that. Just see whether we don't!"

"That's all right with me. . . ."

They parted as hostilely as in November. The attempt to make it up had been a failure. Peter felt resentful and at the same time oddly guilty. It did not help to tell himself that Armbruster was a fanatic and had no idea what things were really like—Armbruster's accusation that he himself was a profiteer kept on rankling.

Two hours later while he was concluding a deal with the Swiss merchant, he felt suddenly driven to raise the price on a case of chisels he had bought for the merchant. The man objected:

"That's high!"

"Very high." He did not care whether he sold the chisels or not.

But there was no satisfaction in the maneuver. The Swiss pulled out his wallet and paid for the order. Peter's irritation turned on the chattering speculators all around them who dealt indiscriminately in everything from platinum to portable smithies. Their parroting talk about steel and machinery annoyed him. *What do they know about steel?* he thought grimly; *they've never unloaded a carload of it in one afternoon! They couldn't tell a lock washer from a trowel!* When one of the men with a notebook came sidling up to him to ask: "You interested in ten bolts of linen?" he turned on him fiercely: "Do I look to you like a huckster?" It gave him some satisfaction to see the man back away hurriedly. But again it was not enough. . . . More and more, in the course of the next few days as he listened to the growing excitement over the election, he felt himself driven to emphasize the distinction that he was not a profiteer, that he was rather a merchant like Herr Straka. Armbruster's vindictive patriotism, he realized, had affected him more than he had been willing to admit. Yet he felt as little inclined to side with the Socialists as he had in November. Almost without being conscious of it, his sympathies drifted toward Herr Straka's party—Poldi's party.

Poldi and the girls in her congregation had been working for weeks distributing handbills and fixing up posters. One evening Poldi put a sheaf of blue handbills on the kitchen table for *her* to hand out in the morning.

She protested: "You leave me alone with your politics. I've got enough to do to try to get a few potatoes and some milk when I go shopping."

"But you can hand out some of these bills to the women you know, can't you? And you've got to vote, too, Mother!"

"Me, vote! I'm too old to bother with any such fool notions."

"Well, do you want the Socialists to get hold of the government? The Socialists are going to confiscate all the church property—and if the Communists win there won't be any churches at all."

"They had to kick out the Kaiser. Now they've got what they wanted: a godless world! God only knows what's going to happen. . . ."

"Nothing is going to happen if everybody goes out and votes. Don't forget to take them with you tomorrow!"

But the following noon the handbills were still on the table where Poldi had left them. Obeying a sudden impulse, he took them with him when he started back to the store and handed them out in the streets. Poldi looked even more surprised when he offered to go electioneering from door to door with her in the evenings. He found that it was almost childishly easy to persuade people to vote for the Conservative party by picturing the Communists as foreign terrorists and by implying that the Socialists were little better. He regretted sometimes that he had to waste his eloquence on no more than two or three people. . . . There were street fights when he went out late at night to help a group of men to stick up posters. Socialist rowdies tried to tear down the posters as soon as they were on the signboards. The battles around the signboards grew more vicious as the election drew nearer.

On election day itself, he worked from early morning until the polls closed, rounding up invalids and old people and bringing them to the polls in a taxi he had hired for the day. Somewhat to his own surprise, he found himself passionately awaiting the results of the election. He felt a mild triumph when they were announced:

the Socialists had won a bare handful more seats than the Conservatives in the new national assembly. The Socialists were far from having complete control of the government, as Armbruster had predicted. . . .

The excitement over the election wore off and with it his satisfaction, but his need to differentiate himself from the flashily dressed speculators with whom he rubbed elbows every day had not diminished. It was largely that need which sent him to the most fashionable tailor shop in the Kärntnerstrasse and made him pick the somber double-breasted model from the English fashion plates and choose a piece of dark-blue cheviot which the tailor had only a few days before imported from Switzerland. The suit was going to be staggeringly expensive—for the same price he could have bought half a dozen of the ready-made suits of which Herr Straka had spoken at Christmas—but its very costliness and the tailor's barely disguised skepticism of his ability to pay, only made him more determined to have it. He counted out the Swiss banknotes and had himself measured for it then and there.

After that, each trip to the Kärntnerstrasse for a fitting became an event. He came to look on the severely plain blue suit as a symbol of his conservatism and proof of his kinship with Herr Straka and Baron Ortner rather than with the brash-mannered, diamond-flaunting profiteers. But as the suit neared completion he took joy in it also for other reasons. The fine wool cloth after the years of wartime substitutes enchanted him. He thought of the charity suits he had worn as a child with so much loathing, and of the made-over suits he had worn lately, Franz's and Father's—now at last he was able to dictate his own mold. Only the best was going to do him now! But it would have to be a best that did not advertise its value, since half the joy would consist in the consciousness of having the best and not caring for people's opinion. . . .

But he could not deny his pleasure at the naïve envy with which Franz, who returned from Vorarlberg on the same day the suit was delivered, admired it and joked:

"Boy, oh boy! Do you suppose Herr Straka would buy me one of those? Perhaps it's not too late for me to become an apprentice at Herr Straka's. . . ."

Chapter Forty-Eight

FRANZ had joked about the new suit, as he occasionally attempted to joke now about other things, but there had been no gaiety in his voice or eyes. There were two heavy lines that ran from Franz's nose to the corners of his mouth, lines which had not been there a year ago and which Peter had first noticed at the hospital in Baden.

Yet the stay in Vorarlberg had worked some improvement in Franz. His hands were not quite so restless as before, and his devoutness had taken a less ostentatious if austerer form. Instead of the black-bound devotional books, Franz now read erudite Catholic periodicals and immersed himself in forbidding-looking philosophical tomes. And he refused to miss even a single one of a series of Lenten sermons given by a Jesuit at the University Church.

From sheer curiosity and because he happened to be in the vicinity, Peter dropped into the church one evening. He was astonished at the number of ex-officers and young professional men. The Jesuit in the pulpit was bald, lean, and had an aristocratic face. In the bleak light of the one electric bulb in the pulpit he seemed strangely impassioned and austere. He spoke of the renunciation by Jesus of the richness of this world and of the ascetic way of life. At times the discourse became so learned that Peter had difficulty in following it. He noted several references to the "City of God." . . . But it was rather the somber earnestness of the men all around him which interested him than the sermon. He wanted to stay and hear the end, but he had an appointment with a merchant and had to leave. On the way to the coffeehouse, it occurred to him that the Jesuit's talk about renunciation and discipline was but another effect of the defeat—different in form but not in origin from Armbruster's railing against the priests and the capitalists. *Not any of these are for me,* he thought. *They are all a sort of running-away from things. If you are successful you don't have to run away.*

He noticed that not even she was altogether easy about Franz's somber devoutness. She said: "Franz has learned what it is to live without God!" and she hastened to attribute his taciturn earnestness to the months he had spent in the trenches; but secretly—Peter was sure of it—she was wishing for Franz to be again as he had been before: rather cavalier about going to church, gay and inclined to tease her about her piety.

For what was most noticeable about Franz was that all his former carefreeness had gone out of him. It showed in the meticulousness with which he now brushed and put away his own clothes, in the way he put on rubbers at the least threat of rain and nearly always carried an umbrella instead of a walking stick, and in the prejudice he had formed against having flowers in his room. When he had first come back from Vorarlberg, she had taken her finest plants and had put them on his window sill. Franz had promptly brought them out into the living room. The next day when she had returned the flowering century plant and the begonias to his window, Franz had pointedly set them on the floor outside his door.

When Peter attempted to fathom Franz's state of mind he could not arrive anywhere. Tucked in among some other papers in Franz's desk there was a whole sheaf of recent letters from Bianca. At least twice a week there was a letter from Hungary. Peter remembered what Bianca had said: "I don't care, I'm going to marry Franz!" What was it, then, that Franz was worried about? It could not just be the constant rumors about the growing power of the Bolsheviks in Hungary. . . .

It was impossible to ask Franz about Bianca, and the very impossibility added to Peter's impatience with Franz. A subtle antagonism had sprung up between Franz and him. When he thought about it, he felt inclined to attribute it to Franz's resentment of his role as go-between when Franz had been sick; it seemed to him that Franz was trying to disown the whole period in Baden by shutting him out from anything where Bianca was concerned. And there was still another reason, Peter was convinced: Franz, who was still waiting for his appointment to a new job in the Ministry of the Interior and who was only having his pitifully small lieutenant's pension in the meantime, was resentful of his large salary and of all the money he was earning outside the store.

There had been several references on Franz's part to profiteering and the amount of trading in stolen goods that was going on. Once, when the newspapers had carried a brief mention of the fact that Herr Breitkopf and two helpers from the store had been convicted of theft and sentenced to the penitentiary, Franz had shoved the paper across to him.

"Did you see that?"

"I knew about that three weeks ago when they were arrested."

A few days later he had more irritating proof of what was in Franz's mind. He had bought several hundred locksmith files one evening and had brought them home and left them there. The following noon when he came home for lunch he saw that the package had been opened and that the files were spread out on the floor. He could tell from her hooded frown what their suspicions were. Franz came out of his room and asked:

"Where did you get those files?"

"I bought them, of course."

He watched while Franz strode up and down in that tense, worried way he had now.

"I'm coming to the store with you after lunch."

Peter tried hard to keep his irritation in check: excitement was bad for Franz! He spoke as calmly as he could:

"They aren't from the store, if that's what you have in mind. They come from an army depot."

"In that case you must have some sort of proof."

Again he forced himself to be calm:

"Look, things nowadays are bought and sold half a dozen times in a single evening. You should come into one of the coffeehouses in the Innere Stadt——"

"Yes, I've heard about that. Stolen goods."

"You don't steal things from the army. They are selling off their supplies. Nobody is going to show you the original bill if he's making two-hundred-per-cent profit over his purchasing price."

Franz looked stubborn and determined. "I'm going to Herr Straka with you after lunch. It's better to do that than to have the police in the house and to have you sent to the penitentiary."

A towering anger seized Peter. He recognized the mood in Franz. It was the same naïve honesty that had made Franz go to Herr

Granini over the few kronen he had taken from her and cause him to be expelled from the choir. . . . He remembered how scrupulously he had paid for the hobnails when he could so easily have made off with them, and he writhed at the humiliation involved in having Franz go to Herr Straka as if he were still a little boy. But there was nothing he could do. As soon as they got up from lunch, Franz asked her: "Have you any paper, Mother, to wrap these up?"

She produced some folded wrapping paper and some string.

Franz spread out the wrapping paper on the floor beside the files.

"We'll each take half," he said.

Peter saw that it was going to be even worse than he had thought. They would arrive in Herr Straka's office, each with a bundle. It was ridiculous.

"Look," he said, "what you are trying to find out is whether these files are from the store. I've been trying to tell you that we don't even handle that make of file. All you have to do is take a single package. It's got the trademark on the wrapper and stamped on every file. You can always get the rest."

Franz hesitated for a second. "All right," he said. He tore off a piece of paper and wrapped up two bundles of files meticulously, the way he did everything nowadays.

They rode together to the Margaretenstrasse without speaking once. But when they walked toward the store from the streetcar stop, Peter said:

"I hope you realize how humiliating this is for me? I am somebody now in the store. You are treating me like a little boy."

"I can't help that. We've always been honest in our family."

"Do you think Herr Straka would have trusted me with tens of thousands of kronen if I weren't honest? The point is that it's humiliating. . . . You could at least go about it in a different way: all you have to do is ask Herr Benesch, who's the head of the file department, and he can tell you whether we handle this make or not."

"How do I know that Herr Benesch isn't in this with you?"

"But if you ask him like a customer, how could he know who you are?"

"I'm afraid that isn't enough."

"All right, then, how about the manager of the store—Herr Emmerich? You don't suppose he's 'in with me' as you put it. He's the general manager and he's got power of attorney for Herr Straka."

"All right, I'll see Herr Emmerich first." Franz's tone made it clear that if he did not think Herr Emmerich important enough, he might still go to Herr Straka.

It was fortunate that there were already several customers and clerks lined up in front of the window in the glass cage. Franz could not help but be impressed by the obvious importance of Herr Emmerich.

It took nearly twenty minutes before Peter could introduce Franz to Herr Emmerich. He explained:

"I bought some files for a man who asked me to get him some. My cousin here is worried that the files are from the store. . . ."

"Yes, I wanted to find out," Franz said and handed the files through the window to Herr Emmerich.

Herr Emmerich glanced at the wrapper. "No, they're not from here. They're a German make——"

Peter could not stay to hear the rest. Herr Lehnert was asking him to help him with a customer in the warehouse yard. When he came back into the store, Franz was gone.

Herr Emmerich stopped him later in the afternoon to ask:

"Are you doing a lot of trading on the side?"

"I've been doing some."

"Well, I hope it's only once in a while. I doubt whether Herr Straka would approve of your making a business of it."

He could see that Franz's anxiety had infected Herr Emmerich, but an hour later Herr Emmerich appeared to have forgotten about the files.

But not Franz. That evening when Peter came home the files were still spread out on the floor. Franz said:

"I put those two bundles back with the rest."

"I hope you're convinced now. As a matter of fact, I paid good hard money for them. And you made me feel like a little boy in coming to the store!"

"I couldn't help that. And in the future you will please not bring any more things to the house. You can keep them somewhere else."

"Then I'll have to rent a room somewhere!"

The incident did not improve relations between them. It seemed as if after that no issue was too small for Franz and him to be immediately lined up on opposite sides. The quarrels were usually precipitated through her. She would complain about the Socialists:

"They say the Reds are going to take away all church property. I wonder who's going to support the hospitals and look after the orphans now!"

He would not be able to resist goading Franz. "The Socialists are going to do it, of course. They don't think that the hospitals have been run so very efficiently in the past."

Franz would already be frowning behind his newspaper.

"And I suppose the Socialists are going to feed us, too?"

"Certainly. The English and the French like the Socialists all right. There's already an Inter-Allied commission reporting on our food shortage. At any rate, the Socialists can't do any worse than the Kaiser and the Christian Democrats have been doing these last few years."

It would be at this point that Franz would flare up:

"You will please watch your tongue when you are speaking to Mother! You are not talking to one of your fellow apprentices now!"

After each set-to like that, Peter would make a point of not coming home for lunch or dinner for several days. Then he would again feel ashamed of showing the power his income gave him and guilty for having excited Franz when Franz was not supposed to be excited. For a few days he would make an effort not to provoke Franz.

They clashed again when the letter from Mizzi came.

It was toward the end of March, only a few days after Franz had obtained his transfer to the Ministry of the Interior and had started on his new job. Franz had already finished lunch and he looked excited and happier than he had for some time. Peter attributed it to the new job and the fact that Franz had only the day before discovered that he had not suffered any loss of seniority through being transferred. He was about to sit down to lunch, when Franz said:

"Look on Father's desk!"

He went and saw the two letters from America, one already

opened and the other addressed to him. He felt pleasurably excited, but some perverse impulse made him pretend not to be interested. He came back to the table and started to eat.

"Aren't you going to look at them?" Franz sounded incredulous and faintly outraged.

"Sure, after I've eaten. There's no hurry."

"I should think you'd be a little more excited than that!"

"What's there to be excited about? It's about time she wrote. The lady I'm taking English lessons from has had letters from her relatives right along. Her relatives simply had sense enough to send them through Switzerland."

"That's quite different. Your teacher probably has some friend in Switzerland who sent the letters on to her."

"Well, that wasn't any trick. It's not so very difficult to find some businessman or some banker in Switzerland who would have done that for her."

"You can be sure that your mother tried everything she humanly could. The mere fact that she tried so hard to have you come to America in 1915 shows that."

"Her trying didn't do me much good."

Franz frowned and went into his room.

She came in from the kitchen and said:

"Your own mother! God has said: 'Honor your father and mother. . . .' "

He did not answer her. When he had finished lunch he opened the letter that was addressed to him. Two snapshots fell out. They were both of a boy and a little girl, one showing them sitting side by side in the bow of a sailboat and the other in bathing suits on a beach. The boy looked rather tall and foreign in his sleeveless sweater and the odd-looking cap. It was rather the little girl who attracted his attention. She was dark and pretty and charmingly solemn-eyed. *So that's my sister!* he thought.

He ignored Mizzi's "My darling Peter—" and skimmed over the letter. Mizzi was still addressing him as if he were years younger than he was, as if he were that boy in the snapshot with the silly cap on his head. He saw that she was calmly assuming that he would be ready to sail "just as soon as we can make arrangements with the American consul in Switzerland and can get a passage. The boats are all terribly crowded. But it'll only be two months at the most, dear Peter. . . ."

He glanced at the other letter addressed to them all: the same solicitude for them because of the war years, and even more detailed information about his trip. There was an inclosed bank draft.

Franz came out of his room and Peter realized that Franz had been watching him from the door.

"Well, aren't you glad?"

"Not particularly."

"Think of it: in another two months you'll be on the high seas, going to America, while we'll still be starving here."

"I'm not so sure that I'm going to go."

"You'll change your mind when the time comes."

"Maybe. I doubt it."

"Don't you realize that there are thousands of people who would give their eyeteeth to go to America and get out of this? Look at all the travel magazines on the newsstands. . . ."

"Well, I'm not one of those thousands. I don't have to go to America to get out of anything. I'm doing quite well right here. Another year and I'll have a small fortune in any currency."

"And I suppose you think that all this profiteering is going to go on forever?"

"Long enough for me. Besides, I'm not profiteering. I'm doing what hardware merchants have always done: I'm selling tools and machinery to the Balkan countries who have always bought them from us. I served an apprenticeship to earn the right to trade."

"If your mother says you're to join her in America, you are going to, whether you like it or not. You may be somebody in the store, as you are always impressing on me, but don't forget that you are still a minor—a seventeen-year-old boy whom nobody has to consult."

It was Franz's parting shot, but it was far from being the last word in connection with the two letters. They continued to lie on Father's desk. The following evening Poldi said:

"I'm going to take the draft to the bank tomorrow and get it cashed."

He could not bear to stand by and let Poldi take the loss involved in cashing the draft at the official rate of exchange.

"If you'll indorse it, I can get at least half again as much as you can at the bank."

"From whom?" Franz asked.

"From every merchant who has to buy things abroad and who needs foreign currency."

"We aren't getting mixed up in anything like that. In case you don't know about it, there happens to be a law against underhand dealing in foreign currency!"

Franz's stubborn guilelessness exasperated him. "Look," he said as patiently as he could, "the draft is for three hundred dollars. That's what you're supposed to get for it. But if you cash it in a bank, you'll only get the equivalent of about a hundred and eighty dollars. What's wrong with selling it to a merchant who needs dollar currency, I'd like to know? Everybody is doing it."

"You may know a lot about commerce, but there are a few other things you don't understand, and one of them is that decent people abide by the law. If our money is losing value every day, it's precisely because there's all that black-market trade in foreign currency."

"I'll see," Poldi said hastily, "whether I can't get part of it cashed in Swiss francs. Then we won't lose so much. . . ."

But the next day when he asked Poldi about the draft, he found that she had had to cash all of it in kronen. She had got the equivalent of a hundred and ninety dollars for it. . . .

Two days went by, and Franz and Poldi and *she* had each written a few pages to Mizzi. Their letter lay reproachfully on Father's desk, all ready to be sealed and mailed. At noon of the third day, Franz asked:

"Have you written your mother yet?"

"No."

"When are you going to?"

"Oh, I will sometime."

"I insist that you write a letter today. You are going to write your own letter, or you are going to add something to our letter. You can take your choice, but you are going to write."

"What am I supposed to say?"

"You can thank your mother for the bank draft and for all she is doing to bring you to her. You can at least show some human decency, if you haven't any other feelings toward her."

"All right. I have to work tonight, but I'll write it when I come home."

He sat down at the kitchen table late that night. He had decided to write in English to impress both Franz and Mizzi. It was hard to write the letter because he did not know what to say. But the snapshot of the little girl gave some validity to the stiff, false-ringing phrases of endearment which he felt the letter called for. He used up most of the space by advising Mizzi not to send any more bank drafts but to put actual banknotes into the letters, because even if half the letters were lost, the rest would still be worth more than a bank draft. He left the letter on the desk for Franz to see.

Franz was markedly conciliatory the next noon, but there was another reason for his change of mood. Three days ago the Bolsheviks in Hungary had seized the government. Franz had been worrying about that. But that morning he had received a telegram from Bianca which had said that Bianca and her mother were arriving by the afternoon train. He spoke to Peter as if they had not quarreled the day before:

"Aren't you glad that you are getting out of this? Just look at what's happening in Hungary! What you can want in staying here when you don't have to is more than I can see. At best, you'll only be a hardware merchant. In America your mother can give you an education and you can be somebody."

"I wasn't going to stay where I was." It was wonderful how quietly he could talk to Franz, now that Bianca was so much closer again! "I was planning to go into the Rhineland where the big steel mills are and learn something about steelmaking there. I've been planning that right along. And after that I'm going to England to the steel mills there and learn all I can. That's why I've been learning English all this time."

"That's very practical and ambitious on your part, but it's still not the same thing as being an engineer. To get somewhere nowadays you need an education."

"I don't know about that. Herr Straka isn't an engineer, and he has the biggest export firm in Central Europe now. You don't know what a demand there is for machines of every sort in the Balkans and in Eastern Europe. And they say that Russia is going to start buying things. I could come back to Herr Straka afterward. There's a career here for me. And I've worked hard to get where I am. . . ."

"Of course, you've worked. But that won't be lost in America either—well, I've got to change my suit. . . ."

"Are you going to meet Bianca at the train?"

"Of course. They're going to have a lot of luggage."

He had hoped for an instant that Franz might ask him to come to the station, but the idea did not seem to occur to Franz.

That evening, although he had an important appointment in the Innere Stadt, he hurried home directly from the store. He found her upset and tight-lipped with fear. Franz had been home for a few minutes in the afternoon, just long enough to change into his army uniform and to announce that he was going to the Hungarian border with Baron Ortner to get Bianca and her mother. It seemed that only an old aunt and one of the servants had arrived on the train and that Bianca and her mother were still on the Hungarian side of the border with a lot of valuables they had brought along.

She scolded angrily:

"When the doctor said he wasn't even to go to a theater because excitement was bad for him, he has to rush off to the border where all this fighting is going on, and all because of that girl!"

Nor was Poldi able to calm her fears. Poldi herself was worried.

They waited all the next day, and *she* spent a second night without sleep. But the second day when Peter came home for lunch, Franz was in the living room. His face looked drawn with fatigue but his eyes shone and he looked gayer than Peter had seen him since he had left for the Italian front more than a year ago.

"I wish you could have been with us," Franz said happily; "you would have known all about wangling things. We didn't dare get on any trains for fear of the Bolsheviks—Heinrich and I were loaded down with silverware and jewelry. I bet I'll never have so many valuables on my person again. Well, we thought at first we'd try to sneak over into Czechoslovakia and we hired a cart and traveled all day yesterday, and then we found out that the Czechs confiscated everything just like the Bolsheviks in Hungary. So we cut south to Sopron and talked a hotel-keeper into letting us hide in his hotel. Heinrich and I told him that Bianca and the *Frau Baronin* were Habsburg princesses and he was so flattered he even got us a guide to help us across the border this morning. And then when we got into Austria we were almost shot by our own soldiers who took us for Bolsheviks."

One thing was clear: Franz had enjoyed the adventure, and Bianca's mother had for the first time been something other than hostile to Franz—"She even condescended to thank me this morning when we got to Vienna," Franz said gaily.

"And Bianca?" Peter asked, because Franz had barely mentioned her.

"She acted like a seasoned cavalry captain—all but wanted to fight the whole Bolshevik gang. Heinrich and I had a hard time to keep her from firing back at them with a little pearl-handled revolver she had brought along when they took a few pot shots at us."

"Dear God!" *she* complained. "When you've been so ill and you know excitement is bad for you."

Franz laughed. "They couldn't have hit us anyway. It was much too dark. We just waited behind some bushes for a while and then we went on. We got across without much trouble, really."

"You'd better get into bed right away!" she commanded.

Franz smiled at her. "All right, Mother, that's one thing you won't have to urge me to do. I'll even drink some of your nettle tea.'"

It was, Peter told himself several times in the next few days and weeks, just like old times. Franz was laughing again. He hummed to himself when he dressed and he joked at meals. The philosophical works were shoved farther and farther back on Franz's desk. He had barely time to glance at the newspapers. He was going out with Bianca nearly every evening now.

Poldi would come home in the evening and would ask: "Where is Franz?" only to have her answer sullenly:

"In the theater again with that girl where he always is!"

"Didn't he come home for supper?"

"If you can call it eating supper: coming home and everything hurry, hurry to get shaved and dressed. All that excitement when the doctor said he was to keep away from that—and then the theater every night: if that isn't excitement!"

"He doesn't go to the theater; he goes to the opera——"

"It's all the same. You can't tell me."

"Well, he can't sit home all the time. You ought to be glad he's getting better."

There was a resentful pause and then she voiced her real fear: "A godless girl like that! He says himself that she only laughs at going to church."

"He didn't say that!"

"He might as well have said it. No good's ever come from marrying out of your class like that. My father always said: Lordling, stick to your castle, and peasant to his glebe."

"We aren't peasants, Mother!" Poldi bridled. "And we're a republic now and there aren't any titles any more. If she doesn't mind, I don't see why you should."

"You and your republic! The Socialists are going to make everything perfect now. I'll only be glad I won't be here to see it. . . ."

But slowly and however reluctantly, she had to yield to the fact that Franz was lighthearted and more nearly like his old self for no other reason but because Bianca was back and because Bianca's mother had withdrawn some of her opposition to him. Franz was already throwing out hints about bringing Bianca home some Sunday afternoon for *her* to meet, but he had apparently decided to win over Poldi first. One morning when Peter was leaving the house with him, Franz said:

"Bianca and Heinrich and I are going to the Opera on Friday night. They are giving *Tannhäuser*. I took tickets for you and Poldi. Do you think you'll be able to get off at the store early enough? I told Poldi last night. . . ."

Chapter Forty-Nine

He left the store at a quarter to five. There was a thrill even in that, just as there was in the new black shoes under his arm. Franz did not know how easy it was for him now to get concessions at the store. Franz still had not got used to the notion that he was not an apprentice any longer, and that he merely had to go to Herr Emmerich in the glass cage and ask, to have Herr Emmerich say with a friendly smile: "Opera, eh? Why, I guess that'll be all right, Herr Domanig."

He tried to make the carton with the new shoes as inconspicuous as possible when he came home. He always felt uncomfortable now when he bought something new which emphasized the gap between his own income and the small incomes of Poldi and Franz.

Poldi was not yet home. Franz was nearly dressed. He was wearing his dress suit, Peter saw with some dismay. Still, he comforted himself, with the new shoes—the first real-leather shoes he had seen in a store in three years—and the new shirt he had bought last week, he himself would be as perfectly dressed as could be. It would simply look as if he were a foreigner who had not brought a dress suit. He noticed that for the second time in one day the notion had struck him that he no longer belonged to Vienna, was here only temporarily.

Franz was adjusting the creamy-colored tie in front of the mirror. He stuck one finger inside the collar and slid it around his Adam's apple as he turned around.

"How's this collar? Does it look all right?"

"It looks fine."

"My neck's thinner. I was afraid all my collars were too large. What time is it?"

"It's not late. It's only half past six. I came early."

But Franz had taken no notice of his being home so early. He made a ball of the blue paper ribbons in which the shirt had been tied by the laundryman and threw the little wad of paper into the basket. Formerly Franz had always left the blue ribbons lying around for her to clean up.

"Well, are you looking forward to tonight?"

"Yes, of course."

She came to the door to look. Franz grinned at her: "My supper ready, *Du Alte?*"

She pretended to scowl a little as she always did when Franz was teasing her. "You'll get to your opera soon enough."

"Next time you'll have to go with us, Mother."

"Me in the Opera! You'll never live to see that day!"

"But if we pick the one with Saint Elizabeth in it, you'd come to that, wouldn't you?"

"I can see Saint Elizabeth in church. Church is my opera," she said gruffly, and yet Peter could see that she was happy that Franz was gay again.

He stayed for a few minutes longer in Franz's room, because it would look silly to seem in an undue hurry to dress when Franz had not even left. Franz had gone out into the kitchen to eat. Peter decided to take his bath. He used Franz's razor, although he had shaved off the fine hair on his cheek only the week before. While he was still shaving, he heard Poldi come in. When he went out to get the hot water off the stove for his bath, Poldi stopped him:

"I have to take my bath first. You wait until I get through!"

He went back into the living room and sat down. Franz was wiping his opera hat with the white silk rag he kept in the hatbox; he flipped the hat open tentatively once or twice, then he came over to the window with a small envelope.

"Here are the tickets, in case we don't meet in the lobby. Now, don't be late, or they won't let you in until after the overture. I've got the house-door key. See you there."

Poldi came out of the bathroom and he went in to take his bath, hurriedly now, because he was haunted by the fear of being late. But there was time enough to get a thrill out of the rough fabric of the blue cheviot suit again as he pulled on the trousers. Then the new shirt and the tie, last of all the new shoes. They were tight, but their very tightness gave him pleasure, because it reminded him of how new they were and how impossible still to get in the shoe shops which were crammed with shoes with wooden soles. He tucked the napkin into his collar when he sat down to eat to make doubly sure of not spilling anything on the good tie. Poldi protested about the napkin when she sat down. He saw that she had curled her hair, and that she was wearing the dark-blue dress with the white lace inset. They had only spinach, which he did not like. The only improvement in their food since the war had ended consisted in the vegetable fat which was suddenly plentiful now.

Then Poldi put on her hat and they left. Until they were on the streetcar and were nearing the Gürtel, they spoke hardly at all. Once Poldi asked: "You're sure you have the tickets?"

"Of course I have."

But in spite of his confidence he felt surreptitiously in his pocket again.

Poldi was excited, too. He could tell by the tense way she sat with her elbows close to her sides. Though Poldi had been to the Opera before. It must be because Poldi was a little uneasy about meeting Bianca, especially after the hostility she had shown when Franz had been ill in Baden.

They were sitting opposite each other on the single seats. When they passed the Neubaugasse, Poldi glanced at him as she had done when he had been small to see whether anything was wrong with his collar or tie. He recognized the look and saw that Poldi's eyes retreated satisfied.

"I don't want to stay late," she said quickly; "in case they suggest going somewhere afterward."

He hadn't even thought of afterward until now. They might go to a restaurant then! The evening still ahead spread out farther. If the opera had seemed like a broad, pleasant mountain until now, there suddenly opened valleys behind it and beyond. But why was Poldi putting a limit on the evening, on herself, really? Was it because of Bianca, or was she uneasy about something else, somebody else? There was not going to be anybody besides Baron Ortner. Could it be that Poldi was in love with Baron Ortner? No, that was too romantic. He had only thought of that because he himself was so excited over seeing Bianca again. Poldi had never shown any interest in Baron Ortner. Perhaps it was only the restraint that had grown over Poldi since Franz had gone to war—no, since Father had been in Steinhof, really—the same restraint that showed in Poldi's clothes: that blue serge dress, for instance, with the poignantly severe white lace inset. Yet above the white lace and under the simple dark blue hat, Poldi's face was pretty—much prettier really than when she had still worn gay clothes. He felt a sudden pride at going to the Opera with her like this. . . .

At the corner of the Ring a group of people was gathered around a man who was haranguing them. Poldi and he threaded their way through the fringes of the crowd and crossed the Ring to the Opera. The large, deep-green leaves of the chestnut trees appeared to float on the air. In another two weeks the blossoms would be out.

It was still light, but all the lights in the huge foyer of the Opera were on and gave a special kind of festiveness to the taxis and the carriages from which people were getting out. He had to fight down a sense of awe as they went up the steps of one of the entrances behind a fat man and his wife in evening clothes.

"Franz said we were to meet by the second cloakroom," Poldi said. "It's over there."

It flattered him that Poldi waited for him to start, instead of going toward it as she formerly would have done. He took her elbow, as he had noticed another man doing with a lady, and steered her through the crowd. Through the confusion of faces he searched for Bianca and Franz. They had not come yet. He waited for Poldi to take the pins out of her hat and hand it to him. Then he stood in line at the cloakroom with it and left it with his own hat and got his check.

They went to one of the Moorish columns to wait. It was amazing how many people were coming in. But he had no eyes for them in his anxiety not to miss Franz. The warning bell went, and Poldi said:

"Don't you think we had better go inside? They may be there already. . . ."

"Let's wait a little longer."

The row of ticket windows was still busy. It occurred to him that Franz must have spent a lot of money to buy orchestra seats for them all. Perhaps, if he could do it gracefully, he could pay the check if they went to a restaurant afterward. . . .

He suddenly saw all three of them at once: Bianca with the velvety, bright-red cloak and the white dress showing underneath, and Franz with his top hat still on, looking a little anxious the way Franz did, and Baron Ortner with a black cane and wearing a soft hat.

He watched them in an agony of impatience while they moved across the huge foyer. Bianca's dark hair was dressed high in front and there were some white stones in it that sparkled across the distance that still separated him from her. He noticed that she looked tall today and that she moved much less spiritedly than when he had seen her in Baden in the tweed suit. His excitement mounted to a climax when they finally came up.

"Are we awfully late?" Franz asked.

"It's my fault," Bianca said. It soothed his tremor that Bianca's voice should be as it had always been, warm and spontaneous, as if she were not aware of the regal appearance she made in the long white dress and the diadem in her hair. She held out her hand:

"How are you, Peter?"

Baron Ortner had come up to Poldi and was talking to her. Then Franz waited for him to answer Bianca, and somewhat hastily, nervously, he said:

"This is Poldi, Bianca," and the two of them shook hands, while Baron Ortner was greeting him:

"The industrialist! Franz tells me you are going to buy the Rathauskeller next week. I'm glad we're related."

Franz had taken Bianca's wrap and had gone to the cloakroom; Baron Ortner followed him. Bianca and Poldi were talking of the Opera, or rather Bianca was talking animatedly as if she felt the need of filling the empty space between them, while Poldi stood by a little stiffly. Bianca turned to him:

"Did Franz tell you about our adventure? It was fun!"

Baron Ortner and Franz returned. They started along the already hushed, sumptuous, curving corridor and then through one of the red-plush-padded doors into the orchestra. The second bell went just as the usher took them down the aisle. The orchestra was already in the pit. The chandelier and the lights around the boxes were being dimmed. The usher had stopped at the fifth or sixth row—Peter could not tell exactly which. People got up. Baron Ortner went in first, then Poldi, and then he—Bianca was sitting next to him! He smelled the subtle perfume, and her nearness would not let him concentrate on either the orchestra or the discreetly gleaming boxes up aloft, or the curtain which already glowed with the footlights.

He was glad that Bianca was whispering to Franz and opening her program. He tried to open his own and to read in the dim light, so as not to think of the exciting nearness of Bianca's bare shoulders and throat, of the line her cheek made as it curved down to the corner of her mouth.

"This is my favorite Wagner opera, next to *Tristan*," Bianca was saying.

He had to keep a wary hold on himself to bring his eyes around slowly to hers. "I hope you like it!"

"I know I will!"

The lean, white-haired conductor had stepped on the podium. He bowed twice to the applause. The lights went down completely.

The somber opening strains flooded out to him and he was grateful for them, yet hardly aware of them either, because Bianca's whisper was still echoing in his ears. Like a bath, the music eddied around the people in the seats, somber and menacing and seductive at the same time, and gradually he felt safe in it and free to steal a glance at Bianca who sat erect and attentive as if she were looking for something in the orchestra, watching rather than listening. He looked once more and this time Bianca was aware of his look, for she turned slowly, much more slowly than he had ever seen her move, and smiled. It would have been an impertinence to look again. And the smile had satisfied him. As the overture gathered into a fortissimo, it seemed already familiar, and he reflected pleasantly that Baron Ortner was also wearing a street suit, double-breasted and blue, though of a smoother cloth than his, so that he need not worry about not wearing a dress suit like Franz. . . .

The overture had finished and the curtain rose. He lost himself in the play. Venus, and the man who wanted to get away from her; he was tired of her, it seemed. The music swirled with a reckless abandon, a seductiveness which came so close to one that one felt uncomfortably singled out by it. . . . So this is Wagner, he thought, detaching himself in reproval from the naked shoulders and arms of Venus on the stage, feeling conscious again of the cool reality of Bianca beside him, but not daring to look at Bianca, not wanting to either because the story and the music bound him and Bianca and Baron Ortner, and Poldi and Franz for that matter, into this pleasant intimacy. . . . Now the knight was singing halfheartedly in praise of Venus and yearning for something else that was pure and chaste, and at once Peter agreed with him and wished that he could get away, and then Venus' threat and the end of the scene.

Bianca bent toward him to ask:

"How do you like it?"

"Very much."

You could not say: it's wonderful, because you are here and because I'm excited and can hardly wait for the next scene; and besides, you did not need to say it because Bianca seemed to sense what he felt and smiled again, so that her smile was like a prelude for the joyous forest scene in which the knight's friends rejoiced at his return, with its news of the *Sängerkrieg*, and Elizabeth, who was beautiful in that stately, chaste, loose-flowing robe. . . . It was a pity that the first act was over so soon.

Yet not a pity, either, because of the joy of applauding and the soft turning on of the lights, the discreet warmth of talk and the stirring in the rows all around. Bianca was bending eagerly toward Franz and not agreeing with something Franz had said about Lotte Lehmann who, it appeared, was playing Elizabeth.

"I don't think so at all," Bianca was saying. "She is in magnificent voice."

People were folding back their seats, walking up the aisle. Baron Ortner was saying:

"What do you say to seeing who's upstairs?"

"Why, whatever you all feel like doing," Franz said, mostly to Bianca.

"After the next act, Franz."

"I'll see if I can get some candy. Will you excuse me, Fräulein Bartsch?" And Baron Ortner went, so that Peter was left alone with Poldi on his left, trying to talk to her, but not paying much attention really because he was waiting for Bianca to turn to him again. And then Bianca did, though she spoke across him to Poldi first:

"Is this a favorite opera of yours, too, Fräulein Bartsch?"

He was too aware of the tenseness between Poldi and Bianca, and too preoccupied with trying to think of something to talk to Bianca about, to listen to Poldi's reply.

"I love Wagner anyway!" Bianca said. "When we were in Budapest this winter I went every day."

Now was the time for him to talk! That temporary connection

between Poldi and Bianca which had been sustained merely by Bianca's liveliness had faltered and snapped, not so much because of any ill-will on Poldi's part, he was sure, as because Poldi was still conscious of the orders she had left in Baden last fall and found it hard to talk. He said quickly: "Did you stay in Budapest long, Bianca?" It was exciting to say "Bianca" in front of Poldi.

"Two months, while my uncle cleared up his army affairs. He doesn't like Vienna much. He's a Hungarian first, you know. Then we went back to the estate until we had to flee. You should have been with us!"

And animatedly, excitingly, she told how they had had to leave. It was much easier now. Poldi listened and Franz half listened and smiled happily now and then, with that same proud smile with which he had told him once how Bianca rode bareback and had said: "You ought to see her!"

Happiness gathered again in Peter as he listened to her thrilling, husky voice. It was as if he owned the whole opera house and as if everything in it contributed to Bianca's account of how they had waded through the swamp at night. Over and over again he waited for the enchantingly foreign way she had of pronouncing some words.

She had started to tell of some ex-soldiers that had raided in the neighborhood of the estate and how the servants had taken guns to drive them off, when Baron Ortner came back. He was carrying two small confectioner's cartons by their strings.

"This is all I could find," he said apologetically, holding out one of the cartons to Franz and bringing the other with him to open for Poldi: "Fruit drops. Not a bit of chocolate to be had!" He shook the carton for Poldi to see inside. "I suppose it'll be months before some chocolate is brought in."

"There's a shop on the Graben that has some Dutch chocolate," Poldi said.

"Oh, splendid!" He spoke across Poldi and him: "Did you hear, Bibi—" So that was what it sounded like when Baron Ortner spoke to Bianca!—"Fräulein Poldi says that she's found a shop on the Graben that has chocolate now. We must get some for Mama!" Then Baron Ortner was talking to Poldi again: "I've been thinking of going on a foraging trip to Switzerland next week. . . ."

The second bell went. Bianca quickly held out the little carton with the fruit drops to him. The outer curtain had gone up and the footlights were on. Then the conductor—applause—the music again.

Joyous, this time. Everything on the stage was joyous, too. . . . The great hall where the knights would compete for Elizabeth's hand. . . . And then, Elizabeth telling the knight of her love, with that wonderful directness that was itself a part of fairyland, then the march as the landgrave came in and started off the song contest of the knights. You had to look first to see who was singing: Wolfram, who sang magnificently—though Peter felt jealous for Tannhäuser—or one of the other men. It was Wolfram all right, and then Tannhäuser, who broke in to sing of the delights of the Venusberg, so that all the other knights—outraged—crowded toward him with bared swords.

But why had Tannhäuser had to sing of Venus anyway, when Elizabeth was so much more beautiful! Peter felt irritated with him, and yet could understand it perfectly. He was Tannhäuser now, and Venus was Herta with her shameless way of standing in her petticoat, and Bianca was Elizabeth—no, that was silly! It didn't fit, for wasn't he conscious of Bianca's beautiful throat and the rise of her breasts? No, Bianca was not like Elizabeth at all, except for the proud way in which Elizabeth shielded Tannhäuser from the other knights. . . .

This time when the curtain came down, he felt relieved that the act was over, but also estranged from Bianca because of his thoughts, and glad that Franz said immediately when the lights went on:

"Well, shall we go out for a stroll?"

They went up the majestic staircase to the lounge. For the first time Peter saw the great windows with their sumptuous red draperies, which he had so often looked at from below on the Ring. He felt at once awed and exhilarated by the luxuriousness of the huge room and by the hum of voices all around. But it surprised him that he should not feel prouder to be here than he did. "After all, why shouldn't I be here!" he protested to himself. "I could afford to come every night!"

They went to the embrasure of one of the glass doors which stood open on the balcony. Franz asked:

"Well, what is it to be? I'm going to try the buffet."

"Something cold, Franz," Bianca said. Poldi agreed.

Franz went off to the buffet. Baron Ortner was bending toward Poldi with the graceful attentiveness he had and was saying something about the Ringstrasse. Bianca was looking over the people still arriving in the already crowded lounge.

There was a surprising number of people not in evening clothes, Peter noticed—some who looked as if they should have been, just like Baron Ortner, but who had decided not to wear them for some secret reason he had yet to probe; some, who to judge by their heavy gold chains and the amount of jewelry on the women were obviously profiteers, because they had not yet reached the point of acquiring evening clothes, although they apparently felt they owed it to their new wealth to come to the Opera. Then there were still other profiteers who had achieved dress suits and evening gowns, but who managed only to look uncouth and ill at ease.

There were practically no Austrian uniforms, except for an occasional officer or two, who had removed the stars or oak leaves from their uniform collars. There were, however, foreign uniforms which Peter could not identify, and there were foreign voices everywhere.

"It's just like Budapest this winter," Bianca said; "all the foreign languages one hears. How are your English lessons coming along?"

"I'm reading Andrew Carnegie's autobiography now."

"Who is he?"

"He's an American steelman."

"Is it interesting?"

"Well, it interests me, because it deals with steelmaking and all that." He did not want to say that it was rather Carnegie's rise to power that had enthralled him in the book.

"And you are really going to stick to machinery and all those things?"

"Yes, I think so. I'd like to learn something about the actual process of making steel."

Franz came with two glasses of soda and raspberry juice for Bianca and Poldi, then went back to the buffet for more. When Franz returned, they moved back still farther into the window embrasure.

"Here we are!" Franz said happily. "Look at all the people who've come!"

"Yes, divine, isn't it?" Bianca said, and Peter was not certain whether she was talking about the soft breeze coming in from the Ring, or about the music, or the spectacle of the crowd in the lounge, or perhaps only about the iced raspberry juice she had drunk thirstily.

"More?" Franz asked.

"Not now, Franz. Later, perhaps."

Baron Ortner, who had been talking to Poldi, looked for the second time across the room at a group of two men and two women who were standing by the entrance from the staircase. "Would you excuse me for a minute?" He made Poldi a little bow, set his glass on the marble table in the center of the window bay, smiled, and sauntered across the room. His limp was barely perceptible when he walked slowly like this, though he still kept his cane with him. Peter watched his back disappear in the crowd, then reappear again. Baron Ortner was bending over to kiss the hand of the woman in the black lace evening gown, then the hand of the stout, white-haired lady in the wine-colored gown. Peter saw him bow to the two men and then say something to the white-haired lady, but he had an odd impression that Baron Ortner was really addressing the slim woman in the black lace dress.

It occurred to him suddenly that that must be the woman—the lieutenant colonel's wife whom Franz had once mentioned with significant abruptness—with whom Baron Ortner was having an affair. Yet Baron Ortner had walked up to her boldly, and in front of her husband, too! Excitement at the risk Baron Ortner was running heightened his pleasure in the group across the room, for a moment took his mind off Bianca even, and yet did not do so altogether either, since Bianca's presence was tied up with that excitement, too.

He could not watch Baron Ortner any longer, because Franz was asking him something about the music. Rather to keep Franz talking and to be free himself to listen to what Bianca was saying to Poldi, than because he was interested, he asked:

"I thought Saint Elizabeth performed a miracle with a basket of roses: is that in the opera?"

"That's another Saint Elizabeth, I think. Anyway, Wagner always took liberties, the way he did with the *Nibelungenlied* when he wrote the *Ring*."

". . . the only thing I really hated about it," Bianca was saying to Poldi, "was my hunter. I couldn't bear to leave him behind with those brutes. They'll probably harness him to a dray. . . ."

Across the lounge Baron Ortner was again kissing the hand of the lady in the low-cut black gown. Then he started to come back but ran into a man he apparently knew well. Peter watched them shake hands. The other man was short, plump and almost stout; his sparse blond hair lay slicked back uncompromisingly on his arrogant, sallow-faced head. He wore a superbly tailored gray suit and a red carnation in his lapel. Baron Ortner was bringing him over with him.

The man bent at once over Bianca's hand. Bianca said, "*Servus*, Kurt," rather indifferently, Peter thought. Baron Ortner introduced them—"Freiherr von Steligerode—Fräulein Bartsch . . ." Freiherr von Steligerode bent briefly over Poldi's hand, then shook hands with Franz and him—a cool handshake that irritated Peter because it seemed to place him as someone of no consequence. The weary superciliousness in the man's face also appeared in his voice; he had addressed himself to Poldi and to Bianca——

"Quite a crush! It is getting so that one daren't dress any more. I have been feasting my eyes on all the butchers that adorn the Opera. But you did right, *ma belle*, to do the honors for us. . . ."

It was cleverly said, Peter was forced to admit; with one stroke the man had managed to compliment not only Bianca but Poldi as well, and he had also explained why Baron Ortner and he had not dressed.

"Just look at that, will you?" Freiherr von Steligerode's eyes focused coldly on a fat, ungainly woman whose hands and throat were dripping with jewelry. The woman's equally fat husband looked stupidly complacent. "Wouldn't you say: just like a Christmas tree?"

"Then we have the gentlemen from Italy!" Baron Ortner fell into the mood of his friend. "Don't forget them!"

"Oh, yes, the museum commission—the *banditti*, to be sure!" Peter followed their eyes to the group of Italian officers and civilians who were laughing together near the buffet.

"They say that the Italians are claiming Dürer's portrait of Maximilian as one of the pictures we've taken from the Uffizi," Franz broke in.

"Yes, isn't it delightful! Pity they can't claim the Stephansdom and the Prater as Italian, too. They have just about cleaned out the Art Museum. Well, to the victor belong the spoils!"

Looking around the room by himself now, Peter's eyes suddenly encountered those of a girl who was so close that he wondered that he had not noticed her before. She was blonde and slim, and she wore a white linen suit which accented her wide shoulders. She was the only woman with a small, rather serious group of foreign-looking men. For just a few seconds their eyes remained locked, then she looked away. He realized that the girl had been surveying them frankly, interestedly.

"And then, we have the Dutch Legation," Freiherr von Steligerode said, his eyes on a paunchy man in full dress with a much taller woman beside him. "Oh, yes, we are getting to be ultra-cosmopolitan again—only our role is that of a starved monkey in a cage."

"Of course, it won't be the same as it used to be," Bianca said indifferently; "but all this sort of thing has always bored me anyway."

Freiherr von Steligerode's shrug implied somehow that Bianca had never really known what it had been like before, and Peter's dislike for him increased.

"And who is that over there?" Franz asked. It was the group with the girl in the white linen suit.

"Ah, *les quatorze point ambulants*—that is the American Food Relief Commission."

Partly because he still chafed under the negligent stare with which Freiherr von Steligerode had dismissed him when he had been introduced to him, and partly because he had been angered by the patronizing shrug with which the man had acknowledged Bianca's remark, but chiefly because he wanted to show off to Bianca that he had caught at least a part of the French phrase about the "fourteen points," Peter said:

"But there aren't anywhere near fourteen!"

Freiherr von Steligerode fixed him with that infuriatingly polite stare of his:

"One more or less—does it matter very much?"

"I thought they had made their report and had left," Franz said.

"The Allied Commission, my dear chap!" It was hard to know

whether Freiherr von Steligerode was sneering at the Americans too, or whether it was merely his habitually scathing tone which colored his words. There were certainly overtones: he seemed to have a caustic resentment of Wilson's Fourteen Points. . . . "These are the Americans who are to put things actually *en train:* Argentine corned beef and salt pork—if and when—"

The warning bell went.

Freiherr von Steligerode excused himself and left. Peter felt relieved. But he realized that in spite of his dislike for Baron Ortner's new friend, he had been impressed by the cynical knowledge he seemed to have of everybody important in the lounge. And he was still nettled by his failure to score with his correction about the "fourteen." He turned to Bianca to ask:

"What did Freiherr von Steligerode mean when he talked about the Americans who were standing over there? I could get that about the 'fourteen points' all right—he was referring to Wilson's Fourteen Points, wasn't he? But I don't know what *ambulants* means, so I missed the rest."

Bianca smiled, then frowned. "It's just one of Kurt's diplomatic corps puns. You know: *ambulants*—walking! He meant that the Americans over there were standing still and not walking around—and he really meant that Wilson's Fourteen Points didn't work and weren't any good. He's always caustic like that. You mustn't pay any attention to him. I—" She did not finish because Baron Ortner had stopped talking to Poldi and Franz, and would have heard. She went and took Franz's arm.

"Let's walk once around the lounge, Franz, before we go inside—shall we?" she asked Poldi and Baron Ortner and him.

They started out. Again, Peter noticed the American girl in the white linen suit. She was standing with her back to him by the buffet with a very tall man. He noticed the fine turn of her neck and the slim waist and her handsome ankles. As if caught in his brief act of disloyalty, his eyes went to Bianca. He felt almost defiantly proud of her. Bianca in her startlingly white gown and the simple diadem in her dark hair was like a princess, representing Vienna against the foreigners who robbed museums and profiteered, and against the butchers and grocers who had got rich out of the war. And it was proper that only Franz who was her escort should be in evening clothes, and that Baron Ortner and Poldi and he should look severely plain as befitted Bianca's retinue.

When they reached the upper end of the lounge, he had a shock. Herr Granini and two younger men whom he remembered from the choir were standing together, talking. Herr Granini had seen Franz, too. His dark eyes flashed. Franz was steering Bianca toward the three men.

It was not something he had reckoned with. At once he felt himself plunged back into that evening so many years ago when Franz had had him expelled from the choir. Nothing had changed about Herr Granini at all. He still had the same dark mane of hair and the same habit of tossing his head to make the black locks fall behind his ear. Only the two other men—he recognized them now—had grown heavier. The tall one with the rounded face was Herr Prohaska, the bass, and the other was Herr Hügel, the engineer.

". . . and you remember Baron Ortner," Franz was saying.

"Of course."

"And my sister—"

"Fräulein Bartsch!" Herr Granini bowed, not from the waist as Baron Ortner did, but merely inclining his head.

"And this is Peter. You remember Peter. . . ."

"No? How he's grown, this fellow! Where have you been all these years? I expected to see you around the Verein with Franz now and again. . . ."

He felt flushed and embarrassed, even though he realized that it was not half so bad as it might have been. Herr Granini's darkly glowing eyes betrayed nothing but pleasure at seeing him again. He might merely have left the choir like any other boy, because his voice had broken at the time.

"He's an industrialist now!" Franz said, and Peter noticed the sudden pride in his voice. "He's the only one in the family who's got any money."

"Well, we'll all come to him."

For a minute they had all looked at him. He was glad when Herr Granini turned to Bianca and Poldi and said something about *Tannhäuser*. The second bell went.

"Sorry we didn't run into each other earlier. Why don't you join us at the Deutschen Haus afterward, Franz? They have fish there tonight."

Franz looked at Bianca and at Baron Ortner. "What do you all think—why, I think that would be very pleasant, Granini."

"All right, we'll see you at the restaurant then. . . ." Herr Granini and the other two men left; they were evidently up in the balcony.

Slowly, pleasantly, they returned with the last stragglers down the stairs. Peter was not sure whether he was pleased over the arrangement Franz had made with Herr Granini or not, but at least Bianca and Baron Ortner would be there, too! They were only just in time in getting to their seats before the conductor raised his baton.

And once more the music engulfed him. Though, this time, the doings on the stage—partly because the setting was the same as in the first act, and partly because the long intermission upstairs in the lounge had broken the spell—seemed less compelling and authoritative, so that he quarreled with the story.

All very fine and romantic, he thought, for Tannhäuser to have gone off to Rome to seek absolution for his offense; but why had he been such a fool in the first place as to tell everybody about his stay at the Venusberg? Now he had neither Elizabeth nor his absolution, and Wolfram was abusing him into the bargain. . . .

He was not sure that he liked Wolfram too well anyhow, in spite of that beautiful song to the evening star. Was—Peter asked himself—Franz like Wolfram: naïvely, exasperatingly honest, with never a hope of winning Elizabeth, and doomed to sing his heart out? No, Franz was better than that: Franz could laugh, and besides, Bianca was in love with him. . . .

But here were the strains that announced the funeral cortege of Elizabeth. Tannhäuser was saved! You could not help but rejoice suddenly that Tannhäuser had escaped the spell of the Venusberg music, which had been so voluptuous and importunate that it had seemed to get under one's clothes and to caress one's very skin with its lasciviousness. It was thrilling now to lend oneself to the thought of Elizabeth. Elizabeth had been pure—not in the silly sense in which people always used the word, since she had shown how passionate she could be, but in a higher, nobler sense which was like his passion for Bianca somehow. He felt a fierce stab of pleasure just as the curtains fell at his own willingness to see Bianca marry Franz.

People were calling "Bravo" and some of them had got to their feet to applaud when Tannhäuser came out to take a bow, then Elizabeth, and then Wolfram. Oh, yes, it was thrilling to be here! Bianca beside him said, "Divine!" neither to Franz nor to him and he could see that she had been as much carried away by the last act as he. Poldi was clapping hard. But Baron Ortner seemed rather in a hurry to get out, just when Peter felt that he wanted to stay forever in this intoxicating atmosphere.

But it was over, finally, irrevocably. Franz was leaning across Bianca to say: "Let me have your cloakroom tickets and I'll go on ahead; you follow slowly in a few minutes."

It was pleasant to watch people streaming out. On the other aisle, he saw now that the Americans and the girl had been sitting in the second row. The girl was talking to one of the men. He followed her for a second with his eyes, in a half-hope that she would turn around.

Bianca sat forward on the edge of her chair—"Cousin Emmi, Heinrich! Do you see her?"

Baron Ortner raised his eyebrows quizzically. "Only too well! I saw her upstairs too, and I took good care that she didn't see me. Our Cousin Emmi—" Baron Ortner explained to Poldi—"used to raise horses, and now that she can't afford to raise them any more, she talks about the ones she used to have—by the hour!"

"That's not what Heinrich has against her," Bianca said to him alone and Peter listened eagerly. "She lives in Heinrich's house on the Rathausplatz and she's always after him to have the elevator fixed—that's why he doesn't like her. But she's very nice!"

"I bet I know why you like her: it's because of the horses!"

Bianca smiled, then instantly was serious again: "She gave me my first hunter, when I was thirteen. Do you like horses?"

"I haven't ever seen any highbred ones, but I like even the heavy drayhorses. In the stable at the store there are some Pinzgauers that are beautiful. They are very intelligent. . . ."

"Oh, but you ought to see my uncle's horses in Hungary! You must come and see those—but with that horrible Bela Kun spoiling everything, you'll never see them now. You'll be gone to America before we can get back to the estate again."

"I'm not gone yet!" he said defiantly.

"Oh, but you will——"

Poldi and Baron Ortner got ready to leave. Far up in the balconies the rows of seats were already deserted, but the warmth of the huge crowd still hung in the auditorium.

Franz was waiting for them with Bianca's wrap and their hats. While Poldi pinned up her hat, Baron Ortner excused himself to Poldi and half to Franz:

"I hope you'll forgive me, Fräulein Poldi, but I have an appointment with von Steligerode. Made days ago, unfortunately! It's been a pleasure, Fräulein——" and he bent over to kiss her hand. "Good-by, Peter. . . . See you tomorrow, Franz. Make my apologies to Herr Granini for me, will you? . . ." And quickly, suavely, he was gone.

Baron Ortner's desertion made a hole in their party, Peter felt. He wondered whether Baron Ortner was meeting the lady in the black lace gown, or whether he was really joining Freiherr von Steligerode. Of course, there was still Bianca, but it would have been so much nicer if they had had Baron Ortner and Freiherr von Steligerode for the rest of the evening, instead of Herr Granini and the two men from the Verein. For, now that they started down the Opera steps, he felt uncomfortable at the thought of seeing Herr Granini again. In spite of the compliments upstairs, Herr Granini had made him feel like a boy.

"We might as well walk," Franz said. "It's only a few steps. . . ."

Halfway up the Kärntnerstrasse, a number of policemen were dispersing a crowd that had gathered around the broken plate-glass windows of a luggage store. Franz had crossed the street with Bianca to see what was going on. There was broken glass all over the sidewalk. "Bolsheviks!" somebody was saying. Some of the men who were always hanging around the Ringstrasse had evidently gone berserk and had smashed the windows; it was, after all, nothing new.

"There isn't anything to see, Franz!" Bianca urged and tugged at his arm. A little reluctantly, Franz came away. Peter remembered that even when he himself had been still quite small, he had already been aware of the naïve curiosity in Franz that always drew Franz toward any crowd to see what was going on. He felt suddenly tender and protective toward Franz.

They reached the Stephansplatz and Franz and Bianca headed for the restaurant on the far side of the square.

Herr Granini and the men were already there. Peter saw that Herr Schmidtmeyer had joined the group. Poldi did not seem to mind, but Herr Schmidtmeyer had flushed to the roots of his hair when Poldi nodded to him.

"We were held up," Franz apologized.

"You mean, you held us up," Bianca teased. "Franz always has to look," she said to Herr Granini and to the other men, who smiled.

"Baron Ortner sent his regrets. He found that he had another engagement."

"Too bad. We shall miss him—Baroness, will you sit here?" Herr Granini had turned to Bianca and was pulling out the chair beside his own. "And you, *Gnädiges Fräulein*—I am afraid we shall have to put you between Herr Prohaska and Herr Hügel—we have to distribute our ladies. . . ."

Herr Granini was gracious and grave and intense, just as Peter had remembered him. There were heavier lines in his dark face, but his black locks still had that tendency to fall forward over his ear, so that he had to brush them back with the swift, familiar motion of his hand. They had all sat down: Bianca on Herr Granini's right, and Franz next to her; Peter himself on Herr Granini's left, because he had happened to be standing by Herr Granini's side and Herr Granini had invited him with a smile to stay where he was. Herr Prohaska and Herr Hügel had both busied themselves gallantly with Poldi's chair. Herr Schmidtmeyer at the other end of the table had looked on helplessly, obviously twitching to be in their place, leaning forward toward Poldi with his pudgy face and thick glasses, and then at last sitting down himself between Herr Prohaska and Franz.

The headwaiter was hovering beside Herr Granini.

"Now, we'll see what we can get! I recommend the fish mayonnaise very highly. . . ."

"Sorry, Herr Granini—but no fish mayonnaise today. We have some sardines that have just come in: real Swedish sardines, with watercress salad."

"*Brötchen?*" Franz asked.

"Sorry, *Gnädiger Herr*; no bread of any sort."

"Well—" Herr Granini frowned and picked up the meaningless menu the waiter had put on the table—"in that case we'll have to try the sardines."

"There is fresh roast pork, if the *Herrschaften* would like that!" the waiter confided. "Fresh in from the country today. And dumplings, and watercress."

"Ah, that's better!" Herr Granini's eyes gleamed. "Will that suit everybody—ladies?" Bianca nodded, and so did Poldi. "Roast pork, then, and some of the Niersteiner—a couple of bottles for a start . . ."

It was exciting to sit beside Herr Granini and to listen to the light, warm talk that wove back and forth across the table. This, Peter told himself, was what he had dreamed of when he had still been in the choir, to sit here like this at one of Herr Granini's supper parties—to take part in the conversation even, as now when Herr Hügel spoke of a rumor that the hotel on the Neuen Markt was to be sold, and he could tell them that it had in fact already been sold to a banker for eight thousand pounds sterling.

No, no use denying it, it was not as he had dreamed it might be! He was really an outsider, because half of the things they were talking about were strange to him. As if to revenge himself for all the easy knowledge they had of music and singers, of books, and of all sorts of things for which he had had no time these last three years, he told himself defiantly: "They may know all these things, but right now I could buy or sell any one of them. Even that hotel they were talking about: in another month or so, if I wanted to go in with the Swiss on it, I could buy that. . . ."

But if, for a minute or two while they started to eat, he felt it necessary to assert the importance of his own world against theirs, he was presently to succumb to Herr Granini's power again, to the spell of Herr Granini's eyes and the melodious gravity of his voice. It started when Franz teased Herr Prohaska about his appointment to the Dresden opera——

"Did you know," Herr Prohaska said, to escape Franz's teasing, "that Jeritza has an offer from Prague, and that Munich is after Schumann?"

"Amsterdam is angling for Lotte Lehmann, I heard today," Herr Schmidtmeyer put in shyly. It was the first time he had spoken all evening; he blushed immediately and looked away from Poldi to whom he had addressed himself.

"Do you think she'll go?" Franz asked.

"What else is she going to do?" Herr Hügel challenged. "We won't be able to support an opera any more, certainly not on the scale we have been doing. A singer has to live, like everybody else. It's just like us engineers—I'm going to Germany, first chance I get. There's no future for me here. We've never been an industrial nation anyway, and we'll be less so now."

"I don't see how Austria can survive anyway," Herr Prohaska said. "Not with Bohemia gone, and Hungary, too. Even the Tyrol wants to become a part of Germany, and Vorarlberg wants to be Swiss. There'll be nothing left but Vienna and a few square miles of land around it. We won't be able to raise enough food to feed Ottakring."

"Our only hope is Wilson," Franz said. "Remember that Wilson has promised to base the peace on the Fourteen Points. He won't let the Italians and the others cut up Austria to the point where the country can no longer exist!"

"If he doesn't, it'll certainly be the end of Vienna!"

Herr Granini's deep-socketed, burning eyes suddenly reminded them of a hundred things of which they were all conscious, but about which they would rather not have thought—of the variegated crowd in the Opera and the profiteers, of the neglected parks and the forests around Vienna which had been cut down by the poor people for firewood, of the thousands of mutilated soldiers in the streets and of the officers who no longer dared to wear their medals or insignia of rank, of the apartment houses in which no one made any repairs because the Socialists had frozen the rents at a ridiculous level so that the landlords could hardly pay the janitors out of the rents, of Herr Granini's own houses and how his income had vanished overnight, and then of the famous supper parties Herr Granini had given before the war, and of the choir he had supported out of his own pocket and of the singers he had trained. . . .

"It takes a thousand years," Herr Granini went on, "to make a city like Vienna and the culture that goes with it. A thousand years of prosperity and security, and the presence of a hundred special factors nobody has ever analyzed. Look at Innsbruck and at Salzburg or Linz: they're all as old as Vienna, but it was Vienna that produced the music and the musicians."

"Of course, there's always an economic basis," Herr Hügel said. "It would be foolish to deny that, but economics alone can't explain a city like Vienna or Paris. Lyon and Bordeaux were as good bets, economically speaking, as Paris to become the seat of French culture. Neither can you say that being the seat of the court accounts for it: Berlin has had a court for a good many hundreds of years, but Berlin is still an upstart culturally. No, it's much more complicated than that. The growth of a city like ours is as unaccountable as the growth of an especially fine blossom on a quite ordinary bush—and as rare. That's why it is so tragic to see Vienna disintegrating around us."

"You're too pessimistic, Granini!" Franz threw in, somewhat desperately, Peter thought. "After all, our great composers weren't all born in Vienna. Look at Beethoven and Mozart and Haydn—they all came from the provinces."

"That is precisely it: they came and they stayed. They had a place to come to. Have you ever heard of a genius in any art flourishing away from the city where his particular art was cherished, was in the very air? That's what a cultural center does for the artist—whether it's Florence under the Medicis, or Vienna and Paris in the last few centuries. It gives the artist the spiritual sustenance he needs: competition, companionship, appreciation!"

"You can't say Schubert got so much appreciation here," Herr Prohaska objected. "Quite the contrary, I should say."

Herr Granini fixed him earnestly. "The kind of appreciation I mean has little to do with what we call 'success.' " In the sense that Schubert needed the city, Vienna made him rich. My grandfather still knew some of the musicians at the old Theater-an-der-Wien; they said that Schubert used to be happier with a simple plate of goulash and a bottle of wine with his friends at the *Heurigen* than any man they had ever seen at a banquet. . . . I doubt whether any great musician ever felt poor in Vienna—any more than a real painter ever did in Paris. The romantic drivel we hear nowadays about Schubert's poverty is due to a few critics with a butcher's way of looking at happiness."

"But why need all that go?" Franz asked. "The city will still be here."

"You mean, the houses and the parks! Have you noticed the faces of people in the street, and our famous humor that isn't there any more? I said that wealth alone won't make a great city, but material well-being is necessary. It's only when there is enough wealth and prosperity so that the temper of a city no longer values material wealth for its own sake, that you get artists and art and that mellowing in people generally which can be called culture. . . . No, Vienna is gone. That's one of the results of this war, and it's much more significant than the fact that the empire has broken up. There have been a good many empires, but very few great cities. Another war—and if I know the Germans, there'll be another war—and Paris will be gone, too, and then there won't be much left of the Europe we know."

"There'll be America, then," Bianca said, and Peter caught her smile.

Herr Granini had not seen her look. "America is a young country, and cities take a long time to grow a soul."

"Well, for once, Granini, I hope you are wrong—about us, at least," Franz said with a grin.

They started to talk about other things, trying to be cheerful again, but Herr Granini's mood had infected them and gave a wistful tinge to everything that was said.

They walked together through the Kärntnerstrasse down to the Ring. When they were almost back at the Opera, Bianca, who had been walking a little ahead with Herr Granini and Franz, dropped back and waited for Peter. She had thrown back her wrap and was exposing her throat to the breeze. She said:

"It's too lovely tonight to think of anything sad. I feel like walking for hours and hours, all around the Ring! By the way, Franz and I are going to Schönbrunn on Sunday. We're walking up to the Glorietta. You must come. . . ."

Chapter Fifty

By Sunday, the evening at the Opera had moved surprisingly far out of his consciousness. It was true that he had been unusually busy on Saturday: first in the store where he had seen to the shifting of all the spring clips and other wagon parts to the new warehouse racks, and then in the Innere Stadt because of a deal which had involved more capital than he had and which he had been determined to carry through—had brought off, in fact, at the very last minute by borrowing five thousand francs at twenty-per-cent interest from the Swiss merchant.

But it was not the agitation over the deal alone which had crowded the opera party into the background, but rather some element in the evening itself which had already given it something legendary and remote. Herr Granini's somberness about Vienna, the supercilious face of Baron Ortner's new friend, the American group whom Freiherr von Steligerode had called *les quatorze point ambulants,* and the blonde girl who had looked at him—all shared in the peculiar static intensity of something lived through a long time ago. Only Bianca's invitation that he join her and Franz in Schönbrunn anchored the evening to this Sunday morning.

He dawdled over getting out of the house to give Franz a chance to speak. When he was about to give up, Franz finally asked:

"Are you going to your lesson in Hietzing?"

"Yes, I am."

"Bianca said something about your joining us. What time do you get through?"

"I can be at the Hietzinger Gate by a quarter to eleven."

"We were going up to the Glorietta. Eleven's pretty late to start. We'll see. We'll meet you by the gate or somewhere along the avenue."

There had not been the same eagerness in Franz to have him

come as Franz had displayed about the opera. There could be no doubt about it: Franz had hoped that the whole thing might fall through, though he had been too honest to let him go out of the house without speaking. But the prospect of seeing Bianca hardened him to Franz's frown. He was restless during his English lesson and so inattentive that Frau Hobbs-Pechlar teased him about it.

When he got to the Hietzinger Gate, Franz and Bianca were nowhere in sight. He started anxiously along the avenue into the park, and he had nearly reached the second intersection when he saw them at last. Bianca waved first. She was in a fluttery white blouse and a dark-blue skirt, and she was carrying her floppy-brimmed straw hat in her hand, swinging it by her side. Franz had been walking several feet away from her, setting down his stick with pensive precision, as if they had had a tiff of some sort. . . .

He was sure of it when he came up to them and they all walked back toward the Hietzinger Gate. Franz was subdued and withdrawn, and Bianca and he were left to talk by themselves.

"How did the lesson go?" Bianca asked.

"All right," he said, and went on to answer Bianca's questions about Frau Hobbs-Pechlar. When they were almost at the gate, he asked:

"I thought you were going to walk up to the Glorietta?"

"No, it's too late. And Franz wants to go to church."

They walked as far as the church just outside the park. Franz stopped:

"Aren't you coming in to Mass?"

"No, Franz. We'll wait for you out here."

"I went to church before the lesson," Peter said hurriedly, before Franz could speak to him. He was glad now that he had never mentioned at what hour his Sunday morning lesson came and that he took two hours on Sunday instead of one.

"It's a Low Mass and it lasts only half an hour," Franz urged.

"It's too beautiful to go inside, Franz." Bianca sounded calm and cheerful, but firm. "We'll meet you out here or just inside the gate somewhere."

Franz looked disappointed as he turned to go into the church. Bianca started back to the park. Peter asked:

"Would you like an ice?"

"After I've just said I wanted to stay outside?" Her eyes danced. "That would be cheating."

"I meant, on the terrace . . ."

"No, let's just walk. It's beautiful today!" She took an exuberant breath. "Glorious!"

They walked for a hundred yards, then Bianca said:

"You know, Franz and I had a spat."

"Yes, I thought—"

"Over nothing at all, really—perfectly silly!" Her right leg thrust forward impatiently and she tossed her head, so that Peter had an impression that she was breasting a storm. He prepared himself to keep up with her quickened stride, but the consciousness of the exquisite peace under the ancient trees and of the gay sunlight on the avenue evidently checked her and made her slow up again.

"I have some jewels and things from my grandmother," Bianca was saying. "If I sold them we could get married right away. Franz doesn't want me to! He insists that we wait until he gets his appointment as bureau head. I know he's been promised the appointment, but goodness knows when it'll go through. It mayn't be until next year—don't you think it's silly of Franz?"

He felt both annoyed and flattered at being taken into her confidence like this. A little painfully, with perverse scrupulousness because of his resentment, he defended Franz:

"Of course, I can see why Franz is touchy about it. Especially since he loves you." It gave him a thrill to add the last few words. It was as if he were speaking for himself.

"I still think it's silly. When two people love each other, what has money got to do with it, or a few stupid jewels I don't care about anyway? Let's turn up here, shall we?"

They started up a narrow path which was enticingly rustic after the formal avenue.

"It does, though," he said stubbornly, less now from any desire to defend Franz than to draw out the delightful mood of intimacy her tone had evoked. But he could not bear to disagree with her, and he added: "Of course, it shouldn't."

"Of course it shouldn't! A little thing like that—any more than I mind about Franz's religiousness. I don't care if he wants to go to church every day. It's just something that's left over from his shell shock, and he'll get better as time goes on. He's much less intense about it already. Don't you think so?"

"Yes, that's true." Peter remembered the Thomas à Kempis book which had been shoved farther and farther back on Franz's desk in the last few months.

"Franz told me himself that he didn't go to Mass any more every day, and twice on Sunday—the way he used to right after he had been ill, when he was so morbid about things. He wouldn't even have thought about it today, if we hadn't quarreled. . . . I know that he was disappointed because we wouldn't go in. But he might just as well learn that I don't like to go to church. I never did—I was simply not born with any talent for religiousness."

"Neither was I," he said happily, delighted to clutch at something he had in common with her, although he felt that what he had said was not altogether true, for he remembered the evenings in the chapel at the Verein when he had sometimes been carried away by an ecstasy of faith. Yet for the moment it seemed utterly true, especially now when she smiled at him.

But the next instant her eyes were serious again:

"Frau Bartsch is very religious, isn't she?"

"Yes, she is."

"I know. Franz told me. That's why she and Poldi don't like me."

"Oh, Poldi is different!"

"Yes, I think she is. I think Poldi and I will get along all right." They had come to a bench under a beach tree. "Shall we sit down for a minute?"

He hastened to brush off some leaves from the bench. A butterfly which had alighted on the ground for a second started up and kept dancing only a few feet away from them in the air.

"I know everything will be all right as soon as I can talk Franz out of his old-fashioned ideas about those bangles. Franz does love me, doesn't he?"

"Yes, he does!" he said—much too seriously, he realized, for her question had been playful and confident. "You know, Bianca, I adore you, too!"

He trembled a little from fear that she might be angry, but it was as if she had expected him to say it. Her fingers touched his hand with the same electrifying lightness as at Baden; only this time they lingered for a few exquisite moments——

"Do you, Peter?"

"Enormously—ever since the time—"

"I know: it was right here in Schönbrunn and you were bringing the book and saying that Franz hadn't been able to come! Was that it?"

"No, it was much earlier than that. . . ." and he told her about the first time Franz had spoken of her at Baron Ortner's lodge, and about the walks when he had slyly managed to make Franz talk about her.

Her eyes glowed with secret, tender depths: "That's the sweetest thing anyone's ever said to me! I like you, too—you know that, don't you? Next to Franz, I like you better than anybody I know. But I love Franz." Her eyes held a softness that intoxicated him with joy, so that he hardly minded the refusal in her words. "It'll be a secret between us, but we'll never talk about it again—promise?"

Because of his happiness, it was almost a joy to say:

"I promise."

She had held out her hand. But instead of shaking it, he raised it to his lips. Again she was not angry; her hand even rose a little toward his face. Then she withdrew it softly and smiled:

"Now we'll go, shall we? Franz will be waiting!"

They started back over the shady path. His exultation made him treasure the silence between them which was so rich with echoes and so full because of all the unspoken words. But when they came to the avenue, Bianca said:

"You'll go off to America, and by the time you come to visit us, I'll be an old married woman and you'll be a famous engineer or something. Franz says you don't want to go, but you are going, aren't you?"

"Do you want me to go?"

"Of course. You'll have a career in America, and your family is there."

"I can have a career here, too."

"It won't be the same thing. You heard what Herr Granini said about Vienna. Franz and I are different. Franz is in the government service, but you like business and things."

"I don't really. I like machinery; I'd like to invent things. I only got into the hardware business because—well, because—" He did not want to mention the cadet school.

"Then there's twice as much reason why you should go to America. They have all the best technical schools and big factories—you'll go, then, promise?"

"All right, I promise," he said for the second time.

"And you'll write Franz and me about all your successes. . . ."

They were approaching the gate out of the park. Bianca suddenly took his arm. A curious ecstasy, compounded of the happiness of walking so close to her that he could feel her body against his and of the aching sweetness her words had left in him, made him feel years older than Franz, when he came striding toward them up the avenue.

"Well, where have you been? I was beginning to think you'd fallen into the goldfish pond, or that the lions had got you!"

As if by a miracle Franz's mood had changed so that it fell in with their own. The worried frown was gone and he looked happy and mischievous.

"We had a fine walk," Bianca said. She had hooked her other hand into Franz's arm, and they walked on to the gate, talking slowly, pleasantly.

"Look at the butterfly!" Franz said once, and they all looked.

"We saw one back in the woods—a yellow one with red dots."

At the streetcar stop, Franz said: "I'm going to take Bianca home. Do you want to come along?"

"I promised to meet somebody before lunch. Up on the Hütteldorferstrasse."

"Good-by, then, Peter." Bianca held out her hand.

He walked away quickly, to store this new sweetness of denying himself the extra few minutes with Bianca for Franz's sake with all the other poignantly sweet treasure he had.

Chapter Fifty-One

IT SEEMED to him as if he had already said good-by to Vienna, and as if the weeks that followed were only a meaningless aftermath to the morning in Schönbrunn. He was suddenly impatient to be gone. Bianca had sent him away. It would be churlish to try to see her again.

The whole morning in Schönbrunn as he looked back on it had a wistful poignancy, a romantic glow of sacrifice on his part, which could still make him happy for minutes at a time. Bianca's sending him away had almost been in the nature of a request. She cared for him: she had said so!

But there was another mood in which he suddenly remembered the curve of Bianca's throat and the touch of her breast against his arm, and then his adoration turned into passion and he became rebellious. He felt that he diminished Bianca in this mood, that he was in danger of losing something that was out of reach and yet of incalculable value to him, so that the future seemed drab and empty without that intactness of Bianca which had sustained him through all the years of his apprenticeship. Yet he could not quiet his passion. Twice, on those occasions, he went to the sergeant's widow whom he had met one night in a theater. She had an exuberant body and she was gay and even amusing, but the visits were without joy and he had a hard time to keep her from seeing how unsatisfied he was afterward and how anxious to get away again.

There was only one advantage to these evenings. Out of his very dissatisfaction with himself, Bianca emerged intact again and as he had always thought of her. He quarreled with her then, and through her with Franz and Herr Granini and especially with that supercilious friend of Baron Ortner's at the Opera: "I'm as good as any of them," he told himself angrily. "They are all full of noble melancholy now, because they aren't in the swing of things any longer, but I am! They can call me a profiteer all they want to, and gloss over what they really think by politely calling me 'the industrialist.' I'm not a profiteer at all, but they don't even know the difference. The fact remains that their world is gone and people like Herr Straka and me are the ones that count now!"

But no matter how much he argued with himself, the feeling of frustration remained. And with it, a sense of unfairness. Even if he had been as old as Franz, Bianca would probably still have preferred Franz. It wasn't his fault that Franz had been to the university and had that lovable light touch with people, and that he himself had been turned down by the cadet school and had had to take this other road. Only, now that he had fought his way up successfully, so that he could afford to go to the best tailors as Baron Ortner had once been able to do, he ought at least to be accepted as their equal. . . .

He emerged from the one-sided debates with a renewed pride in his success. He had made a clear profit of six thousand Swiss francs on a shipment of horseshoes for Rumania, and he had turned around and had risked practically all his capital in a partnership with the Swiss merchant to ship six carloads of tools to Poland. It was a greater risk than any he had yet taken. The tools were to be paid for only on delivery, and the Swiss had charged himself with accompanying the shipment. The danger was that the Czechs might confiscate the tools on some pretext or other, but if the Swiss could get the shipment through to Warsaw their profits would be enormous.

Partly from a superstitious need to assure himself that he was not afraid, and partly from a defiant wish to impress Bianca and Franz, he went back to the English tailor in the Kärntnerstrasse to order another suit. The tailor had just got in some more cloth. There was a piece of precisely the same fine gray cloth that Baron Ortner's friend had worn. He was undecided between it and a tan tweed. In the end, he ordered both. He paid for them out of the little money he still had left.

A week of suspense set in during which he worried about the risk of confiscation and tried to distract himself by thinking about the two new suits. The Swiss was supposed to wire the moment he had got the shipment safely through Czechoslovakia, and again when he received the money. The first telegram was four days overdue. When it finally came, Peter suddenly faced a new worry: hadn't he been a fool to trust all his money to the Swiss? It was true that the Swiss had always shown a metallic scrupulousness in paying him his share, but what was to prevent him now from simply disappearing with this large sum? It was true that he had his address in Berne, but what was to prevent the Swiss from claiming that he had been robbed of the money, or that it had been confiscated by the Czechs or even in Austria—all the countries had regulations now about taking money out.

A whole week went by and still the second telegram would not come. Nor was there any other sign of life from the Swiss. There were more letters from Mizzi with more ridiculous bank drafts which would lose two-thirds of their value if he cashed them here, and a notice from the American consul in Berne to say that his passport was waiting for him. But he hardly glanced at them in his worry over what had become of the Swiss, any more than he had any eyes for the beautiful June days out in the street.

He also attributed it to his anxiety that he had two quarrels at home within one day, first with Franz, and then with Poldi. Franz came up to him one evening while he was glancing over the foreign currency quotations in the newspaper, and said:

"Lend me your blue tie again, will you? I've got to look my best tonight."

It was the second time that Franz was borrowing the tie. He was aware of sounding irritable:

"Look, why don't you keep it for good? I can get another one."

Franz's abruptly creased forehead showed him that he had said the wrong thing. All the gaiety had gone out of Franz's face; he turned without a word and went back into his room. A minute later, Peter followed him. Franz was already putting on one of his own ties.

"I didn't mean to say anything wrong. I just meant that since you liked it . . ."

Franz reached for his vest. "Thank you. I can manage with my old ones."

It was a little thing, of no importance, Peter assured himself, but he was left with an unpleasant feeling of having offended Franz.

The next day Poldi came home rather excitedly:

"We can get our food package tomorrow. I just found out at the Central Market. Letters A through D . . ." And Poldi went to Father's desk and got out the voucher which had come in one of Mizzi's letters. She came and put it on the table beside him. "We've got to get it tomorrow! On Monday they're giving out packages for the next five letters in the alphabet. The inspector said that if we miss our day, we'll have to wait until the very end. There mayn't be anything left then."

"Well, I can't go tomorrow."

"Why can't you? It's Sunday. You haven't anything to do!"

It sounded too trivial to say that he had his English lesson: besides, his real reason for not wanting to go was that he did not want to miss the telegram from the Swiss.

"I can't, that's all. I have something important on and I can't afford to stand in line all day."

"Well, you don't expect Mother to go and bring home a thirty-five-pound package? You ought to be ashamed of yourself! And I've got to work at the relief office in Favoriten!"

"I don't see why Herr Lauber can't get the parcel." Herr Lauber was a war invalid who lived in the next block and who had been doing chores for people in the neighborhood. "I'll simply pay him for the day. He'll be glad to make a few kronen."

But Poldi acted almost precisely as Franz had done the day before—she picked up the voucher angrily and walked away from him.

"What's wrong with sending Herr Lauber, I'd like to know!" he persisted. "I said I'd pay him. My time just happens to be a little more valuable now than to use it to stand in line!"

"We don't need you to pay Herr Lauber. Just forget about it!"

He noticed that they deliberately avoided mentioning the food parcel again the rest of the day. When he failed to see Franz either the following morning or at noon for lunch, he knew that Franz had gone. He felt himself isolated by their opprobrium. He spent the afternoon in the coffeehouse on the Graben in the hope that the Swiss might show up. When he came home, the empty carton of the food parcel was on the floor by the kitchen cabinet. Franz had had to stand in line until five o'clock—seven hours in all. But oddly enough it was Franz who seemed least resentful of having had to stand in line; it was Poldi and *she* who refused to speak to him. He felt like a stranger in the house.

But on Tuesday he heard from the Swiss. Everything was all right. The Swiss wrote from Berne that the Polish syndicate had paid him with a draft on a Swiss bank, and that he had cashed the draft: Peter's share amounted to twenty-seven thousand francs. The Swiss suggested that it would be wise to deposit the money in a bank in Berne, where Peter could always draw on it through the Vienna branch, and that there was grave danger that the money might be confiscated at the border if he attempted to bring it to him in cash. The Swiss asked him to wire what he was to do.

Exultantly, Peter hurried to the telegraph office and wired him to open an account. He scolded himself for ever distrusting the Swiss. And in his jubilant mood it irked him to remember Poldi's distant manner at home: he went to a food store which was getting in more and more things from abroad and bought a whole Dutch cheese, a pound of chocolate, and six tins of sardines—all of them things that Poldi liked. Then he stopped in the haberdashery shop in the Kärntnerstrasse and bought a tie which was the same blue color as the one Franz liked but had a different design, so as not to remind Franz too much of the unpleasant business over the other tie.

He put the food casually on the kitchen table, pretending that he had got it from a customer, and he had the satisfaction of seeing Poldi eat some of the sardines for supper and take a piece of chocolate the next day. But he was aware that neither Poldi nor *she* could be bribed into forgetting about the food parcel so easily. They were still hurt.

With Franz, it was much easier. Franz had taken the tie out of the box delightedly.

"For me? Why, that's a perfect beauty!" And Franz had given him a long look that had shown that he had understood, and had forgiven him. "You must have had a windfall!" Franz had joked. "Did your mother send you some more money? You know, you better save it—you'll need it to travel with."

He had thrust away the suggestion about Mizzi.

"I don't need her money. I can make my own windfalls."

Franz had folded the tie. "Well, it's very fine anyway. Have you told Herr Straka yet about leaving him?"

"Not yet. I will, by and by."

"You oughtn't to wait too long, now that you have your passport and everything. You know what your mother said: that it's only a question now of getting passage for you on a boat!"

"I'll tell him this week sometime. . . ."

He was aware that he had been deliberately putting off the moment of leaving the store. There was not only the feeling every morning now that he no longer needed to go to work unless he wanted to, which gave him a delightful feeling of condescension toward the store, but also the fact that he was exceedingly happy there.

Herr Straka had put him in charge of all the new storerooms that were being built. He loved the discussions with Herr Straka over the architect's and the carpenter's plans, the zest of driving the laborers to shift things to the new racks in record time, the new, efficient arrangement in place of the moldy disorder in the storerooms. And because he spent so much of his time out in the warehouses, he felt a pleasant detachment from the store itself. There had been so many new additions to the clerks that he hardly knew the most recent ones, because he saw them only in the morning and at night for a few minutes in the locker room. There were the two new apprentices who had come in July, the third set since Otto and he had started in at the store. It felt strange to know them only by name this time. He felt a twinge of vindictiveness occasionally when he saw how easy it was for them; they did not have to do any of the things Otto and he had had to do, which certainly *he* had had to do. Laborers now opened the shutters in the morning and closed them at night, and the laborers carried the bolts and rivets into the cellar when they were unpacked. Only now and then he saw one of the new apprentices do some chore for Herr Meier that savored even remotely of the hard work of the war years.

He finally went upstairs to the office to speak to Herr Straka about leaving. Herr Straka was disappointed at the news.

"You could have had a place with us here," Herr Straka said. "You were on your way to a position of responsibility. But if your mother wants you to come—America offers more of a future, of course.... Well, perhaps you may want to come back someday...." Herr Straka had joked.

It was agreed that he would stay on as long as he liked, and he got permission to leave an hour before closing time every evening. He had asked for that so as to get in an English lesson every day.

They could hardly be called lessons any more. They were social calls, during which they discussed the last English or American book he had read—Frau Hobbs-Pechlar filling in the gaps when he was stumped for a word or a phrase, and explaining the sometimes enthrallingly rich background that went with a name or a place or some custom. It was like that he had learned about Philadelphia and about the Quaker villages which had grown into fashionable suburbs around it, and especially about the little town where she had grown up. Slowly, from these accounts his picture of America had filled out, had its own glow from the warm nostalgia with which Frau Hobbs-Pechlar spoke of Philadelphia and of a trip she had once taken as a girl to a ranch in Wyoming, of Boston and New York.

It was almost two years now since he had first come to her. The days when he had worked hard on grammar and had memorized long word lists on the streetcar were far behind. Little by little, he had let her know about his family, just as she occasionally spoke of her dead husband who had been a concert violinist. When she had assumed that his own father was dead, because he had a stepfather, he had let her explanation stand rather gratefully and had not corrected her. But within the limits of that one falsehood, he sometimes felt that she knew him better than anybody. She had, for instance, accepted his ambitiousness as something so natural that it needed no explanation, whereas Poldi and Franz were still puzzled by it. He had grown fond of her. Twice, once at Christmas and once when he had found out from the maid when her birthday came, he had sent her a sheaf of the long-stemmed red roses which she liked to keep on her American cherrywood table in the library. And once, when she had consulted him about exchanging some dollar currency, he had gone out of his way to get her the best possible rate in the coffeehouses near the Exchange. In return, he knew that she was proud of him as her star pupil and liked to show him off to her friends.

Toward the end of one of his Sunday-morning lessons—it was

the first week in July—Frau Hobbs-Pechlar told him about a Quaker Meeting in the Innere Stadt. He discovered that the Canadians and the Americans from the various food relief commissions had been holding the Meetings for several Sundays already, and that that was the reason why she had moved his lessons up from ten to nine o'clock. She invited him to come along.

"You'll meet some of your future countrymen there, and you'll be able to practice your English on them. . . ."

He was glad that he had the new gray suit to wear. They went by streetcar to the Ring and walked over to the Graben. The Meeting was in a clubroom over a bookstore which he had often passed without suspecting the existence of the large room up above. He was a little uneasy as he climbed the stairs with Frau Hobbs-Pechlar. Just what was a Quaker Meeting like? Frau Hobbs-Pechlar had told him about the Quakers, it was true, and about the simplicity of their form of worship, but it was that very difference from a church as he was used to it which alarmed him now, as did the consciousness that presently he would be in a room full of Americans.

It was just half past eleven, but it appeared that they were already late, although the room was completely silent when they entered it. Up front where the windows gave on the Graben, a row of chairs had been lined up against the side walls, he saw with his first nervous glance, and some half-dozen men sat on the right and three women on the left. Several rows of chairs had been placed facing the windows, and there were people sitting on those. Mostly men, it seemed. But again he noticed the division of men and women—the half-dozen women to the left of the center aisle, and the men to the right. They sat mostly with bowed heads, apparently meditating. Nobody turned to look as they came in. Frau Hobbs-Pechlar motioned him to join the men on the right.

From shyness and a need to conform, he bowed his head as he saw the other men doing. He wondered what he was supposed to think about. He forced himself to say an "Our Father" and was aware of the anomaly of praying as he would have done in a Catholic church—*she* would be outraged if she knew that he was sitting in a heretic church! It was the first time in years that he had even attempted to pray and his thoughts persisted in wandering. He noticed that the man's suit just in front of him was tweed, not so very different from the tweed suit he himself had got this week along with the one he was wearing now. Then his eyes noted the lean, angular face of another man in the row ahead. The man was looking at the wall between the windows up ahead. Encouraged, he himself raised his head a little and allowed his eyes to stray over the room. There were some fifteen men in the rows ahead of him, not counting the six who were sitting along the wall. Over in the other corner by the windows, on the left, there was a plump matronly lady, and—next to her, the girl he had seen in the Opera!

The whole quality of the room changed for him. Something of the festiveness of that night seeped into it and leavened its drowsy peacefulness. The girl was looking—appeared at least to be looking—at the wide sunbeam which came in through the middle window and played on the floor. Her eyes held a waiting dreaminess, but her shoulders and her chin had that same vital quality of projecting her forward which he had noticed in the Opera. She wore a dark-blue blouse—or perhaps it was part of an entire dress; he could not tell which, because of the table in front of her—and a straw hat. He felt excited and happy, and he found it almost easy to bend his head again.

The silence over the room no longer seemed so strained. Still, it drew on and on, until suddenly and quite without warning one of the men along the wall got up and started to read from a book. It was a harsher English than Frau Hobbs-Pechlar had accustomed him to, and it took him several minutes to catch on to it: the man was reading the parable about the vineyard. When it was over, the man sat down as abruptly as he had got up and silence reigned once more. Peter looked at the girl again: her eyes were on the floor now where the column of silvery motes made a honey-colored pool of which he could see only a part. He wished that he could see all of it. An elderly and rather stout man got up and spoke for a few minutes. It was rather as if he were speaking to himself than to the rest. He spoke of the man with only one talent and of his duty to his fellowmen.

Peter stole another glance at the girl: she had dropped a glove and her face moved alertly to the right to look down on the floor.

He recognized the quick movement of her head. He had already noticed it at the Opera—not only her eyes moving when she looked somewhere, but her whole head—so that he felt a thrill of familiarity with it. He watched her hesitate, then lean over swiftly to pick up the glove and dust it off in her lap. Then she looked serenely in front of her again. The trivial incident had had a charming frivolity which delighted him. . . .

The man who had read from the Bible said: "Let us pray!" But instead of the loud prayer which Peter had expected, the men in front of him only bowed their heads a little lower, stayed that way for a number of minutes, and then the man who had asked them to pray softly shut the Bible in front of him and got up. Other people around him got up and walked down toward the door. Peter saw the girl and the two women come away from their chairs up by the windows. Frau Hobbs-Pechlar came out of her row and smiled at him, relieving him of his indecision whether to keep on sitting or get up.

Back where the door was, people were talking. They talked quietly, soberly, familiarly. Frau Hobbs-Pechlar left him to join several people, among whom was the stout man who had spoken about the man with one talent. He heard her mention Philadelphia several times. . . . The tall man in the tweed suit suddenly addressed him: the man was inviting him to come again and then introducing himself. It turned out that he was a Canadian and that he had been in Vienna once before the war. While Peter was still talking with him, he saw that the two women and the girl had joined the group around Frau Hobbs-Pechlar. A minute later Frau Hobbs-Pechlar came for him to introduce him to a bewildering number of people, to the plump man who was "Mr. Page," and to the women whose names he could not even remember, and then to the girl who—he noticed with all his senses alert—was "Miss Page."

"Mr. Domanig," Frau Hobbs-Pechlar was explaining, "is really an American. His mother lives in Westchester. He's just about to join her."

"Oh, really," the plump man said. "Are you looking forward to it?"

He said, "Yes, I am," and felt awkward because the girl was looking at him. She had grayish-blue eyes, he saw. One of the women had started to sympathize with him over the war years, a man asked where he was sailing from, and then suddenly he was facing the girl and she said:

"I saw you at the Opera, didn't I, the night they gave *Tannhäuser?*"

It was wonderful that she should have seen him!

"Yes—I saw you, too."

"Wasn't it a marvelous performance! You were with a group of people and that fascinating girl in white. Do you often go to the Opera?"

"No, that was the first time I've ever been. I go to the theater more."

The others were starting downstairs.

"I've been going to the theater, too, although I catch only about one word out of ten." She laughed, and he noticed that her eyes laughed even before her mouth. "But I'm not going to give it up. I'm trying to learn German while I'm here. You speak English awfully well: did you learn it here?"

He felt himself blush at her praise. "Yes, I've been taking lessons with Frau Hobbs-Pechlar. . . ."

"I think you speak it beautifully. I wish I could learn to speak German like that!" The others had started out of the Graben toward the Kärntnerstrasse and he was still with the girl. "I used to have a German governess," she went on, "and I can understand things pretty well, if people talk very slowly. But of course they won't! Maybe Frau Hobbs-Pechlar will give me lessons—I want to learn German and know all about Vienna. I love Vienna! I've seen a lot of it already: Schönbrunn and the Prater, and I want to see Heiligenstadt! That's where Beethoven lived. Do you know Heiligenstadt?"

It was strange to be asked whether he knew Heiligenstadt. Her very question moved it out of the realm of the familiar, so that it was no longer the place where he had gone with Father to the *Heurigen* or the place he had passed on the train dozens of times.

"Yes, I know it," he said and was already frightened by the boldness of what he was about to propose: "If you like, I could show it to you."

"Would you really? I'd love to go with someone who really

knows the city!" Her face and her shoulders had come forward with that crisp eagerness he had first noticed at the Opera. "But I can't this afternoon—I've already promised to help with the food packages. But tomorrow: could you go tomorrow?"

He hesitated for an instant. All he had to do was to ask for the afternoon off at the store—"Tomorrow is fine."

"We're staying at the Hotel Bristol. You know where that is, I suppose? Just a few steps beyond the Opera. . . . We can start after lunch, can't we? Does it take very long to get there?"

"Only about an hour and a half."

"Oh, that's perfect. If we start about half past one, we'll have all afternoon." Her father had turned just then because they had reached the Ring—"Father, Mr. Domanig is going to show me Heiligenstadt—you know where Beethoven made his will—and he's going to teach me German too!"

Her father looked uncertain and Peter shrank a little from his level-eyed scrutiny. "That's fine," he said with friendly deliberateness.

Frau Hobbs-Pechlar was smiling. "But he'll need to practice his English," she said.

"Oh, we can do that, too. We'll talk English for half an hour, and then German for half an hour—won't we? I'll expect you about half past one, then—is that right?"

"Yes, I'll be there." He looked once more into her lively gray-blue eyes, then he said good-by to her father and to the Canadian and the others. . . .

"Well, you didn't have much difficulty getting along with your future compatriots!" Frau Hobbs-Pechlar teased him as they crossed over to the streetcar stop.

Chapter Fifty-Two

HEILIGENSTADT and the road along the Danube where Beethoven had liked to walk, the Prater, the Dutch village behind Neuwaldegg—he took her to see them all. Places which he knew only by name but about which her Baedeker was sternly insistent, places which he knew so well that familiarity had blinded him to them, and places which long ago had held some special significance for him that the years of apprenticeship had dimmed and grayed. It was the last which pleased him most.

They were in the Albrechtsplatz like that—the little square where Father had bent over to tie his shoelaces one evening—and she was looking up at the walls of the old Imperial Palace:

"This is lovely. It isn't ornate at all. I've always thought Baroque had to be gaudy as in Italy. It's even austere. . . ."

"Yes, it's very simple," he had answered happily, delighted once again that she should like a spot that he had once loved, though for entirely different reasons. In a sense she was giving Vienna back to him.

Her zest for seeing the city was endless, and he was happy that there was so much to show. But sometimes her very zest became a reproach. He felt that the city was not at its best and that she was being cheated. He said then, as once in the Prater: "You should have seen all this before the war, during the flower-korso!" and he had gone on to describe the thousands of flower-trimmed carriages and floats, and the gaiety on the first of May.

"It must have been wonderful! But it's still wonderful!"

They had started out to speak English for the first hour, then German for an hour, but nothing ever really came of the German lessons. In the end, she always fell into English again, so that he had protested:

"But you won't learn any German!"

She had merely laughed: "It doesn't matter. I'm taking lessons with Frau Hobbs-Pechlar anyway."

And he had been glad of that too, because in her mouth English was no longer a language a dark ambition had driven him to learn, but a form of music that belonged to her and brought him closer. He had no difficulty in understanding what she said. The puzzling gap that opened between them now and then was due to all the things he did not know about her and she did not know about him.

They would walk through a street just when a group of children with their stockings rolling down for lack of rubber garters would come running out of a doorway——

"Look!" she would say. "Look, isn't that horrible!"

He had seen only the untidy stockings rolling down one little girl's legs. "I guess they are poor."

"But I didn't mean that! Look at their legs—how twisted they are—that's rickets! But we are getting three hundred thousand cans of condensed milk for them next week!"

It was a lordly "we"—impatient and generous, and confident of disposing of all difficulties. He had come to associate it with her and with the whole group of men and women he had seen at the first Quaker Meeting that morning, and with America. She had said when the first news of Communist violence in Hungary had come through: "We'll put a stop to that. We'll get Bela Kun out of there, and fast!" "How?" he had asked at the time. "Why, we'll simply bring pressure to bear on the population, by telling them that we won't send them any food until they get rid of Bela Kun." And she had been perfectly right: in less than two weeks Bela Kun had been glad to flee with a safe-conduct. But he had also noticed that the Rumanians and the Serbs who had invaded Hungary in the name of the Allies, to establish order, had not obeyed the imperious "we" and had marched on Budapest in spite of the protests from Versailles.

But that was niggling, he told himself, and ungenerous on his part; the "we" in her mouth was as generous as her reactions to the misery she saw and as exhilarating as the vitality he loved in her.

In one form or another he was always conscious of her radiant health. In the Burggasse that time, he had been especially conscious of it in contrast with the rickety children and with the slow-moving people with their sallow cheeks. There was as much joy for him in the energy of her wide shoulders above the slim, long waist as in the beauty of her long-browed gray eyes and in the exquisitely bold modeling of her lips and chin.

He had once read in one of the books Frau Hobbs-Pechlar had lent him that both the hero and the heroine were "clean-limbed." The description had puzzled him. Yet now, when he watched her walking toward him in the lobby at the Hotel Bristol, or away from some picture in the museum, he suddenly knew what the term meant. She moved determinedly, eagerly, somehow generously, so that the streets seemed narrower than they really were when she set out to cross them. The grace lay in her freedom from constraint. Poldi had courage, too. It was not that. The American girl simply did not acknowledge any difficulties, and somehow the difficulties disappeared.

Sometimes he attributed all the fascination she had for him to her cool, vibrant air of self-sufficiency. It would not have been possible, he knew, to have spent so many hours with any other girl—except Bianca, because of Franz, and that was over and done with now—without trying to make love to her. But the American girl with her clear-voiced laugh and her frank way of taking his hand when they came to a brook—"Let's do it together: one, two, three . . ."—had tended to discourage him. She had established a titillatingly aseptic mood which at once drew him closer to her than he felt he should have been, and kept him from appoaching as closely as he would have liked. And yet, in speaking of her cousin's marriage and the wedding present they set out to get, she spoke of marriage as something infinitely desirable and understood. She even knew how many children she was going to have. . . . Yet when he had about decided that she was only using him for a guide and looking on him as she might on a cousin, she startled him by explaining what a "beau" was—"Well, like you! You're my beau here, aren't you?" And when he had wanted to make sure just how seriously she had meant it, and had asked: "And in America?" she had said gaily: "Philadelphia isn't so far from Westchester, and I'll be back in January. . . ."

It was like that with other, minor things. He had to grope his way carefully to keep from drawing wrong conclusions. The pitfalls lay in her background in America and all the things he did not know about it. Nothing was entirely as he had expected it. Not even Frau Hobbs-Pechlar was always reliable. It was like that with Sibby's name—she had said on their first trip to Heiligenstadt: "Don't call me 'Miss Page!' That sounds silly. Call me 'Sibby' or 'Sib.' . . ." During his next lesson he had asked Frau Hobbs-Pechlar what "Sibby" stood for. "Sybil, I imagine," Frau Hobbs-Pechlar had said. But it wasn't "Sybil" at all. When he had asked Sibby about it, she had laughed. "I suppose it ought to be 'Sybil,' but it's really Priscilla. The girls in school simply called me 'Sib' and it's stuck."

Another time he was puzzled by her references to her father's "farm." They lived in Philadelphia and her father was a banker, yet there was a farm. When he finally asked her to explain, she countered with another laugh: "Oh, it isn't a farm like that: pigs and chickens and cows. We've got horses and we raise alfalfa for them. Haverford's really more like a suburb of Philadelphia. We stay out there during the summer and fall."

Words, even when he thought he knew what they meant, were only a distorted shadow of the American reality behind. A pharmacy was not a pharmacy, it seemed, but rather a jumble of half a dozen different kinds of stores. It was as if in America an exhilarating anarchy had played havoc with all the rules he knew. You did not, for instance, Sibby said, need to have served an apprenticeship and belong to a merchants' guild to open a shop. Anyone was free to open a shop. . . . Only one thing was clear: that America had much the same quality of galvanizing health and confidence that Sibby had. And it was fun to explore this world, which was strangely enough Mizzi's world, too, because each new bit of information became a bond between Sibby and him. And, too, Sibby was as puzzled about the common, ordinary realities of the life he knew as he was about hers. There was some compensation in that. . . .

"Who was that girl in white at the Opera that time?" Sibby asked on their last afternoon before she had to leave with her father for Budapest to set up the distribution of food in Hungary. They were in the imperial hunting park behind Schönbrunn. The park had only just been thrown open to the public the week before. They had walked for half an hour through a beechwood and had come out on a little meadow at the top of a knoll.

"Baroness Bianca," he said.

"Is that her full name?"

"No, I guess it's Bianca von Ortner."

"Oh, she's the wife of the man who limped—Baron Ortner, you said."

"No, she's his sister."

"But if she's a baroness! In England, I know, the daughter of a baron doesn't really bear any title—only the wife."

"I suppose, that's why she's only called 'Baroness Bianca' and her mother is 'Baroness Ortner.' "

"Anyhow, she's stunning. How did you come to know them?"

He explained about Franz's friendship with Baron Ortner, and then about Bianca and Franz.

"But I thought that class distinctions were so strict in Europe? How is it that your cousin—" she caught herself quickly—"I mean, your cousin doesn't have a title. I thought people with titles all cliqued together?"

"I imagine they do, but my cousin and Baron Ortner simply got to be friends in school."

"But the class distinctions are severe, aren't they?"

It was hard to answer her question. He thought of how little Baron Ortner and Bianca had ever been conscious of their title, but on the other hand there were Baron Ortner's mother and Freiherr von Steligerode! He remembered the rigid distinctions at the store and the line-up outside Herr Straka's office on Christmas Eve: the clerks and the apprentices first, and only then the helpers and laborers. . . . And on the other hand, there had been Herr Straka's simple friendliness to everybody. . . . There was the respect people had for a master locksmith or a master carpenter. . . . Poldi's scorn for what she called a "counterjumper". . . .

"Some people are more aware of them than others," he said evasively, because he himself could come to no conclusion. It was something he had never thought about before.

"And your cousin is going to marry Baroness Bianca?"

"I think so."

"Is she in love with him?"

He told her about Bianca's secret visits to the hospital, and about Bianca's mother and her opposition to Franz.

"You see, that's what I mean! But Baroness Bianca is going to marry him anyway?"

"She said so."

"Of course, your cousin is very handsome. I saw him when he brought the glasses from the buffet."

They had come to the top of the knoll. Sibby turned and looked out over the trees where in the distance one could just make out the spire of St. Stephen's.

"Look, you can see the whole city from here. Let's sit down."

He looked around among the high grass for a smooth place, but Sibby had already found a spot.

"How about right here?" She flung herself down on the grass before he could take off his coat.

"You'll get grass stains on your dress. . . ."

"They won't show. That's the advantage of wearing a green dress."

She sat with her hands clasped around her knees, her face thrust forward dreamily. Then she suddenly unclasped her hands and threw herself back on the grass. "Oh, it's lovely here! When I've finished college, I'm coming back here to live. I'd like to have a house in Sievering where we were yesterday."

"That was Hütteldorf. . . ."

"That's where I mean."

"I thought you were going to get married right after you left college?"

"Well, I can do that, too." She had propped herself up on one elbow and lay looking up at him. "I'd like to have a house here for the summer, and live in the United States the rest of the year. Philadelphia is wonderful during the winter!"

"Why?"

"Oh, there are theaters and the opera and parties. . . . Do you like to dance?"

"I don't know how."

"I love to dance!"

The distance, which all her references to American boys, who could do so many things he had not even known about—play football and polo and tennis, and dance—always seemed to put between them, opened again and grew threatening.

"I thought Quakers didn't approve of dancing and the theater?"

"Oh, it isn't like that. Daddy is a Quaker, but he isn't that strict, and besides my mother is an Episcopalian and I was brought up in an Episcopalian school. It used to be strict like that a long time ago. . . ."

They lay silently for a little while and he watched a bluebell swaying just beside her cheek.

"How did you happen to be apprenticed in a store?" she asked suddenly.

"I couldn't get into a school I wanted to get in, and then I didn't want to go to any other school. I just got mad, I guess."

"Are you sorry you did it?"

"Sorry?" He thought triumphantly of his position now in the store, of what Herr Straka had said, and of the money in the bank in Berne. "No, I'm not sorry at all."

"But wasn't it hard? Daddy says it's frightfully hard to be an apprentice in Europe."

The scars which he still had across his hands where they had been frostbitten that first year seemed very insignificant.

"No, it wasn't so hard."

"I bet you just say that. You know, Daddy has a lot of respect for you. That's why he didn't grouse about my seeing so much of you. Frau Hobbs-Pechlar told us how you used to come and take lessons in the evening when you could hardly keep awake."

He felt himself blushing with the memory of his oil-stained hands and his grimy clothes in those early days, but at the same time he knew a grim twinge at the thought of how easy things had already become even when he had first started his lessons with Frau Hobbs-Pechlar.

"Daddy thought I would be safe with you. He's always warning me about European Don Juans. . . ."

Sibby looked at him with her clear, gray-blue eyes—"Do you know that you've never kissed me?"

All the accumulated feelings of the past few weeks rushed joyously, tremulously through his veins.

"Well, may I—"

Her lips were cool and new and firm. Her free hand had seized his shoulder and she had let herself sink back on the ground. Then her hand pushed him away a little and she was smiling up at him.

He said:

"You are wonderful, Sibby!"

"You're nice, too. . . ." This time her hand drew him as he bent. Adoration for her whipped in his ears as he felt her body yielding for a second or two. Her hand slid to his shoulder, nudged it two or three times, and finally pushed him away.

"We have to go now," she said firmly. Her eyes held him for a second with a new smile. Then she snatched up her hat from beside her in the grass, kissed him quickly on the cheek, and got up.

A delicious silence tied them together as firmly as her hand which was holding his, so that they walked like two children—he felt—back to the forest path. Only after they had entered the woods, he said:

"It'll be awful now without you."

"Are you going to miss me?"

"Every moment."

"It won't be so long. We're only going to stay in Budapest for a few weeks, then Rumania and Turkey. We're going to sail in time for Christmas. I have to be home for the second term."

"May I write you in Budapest?"

"You better!"

They had come out on an avenue and were meeting people now and then. Already she looked so self-possessed and competent again that no passer-by would ever guess—Peter thought happily—that she had trembled a little back there on the meadow when they had kissed.

"And you are going on the French Line?"

"Yes, I am." Nothing could change him now about going through Paris, now that Sibby had told him about the places in Paris she liked. It would be another bond. . . .

He sought to hold back the moments on the way home. Sibby had to be back at the hotel by six. But nothing would hold the minutes back. They passed the Gürtel, then Herr Granini's house—and then the Ring!

She stopped at the desk in the lobby to write out her address in

Budapest. The lanky Canadian walked by and tipped his hat. Two Italian officers sat smoking by a column and were watching Sibby out of the corner of their eyes. He felt jealous of them because they might see her again tonight, perhaps at the dinner she was going to; but the next moment his jealousy was gone because Sibby was handing him the slip with the address in triumphantly full view of the two officers.

"I wish I didn't have to go to that reception. But the Dutch Ambassador is giving it especially for the Commission, and Daddy says I have to go."

They had walked around to the elevators. One of them was sliding down to a halt. Just as the doors opened, Sibby bent forward quickly and kissed him——

"Good-by, Peter. See you in New York. Don't forget to write!"

He watched the elevator disappear up the ornate shaft. He thought exultantly: *Sibby kissed me right in front of the doorman and the elevator boy!* He reached into his pocket and took out a five-franc bill: the doorman scraped and winked. But on his way out of the hotel, his thought took another turn—*I've been kissed by a girl in the Hotel Bristol!* He remembered how he had once longed to be important enough to stay at the Bristol. He smiled at himself as he remembered it. What did it matter where? The trees, and the people walking on the Ring, even the Communists debating on the corner as usual, were all included in his happiness! . . .

There was a rush for the streetcar at the Mariahilferstrasse. He got caught in it without even noticing it. His happiness was like an outer envelope, so that he could afford to lend himself good-naturedly to the shoving and squeezing of the crowd. But just as he was about to get on, a sharp-faced woman ahead of him spun around angrily and started to tug at her pocketbook which had got caught against his arm.

"The nerve of these gangsters nowadays!"

It was only then that he realized that the woman was accusing him of being a pickpocket. The man with her thrust himself forward with an angry scowl. For a moment Peter felt helpless because he had been caught off guard. Several people were staring at him. He said angrily:

"Do I look like a thief!"

"He had his hand on my pocketbook!" the woman charged.

Someone was muttering: "Ought to take him to the police right away!"

He suddenly remembered his passport with the Swiss visa which he had got at the Swiss consulate just before he had called for Sibby. He thought for an instant of taking it out and brandishing it under the woman's nose: "There, I'm going to Switzerland in a few days—maybe tomorrow, if I want to. Do you think I need your money?" But it was silly to pay so much attention to the woman with the hard, vulgar face and to her florid-faced husband—probably a grocer who had done well out of the war. He turned on the man:

"You better be careful whom you call a thief! It isn't my fault if there's a crush."

The man backed down. He muttered: "Not even your life is safe any more in the streets," and hustled his wife up on the car.

Peter looked around haughtily at the two or three people who were still staring at him, then he walked away to the hack-stand and took a cab.

But the incident rankled in him. It was as if his happiness had been soiled. The stupid face of the woman with the pocketbook kept coming between him and Sibby. He resolved suddenly:

I'm going to get out of here! No use waiting here any longer, now that Sibby'll be gone. I'll go to the travel agency first thing tomorrow morning and wire for a reservation on the French Line—I can leave on Monday!

Chapter Fifty-Three

"AND you are really going by way of Paris?" Franz asked.

"Certainly! I talked with the Swiss consul this morning, and he said that there wasn't going to be any hitch about it at all. And I've got the travel agency to wire ahead for a reservation on the French Line. I might have to wait six months before I can get anything on a Dutch boat. Anyhow, it's practically impossible to get anything from here; you have to be on the spot!"

"You seem to be in an awful hurry all of a sudden. That's not the way you talked last winter!"

"It isn't that, Franz. I just feel silly waiting around, after I've quit the store and everything. . . ."

"Perhaps you should have stayed on in the store a little longer. When you've waited this long, a few more months can hardly matter."

"I didn't mean that. I don't need the job in the store. I could make all the money I wanted trading on my own account."

"Well, I don't approve of your going through France at all. Your mother and your stepfather know more about circumstances abroad than you can know here. If they had wanted you to come any other way but through Holland, they would have said so!"

"Well, they did. Didn't you see in the last letter that they were trying to get a passage for me on a Swedish boat? And they don't know about circumstances here in Europe—the way they keep on sending those idiotic bank drafts, after I explained to them that the only way to send money now is in letters, shows that."

Franz had frowned at the "idiotic."

"The fact remains that you are their son and still only a minor. You ought to do what your mother says, not what you feel like doing. Technically, you are still only a child!"

"Oh, am I? I wasn't a child in the store when I had to do a man's work these last three years. I've had to deal with men on an even basis, and I've done pretty well. . . ."

"I know that, and I didn't say—"

"The one thing I want Mizzi to get quite clear is that I'm not a little boy she can boss around. That's the reason I want to pay my own passage and the reason I'm not cashing any more of her bank drafts. She isn't doing me any favors—I would have traveled without her, too."

He could see that Franz was trying hard to avoid a quarrel.

"Of course, I haven't any power to force you not to go to Paris. You are under your parents' jurisdiction now. But you are acting against my wishes, and the least thing you can do is to telegraph your mother first."

"I wrote her last night that the boats were all jammed, and that I couldn't get anything from here, certainly, and that I'd have a better chance in Paris."

"It'll be two weeks before she gets your letter."

"I know it."

For just a moment Franz's eyes crinkled with amused complicity, then Franz became serious again:

"What you don't realize is that you are going into a country with which we've just been at war. The peace isn't even signed yet. It might even be dangerous. Look at the way people here feel about the Italians!"

"I have an American passport and I can speak English. Besides, I'm not afraid."

It annoyed him that nearly everything he had said to Franz so far had sounded like boasting. Franz was looking thoughtful. He pulled out his watch.

"I still have a quarter of an hour—let's go into the Volksgarten."

They entered the park. They had got through early with lunch at the government employees' club where Franz always ate now at noon. It had been a miserable meal: a gristly piece of boiled beef and spinach, and a sirupy corn pudding. The rather handsome dining room had mocked the drab fare and the dignified men who had stood in line at the serving table. Really only a glorified soup kitchen, Peter thought now. He also thought of the good food they could have had in a restaurant. He had asked Franz to come with him to the Rathauskeller, but Franz had turned him down firmly: "You hold on to your dollars. You'll need all the money you've got." He had not dared to insist, for fear of offending Franz's touchiness about money again.

They walked up the main avenue. A few children were playing in the sand pit in front of the Greek temple, where the stamp collectors always loitered with their stamp albums in the late afternoon.

Franz said:

"Own up now: you do feel pretty excited about seeing your mother and your brother and your little sister so soon?"

Franz had adopted a tone of bantering knowingness, obviously induced in him by the summer noonday peace of the park. Peter stiffened himself against it. He was supposed to forget all about the past for the sake of this rich present now! But this present was of his own making—nobody had handed him anything on a silver platter! Not even Franz—in this seductive mood which practically said: "Come, we are both grown up now, walking here under the trees—you know about me and Bianca, and I know all about you—the other was only a childish thing!"—could gloss over that fact.

"Excited? Why should I be?"

"I certainly would be in your place. One's mother is one's mother."

"That's all right for you to say. You aren't—what has she ever done for me?"

"That was due to circumstances beyond her control. When a woman has a family, she can't always do what she'd like. You'll understand that much better when you get there. . . . And what about your little sister? She must be a charming little girl. Don't you feel that you want to see her?"

That was a shrewd thrust! . . . Had Franz sensed that he had been taken by the snapshot of the dark-haired little girl with the pert, serious eyes the first instant he had looked at it, that he had felt proud and excited somehow, and that he had taken more care in answering her childishly scrawled note than he had with all the letters he had written Mizzi?

He tried not to betray what he felt:

"I'll be interested, of course."

"I'm sure you'll feel something stronger than that when you see them all. Your stepfather is undoubtedly a very fine man; I can tell from the letter he wrote you. I still say I envy you."

"Well, we're just different."

They had come to the little grove which inclosed the white marble monument of the Empress Elizabeth. They sat down on a bench near the monument. Franz had taken off his hat and had put it beside him on the bench. He started to draw little patterns in the sand with the tip of his cane. He said suddenly:

"You know, there's a kind of callousness you have developed since you have been in the store. It worries me sometimes."

"That's because I found out that you can't get anywhere in this world unless you are hard-boiled."

"I think that's just a notion you have formed."

"A notion! How do you think I could have lasted at Straka's if I hadn't been hard? I had to fight my way. That's why I finished my apprenticeship half a year ahead of time and why I got more salary than men who had been clerks for years."

"I know all that and we are proud of you. But you were with rough people there and we were in the middle of a war, but that's all over now. There are other things in life that matter a little more than making a bigger salary than the next fellow."

"Sure, I know. But I want to get somewhere first and to do that you've got to be hard." He remembered something he had heard one of the men who harangued people on the Ring say once: "For that matter, that's why we lost the war. Because we weren't hard enough!"

For an instant he thought he had gone too far. He expected Franz to flare up and say something about the hundreds of thousands of men who had given their lives in the trenches and about the thousands of cripples one saw in the streets. But after a little hesitation, Franz merely looked at him, with his pale-blue eyes heavy with seriousness.

"We aren't Prussians. It's better to have lost the war, with all the hardship that's going to mean, than for us to have turned into something we weren't cut out to be. Fortunately!"

"And you don't think that all this suffering is making people bitter?"

"For a little while, maybe. But it just isn't in the Viennese temperament to stay unhappy long. We like to be gay and laugh. The next few years won't be easy, of course. You're lucky you won't have to be here." And as if Franz wanted to brush away the seriousness that had come between them, his face relaxed and he had said quickly, cajolingly: "I don't think you're as hard either as you'd like people to believe. It's just a pose you fell in love with during those hard years. We all know that you have a good heart. Like that new chair for mother! You oughtn't to have done that: you ought to hold on to all your money. You know, mother cried for half an hour the night you brought the chair. You're after all like her youngest to her. . . ."

A woman and a child had come into the grove. The woman had sat down on a bench and the little boy was busily scraping sand together with his shovel. When he had a large enough pile, he shoveled it into his little bucket, then emptied the sand out at a spot near the monument.

They watched him for a while. Franz's eyes finally left the child and traveled over the trees and bushes in the grove, and came to rest on a branch that hung out over the next bench. The branch was studded with bright red berries.

"Do you remember the time you ate all those berries?" Franz asked.

It suddenly came back to Peter. He had been very small, and it was one of those cherished occasions when Franz had brought him along into the Innere Stadt. They had stopped to watch the guards being changed in the Schweitzerhof, and then they had come in here, to this identical spot.

"I thought they were currants," he said, feeling happy and warm with the memory.

"It was this same bush, I'm almost sure."

"No, it was that one over there right next to the monument; I remember your stepping over the bronze chain right there."

"You had your mouth stuffed full of berries," Franz said. "I had to make you spit them all out."

"Worse than that: you made me vomit, and then you bought me some candy on the Ring."

Franz chuckled: "Well, I thought they might be poisonous."

"Are they?"

"I don't know."

This time they both laughed, suddenly very close because of the memory, and because everything in those days had been happy at home.

"Reason I remember it," Franz said, "is that the same thing happened to me with our Father. I'd been eating all the berries I could off some bush and he finally caught me at it, and stuck his finger into my mouth to make me disgorge them. I suppose that's why I did it to you. Only I don't remember his buying me any chocolate afterward—more likely a pretzel I got."

"He was always buying me Salzstangl and raspberry juice and soda at the *Heurigen.* I looked forward all week to Sunday. . . ."

"Remember the chocolate lions for Christmas?"

"Yes, and the sugar-candy icicles. I was almost as fond of those as I was of the chocolate lions."

"He was a good man," Franz said slowly.

"Yes, he was." Peter found it difficult now that he had started to think of Father not to go on remembering.

"And what about your own father—do you still feel about him the way you did that day after the cadet school?"

"If I could have got at him two years ago, I would have killed him."

Franz frowned.

"Stop that! I won't listen to talk like that. Let's walk. . . ."

They started away from the bench. Franz's stride was long, tense, worried. He was carrying his walking stick, holding it below the handle.

"Supposing you did feel like that two years ago. You were still a little boy, and no doubt you had a hard time. If you remember, we didn't approve of all this apprenticeship business! . . . But you certainly don't feel that way now!"

"I wouldn't do the same things I would have done two years ago, if that's what you mean. But my feeling about him hasn't changed. Not one bit. I'm going to make him pay for it, if it's the last thing I do."

"You're talking like a child. We all go through a romantic period like that, when everything is either all white or all black. You're going to change and then you'll see how silly all this talk was."

"Maybe! Only I didn't change any about a man in the store who made life miserable for me the first winter. I had to wait two years until I could get even with him, but I got even with him."

"And you're proud of that?"

"It isn't a question of being proud. It's a matter of—well, of honor."

"Well, I don't believe you. I don't believe that you're really like that. I think I know you better."

It annoyed him that Franz should be so persistent in trying to prove him something he had no desire to be, and should try to browbeat him with his goody-goodness. What annoyed him even more was that there had been some truth in what Franz had just said. He had not thought of his father for months now—really not for two years. But then there had been no need to, he justified himself; the sharp-edged memory of that afternoon in the cellar had always been there, just a little out of focus, but always where he could touch it. You didn't need to think about a sore spot on your arm or leg all the time either to know that it was there. Still, it had been the very fact that he had not thought about his father that had made him sound so artificial just now. He had sensed that himself. He had simply repeated all the phrases that had stayed burned into his brain from that afternoon. . . .

Franz was setting down his walking stick with leisurely regularity again.

"And suppose you meet your father some day and you happen to like him very much. That's not impossible, you know."

"Not likely. I mean, my liking him. Why do you suppose I worked as hard as I did at the store? It's because I was determined to get abroad—and find him!"

He had expected another protest from Franz, but this time Franz walked on quite calmly.

"Perhaps it's a blessing in disguise that you feel the way you do about your father. After all, you aren't going to meet him right away, and by the time you do, I'm sure you'll have changed all your ideas, no matter what you say now. But when people feel as much hatred against somebody as you say you do, they sometimes hate everybody, including themselves. At least, you hate only one person. . . . I don't mind telling you now that I was worried about you that time when you had all that trouble with Mother and when you ran away!"

"You were still worried in February, weren't you?"

Franz took it seriously: "Well, I had to make sure. I was responsible for you. We all make mistakes. But what I was about to say: some people with a hatred like yours turn into criminals, and some into maniacs for power. History is full of people like that. Well, I'm sure that you won't turn out that way. Ten years from now, we'll both look back and laugh about it all. . . ."

"Maybe."

"I've got to get back to work. Which way are you going?"

"Over to the Kärntnerstrasse."

"See you tonight, then. Ten years from now we'll both be wiser." Franz smiled for a moment before he turned to walk down the Ring.

Peter watched him for a little while, then he started toward the Kärntnerstrasse. The conversation with Franz was still running through his head. *Whether his father was nice or not had nothing to do with it. The fact remained that he had an account to settle with him! It was just like Franz, who wasn't happy unless everything was in its place, to talk of Christian charity and sweet forgiveness. But he wasn't built that way!*

At the Opera, instead of turning into the Kärntnerstrasse as he had planned, he continued on down the Ring. The idea had suddenly come to him to call on Aunt Wetti before he left. . . .

It was three years since he had last seen Aunt Wetti and Uncle von Garnhaft in the cemetery at Father's funeral, and more than four years since the time he had secretly gone to see Aunt Wetti. He realized that his sudden impulse to go and see her now was largely due to Franz's talk in the park about Mizzi and about his father, but he was also conscious of a desire to let Aunt Wetti see him as he was now, grown up and in his new English suit, and to impress her with the expansive self-assurance he felt. A tart curiosity, also, to see how Aunt Wetti and Uncle von Garnhaft with his gold-rimmed spectacles and his well-to-do refinement had weathered the war gave an almost vindictive edge to his eagerness as he approached the Kolowrat-Ring.

He happened to glance up at the street sign on the corner house and noticed for the first time how "Kolowrat" was spelled. He had never noticed the 'r' in the word before. At home *she* had always said: "Aunt Wetti there, in her fine apartment on the Kolowat-Ring . . ." and quite unconsciously he had adopted her pronunciation whenever he had thought of the street. *So it was Kolowrat all the time, with an r!* he thought with a rush of tender amusement at *her* idiosyncrasies.

The war had changed nothing about the elegant aloofness of the street, nor about the hallway of the house. The black and gold grill around the elevator was there in back, just as he remembered it. He could ride in the elevator now all he wanted to! He felt himself smiling as he recalled his disappointment when she had refused to take the elevator that day when they had come here after his first communion. Partly to preserve the childish memory intact, and partly because of a certain amount of scorn for the elevator which somehow stood for Aunt Wetti's superiority, he took the stairs.

The same maid, who had received him so patronizingly once, opened the door. He recognized her close-set eyes with their suspicious stare. But her face was thinner, and something about the lines in it spoke of disgruntlement rather than haughtiness. Her small lace apron had been patched a little carelessly in one spot where the lace border had torn loose.

"I came to see Frau von Garnhaft."

She pulled the door open obsequiously:

"Won't the gentleman come in? Whom shall I announce?"

"If you will tell her it's her nephew—Herr Domanig . . ."

The girl returned after a minute. "The *Gnädige Frau* will be right out. If the *junge Herr* will be good enough to wait in the drawing room . . ."

It was all "the young gentleman this" and "the young gentleman that" with her now, Peter thought as he went into the drawing room. Dust covers were over the chairs and the sofa. The French window on the balcony stood open and a bland breeze ruffled the ivory-colored network draperies. Nothing was changed here either, except that the grand piano had been slewed toward the wall, so that it gave the impression of not being played very much. He kept his eyes on the glass doors from the dining room because that was where Aunt Wetti had come in the last time, so that he did not see her until she had already come in through the other door and was closing it softly.

"Well, Peter!" she said excitedly, but he noticed that she kept her voice low for some reason. "So you did come to see your old aunt before you left. I was afraid you might go away without saying good-by."

She had come up to him and had raised her face to his as a matter of course, so that he was forced to kiss her. He felt awkward, and in retaliation he scoffed at her "old aunt!" She was fragrant with the same lilies-of-the-valley scent he remembered from before, and she looked anything but old in the trim muslin dress with the lace collar and the cameo brooch. But her dark hair, he noticed, had a strand of gray over each temple where it was pulled back into the big-looped chignon.

She took her hands from his arms and then took a theatrical step backward——

"How tall you've grown, and how elegant you look! Is that a suit your mother sent you?"

Rather brusquely he said:

"No, I got it myself."

"Well, do come and sit down and tell me all about yourself—over here!"

And just as the last time, she went to the sofa and patted the place beside her. A little reluctantly he went, but he sat at an angle so as not to be too close to her.

"Your uncle saw Franz in March, and Franz told him how well you were getting on in the store. And now you're a full-fledged merchant and going to America. I'm so proud of you!"

Not so fast, Aunt Wetti! he thought. He sensed her desire to pass glibly over all those years when she had not cared what became of him, and he resented her efforts to domesticate both those years and his success.

"And your mother—won't she be proud of you!"

"How is Uncle von Garnhaft?"

He had the satisfaction of seeing her exaggerated enthusiasm—*society manners*, he thought, *you turn them on or off!*—give way to worry in her eyes.

"Your uncle is taking a nap. He doesn't sleep well nights, because his asthma always bothers him at this time of year. He ought to be at the seashore somewhere. We always used to go to Denmark for the summer, but this year, with everything so uncertain—"

He recognized the tune. It was the sort of phrase people who had never had to worry about money before, people whose income had been derived from gilt-edged government bonds and securities, used nowadays to refer to the fact that their incomes had shrunk to next to nothing. He was suddenly aware that there were patches on the dust covers over the chairs, and that the crystal and silvèr *bonbonnière* which had always been full of candied ginger contained only a few small pieces of licorice.

"In a little while," Aunt Wetti said briskly, "I'll go and see whether your uncle is awake. He'll be so glad to see you! You know he was retired in April. He wasn't really of an age to be pensioned yet, but the Socialists want only their own people in the government offices. They did have the grace to retire him with the title of *Regierungsrat*. What they really did was to give him the choice between the larger pension he would have been entitled to five years from now and the title. He took the title, of course. With money losing value every day, what difference did the few hundred kronen make? . . ."

"Of course," he agreed. He realized that, in spite of his initial satisfaction at the hints that Aunt Wetti also was beginning to learn what hardships were, he could not help feeling a little sorry for her. He realized also that somewhere in the back of his mind he had always been proud of Aunt Wetti and of Uncle von Garnhaft on the Kolowrat-Ring.

"And how is Kathi?"

"She is all right."

"And Poldi?"

"She's still in the bank. She's doing a lot of work for some welfare organization out in Favoriten."

"I guess Poldi isn't going to get married!"

"She could if she wanted to!" He was surprised by his own vehemence. "There's a friend of Franz's who has been asking Poldi to marry him for several years. He asked her again just recently and Poldi refused him. He's very nice too."

He remembered the occasion three weeks ago. Poldi had been

abrupt and silent for days. Franz was the one who had spoken of it to *her* one evening. . . . Herr Schmidtmeyer had finally got up his nerve and had proposed, and Poldi had turned him down. According to Franz, the reason Poldi had given Herr Schmidtmeyer was that she had to take care of her mother, now that Franz was getting married. *She* had bridled instantly when Franz had told her of that: "Take care of me? I don't need anybody to take care of me! Not while I've got Father's pension!" But they had all realized that Poldi's reason had merely been an excuse. She did not want to marry Herr Schmidtmeyer. . . .

"But why did she turn him down, then?" Aunt Wetti asked. "If he's as nice as you say. There aren't so many men around nowadays. A girl can't be so particular any more."

"I guess she just didn't want to marry him."

"And Franz is really marrying that young baroness, isn't he? We know all about that: we have some friends who know the von Ortners very well. I imagine Franz is very happy?"

"Yes, I think so."

"That's wonderful!" Aunt Wetti gave him a teasing look—"And pretty soon you'll be thinking of getting married, too! To think how you've grown! Remember the last time you were here?"

He nodded silently.

"How things have changed since then!"

"They haven't changed so much."

Rather hastily, he noted, Aunt Wetti said: "I had the nicest letter from your mother just this week. She's sent us three food packages already. You must be sure and thank her for me. You've been getting them, too, haven't you?"

"Oh, yes."

Three of them! he thought grimly. That was all Mizzi had sent them! Mizzi apparently saw no distinction, then, between Aunt Wetti who had had everything she wanted up until now, and between *her* and Franz and Poldi who had gone hungry all through the war and who had taken care of him all these years.

He realized that his resentment must have shown in his face, for Aunt Wetti lifted her head with a girlish, almost coquettish attempt at gaiety:

"How funny you looked that time you came. You were so

serious and you frowned—like this——" She attempted a scowl.

"It was rather serious to me."

"But don't you think it was funny now?"

"No."

"You don't still feel the way you did then?" She sounded scandalized. "Surely, now that you are older—"

"I know it's the man who's to blame in a case like that—" he sounded stilted even to himself, as if he were rehearsing something he had heard somewhere; he checked himself—"at any rate, you can't expect me to be full of love for her now—and she can't, either. As for my father, I'll settle my account with him sooner or later."

"If I show you something, will you promise never to mention anything about it to your mother?"

"All right."

She got up and went out of the room. When she came back, she was taking a letter out of an envelope. She glanced over it hurriedly, turning the pages until she found the place she was looking for——

"Here—from here on! It's a letter from your mother that came last month."

He read:

> . . . I didn't tell you that G. wrote to me in March. I couldn't tell you then—I was so upset. Can you imagine, after all these years? He wanted to know about Peter and what was I going to do about him—of all the gall! He said that if Peter was still in Austria, he was going to get him, if I had no objection! He had heard that everybody in Vienna was starving. . . .
>
> I was so furious I wasn't going to answer his letter at all. Then I realized that if I didn't, he might really go to Vienna before I could get Peter away. So I wrote and told him that Peter was already on his way over to me, and that his solicitude came a little late in the day. I didn't mince any words, I can tell you. . . . I'm still trying to figure out how he got hold of my address over here. You didn't give it to him? I'd never forgive you, if you did! But I imagine it was Speneder—G. must have written him. They were always as thick as thieves. Speneder swears up and down that he didn't, but I don't trust him. Anyhow, G. had my address, married name and all. He

said that he had been with the army in France and that he was waiting to be demobilized, and that he had been married twice and divorced again—as if I cared!

Peter handed the letter back to Aunt Wetti. He was careful to keep his face blank.

"Now do you see?" Aunt Wetti asked.

"All I see is that she's only been so anxious to have me come to America, because *he's* suddenly shown an interest!"

"Now you know that isn't true! What you probably don't know is that your mother tried everything she could think of to get you to America in 1915. She couldn't come herself and leave two small children at home, and your stepfather wouldn't let her travel, of course, because of the mines. Then it was all arranged to have a friend of your stepfather's bring you with him, and the man was on a ship that actually did run into a mine, and the man was sick for months in a hospital in Sweden. After that, your mother thought it was best to leave you here until the war was over—nobody dreamed that the war would last so long."

"Who is Speneder?" he asked indifferently.

"He's the theatrical manager who took your mother to America. Didn't you know about that?—no, I guess Kathi wouldn't have told you, since it had to do with the theater! It was right after you were born, that same fall. Speneder was getting a company together to tour America. He'd already tried it once and it had been a success. Mizzi wanted to get away from Vienna, and Speneder had been after her, so she went. It wasn't much of a company—mostly popular plays and operettas—but it was good experience for a young actress. She got much bigger parts than she could have got here. Only she never came back: she met your stepfather in a town called St. Louis the next spring, and she got married. Wait—"

He watched Aunt Wetti get up and open the doors of the black-lacquered cabinet with the inlaid gold dragons, and come back to the sofa with a photograph album. Several loose photographs slipped out when she undid the clasp. . . .

"There, that's your mother just before she left——"

He looked, and saw only the quaint style of the blouse and of the long skirt flaring down to the absurd train, and the old-fashioned hat with the roll of osprey feathers around the crown.

"Wasn't she pretty? And here she is as soubrette in a play at the Raimund Theater—and this was taken when she was still at the conservatory—and this—"

There were dozens of photographs of her. He followed Aunt Wetti's finger from picture to picture and recognized Mizzi's face, although his attention refused to stay focused on it and escaped into criticism of the outmoded dresses.

"And this was taken one Sunday when we were all in Rodaun. There's Mizzi, and that's your uncle and me, and those are friends of ours—and do you know who that is: that's your father!"

He felt annoyed with himself at being so startled. In spite of himself, his eyes strained anxiously to make out the features.

"This is a much better picture of him—" Aunt Wetti turned the page—"here he is with your mother. . . ."

Mizzi was holding the handle bars of a two-seater bicycle as if about to get on; the man—his father—was standing beside her, with one hand on the rear saddle of the bicycle. As if he had only one single instant in which to look, his eyes searched the man's face. Dark eyebrows, a rather long face, wide mouth, the head thrust back self-consciously with posing for the camera, the jacket which buttoned almost up to the chin, the black hair parted—*in the same place as his!* Did he look like that! Was there any resemblance?

He could not answer his own question. His mind refused to hold a clear impression of the man's face. Even as he looked, each feature insisted on remaining separate, so that he saw only the eyes or the chin or the flat temple at any one moment.

"Here he is by himself. . . ." Aunt Wetti said.

His eyes followed her hand to the right-hand corner of the page. The same man undoubtedly, if one looked back to the other picture to compare, yet once more he realized that the moment he took his eyes off the picture he would be unable to remember the face. There was some writing across the corner. He twisted his head to read:

For Wetti,
affectionately,
Geoffrey Middlemas

A sort of giddiness seized him. *His name! Here was something to hold on to!* Looking at the pictures had been like thrusting his hand into water, trying to seize an image, but the name—

He made a great effort to sound casual:

"Is that his name?"

"That's his name. But you must never tell your mother that I showed you these!" She shut the album guiltily. "Your mother would never forgive me."

"I won't say anything." He waited until Aunt Wetti had put the album back inside the black-lacquered cabinet. "Do you have his address?"

"Why?"

"Oh, I just wanted to know." His voice had betrayed him. It had shaken ever so little, and Aunt Wetti had noticed it.

"I only have his address in England and that was eighteen years ago. But I won't give it to you. Mizzi made me swear never to answer any letters if he wrote. . . . I couldn't do that, Peter. Maybe later. Besides, it wouldn't do you any good. I doubt whether he still lives there."

"It doesn't matter."

"I'll go and see whether your uncle is awake. . . ."

She came back almost immediately.

"He's still asleep, but he'll wake up in a few minutes."

"I'm afraid, Aunt Wetti, I'll have to go. There are still a lot of things I have to do."

"Can't you stay and have some tea? We don't have any real *Jause* any more, but there is tea and I made some cookies from the flour your mother sent. . . . Your uncle will be so disappointed!"

Her eyes were pleading with him to stay. How things had changed! he thought wryly. Formerly, he would have given anything to spend an afternoon in this nice room with Aunt Wetti. The prospect of tea and cookies would have been irresistible—now she was begging him to stay and he could no longer be enticed by her *Jause* out there in the dining room. *Cookies she made herself* . . . Evidently she no longer had the cook whom he had heard moving so briskly out in the kitchen the last time he had been here. Aunt Wetti was at last feeling the pinch of war. Again he had a moment of vindictive satisfaction, and again he was almost instantly sorry for her.

"I'm afraid I have to. I'm leaving on Monday."

"So soon!"

"Yes, I've got my ticket."

"But surely you can come once more before you go?"

She was the fashionable lady on the Kolowrat-Ring again, bullying him with her society smile and her voice. His latent antagonism rose again.

"I'll try. But in case I can't, will you tell Uncle von Garnhaft that I was sorry not to have seen him? Good-by, Aunt Wetti—"

She embraced him. "Good-by and write us soon! And be sure and give Mizzi our love—and thank her for the food packages. Tell her that now the war is over, she must come and visit us soon. . . ."

Down the elegant staircase, and out into the quiet street—but without that envious constriction around his chest at having to leave the house this time. Yes, he had come a long way! There would be other beautiful streets—in Paris, in New York! It was Aunt Wetti and her fine apartment house who were envious now, who had tried to hold him back. . . .

He felt extraordinarily lighthearted and gay.

Goeffrey Middlemas!

So that was his name! You started to say it and it sang! It echoed from the houses, out of the open windows and from the Venetian blinds, and it whispered in the wheels of the carriage that was coming up the street.

The possession of it gave him a sense of power as if he held in his hand the tiny, precious switch that controlled a huge machine. It was as if something in him that had been frozen ever since that afternoon in the cellar underneath the store had suddenly begun to stir, because now he could afford to let it stir—he was in control!

The address—"but I won't give it to you!" Certainly, Aunt Wetti. It doesn't matter at all. But be sure and keep the red-velvet album tightly closed! . . . There was no hurry now. He would get the address when he was ready for it. *Goeffrey Middlemas* . . . For the present, the name was enough. . . .

Chapter Fifty-Four

It was his last day! he thought on Sunday morning as he looked out on the Ring through the window of the coffeehouse. One more night at home, and then tomorrow at noon, the train!

There had hardly been any need for Franz to remind him of it this morning, when Franz had said: "You are planning to spend a little time with Mother, aren't you? It's your last day. . . ." That's why he was here now in the coffeehouse, wasn't he? And why he had got up early so as to make her think that he was going to church—because of the recent, unwieldy stirring of tenderness toward her.

He had got her the easy chair for the same reason. So far she had preferred her old chair by the sewing machine when she had sat down to read the newspaper. She distrusted new things. It would be some time before she would become accustomed to it. That was the trouble with trying to give her anything: there were so few things that were important to her. Wine—hardly! Every Tuesday when the washerwoman came, *she* bought half a liter of wine for Frau Lang to drink with her lunch; she herself poured out a thimbleful in a glass and after thinning it down with water, drank it. But whether she enjoyed it. . . . Galoshes, there was an idea! In the winter when she went out to early Mass, it would be fine if she had a pair. But he couldn't buy those here. When he got to Switzerland, he would send her a pair—good ones, with fleece-lined uppers. . . .

There seemed to be nothing that he could think of to get her now before he went, and the very thought of her abstemious self-sufficiency sharpened his tenderness toward her.

After lunch, while he was helping her to wipe the dishes, he said casually:

I thought I might go out to the cemetery this afternoon."

She looked up briefly from the dishpan. "I was wondering whether you'd think about saying good-by to Father before you went away."

He could see that she was pleased. He watched her put the accustomed odds and ends which she always took along to the cemetery into her black marketing bag. She had put on her best brown suit, which she wore only three or four times a year, and the beige blouse with the lace ruche which he liked. And she wore the straw hat Poldi had bought her over her protest in June. That was in his honor, too....

They rode out to Baumgarten. Then came the walk up the cemetery road, past the stone carvers, the gardeners, the rustic little inns where people stopped in after funerals. It was a peaceful, autumn-rich Sunday afternoon. Even the one funeral cortege they met inside the cemetery seemed to share in the drowsy, sun-blown peace that hovered over the lush verdure and the orderly avenues. The distance to Father's grave seemed surprisingly short. . . .

It was more than three years since he had been here last, not since he had started his apprenticeship in the store. He looked at the plain granite cross and the black marble plaque set in the pedestal while they stood for a few minutes before the grave to pray, before she started to unpack the gardening tools she had brought. He could see how beautifully the grave was kept. The grass up the sides already had the texture of a fine old lawn; the flowers and shrubs on top were bursting into a second bloom; the two ramblers behind the granite cross were stretching beyond the iron arch to which she had them tied.

She stuck her finger into the soil between two plants——

"That new gardener didn't water again! The lame one was as faithful as could be, but this new one you have to give money every week, or he won't do anything!"

He remembered that she had always kept a watering can hidden behind Frau Wimmer's tombstone.

"Do you have a watering can down here?"

She had already started for the stone and she pulled out a can from behind the ramblers.

"I'll go," he said. He was glad to have something to do. He went down to the intersection of the avenues where the nearest faucet was, and back and forth for water a half-dozen times. She was trimming the grass on the sides, pulling out weeds between the flowers, tying up the new branches of the ramblers. She worked a little on the two adjoining graves and he watered them, too. Then finally she was content. She put her scissors and her old gloves back in the marketing bag.

"I want to see how Frau Wimmer's grave is."

"Do you want me to take the watering can along?"

"No, I've got an old one up there. . . ." Halfway to Frau Wimmer's, she nodded with disapproval toward a black marble stone: "It's all overgrown. You can hardly read the inscription any more. I suppose his wife has forgotten him—a postal inspector from the Kaiserstrasse—only thirty-eight when he died! If she doesn't do something about it soon, I'm going to trim that rambler myself. It's a shame!"

"That one's nice," he said of a miniature rock garden on a grave. . . .

How easy it all was now! He remembered how bitterly he had once hated these trips and how he had writhed at her puttering over strange graves. Yet it was lovely here, profoundly orderly and staid and yet perversely leading one on to prankish thoughts—amusing, for instance, to observe the contradiction between some pretentious stones and the neglect of the graves beneath. Marble angels bending over weeds. . . . She had always sniffed impatiently when she had seen a wife give way to exaggerated grief before an open grave—"carries on like anything!" she had said and had pinched her lips. In the end, he thought, there had always been some grain of wisdom behind her crusty skepticism which had once enraged him so.

Frau Wimmer's grave, and he got water again while she worked with the scissors and the little spade, then Frau Gerstecker's and the two or three others she had taken under her special care. A tilted flowerpot which she could not pass without setting it straight. . . . Then they were back at Father's and he stood beside her while she wiped her eyes. . . . They passed the familiar landmarks on the way back to the gate. He found he remembered them all: the mass grave for the revolutionists of '48, the big tomb for the fourteen nuns who were burned, the towering Christ at the intersection of the main avenues, the tomb of the opera star with the crouching marble figure holding a drooping palm. . . .

When they had started down the cemetery road, he stopped in front of one of the inns:

"Let's go in and have some wine."

"I don't need any wine."

He tried to jolly her: "Oh, but if one comes to the cemetery, one just has to stop at the *Heurigen*. Let's go in and sit down! You must be tired."

"I don't get tired so easily."

But it was not her old stubbornness that spoke. There was a new uncertainty, as if she were afraid of offending him, as if she were almost proud of his insistence and secretly glad to yield to it. For the first time in his life he had taken hold of her elbow, and a little to his surprise she let herself be steered to one of the tables under the trees. Amazing, how like Franz he suddenly felt, cajoling her like this!

When the waiter had brought the wine and the bottle of soda water he had ordered for her, she grumbled:

"Half a liter of wine! Who's going to drink all that? I know I'm not!"

"We'll manage all right. . . ." He felt himself smiling at her. "Now it's just as if Father were here!"

She took a cautious sip from her half-filled glass of watered wine. He heard the shy, gruff humor in her voice:

"Yes, Father never could bear to pass a *Heurigen* without stopping in."

And suddenly Father was very vivid to them both: on a Sunday like this, Father wearing his light-gray suit and the still lighter gray hat, firmly grasping his walking stick as he set out to enjoy the afternoon, striding straight ahead with the peculiar, solid dignity Father had——

"One time in Sievering we were walking through a vineyard: I remember the grapes weren't quite ripe but they had that misty bloom on them, and I remember the huge, dark-green vine leaves and the silvery trail the snails had made on some of the leaves. . . . We went all the way out to Leopoldsdorf that day. . . ."

"He's in Heaven now, I hope," she said. "He won't need any more *Heurigen*."

He had to tease her again: "But how do you know? Heaven's a place where everything's supposed to be perfect—perhaps there are whole rows of *Heurigen* and Father can get all the wine he wants!"

"He drank enough down here!"

She finally emptied her glass, but not without first protesting: "If I drink all that, I'll be tipsy."

"No, you won't! Wine is supposed to give you strength."

"You'll be just like Father," she said, and again something humorous and pleased lurked in her eyes.

They started slowly back to town. When they got off the streetcar, she headed for the Poutongasse for her favorite church. He went along. And he remained uncomfortably on his knees all through the vesper service because she would not get off her knees.

He noticed how crowded the big church was and how urgent the devoutness of the people around him seemed. Still another effect of the war! But with *her* it was different—she had always been devout like this. When she had been worried over Father and in terror because Franz was at the front and then sick, she had come here for comfort and hope; now she came for peace and joy—except during these coming weeks when she would worry over him and pray just as fervently as she once had for Franz. Bianca's phrase, "I simply haven't any talent for religion," came back to him. Neither have I, he thought. But a sudden respect for the unshakable faith of the old woman beside him—she was getting old!—mingled with his tenderness for her. He waited patiently long after the candles on the altar had been put out, until she herself was ready to go. . . .

He knew that he had made her happy. The afternoon, the few trivial gestures of going to the cemetery and then to church, had sufficed to make his peace with her, to round off something that had needed rounding off to fit into her scheme of things. He felt a little guilty when he remembered how easy it had been.

But there was still Poldi—it was not so easy to draw suddenly close to Poldi just because one wanted to!

He had expected her home for supper, but Poldi did not come in until late and then she ate quickly and went immediately to her room. It was almost as if Poldi were avoiding him. . . . How much, he asked himself, did he really know about her? She did not want to marry Herr Schmidtmeyer, and he approved of that. He knew that she was capable in her job at the bank, that she was immensely loyal and proud, that she became restive in the presence of any sort of sentimentality—all that he knew, but beyond that, scarcely anything.

There was still the morning left for him. He made a point of leaving the house with Poldi on the pretext of a last-minute errand in the Innere Stadt. But the streetcar was crowded and when he walked with her to the bank, Poldi was shut-in and defensively matter-of-fact. The sudden puzzle offered by that side of Poldi which he did not know and of which he had only just become aware remained inaccessible. In the end, he tried to console himself, what was there for them to say? Poldi had done things for him because she liked him, but what else had there been? . . .

He walked out from the Innere Stadt over the Margaretenstrasse and went once more to look at the store. He stopped at the upper end of the Kohlgasse where he could watch the drays being loaded in front of the warehouse yard. He did not want to be seen. One of the new apprentices came walking up the Kohlgasse to the warehouse with some papers in his hand. Herr Kropfl came out of the office building and crossed the Margaretenstrasse to the store. . . . It was like a fortress he had taken and which he could now look upon as something vanquished and not even interesting any more.

He did not go to look at the Apprentice Home. That was something he did not want to see again. There had been nothing to conquer there. It had been only something to endure. . . . When he got to the Mariahilferstrasse, he stopped to buy three bottles of the best Riesling wine he could find. He put them on the kitchen table when he came home.

"What's that for?" Her eyes were suspiciously swollen.

"Why, they're for you. To cheer you up, so you won't cry so much!" It did not come off so well. He lacked Franz's light touch.

"I need wine, I do!" And she went on cooking the elaborate lunch in his honor.

He started to close the bag in the living room. She came in with a suit of winter underwear all neatly folded up.

"Here, put that in!"

"But I haven't any more room."

"You can find room for that. It's always cold on the ocean."

"But this is summer!"

"It's always cold on the water."

It was eleven o'clock. Franz came home, and then Poldi. *She* started to serve the lunch. . . .

And then he was at the train with Poldi and Franz.

They were standing on the platform under the gray glass roof of the Westbahnhof, caught up in the peculiar awkwardness—the staccato isolation and the dearth of anything appropriate to do or say—the indecent suspense of waiting for the train to go. There was nothing more to do. Franz had already been in the compartment to inspect his seat, rearrange his bag and the other things in the rack, try the window and point out that he could fold back the armrest of the seat, so that he had felt embarrassed in front of the two Dutchmen who were going to be in the compartment with him. Then Franz had rushed off to the bookstand to buy more newspapers and magazines—"Something for you to read!"

He had them now under his arm.

They avoided looking at each other, yet they were constantly blundering into each other's eyes. Once, Franz spoke to Poldi: "I think I'd better go back afterward to see that Mother is all right!"

It reminded him of the last few moments at the house. She had cried bitterly. "Now you go, too!" she had said. "But it isn't as far as all that," he had joked; "and don't stay awake all night. It'll be weeks before I'll be on the water anyway. I'm only going to Paris first. . . ." She had not clung to him when he had kissed her good-by. Only when she had reached out for the little holy water font beside the door, had her hand been insistent, almost passionate.

No sign from Poldi. Her face and her throat under the white summer blouse looked choked with a dark flush. He must find something especially nice to send Poldi from Switzerland or from Paris.

"Only five more minutes," Franz warned. "You had better get on."

He stalled it off. It was easier to stand out here than to look out through the compartment window. "It's only the warning bell. There's lots of time."

"Here—" Franz pulled out an envelope from his inside coat pocket and handed it to him—"we want you to take this."

"What is it?" He opened the flap. In the envelope were two hundred-franc notes. Wherever had Franz got the Swiss money? He must have borrowed it—from Baron Ortner, or from Herr Schmidtmeyer perhaps. Franz's salary for a whole year would hardly buy that many Swiss francs. He tried to hand it back——

"Look, I don't need it. I've got more than enough."

"You've got to take it. I insist!"

He tried another tack: "They might confiscate it on the border."

"They won't if you show them your passport."

"I'll only send it right back from Switzerland!"

"You can send it back when you are safely in New York, if you want to—not before!"

The conductor was calling, "All aboard."

He moved toward Poldi and kissed her awkwardly. Again she seemed to be holding back. "Good-by, Franz."

"Greet Mizzi from us. You've got your passport and your money where they are safe?"

"Yes, in the little bag around my neck." He could feel the little canvas bag, into which she had sewn a medal of the Virgin, against his chest.

"Don't trust anybody. And take your bag to the sleeping car at night."

"All right, Franz."

"And be sure to write as soon as you stop anywhere. Mother will be worrying."

"I'll telegraph. Good-by. . . ."

A few more minutes at the window of the compartment under the scrutiny of the two Dutchmen who were talking phlegmatically but who were also watching him and Poldi and Franz, and then the train started to pull away from Franz and Poldi. He waved as long as he could see them. Then the train was clear of the station shed and the sun was on every side. He opened one of the magazines Franz had bought him, so as not to be outdone by the two Dutchmen in aplomb, to look worldly-wise and deny Franz's solicitude. . . .

A good thing I'm going away, he thought; *sooner or later, I should have betrayed Franz!*

The two Dutchmen had stopped talking. The one by the door was taking a pair of leather slippers out of his traveling bag and preparing to put them on; the other one was looking out of the window.

As soon as I get to Switzerland, I'm going to send back the money, he thought. *And I'm going to send them things: galoshes for her, and a trench coat for Franz. Franz would like that! Perhaps in Paris it would be easier to find something for Poldi. . . .* He wondered who the two Dutchmen were. Merchants, most likely. . . .

There was Hütteldorf going by! It was strange to start on a journey like this in the very middle of the day. Night would have been much more appropriate—it ought to be dark when you plunged forward into the unknown. . . . The train was going faster now. Purkersdorf! Amazing, how far away from Vienna he already felt, yet Purkersdorf was only ten miles. You could walk back in two hours and a half—half an hour on the suburban train. Yet Switzerland seemed already much nearer than Vienna, just as Paris seemed nearer than Berne. . . .

"Sentimental geography!" was what Freiherr von Steligerode would call that, no doubt. That was the phrase he had used to Baron Ortner about something at the Opera that night. The arid, haughty cynicism of Baron Ortner's friend was suddenly vivid to him again. Only two years ago he would have envied that arrogant manner. But not any more. He had changed! Now he wanted something richer, a unique quality that only he himself could evolve—he felt suddenly strong with power to achieve this exhilarating completeness he sensed. No, he did not want to be like anybody else: not even like Baron Ortner or Herr Granini—he wanted to be himself!

Something Herr Granini had said about Vienna rose in his mind—"The very make-up of the city is changing," Herr Granini had said. Very well, let it! He was going away. . . . "Only the trash has survived, has even come out on top. . . ." He was not trash and he had survived! Still, there was some truth in what Herr Granini had said. Baron Ortner and Herr Granini had lost their wealth and were poor; Freiherr von Steligerode had probably lost his estates and his diplomatic career; Franz had a career but was paid in money that would not allow him to buy a pair of shoes with his salary for a whole month—yet on the other hand, Franz would marry Bianca, a baroness, and that would hardly have been possible if it had not been for the war; and down in Almzell Karl had bought back all the property his father had mortgaged before he had died; all the farmers had got rich in land. . . . No question that everything had changed and you could not say for the better. Yet he had survived, because he had had to survive! He had a purpose. There was one man in the world somewhere he had to convince——

Convince?

What kind of talk was that! His conversation with Franz in the Volksgarten came back to trouble him—"You'll feel differently about all that. You have changed already. You'll change again!"

Something like fear assailed him: Was he going to be cheated out of his revenge by this treacherous change? Did one grow up to one's hatred, outgrow it even? Was it always going to be like this, that he had no sooner attained a goal his hatred had set for him, than there was a new goal farther on, until in the end there would be nothing left of his hatred? He shuddered a little as he thought of it. After all, it was his hatred for his father which had sheltered him through those years in the store, and which had driven him on. No, he must keep the thought of revenge alive—he would keep it alive!

His resolution made him feel happy again. Paris, and then America! It must be a fascinating country from what Sibby had said. There would be Sibby and all the people and things she had talked about.... It would be interesting to see what Mizzi was really like, and it would be nice to have a little sister. "Anne"—the name went well with the grave-eyed little face. It would all be new, new! And he would feel new and rich with this exhilarating sense of adventure——

"Are you going all the way to Berne?" asked the jowly Dutchman who had put on the brown leather slippers.

"I'm going to Berne and then to Paris."

"To Paris!"

He ignored Franz's warning to be careful. He wasn't afraid of these two comfortable-looking Dutchmen. He had done with fear.

"Yes, and to New York."

"That's quite a journey!" the other one said. "Aren't you afraid?"

"No, why should I be! I'm going home...."

THE END

www.ingramcontent.com/pod-product-compliance
Lightning Source LLC
Chambersburg PA
CBHW020926310726
48980CB00005B/409

* 9 7 8 0 8 7 7 9 7 3 6 1 4 *